❀
Peter the First
❀

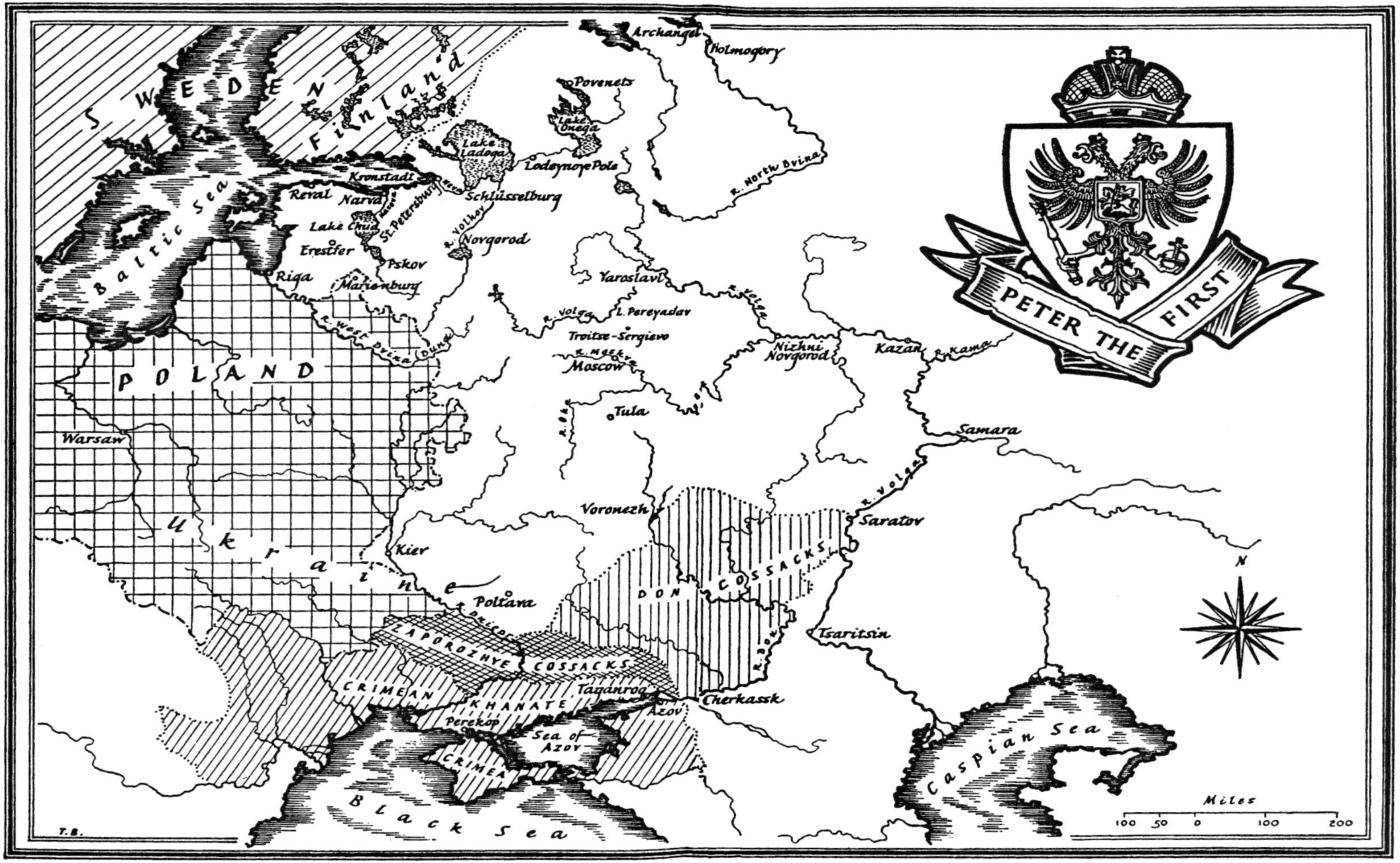
PETER THE FIRST
SWEDEN
Finland
Baltic Sea
Archangel
Holmogory
Povenets
Lake Onega
Lake Ladoga
Lodeynoye Pole
R. North Dvina
Kronstadt
Reval
Narva
Neva
Schlüsselburg
St. Petersburg
Lake Chud
R. Volkhov
Novgorod
Erestfer
Pskov
Riga
Marienburg
R. West Dvina (Duna)
Yaroslavl
R. Volga
L. Pereyadav
Troitse-Sergievo
Moscow
Nizhni Novgorod
Kazan
R. Kama
POLAND
Warsaw
Tula
R. Oka
Samara
Voronezh
Saratov
Kiev
Ukraine
DON COSSACKS
Poltava
R. Dnieper
Tsaritsin
ZAPOROZHYE COSSACKS
R. Don
CRIMEAN KHANATE
Taganrog
Cherkassk
Azov
Perekop
Sea of Azov
CRIMEA
Black Sea
Caspian Sea
N
Miles
100 50 0 100 200
T.B.

Peter the First

by Alexei Tolstoy

University Press of the Pacific
Honolulu, Hawaii

Peter the First

by
Alexei Tolstoy

ISBN: 1-4102-2509-7

Copyright © 2005 by University Press of the Pacific

University Press of the Pacific
Honolulu, Hawaii
http://www.universitypressofthepacific.com

All rights reserved, including the right to reproduce this book, or portions thereof, in any form.

In order to make original editions of historical works available to scholars at an economical price, this facsimile of the original edition is reproduced from the best available copy and has been digitally enhanced to improve legibility, but the text remains unaltered to retain historical authenticity.

Peter the First

BOOK ONE

❊

chapter one

Sanka jumped down from the stove, and bumped open the sagging door with her buttocks. Yashka, Gavrilka and Artamoshka quickly climbed down after her; they all suddenly felt thirsty. They ran out into the dark passage, preceded by a cloud of steam and smoke from the stuffy hut. The faint, bluish light of dawn showed through the snow that covered the little window. It was very cold. The water butt was frozen over, and the wooden dipper was covered with ice.

The children hopped from one foot to the other—they were all barefooted. There was a kerchief tied over Sanka's head; Gavrilka and Artamoshka had only little shirts on, which barely reached their navels.

"The door, you little wretches!" their mother shouted from inside the hut. She was standing in front of the stove. The kindling wood blazed in the hearth and the flames lit up her wrinkled face. Her eyes, sunk and dark-rimmed from much weeping, gleamed terribly, like an icon's. Sanka felt frightened, and banged the door shut with all her might. Then she scooped up some of the evil-smelling water, drank a little, bit on a piece of ice, and gave her brothers a drink.

"Are you cold?" she whispered. "If not, let's run out into the yard and have a look; father is harnessing the horse. . . ."

In the yard their father was harnessing the horse to the sledge. Snow was falling softly, and the sky was thick with snow; crows were sitting on the high fence. It was not so cold here as in the passage. Their father had a tall felt cap pulled down to his stern eyebrows. His wife called him Ivan Artemyich, while everyone else, including himself, called him Ivash, nicknamed Brovkin.* His red beard had not been combed since the feast of the Intercession. His leather mittens stuck out from the breast of his coarse peasant's coat, which was tied low round the waist with bast, and his birch-bark shoes creaked harshly over the dung-strewn snow: he was having trouble with the harness. It was rotten, nothing but knots.

"Be still, you devil!" he shouted at the black horse, short-legged and pot-bellied like himself.

The children relieved themselves near the porch and then huddled together on the ice-covered threshold, although the frost was biting. Artamoshka, the youngest, stammered out:

"Never mind, we'll warm up on the stove."

Ivash finished harnessing the horse and gave it some water from a pail. It took a long drink, distending its shaggy flanks, as if to say: "You starve me for food, but at least I'll have my fill of drink!" Ivash put on his gauntlets, and pulled out the whip from under the straw in the sledge.

"Run into the hut, or I'll give it you!" he shouted to the children. Then he flung himself sideways on to the sledge and making a skidding turn outside the gates, set off at a rapid trot past the tall, snow-covered fir trees towards the homestead where Volkov, the young nobleman, lived.

"Ooh! It's bitter cold!" Sanka said, and the children rushed into the dark hut and clambered up on to the stove, their teeth chattering. Warm, dry smoke curled up to the blackened ceiling and made its way out of the little transom over the door—there was no chimney. Their mother was mixing dough. The family lived fairly well: they had a horse and a cow, and four hens. Ivash was spoken of as "solid".

Sparks from the cresset fell with a hiss into a pan of water. Sanka pulled a sheepskin coat over herself and her little brothers, and under it resumed her stories, told in a whisper, of all manner of terrible things: about those, who must not be named, who rustle under the floor at night.

* From *Brov*—"eyebrow."

"A little while ago—strike me blind, did I get a fright! There was the rubbish heap by the threshold and the broom on it. I looked from the stove—the holy powers be with us! From under the broom—something shaggy, with whiskers like a cat. . . ."

"Oh! Oh! Oh!" The youngsters under the coat were terribly scared.

2

The faintly marked track led through the forest. Age-old pines shut out the sky. Fallen trees and thickets made difficult going. This land had been conveyed to young Vasily Volkov two years ago when he set up independently of his father, a nobleman serving in Moscow. The Chancellery of Estates assigned him twelve hundred acres, along with thirty-seven serfs and their families attached to the land.

Vasily built himself a homestead and having spent all his money was obliged to mortgage half his land with the monastery. The monks lent the money at high interest—twenty kopeks on the rouble. And the estate carried the duty of his presenting himself for service to the Tsar on a goodly steed, in a coat of mail, with sword and arquebus, and to bring with him soldiers—three men, also mounted, in padded coats, with swords and bows and arrows. He barely managed to raise this equipment with the money received from the monastery. And didn't he have to live himself? And feed the house serfs? And pay the interest to the monks?

The Tsar's treasury knew no mercy. Every year brought new orders, new imposts—maintenance-money, travel-money, contributions and quit-rents. Little remained for himself. And the landowner was constantly pressed—why was he slow at squeezing the quit-rent out of the peasant. But you couldn't fleece the peasant more than once. Under the late Tsar Alexey Mihaylovich * the country had become impoverished through wars, disorders and revolts. After Stenka Razin, the accursed robber, had roamed over the land the peasants had forgotten God. If you squeezed them a little tighter they snarled like wolves. To escape the imposts they fled to the Don from where you couldn't get them back either by sword or by decree.

Ivan's horse, covered with rime, kept up a slow jog-trot. Branches caught at the high shaft-bow and showered snow-dust. Bushy-tailed squirrels clung to the tree trunks and watched them pass—the forest swarmed with these squirrels. Ivan lay in the sledge and thought—there was nothing left for the peasant to do but think.

* Second Romanov, father of Peter the First.

"Well, all right. . . . Give this, give that. . . . Pay this one, pay that one. But a State like this is a bottomless well—how could you ever fill it? We don't shirk work, we put up with everything. But now in Moscow the boyars have started driving about in gilded coaches. We must give him money for the coach too, the overfed devil. Well, all right. . . . Make us do things, take what you want, but don't rob us. And it's robbery to fleece us twice over, my lads! We've too many of the Tsar's officials on our backs, damn it—no matter where you turn, there's a clerk, or a collector, or a publican sitting writing. And there's only the peasant to pay. . . . Oh, lads, the best thing is for me to run away—wild beasts will tear me to pieces in the forest—but death's better than this robbery. That way you won't batten on us for long. . . ."

Ivash Brovkin was thinking—perhaps this way, or perhaps not.

Out of the forest there drove on to the track Tsigan, one of Volkov's peasants, very dark, with hair turning grey; he was kneeling on his sledge. He had been a fugitive for some fifteen years, wandering from place to place. But then a decree was issued that all runaways were to be returned to their masters, however long they had been at liberty. Tsigan was caught near Voronezh, where he was working on the land, and sent back to old Volkov. He ran away again, was caught and ordered to be mercilessly flogged and then again imprisoned—and as soon as his skin healed, to be taken out again and mercilessly flogged a second time, and then again imprisoned—to teach him to run away, the rogue, the thief! Tsigan had only been saved by being made over to young Volkov.

"Good day," Tsigan said to Ivan, leaving his sledge and coming to sit in Ivan's.

"Good day."

"Any news?"

"Doesn't seem to be any good news."

Tsigan took off his knitted mitten, passed his fingers through his moustache and beard to mask the sly look on his face, and said:

"I met a man in the forest; he says the Tsar's dying."

Ivan raised himself in the sledge: he felt awed. "Whoa!" He pulled off his cap and crossed himself:

"Who will be made Tsar now?"

"There's no one, he says, but that boy Peter. And he's barely weaned."

"Well, my lad," Ivan drew on his cap and his eyes paled. "Well, my lad. . . . Now the boyars will rule us. We'll be ruined."

"Ruined—or perhaps not, and that's that." Tsigan moved closer to

Ivan and winked. "That man said there'll be a revolt. Perhaps we'll go on living yet and chewing bread, we've been through a thing or two." Tsigan bared his strong teeth in a laugh, and then coughed so loudly that it rang through the forest.

A squirrel sprang down from a tree and leapt swiftly across the track in a flutter of snow that glittered like a swirl of tiny needles in the slanting rays of the sun. The huge crimson sun hung over the hill at the end of the track, over the high palisade, the steep roofs and smoking chimneys of the Volkov homestead.

3

Ivan and Tsigan left their horses at the tall gates, surmounted by an image of the Holy Cross protected by a penthouse. An insurmountable palisade surrounded the whole homestead: good enough to stand up even to the Tatars. The peasants took off their caps. Ivan took hold of the ring in the postern gate, pronouncing the customary formula:

"Lord Jesus Christ, Son of God, have mercy on us."

Averian, the watchman, came out of his hut with a creaking of birch-bark shoes, and peered through a crack: he saw that they were no strangers.

"Amen," he said and began to open the gates.

The men led their horses into the courtyard and stood bareheaded, glancing out of the corners of their eyes at the mica windows of their master's house. A porch with a high flight of steps led up to the dwelling quarters. It was a handsome porch of carved wood, surmounted by an onion-shaped dome. Above the porch rose the tent-shaped roof of the house with two barrelled side-wings and a gilded ridge. The bottom floor, built of huge logs, was a storeroom. Volkov had had it built for storing winter and summer stocks—corn, salted meat and all kinds of preserves. The peasants knew, however, that all his storerooms contained was mice. But the porch—many a prince would be proud of it—the porch was magnificent.

"Averian, why has the boyar summoned us with our horses: is it for some service, or what?" Ivash asked. "There's nothing we're owing that I know of."

"You're to take the men-at-arms to Moscow."

"Crocking up the horses again?"

"What's in the wind?" Tsigan asked, coming closer. "War with someone? Or a rising?"

"That's no concern of yours or mine." The old greybeard bowed his head. "It's ordered—you'll take them. Today they brought in a load of sticks for fellows like you."

Averian shuffled back stiff-legged to the gate-house. Here and there a lighted window gleamed in the winter twilight. The courtyard was crowded with a great many buildings of all kinds—cellars, cattle sheds, huts, a smithy. But half of them were not used. Volkov had only fifteen house serfs, and even those barely kept body and soul together. They worked, of course—ploughed after a fashion, sowed, carted timber—but how was it possible to get a living from this? It was serf's labour they gave. It was said that Volkov sent one of them to Moscow to play the half-wit on a church-porch—that one earned him some money. And that two others went about with baskets, also in Moscow, selling wooden spoons, birch-bark shoes and whistles. But after all it was the peasants who counted: they fed you.

Ivash and Tsigan stood in the courtyard in the twilight, thinking. There was no need to hurry. Nothing good to expect from anywhere. Of course, the old people said that life used to be easier: if you didn't like your master, you left and went elsewhere. Now this was no longer allowed—you had to live where you were told. You're ordered to feed Vasily Volkov—it's up to you to find how. They had all become serfs. And you had to expect that things would get worse.

A door creaked shrilly somewhere and a bareheaded servant-girl, a shameless hussy, ran across the snow to them.

"The master says you're to unharness the horses. You're to stay here for the night. God forbid you should give your horses the master's hay!"

Tsigan moved to slash his whip across the girl's smooth back, but she ran off. They took their time over unharnessing, and went into the servants' hut for the night. Some eight men-servants, having filched a tallow candle from their master, were slapping greasy cards on the table, winning kopeks from each other. They shouted and squabbled; one hid a coin in his cheek and another man tore at his lips. Lazy brutes—but all the same, they were well fed!

On a bench at the side sat a boy in a linen tunic and ragged birch-bark shoes—Alioshka, Ivan's son. Last autumn hunger had driven them to give the boy in perpetual bondage to Volkov: they were in arrears with their dues. The boy had great eyes, like his mother. It was evident that they beat him here. Ivan took a sideways glance at him; he was sorry for him, but said nothing. Alioshka bowed low to his father, without a word.

Ivan beckoned to his son and whispered: "Have they eaten supper?"

"Yes."

"That's bad, I brought no bread from home." This was not true: he had a piece of bread in his shirt, wrapped in a rag.

"You must manage something for me somehow. See here, Alioshka, in the morning I'll go down on my knees to the master—I've a lot to do. Perhaps he'll be merciful—and you'll go to Moscow in my stead."

Alioshka nodded gravely. "Very well, father."

Ivan began to take off his shoes and, in a brisk, sprightly tone, as if he were well-fed and merry, said:

"Do you have such fun every day, lads? Ah, you've an easy life, with plenty to eat and drink."

One of the men, a tall fellow, flung down his cards and turned round:

"And who are you to find fault with us?" he asked.

Ivan did not wait for a box in the ears, but climbed up to the bunk.

4

Mihail Tirtov, the son of a small landowner near by, had remained for the night with Volkov. They finished supper early. Felt rugs, pillows and bearskin coats were piled on the broad benches alongside the glazed stove. But they were young and not inclined for sleep. It was hot there. They sat on the benches in their underclothes, talking in the twilight. Now and again they yawned, making the sign of the cross over their mouths.

"As for you," Volkov's guest said gravely in a low voice, "there are a great many who envy you, Vasily. But put yourself in my place. My father has fourteen of us. Seven of us have been portioned off—and we're struggling on barren soil, some with two peasants, others with three—the rest have all run away. I'm the eighth, and tomorrow I'll be portioned off. They'll give me a burnt-out village and a swamp full of frogs. How am I to live?"

"Times are hard for everyone now," Volkov answered; with one hand he was fingering the beads of a cypress-wood rosary that hung between his knees. "We're all struggling. . . . How are we to live?"

"My grandfather took precedence of Prince Golitsin," Tirtov said. "He watched day and night by Tsar Michael's coffin. But at home we go about in birch-bark shoes. We're hardened to shame. We don't think of honour, but of how to live. Father's forehead is all bruised with bowing in the Chancellery of Estates, making petitions; but now it's no use petitioning empty-handed. Something for the clerk—something for the under-clerk—something for the junior clerk. And they don't always take what you give—they make a wry face. We were asking the under-clerk, Stepka Remezov, to help us in some small business, and sent him presents—ten altyns *—just managed to scrape the money together—and forty pounds of dried fish. He took the money all right, the greedy drunken brute, but ordered the fish to be thrown out into the yard. Others, who are cleverer, manage to gain their ends. Volodka Chemodanov reached the Tsar himself with his petition and got two tidy villages in perpetual ownership. Yet everybody knows that during the last war Volodka ran off the battlefield from the Poles and his father deserted three times from the battlefield near Smolensk. But instead of punishing them by taking away their land and their homesteads, they reward them with villages. . . . There's no justice."

They were silent for a while. Heat flowed from the stove. Crickets chirred drily. It was very quiet and dull. Even the dogs had ceased to yap in the yard. At last Volkov began in a pensive tone:

"If only we could take service with some king—in Venice, or Rome, or Vienna. I'd go without even looking back. Prince Vasily Golitsin gave my godfather a book and I borrowed it to read. All the other nations live in riches and plenty, only we are paupers. The other day I was in Moscow looking for an armourer; I was told to go to the Kukuy suburb, to the foreigners. They're not Orthodox, it's true: God will be their judge. But directly I got inside their palisade I found the streets swept, the houses clean and bright, and flowers in the gardens. I walked along and felt a bit frightened, it was all so wonderful, like in a dream. The people were friendly; and there they live, just at our doors. And their wealth! That Foreign Quarter's richer than the whole of Moscow with her suburbs."

"One could try trading—but money's needed for that too." Tirtov looked at his bare feet. "Join the streltsi † ? Nothing much to be got out of it. They'll break your back before you're a captain. The other day a man called Danila Menshikov, a groom from the Tsar's stables, came to see my father, and he said the treasury owed the strelets regiments two-and-a-half years' pay. And if you make a fuss about it they put you under arrest. Colonel Pizhov sends the streltsi to his

---

* Altyn = 3 kopeks.

† The streltsi (*sing.* strelets) formed the main part of the regular standing army, mostly quartered in Moscow. In peace time they lived in special suburbs with their families, plying various trades and handicrafts. They also acted as garrison, police force and firemen and as bodyguard to the Tsar when he travelled.

Moscow estates and there they work like serfs. When they tried to complain, the petitioners were flogged in front of the courthouse. Oh, the streltsi are very angry. . . . Menshikov says: just wait, they'll show what they can do."

"I've heard say no one in a boyar's coat had better cross the Moskva river."

"What would you expect? Everyone is beggared. There's such a burden of taxes and duties and tolls—enough to make one clear out for good. Menshikov said: it's the foreigners who trade; in Archangel, in Holmogory they've built stone warehouses. They buy abroad for a rouble and sell to us for three. And our merchants just let their goods rot out of greed. Our townsmen are running away from the merciless taxes—some into the provinces, some to the wild steppes. Now they've put on an ice-tax, for cutting holes in the ice on the river. And where does the money go? Menshikov says: Prince Vasily Golitsin has built himself a palace on the Neglinnaya river, with sheets of copper outside and gilded leather inside. . . ."

Volkov raised his head and looked at Tirtov. Tirtov drew his feet back under the bench and stared at Volkov. The meek young man of a moment ago was gone: he was grinning and joggling his leg so that the bench shook under him.

"What's in your mind?" Volkov asked in a low voice.

"Last week, near the village of Vorobiovo, another merchants' train was robbed. Did you hear about it?" Volkov frowned and took up his rosary. "Cloth merchants were taking a rich load to Moscow. They were hurrying to reach the town before suppertime, but never did. One escaped alive and reported what had happened. They set out to catch the robbers, but all they found was their tracks, and those covered with snow."

Tirtov shrugged his shoulders and laughed.

"Don't be alarmed—I wasn't there, I heard it from Menshikov." He bent closer to Volkov. "The tracks, they say, led to the Varvarka —to the house of Stepan Odoyevsky. Prince Odoyevsky's youngest son. He's the same age as we are."

"It's time we were asleep," Volkov said gloomily.

Tirtov gave another mirthless laugh and said: "All right, we've had our joke, let's sleep."

He rose lightly from the bench, his joints cracking as he stretched himself. He poured some kvass into a wooden cup and took a long drink, glancing at Volkov over the brim.

"Stepan Odoyevsky has twenty-five house serfs armed with swords and firearms. They're a desperate lot. He's trained them. For more than a year he never fed them; just turned them out at night to look for loot. . . . They're wolves."

Tirtov lay down on the bench, pulled a bearskin over him and put his hand under his head. His eyes were gleaming:

"Will you go and inform against me for what I've said?"

Volkov hung up his rosary and lay down silently with his face to the pinewood wall on которой beads of resin showed. It was a long time before he answered:

"No, I won't."

5

They passed through the gates of the Earthen Wall and followed a winding route through streets full of potholes, past tall and narrow two-storied houses built of logs. Heaps of cinders, offal, potsherds, discarded rags were lying everywhere; all the rubbish was flung out into the streets.

Alioshka, holding the reins, walked alongside the sledge in which three serfs were seated; they were wearing military caps made of cotton material stuffed with tow and thickly padded, stiff felt coats with high collars—*tegileys*. These were Volkov's men-at-arms. He had not enough money to buy coats-of-mail, so he had dressed them like this, though he was afraid that at the review he might be put to shame and reprimanded: you've not provided the regulation equipment, you're not being honest.

Volkov and Tirtov were in Tsigan's sledge, and servants followed, leading their horses: Volkov's with a Persian saddle and rich saddle-cloth, and Tirtov's spavined gelding with shabby inferior trappings.

Tirtov looked gloomy. Nobles and boyars' sons, in their grandfather's hauberks and cuirasses, and new coats and tunics, rode past them shouting and whipping their mounts: the whole countryside was gathering in Lubiansky Square for the review and the distribution or redistribution of land. Every one of them looked at Tirtov's gelding and laughed: "Hi, you! Are you taking it to the knacker's yard? Take care, or it won't get as far!" And they flicked it with their whips as they passed, the gelding flinching at every blow. Guffaws, laughter, whistling. . . .

They crossed the bridge over the Yaouza where, on the steep bank, hundreds of small windmills were turning. Trotting along in the long line of sledges and supply-carts they passed through a square by a patchy white wall with square towers and guns in the embrasures. At the low Miasnitsky gates there was an uproar—shouting, jostling, cursing—everyone must needs be first through, blows exchanged, caps knocked off, sledges cracking, horses rearing. Over the gates, before an age-darkened icon, shone a lamp that was kept burning day and night.

Alioshka was slashed by whips and lost his cap; it was a wonder he wasn't killed! They drove out into the Miasnitsky street. Wiping the blood from his nose he gazed round in wonder.

Dense crowds pushed along the narrow, dung-strewn street. Shopkeepers leaned out of their wooden booths, shouting, catching at the coats and caps of passers-by, trying to draw them inside. Behind the high fences were stone houses, red or silver high-pitched roofs, church domes of many colours. Thousands of churches. Big ones with five cupolas and small ones at the crossroads, so small that a man could hardly get in at the door and when a dozen were inside they could not turn round. The warm flicker of tapers showed through the open doors. Old women slept as they knelt. Shaggy, terrible-looking beggars shook their filthy rags, clutched at people's feet and whined, exhibiting their bodies covered with blood and dirt. Fierce-eyed roving priests flourished rolls of bread in people's faces shouting: "Come along to church, merchant, or I'll eat this bread and there'll be no mass." Clouds of rooks hovered over the churches.

They barely managed to push their way beyond the Lubianka, where the whole square was thronged with groups of mounted levies. In the distance, near the Nikolsky gates, they could see a boyar's tall, cylindrical sable hat, the clerks' fur caps and the dark long-skirted coats of the elected representatives of the most prominent citizens. From there a tall, lean man with a great long beard shouted something and waved a paper. When he called a nobleman would ride out, richly or poorly equipped, unattended or with his men-at-arms, and gallop up to the table. Then he would dismount and bow low to the boyar and the clerks. These examined his accoutrement and horses and looked up in the rolls how much land he had been granted. There were disputes. The nobleman would call on God to be his witness, tear at the bosom of his coat; some pleaded with tears that they were being ruined on their poor land and were dying of hunger and cold.

Thus, following age-old custom, each year before the spring campaigns the militia, raised by the nobles owing service to the Tsar, was passed in review.

Volkov and Tirtov mounted their horses. The horses were unharnessed from Tsigan's and Alioshka's sledges and two of Volkov's serfs mounted them bareback; the third was ordered to say he was on foot because his horse had gone lame on the way. The sledges were abandoned.

Tsigan caught at Volkov's stirrup and cried:

"Where are you taking my horse? Master! Merciful master!"

Volkov threatened him with his whip: "Only dare make a noise!"

When they had ridden off Tsigan cursed hideously, threw the collar and harness-bow into the sledge and lay down in it himself, angrily burying himself in the straw.

They all forgot Alioshka. He picked up the harness and put it in the sledge. He sat for a while, chilled through, without a cap, in his threadbare coat. Oh well, such was the peasant's lot; he must put up with it. Suddenly his nose caught an appetising smell. A townsman in a rabbit-skin cap was passing him: a fat fellow with small eyes. Baked pies were smoking under the cloth that covered the tray slung across his belly. The sly devil! he glanced at Alioshka and raised the corner of the cloth crying: "Hot! Brown!" The smell drew Alioshka to the pies.

"How much, uncle?"

"A quarter kopek the pair. You'll lick your chops on them!"

There was a quarter kopek in Alioshka's cheek: his mother had given it to him for his bitter luck when he had gone off to become a serf. He grudged the money, but his stomach clamoured.

"All right, give me a pair," he said gruffly. He paid for the pies and ate them. He had never tasted anything like this before. But when he returned to the sledge, there was neither whip, nor collar, nor harness: all had been stolen. He rushed to Tsigan, but he only swore at Alioshka from under the straw. Alioshka's legs gave way, his ears buzzed. He sat down on the edge of the sledge to cry, but immediately jumped up again and began to run from one passer-by to the other asking: "Have you seen the thief?" They only laughed. What was he to do? He ran across the square to find his master.

Volkov was sitting on his horse with one hand on his hip. There was a brass helmet on his head, and the plates of his armour were covered with rime all down the front. He was unrecognisable—he was an eagle! Behind him, on horseback, were his two serfs, like barrels in their quilted coats and with pikes across their shoulders. They realised themselves what sort of warriors they were: it was too silly! They were grinning.

Smearing the tears over his face and whining piteously, Alioshka began to tell of his misfortune.

"It's your own fault!" Volkov shouted. "Your father will flog you. And if he doesn't replace the harness, I'll have him flogged. Clear out, don't wriggle in front of the horse!"

Then the tall, lean clerk brandished his paper and called out Volkov's name. Volkov galloped forward followed by his serfs, who urged their horses on with bark-shod heels, and made for the Nikolsky gates. There, sitting at a table, was the most feared man in Moscow —Prince Fedor Yurievich Romodanovsky. He wore a tall fur cap and two fur coats—one covered in velvet and the other of sheepskin.

What was Alioshka to do now? Cap and harness had gone. He wandered about the square, sobbing quietly. Tirtov, bending down from his horse, called to him and caught him by the shoulder.

"Alioshka," he said—and his eyes were full of tears and his lips trembling—"Alioshka, for God's sake run to the Tver gates and ask for the house of Menshikov, the groom. When you go in, bow three times to the ground. Tell him: Mihail craves a boon from you. His horse has broken down. Say—he's ashamed. . . . Ask him to give me any kind of horse for the day—for the review. Will you remember? Tell him I'll repay the service. I'd kill a man now to get a horse. Beg him, beg him with tears!"

"I'll beg him, but what if he refuses?" Alioshka asked.

"I'll hammer you into the ground up to your shoulders!" and Tirtov rolled his eyes and blew out his nostrils.

Alioshka rushed away in hot haste in the direction which Tirtov had indicated.

Tirtov was freezing in his saddle. He had had no food all day. The sun was setting in a frosty haze and the snow was growing blue. Horses' hoofs crunched more harshly on the hard snow. Dusk was falling, and all over Moscow belfries and bell-towers sent out their summons to vespers. Volkov rode past at a walking pace, with gloomily bent head. Alioshka had not come back. And he never did come back.

6

The lamps burning in front of icons in the low, overheated room lit up the low vaulted ceiling with its dark paintings of birds of paradise and twining foilage. Tsar Fedor Alexeyevich * lay dying on a

* Step-brother of Peter the First.

wide bench under the dark-visaged icons; his wasted body was sunk deep in swansdown featherbeds.

His death had long been expected: he had scurvy and his legs were swelling. That morning he had not been able to stand at matins; he had sat down and had then fallen from his chair. They had rushed to him: his heart was hardly beating. They laid him beneath the icons. His legs, swollen with dropsy, were like logs, and his belly had began to swell. A foreign doctor was summoned. He drew off the water, and the Tsar became still; he was slowly dying. His eye-sockets grew dark and his nose sharpened. Once he whispered something, but no one could understand what he said. The foreigner bent over his bloodless lips: indistinctly, under his breath, Fedor Alexeyevich was reciting Latin verses. The doctor seemed to recognise in the Tsar's whispering a verse of Ovid's. Ovid on his death-bed? Undoubtedly the Tsar was unconscious.

Now even his breathing was inaudible. By the frosted window, in the round panes of which the moonlight glinted, Patriarch Joachim sat, stern and waxen on a folding Italian chair. In his black cassock and cowl bearing a white, eight-pointed cross, he sat bent and motionless, like a vision of death. The Tsaritsa, Marfa Matveyevna, stood by the wall, alone: she was looking through a mist of tears at her dying husband's narrow forehead and pinched nose which showed above the pile of featherbeds. She was only seventeen; she had been taken to the court for her beauty, though her family, the Apraxins, were poor. She had been Tsaritsa for only two months. Her dark-browed, foolish little face was swollen with crying. She sobbed quietly, like a child, and wrung her hands; she was afraid to wail aloud.

At the other end of the room, in the shadow under the vaults, a crowd of the Tsar's relatives stood whispering—sisters, uncles, aunts and boyars of his intimate circle: Ivan Maximovich Yazykov, a small, plump, kindly, unctuous man, extremely shrewd and well-versed in court tactics; Alexey Timofeyevich Lihachev, the lord chamberlain, a learned, ascetic and affable old man; and Prince Vasily Vasilyevich Golitsin, strikingly handsome with his small curly beard parted in the middle, turned-up moustache and hair cut short after the Polish fashion; he was wearing a Polish coat and soft leather boots with high heels, for he was only of medium height. His dark-blue eyes were shining with excitement. It was a decisive moment: the new Tsar had to be proclaimed. Was it to be Peter or Ivan? The son of Narishkina or the son of Miloslavskaya? Both were mere boys;

both had powerful relatives. Peter had a keen intelligence and was physically strong. Ivan was a feeble-minded weakling, you could do anything with him. What was preferable? Which to choose?

From time to time Golitsin turned sideways to the brass-plated door and, pressing his ear to it, listened. On the other side, in the throne room, the boyars were buzzing with excitement. The Narishkins and the Miloslavskys, each with their followers, had been there since the morning, without food or drink, sweating in their fur-lined coats. The room was crowded and they were hurling abuse at each other and recalling old offences: they felt that this day some of them would rise to the top and others be sent into exile.

"What a hubbub!" Golitsin muttered and, walking across to Yazykov, said to him very low in Polish: "Ivan Maximovich, wouldn't you ask the Patriarch which he favours?"

Yazykov, with his luxuriant curly hair and beard, raised his eyes and smiled brightly and sweetly; he was sweating with the heat and smelt of attar of roses.

"His Holiness, and we ourselves, are waiting to hear your opinion, Prince. But for our part, I think our minds are made up."

Lihachev joined them and said with a sigh, gently laying his white hand on his beard:

"In this momentous hour, Prince, we must not be divided. We have reasoned it out like this: it would be difficult to have Ivan for Tsar, and precarious—he's sickly. We need strength."

The Prince lowered his eyelashes and a smile touched the corners of his handsome mouth. He realised that it was dangerous to argue just then.

"So be it," he said, "let Peter be Tsar."

He raised his dark-blue eyes and suddenly they flickered and clouded with tenderness. He was looking at Sophia, the eldest of the Tsar's six sisters, who had just entered the room, not sailing in gracefully like a swan, as a girl should, but impetuously, the skirts of her bright coat—unbuttoned on her full bosom—flying and the red ribbons of her pointed headdress fluttering. Through the rouge and powder that covered her plain face, blotches were showing. She was broad-boned, stocky, robustly built, with a large head. Her rounded forehead, greenish eyes and firmly-set mouth seemed those of a man rather than a woman. Her eyes were fixed on Golitsin; it was clear that she understood what he had just been saying and what answer he had given.

Her nostrils quivered contemptuously. She turned towards the bed where the dying Tsar lay, threw up her hands, then clasped them and sank on to the carpet, with her forehead pressed against the bed.

The Patriarch raised his head and his dull eyes rested on the nape of Sophia's neck, on her hanging plaits. Everyone in the room became alert. The other five sisters of the Tsar began to cross themselves. The Patriarch rose and gazed long at the Tsar. Then he threw back his wide black sleeves and, having made a broad sign of the cross over him, began to recite the prayer for the dying.

Sophia clutched her head and gave a wild, piercing scream, then she began to lament in a low voice. Her sisters also screamed. The Tsaritsa flung herself face down on a bench. Her eldest brother, Fedor Apraxin, went to her and began to stroke her back; he was tall and stout and his long fur-lined coat reached to his heels. Yazykov ran across to the Patriarch, kissed his hand and drew him away. The Patriarch, Yazykov, Lihachev and Golitsin went quickly through the door to the throne room. The boyars crowded round them, waving their sleeves, pushing their beards forward, with shamelessly bulging eyes: "Well, how is it, Your Holiness?"

"The Tsar Fedor Alexeyevich has departed in peace. . . . Let us weep, boyars!"

But they did not listen to him. They were already hurrying to the doorway, pushing past each other. They rushed to the bed, fell on their knees, beat their foreheads on the carpet, then, rising, they kissed the dead man's waxen hands, already folded. The air was so thick that the lamps began to flicker and go out. Sophia was led away. Golitsin disappeared. Two other Golitsins, the brothers Peter and Boris Alexeyevich, approached Yazykov, and, with them, the dark, beetle-browed, formidable looking Prince Yakov Dolgoruky and his brothers, Luke, Boris and Grigory.

"We have coats of mail under our clothes," said Yakov Dolgoruky. "And knives. Well, shall we proclaim Peter?"

"Go out on to the porch, to the people. The Patriarch will come out there and then we'll proclaim him. And if they begin to shout 'Ivan', use your knives on the rogues!"

An hour later the Patriarch came out on to the Red Porch in front of which an enormous crowd had gathered: streltsi, lesser gentry, crown servants, merchants and townsmen. He blessed the crowd and then asked: "Which of the two princes is to be Tsar?"

Bonfires were burning. The moon was setting beyond the Moskva river and its icy light gleamed on the cupolas. Voices from the crowd shouted:

"We want Peter Alexeyevich. . . . !"
Then a hoarse voice:
"We want Ivan to be Tsar. . . . !"
There was a rush towards the man who had said this and his voice was not raised again. The shouts of "Peter! Peter!" grew louder and louder.

7

When Alioshka entered Menshikov's courtyard two chained dogs rushed at him, nearly choking with rage. A little girl with sores on her lips and a coat thrown over her head told him to go up the ice-covered steps to the room at the top; then, with a silly giggle, she slipped into the room under the steps where a wood fire burning in the stove shone in the darkness.

As he mounted the steps, Alioshka listened to someone upstairs screaming frantically. "Well," he thought, "I shan't get out of here alive. . . ." He grasped the wooden peg tied to the latch with string and, with much effort, pulled open the warped door. The warmth of a well-heated room and the smell of radish and vodka met his nostrils. Two men were seated at a spread table under the icons: a priest with his hair in a small plait and a great red, fan-shaped beard, and a short, pockmarked man with a sharp nose.

"Drive wisdom into him through the back door!" they cried, clinking their drinking-cups.

A third man, of heavy build, in an unbelted crimson tunic, held someone fast between his knees and was lashing his bare buttocks with a leather strap. The thin buttocks, covered with weals, wriggled and squirmed. "Oh! Oh!" screamed shrilly the one who was being flogged.

Alioshka was struck numb with horror.

The pockmarked man winked at him with his lashless eyes. The priest opened his great mouth wide and bellowed:

"Here's another boy, beat him too while you're about it!"

Alioshka planted his feet squarely and stretched out his neck. "This is the end of me," he thought. The heavily-built man turned round. From between his legs, a boy, with round, pale-blue eyes, slipped out holding up his trousers. He dashed to the door and disappeared. Then Alioshka did what he had been told to do: he dropped down on his knees and struck the ground three times with his forehead. The heavily-built man picked him up by the collar and held him close to his sweating, copper-coloured face, enveloping him in his hot alcoholic breath.

"What have you come for? To steal? To spy? To rummage round the yards?"

Alioshka, with chattering teeth, began to tell him about Tirtov. The veins swelled on the copper-coloured face: the man did not understand anything. "What Tirtov? What horse? So you've come for a horse, eh? A horse-thief, are you?" Alioshka burst into tears, called on God as his witness and crossed himself with three fingers.* At this the copper-faced man seized Alioshka by the hair and, stamping across the room, dragged him to the door, kicked it open and flung him down the frozen stairs. "Drive the thief from the yard!" he yelled, swaying. "At him, dogs!"

Hunching up his shoulders in the door like a bull Danila Menshikov went back to the table. He snorted, filled the drinking cups and, with his fingers, helped himself to some radish.

"You, priest, you've read the scriptures, you ought to know," he boomed. "My son is completely out of hand. He's taken to thieving, the whore's son. What am I to do, kill him? What do the scriptures say. Eh?"

Filka, the priest, replied solemnly:

"According to the scriptures it is thus: 'Chastise thy son from his youth, and he will solace thy old age. Weary not of beating him with rods: he will not die, but prosper. Multiply his scars, and his soul will be saved from perdition'."

"Amen!" the man with the sharp nose sighed.

"Wait till I get my breath—I'll call him back," said Danila. "Oh, things are bad, my lads. Each year's worse than the last. Children are getting out of hand, there's no more of the old piety. The Tsar hasn't paid our wages for two years. There's nothing to eat. The streltsi are threatening to set fire to Moscow on all four sides. There's great unrest among the people. Soon there'll be an end of us!"

The pockmarked, sharp-nosed scripture-reader, Foma Podshchipayev, said:

"The Nikonites † have broken the old faith, and by that faith"—he raised a finger—"the country lived. There is no new faith. The

---

* According to the rites of the established Orthodox Church, whereas the Old Believers used only two fingers.

† Term used by the Old Believers to designate those who accepted the reforms of Patriarch Nikon.

children are born in sin; even if you beat them to death, what of it? There's no soul in them. They are the children of this age. . . . . Nikonites. A flock without a shepherd, a prey for the devil. Archpriest Avvakum * wrote: 'You, Nikonite, strive to lead astray Christ's followers and deliver them, along with yourself, to your father, the devil.' To the devil!" He raised his finger again. "And further: 'Who are you, you Nikonite? You are dirt, you stink, you are a filthy cur'."

"Curs!" Danila exclaimed, thumping the table.

"The Nikonite priests and archpriests go about in silken cassocks and their cheeks are bursting with fat, the accursed dogs!" the priest Filka joined in.

Foma waited until they had finished cursing and went on:

"And about this, too, Archpriest Avvakum has written: 'My friend Ilarion, Archbishop of Riazan! Remember how Melchisedek lived in the thickets of Mount Tabor. He ate the shoots of trees and for drink licked the dew from the leaves. He was a true priest: he sought not after Rhenish and sweet wines, or vodka and strained wines, or beer with cardamoms. My friend Ilarion, Archbishop of Riazan! Observe how Melchisedek lived. He did not seek pleasure riding in carriages drawn by fine horses. And he was of royal blood. But who are you, priestling? Yet you take your seat in your carriage, swelling like a bladder on the water. You loll on cushions, your hair combed like a girl's, and you drive along exhibiting your face in the public square to win the love of faithless nuns. Oh, poor fellow! It is clear that Satan has blinded you. And you have never seen and do not know the meaning of the spiritual life!' "

The priest Filka closed his eyes and his cheeks shook with laughter. Danila poured out more liquor. They drank.

"The streltsi are already tearing up the Nikonite books and scattering them to the winds," he said. "May God grant that the streltsi rise for the defence of the old faith."

He turned round. The dogs began to bark. The steps of the porch creaked. Someone outside the door recited the customary prayer to Jesus. The three men in the room answered: "Amen!" Menshikov's brother-in-law, Ovsey Rzhov, a tall fellow in the streltsi, entered the room and crossed himself before the icons. He flung his hair back with a jerk of his head.

"Carousing!" he said quietly. "And don't you know what's going on at the top? The Tsar is dead. The Narishkins and the Dolgorukys

* Leader of the Old Believers.

have proclaimed Peter. That's a calamity no one expected. Now we shall all be in bondage to the boyars and the Nikonites."

8

Alioshka rolled down the steps like a tumbler-pigeon and fell into a snowdrift. The yellow-fanged dogs rushed at him. He pulled in his head and shut his eyes. But they did not tear him to pieces. What a miracle—God had saved him! The dogs slunk away growling. Someone was stooping over Alioshka and poking his head with a finger.

"I say, who are you?"

Alioshka uncovered one eye. The dogs, close at hand, began to growl again. The boy who had just been flogged was squatting down on his heels close to him.

"What's your name?" he asked.

"Alioshka."

"Whom d'you belong to?"

"We're Brovkins, peasant people."

The boy was examining Alioshka like a dog, leaning his head from side to side. The moon shining over the roof of a shed lit up his face and his wide eyes. Oh, he must be a bright lad!

"Let's go and warm up," he said. "If you don't come, just see what I'll do! Do you want to fight?"

"No," Alioshka answered, quickly lying down again. Once more they gazed at each other.

"Let me go," Alioshka pleaded. "Don't . . . I haven't done anything to you. I'll go away."

"But where will you go?"

"I don't know myself. They've threatened to hammer me into the ground up to my shoulders. And at home they'll kill me."

"Does your father beat you?"

"Father sold me for life—he doesn't beat me now. The servants beat me, of course. But when I lived at home certainly I was thrashed."

"What are you then, a runaway?"

"Not yet. And you? What's your name?"

"Alexander. We're Menshikovs. My father flogs me twice, sometimes three times a day. I've only bones left on my backside—all the flesh has been thrashed away."

"Oh, you poor fellow!"

"Come on, let's go and get warm."

"All right."

The boys ran into the lower room where Alioshka had seen the fire in the stove. It was warm and dry in there and there was a smell of new bread. A tallow candle was burning in a spiral iron candlestick. Cockroaches were crawling over the smoke-blackened beams of the wall. It would be nice to stay here for ever!

"Vasenka, don't tell father," Alexander said hurriedly to a little woman, the cook. "Take your shoes off, Alioshka." He himself took off his felt boots and both boys clambered up on to the stove which filled half the room. There, in the darkness, Alioshka saw two eyes staring at him without blinking; they belonged to the little girl who had opened the gate to him. She had crept to the farthest end, behind the chimney.

"Let's talk," Alexander whispered. "My mother is dead. Father gets drunk every day. He wants to marry again. I'm afraid of a stepmother. They beat me today, but then they'll tear my heart out."

"They will," Alioshka agreed.

The girl behind the chimney sniffed.

"That's just what I say. The other day I saw a gipsy camp at the Serpuhov gates. They had bears and they were playing pipes, dancing and singing. They wanted me to stay with them. Let's go away with the gipsies and wander about, eh?"

"We'd starve with the gipsies." Alioshka said.

"Or let's hire ourselves out to some merchants on some job or other. And in the summer we'll go away. We might catch a bear-cub in the forest. I know a fellow who catches them. He'll show us how. You'll lead the bear, and I'll sing and dance. I know all the songs. And there's no one in Moscow dances with more dash than I do."

The girl behind the chimney began to sniff more often. Alexander poked her in the ribs.

"Be quiet, will you! I say, we'll take her with us too, shall we?"

"Women are always a nuisance."

"We'll take her in the summer to gather mushrooms. She's a fool all right, but she's clever at finding mushrooms. We'll have some cabbage soup now. Then they'll call me upstairs to recite prayers, then they'll thrash me. Then I'll come back, we'll go to sleep, and at daybreak we'll run away to Kitay-gorod, get across the river and have a look round. I know some people there. I would have run away long ago, but I had no one to come with me."

"It would be a good thing to find a merchant who'd hire us to sell pies," Alioshka said.

The porch door slammed. The guests were leaving and the stairs creaked under their feet. Menshikov's threatening voice summoned Alexander upstairs.

9

On the Varvarka stood a low house with six windows and decorated with carved ridges and cocks: a government tavern. Over the gateway was a sheep's skull. The gates were wide open for anyone who cared to enter. Drunken men were lying in the yard on heaps of dung and snow yellow with urine. Some had battered and bloody faces; others had had their caps or boots stolen from them. Many harnessed sledges—peasants' sledges or merchants', these with high painted backs—stood at the gates or in the yard.

Inside the house the stern black-browed tapster stood behind the bar. Bottles and pewter tankards filled a shelf. In the corner lamps burned before blackened icons. Against the walls were benches and a long table. Another room—the parlour for the merchants—was behind a partition. If any rogue or drunken townsman put his nose in there the tapster would frown and call him back and, if he did not listen to reason, would seize him by the seat of his trousers and fling him headlong out of the tavern.

There, in the second room, the merchants talked sedately over their ginger ale or hot mead. They bargained, made deals and clinched agreements by slapping palm on palm. They discussed the state of business: in those days it was a matter of much perplexity.

In the front room near the counter, there was constant uproar, shouting and cursing. They could drink and enjoy themselves as long as they paid. The treasury was strict. If a man had no money, then he must give up his coat. And if he had drunk away everything, the tapster would wink at the government clerk, who would seat himself at the end of the table, a quill behind his ear and an inkhorn round his neck, and begin to write. Oh, beware, you poor sot! That all-wise clerk will write out a serf's deed for you: though you came into the Tsar's tavern a free man, you may go out a destitute serf.

"It's become easier to drink nowadays," the tapster said, pouring greenish vodka into a pewter mug. "A friend, or a relative, or your wife, comes to fetch you nowadays before you have drunk your soul away. We let such folk go; we don't try to take the last thing from them. Let them go in peace. But in the days of the late Tsar Alexey Mihaylovich it was different. A man might come to fetch his drunken friend away before he had spent his last copper. It would be: Stop! This will be a loss to the treasury. The treasury wants this last copper too. The guard would be called in; they'd take the fellow and drag him to the Criminal Office. And there, after he'd been tried, they'd cut off his left hand and right foot and throw him out on to the ice. . . . Drink up, lads, drink up! There's nothing to fear, we don't chop off hands and feet nowadays."

10

That day the people were climbing over each other outside the tavern and peeping in at the windows. The yard and the porch were crowded. Streltes coats—red, green, purple—were much in evidence. There was jostling and pushing. "What's the matter? Who's been killed? What for?" There, inside the tavern, in the merchants' room, streltsi and merchants stood tightly packed. The air was thick and moisture streamed down the windows. The streltsi had brought in a half-dead man; he lay on the floor, and his groans were heartrending. His clothes were torn to rags, but he looked well-fed. His grey hair was matted with blood and his nose and cheeks were battered.

"The same will be happening to you soon," shouted the streltsi, pointing at the man.

"You're asleep? But they're wide awake in the Foreign Quarter."

"Why should the foreigners beat our people like this, lads?"

"It's a good thing we were passing, we interfered. They'd have beaten him to death."

"Did such things happen under the late Tsar? Did they let the accursed foreigners molest us?"

Ovsey Rzhov, of the Pizhov streltes regiment, restrained his comrades and said to the merchants, bowing low:

"Honourable sirs and eminent merchants, we have come to you because of our poverty. We and our wives and little children are starving. We are beggared. For two years we've had no pay. Our officers have worn us to the bone working on their land. How are we to live? They won't let us trade in the town, and in the suburbs it's crowded with traders. The foreigners have got everything into their hands. Today they've bought up the flax before it's cut and the thread before it's spun. They buy up all the hides and tan them themselves, the devils, in the Foreigners' Quarter. The women won't buy shoes from our suburbs at any price—they ask for foreign ones. Life has become impossible. And if you don't come to our aid, you too, merchants, will be ruined. The Narishkins control the Tsar's treasury now—they're greedy. You can expect such tolls and taxes now that you'll have to give up your last. And still worse, the boyar Matveyev is coming back to Moscow from exile. His heart is bursting with rage. He'll swallow the whole of Moscow."

The man's groans were terrible. And terrible and obscure were the words Ovsey had spoken. The merchants exchanged glances. They were not inclined to believe that the foreigners had beaten this petty tradesman. It was a mysterious affair. Still, what the streltsi were saying was true. Life was hard now; every year it was becoming harder, poorer, less secure. Every ukase issued—"The Tsar has decreed, and the boyars have assented . . ."—brought new calamity: pay, pour your money into the bottomless well. To whom could they turn, who would protect them? The great boyars? All these ever did was to extort money for the treasury—and they did not care how this money was got. Take off your last shirt and give it to them. It was like having the enemy in Moscow.

A stout merchant, waggling his fingers covered with silver rings, pushed his way into the group surrounding the wounded man and said:

"We, that is the Vorobyevs, took raw silk to the Archangel fair. And they, the foreigners that is, agreed among themselves not to buy any of that silk, not even a kopek's worth. And their headman, that is the German Wolff, shouted at us: 'We'll see to it that you Moscow merchants are dragged through the courts for debt and in future force them—that is us, Moscow merchants—to trade only in birch-bark shoes'."

A loud murmur ran round the room.

"What did we tell you?" the streltsi said. "And soon there won't be even birch-bark shoes left!" A young merchant, Bogdan Zhigulin, sprang forward, tossing his curly hair.

"I've come from the Pomorye," he said briskly. "I went for blubber. I came back as I set out—with empty carts. Foreigners, Maxelin and Bierkopf, have bought up all the blubber from the Pomors for ten years ahead. And all the Pomors are up to their ears in debt to them. The foreigners give them a quarter of the right price, and forbid them to sell to anyone else. And the Pomors are beggared, and now they no longer go to sea but have scattered to other parts. We Russians can't even go to the North now."

The streltsi again raised a shout, pulling up their sleeves. Ovsey laid his hand on his sword, rattled it and grinned:

"Give us time to deal with our commanders, and then we'll tackle the boyars. We'll sound the tocsin through Moscow. . . . All the suburbs are with us. But you, merchants, must support us. Well, lads, pick him up, and come on."

The streltsi lifted up the wounded man, who howled, shaking his head: "Oh, they've ki-i-i-lled me!" and dragged him out of the house, pushing through the crowd towards the Red Square, to show him to others.

The merchants remained in the room. Oh, how dark, how dangerous things were! If they allied themselves with the streltsi—well, the streltsi were a reckless lot, they had nothing to lose. And if they didn't, all the same the boyars would swallow them.

11

That evening, after vespers, Alexander was so mercilessly flogged that he could hardly crawl down into the room below. He covered himself up, did not utter a word and ground his teeth. Alioshka brought porridge and milk to him on the stove. He was very sorry for him: "Oh, what have they done to you, poor fellow. . . . !"

For twenty-four hours Alexander lay in the hottest place by the chimney. Then he recovered and began to talk:

"A father like that should be broken on the wheel, the bloodthirsty snake! Alioshka, filch some oil from behind the icons, I'll oil my behind, it'll heal by the morning. Then we'll go. I won't come back, I'd rather die in a ditch."

The storm raged all night outside the log walls. Ghostly voices howled in the chimney. The cook's little girl cried softly. Alioshka dreamed of his mother: she stood surrounded by smoke in the middle of the hut, weeping with her eyes wide open and raising her hands to her head and moaning. Alioshka was racked with misery in his sleep.

Alexander roused him at the break of dawn. "You've slept enough, get up!" Scratching their bodies, they shod themselves with particular care. They found half a loaf of bread and took it. Whistling to the dogs they dragged aside the board under the gate and crawled out of the yard. The morning was quiet and misty. It was damp. Icicles fell with a loud rustle. The winding, log-paved streets were dark. Beyond the wooden town, quite close, the dawn was spreading in misty blood-red streaks.

Sluggish watchmen were clearing away the barriers put up at night in the streets as a protection against tramps and robbers. Beggars, cripples and idiots quarrelled as they shuffled along hastening to take up the best positions on the church-porches. Along the Vozdvizhenka lowing cattle were being driven down the dung-strewn road to the river Neglinnaya to be watered.

The boys followed the cattle as far as the round tower of the Borovitsky gate. A German musketeer in a sheepskin coat was dozing by the iron cannons. "Walk carefully here, the Tsar's not far," Alexander said. Passing along the steep bank of the Neglinnaya, over heaps of cinders and rubbish, they reached the Iversky bridge and crossed it. The day had broken. Grey clouds trailed over the city. A deep moat ran along the walls of the Kremlin. Here and there rotten piles stuck out: remains of water-mills recently demolished. Gallows stood on the edge of the moat, two posts with a cross-beam. A tall man in birch-bark shoes, with his elbows tied back, was dangling from one. His sunken face had been pecked by birds.

"Here are two more," Alexander said. At the bottom of the moat lay two corpses half covered with snow. "They're robbers; that's how they deal with them."

The whole square was empty, right across to the white church of St. Basil with its blue plinth and blue cupolas. A sledge track wound across the square to the Spassky * gates. Above them, over the straddling golden eagle, a huge flock of crows was circling, cawing excitedly, as in spring. The hands on the black clock reached eight, and a carillon rang out a foreign tune. Alioshka pulled off his cap and crossed himself at the tower. It felt eerie here.

"Come on, Alexander, or they'll see us . . ."

"Nothing to be afraid of when you're with me, you fool."

They started to cross the square. On the opposite side wooden booths, shops and tents were huddled together. The shopkeepers were already taking the padlocks off the doors and hanging out their wares on poles. In the bakers' row chimneys were smoking and there was a smell of baking pies. People were coming in from all the side streets.

* Main gates of the Kremlin.

Alexander poked his nose into everything, regardless of blows and curses. He pushed through the crowd to the shops, accosted the shopkeepers, asked the price of things and cracked jokes. Alioshka, open-mouthed, could barely keep up with him. Seeing a fat woman in a cloth coat and fox-fur cap over her head-shawl, Alexander shuffled up to her, dragging one leg, shaking and stammering: "F-f-for God's sake, help a p-p-poor orphan, lady, I'm starving." The merchant's widow raised her skirt and taking two half-kopeks from a purse that hung low under her waist gave them to him and crossed herself gravely. The two boys ran off to buy pies and to drink hot mead.

"I tell you, you'll be all right with me," Alexander said.

The crowd was steadily growing thicker. Some came to have a look at people, and listen to what was being said; others to show off new finery; and yet others to steal what they could. In an alley, where the snow was covered with cut hair as with a felt mat, barbers were clicking their scissors and trying to attract customers. Some were already having their hair cut, seated on billets set upright, with earthenware pots over their heads. The tumult was greatest in the thread row. Here women, shouting as if at a fire, were buying and selling thread, needles, buttons: all the accessories of sewing. Alioshka, afraid of getting lost, kept tight hold of Alexander's belt.

When they got into the open square again someone ran past, people shouted something. A vast crowd was coming up from the Varvarka, yelling and whistling ear-piercingly. Streltsi were carrying a badly beaten man.

"Fellow Christians," they said tearfully to all around them. "See what they've done to this merchant."

The man was placed on someone's birch-bark sledge and Ovsey climbed up on it and began to say the same things all over again: how the foreigners, in their spite, had half-killed this respectable merchant and how the higher boyars would soon farm out all Moscow to foreigners.

The boys pushed through to the sledge. Alioshka, squatting beside the wounded man, recognised him at once. It was the fat pie-man with small eyes and rabbit-skin cap who had sold him the two baked pies the day before in the Lubianka. He smelt strongly of vodka. He was tired of groaning. Lying on his side, his face buried in the straw, he kept saying in a low voice:

"O-oh. . . . For Christ's sake, let me go. . . ."

Ovsey, crossing himself, bowed to the churches and to the people. The streltsi, dispersed among the crowd, were whispering into people's ears. Tempers were rising. Suddenly there was a shout:

"Horsemen! Horsemen!"

Two men were galloping along the sledge track from the Spassky gates. The one in front wore a deep red strelets coat and his cap was pushed to the side of his head. His curved sword, studded with diamonds, flapped against the velvet saddle-cloth. Without slackening speed he dropped his reins and drove into the crowd. Frightened hands seized the horse's bridle. Its rider turned his head rapidly this way and that, baring his yellow teeth; he had a broad forehead, deep-set eyes and a strong small beard. This was Tararuy, as he had been nicknamed in Moscow: Prince Ivan Andreyevich Hovansky, a military leader, a boyar of ancient lineage and a sworn enemy of the low-born Narishkins. Seeing him in their uniform the streltsi cried:

"He's with us, he's with us, Ivan Andreyevich!" and rushed towards him.

The second horseman, who rode up more slowly, was Prince Vasily Golitsin. Patting his horse's neck he asked:

"Rioting, Christians? Who has offended you and how? Speak up, speak up! Our hearts ache for the people day and night. As it is, the Tsar saw you from above and was alarmed—he's very young —and sent us to enquire."

The crowd gazed open-mouthed at his brocaded coat; half of Moscow could be bought for the price of it. They gazed at the jewelled rings on his hand patting the horse; fire flashed from those rings. The people backed away and made no answer. Golitsin rode forward with a smile and pulled up stirrup to stirrup with Hovansky.

"Give us our commanders and we'll judge them ourselves: head downwards from the belfry!" the streltsi shouted to him. "What are the boyars at the top thinking about? Why have they saddled us with a boy for Tsar, with a Narishkin mongrel?"

Hovansky was smoothing his greying moustache with the edge of his leather gauntlet. He raised his hand. All became quiet.

"Streltsi!" He rose slightly in his saddle and his face grew crimson from the effort as his throaty voice carried to the farthest edge of the crowd. "Streltsi! Now you see for yourselves under what an unbearable yoke the boyars are holding you. Now they've chosen God knows what kind of Tsar. It wasn't I who proclaimed him. And you will see: it's not only money you won't get, but even the means to make a living. And you'll work like slaves. And your children will pass into eternal bondage to the Narishkins. Worse than that. . . . They will hand both us and you over to the foreigners. They will destroy Moscow and uproot the Orthodox faith. Ah, there used to be Russian might, but where is it?"

At this the whole crowd gave such a terrible cry that Alioshka was frightened: "Now they'll trample us to death." Alexander, jumping from one sledge to another, put two fingers in his mouth and whistled. And all one could hear was Tararuy, straining every nerve, shouting:

"Streltsi! Cross the river to your regiments; we'll talk there."

12

Only Alioshka and Alexander and unharnessed sledges remained in the square. The wounded man lifted himself up, looked round through his swollen slits of eyes and blew his nose at great length.

"Uncle," Alexander said to him with a wink at Alioshka, "we'll take you home, we're sorry for you."

The man was still dazed. The boys led him away, muttering and stumbling. Now and then he would shout: "Stop!" push the boys away and threaten someone, stamping his felt boots. They went towards the Serpulhovsky gates, on the other side of the river. On the way they learnt that his name was Fedor Zayats. His home on the outskirts was not large; in the kitchen-garden there was one tree with rooks' nests, but the gates and the house were new.

"Here they are, my pies and rolls," Zayats said joyfully when he caught sight of his house. "Here they are, my honeyed beauties, helping me out."

A pockmarked one-eyed woman opened the wicket-gate for them. Zayats pushed past her and the two boys slipped in behind him.

The man turned on them and said angrily: "Where are you going? What do you want?" but suddenly changed his mind and, with a gesture of indifference, went into the house. There he sat down on a bench covered with a new bast mat and began to examine his clothes; they were torn to tatters. He wagged his head dolefully and began to weep.

"They as good as killed me," he said to the one-eyed woman. "I don't remember who beat me and why. Give me some clean clothes."

Then he suddenly banged the bench with his fists and yelled: "Heat up the bath, I tell you, you one-eyed bitch!"

The woman sniffed and went out. The boys huddled against the stove which took up half the room. Zayats began to talk:

"You've saved me, boys. Now ask me for anything you like. My body is bruised all over, I've not a whole rib left. How can I take my tray and go selling pies now? Oh, dear me. . . . ! And business doesn't wait."

Alexander again winked at Alioshka. He said:

"We don't want any reward, only let us stay here for the night."

When Zayats crawled off to the bath-house, the two boys climbed up on to the stove.

"Tomorrow we'll go and sell pies in his place," Alexander whispered. "I tell you, once you're with me, you're all right."

At dawn the one-eyed woman started baking dough-buns, turnovers, biscuits and pies: meatless ones filled with peas, turnips, salted mushrooms for those who fasted, and others with hare's meat, meat or noodles. Zayats lay moaning on his bench, covered with a sheepskin coat; he could not stir a limb. Alexander swept the floor, ran out to fetch firewood and water from the yard, carried out the ashes and slops and sent Alioshka to water Zayats' livestock. He worked with lightning speed and accompanied all he did with a joke.

"A smart lad," Zayats moaned. "Oh, I'd send you to the market to sell pies, but you're sure to make off with the money. You'd steal it, you're much too smart."

At this Alexander began to kiss the cross he wore round his neck, swearing he would not steal the money. He took down from the wall an icon representing forty saints and kissed that too. Willynilly Zayats believed him. The woman packed two hundred pies into trays and covered them with an old cloth. The boys tied on aprons, stuck their leather mittens in their belts, picked up the trays and went out.

"Here are pies, honey-cakes, a quarter kopek the pair, hot from the oven!" Alexander cried in a shrill voice, eying the passers-by. "Hurry, buy them up!"

Seeing a group of streltsi, he called out in a sing-song voice skipping and hopping: "Here, come and buy them: pies fit for Tsars, for boyars! They bought some in the Kremlin, but I caught it in the neck! The Narishkins ate a cake, but it gave them stomach-ache!"

The streltsi laughed, and there was a scramble for the pies.

Alioshka too joined in the patter. Before they reached the river they had to turn back for fresh supplies.

"Boys, God sent you to me!" Zayats exclaimed in wonder.

13

For three weeks Tirtov knocked about Moscow; he had no work and no money. That day in Lubiansky Square the clerks had made fun of him. They gave him neither land nor serfs. Prince Romodanovsky abused him and shamed him and ordered him to come back next year, but this time without cheating, on a good horse.

He left the square and went to a tavern for the night. On the way he met his elder brother who upbraided him for the dishonour and took away his gelding, but he did not bethink him to take Tirtov's sword and their grandfather's belt of striped silk with silver medallions. That same night in the tavern Tirtov, heated by vodka with garlic, pawned both sword and belt to the tapster.

Two sharp Moscow fellows attached themselves to Tirtov: one said he was a merchant's son and the other called himself a clerk, though in truth they were simply tavern riff-raff. They made much of Tirtov, kissed him on the lips and promised to give him a good time. Tirtov spent a week roistering in their company. They took him to a cellar to some Greek to smoke tobacco through a cow's horn filled with water: there they smoked themselves into a trance seeing weird visions and feeling a delicious horror.

They took him to the government baths—a steam bath for the populace on the Moskva river—not so much to bathe as to look on and laugh when, out of the clouds of steam, naked women came darting into the general anteroom, covering themselves up with their bath-brooms. This was to Tirtov no less of a drug than the tobacco.

They tried to persuade him to visit a procuress. But Tirtov was still young enough to fear forbidden fruit. He remembered how his father used to snuff the candle with his fingers after vespers, and open an old leather-bound book with brass clasps, turn over the dog-eared pages and read about women:

"What is a woman? A net of temptations for man. Fair of face, with shining eyes and dancing feet, her sting is terrible, and sends a burning flame through the limbs of man. What is a woman? A slumbering serpent, a disease, a vessel of Satan, a wanton fury, a hellish temptation, the invention of the devil!"

How could he help being afraid? One day they took him to a tavern near the Pokrovsky gates. They had barely sat down when, from behind a bast curtain, a girl skipped out. She was short, her hair was loose, her eyebrows painted black from the bridge of her nose to her temples, her eyes were round and her ears were long, and her cheeks rubbed with beetroot until they were nearly blue. She flung off the patchwork quilt that covered her and, naked, white, fat, began to dance near Tirtov, beckoning him first with one arm then with the other, both covered with copper rings and jingling bracelets.

She seemed to him a she-devil, so horrible, so terrifying was her nakedness. Her breath smelt of wine and her body of hot sweat. Tirtov sprang up, his scalp crawling; he shouted wildly and raised his arm, but did not strike her; he rushed out of the room beside himself.

The yellow spring sunset was fading at the end of the quiet street. The air was intoxicating. Thin ice crackled underfoot. Beyond the blue-grey fortress tower with its small iron flag, from behind a pointed roof, the copper-red disc of the moon climbed, shining into Tirtov's face. He was filled with fear. His teeth chattered, and there was a cold feeling in his chest. The door of the tavern creaked and, like a white shadow, the girl appeared in a lascivious pose on the porch.

"What are you afraid of, dear? Come back!"

Tirtov rushed blindly away.

His money soon came to an end and his companions left him. Filled with regrets for what he had eaten and drunk, for what he had seen and left untouched, he wandered from place to place. He could not bear the thought of going back to his father in the country.

At last he remembered Stepan Odoyevsky, his godfather's son, a man of his own age. He went to his house. The servants gave him a cold welcome; they all looked like brigands. One of them tore off Tirtov's cap—"How dare you mount the porch in your cap?"—but they let him in. In the large warm anteroom the benches were covered with skins of wild beasts; here he was met by a youth as exquisite as a honey-cake, in a satin shirt and fancy morocco boots. Looking insolently into Tirtov's eyes the youth asked in an ingratiating voice:

"What is your business with the boyar?"

"Tell him his friend, Mishka Tirtov, has a request to make to him."

"I'll tell him," the youth drawled, and languidly went away, tossing his silken curls. Tirtov had to wait: poor men are not proud. At last the youth reappeared and beckoned him to follow.

Tirtov entered the audience room. Seized with shyness he crossed himself earnestly, turning towards the corner where icons hung draped with brocade edged with gold lace. He glanced round: so that was how the rich lived! What elegant furnishings! Walls hung with stamped velvet; on the floor rugs and carpets of all hues; velvet covers on the benches; pearl-embroidered coverlets on the window-sills; chests and coffers, covered with silk and velvet, ranged along the walls. Any one of these covers would make a coat or robe such as he had never dreamed of. Opposite the windows was a wooden clock-tower surmounted by a brass elephant.

"Ah, Mishka, I'm glad to see you," Stepan Odoyevsky greeted him, standing in the doorway.

Tirtov went up to him and bowed, touching the ground with his finger-tips. Stepan nodded in reply. But nevertheless he treated him as a noble's son, not as a serf; he gave him his moist hand to shake.

"Sit down, be my guest."

Stepan sat down toying with his cane. Tirtov also seated himself. A skull-cap embroidered with precious stones covered Stepan's shaven head. His forehead was barrel-shaped, devoid of eyebrows, and his eyelids were red, his nose was crooked and his small chin sparsely sown with down. Tirtov thought to himself: "You could snap this shrimp in two with your fingers—a fellow like that to have such wealth!" Humbly, as becomes a poor man, he began to tell Stepan of his misadventures, of the poverty which was ruining his young life.

"Stepan Semenich, for God's sake, tell me, your slave, where to lay my head. It's enough to make one go into a monastery. . . . Or even take to the highroad with a bludgeon. . . ." At these words Stepan jerked his head back to the wall and his bulging eyes grew glassy. But Tirtov's expression did not change, as though he had mentioned the bludgeon casually, out of foolishness. "Stepan Semenich," he went on, "I can't bear this damned poverty any longer."

A silence fell. Tirtov sighed softly, as politeness demanded. Stepan, with a wicked smile, traced the outline of a winged beast on the carpet with the end of his cane.

"What can I advise, Mishka? There are many ways for clever people; and for the fools there's the beggar's bag and prison. Take Volodka Chemodanov, for example; he took two villages away from his neighbour by a lawsuit. Leonty Pustoroslev had a lawsuit and got a fine manor in Moscow from the Chizhovs recently."

"I've heard of it; I was amazed. But how can one start such a lawsuit and win it? It's not easy!"

"Find a village you'd like and then inform against the owner. That's how everybody does it."

"How do you mean, inform?"

"Like this: buy a kopek's worth of paper and ink from the public scribe and write a denunciation."

"But what accusation to make? Denounce what?"

"You're young, Mishka, you haven't been weaned yet. Now Leonty Pustoroslev went to Chizhov's house to a party, but he drank less than he listened and, when necessary, he chimed in. The old Chizhov blurted out at table: 'May God grant health to the great Tsar Fedor Alexeyevich, for people say he will not last till Easter. They say that last night in the Kremlin a hen crowed like a cock.' Pustoroslev seized the opportunity. He jumped to his feet and cried: 'I claim the Tsar's word!' * All the guests, together with their host, were bundled off to the Office of Secret Affairs. Pustoroslev declared that Chizhov had uttered slanderous words against the Tsar. They tied Chizhov's arms and sent him to the rack. And they worked up a whole case about the hen that had crowed like a cock. For loyal service Pustoroslev got Chizhov's manor, while Chizhov himself was sent to Siberia for ever. That's how clever people do." Stepan raised his eyes, unwinking, like a fish's, and looked at Tirtov. "Volodka Chemodanov worked it out even more simply. He complained that they had tried to kill him in his neighbour's courtyard and promised the clerks a third part of the loot. The neighbour was glad to part with his last property to avoid a lawsuit."

Having turned it over in his mind, Tirtov said, twisting his cap:

"I have no experience in legal matters, Stepan Semenich."

"If you had, I shouldn't be teaching you."

Stepan gave such a cruel laugh that Tirtov recoiled, his eyes fixed on Stepan's small, decayed teeth.

"One needs experience to go to the law-courts," Stepan went on. "Or else you may find yourself on the rack. It comes to this, Mishka: don't tackle the strong, but beat down the weak. Now I notice that you came to me without any fear."

"What do you mean, Stepan Semenich? How could I be without fear?"

* Formula imputing high treason, lèse-majesté, etc.

"Hold your tongue! One must learn to keep silent. I am talking to you like a friend, but do you know what happens to others? I may feel bored—I clap my hands—serfs rush in. 'Let me have some fun, my faithful servants.' They'd take you by your white hands and drag you out into the courtyard, to play with you as a cat plays with a mouse." Again he laughed with his mouth only, while his eyes remained lifeless. "Don't be alarmed: I've done nothing but joke since this morning."

Tirtov rose cautiously, meaning to bow himself out. Stepan touched him with the end of his cane and made him sit down again.

"Forgive me, Stepan Semenich, if I have said anything indiscreet out of foolishness."

"You haven't said anything indiscreet, but you are bold above your rank, above your station, above your birth," Stepan said coldly and haughtily. "Well, God will forgive you. But next time wait for me in the antechamber, and when they call you to come here, refuse to enter. When I ask you to sit down, remain standing. And when you bow to me, don't merely bow low, but go down on your knees."

Tirtov's nostrils quivered, but he kept himself under control and began thanking Stepan humbly for his advice. Stepan yawned and made the sign of the cross over his mouth.

"I must do something for you in your poverty. I have only one doubt: can you hold your tongue? All right. I see you are an understanding lad. Sit closer to me." He tapped him with his cane and Tirtov hastily sat down beside him. Stepan looked him over attentively. "Where are you staying—at an inn? Well, come here for the night. I'll give you a coat, a surcoat, trousers and fine boots. Put away your old clothes somewhere. There's a boyarinia who's got to be comforted."

"You mean. . . . ?" Tirtov blushed crimson.

"I mean—make the devil rejoice. You can't fill your pockets with gold unless you give yourself some trouble. There's a certain lady of high birth. She sits on chests full of gold, but the devil torments her. Do you understand, Mishka? If you do what you are told, then your fortune is made. But if you misbehave, I'll have you thrown into the bear-pit and there won't be so much as a bone of you left."

He pushed back his pearl-embroidered cuffs and clapped his hands. The same insolent youth entered.

"Feoktist, take this nobleman's son to the bath. Give him linen and good clothes. And bring him back to sup with me."

14

Tsarevna Sophia was tired when she returned from mass. She had attended two Lenten services that day. All she had eaten was black bread and cabbage, and very little of that. She seated herself in her father's chair—brought from beyond the sea—and laid on her knees a small consecrated loaf wrapped in an embroidered handkerchief. This chair, by her command, had been recently brought from the audience room. When her father's widow, Tsaritsa Natalia, heard of it, she cried: "Soon the Tsarevna will order the throne to be brought to her room!" Let her fume!

The March sun beat hotly in many-coloured shafts through the small panes of two windows. The clean, simple room was fragrant with dried herbs. The walls were whitewashed like a nun's cell. The tiled stove with its tiled couches was well heated. All the furniture, the benches and the table had linen covers. On the tall clock the dial, decorated with a pattern of roses, revolved slowly. A curtain was drawn over the book-case: it was Lent, no time for reading and amusement.

Sophia placed her feet, in felt shoes, on a stool, half closed her eyes and began to sway sleepily. Spring, spring, sin is roving over the world, creeping temptingly into a maiden's chamber. And that during Lent! She ought to draw the curtains over the windows, shut out the bright beams, but she did not want to rise, and she did not want to call a servant-girl. The chants of ancient piety were still ringing in her memory, but her ears strained anxiously: was a board creaking, was the light of her life coming, ah, was sin coming in? Well, if it came, she would atone by prayer, she would make pilgrimages on foot to all the holy monasteries. Let it come!

It was drowsy in the room, only the pendulum ticked. Many tears had flowed in this room. Many times Sophia had paced wildly up and down. She could scream and bite her hands; nevertheless the years were passing and the bloom of her youth fading. A girl, a Tsar's daughter, was doomed to eternal virginity, to the nun's black hood. Only one door led from her room: into the convent. How many tsarevnas had stifled their wild cries in their pillows, tearing their hair! No one saw, no one heard. How many of them had spent wasted lives and had gone to rest under convent tombstones! The very names of these wretched maidens were forgotten. One had been lucky: like a wild bird she had broken out of her maiden's prison. She had told her heart: you may love. And the light of her eyes, handsome Vasily Golitsin, was not like some husband with a whip and big boots, but a lover with sweet words, a gentle and impatient lover. Oh, sin, sin! Laying aside the consecrated loaf, Sophia feebly waved her hands as though to push him away, and, without opening her eyes under the warm rays streaming through the window, smiled at her ardent dreams.

15

A floorboard creaked. Sophia started up looking sharply at the door, as though the destroyer, clad in gold and with flaming wings, were about to swoop in. Her lips trembled. Then again she put her elbows on the velvet arms of the chair and rested her face on the palm of her hand. Her heart beat wildly.

Stooping in the low doorway Vasily Golitsin entered cautiously, and stood there without a word. Oh, she could have wrapped herself round him with her throbbing body, like a wave of the sea! But she pretended to be dozing; it was more decorous: the Tsarevna, tired by standing through the mass, was sleeping with a smile on her lips.

"Sophia!" he called under his breath. He bent over her with a rustle of brocade. Sophia's lips parted. Then his scented moustache tickled her cheeks, his warm lips touched hers and pressed hard against them. Sophia quivered; an indescribable tremor of desire ran down her spine and melted in a hot spasm in her deep belly. She raised her hands to embrace him, but instead thrust him away.

"Oh, leave me . . . What are you doing? It is sinful on a Friday."

She opened her keen eyes and, as always, Golitsin's beauty overwhelmed her. She sensed his eagerness and shook her head, but joy filled her body.

"Sophia," he said, "Miloslavsky and Hovansky are downstairs. They've brought you great news. It's an urgent matter."

Sophia seized his hands, pressed them to her full bosom and kissed them. Her eyelashes were moist with the fullness of her love. She went to the small mirror to arrange her headdress and glanced absentmindedly at her reflection . . . not beautiful, but still, he loved her. . . .

Hovansky and Miloslavsky, Sophia's uncle, were standing by a casement window, their tall fur caps touching the vault of the ceiling. Miloslavsky was wearing a new coat of honour; his slit-shaped eyes peered out of his face with its broad cheekbones, flushed with overeating and excitement.

Sophia went up to him quickly and bowed her head in the fashion of nuns. Miloslavsky thrust his beard and his lips as far forward as his paunch would allow.

"Matveyev is already in Troitsa monastery." Sophia's greenish eyes widened. "The monks welcome him like a tsar. He is expected in Moscow on May 12th. Peter Tolstoy, my nephew, has just galloped here from Troitsa; he says that after mass, before the whole congregation, Matveyev abused us and poured shame on us Miloslavskys: crows, he said, who have flocked to the Tsar's treasury. He said: they want to leap into the palace on the streltsi's pikes. But it won't be, he said; he would crush the rebellion, disperse the strelets regiments to the towns and on the frontiers. He would break the wings of the higher boyars. He swore fealty to the Tsar Peter Alexeyevich. And because of his tender age, let his mother, Natalia Kirillovna, govern the country. And he would not die until all this had come to pass."

A grey pallor spread over Sophia's face. She stood with bent head and drooping arms. Only her pointed headdress quivered and her thick plait stirred on her back. Golitsin stood some way off, in the shadows. Hovansky looked moodily at his feet.

"That is not what will come to pass," he said. "Matveyev won't hold power in Moscow."

"And worst of all," Miloslavsky went on in a hurried whisper, "he abused and upbraided Golitsin: he said Vaska Golitsin was snatching at the crown, and would forfeit his head."

Sophia turned slowly towards Golitsin and met his eyes. He smiled, and a faint pitiful wrinkle hovered at the corner of his lips. Sophia realised that his life was at stake, they were discussing his fate. For the sake of this little wrinkle she would have burnt down Moscow this minute. Mastering her agitation, she asked:

"And what do the streltsi say?"

Miloslavsky breathed heavily. Golitsin stepped softly across the room, looking outside the doors; then he came back and stood behind Sophia. Hovansky tried to speak, but Sophia interrupted him impulsively:

"Tsaritsa Natalia is thirsting for blood. Why? Is it because she can't forget her mean birth—she ran about in birch-bark shoes at her home. Everyone knows that when Matveyev took her out of pity into his palace she had not a shift to change. She had never known women's apartments, she drank wine at the same table with men."

Sophia's plump neck, encircled tightly by the pearl collar of her bodice, swelled with anger and blotches showed on her face.

"The Tsaritsa lived merrily enough with my late father and many were the jokes she had with the Patriarch Nikon too. We, in the women's quarters knew. . . . My little brother Peter—it's a fairy-tale, a miracle—in face and manners he's nothing like his father." Sophia clasped her hands tightly with a clash of rings and pressed them to her breast. "I'm a maiden, it's not my place to speak to you about affairs of State. . . . But if Natalia Kirillovna wants blood, then she'll have it. . . . Otherwise you'll all lose your heads, and I will throw myself into a well."

"It's good, it's good to hear such words," Golitsin said. "You, Prince Hovansky, tell the Tsarevna what's going on in the regiments."

"Except for the Stremianny regiment they are all on your side," Hovansky said. "Every day the men gather in crowds outside headquarters and throw stones and sticks at the windows, and curse their officers in obscene language." At this word Miloslavsky gave a choked cough, Golitsin blinked nervously, but Sophia did not turn a hair. "Colonel Buhvostov and Captain Boborikin, who reprimanded them and tried to stop them, were taken to the top of the belfry and flung down while the crowd cheered. They will not obey orders; and in the suburbs, in Beliy-gorod and Kitay-gorod they gather in groups and incite the people in the markets, and they go to the public baths and shout: 'We don't want to be ruled by the Narishkins and Matveyev, we'll wring their necks!' "

"They're great at shouting, but what we want from them is great deeds." Sophia drew herself up, her eyebrows knitted in anger. "Let them not be afraid to raise Matveyev, Yazykov and Lihachev on their pikes—my enemies, the Narishkins—the whole brood. They must not be afraid to throw out that pup of hers. . . . Stepmother, stepmother! Accursed womb. . . . ! Here, take these. . . . !" Sophia wrenched off all her rings, clutched them in her fist and held them out to Hovansky. "Send them these! Tell them they shall have everything they ask. Pay, land, privileges. But they must not flinch when the time comes. Tell them to proclaim me sovereign."

Miloslavsky, in alarm, could only wave his hands at Sophia. Hovansky, in a growing frenzy of excitement, bared his teeth. Golitsin covered his eyes with his hand; perhaps to hide the look of triumph on his face.

16

Alexander and Alioshka grew fat on pies that spring. They could not have wished for a better life. Zayats too got fat and lazy. "I've worked in my time, now you can work for me, boys." He would sit all day on his porch watching the hens and sparrows. He developed a taste for nuts. Idleness and overfeeding began to make him suspicious: "What if the boys are holding back some of the money? It can't be that they're not stealing, even if it's only a little."

He began, when he counted the takings in the evenings, to question them and find fault, to search their pockets and feel their cheeks for hidden coins. At night his sleep was disturbed by the thought: "A man must steal once he's near money." There was only one thing to do: to drive fear into them.

One evening Alexander and Alioshka came back to supper in high spirits and handed over the takings. Zayats counted the money and claimed that it was a kopek short. They had stolen it, where was it? He had cut a stick that morning and now he caught Alexander by the head and began to beat them, counting the while: one for Alexander, two for Alioshka. After thrashing them, he called for supper.

"So!" he said, stuffing his mouth with meat-jelly, vinegared and peppered. "A lad who's been thrashed is worth two who haven't. I'll make men of you, boys; you'll thank me later."

Zayats ate cabbage soup with pork, chicken giblets with honey and ginger, noodles with boiled fowl, and roast meat. He gulped milk with his porridge. Resting his spoon on the bare table he belched weakly. His cheeks shook with fat, his eyes were mere slits. Unfastening a trouser button, he said:

"You'll be offering prayers for me to God, my dear children. I'm a kind man. Eat, drink; look on me as a father to you."

Alexander said nothing, made a wry mouth and looked away. After supper he said to Alioshka:

"I left my father because he beat me. The more reason to leave this fellow. He'll make a habit of it now, the hog."

Alioshka felt frightened at the thought of leaving this secure life. Of course it was better not to get beaten. But where to find such a place? Everyone beat you. He wept quietly on the stove. But he could not be parted from his friend.

Early next morning, taking their trays with the pies, the boys went out. It was a cool May morning. The puddles were blue, and the leaves on the birches smelled sweet. Starlings whistled, raising their heads to the sun. Outside the gates stood girls, intoxicated by the spring, too lazy to work. Some of them were barefooted, dressed only in long shifts of coarse linen, with birch-bark crowns on their heads and ribbons in their plaits. And their eyes had a wild look. The starlings on the roofs trilled like nightingales, luring the girls into the woods, on to the grass. What a spring!

"Here are baked pies with honey!"

Alexander laughed. "Zayats will have to wait for his money tonight."

"Oh, Alexander, but that's stealing."

"You village idiot! Did the old devil pay us wages? We've been breaking our backs for him these last two months. Hi, strelets, buy a hare pasty—a couple for a quarter kopek hot from the oven!"

They saw more and more women and girls standing outside their gates, and there were crowds at the crossroads. A company of streltsi went past at the double, clanking their halberds. The people made way for them, looked at them with fear. The nearer they got to the Vsehsviatsky bridge, the more streltsi there were, the thicker the crowds. The whole river bank was thronged with people, like flies; they climbed on to dungheaps to gaze at the Kremlin. The green-topped turrets, the battlements of the brick walls and the golden cupolas of the Kremlin churches, chapels and cathedrals were mirrored in the still water, faintly stirred by the current.

But the talk among the crowd was turbulent. Behind the fastness of the walls where the wonderful, rich roofs of the boyars' mansions and of the Tsar's palace showed in a riot of colour, something untoward was happening that peaceful May morning. No one yet knew exactly what. The streltsi were making a stir, but they did not cross the bridge guarded by two cannons on the Kremlin side. Over there were men on foot and mounted men—lesser nobles, members of the Tsar's bodyguard. Over their long white coats swans' wings were slung on their backs on bow-shaped brass supports. There were not many of them, and they were evidently alarmed as they watched the thousands of people streaming in from Balchug.

Alexander kept darting about by the bridge. Alioshka and he had long since sold all their pies and had thrown away the trays. It was no time for trading. It was frightening but it was good fun. People here and there in the crowd began to shout. Everyone was seething with discontent. They were sick of living under such conditions. They made menacing gestures towards the Kremlin. One old man, a townsman, climbed up on a heap of rubbish, took his cap off his bald head and said slowly:

"Under the late Tsar Alexis the people rose. There was no bread, no salt, money was worthless, the Treasury melted down the silver roubles and issued copper money. The boyars ravenously sucked the people's blood. The people revolted, they dragged the Tsar from his horse and tore his coat off his back. Many boyars' mansions were destroyed and burnt in those days, and they killed the boyars. Then in the South rose the great-hearted Cossack, Razin. And there would have been freedom, and the people would have lived in freedom and plenty, but they did not support him. The people are weak, all they are good for is shouting. And today, my lads, unless you are united, you can look forward to the gallows and the block. The boyars will master you."

They listened to him open-mouthed. And things grew even more strange and tense. They understood one thing only: that there was no authority in the Kremlin and the time seemed opportune to rock the fastness that had stood for centuries. But how?

At another point a strelets pushed his way in front of the crowd:

"What are you waiting for? At dawn the boyar Matveyev drove into Moscow. Don't you know Matveyev? So long as the boyars in the Kremlin were leaderless and quarrelled among themselves, life was still possible. Now a real ruler has appeared: he will tighten the reins. He will impose such dues and taxes as have never been known before. We must rise today—tomorrow will be too late."

Such words made heads reel. Tomorrow would be too late. . . . ! Eyes grew bloodshot. The Kremlin, lazily reflected in the river, seemed a mirage: old, forbidding, treacherous, full of gold. Not a gunner by the cannon on the walls. As though all inside were dead. And high above it kites were circling.

Suddenly there was a stir among the winged guard across the bridge, and their faint shouts reached the crowd. A horseman on a white steed appeared in their midst. They would not let him through, waving their broad-bladed halberds. Pressing forward, he made his horse rear and broke through. He lost his cap and galloped madly over the floating bridge. Water spurted up between the planks. The fine-limbed horse shook its mane merrily.

The huge crowd became very quiet. From the other bank a single shot rang out, aimed at the horseman. Cutting into the crowd he raised himself in his stirrups. The skin on his dark, shaven head twitched, his narrow, long-nosed face was aglow with the gallop and he was breathing hard. His brown eyes glittered from under his dark eyebrows, heavy as though they had been drawn with charcoal. He was recognised.

"Tolstoy . . . Peter Andreyevich . . . Miloslavsky's nephew! He's with us! Listen to what he's going to say."

Tolstoy shouted in a high, breaking voice:

"People! Streltsi! A calamity! Matveyev and the Narishkins have just strangled Tsarevich Ivan! Unless you hasten, they will strangle Peter too! To the Kremlin, quick, or it will be too late."

The crowd growled, stirred and shouted and then, with a roar, rushed to the bridge. Thousands of heads swarmed round Tolstoy's white horse. The bridge creaked and sagged: they were running knee-deep in water. Silently, ferociously, the strelets hundreds began to cross, pushing the people aside. Somewhere a bell sounded—boom, boom, boom—more and more rapidly, more alarmingly. Other belfries took it up, bells swung wildly, and all the forty-times-forty churches of Moscow sounded the tocsin.

In the silent Kremlin, here and there, a window banged shut with a brief gleam in the sun, and then another. . . .

17

The strelets regiments broke ranks in their impatience and rushed in a mass to the royal palace and the Cathedral of the Annunciation. Many of them did not get so far, but stayed behind to break open the stout doors of the boyars' mansions, or climbed the belfries to sound the tocsin. The toll bell-tower, called Ivan the Great, boomed out in its terrible bass: the voice of hundreds of tons of metal. In the narrow alleys between the mansions, the stone monastery enclosures and the yellow walls of the long government buildings, lay dead bodies and wounded servants of the boyars crawled about groaning. The people laughed as they caught riderless horses galloping about in terror. They shouted, and smashed windows with stones.

Streltsi, townsmen and flocks of boys (including, of course, Alexander and Alioshka) stared at the bright-hued Tsar's palace that spread over a quarter of the Kremlin grounds: buildings of stone or timber, high attics containing the women's quarters, squat log-houses, passages, towers and turrets, painted red, green, bright blue, weather-boarded or of unadorned logs, all connected by a multitude of passages and stairways; hundreds of different roofs, tent-shaped or domed, with fantastic tops, fluted, barrelled, serrated like a cock's comb, shimmering with silver and gold. Here lived the lord of the earth, the first after God.

It was strangely awe-inspiring. No ordinary mortal dare approach it carrying arms; even the boyars themselves would leave their mounts at the gate and cross the muddy courtyard on foot, hat in hand, glancing apprehensively at the Tsar's windows. The people stood gazing. The voice of Ivan the Great beat agonisingly against their breasts, and they were seized with bewilderment. Then some bold fellows dashed forward:

"Why stand gaping, lads? They've strangled Tsarevich Ivan, they are finishing off Peter. Come on, put up ladders, break into the porch!"

A deep rumble passed through the enormous crowd. Drums beat a sharp tattoo. "Come on, come on!" yelled wild voices. A score of streltsi clambered over the railing, drawing their curved swords. They rushed to the Red Porch and hammered at the copper doors, putting their shoulders against them. A roar ran through the crowd: "Forward! Forward!" Ladders brought from somewhere were passed over their heads and placed against the windows of the royal chambers and the side balustrade of the high porch.

They swarmed up them. They snarled and shouted: "Hand over Matveyev! Hand over the Narishkins!"

18

"They will kill us, they will surely kill us! What's to be done, Artamon Sergeyevich?"

"God is merciful, Tsaritsa. I will go out and speak to them. Has the Patriarch been summoned? Here, send someone else to fetch him."

"Artamon Sergeyevich, it is they, it is my enemies. Yazykov himself saw it: two Miloslavskys disguised, with the streltsi."

"You're a woman; pray, Tsaritsa."

Voices shouted from the ante-chamber:

"He's coming, he's coming!"

The Patriarch Joachim entered, the sharp point of his crozier stabbing the oak floor. His fanatical, dark-hollowed eyes turned towards the low windows under the vaults. From outside the faces of the streltsi who had climbed the ladders pressed against the small coloured panes. The Patriarch raised his dry hand in a threatening gesture and the faces recoiled.

Natalia Kirillovna ran to the Patriarch. Her plump face was as white as the kerchief under her black fox cap. She clung to his ice-cold hand and, covering it with kisses, babbled:

"Save us, save us, Holy Father!"

"Holy Father, things are in a bad way," Matveyev said grimly. The Patriarch turned his dilated pupils towards the speaker. Matveyev shook his greying, square-cut beard. "It's a conspiracy, an open rebellion. They themselves don't know what they are shouting."

Matveyev was calm; with his eagle eyes and thin nose he looked like an icon of the old school. In the course of his long life he had been through much and had many times faced death. Only one passion still burned in him: an arrogant passion for power. Controlling the anger which fluttered his withered eyelids, he said:

"The main thing is to get them out of the Kremlin. After that we'll deal with them."

The blows and shouts outside the windows made a furious sound. Ivan Narishkin, the Tsaritsa's brother, the man whom the streltsi and boyars hated worse than the devil, crossed the room—in at one door and out at another—running on tiptoe. Although only twenty-four, he was already a boyar; he was handsome, and a coxcomb; people said that he had already tried the Tsar's crown on his own head. His small black moustache looked as though it were glued on his livid face; it was as if he foresaw the torture and cruel death that were to be his fate next day at the place of execution. Flapping his Polish sleeves he cried: "Sophia has come!"—and disappeared through the door. His dwarf, no bigger than a child, shuffled after him, holding a fool's cap, his wrinkled face drenched in tears; as if he too foresaw that on the morrow he would betray his master.

Sophia entered with a quick step, and with her Golitsin and Hovansky. Sophia's cheeks were thickly rouged. She was dressed in gold brocade and wore a high pearl headdress. Crossing her hands on her breast, she bowed low to the Tsaritsa and the Patriarch. Natalia started back as though Sophia were a snake and her eyes blinked, but she did not speak.

"The people are angry, and with good reason," Sophia said in a loud voice. "Tsaritsa, you should show yourself to them with my brothers. They are shouting God knows what—that the children have been killed. Speak to them—promise them favours—they may break into the palace at any moment."

Her white teeth clicked as she spoke, and her green eyes were shining with gleeful excitement. Matveyev took a step towards her:

"This is no time to settle accounts among women."

"Then you yourself go out to them."

45

"I am not afraid of death, Sophia Alexeyevna."

"Don't argue," said the Patriarch striking the floor with his crozier. "Show them the children, Ivan and Peter."

"No!" Natalia cried clutching at her temples. "I won't allow it, Holy Father . . . I'm afraid!"

"Take the children out on to the Red Porch," repeated the Patriarch.

19

And so the lock on the copper doors of the Red Porch began to creak and the crowd moved closer, holding its breath and watching eagerly. The drums ceased beating.

Alexander clung with both hands and feet to one of the bellying pillars of the porch. Alioshka kept close to him, although he was very frightened. The doors were flung open and the crowd saw Tsaritsa Natalia, in her black widow's gown and mantle of cloth-of-gold. She looked down at the thousands and thousands of eyes that were fixed on her and swayed. Someone's hands held out to her a boy in a bright, close-fitting coat. With an effort she lifted him and stood him on the balustrade. The cap of Monomach * had slipped over one ear uncovering his black cropped hair. Round-cheeked and short-nosed, he stretched out his neck. His eyes were round like those of a mouse. His small mouth was tightly pursed with fear.

The Tsaritsa wanted to say something but was taken faint and her head fell back. Matveyev came forward from behind her. A deep growl went up from the crowd. He was leading by the hand another boy, a little older than Peter, with a thin, listless face and hanging underlip.

"Who lied to you?" Matveyev began in his still strong old man's voice, drawing together his grey eyebrows. "Who lied that the Tsar and Tsarevich had been strangled? See for yourselves: here is the Tsar in the Tsaritsa's arms, well and happy. Here is Tsarevich Ivan"—he raised the listless boy and showed him to the crowd—"by the grace of God both are living."

People in the crowd began to exchange glances and to say: "It's them all right: there's no deception."

* Emblem of royalty sent to Grand Duke Vladimir of Russia (1113–1125) in memory of his maternal grandfather, the Byzantine Emperor Constantine Monomach, by the Emperor Alexis Comnenus. Used during the crowning of all Russian Emperors.

"Streltsi, go back quietly to your quarters! If you need anything, if you have any requests or complaints to make, send a deputation."

Golitsin and Hovansky came down the steps of the porch. Putting their hands on the shoulders of streltsi and townsmen, they urged them to disperse, but said it as though mockingly. Angry voices were raised again in the crowd, which had seemed to be calming down:

"Well, and what does it matter if they are alive?"

"We can see for ourselves that they're alive."

"All the same, we are not leaving the Kremlin."

"Don't take us for fools, we know your honeyed words."

"And later you'll tear our nostrils in front of the courthouse."

"Hand over Matveyev and the Narishkins to us!"

"Hand over Ivan Narishkin! He tried on the Tsar's crown."

"Bloodsuckers, the boyars. . . . ! Give us Yazykov. . . . ! And Dolgoruky!"

The voices became more and more threatening as they shouted the names of the men they hated. Natalia became deathly pale again and threw her arms about her son. Peter turned his round head from side to side. A voice cried with a laugh:

"Look at him—just like a kitten!"

Then Prince Dolgoruky, the son of the commander of the streltsi, ran down the steps of the porch, with a clatter of weapons. Well-groomed and arrogant, he was dressed in scarlet velvet and sables. He brandished a whip and shouted at the streltsi:

"You're taking advantage, you sons of bitches, of my father lying ill. Away with you! Away with you, you dogs, you slaves!"

At first the streltsi backed away from the lashing whip; but times had changed, and that was not the way to talk to them. They breathed hard, then, with a roar, they reached out towards him:

"You haven't been pitched off a belfry yet? Who are you, you pup? At him, men!"

They seized him by the belt, tore it off, and in a moment his velvet coat was in shreds. He drew his sword and, brandishing it, backed up the steps. Pointing their pikes, the streltsi rushed after him; they seized him. The Tsaritsa screamed wildly. Dolgoruky's spreadeagled body hurtled through the air and was swallowed up by the stamping, tearing crowd.

Matveyev and the Tsaritsa made for the door. But it was already too late. Ovsey and other streltsi rushed out of the anteroom of the royal palace.

"Down with Matveyev!" they shouted.

"That's right! That's right!" roared the crowd.

Ovsey caught hold of Matveyev from behind. The Tsaritsa, her sleeves flying, threw her arms tightly round him. Tsarevich Ivan was pushed aside; he fell and began to cry. Peter's round face was distorted and twisted; he clung with both hands to Matveyev's grey beard.

"Pull him off, don't be afraid, pull him away!" the streltsi shouted, raising their pikes. "Throw him to us!"

The Tsaritsa was dragged away, and Peter flung aside like a kitten. Matveyev's huge body, his mouth hanging open, was suddenly raised, its legs spread wide, then it toppled down on to the raised pikes below.

Then the streltsi, the townsmen and the boys—Alexander and Alioshka among them—burst into the palace and swarmed through its hundreds of rooms. The Tsaritsa and both children were still on the porch; she had swooned.

Golitsin and Hovansky again approached those who had remained in the square, and cries rose in the crowd:

"We want Ivan to be Tsar!" "Let both be Tsar!" "We want Sophia!" "That's right! That's right!" "Let Sophia rule us!" "We want a pillar on the Red Square, a memorial pillar that we shall have freedom for ever!"

chapter two

For some time the streltsi ran wild. They killed many boyars: the Tsaritsa's brothers—Ivan and Afanasy Narishkin—the Princes Yury and Mihail Dolgoruky, Grigory and Andrey Romodanovsky, Matveyev, Peter and Fedor Saltikov, Yazykov and others of less noble birth. They received their soldiers' pay: two hundred and forty thousand roubles, and another ten roubles each as reward. The treasury was obliged to collect gold and silver plate from all the towns, melt it down and mint it in order to pay the streltsi. A pillar was set up in the Red Square. On its four sides were inscribed the names of the boyars who had been slain, with an account of their misdeeds and crimes. The streltsi regiments demanded charters in which the boyars swore, now and in the future, never to abuse them, never to call them rebels or traitors, never to execute or send them into exile without good reason.

When they had drunk and eaten all the stores in the Kremlin, the streltsi returned to their quarters, the townsmen to their suburbs. And all went on again as before. Nothing new had come to pass. The age-old darkness of poverty, slavery and misery still hung over Moscow and the towns, over hundreds of districts scattered through the vast land.

The peasant with flogged back somehow or other scratched the hated earth. The townsman in his cold house howled under unbearable dues and taxes. All the smaller merchants groaned. The noblemen with small estates became impoverished. The land deteriorated:

heaven was to be thanked if the harvest yielded a third. Even the boyars and big merchants complained. In the old days what did a boyar need? A sable-lined coat and a tall cap, and honour was satisfied, while at home he ate his cabbage soup with salt meat, slept and said his prayers. But today his eyes had become rapacious: he wanted to live no worse than the Polish noblemen, or the Livonians, or westerners: he had heard and seen a good deal. Hearts burned with ambition. The boyars set up households with a hundred serfs; and to have them shod, to clothe them in liveries, to feed the whole greedy crew much more money was needed than formerly. It had become indecent to live in wooden houses. Formerly the boyar or his wife drove out in a one-horse sledge, a serf sat astride the horse behind the harness-bow. Fox-tails used to be hung on the horse-collar, the bridle, on the breeching to show off to others. Today you had to order a gilded coach from Dantzig, harness it with four horses; without that you were not respected. And where was the money? Hard to get, very hard. Trade was bad. You could not sell much to your own people, they had no money to spend. And you could not take your wares abroad —there was nothing to take them in. The seas belonged to other nations. All foreign trade was in the hands of foreigners. And when you learned what trade was carried on in foreign parts, it was enough to make you dash your head against the wall. What dark spell held Russia? When at long last would she move forward?

There were now two Tsars in Moscow—Ivan and Peter—and over both, the Regent Sophia. One set of boyars had been exchanged for another. That was all. Life was depressing: time stood still, and there was nothing to look forward to. At the memorial pillar in the Red Square there had once stood on guard a sentry armed with a halberd, but he disappeared. People had heaped all kinds of refuse round the pillar. In the markets people began to murmur again, and rumours were whispered. A doubt crept into the minds of the streltsi: they had not carried things through to the finish last time; there had been much commotion, but little had been gained. Should they not complete the job before it was too late?

The old men said that life used to be good in the old days—it was cheap, there was plenty of food and people behaved more decorously. Robbery was unheard of. Ah, such times had been, and were now past!

One day six Old Believers appeared in the strelets quarters: men versed in theological writings, dry as bones, unshakable in their belief. "The only way to salvation," they told the streltsi, "is to rid ourselves of the Nikonian Patriarch and of the whole Council of Boyars, who have adopted Nikonian practices and Polish ways, and go back to our God-fearing faith and our old way of life."

These Old Believers read out tracts issued by the Solovets monastery which told how to escape the Nikonian temptation and how to save their souls and their lives. The streltsi listened and wept. An Old Believer monk, Nikita Pustosviat, standing on a cart in the market-place, read out to the people from a Solovets tract:

"I, brethren, have seen Antichrist, truly I have seen him. Once, being sad as I thought about the coming of Antichrist, I began to pray, but fell asleep, sinner that I am. And lo, I saw a great multitude of people in a field. And someone stood near me. I said to him: 'Why are there so many people?' And he replied: 'Antichrist is coming, stay, fear not!' I leaned on my crotched staff and stood confidently. And lo, they were leading a naked man; his flesh stank and was hideous to behold, he breathed fire, and from his mouth, his nostrils and his ears issued evil-smelling flames. Behind him came our Tsar and government, and the boyars, and courtiers, and noblemen of the Council. And I spat at him, and I felt sick and full of horror. I know from the Holy Writ that he will come soon. There are already many of his evil creatures, mad dogs. . . ."

Now it was clear what they ought to demand. The streltsi rushed off to the Kremlin. Hovansky, head of the Strelets Office, declared himself for the Old Faith. The six bony Old Believers, and with them Nikita Pustosviat, after three days spent without food or drink, brought lecterns, wooden crosses and ancient books * into the palace and, in the presence of Sophia, cursed and vilified the Patriarch and the clergy. The streltsi gathered at the Red Porch and shouted: "We want the Old Faith, we want the old way of life!" Others said forcefully: "It is time for the Tsarevna to enter a convent, time to cease disturbing the country."

Only one remedy remained and Sophia threatened wrathfully:

"You want to exchange us for six ignorant peasant monks? In that case we, the Tsars, can no longer live here, we shall go to other towns and tell the whole people of our ruin, of your betrayal."

The streltsi realised what Sophia's threat meant and were alarmed:

"What if she brings the nobles' militia against Moscow?" And they desisted and began to negotiate.

Meanwhile Vasily Golitsin had ordered buckets of vodka and beer

* I.e., theological works that had not been emended and corrected by the church council under Patriarch Nikon in 1653.

to be brought out of the royal cellars into the square. The streltsi wavered, became confused in their minds. Someone cried: "What do we care about the Old Faith—that's the priests' business—down with the Old Believers!" One of the bony monks had his head chopped off there and then; two others were crushed to death and the rest barely managed to escape with their lives.

The accursed boyars had befuddled the simple people with drink and saved their own skins. Moscow buzzed like a hive. Everyone shouted his own views. No single leader revealed himself at the time —the rioting was unorganised. They smashed the government taverns. They seized government clerks and tore them to pieces. It was not safe to go about Moscow either mounted or on foot. Boyars' mansions were attacked, and the boyars barely succeeded in driving the people off with gunfire; great and bloody battles took place in those days. Whole rows of wooden houses were burnt down. Dead bodies lay unburied in the streets and market-places. There was a rumour that the boyars had brought the militia close up to Moscow— that they intended to crush the revolt at one blow. And once again the streltsi, with a crowd of runaway serfs, went to the Kremlin with a petition nailed to a pike, asking that every single boyar should be delivered to them for summary justice. Sophia, white with wrath, came out on to the Red Porch:

"They tell you lies about us—the militia did not even enter our thoughts. I swear it on the cross," she cried tearing at the sparkling diamond-studded cross on her breast. "It is Tsarevich Matveyka who is telling these lies about us." And they threw from the porch on to the strelets pikes just the one petty Tatar prince Matveyka: may he choke you!

Matveyka was torn to pieces, the frenzy was appeased, and again the streltsi went away empty-handed.

Moscow was in an uproar for three days and three nights; clouds of rooks, frightened by the incessant ringing of the tocsin, circled high above the city. It was then that in the minds of the most desperate rebels a decision was born: to cut off the head itself—to kill both Tsars and Sophia. But when Moscow awoke on the fourth day, the Kremlin was already empty: neither the Tsars nor the Tsarevna could be found; they had fled together with the boyars. Panic seized the people.

Sophia went to the village Kolomenskoye and sent heralds through the countryside to call up the nobles' militia. Throughout August she circled round Moscow visiting villages and monasteries, voicing her complaints from church porches, telling the people of the insults she had suffered and of her ruin. In the Kremlin there remained Hovansky with the streltsi. They began to think: why not proclaim him Tsar? He was popular, of ancient lineage and a follower of the Old Faith. The common people would have a Tsar of their own.

The nobles mounted their steeds in high fettle in expectation of rich rewards. An enormous militia of nearly two hundred thousand men assembled near the Troitsa-Sergiyevo monastery. Sophia, all the while, circled round Moscow like a bird. In September she sent forward a troop of cavalry, under the command of Stepan Odoyevsky, to attack the village of Pushkino where Hovansky, who with his streltsi had been patrolling the villages on the outskirts of Moscow, was sleeping in a tent pitched on a knoll. The streltsi were sleeping in complete unconcern. They were hacked to pieces as they slept. Hovansky, clad only in his underclothes, rushed from his tent brandishing a halberd. Mihail Tirtov sprang from his saddle on to his shoulders. They tied Hovansky to Tirtov's saddle and brought him to the village Vozdvizhenskoye where Sophia was celebrating her nameday. At the entrance to the village, on benches brought out of the houses sat boyars, helmeted and cloaked as in time of war. Tirtov flung Hovansky from his saddle and Hovansky, half-clothed, knelt on the grass and wept with grief and shame. Shaklovity, a clerk of the Council, read out the list of his crimes.

Hovansky cried out furiously: "Lies! but for me Moscow would have long since been knee-deep in blood!"

It was not easy for the boyars to bring themselves to shed the blood of so ancient a family. Vasily Golitsin sat whiter than snow. Both he and Hovansky were descendants of Gedimin,* and a Gediminovich was now being judged by men of mean lineage, recent upstarts. Seeing this hesitation, Miloslavsky went up to the mounted men and whispered to Odoyevsky. The latter dashed at full gallop through the village to Sophia's silken tent and came galloping back, scattering chickens and children.

"The Regent commands you not to hesitate, but to put an end to the Prince."

Golitsin hurriedly moved away, covering his eyes with a handkerchief. Hovansky gave a wild cry when Tirtov seized him by the hair and dragged him into the dust on the road. There, at the entrance to the village, Hovansky was beheaded.

* Lithuanian prince of the 14th century who formed a vast and powerful state from Lithuanian and Russian territories.

The streltsi were left without a leader. When they heard of the execution they rushed into the Kremlin, closed the gates, loaded the cannon and prepared for a siege.

Sophia hastened to withdraw to the shelter of the stout walls of the Troitsa-Sergiyevo monastery. She entrusted the command of the militia to Golitsin. And thus the two armies confronted each other threateningly, each watching for the other to lose heart. The streltsi lost heart first: they sent a deputation to the Troitsa-Sergiyevo monastery. They made their submission, and thereupon lost their freedom. The pillar in the Red Square was removed. Their charters were revoked. Shaklovity, notorious for his severity, was appointed head of the Strelets Office. Many of their regiments were transferred to provincial towns. The people were cowed. And once more unbroken stillness reigned over Moscow, over the whole land. The years stretched out.

2

In the twilight Alexander was running through the streets along the fences. His heart beat painfully, sweat blinded his eyes. A burning house some distance away shed a sinister light on the puddles in the wheel-ruts. Twenty paces behind him his drunken father, Danila Menshikov, was running, loudly stamping his heavy boots. This time it was not a whip he was holding, but a shining curved knife. "Stop!" he shouted in a terrible voice. "I'll kill you!"

Alioshka had long since dropped behind and climbed up a birch-tree. For over a year Alexander had not seen his father, and now he had come face to face with him by a tavern that had been broken into and set on fire. Menshikov had immediately made chase. All this time the two boys had lived precariously but merrily. They were well known in the suburbs and were willingly given shelter for the night. They had spent the summer roaming through the woods and by the rivers round Moscow. They caught singing birds and sold them to merchants. They stole fruit and vegetables from kitchen-gardens. They were always hoping to catch and train a bear, but the animal was not easy to capture.

They fished. One day, when they had thrown their lines into the quiet clear water of the Yaouza which flowed out of the dense woods of the Losinov island, they saw a boy sitting on the opposite bank with his chin resting on his hands. He was strangely dressed: white stockings and a green coat of foreign cut with red lapels and bright buttons. Close by, on a hillock, the crested roofs of the Preobrazhensky palace showed from behind groves of limes. There had been a time when the whole of it was visible and mirrored in the river, gay and painted in many colours, but now it was screened by thick foliage and was falling into neglect.

Women were running to and fro near the gates and over the meadow calling someone—probably searching for the boy. But he sat sulkily, hidden by burdocks, and paid no attention to them. Alexander spat on his worm and called across the river:

"Hi! You're scaring our fish! Take care, or we'll take off our trousers and swim across, and then you'll catch it."

The boy only snorted. Alexander began again:

"Who are you? Whose boy are you?"

"I'll order your head to be cut off," the boy answered in a somewhat husky voice, "then you'll know!"

Alioshka immediately whispered to Alexander:

"Take care, that's the Tsar."

And he flung down his rod, ready to take to his heels. But Alexander's blue eyes were full of mischief.

"Wait a bit; there's time enough to run away." He cast his line and, laughing, looked at the boy. "D'you think we're frightened of you? Cutting off heads indeed! What are you sitting there for? They're looking for you."

"I'm sitting here to hide from those women."

"Now I look at you—aren't you our Tsar? Eh?"

The boy did not reply at once, evidently amazed at such daring.

"What if I am? What business is it of yours?"

"What business? Now if you were to go and fetch us some honey cakes . . ." Peter looked fixedly and without a smile at Alexander who went on: "Honest, go and fetch some—then I'll show you a trick." Alexander took off his cap and extracted a needle from its lining. "Look—is this a needle or not? If you like, I'll pull the needle, threaded, through my cheek, and it won't hurt me."

"You aren't lying?" Peter asked.

"Look—I'll make the sign of the cross. If you like, I'll cross myself with my foot," and Alexander quickly sat down, seized his bare foot and crossed himself with it. Peter was still more amazed.

"It's not likely the Tsar will run to fetch cakes for you," he growled. "But will you pull the needle through for money?"

"For a single kopek I'll do it three times and won't be hurt."

"You aren't lying?"

Peter began to blink with curiosity. He got up, glanced round the burdocks towards the palace, where some women were still running about and calling him, and then ran along the bank towards the wooden footbridge. He crossed and found himself within a few paces of Alexander. Blue dragon-flies skimmed over the surface of the water, in which clouds and a blasted willow were reflected. Standing under the willow Alexander showed Peter the trick: three times he drew the threaded needle through his cheek, and nothing happened; there was not a drop of blood, only three dirty spots on his cheek. Peter looked on with eyes as round as an owl's.

"Give me the needle," he said impatiently.

"What about the money?"

"Catch!"

Alexander caught the rouble which was tossed to him. Taking the needle from him Peter began to push it through his cheek. He pushed it in, drew it through, and laughed, tossing back his curly head.

"As good as you, as good as you!" he said and, forgetting the boys, ran towards the palace; probably to teach the boyars how to draw needles through their cheeks.

The rouble was a new one: on one side there was the double-headed eagle, on the other the Regent Sophia. The boys had never yet earned so much money. After that they began to haunt the banks of the Yaouza, but saw Peter only in the distance. Sometimes he was riding a small pony, with fat attendants riding behind him; at other times he carried a drum and marched at the head of lads dressed in foreign coats, armed with wooden muskets, with the same attendants fussing round them, waving their arms.

"Spending his time on foolishness," Alexander would say, sitting under the blasted willow.

At the end of the summer he managed at last to buy a bear from some gipsies for half a rouble. It was small and lean with a hump like a boar. Alioshka led it by the nose-ring, while Alexander sang and danced and wrestled with it. But autumn came and the rains filled the Moscow streets and squares knee-deep with mud. There was nowhere to dance. No one would take them in with the bear. And the bear ate a lot; all their money went on feeding it, and it also showed signs of wanting to hibernate. They had to sell it at a loss. During the winter Alioshka dressed himself in pitiable rags and begged for alms. Alexander, bare to the waist, shivered in the frost on church squares, pretending to be dumb and paralytic; he collected a good deal of money given him out of pity. They could not complain; they got through the winter comfortably.

And then once more the earth dried, the woods grew green and the birds began to sing. Their days were full: at dawn to the misty river to fish, during the day to knock about the marketplaces, and at dusk to the woods to set snares. Many a time people warned Alexander: "Take care, your father has long been hunting for you all over Moscow; he says he'll kill you." Alexander only spat through his teeth.

And then suddenly, unexpectedly, he had run into him.

Alexander had raced the entire length of Old Basmannaya street and was beginning to have cramp in his legs. He no longer looked back; he could hear the beat of his father's heavy boots and his hissing breath drawing nearer behind him. Well, this was the end.

"Help!" he cried shrilly.

At that moment a high carriage, swaying on its springs, turned out of a lane into the Razgulay where there stood a well-known tavern. Two horses, harnessed tandem, were trotting briskly, and a foreigner in stockings and a broad-brimmed hat was riding on the leading horse. In a flash Alexander swerved towards the back-wheels, swung himself on to the axle and clambered up to the footboard at the back of the carriage. Seeing this Menshikov roared: "Stop!" but the postillion slashed him with his whip, and Menshikov, cursing and choking with rage, fell in the mud. The carriage drove on.

Alexander sat on the footboard and recovered his breath. He must get away from this place, as far as possible. Beyond the Pokrovsky gate the carriage turned into a smooth road, increased its speed and soon drove up to a high fence. A foreign man emerged from the gate and asked something. A head, with long curls like a priest's, but with a clean-shaven face, looked out of the carriage-window, and replied: "Francis Lefort".

The gates opened, and Alexander was inside the Foreign Quarter, on the Kukuy river. The wheels crunched over sand. Welcoming lights shone from the windows of small houses, lighting up low fences, clipped bushes and glass balls resting on pedestals among sanded paths. Flowers showed white in the gardens in front of the houses and filled the air with scent. Here and there, on benches or porches, sat foreigners in knitted caps, holding long pipes.

"Holy Virgin, how well they live!" Alexander thought, looking about him from behind the carriage. His eyes were dazed by twinkling lights.

They drove past a square pond. Shrubs in green tubs stood on its edges, and between them flares were burning, lighting up several small boats in which women were sitting laughing and singing—in feathered hats, their arms bare to the elbow, their throats uncovered and their skirts drawn up to prevent them from getting creased. Here too, beneath a windmill, in front of a tavern's well-lit door, men and girls were dancing in pairs, holding each other tightly.

Musketeers were strolling about everywhere. In the Kremlin they were grim and silent, but here, unarmed and in unbuttoned coats, they walked arm-in-arm, singing songs and laughing, good-humouredly and peaceably. Everything was peaceful here, and friendly; as though it were not on this earth: enough to make one rub one's eyes.

All of a sudden they drove into a broad courtyard, in the centre of which a fountain played in a small ornamental pool. At the far end there was a house painted red to look like bricks with white pillars stuck on to it. The carriage stopped. The man with the long hair got out and caught sight of Alexander who had jumped off the footboard.

"Who are you? Why are you here? Where have you come from?" he asked pronouncing the words in a funny way. "Tell me, boy, are you a thief?"

"I—a thief? Beat me to death if I'm a thief!" Alexander looked merrily into the clean-shaven face with its snub nose and small, smiling mouth. "Did you see my father running after me with a knife on the Razgul?"

"Ah. So I did . . . It made me laugh: a big one running after a little one!"

"My father will surely cut my throat. Please, take me into your service—please!"

"Service? What can you do?"

"Anything. First, I can sing any song you like. I can play the pipes and the horn and on wooden spoons. I can make people laugh: many's the time I've made people burst with laughter. And dance! I can begin at dawn and go on till dusk, and not sweat a drop. Anything you tell me to do, I'll do."

Lefort took Alexander's sharp chin in his fingers. The boy evidently pleased him.

"Oh, you're a fine lad. You're dirty—get some soap and wash. And then I'll give you some clothes; you shall serve me. But if you start stealing. . . ."

"I don't do that sort of thing—I have more brains," Alexander said with such assurance that Lefort believed him. He shouted some instructions about Alexander to the groom and then went whistling towards the house, turning out his toes with something like a dance-step, probably because on the lake nearby there was music and German women were laughing provocatively.

3

"Surely that's enough, Nikita Moiseyich, the child might get a headache."

No sooner had Natalia said this than Tsar Peter stopped reading the Acts of the Apostles in the middle of a sentence and hurriedly crossed himself with inky fingers. Without waiting for his tutor Zotov to bow to the ground to him, as etiquette demanded, he kissed his mother's hand—which fluttered helplessly in an effort to hold her son for a moment—and dashed off impatiently along the creaking boards of passages and staircases, his heavy footsteps startling the old women dependants in the dark corners of the Preobrazhensky palace.

"Your cap, your cap, the sun will scorch your head!" the Tsaritsa called feebly after him.

Nikita Zotov stood before her respectfully and erect, as in church: clean, with well-kempt hair, in soft boots and a long coat of dark fine cloth with a high collar that stood up at the back higher than his head. His pleasant face with its soft lips and curly beard was turned up earnestly. An excellent man, there was no doubt about it. If you were to tell him: "Fling yourself on a knife, Nikita", he would do so. A man of more than doglike devotion, but too artless, too mild. Not the right kind of tutor for a self-willed boy.

"You should read more religious books with him, Nikita Moiseyich. He is not in the least like a Tsar. Before we know where we are, it will be time to get him married. He has not even learnt to walk with dignity—always running, like a common boy. There, look!"

The Tsaritsa looked out of the window and threw up her hands helplessly. Peter was running across the courtyard, stumbling in his haste. Behind him came tall youths from among the court servants, carrying muskets and small axes on long shafts. On an earthern rampart, representing a fortress, built in front of the palace, peasants brought in from the village stood behind a stockade wearing broad-brimmed foreign hats. They also had orders to keep pipes filled with tobacco in their mouths. Fearfully watching the Tsar coming at a skipping run, they forgot how they should be playing. Peter shouted angrily in a breaking voice. Natalia shuddered to see his furious, round eyes. He climbed up on to the top of the rampart and in his anger struck one of the play-soldiers with a musket. The man drew his head in between his shoulders.

"If it's not done as he wants, he might kill someone," Natalia said. "From whom did he get this hot temper?"

The game began again. As he lined up the long-legged youths with the axes, Peter got angry again because they did not understand what he wanted. The trouble was that when he got excited he began to speak indistinctly, choking with words in his haste, as though he were trying to say much more than he had words for.

"Why has his head started twitching like that?" Natalia said watching her son with alarm. Suddenly she put her fingers in her ears. The peasants on the rampart had rolled forward a wooden cannon—which, in accordance to the Tsaritsa's strict instructions, was loaded with something soft, such as boiled turnips or apples—and fired. Immediately they threw down their weapons and raised their hands in sign of surrender.

"You mustn't surrender! You must fight!" Peter shouted, his head shaking and twitching. "Begin all over again! Everything all over again!"

"Nikita Moiseyich, do shut the window. The noise makes my head ache," Natalia said.

Zotov closed the coloured glass window. Natalia bent her head and lightly fingered the shell beads of her rosary brought from Mount Athos. She was unhappy. Tears and grief had aged her during the past few years. Her eyebrows and her dark, flashing eyes were all that remained of her former beauty. She always wore black, with a black kerchief over her head. This was how the widow of Ivan the Terrible, Maria Nagaya, had lived in Uglich with her ill-fated son Dimitry. Might she be spared a like tragedy! The Regent Sophia dreamt night and day of marrying Golitsin and reigning in her own right. She had already ordered a crown from foreign goldsmiths.

The Preobrazhensky palace was deserted save for the servants, who ran about on tiptoe, and old nurses and gossips who whispered in dark corners. Although the Tsar was still very young, he could not bear the sight of old women. If he saw some old nurse creeping along the wall, her dress spattered with drops of wax from the tapers, he would shout at her so that the old crone could hardly creep to her corner for fright.

The boyars did not come here: there were no honours and no profit to be gained. They all crowded to the Kremlin, nearer to the sun. For the sake of appearances Sophia had ordered four boyars to be in attendance at Peter's court: Prince Mihail Cherkassky, Prince Lykov, Prince Troyekurov and Prince Boris Alexeyevich Golitsin. But what good did they do? They would dismount lazily at the porch, kiss the Tsaritsa's hand, and sit down, saying nothing and sighing. There was not much to talk about with the disgraced Tsaritsa. If Peter ran into the room, the boyars would bow to the Tsar who did not rule, ask after his health and then sigh again, shaking their heads. The Tsar was getting too lively: look at his chapped hands, at the scratches on his cheek. Such things were not decent.

"Nikita Moiseyich," the Tsaritsa said to Zotov, "I have been told of a woman who tells fortunes from kvass dregs—so well, everything happens as she says. I'd like to send for her. But I'm afraid: what if she foretold some evil?"

"Madam, what evil could a low woman, like this Vorobyiha, foretell?" Zotov replied in a sing-song musical voice. "If she did, she should be torn to pieces."

Natalia raised her finger and beckoned. Zotov stepped soundlessly close to her in his soft boots.

"Moiseyich. . . . The other day a strelets' widow brought a sieve full of berries to the kitchen and she said that Sophia had been shouting recently in the palace so that everyone heard her, saying that it was a pity the streltsi had not killed the wolf-cub at the time, together with the she-wolf."

Natalia's lips and her double chin, held in by her black kerchief, were trembling and her great eyes filled with tears.

What could he answer? What consolation could he give? Everyone knew that Sophia had the strelets regiments and the whole of the nobles' militia behind her, while Peter had only a few dozen overgrown boys, who played at soldiers, and a wooden cannon loaded with turnips. Nikita Zotov made a helpless gesture and threw back his head until it pressed against his stiff collar.

"Send for Vorobyiha," the Tsaritsa whispered. "Let her tell me the truth: it's worse not to know."

The summer day was long and dull. White clouds hung over the Yaouza—heat and flies. Through the haze the innumerable domes of Moscow, the tops of fortress towers could be seen; and in the foreground, the spire of the Protestant church and the windmills on the Kukuy in the Foreign Quarter. Hens clucked drowsily. The sound of chopping came from the kitchen.

In the days of Tsar Alexey, Preobrazhensk had been filled with noise and laughter, with crowds of people and neighing horses. There was always some entertainment—hunting, or bear-baiting, or horse-racing. But today, even the drive from the stone gates was overgrown with grass. Life was over: sit and tell your beads.

Something struck the window. Zotov opened it. Peter, standing under a lime-tree, covered with dust and earth and sweat like a peasant-boy, called to him:

"Nikita, write a ukase. My peasants are no good—they're old and stupid. Hurry up!"

"What do you wish me to write, Your Majesty?"

"I want a hundred peasants—young, strong ones. Quick."

"Shall I write what these peasants are wanted for?"

"For my games at soldiers. And let them send muskets, not broken ones, and gunpowder for them. And two iron cannons to fire. Quick, quick! I'll sign it and we'll send it by special messenger."

The Tsaritsa leaned out of the window, pushing aside a bough of the lime-tree. "Peter, my darling, you've had enough fighting. Rest a little—come and sit with me."

"I haven't time, mama. Later on, mama."

He ran off. The Tsaritsa sighed deeply as she watched him go. Zotov crossed himself and took a quill pen from his pocket and also a small knife with which he carefully trimmed the point. Then he tried it on his finger-nail. Then he crossed himself again with a prayer, turned back his sleeve and began to write:

"By the grace of God, We the Most Serene and Mighty Lord, Tsar and Grand Duke Peter Alexeyevich, Autocrat of all the Russias. . . ."

Out of boredom the Tsaritsa picked up Peter's copybook. Arithmetic. The pages were covered with ink-blots, the writing crooked and illegible: "Example of addition. The debt is large and the money I have is less than the debt, and it is necessary to subtract to find how much more there is to pay. And this is put down this way: the debt above, and under it the money, and every lower figure is subtracted from the upper one. For instance: one from two leaves one. And you write two above, and below it one, and under the digit you draw a calculating line; under the calculating line, the number which results, or the calculated number. . . ."

The Tsaritsa yawned; was it hunger she felt, or something else?

"Nikita Moiseyich, I can't remember whether we have had anything to eat or not this afternoon?"

"Madam," Zotov said, laying down his pen, rising and bowing.

"Directly after dinner you were pleased to take a nap, and when you rose you were served with strawberries and cream and pear syrup and monastery honey."

"Yes, that's so. It's almost time for vespers."

The Tsaritsa rose languidly and went to her bedroom. There, in the light of icon lamps—the window was curtained—evil-tempered old women sat on coffers ranged along the wall, whispering abuse at each other. Bonelessly, like rag dolls, they all rose together and bowed to the Tsaritsa. She seated herself under the icons in a high-backed Venetian chair. From behind the bed a bleary-eyed dwarf crept out and, sobbing like a child, curled herself up at the Tsaritsa's feet: the old women had hurt her in some way.

"Well, you silly women, tell me your dreams," Natalia said. "Has anyone seen a unicorn?"

Marking the end of the day the bell in the tower of the palace chapel rang out slowly. The young nobles of poor lineage and small fortune whom Sophia had attached to Peter's court appeared in the passages and on the staircases, rubbing their sleep-swollen eyes. Among them was Vasily Volkov: his father had won this honour for him by endless petitions and solicitations. Life was easy; there was plenty to eat and the salary was sixty roubles a year. But it was dull; the courtiers slept practically day and night.

The bell was ringing for vespers. But the Tsar was nowhere to be found. The courtiers set off to hunt for him in the courtyard in the kitchen-gardens and in the meadow by the river. The Tsaritsa sent out a score of loud-voiced women to help. They searched and called high and low: the Tsar could not be found. Could he, heaven forbid, be drowned? The courtiers were all at once wide awake. Riding bareback, they scattered over the twilit fields, shouting and calling. The palace was in an uproar. The old crones began whispering hurriedly in all the corners: "This is surely her doing—Sophia's. The other day a man was in the grounds near the palace. And people saw he had a knife in his boot. They've killed, they've killed, our kind master. . . ."

Natalia was so alarmed by this sinister whispering that she ran out on to the porch, almost beside herself.

Mist was rising from the dark fields, corncrakes were calling in the damp hollows. Far away a dim cheerless star appeared above the black Sokolniki forest. A sharp pang stabbed Natalia's heart: she wrung her hands and cried:

"Peter, my son!"

Vasily Volkov, galloping along the river bank, came on a group of fishermen round a fire. The men sprang up in alarm, upsetting their iron fish-kettle into the fire. Volkov asked breathlessly:

"Have you seen the Tsar, men?"

"Could it be he who rowed past in a boat a short while ago? They seemed to be making for the Kukuy. Look for him in the Foreign Quarter."

The gates of the Foreign Quarter were not yet closed. Volkov dashed down the street towards a group of foreigners. From his saddle he could see the Tsar and with him a long-haired man of middle height in a short coat, the skirts of which stuck out like a turkeycock's tail. In one hand, held well away from his body, he carried his hat, in the other his cane, and laughing familiarly—the son of a bitch!—talked to the Tsar. Peter listened to him, gnawing his nails. And all the foreigners stood shamelessly at their ease. Volkov sprang from his horse, pushed his way through, and went down on his knees before the Tsar.

"Gracious Sovereign, the Tsaritsa Mother is breaking her heart. God knows what we thought had happened to you. Will it please you to return home; it is time for vespers."

Peter impatiently jerked his head sideways over his shoulder. "I don't want to. Go away!"

And as Volkov, still kneeling, went on gazing earnestly at him, Peter flared up and kicked him with his foot: "Be off, serf!"

Volkov bowed low, a grim look on his face, and, without a glance at the laughing foreigners, rode back at a dignified trot to report to the Tsaritsa. A good-natured German with a pink double-chin, in waistcoat, knitted cap and embroidered slippers—the wine-merchant Johann Mons, who had come out of the tavern to look at the young Tsar—took his china pipe from his mouth and observed:

"His Majesty finds it pleasanter here than at home—we're merrier here."

The foreigners standing around also took their pipes from their mouths and nodded agreement with good-humoured smiles:

"Oh yes, we're merrier here."

And they moved nearer to listen to what the elegant man in a curly wig—Francis Lefort—was saying to the Tsar, this tall boy, with the long, childish neck. Peter had met him on the Yaouza. Peter's servants were clumsily rowing the heavy boat, clanking the rowlocks. Peter was sitting in the bow with his feet drawn up. The tiled roofs, the sharp spires, the tops of clipped trees, the windmills with their weathercocks, the dove-cots of the Foreign Quarter lit up by the setting sun were slowly drawing near. Strange music floated to them down the river. It seemed to Peter as though he was seeing a city of that fairyland about which nurses had mumbled to him when he was in his cradle. On the bank, on a heap of rubbish, he saw a man in a velvet coat with stiff skirts; he was wearing a sword and a black, three-cornered hat. It was Captain Francis Lefort: Peter had seen him at the Kremlin when foreign envoys were received.

Lefort stretched out his left hand which held the cane, and with his right took off his hat; then he took a step backwards and bowed, the long curls of his wig covering his face. Then, just as briskly, he drew himself up and, with a smile playing at the corners of his mouth, said in broken Russian:

"At Your Majesty's service."

Peter stared at him, craning his neck, as at some marvel—so gay, so agile was this man, and so unlike anybody else.

Lefort went on, shaking his curls:

"I can show you a water-mill which grinds snuff, pounds millet, works a weaver's loom and raises water to a huge barrel. I can also show you a mill-wheel turned by a dog running inside it. The wine-merchant Mons has a musical box with twelve cavaliers and ladies on the lid, as well as two birds, completely natural but the size of a finger-nail. The birds sing like nightingales and flap their wings and tails, though it is all done by extremely intricate laws of mechanics. I shall show you a telescope through which you can look at the moon and at seas and mountains on it. At the apothecary's you can see a female infant preserved in spirit: its face is ten and a half inches across, its body is covered with hair and it has only two digits on its hands and feet."

Peter's eyes grew rounder and wider with curiosity. But he kept silent, the lips of his small mouth tightly shut. He felt somehow that if he stepped out of the boat—long-armed and long-legged—Lefort would laugh at him. Out of shyness he snorted angrily and could not make up his mind to get out, although the boat's bows had already touched the bank.

Then Lefort ran down to the water's edge—gay, handsome and debonair—caught hold of Peter's hand, with its scratches and badly bitten nails, and pressed it to his heart.

"Oh, our worthy inhabitants of Kukuy will be enchanted to see Your Majesty. They will show you the most amusing things."

Lefort was clever and artful. Before Peter knew what he was doing, he was already walking along by his side, swinging his arms, towards the gates of the Foreign Quarter. There they were surrounded by the well-fed, red-cheeked inhabitants of the Quarter, each of whom was eager to show his house, his mill turned by a dog, his garden with sanded paths, clipped shrubs and not one superfluous blade of grass. They showed him all the clever inventions of which Lefort had spoken.

Peter was amazed and kept asking: "What's this for? How is that done?" The inhabitants of Kukuy nodded and said approvingly: "Oh, young Peter Alexeyevich wants to know everything; it is good that he should."

At last they came to the square pond. It was already dark. Light from the open door of the tavern fell across the water. Peter saw a tiny boat with a small sail hanging slack. In the boat there was a young girl in a billowing white dress like a rose. Her hair was gathered up and adorned with flowers, her arms were bare and she held a lute. Peter was terribly astonished; he even felt frightened for some reason. The girl turned her face towards him: it looked beautiful in the twilight. She touched the lute strings and began to sing, in a thin treble, a German song that was so moving and lovely, that everyone felt like crying. And the white blooms of the tobacco-plants between the glass balls and clipped shrubs filled the air with fragrance. An emotion that he could not understand made Peter's heart beat wildly. Lefort said:

"She's singing in your honour. She is a very nice girl—daughter of the rich wine-merchant Johann Mons."

Mons himself, pipe in mouth, raised his arm and waved his hand gaily to Peter. Lefort's insinuating voice whispered:

"In a few moments the girls are going to gather at the tavern; there will be dancing and fireworks."

Horses' hoofs came dashing furiously along the dark street. A crowd of the Tsar's equerries made their way through to him with strict orders from the Tsaritsa to go home at once. This time the Tsar was obliged to submit.

4

Foreigners who visited the Kremlin used to declare with surprise that, in contrast to the palaces of Paris, Vienna, London, Warsaw or Stockholm, the Tsar's court was more like a merchant's office than anything else. There was no elegant gaiety; no balls, no gambling, no agreeable musical entertainment. The sole occupation of the gold-coated boyars, haughty princes and famous generals in the low-ceilinged, overheated Kremlin rooms was to discuss deals in hemp, potash, blubber, grain or hides. They argued and quarrelled over prices. They complained that though the land was vast and rich, trade was bad; the boyars' estates were large, but there was nothing from them to sell. Tatars held the Black Sea coast, the Baltic was inaccessible, China was far away and, in the North, the English held everything. They ought to fight for sea-coasts, but this was a task beyond their strength.

Besides, the Russians were sluggish. They lived like bears behind their strong gates and high palisades in their Moscow mansions. They attended three services a day, and ate four solid meals; they slept by day too, for it was the custom and did them good. Little free time was left—for the boyar to visit the palace to await the Tsar's pleasure in demanding service from him; for the merchant to sit by his shop and attract customers; for the government clerk to labour over documents.

The Russians might have gone on scratching their backsides, groaning and complaining for God knows how long but for an unexpected stroke of luck. The Polish king Jan Sobieski sent ambassadors to Moscow to discuss an alliance against the Turks. The Poles said persuasively that it was impossible to allow the heathen Turks to torment Christians, and that it was wrong for Orthodox Russians to be at peace with the Turkish Sultan and the Khan of Crimea. Everyone in Moscow immediately realised that the Poles were in a tight corner and that this was the time to bargain with them. And so it was in fact: Poland, in alliance with the Emperor of Austria, was barely able to beat off the Turks, while in the North she was threatened by the Swedes. The devastating Thirty Years' War was still fresh in all minds, when the Austrian Empire had tottered, Germany was depopulated and Poland had become little more than a Swedish province. The French, the Dutch and the Turks found themselves masters of the seas, while the Swedes held the whole of the Baltic seaboard. What the Poles wanted was clear enough: they wanted the Russian armies to protect the Ukrainian steppes from the Turkish Sultan.

Prince Vasily Golitsin—"Protector of the Great Seal and Comptroller of all Ambassadorial relations and Viceroy of Novgorod"—demanded that the Poles return Kiev to Russia. "Give us back the Tsars' estate from time immemorial, Kiev with its towns, then next year we will send an army to the Crimea against the Khan." For three and a half months the Poles argued: "We would rather lose everything than give up Kiev". The Russians were in no hurry; they stood firm and read out to the Poles all the old chronicles from the time of the conversion of Russia to Christianity. They outdid the Poles in patience and won the day.

Jan Sobieski, defeated in Bessarabia by the Turks, wept but signed an eternal peace with Moscow and returned Kiev with all its towns. It was a great victory; but there was no getting out of it: an army had to be raised to fight the Khan.

5

Opposite the Ohotny Riad, in the Golitsin mansion, everything was clean and well-ordered. The outer walls, covered with copper from roof to ground, glowed warmly. Two tall Swiss musketeers in iron helmets and leather cuirasses, stood on rugs at the entrance. Two others guarded the gilded wrought-iron gates through which the common people, dawdling about the Ohotny Riad, stared at the wellfed Swiss, at the spacious courtyard paved with coloured flagstones, at the magnificent coach, all gilt and glass, harnessed with four chestnut horses, at the glinting copper of the house—the house of the Protector, the lover of the Regent Tsarevna.

Vasily Golitsin himself, in this insufferable heat, was sitting in a breeze by an open window, conversing in Latin with a foreigner, de Neuville, recently arrived from Warsaw. The guest was wearing a wig and French clothes such as had just come into fashion at the court of Louis XIV. Golitsin wore no wig, but his clothes too were French: stockings, red shoes, short velvet breeches with ribbons and a fine lace-ruffled shirt showing under the velvet coat in front and at the sides. He had shaved off his beard but kept his moustache. Rolls and note-books, parchment-bound Latin books, maps and architect's plans were lying before him on a table of French make. On the walls, covered with gilt leather, hung "persons", or, according to the new expression, portraits: those of the Golitsins and, in a magnificent Venetian frame, the image of a double-headed eagle holding in its talons a portrait of Sophia. French tapestried and Italian brocaded armchairs, bright rugs, clocks, Persian weapons, a copper geographical globe, a thermometer of English work, solid silver candle-sticks and candelabra, richly-bound books and the celestial sphere painted in gold, silver and azure on the vaulted ceiling were reflected many times in mirrored panels and mirrors over the doors.

The guest looked with approving interest at these half-European, half-Asiatic furnishings and decorations. Golitsin sat with his legs crossed and played with a quill pen as he said, smiling graciously and only now and then stumbling over the Latin words which he pronounced somewhat Moscow fashion:

"Let me explain, Monsieur de Neuville. Two classes form the basis of our realm: the serving class and the tax-paying class, that is, the nobles and the peasants. Both these classes are greatly impoverished, and therefore the State derives no benefit from them, but only ruin. It would be a great advantage to separate the landowners from the peasants, because today the landowner, from sheer greed, devours the peasant serfs without mercy. That is why the peasant is poor, the landowner is poor and the State is poor."

"Wise and thoughtful words, my Lord Chancellor," de Neuville replied. "But how do you think of solving this difficult problem?"

Golitsin, with a broadening smile, took up a morocco-bound notebook from the table; it was written in his own hand and it was entitled: *Treatise on Civil Life, or How to Improve Matters of Concern to the Common Weal.*

"It would be a great and difficult task to enrich the whole nation," he said and began to read from the manuscript. "Many millions of acres are lying fallow. This land should be ploughed and sown. The number of cattle should be increased. Inferior Russian sheep should be replaced by English sheep with fine wool. The people should be encouraged to take up mining and other industries, giving them a fair profit. Many burdensome taxes, tolls, duties and imposts should be abolished and replaced by a moderate poll-tax. This is only possible if all the land is taken from the landowners, and free peasants settled on it. All existing forms of servitude must be abolished, so that in future no one should be in bondage to any other, except perhaps for a small number of house serfs. . . ."

"Sir," exclaimed de Neuville, "history knows no example of a ruler forming such great and drastic plans." Golitsin lowered his eyes and his pale cheeks flushed. "But will the landowners tamely consent to give the land to the peasants and set the serfs free?"

"In place of the land the landowners will be given salaries. The army will be recruited solely from among the nobility. We shall abolish forced recruiting of serfs and tax-payers. Let the peasants work at their own trade. The nobles will be paid for their services, not in land and serfs, but in an increased salary which the treasury will take out of a general land tax. The revenue of the State will be more than doubled."

"I seem to be listening to a philosopher of ancient times," de Neuville murmured.

"Sons of nobles who are under age must be sent to study the military art in Poland, France and Sweden. Academies and study of the sciences must be introduced. We will enrich ourselves with the beauty of the arts. We will populate our deserts with industrious peasants. We will transform our ignorant people into enlightened citizens, our dirty huts into stone houses. The timorous will become brave. We will enrich the poor." Golitsin glanced at the window through which he saw a cloud of dust and straw being whirled along the street. "Our streets will be paved with stone. We will rebuild Moscow of brick and stone. Wisdom will shine out over the poverty-stricken land."

Still holding his quill pen, Golitsin got up and walked up and down the carpets as he went on imparting to his guest many other extraordinary ideas.

"The English people of themselves destroyed an unjust order of things, but in their rage they committed great crimes—they laid hands on God's anointed. Fearing such horrors, we desire the good of all classes equally. If the nobles are obdurate against our plans, we shall break their age-old obstinacy by force."

Their talk was interrupted. A liveried servant, his eyes round with alarm, approached the Prince on tiptoe and whispered something to him. Golitsin's face grew tense and grave. De Neuville noticed this, and took up his hat and began to make his adieux, backing towards the door. Golitsin followed him, also bowing and making curving gestures from his heart downwards with his ringed hand and lace ruffles.

"I am much grieved, Monsieur de Neuville, I am in despair, that you should wish to leave so soon."

When he was alone he glanced at himself in the mirror, and then, with a hasty tapping of heels, passed into his bedchamber. There, on the double bed, under a canopy of crimson silk surmounted by ostrich plumes, sat the Regent Sophia, leaning her temple against one of the spiral bed posts. As always, she had come secretly, in a closed coach, to the back entrance.

6

"Sonushka, my beloved!"

She did not reply, but raised her sullen face and fixed her green, masculine eyes on Golitsin. Perplexed, he stopped half way to the bed.

"Is anything wrong?—Madam. . . ."

That winter Sophia had secretly had an abortion. Her face, which had grown plumper, with strong muscles on each side of her mouth, had lost its high colour; care, worry and anxiety had lent it a disdainful expression. She dressed elaborately, still as a maiden, but her carriage was that of a portly, self-possessed woman. The need to conceal her love for Golitsin tortured her. Although everyone, down to the last kitchenmaid, knew about it, and although of late a new decent foreign word—gallant—had been found to replace the sinful term "lover", it was nevertheless horrible, wicked to surrender her no longer youthful body to her beloved, without law, without marriage, without benediction. This very spring she would have been giving birth with all the vigour and sweet torment that are a woman's. Because of others she had been forced to have an abortion. And her love for Golitsin too was uneasy, unsuited to her age: to love like that—with constant anxiety, stealthily, with her thoughts ever full of him, at nights burning in her bed—was well enough at seventeen. There were even times when hatred rose like a lump in her throat; for he was the cause of all the torment, he was the father of the unborn child. And he: what did it matter to him? He need not give it another thought.

From the bed where she sat—broad, her feet not reaching the floor, warmly damp under her heavy dress—Sophia looked Golitsin up and down with an unfriendly glance.

"How ridiculously you're dressed," she observed. "What is this you're wearing—French? But for the breeches, it's like a woman's dress. People will laugh at you." She turned away, suppressing a sigh. "Yes, something unfortunate has happened, my friend. Little for us to rejoice about."

When Sophia came to him now she was often gloomy and reticent. Golitsin knew that she had two women jesters in her confidence; they roamed all day about the palace, eavesdropping, listening to what the boyars said or hinted, and then reporting it all to Sophia when she went to bed.

"Idle rumors, Madam," Golitsin said. "People talk all kind of nonsense, don't worry, pay no attention to it."

"Pay no attention?" She tapped the bedpost with her nails and her lips curled angrily. "Do you know what they are saying in Moscow? That we are too weak to govern. That they do not see any great deeds from us."

Golitsin fingered his moustache, shrugged his shoulders. Sophia glanced at him out of the corner of her eyes—ah, how handsome he was! How he tormented her! But he was weak; his nerves were a woman's. He decked himself out in lace.

"That's how it is, my friend. You are clever at reading books and at writing, you have a clear mind—I know that myself. But last night, after vespers, my uncle Miloslavsky said about you: 'Golitsin read me a manuscript about serfs and peasants. I wondered: is the Prince in his right mind?' And the boyars laughed."

Golitsin flushed like a girl and his blue eyes flashed under their long lashes.

"It wasn't written for people with minds like theirs."

"However stupid they may be, we have no servants cleverer than they. I myself have to endure a good deal: I would like to dance, as the Polish queen dances, or to ride out hawking sitting on a horse sideways, in a long skirt. But I keep silent. I can do nothing; they would say I was a heretic. As it is, when the Patriarch gives me his hand he pokes it at me like a spade."

"We live among monsters," Golitsin murmured.

"I tell you this, my friend, you must take off your lace and your pretty stockings, put on your military cloak and take a sword in your hand. Show them great deeds!"

"What? Is there more talk about the Khan?"

"Everyone has only one thought today: to make war on the Crimea. We can't avoid it, my dear man. If you return victorious, then you can do what you please. Then you will be stronger than the strongest."

"But you must understand, Sophia, that we cannot fight. We need money for other purposes."

"The other things will come after the Crimea," Sophia declared firmly. "I have already prepared a ukase: you will be Commander-in-Chief. I shall pray for you day and night, wear out my knees with praying, make pilgrimages on foot to all the monasteries. If you return victorious, who will utter a word of blame then? We will end this shameful concealment. I am confident God will help us against the Khan." Sophia got off the bed and looked up at his averted eyes.

"Vaska, I was afraid to tell you. Do you know what they are whispering? 'In Preobrazhensk a strong Tsar is growing up. The Tsarevna is wasting her time; she will never wear the ermine.' Have pity on my thoughts. Bad thoughts come into my mind." She seized his trembling hand between her hot palms. "He is nearly fifteen already. He's as tall as a post. He has sent a ukase to recruit all grooms and falconers to play at soldiers with him. But their swords and muskets are made of iron. . . . Vasya, save me from sin! They whisper into my ears about Dimitry, about Uglich. . . . That's sinful, isn't it?"

Golitsin jerked his hand out of hers, and Sophia smiled slowly, pitifully.

"I do say it is sinful even to think of such things. . . . That was long ago. . . . All Europe will hear of your great deeds. Then we need not fear him—let him play."

"We cannot go to war!" Golitsin exclaimed bitterly. "We have no proper army, no money. . . . My great projects, all in vain! Who appreciates them? Who understands them? Lord, could I have but three, or even two years without war!" He made a hopeless gesture with his hand in its lace ruffle. To speak, to persuade, to resist was useless.

7

Natalia was scolding Zotov:

"Go after him, find him! He ran out of the palace at break of day, without even crossing himself, without eating anything."

It was not so easy to find Peter, unless the roll of drums or the sound of shooting came from somewhere in the woods: that meant the Tsar was there, sporting with his play soldiers. Zotov had often been made prisoner and tied to a tree to stop him bothering Peter with requests to come to mass or listen to some boyar from Moscow. To prevent Nikita getting bored at his tree, Peter ordered a flagon of vodka to be placed by him. So gradually Zotov became used to the cup, and would himself ask to be taken into captivity under the birch. When he got back to Natalia he would spread his arms in a gesture of distress:

"I can't do anything, Madam. He won't come, our young lord."

Peter was indefatigable in play; he could spend a day and a night without sleep or food, playing at anything, so long as it was noisy, jolly or diverting, so long as guns fired and drums beat. He now had about three hundred play-soldiers, taken from among stable-boys, falconers and even youths of good family. He took them on campaigns to the villages and monasteries round Moscow. Sometimes the monks nearly died of fright when, in the noontide heat, with not a leaf stirring and only the deep hum of bees under the limes breaking the drowsy silence, a crowd in green coats—not Russians by the look of them—suddenly dashed out of the wood with savage yells, and—boom! bang!—fired wooden balls from cannon at the monastery walls. And the monks were still more alarmed when, in the long-legged, restless youth, black with mud and gunpowder, they recognised the Tsar himself.

Service in the play-army was hard. There was no time to sleep or to eat enough. Whether it was wet or insufferably hot, at the Tsar's whim they had to go, the devil only knew where or what for, to frighten good people. Sometimes they would be roused in the middle of the night: "Orders to outflank the enemy, to swim across the river." Some drowned in the river at night.

For laziness or for refusal—when someone, bored with the aimless tramping along the roads, did not appear or tried to run home —they were beaten with sticks. Recently a tried *voivoda*—or, as they now called them, general—had been appointed to the army. He was Golovin, a very stupid man, but one who knew all about drilling and introduced strict discipline. Under him Peter, instead of haphazard play, began to study military science in the first battalion, which was given the name of Preobrazhensky.

Francis Lefort was not in Peter's service—his duties kept him at the Kremlin—but he often rode over to the army and gave advice on organisation. Through him a foreign captain named Sommer was engaged as instructor in fighting with firearms and grenades and was also given the rank of general. Sixteen cannons were delivered by the artillery, and then the play-soldiers were taught to fire iron bombs. The teaching was strict: Sommer did not want to draw a salary for nothing. It was now no longer a game. A number of cattle of all kinds were killed in the fields and a good many people injured.

8

The foreigners on the Kukuy frequently discussed the young Tsar. In the evenings they would assemble in the sanded square, among the clipped trees, and slap the tables:

"Hey, Mons, a tankard of beer!"

Mons, in a knitted cap and green waistcoat, would waddle out of the lighted doorway of the tavern, carrying in each hand five earthenware tankards, with caps of froth. The evening is quiet and pleasant. Stars light up the Russian sky, not as bright and resplendent as in Thuringia, or Bavaria, or Würtemberg—but one can live well enough even under Russian stars.

"Mons! Tell us about when Tsar Peter visited you."

Mons would sit down at a table, joining the good company, take a gulp from someone else's tankard and, with a wink, would begin:

"Tsar Peter is very inquisitive. He heard about the wonderful musical box we have in our dining-room. My father-in-law bought it in Nuremberg."

"Oh, yes, we all know your lovely box," confirmed the others, after exchanging glances and wagging their down-curling pipes.

"I was a little alarmed when one day Lefort and Tsar Peter walked into my dining-room. I didn't know how to behave. In such cases the Russians kneel, but I did not want to. However, the Tsar immediately asked me: 'Where is your box?' I answered: 'Here it is, Your Anointed Majesty.' Then the Tsar said: 'Don't call me that, I'm sick of it at home. Call me as you would if I were your friend.' And Lefort said: 'Oh yes, Mons, we shall all call him Herr Peter.' And all three of us laughed heartily over this joke. Then I called my daughter, Annchen, and told her to wind up the box. Usually we wind it up only once a year, on Christmas Eve, because it's a very valuable box. Annchen looked at me and I said: 'Never mind, wind it up!' So she did, and the ladies and cavaliers danced and the birds sang. Peter was amazed and said: 'I want to see how it's made.' I I thought to myself: my box is done for. But Annchen is a very clever girl. She made a pretty curtsey and said to Peter, while Lefort translated: 'Your Majesty, I also know how to sing and dance, but alas! if you wished to look inside me to see what makes me sing and dance, my poor heart would probably break'. Lefort laughed when he'd translated these words, and I laughed heartily, and Annchen laughed like a silver bell. But Peter did not laugh; he went as red as bull's blood and stared at Annchen as though she were a little bird. And I thought to myself: a thousand devils are in that boy! Annchen also blushed and ran away with tears in her blue eyes."

Mons snorted and took another gulp from the mug. He was an excellent and moving story-teller. A pleasant evening breeze played with the tassels of their knitted caps. Annchen came out to the lighted doorway, raised her innocent eyes to the stars, sighed happily and disappeared. The guests puffed at their pipes and declared that God had given Mons a good daughter. Such a daughter would bring wealth to the house. A bearded, red-faced giant, the blacksmith Herrit Kist, a Dutchman from Zaandam, said:

"I can see that if one sets about it cleverly, much benefit can be got from the young Tsar."

Old Ludwig Pfeffer, a clockmaker, replied:

"Oh, no, there's not much hope in that. Tsar Peter has no power. The Regent Sophia will never let him reign. She's a cruel and determined woman. Just now she is mustering an army two hundred thousand strong to make war on the Khan of Crimea. When the army returns from the Crimea, I wouldn't bet even ten pfennigs on the Tsar."

"You are quite wrong, Pfeffer," Mons replied. "More than once I have heard from General Theodore von Sommer, who until lately was plain Sommer," Mons opened his mouth and bellowed with laughter, and all the others joined in, "I heard him say more than once: 'Just wait, give us a year or two, and Tsar Peter will have two battalions of such soldiers that the French king or even Prince Maurice of Saxony would not disdain to command them. . . .' That's what Sommer said."

"Oh, that's good!" his companions said, looking at each other significantly.

Such was the talk on the neatly swept terrace in front of Mons' tavern door.

9

In the vaulted rooms of the palace Administration it was hot and close. Scribes, with their heads on one side and their hair hanging over their eyes, sat at long tables scratching with their pens. Flies floated in the inkstands. Flies clung to the men's lips and sweaty noses. The clerk, heavy with the many pies he had eaten, dozed on a bench. The scribe Ivan Vaskov copied from a sheet into a ledger:

". . . at the command of the great Sovereigns foreign clothing has been made and sent to the apartments of the Great Sovereign, Tsar and Grand Duke Peter Alexeyevich, Autocrat of all the Russias, and for this purpose the following goods have been bought from General Francis Lefort: two bobbins of gold, paid one rouble, thirteen altyns, one kopek; and nine dozen buttons at six altyns the dozen, and for the undercoat, six dozen buttons at two altyns, two kopeks the dozen; and silk and linen for ten altyns; and false hair for three roubles. . . ."

Blowing at a fly Vaskov raised his drowsy lids:

"Listen, Petruha, how does one write 'false hair'? With capital letters or ordinary ones?"

The under-clerk sitting opposite him answered after thinking it over:

"Write it with small ones."

"Hasn't the young Tsar got any hair of his own?"

"Take care. For such words. . . ."

Bending his head to the left to make writing easier, Vaskov went weak with silent laughter; it seemed too funny to him that they should be buying hair for the Tsar from the women in the Foreign Quarter and paying three roubles for such rubbish.

"Petruha, where will he stick this hair on?"

"That's his royal pleasure. He'll stick it on where he likes. And if you ask me any more questions I'll complain to the clerk."

The clerk was also suffering from the flies. Pulling out a silk handkerchief he waved it about and then wiped his face and thin beard, like a goat's.

"He-e-ey, you're asleep!" he scolded feebly. "What kind of scribes and under-clerks are you? All you want is to grab State money for nothing. You've no wholesome fear, you've forgotten God, you good-for-nothing lazybones. Wait till I have the whole lot of you beaten with sticks, then you'll know how to work with proper care. As it is, there's never enough ink or paper for you. . . . May the lightning strike you, you lazy tribe. . . ."

With another languid wave of his handkerchief the clerk dozed off again. These were dull times: no petitioners, no presents. Moscow was depopulated; the streltsi, the young nobles, the landowners had all left for the campaign in the Crimea. Only flies and dust and petty government matters remained.

"Nice if we could have a drink of kvass," said Vaskov. Glancing over his shoulder at the clerk, he stretched himself till his threadbare coat split at the armpits. "Tonight I'm going to a widow's—that's where I'll drink my fill of kvass." With a shake of his head he went back to writing:

". . . at the command of the G.S.T. and G.D. Peter Alexeyevich, Autocrat of all the Russias, it has been ordered to send to him to the village Kolomenskoye the grooms Yakim Voronin, Sergey Buhvostov, Danila Kartin, Ivan Nagibin, Ivan Eyevlev, Sergy Chetkov and

Vasily Buhvostov. The above-mentioned grooms are to be entered as gunners and given the following pay: five roubles each in cash, forty bushels of rye each and the same of oats. . . ."

"Petruha, aren't some people lucky?"

"Who's that talking again? Hey, you, lazy dogs!" the clerk threatened without quite waking up.

10

It was the equerry Vasily Volkov who received and signed the receipt for the foreign suit and wig and carried both with great care to the Tsar's bedchamber. It was barely dawn, but Peter had already sprung from the bench where he had slept on a felt rug under a sheepskin. He seized the wig first and tried it on; it was too tight. He wanted to shear his dark curls with a pair of scissors and Volkov barely managed to talk him out of it. By dint of effort he finally pulled on the wig and grinned at himself in the mirror. For this once he washed his hands with soap, cleaned his nails and hastily donned the new clothes. He tied the white neckcloth as Lefort had taught him and bound a white silk scarf round his hips, over the coat with full skirts. Volkov, as he waited on him, was surprised: it was not Peter's habit to take such trouble over his clothes. He tried on the narrow shoes and gnashed his teeth. A servant, Stepka Medved, was called in to stretch them. And Stepka, having forced his enormous feet into them, ran up and down the stairs like a stallion. At nine o'clock—according to the new reckoning of time—Zotov appeared to summon Peter to early mass. Peter replied impatiently:

"Tell my mother that I have urgent State business . . . I shall pray alone. And listen: come back here at the double, do you hear?"

He suddenly threw back his head and laughed: his laughter always sounded as though he forced it out of his chest. Zotov realised that the Tsar was again up to something: they were always suggesting things to him in the Foreign Quarter. But he obeyed meekly, hurried away in his soft boots, and soon returned, knowing well that something unpleasant was in store for him. He was right. Rolling his eyes Peter ordered:

"You will go as the great envoy of the Hellenic god Bacchus to pay your respects to someone who is celebrating his name-day."

"Very well, Your Majesty," Zotov replied meekly. Then, following the Tsar's orders, he put on a rabbit-skin coat turned inside out, tied bast round his head, crowned it with birch-twigs and took a goblet in his hands. To avoid vain arguments with his mother, Peter left the palace by the back entrance and ran to the stable-yard. There, amidst shouts of laughter, servants were trying to catch four enormous hogs. Peter joined in, shouting, hitting out, fussing. The hogs were caught and harnessed to a low gilt carriage with carved wheels, which had been a bridegroom's gift from the late Tsar to Natalia. Natalia had ordered it to be carefully treasured, and the head groom's lips quivered to see such ruin and disorderliness. Amid whistling and laughter Zotov was bundled into the carriage and Peter seated himself on the box. Volkov, with belted sword and a three-cornered hat, walked in front throwing carrots and turnips to the hogs, while stable-boys slashed them with whips from the sides.

They set off for the Foreign Quarter. At the gates they were met by a crowd of foreigners. "Good, good, very funny!" they shouted, clapping their hands. "It's enough to split your sides laughing." Peter, flushed, with tightly compressed lips and an angry expression on his face, sat very upright on the box. The whole population of the Quarter came running out. They laughed, holding their sides, and pointed their fingers at the Tsar and the bast-crowned figure in the carriage: Zotov, half-dead with fright. The hogs were straining in all directions and the harness was tangled. Suddenly Peter tore a whip from the hands of a stable-boy and lashed furiously at the hogs. They squealed and dashed off dragging the carriage behind them. Someone was knocked down, another fell under the wheels; women snatched up their children. Peter, standing, his face crimson and the nostrils of his short nose distended, went on lashing. His round eyes were red as though he were trying to hold back tears.

Near Lefort's house the stable-boys managed somehow to herd the hogs together and turn the carriage in through the open gates. Lefort, who was celebrating his name-day, ran across the courtyard waving his hat and cane. Behind him came his guests, gaily dressed. Peter jumped down clumsily from the box and dragged Zotov out of the carriage. Still staring wildly at Lefort as though he were afraid to turn his head and see someone in the crowd, Peter said breathlessly:

"*Mein lieber General,* I have brought a great envoy with greetings from the Hellenic god Bacchus."

Large drops of sweat stood out on his face. Peter passed his tongue over his lips and still looking into Lefort's eyes said:

"*Mit herzlichen Gruss.* In other words he salutes you. He sends the hogs and carriage as a gift." Still clutching Zotov convulsively he said in a whisper: "On your knees! Bow!"

Lefort, handsome in rose velvet and lace, powdered and scented, understood everything at once. Raising his hands high he clapped them, broke into merry laughter and turning alternately to Peter and his guests, said:

"What a delightful joke! I never saw anything more amusing. We thought to teach him a few amusing things, but he can teach us! Hey, musicians, a march in honour of the envoy of Bacchus!"

Drums and cymbals struck up behind some lilac bushes and horns began to play. Peter's shoulders lost their rigidity and the flush faded from his face. He flung back his head and roared with laughter. Lefort took his arm. Then Peter ran his eyes round the assembled guests and saw Annchen; she was smiling at him with a flash of her small teeth. Her shoulders were bare and she looked at though she were straining towards him out of her voluminous flowerlike dress.

Once more an agonising embarrassment choked him. He walked to the house with Lefort in front of the other guests, lifting his feet high, like a stork. A group of singers in crimson Russian tunics stood in the open space in front of the porch. They broke into a dancing song accompanied by whistling. One of them, blue-eyed, impudent, sprang forward and chanting "Ay-dudu-dudu-dudu", began to dance, squatting and leaping, beating a rapid tattoo with his iron-tipped heels, slapping the sand with his palms, turning and whirling like a humming-top: "Ee-eh-ti!"

"Well done, Alexander!"

11

Violins, violas, oboes and cymbals in the gallery played old German songs, Russian dances, stately minuets, lively English dances. Clouds of tobacco smoke hung in the sunbeams which came in through the two tiers of round windows in the room. The guests, their tongues loosened by wine, said such things that the girls blushed scarlet, and red-cheeked beauties with farthingales as hooped as barrels and heavy panniers, laughed wildly. For the first time in his life Peter sat at table with women. Lefort offered him some kümmel: for the first time Peter tasted intoxicants. The kümmel ran through his veins like a flame. He looked at the laughing Annchen.

The music set everything inside him dancing, his neck swelled. Clenching his teeth he struggled against compelling forces of desire which he did not yet understand. Because of the noise he did not hear what the guests were shouting as they held out their glasses towards him. Annchen's teeth gleamed in a playful smile; she did not take her bewitching eyes off him.

The feasting went on as though the day would never end. The clockmaker Pfeffer stuck his nose—as long as a carrot—into his snuff-box and began to sneeze; then he pulled off his wig and waved it over his bald head. It was terribly funny! Rocking with laughter, Peter upset the crockery near him with his long arms. It seemed to him that his arms were so long that he had but to stretch them across the table to plunge his fingers into Annchen's hair, caress her head and taste her laughing mouth with his lips. His neck swelled, and a mist dimmed his eyes.

When the sun sank behind the windmills and the cool air flowed in through the open windows, Lefort offered his hand to the immensely fat miller's wife, Frau Schimmelpfennig, and led her out to dance the minuet. With curving gestures of his arm, he shook his curls dusted with gold powder, bent his knees and bowed, languidly rolling his eyes. Frau Schimmelpfennig, pleased and happy, sailed along in her ample skirts like a forty-cannon ship in full rig. Behind this pair all the guests filed out of the dining-hall into the garden where Lefort's initials had been made in flowers in the beds, and the shrubs and small trees were decorated with bows and flowers of gold and silver paper, and the paths swept in chequer-board pattern.

The minuet was followed by a merry square dance. Peter stood aside, biting his nails. Several times ladies curtsied low before him and invited him to dance, but he shook his head, muttering: "I don't know how, I can't. . . ." Then Frau Schimmelpfennig, accompanied by Lefort, offered him a bouquet which meant that he had been elected king of the dance. It was impossible to refuse. He glanced at Lefort's smiling but determined eyes and clutched the lady's hand convulsively. Lefort ran lightly, turning out his toes, towards Annchen and took his position with her opposite Peter. Annchen, holding a handkerchief in her limp hand, looked as though she were asking for something. The cymbals crashed, the drum boomed, fiddles and flutes sang: the merry music rose to the evening sky, startling the bats.

And again, as earlier in the day with the hogs, all trammels were cast off; he felt hot and wild. Lefort called out:

"First figure—ladies advance and retreat—cavaliers swing their ladies."

Peter seized the miller's wife by the waist and swung her so that her skirts, panniers and train swirled like a whirlwind. *"Ach, mein Gott!"* was all she could say. Leaving her, he began to dance as though the music were twitching his arms and legs. With lips tightly pressed and nostrils distended he executed such jumps and hops that the guests held their sides as they watched him.

"Third figure!" Lefort cried. "Ladies change their partners."

Annchen's cool hand rested on Peter's shoulder. In a moment he was sober, and his violence left him. He was trembling. And as he danced with Annchen, light as a feather, his feet carried him along of their own accord. The lamps between the shrubs shone out, lighted by a train of powder. A rocket soared up with an angry hiss. Two little threads of flame were reflected in Annchen's eyes. "Oh," she whispered faintly, "oh, how lovely! Oh, Peter, you dance beautifully!"

Rockets soared from every part of the garden. Wheels of fire revolved, stencilled pictures lit up. Maroons burst like guns; starshells flared; fountains of sparks played. The evening sky was veiled in smoke. Was it not all a dream he was dreaming in the monotonous boredom of the Preobrazhensky palace? Capering past him with a woman as tall as a soldier, Lefort called out flippantly: "Cupid pierces hearts with his darts!" Annchen, warm from the dance was as fragrant as a flower. "Oh, Peter, I am tired," she moaned in a still fainter voice, hanging on his arm. A rocket rose and broke over their heads and serpents of fire lit up the girl's lovely face, drawn with fatigue. Not knowing how to do it, Peter seized her bare shoulders, shut his eyes and felt the moist touch of her lips. But it was only a touch. Annchen tore herself from his arms. Hundreds of serpents rose in a mad fusillade. Out of the cloud of smoke appeared the rabbit-skin coat and bast-bedecked head of Bacchus's envoy. Completely drunk Nikita Zotov, still holding a goblet, staggered by, mumbling nonsense. He stopped, swaying.

"Here, son, drink!" He offered Peter the goblet. "Drink, for come what may we are both lost. We've lost our souls, feasting on a fast day. Drink to the dregs, Your Majesty of All the Russias. . . ."

He tried to make an admonitory gesture and fell into a bush. Peter flung down the empty goblet. Happiness whirled in him like a firework. "Annchen!" he called, and began to run. Lighted windows, fairy lamps, illuminated pictures all swam round him. He put his hands to his head, planting his feet wide apart.

"Come on, I'll show you where she is," an insinuating voice said in his ear. It was one of the singers in a crimson tunic, Alexander Menshikov with the sharp eyes. "The girl has gone home."

Peter followed him silently at a run into the darkness. They climbed a fence, ran up against some dogs, jumped palings and found themselves in the square near the windmill outside the tavern. One long window in the upper floor was lighted.

Alexander said in a whisper: "She's there!" and threw sand at the window-pane.

The window opened and Annchen—a shawl over her shoulders and her hair in curlpapers—leaned out.

"Who's there?" she asked in a quiet little voice. She peered, saw Peter and shook her head: "You mustn't. Go to bed, Herr Peter."

She looked sweeter than ever in curlpapers. She shut the window and drew the lace curtain. The light went out.

"The girl is cautious," Alexander whispered. Then he looked closely at Peter and, taking him firmly by the shoulders, led him to a bench. "You'd better sit down. I'll bring horses. Can you ride home?"

When he returned leading two saddled horses, Peter was still huddled on the bench, his clenched fists resting on his knees. Alexander peered into his face.

"Have you had too much to drink, or what?"

Peter did not reply. Alexander helped him to mount, sprang lightly into his own saddle and, holding Peter up, rode out of the Foreign Quarter at a walk. A mist lay over the meadows. The autumn sky was ablaze with stars. In Preobrazhensk the cocks were already crowing. Peter's icy hand gripping Alexander's shoulder seemed lifeless. When they had almost reached the palace, Peter suddenly arched his back and began to writhe in his saddle, then he seized Alexander round the neck and pressed close to him. The horses stopped. He was wheezing and his joints were cracking.

"Hold me, hold me tightly," he muttered hoarsely. After a moment his grip slackened and he moaned: "Let's go on. But don't leave me. You'll lie by my side."

At the porch Volkov sprang towards them:

"Sire! Oh heavens! And we. . . ."

Equerries and grooms ran up. Peter, still in the saddle, pushed them away with his foot, and dismounted unaided. Keeping Alexander with him, he went to his apartment. In a dark passage a little old woman rustled and crossed herself; Peter pushed her aside. Another one scuttled like a rat under the staircase.

"Damned whispering hags, blast you!" Peter muttered.

In the bedchamber Alexander took off Peter's shoes and coat. Peter lay down on a felt rug and ordered Alexander to lie beside him. He laid his head on Alexander's shoulder. After a silence he said:

"You'll be attached to the bedchamber. In the morning tell the clerk—he'll write a ukase. It was fun, oh, what fun! *Mein lieber Gott. . . .*"

A few moments later, with a child-like whimper, he fell asleep.

chapter three

All through the winter the nobles' militia was being mustered. It was difficult to bring the landowners out of their distant villages. The Commander-in-Chief, Golitsin, sent peremptory orders, threatening them with disgrace and ruin. The landowners were in no hurry to leave their warm firesides. "What an idea! To make war on the Crimea! Thank God, we've got a treaty of eternal peace with the Khan. We pay him a tribute that's not onerous, then why trouble the nobility needlessly? It's the work of the Golitsins; they want to win honours with other people's hands."

They sent endless excuses: they were ill, or too poor, or absent. Some played impudent tricks; boredom and inactivity in winter time put all sorts of silly ideas into a man's head. The equerries, Boris Dolgoruky and Yury Shcherbaty, unable to avoid taking part in the campaign, dressed themselves and their men-at-arms in black and, mounted on black horses, as though risen from the dead, appeared thus at the army camp frightening everybody out of their wits. "There's bound to be a calamity", the talk went round in the regiments. "We shan't return from the campaign alive."

Golitsin was so incensed that he wrote to Moscow, to Shaklovity, whom he had left as adviser to Sophia: "Have pity, make every effort to obtain a ukase against these men for their offence against me: let them be stripped of their property, sent to a monastery for life and their villages distributed to needy persons, thus giving such an example of severity as to make everyone tremble."

The ukase was prepared, but out of soft-heartedness, Golitsin forgave the offenders who, with tears, implored his clemency. No sooner had the affair been hushed up, than a rumour spread in the army that one night a coffin had been smuggled into the passage of Golitsin's hut. The men shuddered, whispering about this fearful business. It was said that Golitsin had got drunk that day and rushed into the dark passage laying about him with a sword in the black void. There were evil omens. Men who brought in supply-trains had seen white wolves howling horribly on the ancient burial mounds in the steppe. Horses died from unknown causes. During a windy night in March the regimental goat—many heard it—cried out in a human voice: "There will be a calamity!" When they tried to kill the goat with staves, it escaped into the steppe.

The snow melted. A soft wind blew from the South, and willows by the lakes and rivers began to show green. Golitsin went about as black as thunder. Unwelcome news was coming from Moscow. They said that Cherkassky, one of Peter's intimate boyars, had begun to talk loudly at the Kremlin, and that the boyars lent their ears to him and ridiculed the Crimea campaign: "The Khan," they said, "is weary of waiting for Golitsin; in the Crimea, in Constantinople and in the whole of Europe they have dismissed the campaigns from their minds. Golitsin is costing the treasury a fine sum."

Even the Patriarch Joachim, Golitsin's former advocate, had all of a sudden ordered the vestments and coats presented by Golitsin to be thrown out of the church on the Barashi, and forbidden the use of them during the services. Golitsin wrote anxious letters to Shaklovity enjoining him to watch Cherkassky like a lynx and to see that the Patriarch went less often to Sophia's apartments. "As for the boyars, they are a prey to their age-old greed and grudge to part with so much as a penny."

Comfortless news came from abroad. The French King, from whom the great envoys, Yakov Dolgoruky and Yakov Mishetsky, had requested a loan of three million livres, gave no money and did not even wish to see the envoys. Of the ambassador in Holland, Ushakov, it was reported that: "he and his men had become utterly disreputable; they feasted and drank in many places and uttered low words, which brought discredit upon their Majesties".

At the end of May Golitsin at last moved South with his army, a hundred thousand strong, and on the river Samara joined forces with the Ukrainian Hetman * Samoylovich. The army moved slowly,

* Elected chief of the Cossacks.

trailing behind it innumerable baggage-trains. They passed the towns and the last outposts and entered the steppe of Dikoye Pole. A torrid heat reigned over the uninhabited plain where the grass grew shoulder-high. Vultures circled in the hot sky. Mirages shimmered on the horizon. The sunsets were brief in a greenish-yellow sky. The creaking of waggons and the neighing of horses filled the steppe. The smoke of dried horse-dung fires smelt of the melancholy of ages. Night fell swiftly. Terrible stars blazed. The steppe was empty: roadless, trackless. The advance regiments marched far ahead without meeting a living soul. The Tatars were evidently luring on the Russian forces to waterless and sandy wastes. More and more often they came across dried riverbeds. Here only experienced Cossacks knew where to find water.

It was already mid-July, yet the Crimea still remained a dream. The regiments were stretched out from one end of the steppe to the other. The white light, the dry chirring of the grasshoppers made the men's heads swim. Birds swooped down lazily on to the distended ribs of dead horses. Many carts were abandoned. Some peasant drivers remained with the carts, dying of thirst. Some wandered off to the North, to the Dniepr. The army murmured.

Generals, colonels and commanders of "thousands" gathered at dinner-time by Golitsin's canvas tent, gazing anxiously at the drooping banner. But not one had the courage to speak out and say: "We must go back before it is too late. The farther we go, the more terrible it will be. Beyond the Perekop are deadly sands."

During these hours Golitsin rested in his tent. Having taken off his clothes and boots, he lay on rugs reading Plutarch in Latin. The great shades rising from the pages of the book restored courage to his depressed mind. To the tedious accompaniment of the chirring grasshoppers, Pompey, Scipio, Lucullus, Julius Cæsar brandished their Roman eagles. Onward to glory! Onward to glory! Another source of energy was re-reading Sophia's letters: "My beloved, brother Vasenka! May you live, my friend, many years! May God grant you defeat the enemy! But I, my beloved, can hardly believe that you will return to us. I will only believe it when I see you, my beloved, in my arms. Why, my beloved, do you write that I should pray? As though I am really a sinner before God, and unworthy. However, even sinful as I am, I dare hope for His clemency. Indeed, I always pray that I should see my beloved in happiness. May you fare well, my beloved, for endless years!"

When the heat abated Golitsin would don helmet and cloak and come out of his tent. At sight of him the commanders mounted their steeds. Trumpets sounded, bugles sang their long notes. The army was now marching at night before the noontide heat.

It had been the same today. From the height of the ancient burial mound Golitsin looked round at the innumerable camp fires, the dark masses of soldiers, the long lines of baggage-trains fading into the dusk. It was darker than usual. A curtain of dust surrounded the camp. It was difficult to breathe in the still air. The sunset covered half the sky with dark red gloom. Flocks of birds flew past as though fleeing danger. The sun, as it set, swelled, misty and terrifying. The stars had barely begun to twinkle when a film obscured them. Smoky flames glimmered on the horizon. A sultry wind was rising. The dancing tongues of fire shone out more clearly: they formed a ring round the encampment.

A group of horsemen stopped at the mound. One of them galloped heavily up to the tent. He dismounted, straightening his tall cap. Golitsin recognised the fat face and grey moustache of Hetman Samoylovich.

"Disaster, Prince!" he said in a low voice. "The Tatars have fired the steppe."

The hetman's drooping moustache hid a smile and a shadow screened his eyes.

"It's burning all round," he said, pointing with his whip.

Golitsin stared long and intently at the red glow. "Well, we shall put the infantry on horseback and ride through the fire."

"How can we march through ashes? No food, no water. We shall perish, Prince."

"Am I—I—to retreat then?"

"Do as you please. The Cossacks won't go through the burning steppe."

"Drive them with whips!" When angry, Golitsin had no control over himself. He ran backwards and forwards over the mound, his iron heels sinking into the dry earth. "I've noticed for quite a while that the Cossacks are not willingly with us. It is comical to see them: they doze in their saddles. They probably gave more eager service to the Khan of Crimea. And you, Hetman, are not sincere. Take care! In Moscow better men have been dragged to the block by their scalplocks. And you—a priest's son—how long is it since you traded in candles and fish?"

The obese Samoylovich snorted like a bull as he listened to these insults. But he was clever and crafty and so held his tongue. Breathing heavily through his nose he climbed on to his horse, rode down the mound and disappeared behind the carts. Golitsin called for the trumpeters. The trumpets blared harshly over the smoke-veiled steppe. Cavalry, infantry and baggage-trains started to move through the fire.

At dawn it became evident that they could go no farther: the steppe lay black and dead before them. Only whirlwinds moved across it. The south wind grew stronger, driving up clouds of ash. The Cossack patrols could be seen in the distance turning back. At noon the generals and officers assembled at the rear. The hetman, frowning, rode up, pushed his mace into the top of his boot and lit his pipe. Golitsin, laying his beringed hands on his breastplate, said with tears, swallowing his pride:

"Who can go against the Lord? It is written: Man, humble thy pride, for thou art mortal. The Lord has sent us a great calamity. For hundreds of miles there is neither fodder, nor water. I fear neither death, nor shame. Commanders, consider and say what ought to be done."

The commanders and officers considered and replied:

"Retreat without delay to the Dniepr!"

Thus the Crimean campaign came to an inglorious end. The army moved back with all speed, losing men, and abandoning baggage-trains. They did not halt until they reached the neighbourhood of Poltava.

2

The colonels Solonina, Lizogub, Zabela Gamaley, the captain Ivan Mazeppa and the general secretary Kochubey came secretly to Golitsin's tent and said to him:

"The steppe was fired by the Cossacks. It was the hetman who sent them to fire it. And here is a denunciation of the hetman. Read it and send it to Moscow. Lose no time, for we have no patience left to put up any longer with his arbitrary ways: he has enriched himself, ruined the nobles. The Cossack elders dare not keep their caps on in his presence. He insults everybody. He lies to the Russians, he treats with the Poles, but lies to them too, for what he wants is to turn the Ukraine into a private province of his own and deprive us of our liberties. Let them send a ukase from Moscow: that we should elect another hetman, and depose Samoylovich."

"But why should the hetman not want me to defeat the Tatars?" Golitsin asked.

"The reason why he doesn't want it," replied Captain Ivan Mazeppa, "is that so long as the Tatars are strong, you are weak. If you conquer the Tatars, then soon the Ukraine too will become a province of Moscow. But all that is not true. We are the Russians' younger brothers, we are of the same faith, and are all glad to live under the Moscow Tsar."

"Well said!" confirmed the colonels, with their long scalp-locks on blue shaven heads, staring at the ground. "Provided Moscow confirms our nobles' liberties."

Golitsin recalled the black clouds of dust, the innumerable graves left behind in the steppes, the horses' ribs scattered over the roads. With flaming cheeks he remembered his dreams of the campaigns of Alexander of Macedon. He saw in his mind the narrow passages of the Kremlin palace where the boyars—his enemies—would bow to him, with their fingers on their moustaches to hide a mocking smile.

"So it's the hetman who set fire to the steppes?"

"Yes," confirmed the commanders.

"Very well, let it be as you wish."

That same day Mihail Tirtov galloped off to Moscow with a spare mount in lead, and with the denunciation of the hetman sewn in his cap. When the army reached the outskirts of Poltava and encamped, a reply arrived from the Great Sovereigns: "Seeing that Samoylovich is undesirable to the elders and the whole Little-Russian army, let the Great Sovereigns' banner and all military insignia of office be taken from him and he himself be sent under strong escort to the Great-Russian towns. And in his stead let there be installed he to whom the elders with the whole of the Little-Russian army give their preference. . . ."

That night the streltsi brought the waggons close up to the hetman's headquarters. In the morning they seized the hetman in his field-chapel, threw him into a common cart and brought him to Golitsin. There he was questioned. A damp rag was tied round his head and his eyes were inflamed. In terror he kept repeating:

"They are lying, Prince! God is my witness, they are lying! It's the intrigues of Mazeppa, my enemy. . . ." Catching sight of Mazeppa, Gamaley and Solonina who were coming in, he turned purple and shook all over: "So you listen to them? The dogs! All they are waiting for is to sell the Ukraine to the Poles."

Gamaley and Solonina rushed at him with drawn swords, but the strelets officers beat them off. In the night he was taken to the North in chains. There was need to hurry with the election of a new hetman: the Cossacks had broached barrels of spirits in the waggons, killed the hetman's servants and run through the universally hated Gadiatsky commander with a pike. All over the camp there was shouting, singing and musket-fire. The Moscow regiments were also becoming restive.

Without invitation Mazeppa entered Golitsin's tent. He was wearing a long grey Ukrainian coat, a plain astrakhan cap, but a handsome sword hung on a gold chain. Mazeppa was rich; he came from an illustrious family of nobles and had made long visits to Poland and Austria. During the campaign he had let his beard grow—like a Muscovite—and cut his hair Moscow fashion. With a dignified bow —as from equal to equal—he seated himself. Stroking his chin with his long, dry fingers he fixed upon Golitsin his prominent, intelligent eyes.

"Perhaps the Prince would like to converse in Latin?"

Golitsin nodded coldly. Without lowering his voice Mazeppa began to speak in Latin: "It is difficult for you to find your way about in Ukrainian affairs. The Ukrainians are sly and reticent. Tomorrow a new Hetman will have to be proclaimed, and there is a rumour that they want to proclaim Borkovsky. In that case it would have been better not to depose Samoylovich: Moscow has no more dangerous enemy than Borkovsky. I am speaking as a friend."

"You know yourself that we have no wish to interfere in your Ukrainian affairs," Golitsin replied. "Any hetman will do for us, so long as he is a friend."

"It is pleasant to hear wise speech. We have no need to conceal the fact that under the protection of Moscow we are in complete security." Here Golitsin lowered his eyes with a swift smile. "You do not take away the land from us nobles, and you look favourably on our customs. It must be confessed that there are some amongst us who lean towards Poland. But they are those who would destroy the Ukraine for the sake of personal greed. Don't we know that were we to submit to Poland, the Polish nobles would oust us from our lands, build Catholic churches everywhere and turn us all into slaves? No, Prince, we are faithful servants of the Great Sovereigns." Golitsin remained silent and did not raise his eyes. "Well, the Lord has been kind to me. Last year I buried, in a secret place near Poltava, a cask—ten thousand roubles in gold—against a rainy day. We, Little-Russians, are simple folk and would give our lives for a great cause. What do we fear? Only that the mace might go to a traitor or a fool; that's what we fear."

"Very well then, Ivan Stepanovich, may the hour be propitious—

proclaim the hetman tomorrow." Golitsin rose and bowed to his guest. After a pause, he took him by the shoulders and kissed him three times.

The next day, near the field chapel tent there lay on a table, covered with a gold cloth, the mace, the banner and the hetman's insignia of office. Two thousand Cossacks stood round. Out of the tent stepped Prince Golitsin, in Persian armour, wearing a cloak and helmet with a crest of crimson plumes; after him came all the Cossacks elders. Golitsin stood up on a bench, one hand holding a silk handkerchief, the other laid on the hilt of his sword, and said to the Cossacks who moved closer:

"Great Army of Little-Russia, Their Majesties the Tsars permit you, according to the ancient tradition of the Cossack Army, to elect your Hetman. Say whom you want and so it shall be. Whether it is Mazeppa you want, or someone else: it is for you to decide."

Colonel Solonina shouted: "We want Mazeppa!" Other voices took it up, and the whole field began to shout: "Let Mazeppa be Hetman!"

The same day four Cossacks brought a small cask, black with earth and full of gold, into Prince Golitsin's tent.

3

The fortress which had been built two years before on the Yaouza river, below the Preobrazhensky palace, was reconstructed that summer in accordance with plans drawn up by Lefort and Sommer. The walls were made thicker and strengthened with piles, outside deep moats were dug and strong towers with embrasures were erected at the angles. Fascines of plaited willow and sandbags protected a row of bronze cannon, mortars and culverins. A dining-hall that could hold five hundred men was built of logs in the centre of the fortress. A chime of bells was hung in the main tower over the gates.

Games are games, and the fortress might be a toy one, yet in case of need it could withstand a siege. The two battalions—the Semenovsky and the Preobrazhensky—exercised on the wide mown meadow from dawn to dusk; General Sommer spared neither his throat nor his fists. The soldiers marched like clock-work figures, holding their muskets in front of them. "Halt!" The soldiers halted, marking the step with their right feet, and came to a dead stop. "Right shoulder forward—advance! *Vorwärts!* Wrong! *Lumpen!* Rascals! Listen!" The General, red as a turkey-cock, sat on his horse, and even Peter, now a corporal, drew himself up, his eyes bulging with fear, as he passed him.

Two more foreigners had been engaged from the Foreign Quarter: Franz Timmermann, who knew mathematics and the use of the astrolabe, and old Karten Brandt, an expert on naval matters. Timmermann began to teach Peter mathematics and fortification; Karten Brandt undertook to build boats on the model of a wonderful old vessel found in a barn in the Izmailovo village, which could sail against the wind.

More and more frequently boyars rode over from Moscow to see with their own eyes what kind of games were being played on the Yaouza, which cost so much money and took so many arms from the armoury. They did not cross the bridge, but stopped on the farther bank of the river: in front, the boyar sat on his horse, in a handsome overcoat, ample as a featherbed, with a beard like a broad broom and plump cheeks; and behind him, nobles, wearing three or four of their best coats one on top of the other. There they remained by the hour, motionless. On the near bank carts laden with sand or brushwood lumbered by; soldiers hauled logs; on a high tripod a massive hammer rose on pulleys and—thump!—fell on the piles; spades made the soil fly. Foreigners stalked about with plans and compasses; axes rang, saws screeched, overseers ran with measuring rods. And there—oh, God and holy saints!—there was the Tsar himself: not on a golden chair looking on from a height at the diversion, no! the Tsar in knitted cap, Dutch breeches and dirty shirt, trotted along boards trundling a wheelbarrow.

The boyar would take off his cap "of forty sables", the nobles also uncovered themselves and bowed low from the farther bank. And they watched in bewilderment. Their fathers and grandfathers had stood like a solid wall round the Tsar, guarding lest a fly or a speck of dust settle on His Anointed Majesty. On rare occasions they brought him out before the people wellnigh as a god, with all the ancient splendour of Byzantium. But this? What was this Tsar doing? Like a serf among serfs, like a worthless fool, running along boards, the shameless fellow, pipe in mouth, smoking the disgusting weed tobacco. Shaking the foundations. This was no longer a game, an amusement: see how across the river the serfs were grinning!

Occasionally a boyar took his courage in both hands and, shaking his beard, would shout in a trembling voice:

"Punish me, Sire, for speaking the truth, but I am too old to keep silent: it is shameful to see, shameful and monstrous!"

Then Peter, long as a pole, would climb on to the earth wall and, screwing up his eyes, shout back:

"Oh, it's you! I say, what does Golitsin write? Has he conquered the Crimea yet, or not?"

And behind the earth walls the accursed foreigners would start guffawing and roaring with laughter, and the Russians too, who, instead of bawling, should be down on their knees in the presence of a person so close to the Tsars. It also sometimes happened that a boyar—as well be hanged for a sheep as for a lamb—would persist in his exhortations and admonitions: "I dandled your father on my knees, spent night and day by the Sovereign's coffin, my family stems from Rurik, my ancestors have themselves been Grand Dukes. Think of our honour! Leave these games, come to your senses! Go to the bath-house! Go to church!"

"Alexander," Peter would say, "give me the match!" And, taking aim with a twenty-pounder culverin, he would shoot a volley of peas at the boyar. Sommer would roar with laughter, holding his belly, and so would Lefort, while the silent Timmermann would smile good-humouredly. Brandt, short and squat with his face in merry wrinkles, like a baked apple, would shake with amusement. And the foreigners and Russians would jump on to the earth walls to see the high hat knocked off, the boyar, more dead than alive, fall into the arms of the attendant nobles, while the horses reared and plunged. They laughed and talked about it for the rest of the day.

They called the fortress "the Capital City of Pressburg".

4

Alexander Menshikov remained with Peter after that night when he had taken him to his room. He was adroit, the devil, and agile; he divined Peter's wishes: with a shake of his curls he would swing round and rush off—and the thing was done. When he slept was a mystery. He would pass his hand over his impudent face, and then be as though he had washed himself: gay, clear-eyed, full of laughter. He was nearly as tall as Peter, but with broader shoulders and a slender waist. Wherever Peter went, he went too. It was all the same to him to beat a drum, fire a musket or slash a switch with his sword. When he began to play the fool it was enchanting; he would imitate a bear climbing into a hollow tree to get at the honey and being attacked by wild bees; or a priest scaring a merchant's wife to make her order masses; or two stammerers having a quarrel. Peter would laugh till he cried, and gaze at Alexander as though infatuated with him. At first everyone thought Alexander would be the court fool. But he aimed higher; he was full of jokes and fun, but sometimes when generals and engineers were discussing how to do this or that, staring at the plans, while Peter bit his nails with impatience, Alexander would bend over someone's shoulder and, speaking quickly so that they should not have time to send him away, would say:

"Why, that's how it should be done, it's quite simple."

The generals would say: "Oh-oh-oh!" and Peter's eyes would blaze:

"Right!"

If anything was wanted in a hurry, Alexander would take money and fly on horseback to Moscow—through gardens and over fences—and bring what was needed as though by magic. Later, when he presented the bill to Zotov (quartermaster of the palace army) he would sigh meekly and sniff and blink: "Say what you like, but there's not a farthing wrong here."

"Alexander, Alexander!" Zotov would shake his head. "Who ever heard of fir-poles costing three altyns? One at the most. Oh, Alexander!"

"If you're not in a hurry, then it's one altyn; but this was more because it was a rush. I got them quickly—that's what matters—not to keep Peter Alexeyevich waiting."

"You'll be hanged one day for your dishonesty."

"Lord, why do you insult me unjustly, Nikita Moiseyich?" turning his face away and forcing tears into his blue eyes, Alexander spoke plaintively.

Zotov would wave him away with his quill pen:

"All right, go along. I'll believe you this once. But take care!"

Alexander was made Peter's orderly. Lefort praised him to Peter: "The lad will go far; he's as devoted as a dog and as clever as the devil."

Alexander constantly went to see Lefort at his house and never returned without some present. He liked presents hugely, no matter what they were. He wore Lefort's coats and hats, and was the first of the Russians to order a wig from the Foreign Quarter: an immense one, of flaming red, which he wore on feast days. He shaved his lip and cheeks and powdered himself. Some of the servants began to call him "Alexander Danilovich".

One day he brought a modest youth to Peter, dressed in a clean tunic, new birch-bark shoes and linen footcloths.

"*Mein Herz*," he said—Alexander often addressed Peter now in this way—"order him to show you what he can do with a drum. Alioshka, take the drum."

Alioshka Brovkin unhurriedly laid down his cap, took a drum from the table, looked up at the ceiling with a bored expression, and then struck the drum smartly; he rattled out a tattoo, a retreat, a military march and then tapped out a quick dance—it was splendid! He stood like a wooden image, only his hands and his sticks flew—so fast that they were invisible.

Peter rushed over to him, seized him by the ears, looked with wonder into his eyes and kissed him several times:

"Drummer to the First Company!"

So Alexander had his own man in the battalion.

When the days shortened and the earth was frostbound and snow, in hard little pellets, fell from the low clouds, balls and beer parties with music began in the Foreign Quarter. The foreigners sent invitations to Tsar Peter through Alexander: a handsome sheet of paper with the picture of a big-bellied man sitting on a barrel in a frame of columns and vines; above, a naked child shooting from a bow and, below, an old man with a scythe. In the centre were verses written in gold ink:

"With hearty greetings we invite you to a tankard of beer and dancing," but the initial letters read: "Herr Peter."

As soon as it was dusk Alexander would drive a one-horse chaise up to the porch—Peter did not like riding, he was too tall—and the two of them disappeared for a long time into the Foreign Quarter On the way Alexander would say:

"When I called at the tavern, *mein Herz*, to order the small beer you commanded, I saw Anna Ivanovna. She promised to be there tonight without fail."

Peter sniffed and said nothing. A terrible force drew him to these evening parties. The iron-shod wheels thundered over the frozen ruts, the road was barely visible in the darkness, on the dam the wind howled in the bare branches. And then, the welcoming lights. Alexander, peering into the dark would say: "More to the left, more to the left, *mein Herz*, turn into the alley, we won't pass through here." The warm light shone from the low Dutch windows. Through the round bottle-glass panes they could see huge wigs and women's bare shoulders. There was music and couples were dancing. Sconces bearing three candles, with little mirrors behind them, threw droll shadows.

Peter did not enter simply: he always rolled his eyes in some strange way; tall, pale, with his small mouth tightly shut, he would suddenly appear on the threshold and, with quivering nostrils, inhale the sweet scent of the women and the pleasant smells of pipe tobacco and beer.

"Peter!" the host would exclaim in a loud voice. Then the guests jumped to their feet and came towards him with welcoming, outstretched hands; the ladies curtsied to the strange youth, the Tsar of the barbarians, in their low obeisance displaying their plump bosoms, braced high by strong corsets. Everyone knew that Peter would invite Annchen Mons for the first square dance. Each time she flushed with pleased surprise. She grew prettier every day; she was at the zenith of her beauty. Peter knew already a good deal of German and Dutch, and she listened attentively to his jerky, always hurried stories, putting in an apt word now and then.

When, with a jingle of spurs some dashing cavalier invited her to a dance, Peter's face clouded. He sat hunched up on his stool, watching out of the corner of his eyes the billowing of Annchen's skirts, as she danced lightheartedly, the turn of her fair head and the way she inclined her neck—encircled by a velvet ribbon with a little golden heart—towards her partner.

His heart ached: she was so desirable, so tempting, so inaccessible.

Alexander danced with the mature ladies whose age condemned them to be wallflowers; the handsome fellow laboured till he sweated profusely.

Towards ten o'clock the young folk disappeared, and Annchen with them. The important guests sat down to a supper of blood sausage, stuffed pig's head and some wonderfully delicious and satisfying earth-apples called potatoes. Peter ate heartily, drank beer and, having thrown off his love-sick torpor, nibbled radishes and smoked tobacco. Towards morning Alexander helped him into the two-wheeled chaise. Once more the icy wind whistled across the dark fields.

"I wish I had a windmill, or a tannery, like Timmermann," said Peter catching hold of the carriage rail.

"A funny thing to want! Hold tight, here's a ditch."

"Fool! Look how they live; better than we do."

"And if you did, of course, then you could get married. . . ."

"Hold your tongue; I'll hit you."

"Wait a minute; we're off the road again."

"Tomorrow I'll have to render accounts to mama. Go to the bath, go to confession and communion—you have defiled yourself. I must go to Moscow tomorrow: there's nothing I hate more. Put on Tsar's robes, service half the day, and the other half sit on the throne with my brother—below Sophia. Ivan's breath smells horrid. Those sleepy boyars—I'd like to kick them. But I must bear it and keep silent. The Tsar! They'll kill me, I know."

"You've got no reason to think so. It's because you're drunk."

"Sophia is a viper! The Miloslavskys are greedy locusts; I shan't forget their swords and pikes. They'd have thrown me down from the porch, but the people roared at them. Do you remember?"

"I do!"

"Vaska Golitsin has lost one army in the steppe. Now he's been ordered to march on the Crimea again. Sophia and the Miloslavskys are waiting impatiently for him to get back with his army. They've got a hundred thousand men. They'll point me out to them and sound the tocsin."

"We'll shut ourselves up in Pressburg."

"They've already tried once to poison me. Sent a man with a knife." Peter jumped up and looked round him. All was dark, not a light showed anywhere. Alexander grasped him by his belt and drew him back on the seat. "Curse them! Curse them!"

"Whoa! That's where it is, the dam." Alexander struck the horse with the reins. The strong animal carried them out on to the steep bank. The lights of Preobrazhensk showed in the distance. "The streltsi can't be roused by the tocsin nowadays, *mein Herz*. Those times have gone. Ask anyone, ask Alioshka Brovkin, he's been among them. They're none too pleased with that sister of yours."

"I'll fling you all to the devil and run away to Holland. I'd rather be a clockmaker."

Alexander whistled: "Then you'll never see Fräulein Anna again."

Peter bent over his knees. Suddenly he coughed and laughed.

Alexander guffawed gaily and whipped up the horse.

"Soon your mother will get you married. A married man, of course, is independent. Have patience; you've not got long to wait. Ah, it's a pity she's a German, a Lutheran. Else what could have been better, or simpler, eh?"

Peter drew closer to him, his lips trembling with cold, and tried to look into Alexander's eyes in the darkness. "Why is it impossible?"

"Well, what do you think? Fräulein Anna the Tsaritsa? Then you'd hear the tocsin all right!"

5

It was only on Sundays that Annchen's alluring petticoats whirled in the dance: drinking and dancing were only once a week. On Mondays the inhabitants of the Foreign Quarter put on knitted caps and quilted waistcoats and worked like bees. They had the greatest admiration for work: whether a man was a merchant or a simple artisan, they would say of him, raising a respectful finger: "He earns his bread by honest toil."

At break of day on Monday Alexander wakened Peter and told him that Brandt had already arrived, with master-workmen and apprentices. One of the halls of the palace had been transformed into a shipbuilding workshop: Karten Brandt was building model ships from Amsterdam blueprints. The foreign master-workmen and the apprentices, taken by ukase from among the most deft court attendants and play-soldiers, planed, turned, hammered together and caulked small models of galleys and ships, ornamented them with carving, rigged and sewed sails. Here, too, the Russians learnt arithmetic and geometry.

The drowsy palace rang with the sound of hammers, shouts as loud as in the market-place, singing and Peter's strident laughter. The old crones were dumb with fear. Natalia, seeking quiet, moved to the farthest wing, thinking always of Peter and praying for him, in a haze of incense and the flicker of icon lamps.

Through her trustworthy women she knew all that went on in the Kremlin. "Sophia was guzzling fish again on Friday; she's not afraid of sin. They brought her loads of sturgeon from Astrakhan, seven feet long. But she never sent you even a little one, kind Mistress. . . . She's become stingy, she starves her servants." They said that, sadly missing the absent Golitsin, Sophia had admitted a learned monk to her apartments, Sylvester Medvedev, who was something of a cavalier and an astronomer: he wore a silk cassock, a diamond pectoral cross and rings on his fingers; he clipped his beard, which was as black as a crow, and smelt nice. He would enter Sophia's apartment at any hour and they would practise magic. Sylvester would climb on the windowsill, look at the stars through a telescope, write down signs, and putting his finger to his nose read from them, while Sophia would lean over him and ask: "Well, what? What?" The day before he had been seen to bring in the soil from a footprint, and bones and roots; he had lighted three candles, whispered charms and burned someone's hair in the flame. Sophia was trembling, her eyes bulged, and she sat there as blue as a corpse.

Natalia, cracking her fingers, leaned towards her informant and asked in a whisper: "Whose hair did he burn? Was it dark?"

"Indeed, Tsaritsa, it was; as God sees me, it was dark!"

"Curly?"

"Exactly, curly. And we all think: could it be our Master's hair, Tsar Peter's?"

They said of Sylvester Medvedev that he taught the bread-worshipping heresy which stemmed from Simeon Polotsky and the Jesuits. He had written a book called *Manna*, where he stated and upheld that the transubstantiation of the bread takes place not when the priest pronounces the words: "Make therefore," but only at the words: "Take it and eat it." All Moscow—poor and rich, in palaces and market-places—spoke and argued about this one subject, the bread: at which words did the transubstantiation take place? They were completely bewildered, not knowing how to pray in such a way as to be in time for the transubstantiation. And there were many who passed on from this heresy to that of the Old Believers.

The red-haired priest Filka went about Moscow and, when people had gathered about him, would begin ranting: "I have been sent by God to teach you the true faith. The Apostles Peter and Paul are my kin. I am here to bid you make the sign of the cross with two fingers and not three: for in three fingers there abides the Kika-devil, which is the fico; the entire infernal regions are in him—you cross yourself with a fico." Many believed him without more ado and their minds were filled with doubt. And there was no way of laying hands on him.

The taxes levied for the Crimean campaign had impoverished everyone. It was said that for the second expedition people would be stripped of all they had. The towns and boroughs were becoming depopulated. The people fled in their thousands beyond the Ural Mountains, to the Pomorye, to the Volga or the Don. And the others, the Old Believers, were expecting Antichrist; some had actually seen him. Dissenting preachers were going from village to village urging people to burn themselves alive in barns and bath-houses, so that at least their souls might be saved. They shouted that the Tsar, the Patriarch and the entire clergy were emissaries of Antichrist. They shut themselves up in monasteries and fought the Tsar's army which was sent to bring them back in irons. In the Paleostrov monastery the Old Believers had killed two hundred streltsi and, when they could fight no more, had shut themselves up in the church and burnt themselves alive. Near Hvalinsk, in the hills, thirty dissenters barricaded themselves with harrows in a barn, set fire to it and were also burnt alive. In the forests near Nizhni-Novgorod, too, people burnt themselves in log huts. On the Don, on the Medveditsa river, a runaway serf, Kuzma, called himself Pope, crossed himself at the sun and said: "Our God is in heaven, for there is no God on earth any more; on earth there is now Antichrist: the Tsar of Moscow and the Patriarch and the boyars are his servants." The Cossacks were rallying to this Pope and accepting his teaching. The whole of the Don country was mutinous.

Such reports filled Natalia with mortal fear. Peter was amusing himself, unconscious of the clouds gathering overhead. The people had lost all sense of humility and awe. They threw themselves alive into the fire: how could one help being terrified of such people!

Natalia shuddered when she recalled the bloody revolt of Stenka Razin. It seemed as if it were yesterday. Then, too, they had been expecting Antichrist, and Stenka's leaders crossed themselves with two fingers. With a troubled heart Natalia looked at the little flames of the coloured icon lamps, sank groaning to her knees and remained for a long time with her forehead pressed to the worn rug.

"It's time to get Peter married," she thought. "He's grown so tall, he twitches, drinks wine, and all the time he's with foreign women and girls. When he marries, he'll settle down. And then, if only I could go with him and the young Tsaritsa on a pilgrimage to the monasteries, to pray God to grant us happiness, safety from Sophia's witchcraft, strength against the violence of the people!"

Marriage was the one thing needed for Peter. Formerly, when his personal boyars arrived, he would sit for an hour with them on his father's throne in the somewhat dilapidated audience chamber. But now it was always: "I haven't got the time." They had put a vat in the audience chamber holding two thousand buckets of water to sail little boats, blowing the sails with bellows and firing cannon with real powder. The throne had been scorched, a window broken.

The Tsaritsa complained to her brother Leo. He sighed dejectedly.

"Well, sister, get him married; it won't make things worse. The Lopuhins have a girl, Eudoxia, of marriageable age; she's in her prime, sixteen years old. The Lopuhins are loud-mouthed, but there are many of them and they're poor. They will be as faithful to you as dogs."

When the first snow fell Natalia journeyed, on the pretext of making a pilgrimage, to the Novodevichy convent. A trustworthy woman informed the Lopuhins, and some forty of them hurried to the convent. They almost filled the church; all of them were short, lean and fierce; all of them stared fixedly at the Tsaritsa. Eudoxia was brought there too, with great care, in a covered sledge, half dead with fright. Natalia allowed her to kiss her hand, and looked her up and down. She took her to the vestry and there, alone with her, examined her privily all over. The girl pleased her. But on that occasion nothing was said. Natalia left. The Lopuhins' eyes blazed with excitement.

There was only one happy event among all this sadness and anxiety: Prince Boris Golitsin, Vasily's cousin, had returned from the Crimean army near Poltava and, on the Regent's birthday, had attended mass in the Cathedral of the Assumption, dead drunk, under Sophia's very eyes; and later, at table, he had railed against Prince Vasily: "He has disgraced us in the eyes of all Europe. He should not be leading an army; he should be sitting in an arbour writing down his happy thoughts." He denounced and held up to shame the intimate circle of boyars saying: "You think with your bellies, your eyes are sunk in fat; anyone who's not too lazy can take Russia with his bare hands." And from that day he became a frequent visitor at Preobrazhensk.

As he watched the building of Pressburg, and Peter's Semenovsky and Preobrazhensky battalions exercising, he did not shake his head with a sneer, as the other boyars did, but showed interest and was full of praise. When inspecting the shipbuilding workshop he said to Peter:

"When the Romans captured the pirate ships at Actium, they did not know what to do with them, so they cut off the bronze prows, or rostra, and nailed them to columns. But when they had learned to build and rig ships themselves they conquered the seas and the whole world."

He had long talks with Brandt, testing his knowledge, and advised that a shipyard should be built on lake Pereyaslav, some eighty miles from Moscow. He sent a load of Latin books to the workshop with plans, copperplate prints, pictures of Dutch towns, shipyards, ships and sea battles. To translate the books he gave Peter a learned black dwarf, Abraham, and his two companions, also dwarfs, Tomosa and Seka, one twenty-four, the other twenty-seven inches high, dressed in strange coats and turbans with peacock feathers.

Boris Alexeyevich Golitsin was wealthy and powerful, with a particularly keen mind; in learning he was not inferior to his cousin, but by nature he was given to drink and liked above all entertainments and merry company. Natalia was afraid of him at first, thinking he might have been sent by Sophia. For why should such a great noble abandon the strong for the weak? But not a day passed without the roomy carriage drawn by four horses, with two terrifying Negroes at the back, thundering into the courtyard of the Preobrazhensky palace. Prince Boris would come first to kiss the Tsaritsa's hand. He had a high colour and a large nose; under his eyes trembled little puffy pouches, and from his turned-up moustache and his small clipped and parted beard came a scent of musk. One could not help smiling at the sight of his teeth: they were so white and gay.

"How have you slept, Tsaritsa? Did you dream again of the unicorn? Here I am come to visit you once more. But you are tired of my company; forgive me."

"Don't say that, we are always glad to see you. What is there new in Moscow?"

"It's dull, Tsaritsa, deadly dull in the Kremlin. The whole palace is full of cobwebs."

"What a thing to say! Nonsense!"

"In all the rooms the boyars are dozing on the benches. Terribly dull! Things are in a bad way; no respect from anybody. The Regent has not shown her face for three days, she has locked herself in her rooms. I tried to see Tsar Ivan to kiss his hand: His Majesty was lying on a stove-bench in a fox-fur coat and felt boots, very melancholy. 'Why, Boris,' he said to me, 'is it so dull here? The wind howls in the chimneys so fearfully. What does it portend?'"

Natalia guessed at last that he was only joking. She threw him a glance and laughed.

"It's only here with you, Tsaritsa, that one cheers up. You have brought a good son into the world. He'll prove cleverer than all the rest, given time. He has wideawake eyes."

After he had gone, Natalia's eyes would shine for a long time. She would walk up and down her small bedchamber, thinking. So on a rainy day the blue sky will gleam through the scurrying clouds with a promise of sunshine. The throne under Sophia must be tottering if such eagles flew away from her.

Peter liked Boris. On his arrival he would kiss him on the lips, consult him on many things, ask him for money, and the Prince never refused anything. He often enticed Peter with his generals, workmen, orderlies and dwarfs on expeditions and amusements on the Kukuy and invented fantastic entertainments. More than once, heated with wine, he would jump up, one eyebrow lowered, the other cocked high, his teeth gleaming, his nose glowing red, and recite in Latin from Virgil:

"Let us glorify the gods who generously fill goblets with wine the heart with merriment and the soul with delicious food. . . ."

Peter looked at him as one entranced. Outside was the noise of the wind rushing over thousands of miles of plains, wild forests and swamps, only to dishevel the straw on a poor hut, throw a drunken peasant into a snowdrift and clang a frozen bell in a ramshackle belfry. While here were tousled wigs, red faces, smoke billowing from long pipes, crackling candles. Noise. Merriment.

"The drunken council must become permanent!" Peter ordered Zotov to write a ukase: "From this day onwards all drunkards and carousers shall meet on Sundays to pay honour in company to the Greek gods." Lefort suggested they assemble at his house. And so it became a custom. Zotov, the worst tippler of all, was raised to the dignity of archpriest with a flagon hung on a chain round his neck. Alexander, in all his impudent nakedness, would be put astride a beer-barrel and he would sing such songs that the listeners held their sides laughing.

Rumours of these carousals reached Moscow. The frightened boyars whispered: "The accursed foreigners on the Kukuy have made a drunkard of the Tsar; they blaspheme and are possessed by the devil." The respectable old Prince Priimkov-Rostovsky came to Preobrazhensk, made his obeisance and then talked to Peter for an hour, in high-flown Slavonic, about the necessity for observing that Byzantine piety and decorum which were at the foundations of Russia. Peter listened in silence. He had been playing chess with Alexander in the dining-room. Daylight was fading. Then he pushed away the chessboard and began to walk up and down biting a finger. The Prince went on speaking, lifting the sleeves of his heavy fur-lined coat, long-bearded, dry as dust. Not a human being, but a tiresome shade, a toothache, a bore! Peter bent down to Alexander's ear. The other spluttered like a cat and went out laughing. Soon a sledge was brought to the door and Peter ordered the Prince to get in, and took him to Lefort's house.

At the table, on a high chair, sat Nikita Zotov, with a paper crown on his head, holding a pipe in one hand and a goose's egg in the other. Peter bowed to him without a smile and asked his blessing, and the archpriest solemnly blessed him with pipe and egg. Then the score of people present intoned hymns in a nasal chant. The old Prince, fearing to show incivility before the Tsar, furtively spat and crossed himself under his coat. But when a naked man with a cup in his hand climbed on to a barrel, and the Tsar and Grand Duke of all the Russias pointed his finger at him and declared in a loud voice: "This is our god Bacchus to whom we shall make obeisance", Prince Priimkov-Rostovsky turned deadly pale and swayed. The old man was carried out to the sledge in a swoon.

From that day Peter began to call Zotov Most-drunken Pope, archpriest of the god Bacchus, and the gatherings at Lefort's the maddest and most drunken assembly.

News of this reached Sophia. Filled with wrath she sent the boyar Fedor Romodanovsky of her intimate circle to talk to Peter. He returned pensive and reported to the Regent:

"There's plenty of nonsense and fun there, but plenty of serious business too. They're not asleep in Preobrazhensk!"

Hate and fear gripped Sophia's heart. They had hardly had time to turn round, it seemed, and the wolf-cub had grown up.

6

Golitsin arrived from Poltava unexpectedly. Day was only just breaking but already the palace entrance-halls and passages were jammed with people, and hummed like a beehive. Sophia had spent a sleepless night. Her gown, embroidered with gold and covered with a net of pearls, weighing over forty pounds, the short cloak adorned with rubies, emeralds and diamonds, necklaces and a gold chain, pressed heavily on her shoulders. She sat by the window, with lips tightly pressed so that they should not tremble. Verka, one of her near attendants, breathed at the frozen pane:

"Oh, dear Mistress, he's coming!"

She grasped the Tsarevna by the elbow and Sophia looked out: from the Nikolsky gates over the snow that had fallen during the night there advanced a team of six dapple-greys, with plumes on their heads and velvet harness with silver ornamented tassels reaching to the ground; in front of the horses ran van-couriers in white coats who shouted: "Make way! Make way!" At the sides of the low sledge covered with brocade, galloped officers in steel breastplates and short cloaks. The cortège halted in front of the Red Porch. The nobles, crushing one another's ribs in the press, rushed to help the Prince out of his sledge.

Sophia nearly swooned. Verka again held her up: "How she has missed him, poor heart!"

Sophia murmured hoarsely: "Verka, give me the cap of Monomach."

She did not see Golitsin until she mounted the throne in the audience chamber. Wax candles burnt in the chandeliers. The boyars were seated on the benches. Golitsin was standing; he was magnificently attired, yet he looked somehow moth-eaten: he had let his beard and moustache grow long, his eyes were sunken, his face had a yellowish tinge, and his thin hair lay flat on his head.

Sophia could scarcely hold back her tears. She raised her hot plump hand in its tight cuff, lifting it with an effort from the arm of the chair. The Prince knelt and kissed it, barely touching it with his roughened lips. It was not what she had expected, and Sophia shuddered with a foreboding of disaster.

"We are glad to see you, Prince. We want to enquire after your health." She cleared her throat softly. "Was God merciful to our affairs which we entrusted to you?"

She sat, obese, all in gold, with rouged cheeks, on her father's throne inlaid with ivory. In conformity with the rules of court ceremonial, four life-guards—fair and gentle youths, dressed in white, with ermine caps on their heads, holding small silver axes—stood behind her. Like the saints in paradise, the boyars flanked the dais with its three steps carpeted in crimson cloth. Everything proceeded solemnly, in accordance with the ancient ceremonial of the Byzantine emperors. Golitsin listened, on bent knee, with bowed head and lowered, outstretched arms.

Sophia finished her speech, Golitsin rose and returned thanks for her gracious words. Two council ushers gravely set a folding chair for him. The moment had come for the most important matter—the reason for his presence. Golitsin glanced anxiously and distrustfully at the rows of familiar faces—lean, like icons, or copper-red, cruel, bloated with idleness, with wrinkled foreheads, tensed in expectation of what the Prince would say to reach their purses. Golitsin began his address in a roundabout way: "I, your slave and serf, Great Sovereigns, Tsars and Grand Dukes, present a request to you, Great Sovereigns, that you, the Great Sovereigns, should show me, your serf Vaska, and my companions, your favour in future as heretofore and order the image of the Holy, Pure Mother of God, the Merciful Queen and Eternal Virgin Mary, to be sent from the Don monastery to your royal unconquerable and victorious troops in order that the most pure Mother of God should herself lead your armies, protect them from every misfortune and bestow glorious victories and miraculous supremacy over the enemy. . . ."

He spoke at length. The haze caused by the heat and the boyars' sweat made haloes round the guttering candles. When he had finished speaking about the image of the Don Virgin, the boyars conferred for a few moments as a matter of form and decided: the icon should be sent. There were sighs of relief. Then Golitsin, more confident now, turned to the most important matter: the army had had no pay for three months. Foreign officers, for example Colonel Patrick Gordon, were taking offence, refused copper coin and demanded to be paid in silver, or at least in sables. The men's clothes were worn out; there were no felt boots, the whole army was wearing birch-bark shoes, and there was a shortage even of those. Yet they were to take the field in February. Another shameful disaster must be avoided.

"How much money are you asking from us?" Sophia asked.

"Five hundred thousand roubles in silver and gold."

The boyars gasped. Some of them dropped their staffs or canes. They set up a noisy hubbub. Jumping up, they slapped their sides with their sleeves uttering cries of dismay. Golitsin looked at Sophia, and she responded with a burning glance. He went on, even more boldly:

"Two men from Warsaw came to my camp, Jesuit monks. They bore a letter from the French King attesting their trustworthiness. They propose important transactions. You," he half rose and bowed to Sophia, "Most Serene Sovereigns, would draw no inconsiderable profit from them. This is what they say: 'There are today many pirates on the seas, and it is dangerous for French ships to go round the world, much merchandise is lost. But the road to the East over Russian territory is direct and easy—to Persia, and to India, and to China. You yourselves', they say, 'have nothing in which to send your goods, and your Moscow merchants lack money. On the other hand, the French merchants are rich. Instead of closing your frontiers to no purpose, let our merchants through to Siberia and farther—to wherever they wish. They will make roads through the swamps, set up milestones and posting-stations. In Siberia they will buy furs and pay for them in gold; if they find ores, they will work them'."

Old Prince Priimkov-Rostovsky, unable to master his rage, interrupted:

"We don't know how to get away from our own foreign heretics, and you are trying to saddle us with new ones! It means the end of the Orthodox faith!"

"We barely managed to rid ourselves of the English under the late Tsar," cried the council noble Boborikin. "And now we are to submit to the French? Never!"

Another, Zinovyev, said furiously:

"We must stand firm and break the foreigners' long-standing arrogance once and for all, and not hand over our trade and industry to them. They must be humbled. We are the Third Rome." *

"True, true!" clamoured the boyars.

Golitsin looked round him; his eyes gleamed with anger and his nostrils quivered.

"I am no less concerned than you for the welfare of the State," he said, raising his voice. "I beat my breast"—he struck his coat-of-mail with his beringed fingers—"when I heard how the French ministers insulted our envoys, Dolgoruky and Mishetsky. But they went to ask for money with empty hands, that is why they lost their honour." Many of the boyars began to breath noisily. "Had they offered some advantage to the King of France, three million livres would have long since been lying in our treasury. The Jesuits swore on the Gospel: if the Great Sovereigns agree to their proposal and the Council of Boyars assents, they pledge their heads that we shall receive the three million livres before spring."

"Well, boyars, consider it," said Sophia. "It is an important matter."

Easy to say: consider it. There certainly had been a time when foreigners had swooped down on Russia like kites, had seized industries and trade, and undercut the price of everything. The landowners had been obliged to sell flax, hemp and wheat for next to nothing. And it was they, the foreigners, who had taught the Russians the habit of wearing Spanish velvet, Dutch linen, French silks, to drive in carriages and sit in Italian chairs. Under the late Tsar Alexis they had thrown off the foreign yoke. "We'll take our own wares by sea ourselves," they said. They had invited the master-craftsman Karten Brandt from Holland and, at the cost of great trouble, had built the ship *Orel*. But there the business came to a standstill, for no capable seamen could be found. Besides, it was too much effort. The *Orel* rotted away, anchored on the Volga near Nizhni-Novgorod. And now again the foreigners were trying to push their way in and get their arms elbow-deep into the Russian pocket. How to find a way out? Five hundred thousand roubles were needed for the war against the Khan. Golitsin would not go away without it. Clever of him to tempt them with three million! The thought of it made them sweat.

Zinovyev, grasping his beard, said:

* According to Ivan the Terrible, Byzantium was the Second Rome, Moscow was the Third, and there never would be a Fourth.

"Why not put a new tax on the suburbs and settlements? Or, for instance, on salt?"

Prince Volkonsky, a sharp-witted old man, replied:

"There is no tax yet on birch-bark shoes."

"True, true!" the boyars agreed noisily. "The peasants wear out a dozen pairs a year: put a kopek on each pair, and we'll beat the Khan!"

The boyars felt relieved. The matter had been settled. Some wiped off their sweat, others twiddled their fingers and recovered their breath. Others, in their relief, let out foul wind into their heavy coats. They had outwitted Golitsin. But he would not give in and, violating the prescribed order, sprang up shaking his cane:

"Madmen! Paupers! You cast treasure into the mire! Hungry, you push away the hand that offers you bread. What is it? Has God clouded your minds? In all Christian countries—and there are some that are smaller than a province of ours—trade flourishes, the people grow rich, all seek their profit. We alone sleep the sleep of the dead. As in time of pestilence, the people flee and scatter in despair. The forests teem with brigands, and even they take themselves off, no one knows where. Soon Russia will be called a desert! Then the Swede, the English and the Turk can come and take possession."

Tears of extreme mortification sprang into Golitsin's eyes. Sophia, her nails buried in the arms of the throne, leaned forward and her cheeks quivered.

"There is no need to let in the French," Prince Romodanovsky said in his deep voice. Sophia fixed her eyes upon him. The boyars became silent. Swaying his paunch from side to side in order to slide off the edge of the bench, he stood up: shortlegged, with a broad back, his small smooth head set deep between his shoulders. His dark slanting eyes chilled the beholders. He had only lately shaved off his beard; his moustache was turned up and his hooked nose hung over his thick lips. "We don't need French traders: they will rob us of our last shirt. But the other day I visited the Tsar at Preobrazhensk. Fun and play. Quite true. But some games can also be full of wisdom. There are German and Dutch master-craftsmen, shipwrights, officers there; they know their trade. They have two regiments—the Semenovsky and the Preobrazhensky—our streltsi are no match for them. We don't need foreign traders, but we can't do without foreigners. We must set up our own ironworks, linen mills, tanneries, glassworks. We must build mills for sawing timber, as they do in the Foreign Quarter. We must create a fleet; that's what we need. And as for your tax on birch-bark shoes—to the deuce with you, impose it, for all I care."

As though in anger he shook his fat face with its turned-up moustache, backed and sat down on the bench. That day the Boyars' Council came to no final decision.

7

On a frosty evening many guests had gathered at the tavern. The half-witted servant kept putting fresh birch logs on to the open fire. "Oh, it's terribly hot here, Mons!" The guests played dice and cards and sang songs. Johann Mons broached the third barrel of beer. He threw off his padded waistcoat and stood only in his vest. His neck was purple. "Hey, Johann, you'd better go for a spell outside into the frost, you're too full-blooded." Mons smiled uncertainly; he could not understand what was the matter with him. The sound of voices reached him as though from a distance, tears welled up in his eyes. He started to pick up ten tankards of beer, but could not lift them and the beer splashed over. Languor was creeping over his body. He pushed open the door, went out into the frosty night and leaned against a post under the awning. The icy moon stood high surrounded by three great iridescent circles. The air was full of sparkling frosty needles. Snow on the ground, on the bushes, on the roofs. An alien land, an alien sky, death lying on everything. His breath came fast, Something was approaching him with incredible speed. Ah, if he could only look once again on his native Thuringia, where a snug little town lay in the valley between the mountains above the lake! Tears ran down his cheeks. A sharp pang wrung his heart. He groped for the door, opened it with an effort, and the light of the candles and the flickering faces of the guests seemed to him ashen. His chest heaved and, forcing out a terrible cry, he fell to the ground.

So died Johann Mons. The shock of his death filled all the foreigners for a long time with astonishment and grief. He left a widow, Matilda, four children and three establishments: the tavern, a mill and a jeweller's shop. The eldest daughter, Modeste, had been, God be praised, successfully married that autumn to a worthy man, Lieutenant Fedor Balk. The orphaned children who remained were Anna and two youngsters: Philemon and William. As often happens after the death of the head of the family his affairs proved not as good as they had seemed; promissory notes turned up. The mill and the jeweller's shop had to be sold to pay the debts. In these anxious days Lefort did much to help with money and by exerting himself on their behalf. The house with the tavern remained the property of the widow, and there Matilda and Anna now wept bitter tears day and night.

8

"Did you send for me, Mama?"

"Sit down, Peter, my angel."

Peter flopped down on a stool and looked round his mother's bedchamber with an expression of irritation. Natalia, sitting opposite him, smiled affectionately. Oh, how dirty he was! His clothes were torn, there was a rag tied round his finger and his hair was tousled. There were shadows under his restless eyes.

"Peter, my angel, don't get angry. Listen to me."

"I am listening, Mama."

"I want you to marry."

Peter jumped up impetuously and, waving his arms, rushed from the glittering icon lamps to the door, and back again across the room. Then he sat down, and his head jerked. He turned in the toes of his large feet.

"Marry whom?"

"I have found such a lovely little bride for you, a white dove."

Natalia bent over her son, stroked his hair and tried to look into his eyes. His ears burnt red. He dived from under her hand and jumped up again:

"Oh, I haven't the time, Mama. Truly, I'm busy. Well, if you must, then get me married. I have other things on my mind."

He went out, lean and stooping, brushing the doorpost with his shoulder, and raced off along the passages. A door slammed in the distance.

chapter four

Ivash Brovkin, Alioshka's father, drove to Preobrazhensk over the snowy roads, a sledge piled with frozen poultry, flour, peas and a barrel of cabbage. This was the food-tax payable to Volkov; the steward had collected it from the village and, in order that the provisions should not rot, ordered Ivash to take them to the master at the palace where he was serving and where, in his quality of equerry, Volkov had a small room of his own with a closet.

When he drove into the courtyard Ivash was frightened and took off his cap. Many rich sledges, open and covered, stood by the main porch. Groups of smartly dressed servants were chattering in the morning frost. The horses, adorned with wolf and fox tails, were spiritedly pawing the fresh snow; restive stallions whinnied viciously. Sparrows hopped busily on the steaming dung.

Equerries in coats of cloth-of-gold and officers in foreign coats with scarlet lapels and hair curled like a woman's ran up and down the open stairway. Ivash Brovkin recognised his master. Volkov had grown fleshy on the Tsar's victuals, his little beard curled and he stepped out self-importantly, his thumbs in his silk belt.

"Oh, they'll detain me, I've come at a bad time!" Ivash thought to himself. He unbridled his horse and gave it some hay. A palace dog came up, looked at Ivash with unfriendly yellow eyes and growled. He smiled ingratiatingly: "Good doggy, good doggy, what's the matter?" Thank goodness, the over-fed brute went off without biting him. A stalwart groom passed by.

"Here, you tramp, what do you mean by feeding your horse here?"

But at that moment someone called him—praise be to God!—or Ivash would not have got away with a whole skin. He cleared away the hay and replaced the bit. Just then bells started pealing from the palace tower. The servants burst into activity: some sprang on the leading horses, others jumped on the footboards at the back of the carriages, the savage-looking, broad-bottomed coachmen gathered up their reins. Equerries placed themselves on each step of the stairway, with their caps over one ear. A crowd of people belonging to the wedding-train came out of the palace: boys carrying icons, youths with empty dishes; the rich caps, the green, brocaded and red velvet kaftans and long coats made a riot of colour on the snow under the weeping birches powdered with hoar-frost. Knowing the rules of propriety. Ivash began to cross himself. Then boyars came out, and among them a woman wearing several coats, each richer than the last. Under her cuspid headdress, her eyebrows were painted white, her eyelids blue and prolonged to the temples, and her cheeks rouged in large round spots as red as cranberry juice. Her face was like a pancake. In her hand she held a branch of mountain ash. She was handsome and gay, and obviously not quite sober. She was being led down the porch supported under each elbow. Servant girls who ran past Ivash said:

"There's the matchmaker, look!"

"She came to arrange the bridal chamber."

"To make the bed for the young couple."

Grooms shouted, the air resounded with the ringing of harness-bells, sledge runners creaked shrilly, rime showered down from the birches as the cortège took the road across the plain towards the blue mist of Moscow. Ivash stared open-mouthed. A harsh voice called him:

"Wake up, idiot!"

Volkov stood in front of him. As befits a master, he was frowning angrily and his eyes were stern and piercing.

"What have you brought?"

Ivash bowed kneeling in the snow and, taking the steward's letter from his breast, handed it to Volkov. Vasily Volkov stood with one foot set forward and began to read, wrinkling his face: "Gracious master and illustrious lord! We send you the provisions for your honour's store. For God's sake forgive us that it is less than last year: there are fewer geese and no turkeys at all. The people in your honour's village are altogether impoverished, five have run away, we do not know how to excuse ourselves for this. Some are half-dead from starvation, their corn barely lasted them till the feast of Intercession, they are eating goosefeet. That is the reason for the deficit."

Volkov sprang to the sledge: "Show me!"

Ivan unpinned the covering, trembling with fear. The geese were skinny, the fowls blue and the flour lumpy.

"What have you brought? What have you brought, you mangy dog?" Volkov shrieked, beside himself. "Thieves! You are all thieves!" He snatched the whip from the sledge and began to belabour Ivash. Ivash stood there bareheaded, without trying to avoid the blows, and only blinked. He was a cunning peasant; he knew that he was getting off lightly: let him lash away, it didn't hurt through his padded coat.

The whip broke off at the handle. Volkov, in his mounting rage, seized Ivash by the hair. At that moment two men in military coats ran quickly from the palace. Ivash thought: "It's to help him—I'm lost!" The shorter of the two, who was in front, suddenly rushed at Volkov and hit him in the ribs. The master nearly fell and let go Ivash's hair. The other man, the taller one, with a long face and blue eyes, laughed loudly. Then all three began to argue and quarrel. Ivash was seriously alarmed now, and again knelt in the snow. Volkov was shouting:

"I will not suffer such indignity! Both are my serfs! I'll have them flogged without mercy. The Tsar's orders are nothing to me."

Then the blue-eyed one narrowed his eyes and interrupted:

"Wait a bit, wait a bit; will you say that again? The Tsar's orders are nothing to you, eh? Alioshka, did you hear those rebellious words?" Then to Ivash: "Did you hear them?"

"Oh, stop, Alexander Danilovich!" Volkov's anger had suddenly left him. "I was out of my mind when I used those words, I was really. You see, my own serf nearly killed me."

"Let's go to Tsar Peter, we'll get to the bottom of the matter there."

Alexander strode off towards the palace. Volkov followed him and, when they were half-way, snatched at his sleeve. The third man did not go with them; he remained near the sledge and said softly to Ivash:

"Father, it's me. Don't you recognise me? I'm Alioshka."

Ivash was alarmed and perplexed. He looked out of the corner of his eyes. There stood a clean youth, dressed in rich cloth, with bright buttons, a wig with curls down to his shoulders and a sword at his side. All the same, it might be Alioshka. What was he to do? He answered equivocally:

"Of course, how could I not recognise you? A father would."

"Greetings, Father."

"Greetings, good youth."

"How are things at home?"

"God be praised. . . ."

"How are you getting on?"

"God be praised. . . ."

"Father, you don't recognise me?"

"It could be. . . ."

Seeing that there was going to be no more beating and trouble, Ivash put on his cap, picked up the broken whip and angrily began to cover up the load. The youth did not go, would not leave him. Perhaps it really was Alioshka, who had disappeared? Well, what if it was? The bird had risen high. Would it be wise to recognise him? It was more seemly not to. Still, Ivash's eyes narrowed slyly.

"I ought to go to Moscow from here, my old woman told me to buy some salt, but I haven't a copper. If you could give me a couple of altyns, or eight kopeks, you won't be the loser; we're not strangers, I'll pay it back."

"Father, dear Father. . . ."

Alioshka pulled out a handful of money from his pocket—not copper, but silver: three roubles, possibly more. Ivash was dumbfounded. And when he took the money in his palm, as horny as a wooden ladle, he trembled and his knees bent automatically in obeisance. Alioshka waved his hand and ran off. "Oh, my son, my son!" Ivash murmured softly. His narrowed eyes darted swiftly: had any of the servants seen the money? He put two coins in his cheek for safety and the rest in his cap. He quickly unloaded the sledge, gave the provisions to his master's servant and got a receipt and, lashing the horse with the reins, drove off at a rapid pace to Moscow.

Volkov's words: "The Tsar's orders are nothing to me," might have cost him dear: he might have made the acquaintance of the executioners in the department of Secret Affairs. But following Alexander closely into the passage, he clung to his arm, let himself be dragged some distance along the floor and, with tears, implored him to accept a ruby ring which he pulled off his finger.

"Mind, you son of a noble, you cur," Alexander said putting the expensive ring on his middle finger, "this is the last time I will save you. And you must give something to Alioshka Brovkin for insulting him; money or cloth. Do you understand?"

He glanced at the ruby, shook his wig with a laugh and went swaggering off on his high heels. How long ago was it that people in market-places had pulled his hair after smelling the pies of rotten hare's meat? Oh, what power the man was beginning to acquire! Volkov went slowly to his room with hanging head. He unlocked a trunk with a ringing lock and carefully selected a length of cloth. He nearly cried with vexation and resentment. To whom must he give it? To a peasant's son, a serf, who should be getting a lash across his face rather than a present! He lamented for a while, then called a servant:

"Take this to the drummer of the first Preobrazhensky company, Alexey Brovkin. Say that I send it with my greetings so that there should be friendship between us." Suddenly doubling his fist he said wrathfully to the servant: "Don't grin, or I'll hit you. Speak to Alioshka softly, politely, carefully; the scoundrel is dangerous nowadays."

Alexander looked for Peter in all the rooms where servants were spreading rich coverings on the benches and window-sills, putting down carpets, hanging up curtains—creased from having been put away for long years—and draping pearl-embroidered backcloths over the icons. The icon lamps were being refilled. The palace was all noise and bustle.

He found Peter alone in the bridal chamber which the matchmaker had just prepared. This was an outbuilding without a layer of soil in the ceiling, so that the bridal pair should not sleep under earth as in a grave. Peter was in the royal robes he wore for minor ceremonies. He still held in his hand the silk handkerchief given him when he had met the matchmaker. He had torn it to shreds with his teeth. He glanced at Alexander and flushed.

"Lovely decorations," Alexander said in a sing-song voice. "Quite like a paradise prepared for angels."

Peter unclenched his teeth and gave a short laugh. Then he pointed to the bed:

"What nonsense!"

"If the bride turns out agreeable and ardent, then it isn't nonsense. May my eyes burst, there's nothing sweeter in the world, *mein Herr.*"

"You're lying."

"I've known all about it since I was fourteen. And I've had some awful hags. But yours, they say, is a real beauty."

Peter sighed briefly. Again he looked round the bridal chamber; in three of its walls, windows were inserted high up and set with coloured panes. Between the windows hung Persian rugs, and the floor was covered by a carpet with a design of birds and unicorns. In each corner an arrow was stuck into the wall and from each hung forty sables and a small loaf of bread.* Twenty-seven sheaves of rye had been placed on two benches drawn close together and over these seven featherbeds, under a silk spread, with many pillows in pearl-embroidered pillow-cases. A fur cap lay on the pillows. There were marten-fur rugs over the foot of the bed, and near it stood lime-wood barrels of wheat, rye, oats and barley.

"Well, so you didn't see her after all?" Peter asked.

"Alioshka and I bribed the servants and climbed on to the roof. But it was no use. The bride sits in the dark, and her mother doesn't move a step from her side: they fear the evil eye. They don't even allow the sweepings to be taken out of the room. And her uncles, the Lopuhins, patrol the courtyard with muskets and swords, all day and all night."

"Have you heard anything about Sophia?"

"Well, she is in a rage, but she can't stop you from marrying. Listen, *mein Herz*: when you sit at table with your bride, don't eat or drink anything. If you want to drink, look round at me and I'll bring you a cup—drink out of that."

Peter again bit at his torn handkerchief.

"Let's go to the Foreign Quarter. No one will know. For an hour, eh?"

"Don't ask that, *mein Herz*. Don't even think about the Mons girl just now."

Peter stretched out his neck, his nostrils distended and he grew pale:

"You take liberties with me." He seized Alexander by the breast of his coat so that the buttons flew off. "You've grown bold!" With a snort he gave him another shake, but then let go and added more calmly: "Bring me an old coat. I'll go into the garden; bring the sledge there."

2

The wedding was celebrated at Preobrazhensk. Apart from the Narishkins and the bride's relatives few guests were invited; only a few of the personal boyars, including Boris Golitsin and Fedor Yurievich

---

* *Kalach*—a loaf shaped with a handle, like a large padlock.

Romodanovsky. Natalia had asked the latter to stand father to the bridegroom. Tsar Ivan was too ill to come. Sophia left that same day on a pilgrimage.

Everything proceeded according to ancient custom. The bride was brought to the palace in the morning and was robed there. Waiting-maids, washed in the bath-house, wearing head-dresses and warm jackets specially provided for them, sang without ceasing, while the bride was dressed by the court ladies and bridesmaids. They dressed her in a fine shift and stockings, a long red silk chemise with pearl wristbands, a gown of Chinese silk with wide sleeves that reached the ground, exquisitely embroidered with flowers and animals. A shoulder-wide collar of beaver, sprinkled with diamonds, was fastened round her neck, so tightly that Eudoxia nearly fainted. Over the gown came a crimson cloth robe with a hundred and twenty enamel buttons; and, over everything, a mantle of cloth-of-silver, lined with light fur and heavily embroidered with pearls. They covered her fingers with rings and put twinkling pendants in her ears. Her hair was pulled back so tight that she could not blink her eyes, and many ribbons were interwoven in her plait. On her head they set a high coronet representing a town.

By three o'clock Eudoxia was almost dead; she sat like a wax figure on a sable cushion. She could not even look at the sweetmeats which had been brought in an oak casket as a gift from the bridegroom: sugar animals, honey-cakes stamped with saints' faces, cucumbers cooked in honey, nuts and raisins, and crisp Riazan apples. According to custom there was also an ivory workbox and another one of gilded copper, containing rings and earrings. On them lay a bunch of birch twigs: the rod.

Her father, Larion Lopuhin, who by order from that day was to be called Fedor, kept coming in, passing his tongue over his dry lips. "Well, how is it? How is the bride?" His nose with its marked veins looked pinched. After standing about a while, he would remember something and hasten away. The bride's mother had long since swooned and was propped up against the wall. The waiting-maids, who had eaten nothing since dawn, were growing hoarse.

The matchmaker ran in waving her three-yard-long sleeves:

"Is the bride ready? Call the suite. Take the loaves, light the lanterns. Where are the dancing-girls? Oh, how few! At the Odoyevsky's there were twelve, and this is a Tsar's wedding. Oh, my dears, the bride, what a beauty! Where could one find another one like her? There aren't any. Oh, my dears, what have you done? It'll be the death of me! Our bride is not veiled! You've forgotten the most important thing! The veil, where's the veil?"

They then threw a white shawl over the bride's head and made her fold her hands on her breast and told her to keep her head bowed. Her mother began to lament softly. Her father ran in carrying before him—as though preparing for an attack—the icon with which the bride was to be blessed. The dancers waved their handkerchiefs, stamped and began to whirl:

> Mead walks out at festive meetings,
> Mead is full of boasting:
> "There is none so fine as I
> None as Mead so merry!"

Servants held aloft salvers with round loaves of bread. Others followed, carrying mica-sided lanterns on poles. Two candle-bearers carried the bride's wax candle weighing forty pounds. The bride's attendant, her cousin Peter, in a silver coat, with a towel worn as a sash, carried a basin containing hops, silk handkerchiefs, sable and squirrel skins and a handful of gold coins. Then came her two uncles, Lopuhins, the two most capable ones—well-known barrators and informers—to keep the way clear so that no one should cross the bride's path. Then the matchmaker and her assistant came, supporting Eudoxia's arms for, owing to her heavy dress, her fasting and her fright, the poor girl could hardly walk. Two old boyar ladies followed, one carrying a velvet married woman's headdress, the other towels for gifts to the guests, on salvers. Then came Larion Lopuhin, in furs collected from the whole family, and, a step behind, his wife, and finally a crowd of all the bride's relatives, hastily jostling through the narrow doors and passages.

Thus they entered the audience chamber. The bride was seated under the icons. The bowl of hops, skins and coins and the salvers with the loaves were set on a table on which were already salt-cellars, pepper-pots and vinegar-bottles. All took seats according to their rank. Everyone was silent. The Lopuhins' eyes stared glassily: they were afraid of committing some error of deportment. They neither moved, nor breathed. The matchmaker jerked Lopuhin's sleeve:

"Don't keep us waiting!"'

He crossed himself slowly and sent the bride's attendant to tell the Tsar that it was time to join the bride. When Peter Lopuhin left on his errand the shaven, slightly depressed back of his head quivered. The icon lamps crackled, the flame of the candles did not stir. They had to wait for a long time. The matchmaker tickled the bride's ribs from time to time to make her breathe.

The stairs creaked: they were coming. Two young palace guards appeared noiselessly and posted themselves at the door. The honorary father, Prince Romodanovsky, entered, crossed himself, staring with bulging eyes at the gleaming icons, shook hands with Lopuhin and sat down opposite the bride, sliding the fingers of one hand between those of the other. There was another short pause. The Prince said in a deep voice:

"Go, ask the Tsar and Grand Duke of all the Russias to deign to come without delay to attend to his duty."

The bride's relatives blinked, swallowed their saliva. One of the uncles went to meet the Tsar. He was already on his way, with youthful impatience. Clouds of incense poured in at the door. The tall shaggy archpriest of the Annunciation cathedral entered, holding a brass cross containing a relic and swinging widely a censer, while the little-known young palace priest, nicknamed Bitka * by Peter, sprinkled holy water over the red cloth carpet. Between them walked the old, weak-voiced Metropolitan in all the vestments of his rank.

The bride's relatives sprang to their feet. Lopuhin hurried out from behind the table and sank on his knees in the middle of the chamber. The best man, Boris Golitsin, led Peter in, holding his arm. The Tsar was wearing the royal shoulder cloak and his father's golden robes which barely reached his knees. Sophia had forbidden him to have the Monomach cap. Peter was bare-headed, his dark curls parted in the middle; his face was pale, his eyes glassy, unwinking, and the muscles at the sides of his mouth bulged. The matchmaker caught Eudoxia closer and felt her ribs tremble under her hand.

The bridegroom was followed by the master of ceremonies, Nikita Zotov, whose duty was to guard the wedding from the evil eye and sorcery and to see that the proper ceremonial was observed. He was sober, clean and serene. The older Lopuhins exchanged glances: they had not expected this prince-pope, this shameless drunkard, to be entrusted with this post. The Tsarista was led in by her brother Leo and the boyar Streshnev. For this great day she had had her old finery taken out of the coffers: a robe of a charming peach colour and a mantle embroidered with foreign beads in a delicate pattern of grasses. Boris Golitsin approached the Lopuhin who was sitting

* *Bitka*, a bold fellow.

by the side of the bride and, jingling the gold coins in his cap, said in a loud voice:

"We wish to buy that seat for the Prince."

"We will not sell it cheap," Lopuhin answered and, as custom required, protected the bride with his outstretched arm.

"Iron, silver or gold?"

"Gold."

Boris poured the coins on to a plate and, taking Lopuhin by the hand, led him from his seat. Peter, standing among the boyars, smiled; they began to push him gently forward. Golitsin took him by the elbows and seated him by the bride. Peter felt the warm roundness of her thigh and moved his leg away.

The servants brought in and served the first course. The Metropolitan, casting up his eyes, recited prayers and blessed the food and drink. But no one touched the dishes. The matchmaker bowed low to the bride's parents:

"Give your blessing that the bride's hair may be combed and bound."

"God will bless you," the father replied. Her mother only moved her lips voicelessly. The two candle-bearers held a thick shawl between the bridegroom and the bride. The waiting-maids in the doorways, the boyar ladies and their daughters sitting at the table, began to sing the traditional songs—slow, sad songs.

Peter saw out of the corner of his eyes how, behind the stirring shawl, the matchmaker and her assistant were fussing as they whispered: "Take away the ribbons. . . . Lay the plait, twist it. . . . The headdress, give me the headdress." Eudoxia began to cry in a low childish voice. Peter's heart thumped hotly: something forbidden, feminine, feeble was crying at his side, mysteriously preparing for what was sweeter than anything in the world. He moved close up to the shawl and felt her breath. Above him leant the painted face of the matchmaker with merry mouth stretched from ear to ear:

"Have patience, Sire, you have not much longer to wait."

The shawl dropped. The bride sat with her face still covered, but now in a woman's headdress. The matchmaker, with both her hands, scooped hops from the basin and let them fall over Peter and Eudoxia. Then she fanned them with sables, and flung the kerchiefs and gold coins that remained in the basin to the guests. The women broke into merry song, and the dancing-girls began to whirl. Tambourines and cymbals struck up outside the doors. Boris Golitsin cut the loaves and cheese and distributed them, along with towels, to the guests, according to their rank.

Then the servants brought in the second course. None of the Lopuhins ate anything and they pushed the dishes away to show that they were not hungry. The third course was served immediately, and the matchmaker said loudly:

"Give your blessing to the young couple for the wedding ceremony."

Natalia and Romodanovsky and Lopuhin and his wife raised icons. Peter and Eudoxia, standing side by side, bowed to the ground. Having given his blessing, Lopuhin unfastened a whip from his belt and struck the bride three times across the back, so hard that it hurt.

"You, my daughter, have felt your father's whip; I hand you over to your husband. Henceforth not I, but he, will beat you for disobedience."

And he handed the whip to Peter with a bow. The candle-bearers raised their lanterns, the master of ceremonies grasped the bridegroom by the elbows, and the matchmaker took hold of the bride. The Lopuhins guarded their path: one servant-girl who, hard-pressed, wanted to cross it, was pushed away so violently that the servants dragged her away more dead than alive. The bridal procession passed slowly along the passages and stairways to the palace church. It was already after seven.

The Metropolitan conducted the service without haste. It was cold in the church, draughts blew in through the chinks in the log walls. Outside the lattice-work of the frozen windows it was dark. The vane on the roof creaked mournfully. Peter could see only one hand of the unknown woman under the veil: a weak hand with two silver rings and painted nails. It trembled as it held the dripping taper; blue veins, a short little finger, quivering like a lamb's tail. He turned away his eyes and screwing them up looked at the little flames of the low altar-screen composed of icons.

He had not been able to say good-bye to Annchen the day before. The widow Matilda, seeing Peter drive up in a common sledge, flew to him, kissed his hand, and sobbed out that they were poverty-stricken, that they had no fuel or this and the other, and that poor Annchen had been lying for two days delirious with fever. He pushed the widow aside and rushed upstairs to the girl. In the little room an oil lamp burned feebly; a copper basin stood on the floor, and her little slippers lay as she had thrown them off; the air was stifling. Annchen was lying under a muslin curtain, her hair scattered in damp strands over the pillow; a wet towel covered her forehead and eyes, and her mouth was crusted with fever. Peter tiptoed out of the room and poured a handful of gold into the widow's trembling palm: it had been Sophia's wedding gift to Peter. He ordered Alexander to stay on duty day and night at the widow's, in case something was needed from the chemist or the patient asked for some foreign delicacy: he was to get it, even from the bowels of the earth.

The priests were not sparing of incense, and the candles shone through a haze. In a roar, like the trumpets of Jericho, the deacon prayed for a long life for the bridal couple. Peter took another sidelong look: Eudoxia's hand trembled ceaselessly. He felt a cold bubble of anger welling up in his chest. He pulled the taper sharply out of Eudoxia's hand and pressed her frail, delicate fingers. A frightened whisper ran through the church. The Metropolitan's bald head began to tremble, and Boris Golitsin hurried up to him and whispered something. The Metropolitan went faster, and the choir quickened the tempo of their singing. Peter kept his wife's hand in a strong grip, watching her head droop lower and lower under the veil.

They were conducted round the lectern, Peter striding rapidly, Eudoxia supported by the matchmaker, or she would have fallen. They were married. The cold brass cross was given to them to kiss. Eudoxia dropped on her knees and pressed her face against her husband's morocco boots. In a singsong tone, imitating the "angelic voice", the Metropolitan uttered feebly:

"To save her soul, it is meet for the husband to punish his wife with the rod, for the flesh is weak and sinful."

Eudoxia was helped to rise. The matchmaker took hold of the end of the veil: "Look, look, Sire!" and skipping up jerked the veil from the young Tsaritsa. Peter gazed eagerly. The face almost of a child, worn out and drooping; the mouth swollen with crying. A soft little nose. She had been painted and rouged to conceal her pallor. Under the burning round-eyed gaze of her husband she shielded her face shyly with her sleeve. The matchmaker started to pull away her sleeve. "Uncover your face, Tsaritsa. It's not seemly. Raise your eyes!" All those present crowded round the young pair. "She's a bit pale," remarked Leo Narishkin. The Lopuhins breathed gustily, ready to start an argument if the Narishkins dared disparage the bride. She raised her brown eyes veiled with tears. Peter brushed her cheek with his lips; her own moved faintly in response. He smiled and kissed her mouth; she gave a little sob.

Once more they went back to the room from which they had come. On the way the matchmaker scattered flax and hemp over the newly-married couple. A flax seed stuck to Eudoxia's lower lip, and there it remained. Musicians, specially brought from Tver, in clean red tunics, played tambourines and stringed instruments gravely and dispassionately. The dancing-girls sang. Again hot and cold dishes were served, and this time the guests ate heartily. But it was not etiquette for the young couple to touch food. When the third course consisting of roast swans was served, a roast fowl was set before them. Boris Golitsin took it in his hands, wrapped it in a napkin and, bowing to Natalia and Romodanovsky and the bride's parents, said gaily:

"Give your blessing for the young couple to retire to their bedchamber."

The whole crowd of guests and relatives, all feeling the effects of drink, led the Tsar and Tsaritsa towards the bridal chamber. On the way some woman in a fur coat turned inside out, again scattered flax and hemp over them out of a pail, laughing loudly the while. Zotov, holding a naked sword, stood at the open door. Peter took Eudoxia by the shoulders. She closed her eyes and drew herself back, resisting. He pushed her inside and turned sharply to the guests. Their laughter died away when they saw his eyes, and they retreated. He slammed the door behind him and, staring at his wife who stood by the bed with her little fists pressed to her bosom, began to bite his nails. It had been devilishly unpleasant and all wrong; he was seething with annoyance. That accursed wedding! They had amused themselves with the old customs. And here was the girl now, shaking like a sheep. He threw the cloak off his shoulders, pulled off his robes, dragging them over his head, and flung them on a chair.

"Sit down, Eudoxia. What are you afraid of?"

Eudoxia nodded meekly and obediently, but she could not climb on to that mountainous bed and did not know what to do. She sat down on a barrel of wheat, glanced sideways at her husband with frightened eyes and blushed.

"Are you hungry?"

"Yes," she answered in a whisper.

The roast fowl was now on a dish at the foot of the bed. Peter tore off a leg and at once began to eat it, without bread or salt. He tore off a wing: "Here you are!"

"Thank you."

3

At the end of February the Russian army was again moving towards the Crimea. The cautious Mazeppa advised them to march along the bank of the Dniepr, building fortified points, but Vasily Golitsin would not hear of slowing down: he wanted to reach Perekop as soon as possible to wipe out his dishonour in battle.

In Moscow people were still driving in sledges, but here the ancient burial mounds were covered with celandines as with velvet, the wide plain showed green and the wind rippled the surface of the spring-flood lakes. The horses advanced through them with water up to their knees. Blinding shafts of sunlight frequently pierced the spring clouds. Oh, what soil there was here: black, rich, a gold mine! If it could be peopled with peasants from the swamps and forests, they would walk up to their ears in corn. But the only signs of life were the triangular flocks of cranes flying high above with long-drawn cries. These steppes had been watered with the tears of captives; century after century millions of Russians had passed here, led into slavery by the Tatars, to the galleys of Constantinople, to Venice, Genoa, Egypt.

The Cossacks praised the steppe: "The harvest here is a twentieth; you only have to spit, and a tree grows on the spot. If it weren't for the accursed Tatars, we'd have covered the land with farms." Soldiers from the northern provinces wondered at such rich soil: "This is a just war," they said. "How can such land lie without being any use to anybody?" The landowners of the militia selected sites for manors, quarrelled over the sharing out and hurried to Golitsin's tent with requests: "If God helps us to conquer these parts, would the Tsar graciously bestow that particular plot of land from such and such gulley to the hillock with a stone image on top. . . ?"

In May the Moscow and Ukrainian armies, a hundred and twenty thousand strong, reached the Green valley, rich in water and grazing grounds. Here the Cossacks brought a prisoner to Golitsin: a sturdy, red-bearded Tatar, with tanned and glistening skin, in a long padded coat. Golitsin pressed a handkerchief to his nose to keep out the Tatar smell of sheep, and ordered him to be questioned. They tore off his padded coat and the Tatar, baring his small teeth, turned and twisted his closely-shaven head. A grim Cossack slashed him across his swarthy shoulders. "Master, Master, I'll tell everything!" the Tatar began to babble. The Cossacks translated: "The naked-headed fellow says the Tatar army is encamped not far from here, and the Khan himself is with it." Golitsin crossed himself and sent for Mazeppa. Towards evening the deployed army, with cavalry on its right and left flanks, and baggage-train and guns in the centre, moved to attack the Tatars.

The sun, like an orange loaf, had barely risen over the low trampled plain, when the Russians came within sight of the Tatars. Standing on a cart Golitsin examined through a telescope the many-coloured coats, the spiked helmets, the merry, evil faces with high cheekbones, the horses' tails on the spears, the solemn mullahs in green turbans. This was the Tatar vanguard.

Detachments of horsemen wheeled, converged, gathered into a close mass. Dust rose. They were coming, fanning out as they galloped forward. Piercing yells rang out. Then they were hidden by the dust as it was swept into the faces of the Russians. The telescope wavered in Golitsin's hands. His horse, tied to a cart, shied, tearing the bridle—a feathered arrow stuck in its neck. At last! Guns thundered, muskets cracked; everything disappeared in clouds of white smoke. The iron barb of an arrow rang against Golitsin's breastplate just above his heart. He shuddered and made the sign of the cross over the place.

The engagement lasted more than an hour. When the smoke cleared a few horses were writhing on the plain where some hundred dead bodies lay. The Tatars, beaten back by the guns, were retreating beyond the horizon. Orders were given to cook food and to water the horses. The wounded were placed on carts. Before sunset the army set out again very cautiously towards the Black valley, where the Khan was encamped with his army on the river Kolonchak.

During the night a strong wind came up from the sea. The stars clouded over. Thunder rumbled in the distance. Extraordinary flashes of lightning broke through the black clouds, lighting up the grey plain: sand, wormwood bushes and salt marsh. The army advanced slowly. Soon after four o'clock the sky split and a column of fire fell on the baggage-train, melting a cannon and killing a gunner. A whirlwind struck them, knocking men down, tearing off caps and cloaks and blowing the hay from the carts. Blinding lightning flashed. Orders were given to bring out the icon of the Holy Virgin of the Don and carry it round the army.

The downpour came at dawn. Through the driving rain the Tatars could be seen on the right flank: they were approaching in crescent formation. Before the Russians had time to realise what was happening, the cavalry was routed and the vanguard regiments driven back on to the baggage-train. The slow-matches would not burn, the gunpowder on the priming-pans was damp. The splashing of rain drowned the cries of the wounded. But the Tatars were stopped at the triple row of waggons. Their bowstrings were wet and their arrows fell without force.

Golitsin, on foot, rushed about the baggage-train, lashing the gunners with his whip, seizing hold of wheels, tearing the slow-matches out of the men's hands. The wind drove into their eyes and mouths. But the gunners won through at last. They covered themselves with their sheepskin coats, sparked their flints, added some dry gunpowder, and leaden grapeshot from the cannon hurtled among the Tatar horses. On the left wing the Cossacks with Mazeppa were fighting desperately with their swords. Suddenly a long-drawn-out call came from the mullahs; the Tatars retreated, disappearing in the stormy darkness.

4

"To my lord, my joy, Tsar Peter! May my dear one prosper for many years. . . ."

Eudoxia was worn out with writing. Her thumb and two fingers, with which she gripped the quill pen close to the very point, were smeared with ink. She was spoiling the third sheet of paper: either the letters came out wrong, or she made blots. And she wanted to write such a nice letter that Peter would be pleased.

But how can you say what fills your heart, on paper with ink? Outside it was spring; April. The birches showed green, like down. White clouds with blue linings floated across the sky. Eudoxia looked at them, looked, and tears hung on her eyelashes. How silly! She glanced at the door; she did not want her mother-in-law to come in and see her. She wiped her eyes with her sleeve and frowned.

What else could she write to him? He had gone, her darling, to Lake Pereyaslav, and did not write to say when to expect him back. It would have been nice to attend the Lenten services, confession and communion together; also Easter night service, and the supper to break the fast afterwards. Here Eudoxia remembered the chicken which they had eaten after the wedding, and blushed and laughed to herself. On Easter Day one could call in some girls and play games and roll eggs. Have songs and dancing. Get on the swings and laugh, run about at a game of blind-man's-buff. Should she write about all this? Peter, my dear, my darling, do come back, I miss you so! But how could one write that? There were not even the letters for it.

She took up the quill again and, moving her lips, wrote:

"We beg your favour, pray, dear Lord, do not delay your return. Your little wife Eudoxia greets you."

She re-read the letter and was pleased: it was well phrased. But alas, she had not mentioned her mother-in-law! Now she would have to write the letter a fourth time. For mother-in-law Natalia Kirillovna was strict. No matter how much you tried, she always found something wrong. Why was she so thin?—She wasn't at all thin; all that should be was nice and round. "Why has Peter dashed off to Lake Pereyaslav two months after the wedding? What's the matter with you? are you frowsty, or are you such a dull fool that your husband must flee to the ends of the earth, as from the pest?" She was not a fool, nor a pest. It was their own fault: why had they allowed Lefort to be with him, and Alexander too and the foreigners? It was they who had enticed her darling away to the lake, and they would entice him to some worse place soon.

Eudoxia dipped her pen angrily. But she raised her eyes. A pale light filtered in at the window through the green birches. On the sill a pigeon was strutting, puffing out its neck, and other birds were singing. There was a smell of meadows. A great tear fell suddenly on the fourth clean sheet. How tiresome!

5

Not a day passed but brought a letter from wife or mother: "Without you it is dull here, are you coming back soon? We could make a pilgrimage to Troitsa monastery . . ." Old-fashioned nonsense! Peter had not time even to read these letters, still less to answer them. He lived in a newly-built log-house on the wharf on the shore of the wide Pereyaslav lake, where two nearly completed vessels stood on the slips. The decks were being covered and wooden faces were being carved on the poops. A third ship, *The Capital City of Pressburg,* was already launched. It was thirty-eight paces long, with a steeply curved prow ornamented with a gilded mermaid, and a high poop with a ward-room built at the top. On its flat roof, guarded by carved rails, was an admiral's bridge and a large glass lantern. Under the top deck eight guns protruded through open port-holes on each side. The curved sides gleamed black with tar.

In the morning, when a light mist covered the lake, the three-masted ship seemed to be suspended in the air, as on the wonderful Dutch pictures Boris Golitsin had given him. They were only waiting for a wind to make the trial run. But as though to spite him, for over a week not a leaf stirred. Blue-lined clouds floated lazily over the lake, and the spread sails hung limp, barely flapping. Peter never left Brandt's side. The old man had been ailing since February; his chest was torn by a hacking cough. Nevertheless, wrapped in a sheepskin coat, he spent all day on the wharf, shouting, scolding, and sometimes even giving blows for idleness or stupidity. By special ukase some hundred and fifty monastery serfs had been brought to the wharf: carpenters, sawyers, smiths, common laborers, and a number of capable women to make the sails. About fifty play-soldiers, taken from their regiments, were learning seamanship here: to pay and belay ropes, climb the masts and obey orders. Their instructor was a foreigner, a Portuguese, Pamburg, hook-nosed, with a bristly black moustache; a cruel devil, a pirate. The Russians said about him that he had been more than once hanged for his deeds, but that Satan had come to his aid; he had survived and here he was now.

Peter was wild with impatience. The workmen were roused at dawn by a drum. Spring nights are short; many dropped from fatigue. Nikita Zotov could hardly keep up with the orders he had to write, in the name of the G.S.T. and G.D. of all the R.s, to the neighbouring landowners to supply and deliver at the wharf corn, poultry, meat. The terrified landowners obeyed. It was harder to obtain money. Although Sophia was delighted that her brother had buried himself still farther from Moscow—"may he drown in one of his play-ships" —the treasury of the Great Palace was empty; the Crimean war had swallowed everything.

When Lefort was able to get away from his work and visit the Pereyaslav wharf, merrymaking began. He would bring wine, sausages, sweetmeats and—with a wink—greetings from Anna Mons; she had recovered, was prettier than ever, and begged Herr Peter graciously to accept her gift of a couple of lemons.

At dinner and supper in the new log-house glasses were generously raised to the great Pereyaslav fleet. A special flag had been designed for it, made up of three stripes—white, blue and red. The foreigners told stories of former voyages, storms or sea battles. Pamburg, straddling his legs and working his moustache up and down, shouted in Portuguese as though he really were on a pirate ship. Peter drank it all in, all eyes and ears. How was it that he, a landsman, should love the sea? But at night, lying on the bunk by Alexander, he dreamed of waves, dark clouds above a watery expanse and phantom ships swiftly gliding past.

Nothing could tempt him back to Preobrazhensk. When they importuned him too much with their letters, he wrote back:

"To my beloved Mother, dearer to me than my earthly life, Tsaritsa Natalia Kirillovna, from your unworthy son Peter, busy at work. I beg your blessing and desire news of your health. As for your orders to return to Preobrazhensk, I would be ready to do so, but indeed there is business to be done: the vessels are nearly completed, what we are waiting for is rope. I beg your favour that this rope be sent without delay from the arsenal. Then we shall be able to get on. I beg your blessing. Your unworthy Petrus."

6

Nowadays people took off their caps when they passed Ivash's hut. The whole village knew that "Ivash's son is powerful—he's the Tsar's right hand. Ivash need only wink, and he gets all the money he wants". With Alioshka's money—three and a half roubles —he had bought a fine heifer for one and a half roubles, a ewe for thirty-five kopeks, four piglets at nine kopeks each; he had also got fresh harness, put up a new gate and rented twenty acres of land for summer crops from other peasants, having given them one rouble in money and a pail of vodka and promised them a fifth of the harvest.

He was a made man. He no longer belted his coat with bast tied low on his hips, but wore a Moscow sash high above the waist so that his well-fed belly should stand out. He wore his cap pulled down to his very eyebrows and stuck his beard in the air. One had to bow to a man like that. He also said: "Wait a bit, in the autumn I'll visit my son, get some money from him and then I'll put up a mill." Volkov's steward no longer addressed him in the familiar person or called him Ivashka, but spoke to him noncommittally as Brovkin. And he relieved him of the corvée.

His sons—his helpers—were growing up. Yashka had been going all last winter to the sexton in the neighbouring village to learn his letters; Gavrilka was becoming a handsome lad, and the youngest, Artamoshka, a quiet boy, was also not without brains. His daughter, Sanka, had already been asked in marriage, but with things as they were, one would think twice about giving her away to a peasant like oneself.

In July there was a rumour that the army was returning from the Crimea. They began to expect the warriors home, sons and fathers. In the evenings the women would go out on to a hill to watch the road. From a wandering pilgrim they learnt that the men had really returned to the neighbouring villages. The women began to weep: "Ours have all been killed. . . ." At last one warrior returned—Tsigan—his face smothered in a tangle of grisly beard, one eye gone, his shirt and trousers rotted on his body.

Brovkin and his family were having supper in the yard—cabbage soup with salt beef—when somebody knocked at the gate: "In the name of the Father, the Son and the Holy Ghost!" Ivash lowered his spoon and looked suspiciously at the gate.

"Amen!" he replied. And then louder: "Look out, we've got fierce dogs, take care!"

Yashka drew back the bolt and Tsigan came in. He looked round the yard, at the family and, opening his gap-toothed mouth, said loudly in a hoarse voice:

"How d'you do?" He sat down on a block of wood by the table. "Having supper in the cool? Is it that flies pester you indoors?"

Ivash moved his eyebrows. But here Sanka of her own accord pushed a bowl of cabbage soup towards Tsigan, wiped a spoon on her apron and handed it to him:

"Share our meal, friend."

Ivash was astonished at Sanka's boldness. "All right," he thought. "Later on I'll pull her hair. Giving our food away to anyone she sees!" But he refrained from arguing with her.

Tsigan was hungry; he ate screwing up his one eye.

"Been at the war?" Ivash asked.

"Yes. . . ." And Tsigan went back to the soup.

"Well, how did you get on?" Brovkin asked again after shifting about on the bench.

"As usual. Fought as people fight."

"Beat the Tatars, eh?"

"We did. . . . Lost twenty thousand of our men at Perekop, and as many on our way back."

"Ah, ah!" Brovkin wagged his head. "And here they say the Khan has submitted to us."

Tsigan showed his few yellow teeth.

"Ask those we left to rot in the Crimea how the Khan submitted to us. Heat, no water, a putrid sea on the left, the Black Sea on the right: you can't drink that. The Tatars filled up the wells with carrion. There we were at Perekop—neither forward nor backward. Men and horses died like flies. Yes, we've fought. . . ."

Tsigan combed his moustache with his fingers, wiped his mouth, and looked at Sanka with his one bloodshot eye: "Thank you, girl." He leaned on his elbows.

"Ivash, when I left I had a cow. . . ."

"Yes, we asked the steward: what'll he do without a cow when he comes back? But he wouldn't listen, and took it."

"So! And the pigs? A hog and two sows. I asked the village to look after them."

"We did, friend, we did. But the steward pressed us hard for the maintenance tax. We thought perhaps you'd be killed."

"So Volkov bolted down my pigs?"

"He ate them, he ate them."

"So!" Tsigan pushed his fingers into his wiry uncombed hair and scratched his head. "Very well. Ivash!"

"Well?"

"Don't say I came to see you."

"Whom should I tell? I always keep my mouth shut."

Tsigan got up. He glanced at Sanka, and then went slowly to the gate. There he said threateningly:

"Mind, keep it quiet, Ivash. Goodbye." And he vanished. From that day on he was never seen again in the village.

7

Ovsey Rzhov stood unsteadily at the tavern door, on the Varvarka, counting money in his palm. Two lower officers of the streltsi, Nikita Gladky and Kuzma Chermny, came up to him.

"How are you, Ovsey?"

"Stop counting your coppers, come with us."

Gladky whispered: "We've something to discuss. We've heard some evil news."

Chermny jingled some silver in his pocket and broke out into a laugh: "Enough to have a good time."

"You didn't rob anyone, did you?" Ovsey asked. "Oh, streltsi, what are you doing?"

"Fool!" Gladky said. "We were standing on guard at the palace. D'you understand now?" And they both laughed again.

They took Ovsey inside the tavern and seated themselves in a corner. The sombre publican brought them a flagon of wine and a candle. Chermny at once blew out the candle and bent over the table listening to what Gladky whispered.

"A pity you weren't on guard with us. We stood there—and out came Shaklovity. 'The Tsarevna,' he said, 'grants you five roubles each for your faithful service.' And he gave us a bag of silver. We said nothing. What was he driving at? And he gave such a bitter sigh: 'Oh,' he said, 'streltsi, faithful servants, you won't have much longer to live with your wives in your comfortable houses across the river'."

"What did he mean by 'not much longer'?" Ovsey asked in alarm.

"It's like this. 'They want,' he said, 'to transfer you and scatter you through the smaller towns, to turn me out of the Strelets Office and send the Regent to a convent. It's the old Tsaritsa Natalia who's stirring up the trouble. That's why she got Peter married. It's at her bidding,' he said, 'that servants—only we can't find out which —are giving Tsar Ivan slow poison; they've barricaded his room with logs and firewood, and he uses the back door. Tsar Ivan isn't long for this world. Who will look after you, streltsi? Who will protect you?' "

"And Vasily Golitsin?" Ovsey asked.

"He's the only man they feared. But now the boyars want to make him pay with his head for the Crimean disgrace. They'll hang Peter round our necks."

"We'll see about that. They'll have to wait! It won't be the first time we've sounded the tocsin."

"Don't shout so loud." Gladky pulled Ovsey closer to him by the collar and said, barely audibly: "The tocsin alone won't save us. Even if we kill everyone, as we did seven years ago, the root will remain. We must do away with the old she-bear. And why spare the cub? What's to prevent us? On the bear-spear with him—we must save ourselves, my lads."

Gladky's words were dark and terrible. Ovsey shuddered. Chermny poured out some wine into the pewter mugs.

"This business must be done quietly. We must pick out fifty trustworthy fellows and fire Preobrazhensk at night. We'll get them with our knives during the blaze; neatly."

8

The streltsi regiments had long since returned to their quarters, and the landowners of the militia to their estates, but along the Kursk and Riazan roads wounded men, cripples and deserters were still straggling back to Moscow. Crowding on the church porches, they exhibited hideous sores and wounds and howled as they stretched out the stump of an arm towards kindhearted people, or plucked at their empty eyelids.

"Feel, good Christians, here it is, the arrow, in my chest. . . ."

"Kind people, both my eyes are gone, they beat me mercilessly over the head with a stick, ah-ah-ah!"

"Smell it, sir, look, my arm has rotted away to the elbow."

"And here they cut strips from my back. . . ."

"Sores from drinking mare's milk. . . . Pity me, kind people!"

The good parishioners were horrified by such appalling injuries and gave alms. And at night bodies with their heads cut off were found in lonely spots. There were robberies on the roads, on bridges, in dark lanes. Crowds of maimed soldiers drifted towards the Moscow market-places.

But in Moscow itself there was no abundance either. Many shops had closed. Taxes had ruined some merchants, others hid their wares and money until better times. Everything grew dear. Nobody had any money. The corn that was brought in was mixed with rubbish, and the meat maggoty. Even the fish seemed to have grown smaller and thinner since the war. The pie-man Zayats, known to everyone, brought out such rotten stuff on his tray that it made you sick. And a sinister fly made its appearance: its sting made people's cheeks and lips swell. There was a dense crowd in the market-places, but when you looked, you saw they were selling nothing but birch-brooms for the steam-bath. The vast city was buzzing angrily with idleness and hunger.

9

Tirtov reined in his horse and set his cap straight. He looked handsome and was richly dressed; the collar of his coat was higher at the back than his head, his lips were painted and lines were pencilled round his eyes, prolonging them to his temples. His curved sword rang against his Persian stirrup. Stepan Odoyevsky leaned over to him from the porch:

"Listen to what the people are saying. Don't begin till you've heard them."

"All right."

"Then give it them from the shoulder: the Tsaritsa Natalia and her brother Leo have bought up all the corn, they're deliberately starving Moscow. And don't forget the poisonous fly: say it's their magic."

"All right."

Tirtov glanced coldly between the ears of his stallion, bent forward in the saddle and set off at full gallop through the open gates. A wave of dust and stench met him in the street. A tramp, bare to the waist and covered with purple blotches, screamed and pushed his way through the crowd to throw himself under the horse's hoofs. Tirtov slashed him with his whip. From all sides the crowd pressed in on the rich boyar, stretching out their dirty, scabby palms. Frowning, hand on hip, Tirtov made his way slowly through the throng.

"Fine sir, share with us. . . ."

"Throw a copper. . . ."

"I'll catch it in my mouth. . . ."

"Give us a coin, give, give. . . ."

"Look out, or I'll smear you with dung; better give something."

"I'll sell you a handful of lice! Buy it, or I'll give it for nothing!"

"Trample me down, trample me down, I'm starving. . . ."

The horse champed its bit nervously, casting proud glances at the waving tatters, the tousled heads, the terrible faces. The beggars and tramps grew bolder and bolder. At last Tirtov reached the end of the Ilyinka. Here a proclamation was nailed to a post under a small icon, and a respectably dressed man, shouting to make himself heard above the noise, was reading:

"We, the Great Tsars, to you, great boyar and protector, Prince Vasily Vasilyevich Golitsin, for your abundant and zealous service, in that you laid low such fierce and hereditary foes of the Holy Cross and of all Christendom, *not fortuitously and in a manner never yet witnessed,* pursued them to their heathen homes and defeated and routed them. . . ."

A hoarse voice came from the crowd:

"Who was defeated and routed? We or the Tatars?"

The crowd at once began to hum angrily:

"Where did we lay low the Tatars and when?"
"We didn't even see them face to face in the Crimea."
"We saw them when we ran for our lives!"
"Who's the fool who's reading the proclamation?"
"A clerk from the Kremlin."
"Golitsin's serf, his faithful dog."
"Well, then, pull him down by his coat."

The respectable-looking man went on reading, straining his voice:

". . . the Tatars destroyed their own dwellings; in Perekop they fired towns and villages and, filled with horror and despair, their heathen hordes fled, not daring to face you. And for returning safe to our frontiers with your army, bringing the above-mentioned victories, glorious throughout the world, no less than Moses who led the people of Israel out of the land of Egypt, for this we graciously and liberally commend you. . . ."

A one-eyed man with grisly hair shouted again:
"Say, reader, is there nothing about me in the proclamation?"

There was a hoot of laughter. Some cursed and moved away. A lump of mud struck the proclamation. "Guards!" cried the clerk, shielding himself with his hand. Tirtov, pushing his horse through the crowd, began to make his way towards the one-eyed man. But Tsigan only bared his broken fangs at him and disappeared. A man seized Tirtov's bridle: "Here's someone who should be stripped!" Another man pricked the horse with an awl. It struggled, snorting, and reared. Wild whistling sounded. A stone grazed Tirtov's cheek. He shot out of the crowd pursued by roars, yells and whistles.

Near the Nikolsky gates he saw two horsemen: Odoyevsky and a pale, aquiline-nosed man with a small, elegant moustache. The stiffness of his surcoat showed that he was wearing a coat of mail under it. Tirtov snatched off his cap and bowed as low as the horse's mane. It was Fedor Leontyevich Shaklovity. His intelligent face was gloomy, and his lower lip tightly covered the upper. He eyed the crowd malevolently through narrowed eyes.

Odoyevsky asked:
"Did you shout to them?"
"Go and shout yourself. . . ." Tirtov's cheeks were burning. "The hungry devils don't care whether it's Sophia or Peter. We ought to bring a couple of hundred streltsi and disperse the scum; that's all the talk that's needed."

"We must send some really able man," Shaklovity said through his teeth, "to egg them on to Preobrazhensk demanding bread. Let the play-soldiers deal with them. And we'll tell them that it's by Peter's orders that Germans are beating Russians." Odoyevsky laughed. "Go without delay, rub it into the streltsi. And I'll send reliable men to the market-places. We must get the mob away from Moscow; we don't need a general rising, the streltsi can manage it alone."

10

A travelling carriage, covered with dust and drawn by four horses of different colours, emerged from the forest by the shore of Lake Pereyaslav. The stolid coachman and the barefooted peasant astride the near leader looked round them. Logs and boards, chips and broken tar-barrels were scattered everywhere. And not a soul to be seen, though heavy snores were coming from somewhere. Near the shore rode four tarred ships; their high poops decorated with wood carvings, with small square portholes, were mirrored in the greenish water. Seagulls flew in and out between the masts.

Leo Narishkin climbed out of the carriage and rubbed his back with a grimace; the journey had given him cramp. Although he was not yet old, he was obese from drink. He waited for someone to come up and grunted, too lazy to call out himself. Squinting at the sun the coachman said:

"They're resting. It's the dinner hour."

And indeed, in the shade, from behind logs and barrels they could see feet in birch-bark shoes, or a dirty shirt rucked up over a naked back, or an unkempt head. The outrider, coming to the aid of his lazy master, called out briskly:

"Ho, Christians, anyone alive here?"

At this an inebriated, non-Russian face, with black moustaches stretching a foot across, reared itself from behind some ropes near the carriage and growled in broken Russian:

"Why do you shout, you fool?"

The coachman looked back at his master: should he give this fellow a taste of his whip? But Leo shook his head. Who could tell? Tsar Peter had even generals lying around drunk. He asked, without shedding his dignity, where the Tsar was.

"The devil only knows," the moustached head replied and once more fell back on to the ropes. Leo went along the shore, looking for someone of Russian aspect, and when he came upon a man in birch-bark shoes he had no hesitation in stirring him with his foot. The man, a carpenter, jumped up, blinking:

"In the morning the Tsar was sailing and firing guns. I expect he's tired and resting now."

They found Peter in a boat. He was asleep, with his head wrapped in a short coat. Leo sent all the others away from the boat and waited for his nephew to regain consciousness. Peter snored happily. His thin bare legs, with stockingless feet thrust into shoes, protruded from his broad Dutch breeches. Once or twice he rubbed them together, brushing off flies in his sleep. This particularly depressed Leo. The fate of the realm was hanging by a thread, while here the Tsar was brushing off pestering flies.

Nowadays the boyars were saying openly at the Kremlin: "The right place for Peter is the monastery. He's a soak who hobnobs with soldiers, he'll gamble away his crown at dice in the tavern." Once more drunken streltsi wandered about the Kremlin, standing insolently arms akimbo when any of the nobles passed. Sophia, made dangerous by these drunken swords, was in a frenzy. That inglorious warrior, Golitsin, sombre as a raven, stayed in his copper-plated palace and admitted only Shaklovity and Sylvester Medvedev into his presence. It was clear to everyone that the only choice for him now was to retire with ignominy or try to seize the throne at the price of bloodshed. A thundercloud was gathering over the Kremlin. . . .

And here the Tsar was sleeping in a boat as unconcernedly as you please.

"Ah, Uncle Puss Kirillich, how are you?"

Peter seated himself on the edge of the boat, sunburnt, dirty, happy. His eyes were slightly puffed, his nose was peeling, and the ends of his budding moustache were twisted.

"Why have you come?"

"To fetch you, Sire," Leo replied in a tone of severity. "And not for some favour or other, but because things have reached such a pass that you must at all costs come to Moscow. I shall not return without you."

Leo's fat face trembled, and beads of sweat stood out on his temples. Peter gazed at him in amazement. Things must indeed be pretty bad in Moscow if his lazy uncle was so agitated. He bent over the edge of the boat and drank out of the hollow of his hand. Then he hitched up his breeches.

"All right, I'll come one of these days."

"Not one of these days, but today. There is not an hour to lose."

Leo moved closer, barely reaching up to Peter's ear. "Last night, close to Preobrazhensk, across the Yaouza, an ambush of over one hundred streltsi was discovered." Peter's ear and neck instantly flushed. "Our sentries of the Preobrazhensky battalion kept their slow-matches burning and blew horns all night. So the streltsi didn't dare cross the river. And afterwards the strelets Ovsey Rzhov was heard to say in Moscow that they planned it like this: directly cries were heard at night in the Preobrazhensky palace, the streltsi were to be ready to cut down anyone who came out, no matter whom."

Peter suddenly covered his eyes tightly with his hand. Leo went on to tell how Shaklovity was sending agitators to the market-places to incite the hungry mob to go and attack Preobrazhensk.

"The people are desperate—their one thought is plunder and pillage. A new rising is just what Sophia is waiting for. Her most trusted streltsi have already tied a rope to the bell on the Spassky tower. They would have sounded the tocsin long ago, but the strelets regiments, the tradesmen and the townsfolk are hesitating: they are all tired of the tocsin. Things have reached such a pass that the boyars keep to their mansions, as if besieged. And as for my sister, Natalia Kirillovna, she is nearly out of her mind." Leo laid his face against Peter's shoulder and gave a sob. "Peter, my dear boy, we implore you for God's sake, come and show you are Tsar, call them to account. They miss the Tsar's authority; stamp your foot, and we'll support you. Not only we; our enemies too are tired of Golitsin, and Sophia sticks in everyone's throat."

Peter had often listened to such speeches, but today his uncle's tearful whispering alarmed him. He seemed once again to hear cries that made his hair stand on end, to see distorted open mouths, swollen necks, the blades of raised pikes, and Matveyev's body falling heavily on them. The physical horror of those days of his childhood! . . . His own mouth became distorted, his eyes bulged, a phantom blade pierced his neck under the ear.

"Peter! Sire! What is the matter?" Leo grasped his nephew's heaving shoulders. Peter struggled in his arms, his mouth foaming. Rage, horror and fear were in his incoherent cries. People ran up and surrounded the convulsed Peter in alarm. Pamburg with the moustaches brought some vodka in a broken earthenware pot. Like a small child, Peter merely sputtered without drinking; his teeth were so tightly clenched. They dragged him towards Leo's carriage, but he kicked and demanded to be laid on the grass. At last he grew quieter. Then he sat up and clasped his arms round his bony knees. His eyes were on the pale surface of the lake where seagulls were circling over the ships' masts. Nikita Zotov appeared from somewhere, staggering along. For the occasion of the morning's sham battle he was wearing his pope's mantle; his hair was dishevelled and there were wisps of hay in his beard. He sat down by Peter, looked at him pityingly, like a bearded old peasant woman, and said:

"Peter listen to me, fool though I am."

"Go to the devil!"

"I'm going, Sire. That's what our games have brought us to. It's time to stop. These are child's games."

Peter turned his head, Zotov crawled on his knees to look into his face from the other side. Peter pushed him away and, without a word, got into the carriage. Leo hastily crossed himself as he followed.

11

The mass was just ending in the Cathedral of the Assumption. The Patriarch's choir on the left and the choir of the palace staff on the right alternately filled the golden-dark vaults with sweet boyish voices and the stentorian tones of powerful throats. The bunched tapers gently crackling before the gold-mounted icons lit up the heated faces of the boyars. The service was conducted by the Patriarch, who looked like a martyr descended from an icon of the Suzdal school; all that was alive were his eyes, his feeble hands and his narrow beard that reached his navel and slid over his heavy vestments. Twelve gigantic deacons, with great heads of hair and of ferocious aspect, jangled ponderous censers. The Patriarch and the Metropolitan and the archpriests on each side of him swam in clouds of incense. The invocations of the archdeacon filled the whole cathedral as with a strong wine. This was the Third Rome. The proud Russian heart rejoiced.

On the royal dais, under a crimson canopy, stood Sophia. Tsar Ivan stood at her right hand; there were burning spots on his cheekbones and his eyes were half-shut. Peter, long and lank, stood at her left; he looked like a peasant dressed up for Christmas Eve in Tsar's clothes that were too short for him. The boyars smiled as they glanced at him and covered their mouths with their handkerchiefs: a clumsy youth who didn't know how to stand, shuffling, with his toes turned in like a goose. Sophia at least knew how to maintain royal dignity. She stood on a hassock to appear taller. Her face was calm, her hands folded together on her breast, and hands, breast, shoulders, ears and headdress sparkled warmly with gems. It was as though Our Lady of Kazan herself were standing under the canopy. But that other one, the sot from the Foreign Quarter, had knots of muscles bulging at the corners of his mouth as if he were going to bite; yes, but his bite would be weak. His eyes were cruel and proud. And all could see that there was no reverence in his thoughts.

Mass was over. The church attendants bustled about. Banners, mica lanterns, crosses and icons were raised, and the procession passed through the rows of boyars and nobles who stood aside. The Patriarch, supported by deacons, bowed to the Tsars, asking them as usual to carry the icon of Our Lady of Kazan and to walk through the Red Square to the Kazan cathedral. The Metropolitan of Moscow offered the icon to Ivan, who clutched his thin little beard and looked at Sophia. She stood as still as a graven image, gazing at a ray of light shining through the mica of a small window.

"I can't carry it so far," Ivan said timidly. "I'll drop it."

Then the Metropolitan, passing over Peter, offered the icon to Sophia. She unclasped her hands, heavy with rings, and grasped the icon firmly, greedily. Still looking at the ray of light, she stepped off her hassock. Vasily Golitsin, Shaklovity, Ivan Miloslavsky, all wearing sable coats, immediately drew near her. The cathedral was very still.

"Give it to me!" Everyone heard the harsh, indistinct voice.

"Give it to me!" The voice was louder, more hostile, and when they looked they realised that it was Peter speaking. His face was crimson, his eyes as round as an owl's. He was clutching the spiral pillar of the canopy and it was tottering.

But Sophia made only the smallest of pauses; she did not turn round, nor show any agitation. Abruptly, coarsely, so that the whole cathedral heard, Peter said:

"Ivan is not going, I shall go. Go to your apartment. Give me the icon. It's not for a woman to do. I won't allow it."

Raising her eyes, Sophia said in a voice of unearthly sweetness:

"Choristers, sing the Great Exodus!"

And stepping down, short and resplendent, she walked slowly along the rows of boyars. Peter gazed after her, with neck outstretched. The boyars sniggered in their handkerchiefs: it was funny though also sad. Ivan, stepping down cautiously after his sister, whispered:

"Don't be angry, Peter, make it up with her. Why should you quarrel? What is it you cannot share?"

12

Leaning forward in his chair, Shaklovity stared fixedly at Vasily Golitsin. Sylvester Medvedev, in a crimson silk cassock, also looked at Golitsin, gently gathering in his hand and nibbling his well-kept beard as black as a raven's wing. In the bedchamber a single candle burnt on the table. The ostrich feathers on the canopy of the bed cast shadows over the whole ceiling, where winged horses, cupids and barefooted maidens were crowning a hero with a face like Golitsin's. Golitsin himself was lying on a bench spread with bearskins. He was shivering with fever caught during the Crimean campaign. He was muffled up to the nose in a squirrel coat and his hands were tucked into the sleeves.

"No," he said after a long pause. "No, I cannot listen to such talk. God gave life, God alone can take it from him."

Shaklovity struck his knee with his cap in vexation, and glanced at Medvedev. The latter did not hesitate:

"It is written: 'I will send an avenger'. This must be understood: God does not take life, but by His will it is taken by the hand of man."

"He shouts in church as in a pothouse," Shaklovity added hotly. "Tsarevna Sophia has hardly recovered yet, he so alarmed her. They've reared a wolf-cub; he'll only find the first step hard. You can expect him in Moscow with his play-soldiers, there are three thousand or more of them. They're as restive as stallions. Am I right, Medvedev?"

"He will bring ruin to mankind, wounds to the Orthodox church and rivers of blood. When we were casting his horoscope, my hair stood on end: words, numbers, lines swollen with blood. It's true. It has long been said: wait for this horoscope."

Golitsin, pale as ashes, raised himself on his elbow:

"You aren't lying, priest?" Medvedev raised his pectoral cross. "What is this you are talking about?"

"We have been awaiting this horoscope for a long time," Medvedev repeated in so strange a tone that a cold, feverish shudder ran down Golitsin's spine. Shaklovity sprang up, his silver chains jingling, and thrust his sword and cap under his arm.

"It will be too late, Prince. Take care, or our heads will be stuck on poles. You tarry, you hesitate, you tie our hands."

Closing his eyes, Golitsin murmured:

"I am not tying your hands."

They could not get another word from him. Shaklovity left and they could hear him gallop furiously out of the gate. Seating himself by Golitsin's head, Medvedev began to speak of the Patriarch Joachim: he was, he said, hypocritical, stupid, weak. When they robed him in the vestry the Metropolitans pushed him for fun, showed ficos at his back. What was needed was a young and learned Patriarch so that the church should flourish joyfully, like a vineyard.

"It would wreathe your crown, Prince, with these divine grapes." He tickled Golitsin's ear with his beard drenched in sandalwood and attar of roses. "Take me for instance: no, I would not refuse the Patriarch's robe. We would blossom out. Vaska Silin, the seer, looked from the belfry of Ivan the Great through his fingers at the sun and saw all this in its signs. Have a talk with Silin. As for Joachim, why, every Saturday they bring him secretly four pails of crucian carp from Preobrazhensk. And he accepts them."

Medvedev also left. Then Golitsin opened his dry eyes and listened. His body servant was snoring outside the door. In the courtyard the men on guard were pacing the flagstones. Picking up the candle Golitsin opened a small secret door hidden by the curtain of his bed, and began to descend a steep winding staircase. Fever sent shivers through him, his thoughts were confused. From time to time he paused, raised the candle above his head and looked fearfully down into the dark.

Give up his great plans and retire to his estates? Let the troublous times pass; let them tear each other and vent their rage without him? Yes, but the shame, the ignominy of it. They would say: there was a time when he led armies, and now he is pasturing geese, this Prince Vasily. The candle trembled in a hand that had grown cold. He stretched out his hands for the crown, and now he's chasing chickens. He clenched his teeth and ran down a few steps. "What remains then: what Sophia wants, and Shaklovity and the Miloslavskys? To kill! If we do not kill Peter, then he will kill us! And what if we do not overcome him? An obscure business, a baffling business, an uncertain business. . . . Oh Lord, enlighten me!" He crossed himself, leaning against the wall. If he could but fall sick with brainfever during this time.

At the foot of the stairs Golitsin pushed back an iron bolt and entered a vaulted cellar where, in a corner, on a felt rug lay the sorcerer Vaska Silin, chained by the leg.

"Merciful boyar, why have you done this to me? I have done my best. . . ."

"Get up."

Golitsin set the candle on the floor and wrapped himself tighter in his fur coat. A few days ago he had given orders to take Vaska Silin, who lived in Medvedev's house, and chain him up. Vaska had begun to talk too much about powerful people who got love potions from him and used them for a person of whom one dared not speak; and that for this he was going to be given a house in Moscow and the privilege of drinking, free, in the government taverns.

"Did you look at the sun?" Golitsin asked.

Vaska fell muttering to his knees and greedily and noisily kissed the ground under the prince's feet. Then he got up again: short, thick-set, with a bear's nose and bald head; over his nose thick eyebrows slanted up to the curly hair on his temples; his deep-set eyes burned with wild impudence.

"They took me early in the morning up to the belfry, and again at the stroke of noon. I won't conceal what I saw. . . ."

"It's doubtful," Golitsin said. "What signs can there be on a celestial body? You're lying. . . ."

"There were signs; there were. I'm accustomed to look through my fingers, and it's a matter of prophesying that comes through me, I look as into a book. Of course, there are others who see in kvass lees, or in a sieve held up against the moon. Why not, if one knows how? Ah, Prince!" Vaska suddenly sniffed with his bear's nose and, rocking to and fro, looked sharply at the prince. "Ah, merciful Prince! I've seen everything. I know everything. There stands one Tsar, tall, dark, and his crown hangs down his back. Another Tsar, fair—oh, it's terrible to say!—three candles are in his head. And between the Tsars a couple is holding each other tight, going round and round like a wheel, as though they were husband and wife. And both are wearing crowns, and the sun burns hot between them."

"I don't understand your babbling," and, taking up the candle, Golitsin backed away.

"Everything will happen as you wish it. Fear nothing! Stand firm! And go on giving her my herbs; it will make things more certain. Don't leave the woman alone, feed her passion, feed it!"

Golitsin was already at the door.

"Merciful master, tell them to take the chain off." The man wrenched at it like a tethered dog. "Master, order them to bring me food. I haven't eaten since yesterday."

When the door was shut, he howled, clanking the chain and clamouring wildly.

13

The commanders Chermny, Gladky and Petrov wore themselves out trying to make the streltsi rise. They would go to the men's houses, violently flinging open the doors: "Why are you here sleeping with your women—we'll all lose our heads soon." They shouted frenziedly in front of the guardhouse: "We'll mark the boyars' and merchants' houses with tar; we'll plunder their shops and share their goods and chattels. Nowadays there's freedom again." They scattered anonymous letters in the market-places and, then and there, cursing savagely, read them out to the people.

The streltsi, however, like damp wood, only hissed but did not catch fire. The red blaze of revolt did not flare up. Besides, they were afraid: "See what a lot of rabble there is in Moscow; sound the tocsin and they'll smash everything, we shan't be able to protect our own property."

One day, early in the morning, four strelets sentries were discovered near the Miasnitsky gates, unconscious, with broken heads and hacked limbs. They were hauled to the guardhouse of the Stremianny regiment, and Shaklovity was sent for. In his presence they told their tale:

"We were standing guard by the gates and, heaven is our witness, we were stone sober. It was just at dawn. Suddenly from out of the waste ground horsemen rode down upon us and, without rhyme or reason, fell on us with bludgeons, whirlbats and maces. The worst of all was a stout fellow in a white satin coat and a boyar's cap. The others tried to stop him: 'Stop hitting, Leo Kirillovich, you'll beat them to death!' But he shouted: 'There's worse coming, I'll pay the accursed streltsi for my brother'."

Shaklovity listened with a smile. He examined the wounds and, displaying a severed finger from the porch to the onlookers and other streltsi, said: "Yes, it looks as though soon you too will be dragged off by your feet."

It was very strange. People found it difficult to believe that Leo Narishkin had suddenly taken to such violent deeds. But Gladky, Petrov and Chermny were already carrying the news to the suburbs that Leo Narishkin and his companions were riding out at night scanning faces, and when they recognised someone who seven years ago had taken part in the rioting in the Kremlin, they beat him to death. "Naturally," the streltsi replied mildly, "they don't pat people on the head for rioting."

Some three days passed and again, at the Pokrovsky gate, the same horsemen attacked a post with bludgeons, whips and swords, wounding a number of men. In some of the regiments the tocsin was sounded, but the streltsi were so frightened that they did not come out. At night men on guard began to leave their posts. They demanded to be sent on detail duty in detachments at least a hundred strong and with a cannon. It was as though an evil spell had been put on the streltsi; they were completely cowed.

Later a rumour spread that some of these wicked horsemen had been recognised. They were Odoyevsky, Tirtov, who lived with him as a paramour, Peter Tolstoy; and the one in the white coat was even said to be no boyar, but the under-clerk Matthew Shoshkin, belonging to Tsarevna Sophia's close circle. People asked in perplexity: what were they hoping to gain by this lawlessness?

These were distressing times in Moscow, full of anxiety. Every night a detachment of five hundred men was sent to the Kremlin. They returned drunk. People were afraid they would start fires. It was said that cunningly-made grenades had been prepared, and that Gladky had taken them secretly to Preobrazhensk and placed them on the road where Tsar Peter passed, but they did not explode. Everyone waited for something to happen and lay low.

At Preobrazhensk, since Peter's return, cannon were fired incessantly. Clean-shaven soldiers, with hair like women's, in hats and green coats, were posted behind barricades along the roads. Several times tramps, after shouting themselves hoarse in the market-place, started off to plunder the barns at Preobrazhensk, but before they reached the Yaouza they ran into soldiers, who threatened to shoot. Everyone was weary; the sooner one of them destroyed the other, the better: Sophia or Peter, Peter or Sophia. Either of them, so long as something was firmly established at last.

14

Volkov was riding down Miasnitskaya street picking his way through the barricades. He was challenged at every step and he replied: "Equerry of Tsar Peter, bearing the Tsar's ukase." In Lubiansky Square the gleam of camp-fires lit up the squat tower, the peeling, battlemented walls receding into the darkness towards the

Neglinnaya river. This gleam made the sky with its August stars seem blacker, and the trees behind the palings and fences round the square thicker. The crosses on the small low churches glittered. At this late hour many trading booths were empty. To the right, in front of the long guardhouse of the Stremianny regiment, sat men with pole-axes.

Volkov had orders, under cover of a specious mission to the Kremlin, to see what was going on in the town. Boris Golitsin, who now spent day and night at Preobrazhensk, had sent him. The old drowsy life there had come to an end. Peter had rushed up from Lake Pereyaslav a changed man. Former amusements were not even to be mentioned. When on the day of the celebration of Our Lady of Kazan he returned home, he was so convulsed with rage that they had great difficulty in calming him by making him drink holy water. His closest counsellors were now Leo Narishkin and Boris Golitsin. He was constantly shut up with them, holding whispered consultations, and he took their advice. The play-soldiers' rations were increased, they were given new belts and gauntlets, for which the money was borrowed in the Foreign Quarter. Peter never went out into the courtyard or the field without a dozen armed equerries. And all the time he seemed to be looking over his shoulder, as though he did not trust them, and he scrutinised everyone sharply. That day, as Volkov was mounting his horse, Peter shouted from a window:

"If Sophia asks about me, keep silent. If they put you on the rack, keep silent."

Glancing round the deserted square, Volkov put his horse to a gentle trot.

"Hi, stop!" came a terrible shout out of the darkness. Running across his path was a tall strelets taking an arquebus from his shoulder. "Where are you going?" He seized the bridle.

"Ho, there, take care! I'm an equerry of the Tsar."

The strelets put two fingers in his mouth and whistled. Five others ran up. "Who is he?" "An equerry?" "That's the man we want." "He came our way of his own accord." They surrounded him and led him towards the guardhouse. There, by the light of the camp-fire, Volkov recognised in the tall strelets Ovsey Rzhov. He drew himself up. Things looked bad. Still holding the bridle Ovsey said:

"Here, someone who's nimble-footed, run and find Gladky."

Two men went off unwillingly. Streltsi got up from the camp-fire, from the bench in front of the guardhouse and from carts, throwing back the bast matting. About fifty of them gathered round. They stood there quietly, as if it was none of their business. Volkov said boldly:

"You're not behaving well, streltsi. Is it that you've each got a head to spare? I am carrying the Tsar's ukase. To seize me is robbery, treason."

"Hold your tongue!" Ovsey made as though to strike him with his arquebus.

An old strelets restrained him:

"Don't touch him: he has to obey orders."

"That's it—I have to obey orders. I am a servant of the Tsar. And whose servants are you? Take care, streltsi, don't make a mistake! Hovansky was in high favour but what became of him? You were in high favour, but where's the pillar in the Red Square, where are your liberties?"

"Stop lying, you swine!" Ovsey shouted.

"I'm sorry for you. Didn't you have enough of Golitsin dragging you over the steppes? Help him, support him, and he'll lead you on a third campaign. You'll end by begging crusts at people's doors." The silence of the streltsi became still more gloomy. "Tsar Peter is no child. The time is past when he was afraid of you. You may have cause to be afraid of him. Oh, streltsi, put an end to this lawlessness!"

"Hi-eh!" someone yelled so wildly that the streltsi started. Volkov groaned hoarsely, raised his arm and fell. Gladky at a run had sprung on to his horse from behind and seized his neck. Both fell together to the ground. Turning Volkov over, Gladky sat on him, hit him in the mouth, knocked his cap off and tore off his sword. Then he jumped up roaring with laughter and brandishing the sword:

"See, here's his sword. I'll strip Tsar Peter like that too! Take him and haul him off to the Kremlin, to Shaklovity."

The streltsi raised Volkov and led him down the hill along the Kitay-gorod wall, past gnarled old willows full of crows' nests that spread their branches along the bank of the stagnant Neglinnaya, past gallows and wheels on poles. Gladky, reeking of stale spirits, walked behind. They entered the Kremlin by way of the Kutafya tower. Camp-fires burned inside the gates. Several hundred streltsi were sitting against the palace wall, lying on the grass, wandering about. They dragged Volkov along a dark passage and pushed him into a low-ceilinged room lit by icon lamps. A quiet, wrinkled sentry posted himself at the door. Leaning on his pole-axe he said in a low voice:

"Don't be angry; we too are in a tight corner. If they give the order, we strike. Hungry times, boyar. There are fourteen of us at home. We used to make a bit by trading, but today we live on what they give us. Don't think we are against Tsar Peter. Anyone who wants can rule us; that's how it is nowadays."

Sophia came in, bareheaded like a maiden, in a wide-sleeved coat of black velvet trimmed with sables. She sat down at the table, frowning. Behind her came the handsome Shaklovity, with a smile showing his white teeth. He was wearing a green strelets kaftan. He sat down by her. Gladky, somewhat affectedly—the faithful servant —leaned against the door. Shaklovity was turning over Peter's letter, taken from Volkov's pocket.

"The Tsarevna has read this letter, it deals with a trifling matter. Why were you sent so urgently in the night?"

"A spy," Sophia said through her clenched teeth.

"We are pleased to talk to you, equerry of the Tsar. Is he in good health? Is the Tsaritsa in good health? Do they intend to remain angry with us long?" Volkov remained silent. "You'd better answer, or we shall make you."

"We shall make you," Sophia repeated in a low voice, looking at him with a dull, peasant's glance.

"Is the play-army well provided? Do they lack anything? The Tsarevna wishes to know everything," Shaklovity went on. "Why do you post pickets on the roads? For fun, or are you afraid of someone? Soon there will be no thoroughfare to Moscow because of you. You seize corn waggons; is that right?"

Following his instructions Volkov remained silent, with bowed head. It was terrible to keep silent. But the more impatiently Shaklovity questioned him and the more menacingly Sophia frowned, the more obstinately he compressed his lips. He took no pleasure in his daring. He had gained much strength during his lazy life at Preobrazhensk, and his heart grew hot: torture me, go on, torture me! I won't tell anything. Had Shaklovity rushed at him with a knife to cut strips from his back, he would have looked him in the eye with gay insolence. And he raised his head and looked at them like that now. Sophia paled and her nostrils dilated. Shaklovity sprang up and stamped furiously.

"Do you want to answer on the rack?"

"I have no answer to give you," Volkov said, to his own horror, standing at ease and shrugging his shoulders. "Go to Preobrazhensk yourself, you've probably got enough streltsi to escort you."

Shaklovity struck him in the pit of the stomach with all his strength. Volkov gulped and backed, and saw Sophia rise from the table, her fat face shaking with anger.

"Cut off his head," she said harshly.

Gladky and the sentry dragged Volkov into the yard. "Headsmen!" Gladky shouted. Volkov drooped lifelessly on their hands. They let go and he fell on his face. Some of the streltsi came up and asked who he was and why he was to be beheaded. Laughing, they began to shout from one to the other across the dark square, calling for a volunteer headsman. Gladky made a movement to draw his sword, but the others said: "It's rather shameful, Nikita Ivanych, to redden your sword in this way." Swearing, he rushed back to the palace. Then the old sentry bent over the benumbed Volkov and touched his shoulder:

"Go, and good luck. Don't try the gates; run along the wall and climb over somewhere."

The camp-fires in Lubiansky Square had died down—one still smouldered by the guardhouse—no one wanted to haul wood however much Ovsey stormed. In the dark many of the streltsi had gone off to their homes. Others slept. A group of five was standing close to a fence, under the shelter of overhanging lime-trees, and talking in low voices.

"Gladky says: at the Riazan inn Boris Golitsin has hidden sixty clinking silver chains. He said we'd divide them and sell them."

"All Gladky thinks of is robbing, but he won't get many to go with him."

"They're not to be trusted: they plunder, and it's we who answer for it."

"The equerry was right when he said we might soon have cause to fear Tsar Peter."

"Not much needed to feel afraid."

"And this Tsarevna of ours; some she rewards with money, and others have to stand guard day and night, while at home all goes to wrack and ruin."

"As for me, I'd just as soon go straight off to join the play-army."

"You know, my lads, he'll come out on top."

"Very likely."

"There's no purpose in our waiting here. All we'll get is a rope round our necks."

They fell silent and turned round. From the direction of the Kremlin someone was galloping at full speed. "Gladky again. . . .

What makes the devil rush about so?" Drunkenly urging his horse into the camp-fire, Gladky dismounted and yelled:

"Why aren't the streltsi mustered? Why haven't they been sent to the gates? In the Kremlin everyone's ready, while here even your camp-fires aren't burning! Sleeping! Devils! Where's Ovsey? Send to the strelets' suburbs! When we ring the bell on Spassky tower, all to arms!"

Swearing, Gladky ran straddling into the guardhouse. The men standing under the lime-trees said to one another:

"The tocsin. . . ."

"Tonight. . . ."

"They won't muster the men."

"No. . . ."

"And what, my lads, if . . . eh?" Their heads came closer together and they spoke under their breath:

"They'll thank us there. . . ."

"Of course. . . ."

"A reward and all that. . . ."

"It's no good here, lads."

"We know. Who'll go? There should be two. . . ."

"Well, who?"

"Dmitry Melnov, will you go?"

"Yes."

"Yakov Ladygin, will you?"

"I? All right, I'll go."

"Try to get to him, himself. Throw yourselves at his feet and explain how it is. Say: 'Murder is planned against you, Great Lord'. Say we are his faithful servants, because we kissed the cross."

"You don't have to teach us. We know."

"We'll say it."

"Come on, lads!"

15

It was impossible even to think of fighting with the two battalions: the Preobrazhensky and the Semenovsky. Thirty thousand streltsi, the Kremlin guard, the foreign infantry, General Gordon's regiment: they would wipe out the play-army like flies. Boris Golitsin insisted that they wait quietly till the spring. Soon the autumn mud would come, and the frosts, and then you would not be able to make the streltsi leave their warm stoves to fight, even with bludgeons. In the spring they would see. It could not be worse for them, but it might be worse for Sophia and Golitsin: during the winter the boyars would all finally quarrel amongst themselves and would begin to come over to Preobrazhensk; the streltsi would not be paid—the treasury was empty. The people were hungry, the townspeople and craftsmen were ruined, the merchants were groaning. But if, nevertheless, Sophia sounded the tocsin and raised the army, it would be necessary to go with the play-soldiers to Troitsa-Sergiyevo to shelter behind its impregnable walls; it had stood the test, one could hold out there for a year or more.

On Boris Golitsin's advice presents were sent secretly to Troitsa, to the Archimandrite Vikenty. Boris Golitsin made the journey there twice and talked to the archimandrite, asking for protection. Every day General Sommer held reviews and manœuvres; the cannon-fire had broken almost every window in the palace. But when Peter mentioned Moscow, Sommer only snorted gloomily into his moustache: "Well, we'll defend ourselves." Lefort came sometimes, but not often. Sober, urbane, with a nervous smile, his manner alarmed Peter more than anything else. He no longer trusted even Lefort. He would often wake Alexander in the night, and they would fling on their coats and run round to inspect the sentry-posts. Peter would stand in the damp night on the bank of the Yaouza and look intently towards Moscow: darkness, not a light showing, a sinister silence.

With a sudden shiver from the cold, he would sullenly call Alexander and slowly go back to bed.

He slept with his wife only for the first few nights after his return. Then he ordered his bed to be made in an annexe of the palace, a low room with one window, like a closet; the Tsar slept on a bench, Alexander on a felt rug on the floor. Eudoxia had cried her eyes out waiting for the return of her beloved—she was in the fourth month of her pregnancy—and now that she had got him back, she was weeping again. She had wanted to run out into the road to meet him, but the old women would not let her. She had torn herself free and rushed to her dear husband in the hall. He came in, long, lean, something of a stranger, and she pressed her face, her arms, her breasts, her body against him. Her beloved kissed her with rough lips—he reeked of tobacco and tar. Then, passing his hand over her belly which was beginning to swell, he asked only: "Well, well, why didn't you write to me about a thing like that?" and for a moment his face softened. He went with his wife to pay his respects to his mother.

He spoke abruptly, incoherently, twitching his shoulder and scratching himself. At last Natalia said:

"My dear Peter, the baths have been heated since this morning."

He looked strangely at his mother: "Mother, I'm not itching from dirt." Natalia understood and tears rolled down her cheeks.

Only for three nights could Eudoxia entice him to her room: how she had pined for him, loved him, longed to show him tenderness! But she felt shy, worse even than on their wedding night; she did not know what questions to put to her beloved. And she lay on the pearl-embroidered pillows like a fool. He kept starting and scratching in his sleep. She was afraid to move. And when he went off to sleep in his closet, she could not look people in the face for shame. But Peter seemed to have forgotten his wife. He was busy all day running about and whispering with Boris Golitsin.

So August began. In Moscow the atmosphere was ominous. Preobrazhensk was on guard and full of apprehension.

16

"*Mein Herz,* what if you wrote to the Roman Emperor and asked him to give you an army?"

"Idiot!"

"Who—I?" Alexander raised himself nimbly on all fours on his felt rug and crawled to Peter. His eyes danced. "What I'm saying isn't at all foolish, *mein Herz*. You must ask for ten thousand infantrymen. Not more. Talk to Boris Alexeyevich about it."

Alexander squatted down by the head of the couch. Peter lay on his side, with his knees drawn up and the blanket covering his head. Alexander gnawed his lip.

"Of course we have no money for it, *mein Herz*. We need money. But we'll fool him. Surely we can fool the Emperor? I'd make a quick journey to Vienna myself. Oh, how we'd strike at Moscow and the streltsi, my word!"

"Go to the devil!"

"All right, then." Alexander just as nimbly slipped back under his sheepskin coat. "I don't suggest going begging to the Swedes or the Tatars. I understand how things are. But if you won't, you needn't. It's your business."

Peter, from under his blanket, said indistinctly as if speaking through clenched teeth:

"You've thought of it too late."

There was silence. It was hot in the closet. A mouse was scratching under the stove. "On guard!" came a distant cry from the sentries on the Yaouza. Alexander's breath began to come evenly.

All these nights Peter had been suffering from insomnia. No sooner did his head sink into the pillow than he would hear the soundless cry of "Fire! Fire!" And his heart would flutter like a lamb's tail. Sleep would be gone. He would calm down, but listening intently he would seem to catch the sound of someone weeping in the house behind the log walls. He thought much during these nights. He looked back on the years spent at Preobrazhensk, which, despite mortifications and obscurity, had been carefree, noisy, confused and happy-go-lucky. And he had ended up a stranger to everyone. A wolf-cub, a soldier's boon-companion. He had danced and played; now the murderer's knife was at his heart.

Once more he was wide awake. He curled himself up more tightly under the blanket. That sister, that sister of his! Shameless, bloodthirsty! Broad-hipped with a fat neck. He recalled how she had stood under the canopy in the cathedral. A painted peasant face, a butcher's wife! She had ordered grenades to be placed on his path. She sent men with knives. Yesterday a keg of kvass had turned up in the kitchen; a good thing they gave some to a dog first—it died.

Peter tried to chase away his thoughts. But anger throbbed through the veins on his temples. Take his life! But no beast, no man, wanted so greedily to live as did Peter.

"Alexander! Asleep, you devil? Give me some kvass."

Alexander, stupid with sleep, jumped up from under his sheepskin coat. Scratching himself he brought some kvass in a dipper and handed it to Peter, first tasting it himself. They talked for a while. "On guard!" came the melancholy, sleepless call from the distance.

"Let's sleep, *mein Herz*."

Peter lowered his bare, thin legs from the bench. It was not fancy: heavy footsteps were hurrying along the passages. Voices, cries. Alexander, in his underclothes, stood at the door with a pistol in each hand.

"*Mein Herz*, they're coming here."

Peter stared at the door. They were running up—they stopped at the door—a trembling voice said:

"Sire, wake up, disaster!"

"*Mein Herz*, it's Alioshka."

Alexander drew the bolt. Breathing heavily, Zotov—barefooted and with frightened eyes—entered, followed by men of the Preobrazhensky battalion. Alioshka and the moustached Buhvostov dragged in two streltsi like boneless sacks. Their hair and beards were tousled, their mouths hung open, their gaze was vacant.

Zotov, voiceless with fear, wheezed:

"Melnov and Ladygin, of the Stremianny regiment, they ran all the way from Moscow."

The streltsi fell on their knees at the door, their beards touching the felt rug, and shrieked wildly, to inspire as much alarm as possible:

"Oh, oh, Lord Tsar! You are lost! Oh, oh! They plot against you, our merciful Father; an immense horde is mustering, they are sharpening their steel blades. The tocsin is sounding on the Spassky tower and people come running from all sides!"

Trembling from head to foot, shaking his matted curls, his left foot twitching convulsively, Peter cried out in a voice even more terrible than that of the streltsi, pushed Zotov aside and just as he was, in only his shirt, fled down the passages. Everywhere frightened old women peered out.

Terrified servants swarmed round the back porch. They saw someone rush out, white and tall, with hands outstretched, as if blind. "Heavens, the Tsar!" Some fell to the ground with fright. Peter pushed through them, seized reins and whip from an officer of the watch, sprang into the saddle, his feet missing the stirrups and, slashing the horse, galloped off to disappear behind the trees.

Alexander kept his head; he took time to put on his coat and boots and, shouting to Alioshka: "Take the Tsar's clothes and catch up with us!" galloped off after Peter on another officer's horse. He overtook Peter, riding headlong without reins or stirrups, in the Sokolniki grove.

"Stop, stop, *mein Herz*!"

Stars were shining with autumn brightness through the tall treetops. They could hear rustling. Peter glanced round, shuddering, and kicked the horse with his heels to make it gallop on. Alexander seized the reins and repeated in an angry whisper:

"Wait a bit, where are you off to without your trousers, *mein Herz*?"

Something swished noisily in the bracken and a blackcock shaking its wings free rose and flew like a shadow across the stars. Peter only pressed his hands to his bare chest. Alioshka and Buhvostov rode up bringing the clothes. The three of them dressed Peter hurriedly.

A score of officers and equerries galloped up to join them. They made their way cautiously out of the grove. A faint glow showed over Moscow and it seemed to them that they could hear the tocsin. Peter said through clenched teeth:

"To Troitsa!"

They rode swiftly along cart-tracks and deserted fields to the Troitsa road. Peter galloped with slack reins, his three-cornered hat pulled over his eyes. From time to time he lashed his horse's neck furiously. Twenty-three men rode in front and behind them. The horses' hoofs rang loudly on the dry road. Knolls and hillocks, thickets of aspen and birch were left behind. The sky took on a green tint in the East. The horses snorted; wind whistled in their ears. At one point a shadow darted across the road—they could not make out whether it was a beast or a peasant come to pasture horses in the night—it threw itself into the grass, mad with fear.

They must reach Troitsa before Sophia. The dawn broke, yellow and clear. Several horses fell. At the first post they re-saddled and, without resting, galloped on. When the pointed roofs of the fortified towers rose in the distance and the flaming dawn lit up the domes, Peter reined in, turned round and bared his teeth. They rode through the monastery gates at a walk. The Tsar was lifted from his horse and carried, half dead with shame and fatigue, to the archimandrite's cell.

17

Neither in Moscow nor in Preobrazhensk had they anticipated what actually happened: Sophia was unable to raise the streltsi and the tocsin on the Spassky tower was not sounded. Moscow slept unconcernedly through that night. Preobrazhensk was abandoned. Everyone—Natalia with her pregnant daughter-in-law, the boyars, the equerries, members of the household and servants, and both play-regiments with cannon, mortars and ammunition—went to Troitsa.

Next day, when Sophia was at mass in the palace chapel, Shaklovity pushed his way through the boyars. His face was terrible. Sophia raised her eyebrows in surprise. With a crooked smile he bent down to her:

"Tsar Peter has been driven out of Preobrazhensk. He went off in his nightshirt, the devil knows where."

Sophia pursed her lips and said sourly:

"He can please himself; running away in a rage."

It seemed as if nothing of any importance had happened. But that same day it became known that the strelets regiment of Lavrenty Suharev had gone to Troitsa, though no one could make out when or who had persuaded them to go: probably Boris Golitsin, Suharev's boon-companion of long standing. Rumours began to fly round Moscow. Gates creaked at night; here and there a boyar's carriage drove out and, rumbling over the log-paved streets, dashed at full speed on to the Yaroslav road.

Vasily Golitsin spent his nights with Medvedev, trying to foretell his future by magic. And by day he wandered somnolently through the palace, agreeing with every proposal made. Shaklovity dashed from one regiment to another. Sophia, concealing her fury, waited.

Suddenly Ivan Tsikler went off to Troitsa with all his officers and many of his men. It was he who seven years earlier had dragged Ivan Narishkin, the Tsaritsa's brother, from his hiding-place under the altar. He had been in Sophia's confidence and, of course, when begging Peter for forgiveness, he disclosed all Sophia's plans.

Sophia was at her wits' end when she learnt about Tsikler. Whom could she trust if even such faithful dogs deserted? And now messengers from Troitsa began to arrive at all the nineteen strelets regiments carrying rescripts, written in Boris Golitsin's hand and bearing slantwise the spluttering signature "Ptr". These rescripts ordered commanders of regiments and other officers to go without delay to Peter on important State business.

The messengers were beaten at the city gates and their papers taken from them, but some of them managed to get through to the regiments and read out the ukase. Then Sophia ordered a proclamation to be made that anyone who dared go to Troitsa would be beheaded. At this the commanders of regiments said: "All right, we won't go." Vasily Golitsin had the idea of sending reliable men to the wives of those streltsi who had gone over to Peter to frighten them into writing to their husbands to come back. This was done, but little came of it.

They sent the Patriarch Joachim to Troitsa to propose a reconciliation. He went willingly but there he stayed and did not even write to Sophia. New rescripts came from Peter to the regiments, the merchants' and people's militia, to the suburbs and settlements: "Present yourselves without fail at the Troitsa monastery; those who do not appear incur the death penalty." So you lost your head either way: whether you went or whether you stayed. The commanders

Nechayev, Spiridonov, Normatsky, Durov, Sergeyev, five hundred officers, a large number of rank and file streltsi, together with representatives of the merchants and townsmen, filled with great fear, set out for Troitsa. Tsar Peter, clad in Russian dress, stood on the porch with Boris Golitsin, both the Tsaritsas and the Patriarch, and offered a cup of vodka to the men who presented themselves. They implored him with tears to put an end to the disorder. And that same day the Suharev regiment shouted: "Let's go to Moscow to catch the rogues!"

Vasily Golitsin gave out that he was ill. Shaklovity, afraid now to show himself, remained concealed in the palace. Gladky with his companions lay hidden in Medvedev's cloister. All the Kremlin gates were closed and cannon were wheeled out on to the walls. Sophia wandered restlessly through the deserted rooms with heavy steps and hands tightly clasped below her breasts. Better open fighting, rebellion, massacre, than this deathly silence in the palace. Power and life were ebbing from her as a dream fades from the memory.

But in the town all seemed quiet. The squares and market-places buzzed as usual. At night the watchmen's rattles were heard and the crowing of cocks. No one wanted to fight. Everyone seemed to have forgotten Sophia, entrenched alone behind the Kremlin walls.

At last she made up her mind, and on the 29th of August, accompanied only by her maid Verka and a small escort, she set out in a carriage for Troitsa.

18

Day and night dust hung over the Yaroslav road: carriages, horsemen and men on foot were streaming out of Moscow. Under the walls of the Troitsa monastery, waggons thronged the villages and fields, camp-fires smoked, noise and disputes broke out constantly for position, for bread, for fodder. The monastery had not expected such an invasion, and its granaries were soon emptied, its hay stacks pillaged. Yet the streltsi and militiamen had to be well fed. Detachments were sent to the neighbouring villages for food, but there too soon not a chicken was left. And still Troitsa was overcrowded and hungry. Many high-born boyars lived in tents, some in the yard, others out in the open. They sat, waiting for the Tsar to appear, on the porch steps in the heat of the sun, and ate there too with nothing to wash the food down. It was hard to exchange the comfortable Moscow houses, where even a strange bird could not fly in, for such a jostling press. But everyone realised that a great event was taking place: power was changing hands. And would it be for the better? It seemed as though it could not be worse than at present: the whole of Moscow, the whole people, the whole of Russia were covered with sores, clad in rags, beggared. In the evening, sitting round the camp-fires, lying under carts, people talked freely and to their hearts' content. The hum of voices and the red glow of camp-fires filled the fields round the monastery. Men, versed in magic, appeared from nowhere, winking mysteriously and shaking beans in their caps, ready to tell anyone his fortune. They would squat down, spread a kerchief on the ground, pour out the beans in three heaps, pass their fingers over them and hold forth in a soft, quiet voice:

"What you want, you'll obtain, have no doubts about what is in your thoughts. Be warned against him who does not wear birch-bark shoes or a sheepskin, and whose face is white. Do not walk past the third house, do not relieve yourself under three stars. What you want will come, perhaps soon, perhaps not. Amen. Do not thank me, give me the coin in your cheek."

Crawling among the carts in the dark these soothsayers spread strange rumours:

"The Tsarevna's spinal marrow is failing," they whispered. "Prince Vasily Golitsin will not live till the first snow. Those who left them were wise. Tsar Peter is still green, but the Tsaritsa and the Patriarch think for him, they are the crown of the whole matter. They stand for the real substance, and the substance is this: the boyars will be forbidden to ride in carriages and each of them will be allowed only one house to live in. And the merchants and the elected delegates of the townsmen will go to the palace and say with assurance: 'do this', or 'that is not to be done'. They will drive all foreigners out of Russia and their houses will be given over to pillage. Peasants and serfs will be free to live where they like, without servitude or taxes."

So spoke the soothsayers, and so thought those who listened to them. Festive chimes rang continuously from the monastery. Cathedrals and churches were open and lit with candles, and the austere monastic chants sounded day and night.

At dawn Tsar Peter, with the Tsaritsa mother on his right and the Patriarch on his left, came down the steps to attend mass. Later, appearing to the people, the Tsaritsa herself offered a cup of vodka to newcomers; the Patriarch, withered by prayer and fasting, but elated in spirit, would say:

"It is pleasing to God that you have abandoned the rebels, and fear the Tsar."

And his eyes would flash towards Peter. The Tsar was clad in

Russian dress, with a silk handkerchief in his clean hands; he was meek, his head was bowed and his face was thin. For over a fortnight he had not smoked a pipe or tasted wine. Whatever his mother, or the Patriarch, or Boris Golitsin told him to do, he did, and he never went outside the monastery walls. After the mass he sat under the icons in the archimandrite's cell and gave his hand to the boyars to kiss. He no longer spoke rapidly or stared, but answered with quiet dignity, not according to his own mind, but as advised by his elders. Natalia kept telling the personal boyars:

"I don't know how to thank God: the Tsar has come to his senses; he's grown so composed, so dignified."

The only foreigner permitted to see him was Lefort, and that not at meals or receptions; he would come in the evening to the Tsar's cell so that the Patriarch should not see him. Peter would silently take Lefort's cheeks in his hands, kiss him and sigh with relief. He would sit close to him, and Lefort, whispering in broken Russian, would tell him about this and that, amusing and encouraging him, and introducing practical ideas between his jokes.

He realised that Peter was painfully ashamed of his flight in a shirt, and he recounted examples from *The History of Bronnius* of kings and famous generals who had saved their lives by a ruse. "One French duke was obliged to dress up as a woman and get into bed with a man, but on the next day he captured seven towns. . . . The general Nectarius, seeing that the enemy were gaining, frightened the foe with his bald head and put them to flight; but later on he did not avoid dishonour and decorated his bald head with horns, although this did not diminish his fame, Bronnius says. . . ." Laughing, Lefort warmly pressed Peter's hands covered with drops of wax from the church tapers.

Peter was inexperienced and impetuous. Lefort insisted that, above all, caution was needed in the struggle with Sophia: that he must not rush into a fight—everyone was tired of fighting—but, to the blessed ringing of the monastery bells, promise peace and plenty to the people who swarmed from Moscow. Sophia would fall of herself, like a rotten post. Lefort whispered:

"Walk with dignity, Peter, speak meekly, look mildly, attend divine service as long as your legs can stand it; you will make everyone like you. This, they will say, is the kind of master God has sent us, with a master like that we shall have a respite. As for shouting and fighting, let Boris Golitsin do it."

Peter marvelled at the good sense of his bosom friend.

"The French call it politics," Lefort explained, "to know what is to your advantage. The French King Louis XI would visit a low peasant if he needed him and, when necessary, would mercilessly behead a famous duke or count. He did not fight so much as practise politics; he was a fox and a lion, he ruined his enemies and enriched his country."

It was wonderful to listen to him: a dancer, a rake and a jester, yet here he spoke of things no Russian even mentioned.

"With you everyone pulls his own way, and no one has a thought for the State: one wants profits, another honours and a third thinks only of filling his belly. Only perhaps in Africa could you find such a savage people. No industry, no army, no fleet. All you know is how to fleece—and the fleece itself is poor."

He uttered such words boldly, without fear that Peter would take up the defence of the Third Rome. It was as if he were taking a light into the thickets of Peter's wild, eager, apprehensive mind. The oil lamp before the icon of St. Sergius was burning low, and outside the window the watchmen's footsteps were no longer heard, but Lefort would make Peter laugh, and begin again:

"You are very clever, Peter. I've knocked about the world a lot and have seen all kinds of people. I offer you my sword and my life." He looked affectionately into Peter's brown, prominent eyes, so subdued now, as though he had lived through many years in these last few days. "You need trusted and intelligent men who will go through fire, spare neither father nor mother, for the sake of your word. As for the boyars, let them quarrel among themselves for place and honours. You can't put new heads on them, and it's never too late to chop them off. Wait, get stronger, you're still too weak to fight the boyars. We'll have plenty of fun and jollity and pretty girls. Enjoy life while the blood is hot; there'll be money enough; you're Tsar."

His thin lips whispered closely, his curled moustache tickled Peter's cheek, his eyes, in turn tender and firm, looked intelligent and dissipated. This man he loved read Peter's thoughts, put into words the things which went through his mind as vague yearnings.

Tsaritsa Natalia kept wondering how Peter had acquired so much prudence. She took endless joy in his sedate behaviour: he showed respect to his mother and to the Patriarch, listened to the boyars of his council, slept with his wife and went to the bath. Like an autumn rose, Natalia blossomed out in the monastery: she had lived fifteen years in neglect, and now once again high-born princes jostled one another to pay homage to the Tsaritsa Mother; the boyars and courtiers hung on her word to rush off on some errand. At mass she stood in the place of honour and to her the Patriarch presented the cross first to be kissed. When she appeared in public the crowd fell on their knees, the idiots, cripples and beggars yelled their praises of her and strained to touch the hem of her robe. Natalia's voice had become calm and measured, her glance regal. In her cell boyars, rendered motionless by the heat, sat on benches and coffers in their State robes of fur: Tihon Nikityevich Streshnev, the most intimate of all, who at the time of Peter's infancy had been his under-tutor, a serene smile on his lips, eyebrows beetling so that people could not judge whether he was sly or clever; the stern, red-haired, broad-faced Prince Ivan Borisovich Troyekurov; Peter Abramovich Lopuhin, a relative by marriage, the tightly-stretched skin over his cheekbones inflamed and his lashless eyelids red, so impatient was this small, dry old man to reach power; and, leaning against the stove, Prince Mihail Alegukovich Cherkassky, dozing with hands calmly folded, hawk-nosed, gipsy-like. In the middle of the month Fedor Yurievich Romodanovsky arrived and he, too, took to sitting in the Tsaritsa's cell, stroking his moustache, rolling his glassy, protuberant eyes and sighing till his great paunch heaved.

When the Tsaritsa entered the cell she greeted each one by name and seated herself on a simple chair, holding a small consecrated loaf in her hands. By her side sat her brother Leo Narishkin, red-cheeked, obese, dignified, and the boyars discoursed unhurriedly with him about State affairs: how to deal with Sophia, what to do with Miloslavsky, who should be sent into exile, who to a monastery and which of the boyars was to be put in charge of which government office.

Boris Golitsin showed himself at the Tsaritsa's seldom and only in extreme necessity; he was ashamed for his cousin and, besides, he was pressed for time: day and night he wrote rescripts, parleyed with Moscow, persuaded regiments to come over, conducted examinations, arranged for the feeding of the troops. He would take no one's advice: he was prouder and more arrogant than his cousin Vasily. In a light, gilded cuirass and Italian helmet with red plumes, magnificent, flushed with wine, he made the round of the regiments on a high-spirited mare, whose mane and tail were laced with gold cords. Bending down from his velvet saddle he kissed the newly arrived commanders of regiments. With his hands on his hips he would stride briskly up to the streltsi who fell to their knees like mown grass.

"Welcome, fine fellows!" he shouted hoarsely and the parting in his beard reddened. "God will forgive you, the Tsar will be merciful. Unharness the waggons, cook your dinner, your Sovereign makes you a present of a barrel of vodka."

"A merry fellow, this Boris," the streltsi told the women in the baggage-train. "Things must be going well here. A good thing we came."

Boris Golitsin managed everything alone. The boyars were glad enough to be left in peace; it was more restful to sit in the Tsaritsa's cell and ponder. Only the Dolgorukys, Yakov and Grigory, who lived in a tent of carpets in the Metropolitan's courtyard, were resentful: "Seven years we had to put up with Vasily, and now here's Boris lording it over us! Out of the frying-pan into the fire." Nor did the Patriarch like him, because of his carousing with Peter in the Foreign Quarter, because of his Latin and his love of foreign things. But the Patriarch also bided his time in silence.

On the 29th of August a strelets galloped up to the iron gates of the monastery. He was bareheaded, his coat was loose and only the protruding whites of his eyes showed in his dusty face. He raised his thin tousled beard towards the gate-tower and cried in a terrible voice:

"On the Tsar's business!"

They opened the creaking gates and helped the strelets off his winded horse. He was a strong man but behaved as though he could not walk, exhausted by his haste on the Tsar's business, so they led him to Boris Golitsin, carefully holding him by his arms. The man went shaking his head. At the sight of Boris on the porch he fell at the prince's feet:

"Sophia is five miles away, at Vozdvizhensk."

19

The outpost in the village of Vozdvizhensk stopped the Regent's carriage. Sophia opened the glass door and, recognising some of the streltsi, began to call them traitors and Judases, shaking her fist at them. The streltsi were frightened and took off their caps; but when the carriage began to move on, they barred its way with the shafts of their halberds and caught hold of the horses. Then it was Sophia who was alarmed; she ordered the carriage to be driven to any house near by.

Men and women peered out of their gates, boys climbed on to

the roofs to stare and dogs snarled at the carriage. Sophia leant back pale and exhausted with shame and anger. Verka pressed close to her feet, and the misshapen dwarf Ignashka, three feet high, in a cap with falcon-bells, who had been brought to amuse her on the way, screwed up his little face and wept. They drove to a rich exciseman's house. Sophia ordered the owners to keep out of the way and went into a bedroom, where Verka immediately covered chests, benches and bed with royal shawls. She also lit the icon lamps and Sophia lay down. Forebodings of misfortune gripped her head like an iron band.

Before two hours had passed, the sound of horses' hoofs was heard and the ring of sword on stirrup. Without asking permission, as though entering a tavern, the equerry Ivan Buturlin strode into the bedroom, with his cap on one ear and his hands in his pockets.

"Where is the Tsarevna?"

Verka rushed at him with fingers outspread and pushed him back:

"Go away, go away, you shameless fellow! She's sleeping. . . ."

Sophia sprang up and fixed her eyes on Buturlin until he pulled off his cap.

"I am on my way to Troitsa. Tell my brother I am coming."

"It's your business. But the Tsar orders you to await his envoy, Prince Troyekurov, without whom you must not leave here."

Buturlin departed. Sophia lay down again. Verka covered her with a fur coat to stop her shivering. The light in the mica window faded, they heard the shepherd's whip cracking, cows lowing, gates creaking, and then all was silent. The bells on Ignashka's cap jingled plaintively; the little jester sat dismally on a coffer, his legs dangling. "He too is preparing to bury me. . . ." Sophia was convulsed with rage. If her hand could have reached him he would have gone flying off the coffer. But her arms were like lead.

"Verka," she called in a low voice. "Don't forget to remind me about Buturlin when we are in the monastery."

Verka's cold lips touched her hand. In the grey twilight she pictured Buturlin's naked back, his bluish arms tightly bound, the flash of steel, his shoulder-blades swelling and drooping and in place of his head a bloody bubble appearing. . . . That's to teach you manners! Sophia drew her breath slowly.

So Troyekurov was on his way. A fortnight ago she had sent him to Peter from the Kremlin; he had returned without having settled anything. Then in her anger she had refused to give him her hand to kiss. Had he taken offence or turned coward? He was not very intelligent; it was only his appearance that was formidable. Sophia lowered her plump legs from the bed and straightened her skirt over her velvet shoes:

"Verka, give me the casket."

Verka set a metal-bound box on the featherbed and stuck a wax candle at the corner. She tried for a long time to strike the flint; Sophia's shoulders shook again with impatience. The tinder began to smell; she lit a piece of paper and then the candle. Sophia bent over in its light, pushing back the hair that fell on her cheeks. She re-read the letter her ailing brother, Tsar Ivan, had written to Peter begging a reconciliation—enough blood had been shed—and imploring the Patriarch to intercede mercifully and soften the hardened hearts of Peter and Sophia.

She smiled grimly as she read. Never mind; she would endure this humiliation too. Anything to lure the wolf-cub out of Troitsa! She was so deep in reverie that she did not hear riders come through the gates. When Troyekurov's deep voice enquired for her in the passage, she seized a black shawl off the bed, put it over her head and stood up to receive the prince. He came in sideways through the narrow door, bowed to her, touching the floor with his fingers and straightened up, copper-faced, his head reaching the ceiling, his eyes shadowed and only his great nose gleaming in the candle-light. Sophia asked after the health of the Tsar and the Tsaritsa. Troyekurov boomed out that, thank God, they were all well. He passed his hand over his beard, scratched his chin and still did not ask after Sophia's health. Realising what this meant, she went cold. She ought to sit down and not humiliate herself further, yet she remained standing. She said:

"I wish to spend the night at the monastery. It is uncomfortable here and there is no food." She kept trying to look into his eyes through the shadows. Her pride was crying out that she, the Regent, was afraid of this fool in three coats, that the long-forgotten feeling of a woman's fear was making her shrink as if in expectation of a blow.

Troyekurov said: "It was unwise of the Tsarevna to set out without an armed guard, without troops. The roads are unsafe."

"It is not I who need be afraid. I have more troops than you have."

"But of what use are they?"

"The reason I came without an armed guard is that I do not want bloodshed—I want peace."

"Of what bloodshed are you speaking? There won't be any bloodshed. Perhaps that rebel Fedka Shaklovity and his companions still thirst for blood, well, we shall deal with them."

"Why have you come?" Sophia cried in a strangled voice. He drew out of his pocket a roll of paper from which dangled a red seal. "You've brought a ukase? Verka, take the ukase from the boyar. And my ukase is this: order the horses to be harnessed—I will pass the night at the monastery."

Pushing aside Verka's hand, Troyekurov slowly unrolled the document and without haste began to read solemnly:

"By order of the Tsar and Grand Duke, Autocrat of all the Russias, you are commanded to return to Moscow without delay, there to await his royal pleasure and dispositions with regard to yourself. . . ."

"You dog!" Sophia tore the paper from his hands, crumpled it up and flung it down. The black shawl fell from her head. "I will return with all my regiments, and your head will be the first to fall!"

Troyekurov bent down with a grunt, picked up the ukase and finished sternly, taking no notice of Sophia's rage:

"And if you persist in trying to reach the monastery, orders have been given to use force . . . So!"

Sophia raised her hands, dug her nails into the back of her head and fell headlong on the bed. Troyekurov carefully laid the ukase on the edge of a bench and scratched his beard again, considering how he, as an envoy, should act in such a case: to bow or not to bow? He glanced at Sophia: she was lying face down and her velvet-shod feet protruded from her skirt, like those of a corpse. He put on his cap slowly and squeezed himself through the door, without bowing.

20

". . . And nothing could be worse than delay in such an important matter."

The letter trembled in Vasily Golitsin's hand. He moved the candle nearer and peered closely at the hastily scribbled words. He read and re-read them, trying to comprehend their meaning, to collect his thoughts. His cousin Boris had written: "Colonel Gordon brought the Butyrsky regiment to Troitsa and was admitted to the Tsar who embraced him and kissed him many times with tears, and Gordon swore to serve him to the death. . . . The foreign officers and dragoons and cavalry came with him. Whom have you left?

A small part of the streltsi who do not want to leave their shops and trades and public baths. Prince Vasily, it is not yet too late, I can save you. But tomorrow it will be too late. Tomorrow we shall break Shaklovity on the rack."

Boris had written the truth. From the day when Sophia had been refused admittance to the monastery, nothing could stem the flight of soldiers and officials from Moscow. Boyars left brazenly, in full daylight. The stern and incorruptible warrior Gordon had come to Vasily Golitsin and shown him Peter's ukase to come to Troitsa:

"My head is grey and my body is covered with wounds," Gordon had said frowning and wrinkling his shaven cheeks. "I swore on the Bible; and I faithfully served Tsar Alexey and Tsar Fedor and Tsarevna Sophia. Now I go to Peter." He grasped the hilt of his long sword in his gloved hand and struck the ground with it. "I do not wish to lose my head on the block."

Vasily Golitsin did not argue; it was useless. Gordon had realised that in the struggle between Peter and Sophia, Sophia had lost. And that same day he had left, with banners flying and drums beating. That was the last and hardest blow.

Golitsin had been living for some days now as if in a nightmare: he saw Sophia's vain efforts, yet could neither aid nor leave her. He feared dishonour but felt that it was near and as inevitable as the grave. With his authority as Guardian of the Throne and Commander-in-Chief he could have called out no less than twenty regiments and gone to Troitsa to parley with Peter. But doubts assailed him: what if, instead of obeying, the regiments shouted: "Brigand! Rebel!" Torn by doubt, he took no action, and avoided seeing Sophia alone by giving out that he was ill. Several times he secretly dispatched a reliable messenger with letters written in Latin to his cousin Boris at Troitsa, begging him not to start military action against Moscow, suggesting various ways of reconciling Peter and Sophia and laying stress on his own achievements and sufferings in the Tsar's service.

But it was of no avail.

It was like a nightmare in which someone visible yet obscure was pinning him down; and though his soul groaned with horror he could not stir a limb. A fly flew into the flame of the half-spent candle; it fell, spinning. Golitsin put his elbows on the table and clutched his head with his hands.

The night before he had ordered his son and his wife (long living in neglect and forgotten) to leave immediately for his estate Medvedkovo, near Moscow. The house was empty. Shutters and porches were nailed up. But he himself lingered. There was one day when it seemed the tide would turn. Sophia, returning from Troitsa, before so much as washing her hands or touching food, ordered heralds and criers to summon to the Kremlin all the streltsi, merchant militia, townspeople and all good citizens. She led Tsar Ivan out on to the Red Porch—he could not stand and seated himself by a pillar smiling piteously: everyone saw that he had not long to live. She herself, with a black shawl over her shoulders and untidy hair, just as she was from the journey, began to speak to the people:

"Peace and love are dearer to us than all else. Our letters are not read at Troitsa, our envoys are driven away. So, having prayed, I went myself to discuss matters peaceably with my brother Peter. I was allowed to go only as far as Vozdvizhensk. And there they reviled and shamed me, calling me a wench, as though I were not the daughter of a Tsar. I do not know how I got back alive. In four and twenty hours I ate only the tiniest morsel of holy bread. All the villages round have been plundered by order of Leo Narishkin and Boris Golitsin. They have made my brother a drunkard: all day he lies drunk in a closet. They want to attack Moscow and behead Prince Golitsin. Our days are numbered. If you say you do not need us, I shall go hence with my brother Ivan and seek a cloistered refuge."

Tears fell from her eyes. She could speak no more, but raised a cross with a holy relic high above her head. The people stared at the cross, at the Tsarevna weeping loudly, at Tsar Ivan drooping, with his eyes narrowed. They took off their caps and many sighed and wiped their eyes. When the Tsarevna asked: "Will you go to Troitsa, or can I rely on you?" they replied: "You can, you can, we won't betray you!"

The crowd dispersed. Thinking over what the Tsarevna had said they made wry faces. Of course they ought to stand up for her, but how could they do it? Bread had become scarce in Moscow; the supply carts turned off to Troitsa; there was robbery in the town and no order; in the markets people thought of other things than trading. Everything was at a standstill and sedition was rife. They were tired of it; it was time to end it. And whether it was Vasily or Boris Golitsin, it made no difference.

That day some ten thousand people had crowded into the Kremlin, waving copies of Peter's edict telling them to seize the rebel and brigand Shaklovity with his confederates and bring them in chains to the monastery. "Give us Shaklovity!" They shouted and climbed on to the porch and up to the windows, just as they had done many years earlier. "Give us Gladky, Chermny, Petrov, the priest Sylvester Medvedev!" The guards flung down their arms and fled. The court servants, women, maids, fools and dwarfs hid under the stairs and in cellars.

"Go out, tell the beasts I won't give up Shaklovity," Sophia said, gasping for breath, and pulled Golitsin by the sleeve towards the door. He did not remember how he had gone out on to the Red Porch; the breath of the people closing in came hot, smelling of garlic and laden with hatred; his eyes were dazzled by the threatening points of pikes, swords and knives. He shouted—he could not remember what—and backed slowly into the passage. Immediately the door began to give under vigorous shoulder thrusts. He saw Sophia's white face and staring eyes. He said: "We can't save him. Give him up!" The door burst open with a crash and people poured in. Sophia pressed back against him, and her body sagged more and more heavily. He wanted to hold her up, but with a low wail she pushed him away and fled. When they stood in the audience chamber, they heard Shaklovity's appalling shriek. He was captured in the royal bath-house.

And yet Golitsin delayed his flight. His travelling-carriage had been ready waiting at the back porch since the night before, and his steward and several old servants were dozing in the hall.

Golitsin sat before the candle with his head in his hands. The fly with scorched wings was lying with its feet in the air. The great house was silent, dead. The signs of the zodiac glimmered faintly on the ceiling, and the Greek gods looked through the darkness at the prince. Only the regrets tormenting Vasily Vasilyevich were alive. He could not understand how it had all happened. Who was to blame? Ah, Sophia, Sophia! At this moment he no longer deluded himself. Out of the forbidden inmost recesses of his heart there rose the heavy, unloved face of the woman as she was: the greedy mistress, despotic, gross, horrifying. The face of his glory!

What would he say to Peter, what answer give to his enemies? He had gained power by sleeping with a woman, had dishonoured himself in the Crimea and had written a manuscript: *Treatise on Civil Life, or How to Improve Matters of Concern to the Common Weal.* Clenching his fists he struck the table. Shame! Shame! Of his recent glory, nothing left but shame!

Through a chink in the shutters a dim redness showed. Could it be dawn already? Or had a bloody moon risen over Moscow? Golitsin rose and looked round the glimmering twilight of the vaulted chamber with the signs of the zodiac over his head. Astrologers, soothsayers, magicians had deceived him. He could expect no mercy. He slowly pulled his cap down to his eyebrows, put two pistols in his pocket and still watched the candle burn down in the candlestick: the wick fell into the melted wax, sputtered and went out.

In the dark courtyard people with lanterns began to bustle about. Through the distant glow dawn was just breaking. Taking his seat in the travelling-carriage Golitsin handed a key to his steward:

"Fetch him. . . ."

Valises were stored in the carriage and boxes tied to the back. The steward returned, pushing in front of him Vaska Silin with his clanking chain. The wizard groaned loudly and crossed himself in all four directions and towards the stars. The servants flung him in under Golitsin's feet.

"Let go then," the coachman said slowly and impressively, "and God speed!"

The six restive horses came out at a spanking trot on to the log-paved road. They turned uphill along the Tverskaya. There were as yet few people in the streets. A cow-herd was sounding his horn as he walked slowly in the dust past gates from which lowing cows emerged. Beggars on church porches were waking up, stiff with cold, scratching and quarrelling. Here and there a yawning sexton opened a low church door. In an alley a peasant on a cart with charcoal cried his wares. Women were emptying slops and ashes into the road, and all stared open-mouthed at the snow-white horses dashing past, at the outriders with peacock feathers in their caps, bouncing in their high saddles, at the savage-looking coachman who held twelve white silken reins in his great outstretched hands, and at the two giants with drawn swords on the footboard at the back of the carriage. The pails dropped from the women's hands, passers-by doffed their caps and some, to be on the safe side, went down on their knees.

Thus Vasily Golitsin drove for the last time through Moscow. What would the morrow bring? Exile? A monastery? Torture? He hid his face in the collar of his travelling sheepskin coat. He appeared to be dozing, but when Vaska Silin tried to move, the prince gave him a violent kick.

"Ho, ho!" Vaska was astonished. The prince's cheek twitched under his closed eye. As they drove out of the town gates, Golitsin said in a low voice:

"Your divination is all lies, cheating, banditry. You're a cur, a bastard, a swindler! To flay you with a whip would be less than you deserve."

"Don't, don't, don't doubt, kind Master. You'll have everything, everything, even the royal crown!"

"Hold your tongue, you rogue!"

Golitsin threw himself back and furiously kicked the soothsayer until he groaned.

Half a mile from Golitsin's estate a peasant on the lookout waved his cap as soon as he caught sight of the carriage; at the edge of a birch copse another passed on the signal to a third, on the rising ground across a ravine. "He is coming!" About five hundred servants received the prince on their knees, bowing down to the grass with frightened faces and inquisitive eyes. Golitsin scowled at them: they bowed too low, bustled and fussed too much. He looked at the small panes of glass in the six windows of the log-built house under its four-sided Dutch roof, with its open porch and a double semi-circular flight of steps. The wide courtyard was surrounded by stables, cellars, linen-weaving rooms, hothouses, poultry-runs and dovecots.

"Tomorrow," Golitsin thought to himself, "officials will come, make an inventory, seal up everything, despoil everything. All will go to wrack and ruin."

He went into the house, walking with unhurried dignity. His son Alexey rushed out to meet him in the hall; he was a tall youth, very like his father in build and face. He pressed his trembling lips to Golitsin's hand; his nose was cold. In the dining-room Golitsin, as though reluctantly, made a perfunctory sign of the cross, and sat down at the table facing a Venetian mirror which reflected the smoothly-planed walls, with tapestries and shelves holding valuable porcelain between the windows. All would go to wrack and ruin! He poured himself a goblet of vodka, broke off a piece of black bread and dipped it in the salt, but forgot to drink or eat. He put his elbows on the table and bowed his head. Alexey stood by him, holding his breath, bursting with the news he had to impart.

"Well?" Golitsin asked harshly.

"Father, they have already been here."

"From Troitsa?"

"Twenty-five dragoons with a lieutenant, the equerry Volkov."

"What did you say?"

"We said you were in Moscow and had no intention of coming here. The equerry said: 'Let the Prince hasten to Troitsa if he does not desire dishonour!'"

Golitsin gave a wry smile. He drank the vodka and munched the bread: there was no savour in either. He saw that his son could scarcely control himself: his shoulders drooped, his feet turned in like a serf's, and the floorboard beneath him shook. Golitsin was on the point of shouting at him, but when he glanced at his frightened face he felt sorry for him.

"Your knees are trembling, sit down."

"They ordered me too, Father, to go with you to Troitsa."

At this Golitsin flushed and he half rose, but again pride restrained him. He lowered his eyes, refilled his goblet and cut a slice of jelly with garlic. His son hastily pushed the vinegar towards him.

"Get ready, Alexey," he said. "I will rest, and at nightfall we will start. God is merciful." As he chewed, his thoughts were bitter. Suddenly his forehead grew damp and his eyes darted about. "Here's something you must do, Alexey: I've brought a man with me. Go, see that they take him to the bath-house by the river and lock him up and guard him as the apple of their eye."

After Alexey had gone, Golitsin lowered the knife with the piece of jelly that trembled on its tip, and his whole body sagged; he frowned, pouches swelled under his eyes and his lip hung loosely.

Vaska Silin sat in the small bath-house by the river, over the steep bank. All day he had yelled and howled for food. But only the bushes around rustled desolately, small fish splashed in the river escaping from pikes, and a flock of starlings, preparing for migration, flew to and fro, their wings shimmering in the blue sky that the soothsayer could see through the sash-window. Wearied, the birds perched themselves on a hazel-bush, twittering and whistling, fearless of human sighs.

"Oh, my dear Poltava!" the soothsayer murmured. "The devil brought me to accursed Moscow! Plague take you, may you all be scattered to hell and all your towns fall in ruins!"

The setting sun lit up the narrow window and sank behind the tree-tops of the forest. Vaska Silin realised that he was not going to get food and lay down on the cold bench with a bath-broom for a pillow. He dozed off but suddenly sprang up thrusting out his beard in terror: Golitsin stood on the threshold. He wore a black three-cornered hat and, under his travelling-coat, a black suit of foreign cut; a sword stuck out like a tail.

"What do you say now, soothsayer?" the prince asked in a strange voice.

Vaska Silin lost his head; he began to shake and tremble. He ought to have realised that the prince still retained some faith in his art of seeing into the future. He should have gripped the prince's hands and yelled: "You are going to the Tsar to face the martyrdom of death! Go, fear not. . . . ! Four beasts have loosened their claws. . . . ! Four ravens have flown away. . . . Death has retreated. . . . I see it, I see it all!" Instead, out of fear and hunger, Vaska babbled the old nonsense about royal crowns, and then broke into weeping and begged:

"For God's sake, let me go back to Poltava! I will do no harm, no denouncing. . . ."

Golitsin stared at him from the threshold with blazing eyes. Suddenly he rushed out, braced a log of wood against the door from the little passage outside, and padlocked it. Hearing him running about round the bath-house Vaska realised that he was piling up brushwood. "Don't!" he yelled. The prince replied: "You know too much, to the devil with you!" and coughed as he blew on the tinder. There was a smell of burning. Vaska seized a bucket and smashed it against the door but the door did not give. He pushed his head sideways out of the sash-window and shouted; smoke choked him. The brushwood crackled and roared as it caught fire. The chinks between the logs lit up. The fire rose in a roaring wall. To save himself from the heat Vaska crawled under the bench. The roof buckled. The walls blazed.

In the windless night, a flame surged high above the river, extinguishing the stars. And for a long time the reddened shadows of six white horses and a black leather coach, travelling fast over the Yaroslav road, flew over the fields, spread into the depth of a damp ravine, and climbed low hills, gliding across and breaking on the trunks of a birch-copse.

"Where is the fire? Father, is it at our place?" Alexey asked more than once.

Golitsin did not reply as he dozed in a corner of the coach.

21

Carpenters were busy clearing a space under the low beams of a cellar in the cattle-yard. In troubled times this cellar had been used as a powder magazine, but now it was a storeroom for the monks' provisions. The carpenters placed a cross-beam between two brick pillars and fastened to it a block with a noose and, under that, a log with a collar at one end. This was the rack. Then they put a bench and a table for the scribe who would record the depositions and a second bench, covered with brocade, for those of high rank. Finally they mended the steep steps from the cellar to the barn in which Shaklovity had been confined for the last two days.

Boris Golitsin conducted the examination. Sviezhev, renowned for being able to make anyone speak with the first touch of the whip, had been brought from the brigands' prison in Moscow. At public whippings at the post he could lash mercifully but, if he chose, he could break a man's spine with his fifteenth stroke.

Many had already been examined. Some came of their own accord and gave information. But Gladky and Medvedev had not been caught. Orders to seize them were sent all over the country.

It was Shaklovity's turn. The day before he had replied hotly to everything: "It is a libel. My enemies want to destroy me, but I am guilty of no crime." Today they had Sviezhev ready for him, but he did not know this and intended again to deny everything, to deny that he had instigated rebellion or plotted against the Tsar's well-being.

At first Peter was not present at the examinations. Boris would come to him in the evenings with the scribe, who would read out the depositions. But when Sophia's confidential agents were examined, Peter wished to hear their statements himself. A chair was brought to the cellar and he sat at the side, under the mildewed beams. With his elbows on his knees and his chin on his fists, he would sit there listening, never asking a question himself. When the rack creaked for the first time and the victim's broad-shouldered body, naked to the waist, hung from it, his face grey and his teeth grinding with pain, Peter drew back into the shadows behind the brick pillar and sat motionless throughout the torture. All that day he was pale and pensive. But each time he got more used to it and no longer hid in the background.

That morning Natalia had detained him after early mass and the Patriarch congratulated him on the successful ending of the troubles. And, in fact, although Sophia was still in the Kremlin, she was powerless. The regiments which remained in Moscow sent deputations to beg forgiveness and mercy; they were ready to go to Astrakhan or to the frontiers if their lives and their families and trades were spared.

Peter left the cathedral on foot. The cattle-yard was full of streltsi, who called out to him: "Sire, hand over Shaklovity to us, we'll talk to him ourselves!" He waved them aside and, with bowed head, hurried past them to the old barn, stumbling down the steps to the dark cellar. It smelt of mildew and mice. Passing between sacks and barrels, he pushed open a low door. The candle on the scribe's table threw a yellow light on the cobwebs on the beams, the rubbish on the earth floor and the newly-cut logs of the rack. The scribe and the others sitting on the bench—Boris Golitsin, Leo Narishkin, Streshnev and Romodanovsky—rose and bowed. When they sat down again Peter saw Shaklovity: he was on his knees near them, his curly head drooping, the rich coat in which he had been captured torn and splashes of mud on his shirt. He raised his haggard face slowly and met the Tsar's eyes. His pupils gradually dilated and his handsome lips were tight-drawn and quivering, as if he were crying. He leaned forward, not taking his eyes off Peter.

Boris also glanced at the Tsar and, with a cautious laugh, asked: "Do you command us to continue, Sire?"

Streshnev said through his clenched teeth: "You knew how to commit crimes and you ought to know how to answer: why waste time? The Tsar wants to know the truth."

Boris said in a louder voice: "He has but one answer: 'I never said such words or did such deeds'. But the investigation shows that he is implicated. We must use torture."

As if he had been pushed, Shaklovity moved sideways on his knees, like a mouse trying to hide itself behind a bale of skins or a barrel of salt fish. Then he fell over and lay still. Peter strode across to him and saw at his feet Shaklovity's shaven neck with a deep furrow. He put his hand into the pocket of his brocaded coat and, sitting down, said haughtily and contemptuously in his high-pitched, youthful voice:

"Let him tell the truth."

Boris called Sviezhev. A tall, narrow-shouldered man in a red tunic down to his knees came out from a pillar behind the rack. Shaklovity had evidently not expected him so soon; he squatted on his heels and hunched his shoulders, staring at Sviezhev's horse-like, unconcerned face: it had almost no forehead—a mere line above the eyebrows—and an immense jaw. He went up to Shaklovity, picked him up as if he were a child, shook him, and stood him on his feet. Then he carefully and skilfully gripped Shaklovity's sleeve and pulled off his coat, tore his white silk shirt with a finger-nail and ripped it, leaving him naked to the waist. Shaklovity tried to speak firmly, but his voice was hoarse and inarticulate as he cried:

"Gentlemen, I will tell everything."

The boyars on the bench shook their heads, their beards and their cheeks. Sviezhev tied Shaklovity's hands behind his back, fastened the leather noose round his wrists and pulled the other end of the rope. Shaklovity stood there astounded. The block creaked and his hands began to rise behind his back. The muscles strained, his shoulders swelled and he bent forward. Sviezhev gave him a hard blow in the small of his back and, sitting down, raised Shaklovity from the ground. The twisted arms were wrenched from the sockets and raised above his head. He gave a stifled groan and his body, with open mouth and staring eyes, hung a yard from the ground. Sviezhev fastened the rope and took a short-handled whip from a nail. At a sign from Boris, the scribe put on his iron-rimmed spectacles and, with his thin nose close to the candle, began to read:

"And further, at the examination Captain Sapogov said: 'Last year, on a day he could not recall, Tsarevna Sophia went to the village of Preobrazhensk and at that time the Great Tsar Peter was not there, and the Tsarevna remained only till noon. And Shaklovity and many others from various regiments were with her, and Shaklovity had brought them to kill Leo Narishkin and Tsaritsa Natalia. At that time Shaklovity came out of the palace and said to him, Sapogov: "Listen until you hear cries in the palace"—and at that moment there was uproar in the palace, for the Tsaritsa was upbraiding Tsarevna Sophia—"And when you hear cries, be ready, and beat to death all those whom we pass out to you'."

"I said no such words. Sapogov lies," Shaklovity said, choking.

Boris gave a sign and Sviezhev stepped back, measured the distance with his eye, drew himself taut, swung the whip and, lunging forward, brought it down with a hiss. Shaklovity's soft body gave a convulsive shudder and he cried out. Sviezhev struck him a second time. Boris said: "Three!" and he struck a third time. Shaklovity howled and, sputtering foam, shrieked: "I was drunk! I said it when I was drunk, I didn't know what I was saying."

"And further," the scribe continued when the cries died down, "he spoke slightingly of Tsar Peter, saying: 'He goes to the Foreign Quarter and drinks and nothing can sober him, for he drinks himself dead drunk. And it would be good to place hand-grenades in his carriage so that they should kill him, the Tsar'."

Shaklovity did not speak. "Five!" Boris ordered in a savage voice. Sviezhev raised the whip and brought it down with terrifying force. Peter sprang towards Shaklovity and looked into his wild eyes: Peter was so tall that their eyes were level. His back, his hands, his neck were twitching.

"Tell the truth, you dog!" He caught him by the ribs. "Are you sorry you did not kill me when I was little? That's so, isn't it? Who wanted to kill me? You? No? Then who? You sent men with grenades? Whom? Name them? Why did you not kill me, murder me?"

Shaklovity, his muscles growing taut with the effort of speaking, muttered into Peter's face:

"I do remember these words only: 'Why were the Tsaritsa and her brothers not done away with earlier?' But as for knives and grenades, I remember nothing of these. It was Golitsin who said it of the Tsaritsa."

When he mentioned Golitsin's name, Boris jumped up from the bench and shouted wildly:

"Lash him!"

Sviezhev, taking care not to hit the Tsar, brought down the whip between Shaklovity's shoulders, tearing the flesh. Shaklovity shrieked. At the tenth blow his head sank on his chest.

"Take him down," said Boris, wiping his lips with his silk handkerchief. "Take him upstairs carefully. Wipe his back with vodka and look after him like a child. Tomorrow he must speak."

When the boyars left the cellar and came into the cattle-yard, Streshnev asked Leo Narishkin in a whisper:

"Did you see Prince Boris, eh?"

"No. What do you mean?"

"How he jumped up. To shut Shaklovity's mouth."

"Why?"

"Shaklovity said too much. They're of the same blood, Boris and Golitsin. Blood is dearer to them, it seems, than the Tsar's affairs."

Leo Narishkin stopped by a dung-heap, raised his hands and slapped his thighs. He was astounded.

"Oho! And we are trusting Boris!"

"Trust him, but keep a watch on him."

"Ah!"

22

The stove was burning in the hut; there was no chimney and the smoke filled the upper part so that the bunks were completely invisible and people standing could only be seen up to their waists. The flame of the cresset light glimmered feebly, and the sparks hissed as they fell into a small wooden trough of water. Pot-bellied children with running noses and dirty buttocks ran about, falling now and again and howling. A pregnant woman with a bast rope holding up her skirt dragged them outside the door, saying: "There's no peace with you, you'll be the death of me, you little wretches!"

Golitsin and his son Alexey had been in this hut since the day before; they had been refused admittance at the monastery gates: "The Great Sovereign orders you to remain at hand until required." They were waiting for their time to come. They could hardly swallow food and drink. The Tsar had declined to listen to any defence. Golitsin had expected anything and on the way had steeled himself for the worst; but he had not foreseen this smoky hut.

During the day Colonel Gordon had come in, cheerful and honest; he had expressed his sympathy, clicked his teeth commiseratingly, and patted Golitsin's knee as equal to equal. "Never mind," he said, "don't be downcast, Prince; things will blow over." And he had gone off, free—the lucky man—jingling his big spurs.

There was no one to send to the monastery to find out how things stood. The local people did not even doff their caps to the Tsarevna's former lover. He was ashamed to go out into the street. His head ached with the stench and the squalling of the children and his eyes smarted with the smoke. And more than once, for some reason, he suddenly remembered the accursed soothsayer, and his ears rang with the man's cry: "Open the do-o-or! You'll perish, you'll perish!"

Late that night a non-commissioned officer with several men entered unceremoniously and, coughing with the smoke, asked the pregnant woman:

"Is Vasily Golitsin here?"

The woman thrust out her ragged elbow: "There he is."

"You are ordered to go to the palace. Get ready, Prince."

Golitsin and his son Alexey entered the monastery gates on foot, like tramps, surrounded by guards. The streltsi recognized them, and sprang up, laughing: one pulled his cap over his eyes, another caught hold of his beard, still others took up ribald postures:

"Stand up smarter! The Commander-in-Chief is riding in on two hoofs!" "And where's his horse?" "Between his legs of course. . . ." "Oh, I'm afraid the Commander-in-Chief may fall into the mud. . . ."

The humiliating ordeal was over. Golitsin ran up the steps of the Metropolitan's porch, but an unknown clerk in shabby clothes came importantly out of the door to meet him and stopped him with a sign. Opening out a roll of paper, he read loudly and slowly— each word striking the prince like a blow on the head:

". . . for all the above-mentioned misdeeds the Great Tsars Peter and Ivan have decreed that you, Prince Vasily Golitsin, shall be deprived of your honours and boyar rank and be sent, together with your wife and children, to perpetual exile in Kargopol. And your estates, manors and Moscow mansions and livestock will be confiscated and taken by the Great Tsars for their own. Your people, serfs and bondsmen, except the peasants and their children, are to be granted their liberty."

When he had finished reading the long document, the clerk rolled it up, turned to the officer of the guard and said, pointing to Golitsin who, bareheaded, could hardly stand on his feet, while Alexey held him up by the arm:

"Arrest him and act in accordance with this order."

They took him and led him away. Outside the church gates they put both father and son in a cart, on bast mats; then the officer and a dragoon jumped up behind, and the driver, in a ragged coat and birch-bark shoes, gathered up the reins. The sorry nag dragged the cart slowly out of the monastery into the fields. It was night and a damp mist veiled the stars.

23

The Troitsa campaign was over. Once again, as seven years before, they had held out in the monastery against Moscow. The boyars, the Patriarch and Natalia took counsel and wrote in Peter's name to Tsar Ivan:

". . . And now, my Lord Brother, the time has come for us two ourselves to rule the realm entrusted to us by God, for we are now of age and are no longer willing to allow a dishonourable third person—our sister—to share with our two male persons the titles and the administration of affairs."

Sophia was taken in the night, without much fuss, from the Kremlin to the Novodevichy convent. Shaklovity, Petrov and Chermny were beheaded. The other rebels were flogged in the public square, in the strelets suburb, had their tongues cut out and were exiled to Siberia for ever. The priest Medvedev and Gladky were caught later by the governor of Dorogobuzh. They were cruelly tortured and then beheaded.

Those who had come over to Peter were rewarded with land and money in accordance with their rank. The boyars received three hundred roubles each; the courtiers, two hundred and seventy; nobles of the council, two hundred and fifty. The equerries who had accompanied Peter to the monastery received thirty-seven roubles each, and those who had followed later thirty-two; those who had arrived before August 10th got thirty, and those before August 20th, twenty-seven. The town nobles each received, in the same order, eighteen, seventeen and sixteen roubles; the rank and file streltsi getting for their loyalty one rouble each, without land.

Before returning to Moscow the boyars divided the various offices among themselves. The first and most important—the Ambassadors' Office—was given to Leo Narishkin, but without the title of "Protector". Now that his military and other use was past, Boris Golitsin could have been completely dispensed with—there was much the Patriarch and the Tsaritsa mother could not forgive him, and in particular the fact that he had saved his cousin Vasily from the whip and the block—but the boyars found it unbecoming to deprive so noble a family of honours: "If we do this, the offices will soon be taken away from us: merchants, low-born clerks, foreigners and other common people are all crowding to Tsar Peter for gain and place." Boris Golitsin was given, for the benefit of the income and honour, the office of the Kazan Palace. When he learnt this, he spat, got drunk and shouted: "To the devil with them! I'll do with what I've got." And, drunk as he was, he drove post-haste to his estate near Moscow to sleep it off.

The new Ministers—as foreigners now began to call them—turned out one set of clerks and scribes and put in another set, and then began to think and govern in the old way. Little was changed: only now Leo Narishkin, instead of Ivan Miloslavsky, strode about the Kremlin in black sables, slammed doors with authority and titupped mincingly.

They were all old men, all well known, and there was nothing to be expected from them but ruin, bribery and disorder. In Moscow and in the Foreign Quarter, merchants of all guilds, excisemen and artisans, Dutch, Hanoverian traders and English sea-captains, were all impatiently awaiting new men and a new order. Many rumours about Peter were circulating, and many put all their hopes on him. Russia, a gold mine, lay buried under age-old slime. If the new Tsar could not revive the country, who could?

Peter was in no hurry to go to Moscow. He marched his army from Troitsa to Alexandrovsk village where the ruins of Ivan the Terrible's dreaded palace were still rotting. Here General Sommer organised a sham battle, which went on for a whole week—as long as the gunpowder lasted. And here too Sommer's career ended: he fell, poor fellow, from his horse and was badly crippled.

Peter went to Moscow in October, taking with him only the regiments of his play-army. Some six miles from the city, in the village of Alexeyevsk, huge crowds of people met him, carrying icons, holy banners and loaves of bread on salvers. Logs and blocks with axes stuck into them had been placed on each side of the road. Streltsi—deputies from those regiments which had not gone to Troitsa—lay on the damp earth with their heads on the blocks. But the young Tsar did not cut off any heads: he was not angry, though neither did he show himself gracious.

chapter five

Lefort was becoming a person of importance. The foreigners who lived in the Foreign Quarter, as well as those who came there on business from Archangel and Vologda, spoke of him with great respect. Agents from Amsterdam and London wrote to their establishments about him and advised sending him small presents—preferably some good wine—if there was any question of business. When, after the Troitsa campaign, the rank of general was conferred on him, the inhabitants of the Foreign Quarter clubbed together and presented him with a sword. As they passed his house, they exchanged meaning winks and said: "Ah, yes!" His house was not large enough now: so many people wanted to shake hands with him, exchange a few words, or merely remind him of their existence. In spite of the late autumn, work was hurriedly begun on rebuilding and extending his mansion: a stone porch with wings was added and the façade decorated with columns and stucco figures. On the courtyard site, where formerly a fountain played, they dug a pond for aquatic and firework entertainments. On either side guardhouses for musketeers were being built.

Perhaps Lefort himself would not have cared to embark on such expense, but it was the young Tsar's wish. During his stay at Troitsa Lefort had become as necessary to Peter as a wise mother to a child. Lefort understood his wishes at the slightest hint, warned him of dangers, taught him to see advantages and disadvantages and, to all appearances, was himself deeply attached to Peter. He was constantly with him; not, like the boyars dully thumping their heads on the ground at his feet asking for villages and peasants, but in order to discuss their joint affairs and amusements. He was elegant, a ready talker and good-natured and, when he entered Peter's bedchamber, bowing and smiling, he was like the morning sun at the window; the day began with merriment, pleasant activity and happy expectations. Peter loved in Lefort his own thrilling dreams of foreign countries, beautiful cities and harbours full of ships with courageous captains reeking of rum and tobacco: everything that since his childhood he had imagined, looking at the pictures and prints brought from abroad. Even Lefort's clothes had a smell that was not Russian, but something different and extremely pleasant.

Peter wanted his favourite's residence to become an enclave of this alluring foreign life; it was for the Tsar's pleasure that Lefort's mansion was being enlarged and embellished. All the money he could get out of his mother and Leo Narishkin was spent on it unstintingly. Now that his supporters were supreme in Moscow, Peter threw himself heart and soul into enjoyment. He flung restraint to the winds, and this made Lefort particularly necessary to him; without Lefort he did not know how to satisfy his desires. What counsel could his own, Russian, people give him? Well, to go on hawking expeditions or call in blind men to sing. But a hint conveyed what he wanted to Lefort, who was like leaven in the dough of Peter's passions.

Simultaneously work was resumed on the capital city of Pressburg; the little fort was being made ready for the play-army's spring manœuvres. The regiments were issued with new uniforms: the Preobrazhensky regiment with green coats, the Semenovsky with blue, and General Gordon's Butyrsky regiment with red ones. The whole autumn was spent in feasting and dancing. And in the intervals between the entertainments in Lefort's mansion, the foreign merchants and traders were forwarding their interests.

2

The newly-built ballroom was still damp; the high, semi-circular windows and the mirrors on the blank wall opposite, made to look like windows, were sweating with the heat from two enormous fires. The parquet oak floor was freshly polished with wax. The candles in their three-branched sconces, fitted with reflectors, were lit, although dusk was only just beginning to fall. Soft snow was drifting down. Sledges were driving into the courtyard between heaps of clay and wood-chips, dusted over with snow: Dutch sledges shaped like swans and painted black and gold; Russian sledges—long and box-like—piled with cushions and bearskins; heavy, covered sledges drawn by six horses tandem; and common hired sledges in which sat some laughing foreigner with his knees drawn up, driven by a peasant who had brought him from the Lubianka to the Foreign Quarter for the sum of two kopeks.

The guests were welcomed on the stone porch by two dwarf buffoons, Tomosa and Seka, who stood on a carpet sodden with snow from the guests' boots; one of them wore a short black Spanish cloak and a straw hat with raven's wings, the other was dressed as a Turk, in a six-foot-high bast turban adorned in front with a pig's ear. The Dutch merchants were particularly delighted with the dwarf in Spanish costume—they flipped his nose and enquired after the health of the King of Spain. Coats and hats were handed to liveried footmen in the well-lit hall, whose oak-panelled walls were hung with blue Delft dishes. Lefort met his guests at the ballroom door; he was dressed in a white satin coat laced with silver, and a silver-powdered wig. The guests gathered round the blazing hearths, drank Hungarian wine and lit their pipes.

As few of the Russians could yet speak enough Dutch, English or German to converse with the foreigners, they arrived late, only for the banquet. The guests stood at ease in front of the fire, warming their posteriors and legs in tight-fitting hose and discussed business, while the host flitted like a butterfly from one to the other, swinging his flared coat-tails, introducing people, enquiring after their health or their journey, whether they had found comfortable inns and warning them against thieves and robbers.

"Oh, yes, I've heard a lot about the Russian rabble," one guest replied. "They are much inclined to rob and even murder rich travellers."

The English timber-merchant Sidney drawled:

"A country whose population gets its living by cheating is a bad country. Russian merchants ask God to help them to swindle better, they call that skill. Oh, I know this damned country well. It's best to come here secretly armed."

A modest trader of the Foreign Quarter—grandson of Lord Hamilton who had fled to Russia from Cromwell's terror—approached the group and said deferentially:

"Even I, who have had the misfortune to be born here, find it difficult to get used to Russian coarseness and dishonesty. They all seem to be possessed by the devil!"

Sidney glanced at this émigré who spoke English with a strong accent and whose clothes were rough and old-fashioned, and pursed his lips contemptuously; but out of respect for their host he replied:

"We don't intend to settle here. And Russian dishonesty has little importance to a great wholesale trade like ours."

"You trade in timber, sir?"

"Yes, sir, I trade in timber. We have bought a large forest concession near Archangel."

Hearing the words "forest concession", van Leyden, a Dutchman, thrust his red face with lashless eyes and short pointed Spanish beard into the group; his three chins rubbed against an enormous starched collar.

"Oh yes," he said, "Russian timber is good, but the devilish winds in the Arctic Ocean and the Norwegian pirates are fearful." He opened his mouth and his face flushed even redder as he laughed till two tears were squeezed out of his screwed-up eyes.

"Never mind," replied the tall, bony, sallow Sidney. "Mast trees cost us twenty-five kopeks here, and we sell them in Newcastle for nine shillings.* We can afford to take risks."

The Dutchman clicked his teeth: "Nine shillings for one tree!"

He had come to Moscow to buy linen yarn, linen cloth, tar and potash. Two of his ships were wintering at Archangel. Business was hanging fire: the Tsar's agents—important Moscow merchants who were buying goods for the treasury—had heard of his two ships and raised their prices absurdly. The stuff offered by the small middlemen was not worth having. But if this Englishman was speaking the truth, he must be doing good business. It was very vexing. Glancing round to see that there were no Russians within hearing, van Leyden said:

"The Russian Tsar owns three-quarters of the tar in the world, the best spar timber and all the hemp. But it's as hard to get as if it were in the moon. Oh no, sir, you won't make much on your concession. The North is not populated—you can't teach bears to fell timber. Besides, two out of every three of your ships will be sunk by Norwegians or Swedes, and the third will be crushed by ice-floes." He laughed again feeling that he had annoyed the arrogant Englishman. "Yes, yes, this country is rich, just as the New World is richer than India, but so long as the boyars rule we shall suffer one loss after the other. The Muscovites don't understand where their own advantage

* Four roubles and fifty kopeks. (*Author's note*)

lies; they trade like savages. Oh, if they had ports on the Baltic, and good roads, and traded like honest citizens, then one could do a thriving trade here."

"Yes, sir," Sidney answered stiffly, "I have listened to you with pleasure and I agree with you. I do not know what things are like with you, but I imagine that you in Holland too, as in England, no longer build small ships. Our English shipyards lay down no ship smaller than four or five hundred tons. We require five times as much timber and flax nowadays. Each ship needs no less than ten thousand yards of sailcloth."

"O-o-o-oh!" gasped those who heard.

"And hides, sir; you are forgetting the demand for Russian leather," Hamilton interrupted him.

Sidney glared indignantly at the ill-mannered fellow. He wrinkled his bony chin, and gazed at the fire for some time through narrowed eyes.

"No," he rejoined at last, "I am not forgetting Russian leather, but I don't trade in it. Swedish merchants export it. Thank the Lord, England is growing richer, and we need vast quantities of building materials. And we shall have them. When the English want something, they get it."

He closed the conversation by sitting down, putting his heavily-shod foot on the fender and paying no further attention to anyone. Lefort hurried up with his arm through Alexander's. Alexander was wearing a green cloth coat with scarlet lapels and brass buttons, there were enormous silver spurs on his top boots. His face, framed in a luxuriant wig, was powdered, and a diamond pin was stuck in his lace cravat. His clear, merry eyes glanced boldly round the guests. He bowed gracefully and, standing with his back to the fire, took up a pipe.

"The Tsar will be pleased to arrive in a moment."

The guests began to whisper, and the more important ones moved forward, facing the door. Sidney, who had not understood what Alexander had said, opened his mouth with astonishment at this young fellow who had carelessly pushed respectable men away from the fireside. But Hamilton whispered to him: "The Tsar's favourite; quite recently raised from orderly to officer's rank. A very useful person."

At this Sidney turned to Alexander with a smile that brought good-natured wrinkles round his eyes:

"It has long been my earnest wish to have the happiness of meeting the great Tsar. I am only a humble trader and I thank the Lord for the unexpected opportunity. It will be something to tell my children and grandchildren."

Lefort translated, and Alexander replied:

"We'll show you, we'll show you!" And he laughed, showing his even white teeth. "And if you can drink and crack a joke, then you can have fine times with him. That will be something to tell your grandchildren about." He turned to Lefort: "Ask him what he trades in. Oh, timber! I suppose he's come to ask for men, woodcutters?" Lefort translated the question and Sidney nodded. "Why not, if the Tsar gives him a note to Leo Kirillovich? Let him try."

Suddenly Peter appeared in the doorway; he was wearing the same Preobrazhensky uniform coat—narrow in the shoulders and chest— as Alexander, and was powdered with snow. His ruddy cheeks were dimpled, his lips compressed, but his dark eyes were dancing. He took off his three-cornered hat and stamped, shaking the snow from his rough square-toed top boots.

"*Guten Tag, meine Herrschaften!*" he said in a youthful bass.

Lefort flew up to him and bowed with one hand outstretched and the other resting on his heart.

"I'm very hungry. Come, let's get to the table."

With a wink at the foreigners who stood with bated breath, Peter turned round, slightly stooping and nearly as high as the door and, crossing the hall, passed into the banqueting-room.

3

The faces of the guests had already become flushed and their wigs were awry. Alexander, having taken off his sash, had spiritedly performed the Russian national dance, and was drinking again. Wine only made him grow pale. The buffoons, pretending to be more drunk than the guests, played at leap-frog and slapped the guests' heads with inflated bladders in which dried peas rattled. Everyone talked at once. The candles had burnt halfway down. The ladies from the Foreign Quarter would soon arrive for the dancing.

Sidney, erect and composed, but with eyes slightly bloodshot and squinting, was talking to Peter, while Hamilton, standing behind their chairs, interpreted:

"Sir, tell His Majesty that we English consider our fortune lies in the success of our seaborne trade. War is a costly and grievous necessity, but trade is a blessing from God."

"Quite so," Peter agreed. He was enjoying the clamour and the arguments around him, and was particularly amused by the foreigner's strange discourses on the State and trade, and what was beneficial and what harmful. About fortune too. It was very odd! "Well, go on, I am listening."

"His Majesty the King of England and the honourable Lords would never pass a law which was harmful to trade. That is why His Majesty's treasury is full. An English merchant is respected in his own country, and we are all ready to shed our blood for England and for the King. I trust His Majesty the young Tsar will not be angered if I say that there are many bad and useless laws in Russia. Oh, a good law is a great thing! We too have harsh laws, but they are good for us and we respect them."

"The devil knows what he's saying!" Peter said with a laugh as he drained a tall goblet with a foot shaped like a bird's. "If he were to talk like this in the Kremlin—I say, Franz—wouldn't they all have fits? All right then, tell us what's wrong with us! Hamilton, translate."

"Oh, that is a very serious question, and I am not sober," Sidney replied. "If His Majesty permits, tomorrow, when I am in full control of my faculties, I would tell him of evil Russian customs and also what makes a State rich and what is necessary to that end."

Peter stared into his squinting, alien eyes. Could the merchant be making fun of those fools of Russians? But Lefort bent quickly over his shoulder and whispered:

"It would be interesting to hear—this philosophy of how to make a country rich."

"Very well," Peter said. "But let him say now what is wrong with us."

"All right." Sidney drew his breath, mastering his intoxication. "On the way to our most amiable host's I drove through a square where there was a gallows. There a small space is cleared of snow and one solitary soldier is standing guard."

"Beyond the Pokrovsky gate," Alexander added, drawing up his chair.

"Yes. Suddenly I noticed a woman's head sticking out of the ground and blinking its eyes. I was very much alarmed, and asked my companion: 'Why is the head blinking?' and he answered: 'She is still alive. This is a Russian form of execution; for killing her husband the woman is buried in the ground and after a few days, when she has died, they hang her up by the feet'."

Alexander guffawed. Peter looked at him, then at Lefort, who was smiling gently.

"Well, what of that? She is a murderess. They have been executed like that for centuries. Do you expect her to be pardoned?"

"Your Majesty," Sidney replied, "ask this unfortunate woman what led her to commit this frightful crime, and she will surely soften your generous heart." Peter smiled. "I have heard and observed a few things in Russia. A foreigner's eyes are sharp. The life of a Russian woman in the women's quarters is like an animal's." He passed his handkerchief over his sweating forehead, feeling that he was saying too much; but conceit and drink had loosened his tongue. "What an example for a future citizen for his mother to be buried alive and then hung up by the feet! One of our writers, William Shakespeare, touchingly describes in a beautiful comedy how the son of a rich Italian merchant poisoned himself for love of a woman. But the Russians beat their wives with whips and sticks till they are half dead, and the law even encourages it. When I return to London, to my home, my good wife will greet me with a loving smile and my children will run to me without fear, and I will find peace and order in my home. It would never occur to my wife to kill me since I am kind to her."

The Englishman, overcome with emotion, fell silent and bowed his head. Peter gripped his shoulder.

"Hamilton, translate to him . . ." and he shouted in Russian into Sidney's ear:

"We ourselves see all this. We don't boast that all is well. I have been telling my mother that I want to send fifty equerries, the cleverest of them, abroad, to learn from you. We have to start with the ABC; that's what we must do. You accuse us of being savages, beggars, fools and beasts. Damn it, I know it myself! But wait, wait. . . ."

He rose and hurled a chair out of his way.

"Alexander, horses!"

"Where to, *mein Herz*?"

"To the Pokrovsky gates."

4

"Where is she?" Peter asked in a loud voice. "I don't see her. Have the dogs eaten her?"

"Sentry, are you asleep? Guard!" the people round the sledge shouted.

"Here!" a drawling voice answered, and the sentry ran up through the falling snow, stumbling over his sheepskin coat. Then softly, like a bear, he fell at Peter's feet and remained kneeling.

"Is it here a woman is buried?"

"Here, Lord Tsar!"

"Is she alive?"

"She is."

"Why is she being executed?"

"She killed her husband with a knife."

"Show me."

The sentry ran a few paces, then bent forward and carefully brushed the snow from the woman's face and frozen hair.

"She's alive, Tsar. Her eyes blink."

Peter, Sidney, Alexander and four or five of Lefort's guests went towards the head. Two musketeers held up torches. Their helmets glittered. Big, sunken eyes gazed up at them from the snow; the woman's face was as white as the ground round it.

"Why did you kill your husband?" Peter asked.

She said nothing. The sentry touched her cheek with his felt boot.

"The Tsar himself is asking, fool."

"Did he beat you? Was he cruel?" Peter asked, bending over her. "What's her name? Dasha? Well, Dasha, tell me!"

She remained silent. The sentry sat down and whispered into her ear: "Confess! Perhaps he will pardon you. You're making things awkward for me, little woman."

Then the head opened its black mouth and, in a hoarse, deep voice filled with hatred, it said: "I killed him. And I would kill him again, the beast!"

The eyes closed. No one spoke. Drops of resin fell from the torches with a hiss. Sidney began to talk rapidly, but no one would translate. The sentry again touched her with his felt boot; the head rolled over, as if the woman was dead. Peter coughed harshly and went to his sledge. He said in a low voice to Alexander:

"Order her to be shot."

5

Silent and chilled through, Peter returned to Lefort's brightly lit house. Musicians were playing in the ballroom gallery. The gaily-coloured clothes, the faces and the candles were multiplied in the mirrors. Through the warm haze Peter caught sight at once of fair-haired Anna Mons. The girl was sitting by the wall; her face was pensive and her bare shoulders drooped.

At that moment the musicians, playing a slow dance, sounded a long-drawn-out blare of brass trumpets from the gallery and seemed to sing to him of Annchen, of her billowing pink dress, of her innocent hands lying in her lap. Why, oh why was his heart bursting with such unbearable sadness? It was as if he himself were buried in the ground up to the neck and was calling his love to him through the snowstorm from an impossible distance.

Annchen's eyes flickered; she was the first to see him in the doorway. She rose and flew across the polished floor. And now the music was singing merrily of good old Germany, where, in front of very, very clean little windows, good papa and mama look with loving smiles at Hansel and Gretel standing under the pink blossoms of an almond-tree which means love for ever and ever; and when their sun sets in the blue of the night, they will both go with a peaceful sigh to their graves. Oh, how impossibly far away!

Peter put his arm round Annchen's waist, warm under the pink silk, and danced with her in silence and for so long that the musicians began to play out of tune.

He said: "Anna?"

She looked up at him with pure, clear and trustful eyes:

"You are not happy today, Peter?"

"Annchen, do you love me?"

Annchen only bowed her head quickly; a velvet ribbon was tied round her neck. All the ladies present, those who were dancing and those who were sitting round, understood both what the Tsar had asked and what Anna Mons had replied. As they went round the ballroom, Peter said:

"With you I am happy."

6

The Patriarch Joachim entered supported on each side. As he blessed the old Tsaritsa with her brother and the boyars, he sternly pushed the knuckles of his ascetic's hand against their lips. Tsar Peter had not yet arrived. Joachim seated himself on a hard chair with a high back and bent low, his face hidden in his cowl. The beams of the sun beat strongly through the deep embrasures of the windows under the brightly painted vaults of the audience chamber. Everybody was silent, with hands crossed and lowered eyes. Only the winged shadow of a pigeon that came to perch on the snow-covered windowsill outside disturbed the quiet. Heat streamed from the blue-tiled stove, and there was a smell of incense and wax. The first and most important matter was to sit like this in dignified silence, preserving ritual and tradition. Let the waves of humanity—vanity of vanities—break upon this unshakable fastness! There had been enough temptations and innovations. The bulwark of Russia was here; we might be poorer, but we were nearer the truth. For the rest, God would help us.

They remained silent awaiting the Tsar's arrival. Tsaritsa Natalia dozed piously; during the last few months she had grown stouter and her health was failing. Streshnev, with a groan, picked up the beads which had fallen from her knees on to the carpet. In Sophia's time a clock in a tall case had stood in the audience room, but orders had been given to have it removed: the ticking was irritating and, besides, it has been said: "None knows the hour. . . ." To count the time was to delude oneself. Let it fly more slowly over Russia, and more quietly.

From outside came the sound of banging doors and frosty voices shattering the languid silence. The Tsaritsa, stifling a yawn, made the sign of the cross over her mouth. A bodyguard, a gentle youth, meekly reported the Tsar's arrival. Without haste the boyars took off their tall caps. Tsaritsa Natalia wrinkled up her face with her eyes on the door, but thank the Lord, Peter was in Russian dress. He had stopped laughing and he made a decorous entrance. "He's got legs like a stork, it's difficult for the dear boy to walk in a dignified manner," the Tsaritsa thought to herself. Her face lit up in welcome. He went up to the Patriarch to receive his blessing and enquired after the health of his ailing brother.

He needed money urgently, which was why he had come obediently to listen to Joachim in response to his mother's letter. He took his seat on the throne and the sleepy silence of the room enveloped him like a feather-bed; with his elbows on the arms of the throne he covered his mouth with his hand, in case a fit of yawning were to steal upon him.

Joachim brought out from under his black mantle a sheaf of papers sewn together and slowly turned a page with a shaky hand. Then he raised his eyes, pressed his fingers for a long time to the eight-pointed cross on his cowl and, having crossed himself, began to read with slow distaste in a low, drawling voice:

". . . Do not delude yourselves that, having rooted out sedition, you have brought peace to the land and the people. My soul grieves to see no unity of thought and no prosperity among nations. In the capital city idle monks and nuns, priests and deacons, lacking propriety and discretion, as well as various worthless people—their name is legion—having bandaged their arms and legs, and some also having veiled or shut their eyes, tramp the streets and beg for alms with deceitful cunning. Is this the flourishing vine? And, further, I see drunkenness, dream-reading, sorcery and unbridled lechery in the homes. The husband tears out his wife's hair and throws her naked into the street, and the wife murders her husband, while the children, like creatures bereft of their senses, grow up like weeds. Is this the flourishing vine? And further I see a boyar's son, a craftsman, a peasant, take up bludgeons and, having set fire to their homes, go off into the forest to indulge their ferocity. Peasant, where is thy plough? Tradesman, where is thy measure? Boyar's son, where is thine honour?"

Thus he read about the evils which were rife throughout the country. Peter no longer felt like yawning. Natalia, in perplexity, looked from her son to the boyars, while they, as custom demanded, remained silent, sunk in their beards. Everyone knew that the affairs of the realm were in an extremely bad way. But what could be done? There was nothing for it but to endure. Joachim went on:

"We, with our feeble mind, have decided to tell you, the Great Tsars, the truth. There will be no order and no plenty in the land so long as there exist in it godlessness and the detestable Latin, Lutheran, Calvinistic and Jewish heresies. We are suffering for our sins. We were the Third Rome and have become Sodom and Gomorrah. Great Tsars, it is necessary to forbid heretics to build their prayer-houses, and to destroy those which have already been built. Not to allow accursed heretics to be officers in the regiments. What help can they be to the Orthodox army? They only bring down divine wrath. Wolves are in command over lambs! Orthodox people must be forbidden to befriend heretics. Foreign customs and garments must not be introduced. And after we have gradually recovered and raised the spirit of Orthodoxy, the foreigners must be expelled from Russia, and the Foreign Quarter, that Gehenna and seat of temptation, must be burnt down!"

The Patriarch's eyes were blazing, his face quivered, as did his narrow beard and bluish hands. The boyars hid their eyes; the Patriarch was putting it too strongly, one should not go full tilt at such a matter.

Romodanovsky's eyes bulged like a lobster's. Natalia, who had not understood anything, nodded and smiled, even after the reading was over. Peter was sprawling on the throne, his lips pouting childishly. The Patriarch put away the papers and said, passing his fingers over his eyes:

"Let us begin the great task with a small matter. In the days of Tsarevna Sophia, at my humble entreaty they seized the vile heretic Quirin Kuhlmann in the Foreign Quarter. During his questioning he said that in Amsterdam he had had a vision of a man in a white robe who commanded him to go to Moscow where people were perishing in the darkness of impiety." Joachim made a pause, overcome by the violence of his feelings. " 'And you,' he said at the questioning, 'are blind: you do not see that there is a halo over my head and that the Holy Ghost speaks through my mouth.' And he quoted texts from the false teachings of Jacob Bohm and Christopher Bartut. Nevertheless he himself seduced the girl Maria Selifontova in Moscow, dressed her in man's clothing, for fear of being found out, and she lives at his house in a closet. Every day both of them are drunk, they play the fiddle and the cymbals, and he puts his head out of the window and shouts in a wild voice that he is possessed by the Holy Ghost. To those who visit him he makes prophecies and forces them to kiss his belly. Lord, how can one be calm for a single moment when Satan is already triumphant here! I beg the Great Tsar to issue a ukase condemning Quirin Kuhlmann to be burnt alive, together with his books."

All turned their heads towards Peter, and he realised that the case of Quirin Kuhlmann had long been decided. He read it in his mother's calm eyes. Alone Romodanovsky twitched his moustache disapprovingly. Peter sat up straight and made an involuntary movement with his hand, to bite his nails. For the first time in his life he was being called upon to make a decision as a ruler. He felt nervous, but cold anger was already closing round his heart. He recalled the recent conversations at Lefort's, the dignified, intelligent faces of the foreigners. Polite contempt: "Russia has been too long an Asiatic country," Sidney had said the next day. "Your people fear the Europeans, but you are your own most dangerous enemies." He remembered how ashamed he had felt as he had listened. He had ordered

Sidney to be given a sable coat and told not to visit Lefort any more, but to proceed to Archangel. What would the Englishman have said now hearing such words? To destroy the Protestant and Catholic churches in the Foreign Quarter? His memory evoked the tinkling of the bells of the German church that could be heard through the open windows in summer. Those early chimes spoke of honesty and order, of the smell of the well-kept little houses on the Kukuy, of the lace curtain on Anna Mons' window. You would like to burn her too, you living corpse, you black raven! You would leave a mound of ashes on the Kukuy! Now it was Peter's burning eyes that glared at the Patriarch. But stronger than rage—was it the result of Lefort's teaching?—there arose in him stubbornness and cunning. Very well, boyar-rulers, long-beards! It would be easy to shout at them; they would fall on their faces on the carpet, his mother would burst into tears, the Patriarch would bury his nose in his knees, but after that they would nevertheless have it their own way, and in addition make difficulties over money.

"Holy Father," Peter said with dignified wrath, at which Tsaritsa Natalia's eyebrows rose in amazement, "it is bitter that we should not think alike on this matter. We do not interfere in your Christian affairs, but you interfere in our military ones. We may have great plans: what do you know of them? We want to conquer the seas. We consider that the happiness of our country lies in the success of seaborne trade. It is God's blessing. I cannot do without foreigners in military affairs. If you touch their churches, they will all flee. What does this mean then?" He looked at the boyars one by one. "Do you want to clip my wings?"

The boyars were astonished to hear Peter speak in so manly a fashion. "Oho!" said the glances they exchanged, "that's how he is! Pretty high-handed!" Romodanovsky nodded full approval. The Patriarch stretched his thin nose towards the throne and cried vehemently:

"Great Tsar! Do not take from me the devilish heretic Quirin Kuhlmann!"

Peter knit his brows. He felt that in this he ought to make a concession to the longbeards. Tsaritsa Natalia murmured: "My dear Lord!" and folded her palms together beseechingly. Peter stole a glance at Romodanovsky who made a slight gesture of resignation.

"Kuhlmann does not concern us," Peter said. "You can have him to deal with as you please." The Patriarch sat down and closed his eyes in exhaustion. "And now, this is what I have to say, boyars:

I need eight thousand roubles for military and shipbuilding purposes."

As he left the palace Peter took Romodanovsky into his sledge and drove to his house on the Lubianka to dine there.

7

The woman Vorobyiha was brought from the village of Mytishchi to the Kremlin palace for the young Tsaritsa. Eudoxia was so pleased that she ordered her to be brought straight away to her bedchamber. This small chamber was in a log-walled apartment over the main body of the building. Its two small windows were curtained to keep out the sun. A midwife, constantly in attendance, dozed in felt boots and warm coat on the stove-bench. Eudoxia's labour was hourly expected and for several days now she had not risen from her swansdown feather-bed. Of course she would have liked a change from the stifling heat: a sledge drive through snow-covered Moscow, with the sun low on the horizon, blue smoke rising and drooping silver branches in the lanes brushing the high harness-bow. But the old Tsaritsa and all the women around her would not hear of drives: Lie still, do not stir, guard your belly: it's a Tsar's child you are bearing! All she was allowed to do was listen to stories with a pious ending. She was not even allowed to cry; it would upset the child.

Vorobyiha came in respectfully but briskly. She was clean, and wore new birch-bark shoes. A bunch of sage was fastened under her coarse linen skirt to give her a pleasant smell. Her lips were soft, her eyes like a mouse's; her face, though old, was rosy and she chattered incessantly. As she came in she looked sharply round the room, taking in everything; then she fell on her knees beside the bed, and was graciously received: the young Tsaritsa held out her damp hand to her.

"Sit down, Vorobyiha. Tell me something, amuse me."

Vorobyiha wiped her clean mouth and began telling a story about the old man and woman, the priest's daughters and the goat with the golden horns.

"Wait a minute, Vorobyiha!" Eudoxia half rose and looked to see whether the midwife was asleep. "Tell my fortune."

"Oh, light of my eyes, I don't know how to."

"That's not true, Vorobyiha. I won't tell anyone. Do, if only by beans."

"Oh, even for beans they take the skin off your back with a whip nowadays. Well, perhaps with oatmeal, mixed with holy water, not too thick."

"When will it begin with me? Soon? I'm frightened. At night my heart falters, falters, and stops. I start up—is the child alive? Oh, Lord!"

"Does it kick out with its little feet? Whereabouts?"

"Here. It turns, just as if it were rubbing with its knees and elbows, very softly."

"Does it turn widdershins or the other way round?"

"This way and that. It's playful."

"It's a boy."

"Oh, are you sure?"

Vorobyiha screwed up her mouse-like eyes ingratiatingly and whispered:

"About what else shall I tell your fortune? I see, my lovely beauty, there's some secret there that's asking to be told. Say it in my ear, Tsaritsa."

Eudoxia turned away to the wall, and her face with its brown patches on forehead and temples and its slightly swollen lips, flushed.

"Perhaps it's because I've become ugly; I don't know. . . ."

"Such beauty, such wonderful. . . ."

"Oh, hold your tongue!" Eudoxia turned round; her hazel eyes were full of tears. "Does he feel sorry for me? Does he love me? Find that out. Go, fetch the oatmeal."

Vorobyiha had come well provided: in a bag she had an earthenware saucer, a phial with water and a dark powder. "Fern-seed, gathered on St. John's Eve," she whispered. She diluted it with water, set the saucer on a stool by the bed and, muttering something incomprehensible, took Eudoxia's wedding ring. This she laid in the saucer and told Eudoxia to look:

"Think your secret thought. Aloud, if you like, or just as you please. What is it that's making you doubt?"

"After his return from Troitsa, he changed," Eudoxia said barely moving her lips. "He doesn't listen to me when I speak, as though I were the worst of fools. He says: 'Why don't you read something on history? Learn Dutch or German?' I tried to, but I don't understand anything. After all, men love their wives without any books."

"How long since you slept together?"

"Over two months. Natalia Kirillovna has forbidden it. She's afraid for the child."

"Look inside the ring, my lovely angel. Do you see something misty?"

"It looks like a face."

"Go on looking. A woman's face?"

"It looks like it. A woman's."

"It's she." Vorobyiha pursed her mouth knowingly, and her beady eyes looked as though they were peeping out of a mouse-hole. Eudoxia, breathing heavily, raised herself and her hand slipped off her rounded belly under her breast where her heart fluttered like a captive bird.

"What do you know? What are you hiding from me? Who is she?"

"Who? Why, the snake in the grass, the German woman. All Moscow is whispering about it, only they're afraid of saying it out loud. They are poisoning him in the Foreign Quarter with love potions. Don't distress yourself, dear heart, it's too early to grieve. We shall help. Take this needle. . . ." Vorobyiha quickly pulled a needle out of her headdress and gave it with a whisper to the Tsaritsa. "Take it in your fingers, don't be afraid. Repeat after me: 'Go away, go away, wicked, cruel snake Anna, crippled and sickly, rheumatic and consumptive, go without looking back beyond the Fafer hill, where the sun does not shine, where the dew does not fall; disappear into the damp earth, three fathoms deep, there wicked, cruel snake Anna, is the unhallowed place for you till the end of time, amen!' Prick the needle right inside the ring, prick it into her face."

Eudoxia went on pricking until the needle broke against the saucer. She dropped back, covered her eyes with her arm and her puffy lips trembled with weeping.

That evening the wet-nurses and maids, the midwives and palace fools began to bustle about, making the doors and floorboards creak: "The Tsar has come." Vorobyiha threw a grain of incense on the candle to sweeten the air and hurried away. Peter ran up three steps at a time. He smelt of frost and wine as he bent over his wife's bed.

"How are you, Eudoxia? Not through with it yet? I thought. . . ."

He smiled a far-away, gay smile; his round eyes were like a stranger's.

Eudoxia's heart grew cold. "I would be glad to please you," she said distinctly. "I can see that everyone is tired of waiting. I am sorry."

He frowned in an effort to understand what was the matter with her. He pulled up a stool and sat down, scratching the carpet with his spur.

"I dined at Romodanovsky's. And they said it would be any moment; I thought it had begun."

"I shall die in childbirth. You will know then. People will tell you. . . ."

"Nonsense, people don't die of that."

Then, with all her strength, she threw off the blankets and sheet and showed her belly:

"Here it is, you see—I, not you, will suffer and scream. People don't die? You'll be the last to hear about it! Go, laugh, amuse yourself, drink wine! Go, go to your accursed Foreign Quarter!" He gaped and stared at her. "It's a public scandal—everyone knows."

"What does everyone know?"

He drew up his legs, looking like a cat in his anger. Now she felt that nothing mattered. She screamed out:

"About that heretic of yours, the German, the tavern wench! What philtre has she made you drink?"

At this his face flushed so hotly that beads of sweat stood out. He flung the stool aside. He looked so terrifying that Eudoxia involuntarily put her hand up to her face. He stood there looking at his wife with fiendish eyes.

"Fool!" was all he said.

She threw up her arms and caught her head in her hands, shaking with silent sobs. The child in her womb turned gently, impatiently. A sundering, dragging, terrible pain encircled her body with incomprehensible force.

Hearing the low animal wail, the maids and nurses, midwives and crones ran into the young Tsaritsa's bedchamber. She was screaming, wild-eyed, her mouth hideously distorted. The women began to bustle about. Icons were taken down and icon-lamps lighted. Peter left the room. When the first pangs had passed, Vorobyiha and the midwife led Eudoxia into the steaming hot bath-room to give birth to her child.

8

A light-eyed jackdaw, scared by something, flew out from under the straw eaves and perched on a tree; hoar-frost showered down. One-eyed Tsigan raised his head; the winter dawn was spreading red behind the snow-covered branches. Housewives were lighting their stoves and the smoke rose slowly. All round were the sounds of felt boots crunching, of coughs, of wicket-gates creaking, of the ringing of an axe. The high-pitched roofs stood out more clearly between the silver birches and the whole district across the river—the sturdily-built houses of the streltsi, the tall warehouses of the merchants, the modest dwellings of all kinds of townsfolk, tanners, stocking-makers, kvass-brewers—sent up columns of pink smoke.

The lively jackdaw hopped from branch to branch sending the snow into Tsigan's eyes. He waved at it angrily with his leather mitt. He pulled the ice-covered bucket out of the well and poured the fetid water into the trough. This radiant Sunday morning made his heart ache with bitter resentment. Accursed fate! He had been beggared. For them man or beast were all one. He could have managed his own property no worse than they did theirs. The bucket rang with a clink of iron, the pole creaked, and the wheel tied to its end as a counterweight swung to and fro.

His master, the strelets Ovsey Rzhov, came out on to the porch. His short sheepskin coat was belted with a red sash. He grunted at the frost and, settling his cap deeper on his head, drew on his knitted gauntlets and rattled his keys.

"Have you filled the trough?"

Tsigan only flashed his single eye; his birch-bark shoes slipped on the ice bank by the trough. Ovsey went to open the cattle shed: a good master must water his livestock himself. On the way he kicked a pole that had not been put away with his felt boot.

"Shall I give you a taste of this pole, you whore's son? You've left things lying all over the yard again."

He unbolted the door, propped it open with a peg and led out two well-fed geldings. He stroked them and whistled to them and they drank the icy water, raising their heads and looking at the dawn, while the water dripped from their warm lips. One of them neighed and its body quivered. "Whoa, whoa!" said Ovsey gently. Then he drove the cows and a young grey-blue bull out of the shed; after them, huddling close together, the sheep ran out with a scrunching of hoofs. Tsigan was still drawing water with painful effort; his trousers were splashed. Ovsey said:

"There's little good in you, and a lot of wickedness. You're never kind to the cattle, all you can do is to glare at them with your one eye. I don't know what kind of man you are."

"I work in the way I know."

Ovsey sneered: "Well, well!" He ordered Tsigan to give the horses fodder and bring them fresh litter while he watched. Tsigan made a number of journeys to the far end of the yard, to the snow-covered ricks, where sparrows hopped about in the scattered chaff. He chopped and hauled in firewood. Against the deep blue of the sky the sun lit up the snowy tops of the birches. Church bells began to ring. Ovsey solemnly crossed himself. A small girl with a round face and pale blue eyes, like a jackdaw's, ran out to the porch:

"Father, come in and eat, quick."

Ovsey knocked the snow off his felt boots and stepped through the low door, slamming it behind him with proprietorial force. No one called Tsigan. He waited a while, blew his nose, and wiped it for a long time with the tail of his ragged coat; at last he went, un-invited, to the warm, dim basement where his employers were eating, and edged on to a bench near the door. There was a smell of cabbage soup with meat. Ovsey and his brother Constantine, also a strelets, were dipping their spoons unhurriedly into a wooden bowl. The food was served by a tall, stern old woman with a lifeless expression.

The brothers owned a shop for bast articles, a public bath on the Balchug and a windmill and, in addition, they rented thirty acres of arable and meadow land from Prince Odoyevsky. Formerly they had worked it themselves (they had not taken part in the Crimea campaign, but now Tsar Peter gave them no respite: every day they had to expect either detail duty, or drill. Streltsi were forbidden to carry on their business personally in shops and public baths. Hired help was not to be trusted. The work had to be done by wives and daughters—in a word, by women—while manpower was used for the Tsar's amusement.

"I can't see how we'll deal with the harvest this summer," Ovsey said. He held the big round loaf close to his chest; it rasped against his coarse linen shirt as he cut slices off for himself and his brother. They sighed, took a bite and once more began to lap up the soup, jogging the meat in their spoons.

"It's no longer safe with hired men," said Constantine. "There's a new ukase to report all tramps, those who live without guarantee in suburbs or taverns, in bath-houses and brick barns."

"But what if they're working?"

"Well, you'll have to answer for them as you would for a brigand. Did you get a written guarantee from Tsigan? What is he?"

"The devil knows. He doesn't say anything."

When Tsigan entered and fixed the brothers with his eye, as he plucked the ice from his beard, Ovsey said purposely in a loud voice:

"I'm tired of him as it is."

There was a silence while they went on eating. Tsigan quivered at the smell of the bread and the cabbage soup. Throwing an icicle under the door, he said hoarsely:

"So you're talking about me?"

"And what if we are?" Ovsey laid down his spoon. "For more than six months you've been eating our food, but the devil alone knows who you are. There are many of your kind, men without a name, tramping round."

"What d'you mean, without a name? Have I stolen from you?" Tsigan asked.

"I can't say yet—"

"That's it, you can't say."

"It might be better if you did steal. Why did two of my ewes die? Why do my cows mope and why does their milk smell so that you can't bear to taste it? Why?" Ovsey leant against the edge of the table and hammered with his fist. "Why did our women have pains in the stomach all through the autumn? Why? There's some bewitchment here? The evil eye—"

"Do stop raving, Ovsey," Tsigan said wearily. "A clever man like you."

"Constantine, did you hear him abuse me? Raving?" Ovsey pushed himself away from the table and flexed his fingers, clenching them. Tsigan could not argue: the brothers were strong fellows and they had had a solid meal. He got up cautiously.

"A man's not liked because he's good, but good because he's liked. . . . I've sweated enough working for you, Ovsey; thank you." Tsigan bowed to him. "Think evil of me, if you wish; it's all one to me. Only pay me the money I've earned."

"What money d'you mean?" Ovsey turned to his brother, then to the grandmother who watched the quarrel with her lifeless eyes. "Did he give us his money to keep for him? Or did I borrow money from him?"

"Ovsey, have you no conscience? Fifty kopeks a month; two and a half roubles are mine, I've earned them."

At this Ovsey lunged at him yelling furiously:

"Give you money? D'you hope to get away alive? Take that, you whore's son!"

And, gripping Tsigan by his coat, he struck him on the ear, gave a wild shout and, had not Tsigan ducked, would have killed him with a second blow. Constantine, restraining his brother, seized his heaving shoulders, while Tsigan tottered out of the room. Constantine came after him and pushed him out into the street prodding his back. Tsigan stood for a long time looking at the gates with his one eye: if he could, he would have burnt a hole in them. "All right, just you wait!" he muttered darkly. He passed his hand over his cheek and felt the blood on it. People were passing by; they turned round and laughed. He threw back his head and, tramping heavily in his birch-bark shoes, trudged away—anywhere.

9

"Shove hard, shove, push. . . !"
"Where are they all running?"
"To see a fellow being burnt."
"Is it an execution?"
"Well, he didn't ask for it."
"There are people who burn themselves."
"That's for their faith: the Old Believers."
"And what about this one?"
"He's a foreigner."
"Thank God, they're dealing with them too at last!"
"It's about time; the damned tobacco-smokers. They've grown fat on our sweat."
"Look, it's smoking already!"

Tsigan, too, made his way to the bank where people were crowding on heaps of cinders. He had had his eye on two men, tramps like himself, for some time. He tried to keep close to them: perhaps something might turn up in the way of food. The men seemed to have been through trials and torture. One of them, with a pockmarked face, had a rag bound over his cheek to hide a brand made by a hot iron. His name was Judas. The other was bent nearly double and leant on two short crutches, though he walked briskly enough, thrusting out his small beard, and his eyes were merry. Over his patched coat he was covered with a piece of bast matting. He was called Ovdokim. Tsigan took a particular fancy for him. Ovdokim was not slow to notice that a dark, one-eyed fellow with a bruised face was hanging round them. He raised himself on his crutches and said mildly:

"There's nothing to be gained from us, dear fellow. We ourselves live by stealing."

Judas said out of the side of his mouth:

"There was a fellow from the Secret Chancellery who hung round; he got shoved under the ice."

"Oho!" Tsigan thought to himself. "They're bold fellows." And his desire to take up with them grew.

"Death, curse it, won't take me," he said blinking his eyelashes covered with rime, "so I've got to live somehow. Won't you two take me along with you? It's easier working together."

Judas said again through his teeth to Ovdokim:

"Could it be the 'dark eye'? Eh?"

"No, no, evidently not," Ovdokim said in a sing-song voice, and twisting his head looked up into Tsigan's eye.

They said no more. Down below, on the ice, streltsi, chilled with the cold, were pacing about stamping their feet and slapping their gauntleted hands. In their midst stood a roughly-made square of logs filled with fire-wood. Nearby was a pillar for public executions, and a fire, in which iron was being heated, sent up white plumes of smoke. The waiting crowd was beginning to feel the cold.

"Here they come, here they come. . . . Shove! push!"

From the direction of the town mounted dragoons appeared. They rode down on to the ice. Behind them came a plain sledge in which sat, with their backs to the horses, a foreigner and a woman wearing a man's cap. Next came a boyar, equerries and a clerk on horseback, and last in the procession was a cumbersome covered sledge of black leather.

The streltsi made way for the procession. The clerk got off his horse. The covered sledge halted as it reached the spot, but no one got out of it. All eyes were on this sledge and a whisper ran through the crowd.

From behind the log structure appeared Yemelian Sviezhev in a red cap with a whip over his shoulder. His assistants took the woman out of the sledge, pushed her towards the pillar and tied her arms round it, after tearing off her coat. The clerk was reading in a loud voice from the unrolled scroll with its dangling seals, but his voice was barely audible in the hard frost and all the crowd could make out was that the woman was Mashka Selifontova and the foreigner Kulkin, or something like that. His hunched shoulders and bald nape could be seen in the sledge.

Yemelian's horse-like face bore a fixed smile. He walked unhurriedly to the post and grasped his whip. All they heard was a sharp swish, and all they saw was a red diagonal weal on the woman's bare back. She squealed like a pig. They gave her five lashes and not with full force. Then they untied her and led her, tottering, to the fire. Yemelian seized the iron out of the fire and pressed it to her cheek. She screamed, sank down and began to throw herself about. They raised her, put on her clothes, laid her in the sledge and drove her away at walking pace along the Moskva river, to a convent.

The clerk was still reading the document. Now they tackled the foreigner. He got out of the sledge, small and sturdy, and walked to the log structure. Suddenly he joined his palms, lifted up his swollen face overgrown with dark stubble and—this whore's son of a foreigner—began to mumble and mutter and burst into noisy weeping. They seized him and dragged him to the logs. There Yemelian tore off his clothes and threw him down naked. On his fat, pink back he laid his heretical books and papers and set fire to them with a fire-brand handed to him from below. So it was directed in the ukase: the books and papers to be burnt on his back.

From the bank, where Tsigan was standing, someone shouted:

"Have a good warm-up, Kulkin!"

But the people round turned on the speaker, a thick-lipped lad:

"Shut up, you shameless fellow! How would you like to warm yourself like that?"

The thick-lipped youngster immediately made himself scarce. From the pyre, fired on all four sides, grey smoke rolled. The streltsi stood, resting on their pikes. All was silent. The smoke slowly drifted up to the sky.

"He'll stifle first, the firewood's damp."

"A foreigner, a foreigner! But to burn him alive. . . . Oh Lord. . . . !"

"He learnt to read, wrote books, and now this. . . ."

Out of the covered leather sledge—now everybody could see it —through the small window, there peered at the smoke, at the rising tongues of flame, a lifeless face, as though it had come down from an ancient icon.

"Look how his eyes glare; it's frightful!"

"It's not seemly for the Patriarch to go to executions."

"To burn people for their faith . . . oh, you priests!"

This last was uttered by Ovdokim, loudly, fearlessly. All those who stood near him moved away; only Judas and Tsigan stayed by him. Tapping his crutches he began again:

"What of it if he is a heretic? He believes as he thinks best. Supposing our way doesn't suit him? And for that he's got to burn. We live in suffering, in torture."

The great fire was roaring and crackling; sparks and smoke spiralled upwards. Some alleged that through the flames they could see the foreigner still moving. The covered sledge drove away at a trot. The crowd slowly dispersed. Judas kept saying:

"Come on, Ovdokim."

"No, no, my lads!" His eyes were laughing, but his red face, clean as though straight from the steam-bath, was weeping and his wispy beard trembled. "Do not seek the truth! Priests and rulers, toll-gatherers, jingling their gold, all have donned the robes of their wicked fury. Flee, my lads, flee, tortured ones, branded, broken on the wheel, flee in all haste to the thickets of the forest!"

Only with difficulty did they succeed in leading Ovdokim away. The three of them went into a side street, to a tavern.

10

At last Tsigan held a spoon in his hand, his hand which trembled as he carried the meatless cabbage soup to his mouth, dripping on a slice of bread. He had been very afraid that they would not take him along to the tavern and, on the way, complained about life and wiped his eyes on his leather mitt. Ovdokim, not saying a word, scurried along on his crutches, like a beetle. At the gates he suddenly asked:

"Can you steal?"

"Why, if it's in company, I'd even go into the forest with a bludgeon."

"Oh, you're a bold fellow."

"What sort of people do you think we are?" Judas asked.

Tsigan thought unhappily: "They want to get rid of me." He looked longingly at the lopsided gates, at the snowdrift in the yard, iced over with slops, at the bast-covered door, from where there came such an appetising smell that it made his head swim. He said in a low voice:

"You are just men. What if you steal? You do it from need, it's no fault of yours. Half the people go away into the forests nowadays. . . . Dear people, don't send me away, give me something to eat!"

"We, sir, are sometimes kind and sometimes merciless," Ovdokim said. "Mind!" and taking both crutches into his left hand he shook them at Tsigan. "Now you've joined up with us, don't back out. Judas, friend, got any loot?"

Judas pulled a purse out of his pocket and spilt some coppers on to his palm. The three of them counted the stolen money.

Ovdokim said gaily:

"The bird does not reap, neither does it sow, and the Lord provides for it. We don't want much; only enough for our food. Come on, you one-eyed fellow!"

In the tavern they found seats in the farthest corner which the light of the tallow candle on the counter barely reached. There were a good many people in the place; some had unfastened their steaming padded coats and were noisily drunk, others slept on the benches. Ovdokim asked for half a bottle and a pot of cabbage soup. After they had been served he rapped with his spoon:

"Eat, one-eyed fellow, this is the Lord's."

He took a drink from the bottle and began to munch fast, like a rabbit. His eyes danced with laughter:

"I'll tell you a parable, my lads. Will you listen or not? There were two men, one merry, the other gloomy. This merry fellow was poor. All he had had been taken from him by the boyars, the clerks and judges; they tortured him for various antics and broke his back on the rack, so that he walked bent. Very well. . . . And the gloomy fellow was a boyar's son, rich and mean. His servants were kept so hungry that they left him, and his yard was overgrown with pigweed. He sat all day long alone on a chest full of gold and silver. And so they lived. The merry fellow had nothing; he washed with dew, crossed himself at a tree stump; when he was hungry, he stole or begged in Christ's name: those who aren't rich always give something —they understand. And so he went about cracking jokes, as blithe as the day was long. But the gloomy fellow did nothing but worry about not losing his money. And also, my lads, he was afraid of dying. Oh, it's terrible for the rich to die! And the more money he had, the less he wanted to die. He bought forty-pound candles for the church and valuable mounts for icons, thinking that God would postpone the hour of his death."

Ovdokim broke into laughter, rubbing his beard on the table. He stretched out his long arm, took a mouthful of soup and went on:

"Now this rich fellow was the very same man who had tortured the merry one and ruined him. One day the merry fellow got into his house to steal and took a cudgel with him. He went from room to room and saw the rich fellow sleeping on a bench, with a coffer under it. He didn't notice the coffer; he seized the rich fellow by the hair and said: 'You once robbed me of all I had, now give me something for my food'. The rich fellow was afraid to die but he didn't want to part with his money, so he kept saying he hadn't any. Then the merry fellow took up his cudgel and began to belabour his sides and ugly face." Judas grinned and chortled with pleasure. "Very well. . . . He beat him and beat him until it made him laugh. 'All right,' he said, 'I'll come some other night, and you—have a capful of gold ready for me'. The rich fellow was no fool. He wrote to the Tsar, and the Tsar sent him some guards. But the merry fellow was cunning. He dodged the guard, got into the house and seized the rich fellow by the hair: 'Have you got the money ready?' The other trembled and swore that he hadn't any. Again the merry fellow gave him a drubbing; beat him within an inch of his life. 'All right,' he said, 'I'll come a third time, and you better have a coffer of money ready for me'."

"That's just," Tsigan said.

"He'd already given him a drubbing," Judas laughed.

"Very well. This time the Tsar sent a regiment to guard the rich fellow. What was to be done? But the merry fellow was cunning. He dressed up as a strelets, came to the rich man's house and said: 'Guards, whose property are you guarding?' They replied: 'The rich man's, on the Tsar's orders.' 'And have you been paid much for doing it?' The others said: 'Nothing!' 'Well,' said the merry fellow, 'you're fools: you're guarding someone else's property for nothing, the rich fellow will die like a dog on that money, and you won't see any of it'. And he got them so wrought up that these soldiers went and tore the locks off the cellars and storerooms, and began to eat and drink until they got drunk. And of course they felt cheated, so in the night they broke open the doors and found the rich fellow shivering on his coffer, all battered and filthy. Here our nimble strelets caught him by the hair and said: 'You didn't give me what was mine when I asked you, now you'll give up everything'. And he threw him to the soldiers who tore him to pieces. Then the merry fellow took what he needed for his living and went off quietly."

While Ovdokim was telling his story people kept coming up and seating themselves at his table, and expressed their approval as they listened. One man, who seemed either drunk or not quite in his right mind, kept sobbing, waving his arms and clutching at his big bald forehead. When they let him speak, he gabbled so hurriedly that

it was impossible to understand what he said. The others laughed:
"Kuzma's been visiting the boyars. They knocked wisdom into him through the back gate."

At the counter someone snuffed the candle so that people could see better to laugh. Kuzma's snub-nosed face with its bushy beard was bloated: evidently the poor man had been drinking continuously. All he had on was a pair of trousers and a torn shirt without a belt.

"He even pawned his cross for drink."

"He's been hanging round here for a week."

"Where could he go barefoot in this frost?"

"My trouble is the whole people's: here it is!" Kuzma cried clutching at his trousers. "Boyar Troyekurov gave it his signature." Quickly he pulled his trousers down and exhibited his swollen buttocks covered with blue weals and bruises. All those present burst into a roar of laughter. Even the potman snuffed the candle again and leant over the counter. Kuzma went on:

"Do you know the smith Zhemov, the smithy by the church of St. Barbara the Martyr? I've been there fifteen years. Smith Zhemov! There hasn't been a thief yet who could open my locks. My sickles have been sold as far as Riazan. Whose sickles? Zhemov's. Bullets could not pierce breastplates of my workmanship. Who shoes horses? Who pulls out teeth for men and women? Zhemov! Do you know that?"

"We do, we do!" came the laughing reply. "Go on with your story."

"But what you don't know is that Zhemov doesn't sleep at night." He clutched at his bald pate. "Zhemov's got a bold mind. In another country they would have honoured me. But here my mind is only good to feed pigs with. Yes, you'll remember it some day!" Clenching a broad fist he shook it at the streaming window with its four little panes, at the winter night. "Your graves will be overgrown with nettles. But Zhemov will be remembered."

"Wait a bit, Kuzma, why were you flogged?"

"Tell us . . . we aren't laughing."

He looked with surprise—as though he had only just noticed them—at the shiny noses, the tangled beards, the gaping mouths ready to burst into guffaws, at the dozens of pairs of eyes greedily waiting for some spectacle, which surrounded him on all sides. He saw them as through a haze.

"Look, fellows. On one condition: don't laugh. After all, it's my heart that's aching."

He fumbled for a long time, pulling a folded paper out of his tobacco pouch. Then he spread it on the table. They brought the candle from the counter. With his nail he pinned down the scrap of paper on which two wings were drawn, like those of a bat, with loops and levers. His bloated cheeks swelled.

"It's a wonderful and amazing mechanism," he began self-confidently. "Mica wings, each three yards long, and a yard and three-quarters wide. They flap like a bat's by means of levers, worked by the feet and also by the hands. I'm certain man can fly. I'll run away to England. I'll make these wings there. I'll jump off a belfry without hurting myself. Man will fly like the crane." Again he said furiously to the damp window: "Troyekurov has made a mistake there, the boyar! God made man a crawling worm, but I shall teach him to fly. . . ." *

Reaching out, Ovdokim patted him gently:

"Tell us all in order, friend. How did they hurt you?"

Kuzma frowned and breathed heavily through his nose:

"I made them too heavy, by a slight miscalculation. . . . I'm a poor man. I'd made a pair of small wings out of scraps—birch-bark, leather. In the yard I jumped off the roof wind astern; they carried me some fifty paces. My brain was already on fire. People advised me; I went to the strelets headquarters and shouted: 'Guards!' They seized me and naturally started to beat me. 'No,' I said, 'don't beat me, but take me to a boyar, I have some Tsar's business on my mind.' So they took me to him. There he sat, the devil, with a face as fat as a pig's, this Troyekurov. I said to him: give me twenty-five roubles or so and some mica, and in six weeks' time I'll fly. He wouldn't believe me. I told him: send a clerk to my house, I'll show him my small wings, only it's not seemly to fly with them before the Tsar. He tried to dodge, but there was no getting out of it; everybody had heard me cry: 'Guard!' He cursed me, grabbed me by the hair, made me kiss the Gospel and swear I wouldn't cheat him. And he gave me eighteen roubles. I made the wings sooner than I'd promised. They turned out too heavy. It's only here, in the tavern, that I've come to see it. After I got drunk I understood it. Mica won't do, what is needed is parchment on a wooden frame! I brought them to the Kremlin to try them out. Well, I didn't fly; I smashed my face. I told Troyekurov the experiment had failed and asked him for another five roubles, and then I would fly, he might cut my head off if I didn't. The boyar wouldn't believe a word: 'Thief,' he shouted, 'Swindler! Heretic! You want to be cleverer than God Himself.' He

* The scene described here took place in 1694 in Moscow. (*Author's note*)

ordered me to be beaten in his presence. Two hundred blows with a stick. I stood it—the whole two hundred—only gritted my teeth. And I'm ordered to repay the eighteen roubles, sell my smithy, my tools and my house. What am I to do, naked as I am? Go to the forest with a bludgeon?"

"Nothing else for it, poor fellow," Ovdokim said in a low, clear voice.

Kuzma Zhemov joined Ovdokim's band. They bought him a pair of felt boots and a coat in the second-hand clothes market. Now there were four of them going about Moscow: to the market-places, the public baths, the narrow side streets of Kitay-gorod. Judas specialized in picking pockets. Tsigan was taught to roll up his eye, so that the eye-ball started horribly out of its socket, and to sing plaintive songs. They put a rope round Kuzma's neck and Ovdokim led him about as a lunatic and epileptic: "Give something to the mad fellow; make way, make way, or he might attack someone." At the end of the day they would have collected enough for food, and sometimes to buy a bottle. It meant a lot of work, and even more fear, for, by the Tsar's ukase, such men were now seized and taken to the Office for Criminal Affairs.

Lent was coming to an end. The spring sun rose higher over Moscow. Where the sunbeams reached, there was thawing and dripping and smells began to rise. The snow, mixed with dung, no longer crunched under the sledge-runners. One night, at the tavern, Ovdokim began:

"Isn't it about time, friends, to be on our way? There's nobody here we'd grieve to part with. We'll just let the high ground dry a little. We'll get out into the open."

Judas tried to object:

"There are too few of us. Without weapons we'll starve in the forest."

"But before we go, we'll carry out a wicked deed," Ovdokim said, and the others looked at him with apprehension. "We'll get all we need. One sin won't surpass all our sufferings. But even if it does, well, then it will mean that there's no justice in the Scriptures. Don't be afraid, my friends, I take all the responsibility for it."

11

It began in the spring: fun for the cat, tears for the mice. War was declared between two kings, the King of Poland and the King of the Capital City of Pressburg. The Pressburg monarch had the play-battalions, the Butyrsky and Lefort's regiments, and the Polish king had the best contingents from eight strelets regiments, the Stremianny, the Suharev, those of Tsikler, Krovkov, Nechayev, Durov, Normatsky and Riazanov. Romodanovsky was made King of Pressburg, with the name of Frederick, and Buturlin King of Poland. Buturlin was a drunkard, full of malice and greedy for bribes, but ready for any fun or revelry. His capital city was to be the Falconry on the Semenov field.

At first everyone thought this was one of Peter's old games. But every day brought fresh ukases, each more disquieting than the last. Boyars, courtiers and equerries were appointed to the suites of the two kings. Peter's games were beginning to overstep the bounds of decency. Many boyars felt dismayed: playing with rank and dignity had no precedent. They went to Natalia and made cautious complaints against her son. She raised her plump hands in bewilderment: she could make nothing of it. Leo Narishkin said irritably: "What can we do? A ukase has come from the Great Tsar, with official seals. Go to him yourselves, ask him to revoke the order."

However, they were too prudent to go to Peter; they hoped the matter would drop. But Peter would not let it drop. Soldiers appeared suddenly at some of the boyars' houses, forced their way in, compelled them to put on court dress and carried them off to Preobrazhensk for fool's service. Old Prince Priimkov-Rostovsky lost the use of his legs. Others tried to pretend they were ill; but it was of no avail. There was no escape. They had to endure the shame and disgrace.

Pressburg with its octagonal log towers, its glacis dominated by cannon, the white tents all round, visible from afar, was enough to drive a Russian mad. It was like some incongruous dream; a game yet not a game, where everything was done in earnest. In a brightly painted room King Frederick sprawled on a gilt throne under a red canopy, a brass crown on his head, stars pinned to his white satin coat, a mantle lined with hare-fur on his shoulders, jingling spurs on his topboots and a pipe between his teeth. His eyes flashed like a king's, but if you looked closer you saw it was Romodanovsky. It made you feel like spitting in disgust, but that was dangerous. Zinovyev, a noble of the Council, did spit in abhorrence, and that same day he was sent to exile in a peasant's cart and deprived of all his honours. Natalia had had to go in person to Preobrazhensk and beg that he might be pardoned and brought back.

And Tsar Peter—it was deplorable!—had no rank at all and went about in a soldier's coat. When he approached Frederick's throne, he went down on bended knee, and that damned king would shout at him sometimes as if he were a commoner. Boyars and court nobles sat conferring in the make-believe council, received ambassadors and issued Pressburg ukases, burning with shame.

And at night there was feasting and drinking in Lefort's mansion, where the second, the night monarch held sway: that ungodly man, whose very sight was hateful, Nikita Zotov, the All-Fools' Prince-Pope of the Foreign Quarter.

And then—the damned foreigners must have suggested it to complete the horror—about a thousand of the younger clerks and scribes were picked out from various offices and brought from Moscow. They were given arms, put on horseback and mercilessly drilled. Frederick said in the council: "We shall soon lay our hands on everybody. The cockroaches won't be able to hide in their cracks much longer. We'll make everyone eat soldiers' porridge."

Peter, who was standing by the door—he dared not sit down in the royal presence—laughed loudly at these words. Frederick furiously rattled a spur at him, and the Tsar shut his mouth. At this they should have wept, repented of their sins and fallen with a prayer at the Tsar's feet: "Behead us, torture us, be cruel if you must have your fun. But you, heir of the Byzantine Emperors, into what abyss are you dragging Russia? Can it possibly be that the shadow of Antichrist is rising behind you?" Yet their courage failed them and no one said it.

The Polish King, Vanka Buturlin, held another such court in Semenovsk. But there at least there was no need to exert themselves, the service was easy: the boyars and court officials sat on benches along the walls of the council chamber, yawning into their sleeves until dusk showed blue in the windows, and then they would drive back to Moscow for the night. The King, that abominable Vanka, maliciously tried to make them speak Polish, but he could not break down their stubborn resistance and finally tired of the game and let them doze in peace.

No sooner had they got used to all this than there came a new upheaval: the woods had barely begun to wrap themselves in a green haze when Buturlin sent an envoy to King Frederick with a declaration of war and set out for Pressburg with his regiments, baggage-train and boyars. The streltsi were already angry when the campaign began: it was the season for sowing, every day was precious, and here the devil had put it into the Tsar's mind to amuse himself.

The siege had to be conducted according to rule: trenches and approaches were dug, mines laid and assaults made. It was not an easy game. Gunpowder was not spared. Earthenware pots which burst like bombs were fired from mortars. The defenders poured muddy water and muck on the attackers, poles with burning tow tied at the end were thrust at them, both sides slashed with blunt swords. Faces got burnt, eyes poked out, bones broken. It cost nearly as much money as a real war. And this lasted for weeks; the whole spring.

During the respites both kings feasted with Peter and his favourites.

When summer was drawing to its close, Buturlin, having failed to take Pressburg, retreated some twenty miles into the forest and there entrenched himself in a fortified camp. Then Frederick in his turn went over to the attack. The streltsi, infuriated with this kind of life, fought in real earnest. The dead were counted in dozens. General Gordon's head was hit by a pot from a mortar and he barely recovered. Peter's face and eyebrows were singed, and he went about patched up with plaster. Half the army was suffering from dysentery. And only when all the gunpowder had been used up and the weapons broken, when the soldiers and streltsi were in rage and when Leo Narishkin drove into the camp with a letter from the old Tsaritsa and, with tears, implored Peter not to demand more money, for the treasury was empty as it was, only then did Peter calm down and the kings order their armies to disperse to their quarters and homes.

The mock campaigns were much discussed among the people: "Surely they wouldn't waste all that money on a mere game. There's something behind it. Peter is still young and foolish; he does what others prompt him to do. Someone clearly hopes to make profit out of this waste."

12

Life was hard and dull. In Sophia's time there had been some sort of restraint. But now the strong and the mighty shook the soul out of the common man. There was no justice in the courts; there were widespread bribery and corruption and defrauding of the State. Many fled into the woods and became robbers. Others went into the virgin forests on the northern rivers to escape from the oppression of the crowd of governors, land-owners, clerks and scribes, publicans and other officials who mercilessly and unlawfully sucked their blood.

There, in the North, they lived forgotten; the river and forest provided their sustenance. They made clearings in the forest and sowed barley. They built their homes of age-old pines, raised on piles, spacious and far apart; peasants' palaces. From the places they had left forever they brought with them into this isolation only their folktales, their legends and their mournful songs. They believed in the house-spirit and the old-man-of-the-forest. They went to the stern old dissenters for prayers and received communion in flour and cranberry juice. "Antichrist is abroad in the world," said these elders. "Only those shall be saved who have fled from the Tsar and the Patriarch."

But it so happened that Antichrist's servants, sent to seek out the disobedient and discontented, managed to make their way even into these dense forests, to this extreme edge of the land. Then the peasants, with their women and children, abandoning their houses and cattle, assembled in the elder's yard or in the church, and fired on the soldiers. And if they had nothing to fire with, they simply abused them and defied them and, rather than fall into their hands, burned themselves to death in their homes or in the church, yelling and chanting wildly.

Those who were not burdened with property or family and fled from poverty and bondage to become robbers in the forests, pressed on gradually to where it was warmer and food more plentiful, on to the Volga and the Don. But even there they were not quite out of reach: the Tsar's ukases and belligerent Orthodox priests would come; so many of the armed gangs went farther still: to Daghestan, to Kabarda, beyond the Terek, or they would offer to serve the Turkish Sultan with the Tatars in the Crimea. In the free South they did not believe in the shadowy house-spirit, they believed rather in the curved sword and a good horse.

Unloved and comfortless was the Russian land—worse than any bitter bondage—the land trodden for a thousand years by birch-bark shoes, resentfully scratched by wooden ploughs, covered with the ashes of ruined villages and nameless graves: misery, wilderness.

13

"Father, what does it mean? The bells aren't tolling right."
"How can they toll wrong?"
"Oh, Father, not like this. They ought to ring slowly, but this. . . . Father, hadn't we better go before something happens?"

"Wait, you fool."

Ivan Artemyich Brovkin (people had forgotten that they ever called him Ivash) stood at the entrance of a small, very old church on Miasnitsky street. His new, short sheepskin coat, covered with dark blue cloth, bulged stiffly; his new felt boots were straight from the last and his new woollen scarf was wound so tightly that he could not bend his head. A searching wind blew cuttingly into people's faces. With a hiss it chased the hard-grained snow along the black street and piled it into the frozen ruts. Crowds of people were clustered round the shops, listening: from every church the small bells pealed, discordantly and out of rhythm, rung anyhow, as if in a fit of temper.

Sanka Brovkina was now in her eighteenth year; well-dressed, handsome, plump, fit to become a bride. She again pulled her father by the sleeve, urging him to go: she seldom came to Moscow, and when she did her heart fluttered; she was afraid of being assaulted. Today she had come with her father to buy down for a featherbed, for her dowry. Matchmakers hung round Brovkin's house, but he, as time went on, aimed higher and higher for her. His son, Alioshka, was already Chief Bombardier and well known to the Tsar. Volkov's steward visited the Brovkins in their new, rich house. Ivan rented meadows and plough land from Volkov, and he traded in timber. He had recently built a windmill. His cattle herded separately from the village cattle. He sold poultry to Preobrazhensk for the Tsar's table. Everyone in the village bowed low to him; everyone was in his debt; some he let off, but others he did not, and half a score of peasants were working for him on bond receipt.

"Well, what are we waiting for?" Sanka asked.

At that moment the red-bearded priest Filka came up. In the past ten years he had grown so stout that his fur-lined cassock stretched at the seams. He was pushing in front of him a weedy sexton with a drooping nose:

"Come on, you psalm-peddler, come on, Beelzebub. . . ."

The sexton stumbled, caught hold of the padlock and started to unlock the church door. Filka kept pushing him:

"Your hands are shaking, you wretched drunkard. I told you last night, last night, last night"—he emphasised his words by thumping the sexton's back—"you were to come and ring the bells. You'll get me into trouble again."

The sexton pushed through the slightly opened half of the iron door and started to climb up to the belfry. Filka remained on the porch. Ivan took off his cap with both hands—they were encased in new leather gauntlets—and bowed gravely.

"Is it some sort of holiday today? My daughter and I can't make it out. Be so kind as to tell us, Father."

Filka narrowed his eyes and looked along the street into the snow-laden wind which was blowing his beard about, and said in a loud voice so that many people should hear him:

"The advent of Antichrist!"

Ivan staggered back in his new felt boots. Sanka clasped her hands to her breast, then began to cross herself, and went quite pale: all she had understood was that it was something terrible. A crowd poured out of the Miasnitsky gates, shouting, whistling and laughing wildly. The people in the street looked on in silence. Shops were closed. Ragged beggars, palsied, naked to the waist, noseless, crawled out from nowhere. A grizzled half-wit, rattling the chains and padlocks on his chest, yelled: "Nebuchadnezzar! Nebuchadnezzar!"

Ivan's heart sank into his boots. Sanka, catching her breath in fright, leant against the barred church window under a permanently burning icon lamp. The girl was far too high-strung.

And then they saw it. Stretching all down the street a procession advanced slowly: carts drawn by six pigs each; sledges drawn by cows, tarred and feathered; low carriages drawn by goats and dogs. In every vehicle there sat men in bast hats, matting coats, straw boots and mouse-skin gloves. Some had coloured patchwork coats trimmed with cats' tails and paws. Whips cracked, pigs squealed, dogs barked, the masqueraders mewed and bleated; they were all drunk and their faces were scarlet. In the middle of the procession came a gilded royal carriage drawn by miserable piebald nags with birch bath-brooms hanging from their necks. Through the window the crowd could see the young priest Bitka, Peter's boon-companion, on the front seat, fast asleep. A long-nosed man in a rich coat and a cap with peacock's feathers lolled in the back seat, and at his side was a round, plump woman, painted and powdered, covered with jewels and sables; in her hands she held a bottle. These were the new court fools, Yakov Turgenev—a former equerry of Sophia's, who had exchanged exile for a jester's cap—and the woman Shushera, a scribe's widow, whom he had married two days before, since when they had been taken on a ceaseless round of visits. Behind the carriage walked the two kings—Romodanovsky and Buturlin—and, between them, the prince-pope, "the most holy Lord Ianikita of Pressburg", in a tin mitre and red cloak carrying two pipes in the form of a cross. They were followed by a throng of boyars and courtiers from the suites of the two kings. People recognised the Sheremetevs, the Trubetskoys, the Dolgorukys, the Boborikins. Since its foundation Moscow had never witnessed anything so shameful. The people pointed at them, crying out in surprise and horror. Some went up close and bowed impudently to the boyars.

After the boyars came a boat on wheels, its masts swaying in the blustering wind. Peter was walking in front of the horses drawing it; he was in the uniform of a bombardier. With his chin jutting forward and his round eyes rolling at the people, he was beating a drum. They were afraid of bowing to him: what if there were orders not to? The half-wit, seeing him with a drum, yelled again: "Nebuchadnezzar!" but people pressed the simpleton into the crowd and hid him. On the boat, dressed as Dutch sailors, stood Lefort, Gordon, the bewhiskered Pamburg, Timmermann and the newly-commissioned colonels Weide, Mengden, Grage, Bruce, Livingstone, Salm and Schlippenbach. They laughed as they looked down on the crowd and puffed at their pipes and stamped their feet with the cold.

When Peter came level with the church, Ivan nudged the benumbed Sanka and fell on his knees. "Kneel, you fool!" he whispered hurriedly. "It's no business of yours or mine." Filka opened his great mouth and roared with laughter, so that even the Tsar turned to look at him. Then, still laughing, he raised his arms, turned his back and went into the church.

The procession had passed. Ivan rose from his knees, and pulling his cap well down over his ears said thoughtfully:

"Yes. Of course. Yes. But still, Oh, dear! Oh, well!" And then angrily to Sanka: "Now then, that'll do, wake up! Come along, let's go and buy the down."

14

Everyone wondered where the young devil got his strength from. Anyone else, even an older and stronger man, would have given up the ghost long ago. At least twice a week he was brought home drunk from the Foreign Quarter. He would sleep it off in four hours, and then think of nothing but some new entertainment.

On Christmas Eve he conceived the idea of having surprise parties: he took the prince-pope, the two kings, his generals and boyars (these last again by order of a strict ukase) to visit in turn the most aristocratic houses. All were in fancy dress and masked. As leader of the party they chose a Moscow noble, Vasily Sokovkin, a man prone to every kind of vice, a pettifogging and malicious backbiter. He was given the title of "prophet" and dressed as a Capuchin, with a slit in the seat of his habit. On that Christmas Eve the noble houses were finally insulted and humiliated, especially those of the princes and old boyars. About a hundred revellers whistling and yelling wildly, playing stringed instruments, pipes and kettledrums, would burst in, and their God-fearing host's hair would stand on end as he watched their antics and grinning faces. They recognised the Tsar by his height and his costume, that of a Dutch skipper: wide cloth breeches tied at the knee, woollen stockings, clogs and a round cap, something like a Turk's. His face was either bound up with a coloured kerchief or adorned with a long false nose.

There were music, stamping, laughter. The whole company, heedless of precedence, would rush to the tables, calling for cabbage, baked eggs, sausages, vodka with pepper, and dancing girls. The house was turned upside down and the guests drank themselves silly in the sweltering rooms filled with tobacco smoke. The host had to drink twice as much and, if he could not, they forced it down his throat.

The Christmas fun was so appalling that many prepared for those days as though they were to be their last on earth.

Only in spring did things grow a little easier. Peter went off to Archangel. The Dutch merchants van Leyden and Henry Peltenburg were there. They were buying twice as much as the year before. From the government they bought pressed caviare, frozen salmon, furs, fish-glue, raw silk and, as before, tar, hemp, coarse linen and potash. From handicraftsmen they bought leather work and carved bone articles. Leo Narishkin, who had bought the Tula arms works from the foreigner Marcelis, pressed chased steel weapons on the Dutchmen, but he asked such high prices that they refused to buy.

Towards spring six ships were loaded, only waiting for the ice to shift in the North Sea. Suddenly Lefort, at the Dutchmen's request, hinted to Peter that it might be a good thing to make the trip to Archangel and see real seagoing ships. The very next day relays and officials carrying orders to governors were despatched post-haste along the Vologda road. Peter set off with his usual company: the prince-pope Zotov, the two kings and their suites and Lefort, but besides these he also took men experienced in State affairs: the council clerk Vinius, Boris Golitsin, Troyekurov, the late Tsar Fedor's brother-in-law, Apraxin, and fifty soldiers under the command of the dashing Alexander Menshikov.

They drove as far as Vologda, where the local priests and merchants came out to meet them on the outskirts of the town. But Peter was impatient, and that same day they embarked in seven rowing boats and travelled by the Suhon to Ustug Veliky, and from there by way of the Northern Dvina to Archangel.

It was the first time Peter had seen such vast stretches of flooded rivers, such illimitable forests. The land spread out before his eyes to boundless distances. Lowering banks of cloud sailed overhead. Flocks of wild fowl rose from the water at the approach of the boats. Rough waves beat against the sides, sails billowed in the wind, masts creaked. The riverside monasteries rang out a welcome. And from the forests, peering through the thickets, the unsleeping eyes of the dissenters watched the boats of Antichrist.

15

Two candles guttered on the table which was covered with a rug. Drops of resin trickled slowly down the freshly-planed planks of the walls. Wet footprints—from corner to corner, from window to bed—stained the well-scrubbed floor. One muddy shoe lay in the middle of the room, the other under the table. An unfamiliar rain-laden wind rustled outside the windows, in the starless half-dusk of the short northern spring night. Waves lapped the beach close by.

Peter was sitting on the bed, with his bare toes turned in; his pants were wet to the knee. With his elbows on his knees and his small chin resting on his fists he stared with unseeing eyes at the window. Behind a partition, the two kings snored in competition with one another. People were sleeping everywhere in the house, which had been hurriedly built for the Tsar on Maseyev island. Peter had worn everyone out that day.

They had reached Archangel at dawn. For nearly all of them it was their first visit to the North. They stood on deck, watching the strange dawn spread behind the layers of dark cloud. The sun rose, extraordinarily large, over the dark edges of the forest, its rays flooded the sky and lit up the shore, the boulders and the pine trees. Round the bend of the Dvina, towards which the boats were being laboriously rowed, there came into sight a long building, not unlike a fortress, with glacis and palisade and six towers: a foreign warehouse. Within the rectangular courtyard there were strong barns and neat houses with tiled roofs; guns and mortars showed on the ramparts. Along the bank stretched landing stages on piles, wooden quays, awnings over mountains of bales, sacks and barrels. There were coils of rope and stacks of sawn timber. A score of seagoing vessels were moored to the quays, and three times as many were anchored farther out in the roadstead. The tall masts with their network of rigging rose like a forest, and the high carved poops rocked. Dutch, English and Hamburg flags drooped almost to the water. On the tarred sides, with their broad white band, guns showed through the open port-holes.

On the right—the eastern bank—a bell rang out in welcome. It was the same old Russia there: belfries, huts scattered about as though aimlessly, out of sheer laziness, fences, dung-heaps. Hundreds of small boats and barges laden with raw material and covered with bast matting were moored near the shore. Peter stole a glance at Lefort who stood at his side at the stern. Lefort, as usual elegantly dressed, tapped with his cane; under his small moustache a suave smile lingered, there were also a smile in his puffed eyelids and a dimple on his powdered cheek. He was pleased, gay and happy. Peter breathed heavily through his nose: he felt he would like to hit his bosom friend Francis in the face. Even the shameless Alexander, sitting on a thwart at Peter's feet, wagged his head and exclaimed deprecatingly. Rich and important, menacing with its gold and its guns, the European bank seemed to be gazing in contemptuous perplexity, as it had gazed for over a century, at the eastern bank; as a master looks at his slave.

A cloud of smoke billowed from the ship nearest them and a prolonged roar drowned the ringing of the church bells. Peter rushed from the stern, trampling on the oarsmen's feet, dashed to the little three-pounder and seized the slow-match from the gunner. The shot resounded; but how could it be compared with the thunder of a naval gun? In answer to the Tsar's salute, all the foreign ships wrapped themselves in smoke. It seemed as if the river-banks were shaking. Peter's eyes blazed and he kept saying: "Splendid! Splendid!" It was as if the pictures in the books of his childhood had come to life. When the smoke had cleared he could see foreigners on the quay of the left bank, waving their hats. They were van Leyden and Peltenburg. Peter tore off his three-cornered hat, waved it gaily and shouted a greeting. But, catching sight of the tense faces of Apraxin, Romodanovsky and the clerk Vinius, he turned angrily away.

Now he was sitting on the bed, gazing at the grey twilight outside.

In the Foreign Quarter on the Kukuy he had his own tame foreigners. But here it was not clear who was master. How miserable his homemade boats seemed as they passed the high sides of the seagoing vessels! The shame of it! Everybody had felt it: the boyars, whose faces had clouded, the polite foreigners on the bank, the captains, and the old seamen, weatherbeaten by the ocean winds, ranged on the quarterdecks. Ridiculous . . . Shameful . . . The boyars, and perhaps even Lefort—who could guess what Peter must be feeling—had only one wish: to maintain their dignity. They had drawn themselves up haughtily to show, if only in this way, that the Tsar of all the Russias could not be very interested in the sight of a few trading vessels. If need be, he would have his own; there was nothing in it. And if in future he didn't want these ships to enter the White Sea, they would be helpless; it belonged to Russia.

Had Peter not come in boats, he too perhaps would have been infected with the same conceit. But he remembered well and could still see the haughty contempt, veiled by courteous smiles, of all these people from the West: from the grey-bearded, gap-toothed sailor to the merchant dressed in Spanish velvet. There, on the high poop, near the lantern stands a stocky, brown, stern man in gold braid, with an ostrich plume in his hat, and silk stockings. In his left hand he holds a telescope pressed to his hip, his right hand rests on a cane. This is a captain who has fought corsairs and pirates on all the seas. He looks down calmly from his height at the tall, awkward youth in a clumsy boat, at the Tsar of the barbarians. So he must have looked down somewhere in Madagascar, in the Philippines, after giving orders to load the guns with grapeshot.

And Peter had sensed, with Asiatic cunning, how he must show himself to these foreigners, what was the only way to impress them. He must astonish them, show them something so spectacular that they would take back a story about the extraordinary monarch who did not care a rap about being Tsar. Let the boyars give themselves airs; so much the better. But he was Peter Alexeyev, mate in the Pereyaslav fleet, and would behave accordingly: we are working men, poor but clever, and have come to you with a request from our poverty: please, teach us how to hold an axe.

He had ordered the boat to be rowed ashore and was the first to jump out up to his knees in water; then he scrambled on to the quay, embraced van Leyden and Peltenburg, and shook hands with the others, patting them on the back. Mingling German and Dutch words he told them about the voyage and laughingly pointed to the barges where the boyars were still standing like graven images. "In your parts such poor boats have probably never even been dreamed of." He expressed exaggerated admiration for the ships with their many guns, stamped his feet, slapped his lean thighs—"Ah, if we could have a couple of ships like that!"—and mentioned in passing that he was going to lay down a shipyard in Archangel without delay: "I'll do some carpentering myself and make my boyars hammer in the nails."

Out of the corner of his eye he saw the hypocritical smiles vanish; the respectable merchants were indeed amazed; they had never seen anything like it before. He invited himself to dine with them, saying with a wink: "If you give me a good dinner, we'll discuss business to advantage." He leapt down into his boat and made for the newly-built house on Maseyev island where the governor Matveyev met him in great awe. But with him Peter conversed quite differently: half an hour later he pushed him furiously out of doors. (Already on his way he had received a report denouncing Matveyev for extorting money from the foreigners.) After that, accompanied by Lefort and Alexander, he sailed round inspecting the ships. In the evening they feasted in the foreign settlement. Peter danced so enthusiastically with the English and Hanoverian ladies that his heels came off. Yes, the foreigners had never seen anyone like him in all their lives.

And now a sleepless night. He had succeeded in astonishing the foreigners, but what of it? Russia remained as before: sleepy, poverty-stricken, stagnant. Shame? No. Only the wealthy, the powerful could feel shame. But in this case it was impossible to see what would awaken the people, open their eyes. Were they human beings, or had they, after shedding blood and tears for a thousand years, lost faith in justice and happiness and rotted like a tree sinking into the moss?

Why the devil had he been born Tsar of such a country?

He recalled how, on an autumn night, he had shouted to Alexander, choking with the icy wind: "Better to be an apprentice in Holland than a Tsar here." But what had he done in all these years? Not a cursed thing: he had played the fool. Vaska Golitsin had built stone houses, led campaigns—even if inglorious ones—had negotiated a peace with Poland. It was as if claws were tearing at his heart, so sharply did he feel remorse and resentment at his own people, the Russians, and envy of the self-satisfied merchants: they would spread their free sails and be wafted home to wonderful countries, while he would return to the squalor of Moscow. Should he perhaps proclaim some terrible ukase? Hang a lot of people, flog them? But whom, whom? The enemy was invisible, intangible, the enemy was everywhere; the enemy was in himself.

Peter impetuously opened the door to the small adjoining room:

"Francis!" Lefort sprang off the bench and stared with puffy eyes. "Are you asleep? Come here."

Lefort, clad only in his shirt, sat down on Peter's bed.

"Are you feeling unwell, Peter? Perhaps you'd better vomit?"

"No, it isn't that. Francis, I want to buy two ships in Holland."

"Well, that's all right."

"And we'll build some more here. To carry our own goods."

"Excellent."

"What else would you advise?"

Lefort looked into his eyes with amazement and, as always, understood, better than Peter himself, the tangle of his hurried thoughts. He smiled:

"Wait, I'll put on my trousers and bring pipes." As he dressed in the closet, he said in a strange voice: "I've long been expecting this, Peter. You have reached the age for great deeds."

"What deeds?" Peter shouted.

"The Roman heroes, who still serve as models. . . ." He returned, straightening the curls of his wig. Peter watched him with smouldering eyes. "The heroes considered that their glory lay in war."

"With whom? March on the Crimea again?"

"You can't live without the Black Sea and the Sea of Azov, Peter. This evening Peltenburg whispered in my ear asking whether the Russians still paid tribute to the Khan of Crimea." Peter's eyes flickered, then the pupils rested like pin-points on his dear friend. "Nor can you do without the Baltic, Peter. If you don't do it of your own accord, the Dutch will make you. They say they would export ten times as much if you had ports on the Baltic."

"Fight the Swedes? You're mad! You're joking, aren't you? No one in the world can beat them, and you. . . ."

"But it hasn't got to be done tomorrow, Peter. You put a question to me, and my answer is: aim at the great things; if you strike out at little things you'll only hurt your fist."

16

"To merchants of other towns and merchant guilds, and to all townsmen, tradesmen and craftsmen losses and ruin are occasioned in their deals and in all kinds of business by the many official delays due to governors, clerks and other official persons. Like lions, like wolves they devour us with their jaws. Have mercy, Great Tsar. . . ."

"Another complaint against the governors?" Peter asked.

He was eating seated at the edge of the table. He had just returned from the wharf and had not even turned down the sleeves of his tar-smeared linen shirt, which he had rolled up to his elbows. He was dipping pieces of bread into an earthenware dish with roast meat and chewing rapidly, glancing the while, now at the foam-crested choppy waters of the leaden Dvina, now at the portly clerk Andrey Andreyevich Vinius with his white face and fair beard, who sat at the other end of the table.

Vinius was reading the mail from Moscow. Round spectacles sat on his firm nose, and his wide-set blue eyes were cold and intelligent. He had lately come to play an important rôle, especially since Peter, after his conversation in the night with Lefort, had ordered the Moscow mail to be read in his presence. Formerly all the paper business used to pass through Troyekurov, and Peter did not interfere. But now he wanted to hear everything himself. The letters were read to him while he dined: there was no other time. He spent all day on the wharf with foreign craftsmen taken from the ships. He worked as a carpenter and as a smith, to the astonishment of the foreigners; he questioned them with savage eagerness about everything and quarrelled and fought with everyone. There were already over a hundred workmen on the wharf. They had been sought out and brought from all the villages and hamlets, honourably—for wages—if they came willingly, and if not, they were brought without honour in chains.

In the dinner hour Peter, hungry as a wolf, sailed back to the Maseyev island. In a solemn voice Vinius read out to him ukases, sent for the Tsar's signature, petitions, complaints, letters. The flowery language of these edicts breathed the dreariness of ages; the complaints wailed with the moans of slaves. Age-old Russian officialdom lied, thieved and oppressed, and covered it up with reports written in archaic script, while the inert mass of the people groaned, devoured by lice and cockroaches.

"A complaint against a governor," Vinius replied. "Stepan Suhotin again."

Straightening his spectacles he went on reading the doleful outcry against the governor of Kungar. He was ruining trade by imposing taxes for his own benefit; he held merchants and townsmen imprisoned in his house and beat them with his stick, thus causing the death of one innocent man. He levied tolls from supply-trains for his own pocket, eight kopeks from each waggon in winter, one altyn in summer from each barge. He tormented the wealthy manufacturer Zmiev by keeping him shut up in a chest with holes bored in the lid to prevent him from stifling. And he took land-tax and excise money for himself and threatened to destroy the whole of Kungar if any complaint was lodged against him.

"Hang the cur in the Kungur market-place!" Peter cried. "Write the ukase!"

Vinius looked sternly at him over his spectacles:

"It doesn't take long to hang a man, but it won't help to bring them to their senses. I have long said, Peter Alexeyevich, that no governor should be left more than two years at his post. They get used to the place and learn the ropes. Whereas a new governor robs with a lighter hand. Peter Alexeyevich, you must give your protection first and foremost to the merchants. They will give you much if you lift the intolerable burdens from them. Why, some dare not bring two pairs of birch-bark shoes to the market—they'd be seized, and beaten and robbed of their money. And where will you get any wealth if not from the merchants? There's nothing to be had from the nobles; they eat all they've got. And the peasant has long been stripped to the skin. Here, listen."

After searching among the papers Vinius began to read:

". . . And by the will of God our harvest is always poor, the frost always ruins our fields, and today we have neither bread, nor firewood, nor cattle, and we are perishing from cold and starvation. Take pity, Great Tsar, on our scarcity and poverty and order us to be put on the quit-rent to help us in our indigence. Poor and helpless as we are, we have nothing from which to provide our landlord with pork and meat and poultry and other provender. We feed on pigweed and our bodies swell. Take pity on us!"

Peter, as he listened, angrily struck the steel against a piece of flint, cutting his finger so that it bled, and as his pipe started to draw, inhaled the smoke deeply. Immovable, age-old stagnation! Breaking through the flying clouds the sun danced on the river that had now turned blue. The ribs of a new ship rose above the slips on the far side of the stream. Axes rang, saws rasped. Over there the air smelt of tobacco, tar, wood shavings, hemp ropes. The wind from the sea refreshed the heart. That night Lefort had said: "Peter, Russia is a terrible country. It must be turned inside out, like a fur coat, and remade."

"Abroad people don't steal, don't plunder," Peter said gazing with narrowed eyes at the choppy water. "Are people there of some different breed?"

"The people are the same, Peter Alexeyevich, but thieving doesn't pay, honesty pays better. They look after the merchants, and the merchants look after themselves. My father came to Russia under the late Tsar. He built a factory in Tula and wanted to work honestly. They wouldn't let him; they ruined him by all kinds of obstruction and delay. Here if a man is not a thief, then he must be a fool, and honour lies not in being honourable, but in being exalted above others. Yet we too have clever men."

Vinius's white plump fingers seemed to be weaving a web; the sun was reflected in his glasses, and he spoke softly and smoothly: "Honour the traders, pull them out of the mire, give them power, and their word will be their bond; you can safely depend on them, Sire."

Sidney, van Leyden, Lefort, had all said the same. Peter began to feel as if this was the firm ground his feet were seeking. This was no longer a matter of three play-regiments, but stability, power. With his elbow on the windowsill he gazed at the waves glinting like oil in the sun, at the wharf where a sledgehammer beat down noiselessly on a pile, the sound of the blow coming to him only much later. He blinked and blinked, and his heart beat with assurance, with happy excitement.

"The Vologda merchant Zhigulin has brought a petition in person and begs to be allowed to present it himself," Vinius said with particular emphasis.

Peter nodded. Vinius, carrying his portly person lightly, went to the door, called to someone and quickly resumed his seat. He was followed by a big, broad-shouldered merchant, with his hair cut straight across the forehead in Novgorod fashion. In his strong face his eyes looked sharply from under beetling brows. He crossed himself with a sweeping gesture and bowed to the ground. Peter pointed with his pipe to a chair:

"I command you to sit down." Zhigulin raised his eyebrows slightly and sat down gingerly. "What do you want? Speak out!"

Zhigulin apparently realised that here it was not a matter of banging the ground with his forehead, but of exhibiting the length of his purse. He smoothed his moustache with dignity, glanced down at his kid boots and coughed deeply.

"We come to petition the Great Tsar. When we heard you were building ships on the Dvina our joy was great. We wish you to order us not to sell our goods to the foreigners. Truly, we give them to them for nothing, Sire! Blubber, sealskins, salted salmon, walrus tusks, pearls. Order us to bring them to your ships. The English have completely ruined us. Have mercy on us! And we shall do our best: serving our own Tsar rather than foreign kings."

Peter's eyes shone as he looked at him. Stretching out he clapped Zhigulin on the shoulder with a happy grin:

"I shall have two ships built by autumn and a third has been bought in Holland. Bring your goods; but mind, no trickery!"

"But we, good God, we. . . ."

"Will you take the goods yourself? Be the first commercial representative? Sell them in Amsterdam?"

"I don't know foreign languages. But if you command me, why not? I'll trade in Amsterdam, I won't let myself be swindled!"

"Good man! Vinius, write a ukase. To the first merchant-navigator. What's your name, Zhigulin—Ivan—and your patronymic?"

Zhigulin gaped; he rose, his eyes bulged and his beard shook.

"You will write me down with my patronymic? Why, for that I'll do whatever you ask!"

And he fell at the Tsar's feet, as he did before the icon of Christ to whom he prayed for success in his affairs.

Zhigulin left. Vinius's quill scratched. Peter paced up and down the room, grinning. Then he stopped:

"Well, what else have you got there? Read! But make it short."

"Robbery again. On the Troitsa road a waggon-train with money was robbed, two men were killed. After investigation they arrested Stepan Odoyevsky, youngest son of Prince Semyon Odoyevsky, and brought him in a common cart to the Office for Criminal Affairs. There he confessed and sentence was imposed that he was to be whipped in the basement of the building, and to have his Moscow house and four hundred peasant families confiscated. His father, Prince Semyon, has taken him on bail. Fifteen of his house serfs have been hanged."

"There they are, Vinius, the princes and the boyars! Taking to bludgeons, robbing."

"Yes, it is a fact; they are robbing, Sire."

"Parasites, longbeards! I know, I remember. . . . Every one of them has a hidden knife for me." His neck twitched. "But I've got an axe for each of them." He spat and jerked his leg. With outspread fingers he clutched at the tablecloth and pulled. Vinius hastily steadied the inkpot and papers. "I've got power now. We'll clash. . . . Without mercy. . . ." He moved towards the door.

"Forgive me, Sire, there are two more letters. From the Tsaritsas."

"All right, read on."

Peter returned to the window and fiddled with his pipe. Vinius made a slight bow and began to read:

"Greetings, my beloved father Tsar Peter Alexeyevich, may you prosper for many years. . . ." Peter turned an astonished eyebrow towards him. "Your little son Alexey begs for your blessing, light of my eyes. Do not delay your return, our joy, our Sovereign. I beg this favour of you because I see the Tsaritsa, my grandmother, in great sorrow. Do not be distressed, my beloved lord, that this letter is poor: I have not yet learned to write, my lord."

"Whose writing is it?"

"It is in the hand of the Great Tsaritsa Natalia, very shaky, hardly legible."

"Well, write something in reply. Say I'm waiting for ships from Hamburg. That I'm well and don't go to sea, that she need not worry. And say they mustn't expect me back soon, do you hear?"

Vinius said with a gentle sigh:

"The Tsarevich Alexey has personally put his inked finger to the letter."

"Oh, all right, all right! His finger!" He snorted and took the second letter from Vinius. "His finger, indeed!"

He read his wife's letter in the boat. A fresh breeze filled the sail, and the little boat dived and rose like a living thing, foam-crested waves lashed its sides and spray flew up from the bow. Peter sat at the helm and read the short letter, holding it down on his knee as the spray splashed it.

"Greetings, my dear one, may you prosper for many years. I beseech you, my light, my dearest, to gladden my heart with news of your health, so that I may have some joy in my desolation. You have not written me a single line since it pleased you to depart. I am the unhappiest creature on earth because you do not come and do not write to me of your health. Please, my joy, write and tell me how you feel towards me. As for me and little Alexey, we are alive. . . ."

The boat shipped water. Peter hastily put the tiller over to port; a large wave, hissing with foam, hit the side of the boat and drenched him from head to foot. He laughed. The unwanted letter, torn from his knees by the wind, fluttered up and vanished in the waves far astern.

17

At last Natalia saw her son. It was on the day when she felt as though a nail had been driven into her heart. Propped high on swansdown pillows, she stared with dilated pupils at the wall, at a golden spiral on the stamped leather. She was afraid of shifting her eyes, of making the slightest movement. The empty feeling in her breast was more painful than any thirst could be; she lacked air, but when she tried to take a breath, her eyes bulged with terror. Every now and again Leo Narishkin would enter the bedchamber on tiptoe and ask the ladies in attendance:

"Well, how is she? Oh, my God, oh, my God! do not let this happen!"

Swallowing his saliva, he would seat himself on the bed and speak to his sister. But she did not reply. The whole world seemed to her unreal. The only thing she felt was her heart with the nail driven into it.

When look-out men on foam-flecked horses dashed into the Kremlin yelling: "He's coming, he's coming!"; when sextons crossed themselves and climbed to the belfries; when the doors of the Archangelsky and Uspensky cathedrals opened, and priests and deacons hastily pulled their hair free of the chasubles they were donning; when the courtiers assembled on the steps and barefooted runners scattered through Moscow to inform the important people, then Leo Narishkin leant, panting, over his sister and said:

"He's come, the light of our eyes!"

Natalia drew a sudden breath, her plump hands plucked at her nightdress, her lips went blue and she collapsed. Leo himself began to gasp, unconscious of what he was doing. The ladies ran for the confessor. In nooks and corners the poor dependents groaned. The whole palace was filled with alarm.

And now Ivan the Great lifted its brazen voice, the bells of churches and monasteries began ringing, the servants set up a noisy bustling and, above the turmoil and shouting, sounded the harsh voices of the foreign officers: *"Achtung!* 'Shun! Order arms!" Carriages and coaches dashed at full speed to the Red Porch past the troops and the crowding people. They sought the Tsar with their eyes, but did not catch sight of him among the rich coats, the generals' cloaks and plumed hats.

Peter ran straight to his mother; the people thronging the passages could barely get out of his way. Sunburnt, thin and close-cropped, in a tight black velvet jacket and full knee-breeches, he flew up the stairs and some of those who saw him took him for the doctor from the Foreign Quarter, and later, having recognised him, crossed themselves in fear. He took everyone by surprise when he tore the door open and rushed into the low, stuffy bedchamber panelled with Spanish leather. Natalia raised herself on her pillows and fixed her shining eyes on this lean Dutch sailor.

"Mama!" he cried, as in his far-away childhood. "My darling!"

Natalia stretched out her hands:

"Peter, my dear, my son!"

With her mother's love she overcame the nail that was piercing her heart, and did not breathe while he, hanging over her, kissed her shoulder and face; only when a mortal pang tore at her chest she loosened her hands from his neck.

Peter sprang up and looked, as though with curiosity, at her turned-up eyes. The ladies, afraid to wail, stuffed their handkerchiefs into their mouths. Leo Narishkin was trembling. But suddenly Natalia's eyelashes fluttered. Peter said something hoarsely—no one understood what—and, rushing to the window, shook the leaden frame, so that the round panes fell out with a rattle.

"Fetch Blumentrost from the Quarter!" And when again they did not understand him, he seized one of the ladies by the shoulders: "Fool! Fetch the doctor!" and pushed her out of the door.

Half dead, the lady went pattering down the stairs, clucking: "The Tsar has ordered! The Tsar has ordered!" But what he had ordered she was unable to say.

Natalia recovered from the attack and, two days later, was even able to attend mass and had a good appetite. Peter went off to Preobrazhensk where Eudoxia was living with the Tsarevich Alexey; she had gone there in the spring to be farther away from her mother-in-law. She was not expecting her husband for some days, and she was not prepared and not in full toilet when Peter suddenly appeared on the sandy path in the garden, where they were making apple jam in the shade of the limes. Court maids, one prettier than the other, with long plaits, wearing low headdresses and pink wide-sleeved gowns, were peeling apples under the supervision of Vorobyiha, while others carried brushwood to the little stove on which the copper pan boiled appetisingly, or, seated on a rug, tried to amuse the Tsarevich, a thin child with a high forehead, dark, unsmiling eyes and a petulant mouth.

Nobody could understand what he wanted. The broad-hipped girls mewed like cats, barked like dogs, ran about on all fours, and were themselves quite weak with laughter, but the child looked at them sullenly, on the brink of tears. Eudoxia said angrily:

"You silly fools, you're thinking of other things. Steshka, pull down that skirt! A few strokes with a switch on those parts would do you good. Vasenka, show him how a goat butts. . . . Go, find a beetle, stick a straw into it! Use your imagination. Here I've got to feed the lot of you, and you don't even know how to amuse the child."

Eudoxia was feeling the heat and the autumn flies pestered her. She took off her headdress and ordered the girls to comb her hair. The air was limpid and the sky stretched serenely blue above the limes. If the Saviour's Day had not already passed, it would have been nice to go for a bathe, but the stag had already wetted its horns, so it was too late and sinful.

Suddenly a tall, sunburnt man, dressed all in black, appeared on the path. Eudoxia clapped her hands to her cheeks. Her heart thumped so that she could not think. The maids gasped and fled, with plaits flying, behind lilac and wild-rose bushes. Peter came up, took Eudoxia under the arms, and kissed her hard on the mouth. She screwed up her eyes and did not respond. Through her unbuttoned gown he kissed her damp breast. Eudoxia caught her breath and, flushing with shame, trembled all over. The child, left alone sitting on the rug, began to whimper like a little hare. Peter lifted him up and tossed him in the air; the boy burst into noisy tears.

The reunion was not a happy one. Peter asked questions and Eudoxia answered at random. Her hair uncovered, her dress in disorder, the child smeared with jam. And, of course, after a while her husband went away to the palace where he was surrounded by craftsmen, merchants, generals, boon-companions. She could hear his abrupt laughter in the distance. Then he went to the river to inspect the Yaouza fleet. And from there to the Foreign Quarter. . . . Oh, Eudoxia, Eudoxia, you've let your happiness slip through your fingers!

Vorobyiha said that things could be put right. She set to with a will. She sent maids to heat the bath and ordered the nurses to take the child away and wash and change him.

"Don't lose your head when night comes, my pretty," she whispered to the Tsaritsa. "In the bath-house we'll steam you in our own, the peasant way, throw kvass on the hot stones, wash you with benjamin, to make you smell sweet. And for men a sweet smell is the most important thing. And then, my beauty, laugh all the time in answer to what he says, so that your whole body quivers, laugh low, trillingly, with your breast. It's enough to drive a dead man crazy."

"Vorobyiha, he's gone to his foreign woman."

"Oh, Tsaritsa, don't even mention her. What is there so wonderful about her? She's frisky, her mind is grasping, her soul black and her skin clammy. But you, like a lovely swan, welcome him to your bed with tenderness and gaiety; how can that foreign woman compare?"

Eudoxia understood and began to hurry. The bath-house was very hot. The maids, together with Vorobyiha, laid the Tsaritsa on the high bench and fanned her with bath-brooms dipped in mint and benjamin. Then they led her, mellow and languid, to the bedchamber, combed her hair, rouged her cheeks and painted her eyebrows. After that they put her to bed and drew the curtains, and Eudoxia waited.

Mice scratched. Night fell. The palace grew silent. In the yard the watchman tapped sleeplessly, and her heart knocked against the pillow. Still Peter did not come. Keeping in mind what Vorobyiha had told her, she lay in the dark smiling, though hatred of the foreign woman made her belly tremble and turned her feet to ice.

And now the watchman had ceased his tapping, the mice were quiet. Tomorrow she would be ashamed to show herself even to her maids! Still Eudoxia tried to take heart until she remembered how, on their first night, she and Peter had eaten the chicken: then she wailed and, pressing her face into the pillow, wet it with her tears.

A hot breath awakened her. She started: "Who's there? Who's there?" Confused with sleep she did not realise whose body was crushing hers. When she did, she sobbed with her still fresh hurt, and pressed her fists to her eyes. There was nothing human about Peter; drunk, reeking of tobacco, he had come straight from the foreign strumpet to her, who had waited for him with such longing. He did not caress her, but raped her silently, frighteningly. Was it worth her while to have washed herself with benjamin?

Eudoxia moved to the edge of the bed. Peter muttered something and fell asleep like a drunken peasant in a ditch. The light showed blue between the curtains. Ashamed of Peter's long bare legs, Eudoxia covered him up and cried softly. Vorobyiha's good advice had been wasted.

A messenger galloped in from Moscow; Tsaritsa Natalia was again very ill. They hurried off to find the Tsar. He was at a christening in the soldier Buhvostov's house in the newly built suburb of Preobrazhensk.

They were eating pancakes. There were no strangers. The company consisted of Lieutenant Alexander Menshikov, Alioshka Brovkin, recently taken by Peter as his orderly, and Zotov. They were joking and enjoying themselves. Menshikov was telling them how, twelve years ago, he and Alioshka had run away from home, how they lived with Zayats, tramped and thieved, and how they had met the boy Peter on the Yaouza and taught him to draw a needle through his cheek.

"So it was you?" Peter cried in amazement. "Why, after that I searched for you for half a year. I love you for that needle, Alexander!" And he kissed him on the lips.

"And do you remember, Peter Alexeyevich," asked Zotov shaking his finger at him, "do you remember my whip, how I flogged you for your pranks? You were a mischievous lad. . . . Why. . . ."

And Nikita Zotov embarked on a story of how Peter—just a tiny little fellow, a few inches from the ground—was already possessed of great intelligence. He would put some question to the boyars, and they would sit thinking and thinking without being able to answer. And then he would just wave his hand, and give the answer pat. It was wonderful!

All those at the table listened to these wonderful tales openmouthed and although Peter could not remember anything of the kind himself, if others believed it, he was ready to chime in.

Buhvostov kept the goblets filled. He was a man of some cunning, although he looked simple and disinterested. He understood Peter both drunk and sober, but of course he could not keep pace with Alexander: he was no longer young enough, nor was his mind sufficiently nimble. He smiled, hospitably invited his guests to eat and drink and did not try to enter the conversation.

"And now," Menshikov said, his gold embroidered red cuffs scratching the tablecloth (he sat upright, ate little and wine had no effect on him, except to make his eyes bluer), "and now we have learnt that the Tsar's orderly, Alioshka Brovkin, has a beautiful sister of marriageable age. This is a matter in which we ought to take a hand."

The stolid Alioshka blinked and suddenly grew pale. They began to badger him with questions and he confirmed that it was true, his sister Alexandra was of marriageable age but there was no suitable bridegroom. His father, Ivan Brovkin, had become so proud that he would not even look at merchants of ordinary means now. He had got himself some savage dogs, so that people were afraid and gave his house a wide berth. He turned matchmakers away without ceremony. He had brought Sanka to such a state that she cried day and night: she was at the flower of her age but was afraid that instead of a wedding crown it would all end with a nun's cowl because of their father's conceit.

"How's that? No bridegroom?" Peter cried hotly. "Lieutenant Menshikov, be so good as to marry."

"I can't, I'm too young. I couldn't cope with a woman, *mein Herz.*"

"What about you, Most Holy Prince-Pope? Do you want to get married?"

"I'm a bit too old, my son, for a young girl. I mostly keep company with whores."

"All right, you drunken devils. Alioshka, write to your father and tell him I myself shall be the matchmaker."

Alioshka took off his great black wig and solemnly bowed to the ground. Peter wanted to start immediately for the village where the Brovkins lived, but just then the messenger from the Kremlin entered and handed him a letter from Narishkin. The Tsaritsa had died. All rose from the table and removed their wigs while Peter read the letter. His lips went slack and began to tremble. He took his hat from the windowsill and pressed it down over his eyes. Tears ran down his cheeks. He went out silently and strode down the street, raising the dust with his shoes. His carriage met him half-way to the palace; he got in, and they went off at a gallop to Moscow.

While the others talked and discussed what would happen now, Alexander Menshikov was already at Lefort's with the great news: Peter would now be sole master. Lefort was overjoyed and embraced Alexander; they whispered together that Peter must no longer evade State affairs: the whole of the treasury and the army were in his hands and no one must be allowed to influence him except those who were closest to him. The court must be moved to Preobrazhensk. And Anna Mons must be told to stop dilly-dallying and to give herself to the Tsar without reserve. It was necessary.

No one touched Natalia before the Tsar arrived. She lay with a look of surprise on her face, blue like that of someone who had been stifled; her eyes were tightly closed and her swollen hands held a small icon.

Peter looked at her face. It seemed as though she had gone so far away that she had forgotten everything. His eyes sought: perhaps at the corner of the mouth a little love lingered. No. No. Never had these lips been folded together with such estrangement. And yet, only this morning she was still calling as she fought for breath: "Peter . . . to bless him. . . ." He felt that now he was alone, surrounded by strangers. He became mortally sorry for himself, who had been left abandoned.

He hunched up his shoulders, frowning. In the bedchamber, apart from the tearful ladies-in-waiting, were the new Patriarch Adrian—a small man with fair hair, who looked at the Tsar with foolish curiosity—and Peter's sister Tsarevna Natalia, a year younger than he, a tender and gay young woman. She stood in a peasant woman's mournful posture, her cheek on her hand, and a mother's compassion shone in her grey eyes.

Peter came up to her.

"Natasha. . . . Poor Mama. . . ."

His sister took his head in her hands and clasped it to her bosom. The ladies began to wail softly. The better to see the Tsar crying, the Patriarch Adrian turned his back on the dead Tsaritsa and half-opened his mouth. Leo Narishkin entered unsteadily, his beard wet and his face swollen like a lump of raw meat. He fell on the ground before the dead body of his sister and lay motionless save for the spasmodic jerking of his behind.

Tsarevna Natalia took her brother upstairs to her room during the time they washed and arranged the body. Peter seated himself at the window with its small coloured panes. Nothing had changed here since his childhood. There were the same little coffers and rugs, the silver, glass and stone animals on the low cupboards, the heartshaped mirror in a Venetian frame, the coloured prints from the Scriptures, the exotic seashells.

"Natasha," he asked in a low voice, "where is that Turk you had, you remember, the one with the terrible eyes? His head had got broken off."

Natalia Alexeyevna pondered a little, then opened a small coffer and from the bottom of it brought out the Turk and his head. She showed it to Peter and her eyebrows quivered. She sat down beside him, clasped him tightly in her arms and they both wept.

In the evening Tsaritsa Natalia, robed in cloth-of-gold, was laid in the audience chamber. Peter stood at a lectern by the coffin and, his head bowed between the candles, read in his slightly hoarse, youthful bass. Two palace guards, in white, with short halberds on their shoulders, stood at each of the two doors and shifted their weight noiselessly. Leo Narishkin knelt at the foot of the coffin. Everyone in the palace was sleeping, worn out with emotion.

At the dead of night the door creaked and Sophia entered, wearing a stiff black habit and a nun's small black cap. Without glancing at her brother she touched Natalia's blue forehead with her lips and knelt down. Peter turned the pages, stuck together with wax, and read on in a low voice. The chimes of the Kremlin clock sounded at long intervals. Sophia stole glances at her brother. When light began to show through the window, she rose softly and went to the lectern.

"I will take your place. You rest," she whispered.

His ears pricked involuntarily at the sound of her voice. He broke off, shrugged his shoulders and drew aside. Sophia took up the reading from the middle of a sentence and, as she read, snuffed the candle with her fingers. Peter leant against the wall; the vault made it uncomfortable for his head and he sat down on a coffer, with his elbows on his knees and his face in his hands. He thought to himself: "All the same, I won't forgive her."

Thus passed the last night of time-honoured tradition in the Kremlin palace.

Three days later Peter returned to Preobrazhensk straight from the funeral and lay down to sleep. Eudoxia followed later, accompanied by a suite of court ladies whose names she did not even know. Now they called her Mother Tsaritsa, fawned upon her, flattered her and begged to be allowed to kiss her hand. She could hardly get rid of them. She went first to the nursery, and then to the bedchamber. Peter was lying on the white satin bed just as he was, and had only thrown off his dusty shoes. Eudoxia made a wry face: "Oh, these Foreign Quarter habits! They drink and then drop down anywhere." She seated herself in front of the mirror and began to undress; she would rest before dinner. Her mind was full of the court ladies, of their flattering speeches; and then suddenly she understood: she was now the all-powerful Tsaritsa. She narrowed her eyes and pursed her lips in a queenly manner. "First thing, send Anna Mons to Siberia for life." Then she must take her husband in hand. Her late mother-in-law had hated her, of course, and was always setting him against her. Now things would be different. Yesterday she was only Eudoxia, today she was Tsaritsa of All the Russias. She pictured herself leaving the Cathedral of the Assumption, in front of the boyars, to the ringing of bells, to appear before the people. It took her breath away. New royal robes for State occasions would have to be made; she would not wear Natalia's cast-off things. Peter was always away somewhere, she would have to rule. What of it? Sophia had ruled, and she was not much older. If there was any thinking to be done, well, the boyars were there for that. She smiled suddenly, recalling Leo Narishkin. Formerly he had hardly noticed her, looked past her, but today at the funeral he had supported her by the elbow and looked at her beseechingly. Oh, the fat fool!

"Eudoxia!" She started and turned round. Peter was lying on his side, propped up on his elbow. "Eudoxia, Mother is dead." Eudoxia merely blinked. "Life seems so empty I dropped off to sleep. Oh, dear Eudoxia!"

He seemed to expect something from her. His eyes were sorrowful. But she was already carried away by her thoughts and became quite bold:

"It was God's will. We must not repine. We have wept for her, and life moves on. After all, we are Tsars. We have other cares."

He slowly unbent his elbow and sat up, his legs dangling. There was a hole in his stocking at the big toe.

"And another thing," she went on, "it's not decent, not nice to lie down on a satin coverlet in your clothes. You spend your time with soldiers and peasants, and it's about time. . . ."

"What? What?" he interrupted and his eyes flashed. "Have you been eating toadstools, Eudoxia?"

His glance made her flinch, but she went on, though in a different voice, talking the same nonsense which to him was incomprehensible. When she blurted out: "Your mother always hated me, from the day of our wedding. The tears I have wept. . . ." Peter bared his teeth savagely and began to put on his shoes.

"Peter, there's a hole in your stocking; look! For goodness sake change it."

"I've known fools," he said, and his hands were trembling, "but such a fool. . . . Well, well. . . . I'll never forgive you this, Eudoxia; my mother's dead, and for once in my life I turn to you. . . . I won't forget!"

He went out and slammed the door so violently that Eudoxia cringed. And she sat for a long time in front of her mirror, wondering. What had she said that was so awful? He was mad, absolutely mad.

Lefort had long been waiting for Peter in the passage outside the bedchamber. At the funeral they had seen each other only at a distance. Now he seized Peter's hand impulsively and said:

"Oh, Peter, Peter, what a loss!" Peter was still rather stiff. "Allow me to express my sympathy for your grief. *Ich kondoliere, ich kondoliere. Mein Herz ist voll Schmerzen.* Oh! My heart is full of *Schmerzen.*" As usual when he was excited he began to speak in broken Russian and this particularly affected Peter. "I know that consolation is vain. But take my life, take it, Peter, do not suffer—"

Peter embraced him with all his strength and laid his cheek against the scented wig. Here was a true friend. Lefort said in a whisper:

"Come to my house, Peter. Dispel your sorrow. We shall amuse you a little, if you wish. Or—*zusammen weinen*—weep together—"

"Yes, yes, let's go to your house, Francis."

There everything was ready. A table was laid for five in a small room with a door opening into the garden, where musicians were concealed behind bushes. The dwarfs, Tomosa and Seka, in Roman coats and with maple-leaf wreaths on their heads, served them. The whole room was decorated with garlands of roses. They took their seats at the table: Peter, Lefort, Alexander and Zotov. There was no vodka nor the usual snacks that accompany it. The dwarfs brought in sparrow and quail pies on gold dishes held high above their heads.

"For whom is the fifth place?" Peter asked.

The corners of Lefort's lips lifted in a smile:

"Tonight we are having a Roman supper in honour of the goddess Ceres, renowned for the edifying story of her daughter Proserpine."

"What's the story?" Alexander asked. He was wearing a silk coat and a wig that reached his waist, and was languid in the extreme. Zotov was dressed in the same way.

"Proserpine was carried off by Pluto, god of the underworld," Lefort said. "Her mother grieved. One might think this would be the end of the story. But no; there is no death, only eternal growth. The unfortunate Proserpine grew up through the earth as a wonderful pomegranate fruit and thus appeared to her mother to comfort her."

Peter was quiet and sad. It was dark and damp in the garden. Stars showed through the open door. Now and then a withered leaf fell in the beam of light from the door.

"Then for whom is the place?" Peter asked again.

Lefort raised a finger. The sand in the garden crunched. Annchen entered the room. She was dressed in a full-skirted gown; a sheaf of corn rested on her left arm and her right hand held a dish with carrots, lettuce, radishes and apples. Her hair was gathered into a high knot and there were roses in it. Her face was bewitching in the candlelight.

Peter did not rise; he only sat bolt upright gripping the arms of his chair. Anna set the dish before him and curtsied. Apparently she had been taught a little speech, but she said nothing and became confused; and this was even more effective.

"Ceres brings you fruit, which means: there is no death! Take it and live!" Lefort cried, moving a chair up for Annchen. She sat down next to Peter. Sparkling French champagne was poured out. Peter did not take his eyes off Annchen. But a certain constraint still made itself felt at the table. She laid her fingers on his hand:

"Ich kondoliere, Herr Peter—" Her large eyes filled with tears. "I would give everything to comfort you."

Warmth flowed from the wine, from Annchen's closeness. Zotov was already winking. Alexander was bursting with fun. Lefort sent a dwarf into the garden and tambourines and string instruments struck up. Annchen's dress rustled, her eyes had dried like the sky after rain. Peter threw off his sadness:

"Champagne, Francis, champagne!"

"That's right, my son," Zotov said, beaming with wrinkles. "It's easier with Greek and Roman gods!"

18

In the thick forests beyond the Oka, where they spent the whole summer, the cripple Ovdokim was in his element; he was successful and bold. He picked a small band of experienced men who had known torture: they feared neither death nor blood, and did not indulge in unnecessary depredations. Their camp was in the marshes, on an island which neither man nor beast could reach except by a single shaky path. There they brought their loot: bread, poultry, vodka, clothes, silver from robbed churches. A lookout post was arranged on a venerable pine; Judas climbed it to survey the surrounding country.

Altogether there were nine robbers on the island, and two others— the most desperate ones—wandered as scouts along the roads and in the taverns. If a merchant's goods train was going from Moscow to Tula, or a boyar was on his way to his country estate, or a publican in his cups had boasted of buried treasure, immediately a village boy, with a whip or a basket, went off to the dark forest and, once there, ran as fast as his legs could carry him to the marsh. There he whistled. From his lookout post Judas whistled in reply. Out of a mud-hut crawled the crook-backed Ovdokim. The boy was led across the marsh to the island and there questioned. In all the villages near the highway Ovdokim had such messengers. They could be cut to pieces, but they would hold their tongues. Ovdokim treated them kindly, fed them, gave them a kopek, would ask after their fathers and mothers, but both children and grown-ups feared him: he was quiet and serene, but even his friendly manner inspired terror.

Life on the marsh was gloomy. In the evening the mist rose as thick as milk. Bones felt the damp, old wounds hurt. Ovdokim did not allow fires to be lit at night. Once a robber protested noisily: the night was like being in a cellar; it wasn't enough that they had governors and landowners over them; they'd put one more devil on their backs. And he started to kindle a fire. Ovdokim went mildly up to him, put his crutches into his left hand and took him by the throat. The man's tongue and eyes protruded; they threw him into the marsh.

The sun rose yellow and without warmth. The trees stood veiled in a misty vapour. The robbers coughed, scratched their flogged behinds, re-shod themselves, heated kettles.

There was no real work. It was lucky if a messenger whistled from the forest. Otherwise there was nothing to do but to sleep all day. Out of boredom they told fairy-tales and sang convict songs that filled the heart with melancholy. They seldom spoke about their past, and then little. Apart from Judas and Zhemov they were all peasants who had fled from their landlords; they had been caught, put in chains and had escaped again out of the prisons.

Often Ovdokim, seating himself on a mossy stone, would start a story. They listened to him sombrely in the sleepy forest silence; they did not know what Ovdokim was leading up to. They would have preferred if he had simply told lies like some others, saying for instance: "Listen, lads, soon they'll find a golden Tsar's ukase and there'll be freedom for everybody: live as you please, in quiet, plenty and oblivion." A fairy-tale, of course, but it was pleasant to think about to the damp rustling of the pines. But no, he had never anything consoling to say.

"There was a time once, my lads, but it is past, though only for the moment. I used to go about in a cloth coat, with a sharp sword at my side and rousing letters in my cap. A time like that will come back, my lads; that's why I'm keeping you in the forest. The poor, the destitute were gathering, like ravens flocking together, in clouds, innumerable. They carried a golden ukase, it was sewn in the coat of the cossack, Stepan Razin. The ukase was written in blood, the blood was taken from our wounds and written with a sharp knife. It said: 'There must be no mercy: all the rich, all the high-born, together with the estates, the towns and the suburbs, with the capital city of Moscow, must be utterly destroyed. And on the waste land a free Cossack camp must be set up—' Ah, this couldn't be accomplished, dear lads. And yet it must and shall be. For so it is written in the Dove Book."

His narrow little beard pressed on a crutch, he gazed with his watery eyes at the slushy surface of the marsh, squashed a mosquito on his cheek and smiled.

"We'll be able to live here till Intercession Day, there are plenty of mushrooms. And when the first snow falls, I shall lead you on, my lads, but this time not to Moscow. Life has become very hard there. Prince Romodanovsky has been put at the head of the Office for Criminal Affairs, and they say of him: 'On a day when he has drunk blood, he is merry; but on the day when he has drunk none, then even bread sticks in his throat.' So I'm going to take you to the river Vyga, in the farthest thickets of the forest, to a dissenters' stronghold. There a great cell stands with tiers of bunks, and windows have been made in it out of which to defend oneself against the Tsar's men. They have plenty of guns and powder there. In that cell lives a monk, he is small, his hair is grey and he is old. He has altogether about two hundred dissenters who live scattered on the Vyga. Their huts are built on piles, and they plough without horses; they do all this monk tells them to do, and their number increases all the time. And nobody can keep anything to himself; they go to him for confession every week, and he, taking some cranberries and rye or barley flour, mixes them together and gives them this for communion. To that twilit vineyard I will take you by secret paths, and there, my lads, we shall rest from evil-doing."

The bandits sighed as they listened, but few of them believed that they would reach the Vyga alive. This was only another fairy-tale.

Ovdokim seldom took part in robberies, but remained alone on the island, cooking their food and washing their trousers and shirts.

But whenever he did go out himself, with his chased flail stuck through his belt at the back, then they knew that the affair would be a hot one. Although a cripple, he showed himself as agile as a spider when, in the night, whistling so that it made one's hair stand on end, he threw himself at the horses and struck them on the forehead with his flail. If the traveller was some noble or a wealthy man, he knew no mercy and finished him off himself. The underlings he let go, after giving them a good scare, but woe to anyone who happened to recognise him!

This sinister work on the Tula road was known in Moscow, and several times soldiers under the command of a lieutenant were sent to wipe out the gang. But not one of them returned from the forest, and only the marshy bog, whither Ovdokim had enticed them, knew the soldiers' sad fate.

So they lived more or less in plenty. Towards the end of the summer Ovdokim put together some clothes and furs and sent Tsigan, Judas and Zhemov to the great market in Tula to sell them.

"You'd better come back with the money, dear lads," he told them. "Don't saddle your conscience with a sin. Besides you wouldn't have long to live; no, I'd find you."

A week later Judas returned alone with a broken head, without the things and without any money. The island was deserted: nothing but the cold ashes of the camp-fire and some scattered rags. He waited and called. There was not a soul. He began to look for the spot where Ovdokim buried money and ingots of silver but he did not find the treasure.

The forest was yellow and red; gossamer threads floated in the air; withered leaves fluttered down. Judas felt sick at heart. He collected some dry crusts and started off he knew not whither; perhaps to Moscow. And immediately beyond the marsh, in the pine forests, he stumbled across one of his comrades, Fedor Fedorov, one of Narishkin's bonded peasants.

Fedor was a quiet man with a large family. He worked under the heavy burden of his quit-rent as resignedly as a horse, and it could be said that he fed his numerous progeny with his body. What led him into trouble was that drink went to his head, and then he would go about the village with a stake and threaten to break the Narishkin steward in two. Whether it was he who killed the steward, or some other man, Fedor swore to his children before God that he was innocent and ran away. And now he was hanging from a pine-branch, his arms tied behind his back and his head twisted to one side. Judas did not try to look at his face. "Ah, friend, friend!" he said and wept, and left those parts, keeping to the thickets.

19

If the upper boyars, who pondered on State affairs in the Tsar's Council in the Kremlin, still hoped to live somehow—"the young Tsar will sow his wild oats, things will straighten out, there's no need to worry, for no matter what happens, the peasants will always feed us"; if, in Preobrazhensk, Peter, in company with all kinds of new greedy men, merchants and nobles, who had traded their ancestors' honour for a curly wig, was now quite unrestrainedly exhausting the treasury on military and other games, on the building of ships, on soldiers' quarters and palaces for his favourites, and was lightheartedly and unashamedly amusing himself; if the State was creaking as of old like a cart stuck in a bog, affairs in the West—in Venice, in the Roman Empire and in Poland—had taken such a turn that the torpor and duplicity of Moscow could no longer be tolerated.

The Swedes were masters of the North Sea and the Turks of the Mediterranean, with the secret support of the French king. The Turkish fleet seized Venetian trading vessels. Turkish janissaries were devastating Hungary. The Crimean Tatars, vassals of the Sultan, roamed over the southern steppes of Poland. But the Moscow government, pledged by treaty to fight Tatar and Turk, merely wrote notes, procrastinated and made excuses: "Twice we sent armies to the Crimea, but our allies gave no support, and this year's harvest is poor; it is better to wait till next year. We do not refuse to fight, but we are waiting for you yourselves to begin, and we swear we shall support you."

The Crimean Khan's envoys were in Moscow, distributing lavish gifts to the boyars, trying to persuade them to conclude a perpetual peace with the Crimea, swearing never to raid Russian territory or to demand the former humiliating tribute. Leo Narishkin wrote to the Russian envoys in Vienna, Cracow and Venice, instructing them not to trust the promises of emperor, king or doge and to be vague in their commitments. This procrastination had been going on for over two years. The Turks threatened to put the whole of Poland to fire and sword, and to hoist the crescent over Vienna and Venice. At last the emperor's envoy, Johann Curtius, arrived in Moscow from Vienna. The boyars were alarmed; some decision had to be made. They received him with great pomp, drove him to the Kremlin, housed him in a luxurious suite and allotted for his maintenance twice as much as other envoys; and then they began to temporise, lie and delay, on the excuse that the Tsar was away at manœuvres and they could settle nothing without him.

But all the same they were forced to negotiate. Curtius pinned them down to the old treaty and succeeded in making them decide for war and kiss the cross on it. Then he departed, overjoyed. The Roman Emperor and the Polish King sent letters of thanks in which Peter was styled "Majesty" and accorded his full titles, even to "lord of the lands of Iberia, Georgia, Kabarda and the provinces Dedich and Otchich". After that they managed to procrastinate again for a time, but it was already clear that war was inevitable.

20

After carnival week, when the Lenten chimes sounded over Moscow, stilled now in the soft dawn, talk about war sprang up in all the market-places, suburbs and settlements. It was as though overnight someone had whispered to the people: "There will be war, and we will get something out of it. If the Crimea becomes ours, we shall be able to trade with the whole world. The sea is immense; there no tax-collector's agent will poke into a man's cheek to get at his kopek."

Peasant-farmers and petty landowners, sunk to peasants' condition, who brought in grain-waggons from Voronezh, Kursk and Belgorod, said that in the steppes the people were eagerly waiting for war with the Tatars. "Our steppe stretches for thousands of versts to the South and East. The steppe is like a woman in her prime: only touch her, and we'd be up to our necks in wheat. The Tatars won't let us. And how many of our people have been carried off to captivity into the Crimea! Oh! And the freedom of the steppes, that's real freedom! Not to be compared to what you people have here in Moscow."

More than anywhere else the war was argued about and discussed among Peter's entourage. Many were against it: "We don't need the Black Sea. You can't sell timber, tar or blubber to the Turks or to Venice. We must conquer the northern seas." But the military, especially the younger ones, were heartily in favour of the war. That autumn they had marched with two armies to the village of Kozhuhovo and there, as they had not done in previous years, they had fought according to all the rules of military science. The foreigners said that the Lefort and Butyrsky regiments, the Preobrazhensky and Semenovsky play-battalions, now given the title of Life Guards, were not inferior to the Swedes or the French. But the glory of the Kozhuhov campaign could be vaunted only at festive tables, to the sound of toasts, kettledrums and gunfire salutes. People shouted after officers in raven-black wigs, silk scarves that swept the ground and enormous spurs: "Kozhuhov heroes! You're brave enough fighting with paper cannon balls. Try what a Tatar bullet tastes like!"

Only those belonging to Peter's most intimate circle felt hesitant: Romodanovsky, Artamon Golovin, Apraxin, Gordon, Vinius, Alexander Menshikov. To them the undertaking seemed formidable. What if they were defeated? In that case no one would escape destruction; the outraged mob would sweep them all out of existence. But not to go to war would be even worse, for already there were murmurs that the Tsars had been enticed by the foreigners: they'd poisoned their minds, a mint of money was being spent on frivolities, the people were suffering, and no great deeds were forthcoming.

Peter kept his own counsel and gave ambiguous replies to the talk of war: "All right, all right! We've had our fun at Kozhuhovo, now we'll go and play with the Tatars." Only Lefort and Menshikov knew that secretly Peter felt fear, the same fear as during the memorable night of the flight to Troitsa. But they also knew that nevertheless he would make up his mind to fight.

Two dark-visaged monks brought a letter from Dosivius, Patriarch of Jerusalem. The Patriarch wrote in plaintive terms that a French envoy had arrived in Adrianople with a letter from the King concerning the Holy Places. He had made a gift of seventy thousand pieces of gold to the Grand Vizier, and ten thousand to the Khan of Crimea who happened to be in Adrianople at the time, asking the Turks to give the Holy Places to the French. "And the Turks have taken the Holy Tomb from us, the Orthodox, and have given it to the French. The French have taken from us half of Golgotha, the whole church of Bethlehem and the Holy Cave; they have destroyed all the ancient groups of images, dug up the hall where we distribute the holy light, and have done worse things in Jerusalem than the Persians or the Arabs ever did. If you, the anointed Autocrats of Moscow, forsake the Holy Church, how will your names be revered? Force the Turks to return the Holy Places to the Orthodox; make no peace with them unless they do so. Should they refuse, make war on them. It is a propitious moment: the Sultan has three great armies fighting in Hungary against the Emperor. Take the Ukraine, and then Moldavia and Wallachia. Take also Jerusalem and only then conclude peace. Did you not pray to God that there should be war between the Turks and Tatars and the Emperor? Now the time is favourable, yet you hold back! See how the Muslims laugh at you: the Tatars, they say, are the pride of the people and boast that they make you pay tribute; and the Tatars are vassals of the Turks, hence it follows that you too are subject to the Turk."

It was humiliating to read this letter in Moscow. The Great Council of boyars assembled. Peter sat on the throne, silent and sombre, in royal robes and regalia. The boyars relieved their feelings in florid speeches, quoting ancient chronicles and bewailing the desecration of the Holy Places. Already the night showed deep blue in the windows, the lamps in the icon corner lit up their faces, and still the boyars, rising in order of rank and birth, threw back their heavy sleeves and talked and talked, gesturing with their white fingers. Their proud foreheads, beaded with sweat, their stern eyes, their well-groomed beards and empty speeches, which beat the air like the sails of a toy windmill in the wind, filled Peter with bored distaste. None of them spoke directly of war, but all, glancing from time to time at Vinius, the clerk of the council, who with two scribes was recording the speeches, kept beating about the bush. They feared to say the word—war—and shatter their peaceful existence. It might lead once more to rebellion and ruin. They were waiting for the Tsar's word, and it was clear that his decision would be theirs.

But Peter too felt awed at the thought of taking the responsibility for so momentous a decision: he was still young and had had fear driven into him from childhood. He waited, and screwed up his eyes. At last the boyars of his intimate circle began to speak and in a different tone, straight to the point. Tihon Streshnev said:

"Of course, it is for the Tsar to decide. But we, boyars, must give our lives for the Sepulchre of our Lord that has been profaned, and for the honour of the Tsar. They are mocking us in Jerusalem, could shame go deeper? No, boyars, prepare to summon the militia."

The slow-witted Leo Narishkin began with the conversion of Russia under Vladimir but, after a glance at Peter's wry face, made a gesture of acceptance:

"After all, boyars, we have nothing to fear. Vasily Golitsin burnt his fingers in the Crimea. But how was his militia armed? With staves! Now, praise be to God, we have arms enough. Take my factory in Tula: we make cannon as fine as the Turkish ones, and as for muskets and pistols, mine are better. If the Tsar commands, by May I can supply spear points and swords for a hundred thousand. No, we cannot draw back from war."

Romodanovsky cleared his throat and said:

"If we were living in isolation, we would think twice about it. But Europe has its eyes on us. If we mark time, ruin is inevitable. These are not the days of Gostomysl, cruel times are before us. And our first task is to beat the Tatars."

There was silence under the low red vaults. Peter bit his nails. Boris Golitsin entered—cheerful, clean-shaven, but in Russian dress —and handed Peter an open scroll. It was a petition from the merchants of Moscow, praying Peter to protect Golgotha and the Holy Sepulchre, to clear the southern routes of Tatars, and, if possible, to build towns on the Black Sea. Vinius, pushing his glasses on to his forehead, read the document in a clear voice. Peter rose, and the Monomach cap on his head touched the canopy:

"Well, boyars, what is your decision?"

And he looked harshly at them with his lips tightly pursed.

The boyars rose and bowed:

"May it please Your Majesty, summon the militia!"

21

"Tsigan, listen to me."

"Well?"

"Tell him you were my assistant in the smithy. And kiss the cross on that."

"Is it worth while?"

"Of course. We'll live some time yet. It's a wonderful piece of luck!"

"I'm tired of it all, Kuzma. I'd rather they finished us off, the sooner the better."

"Finish us off? You can whistle for that. They'll tear your nostrils, flog you to the bone and send you to Siberia."

"Yes—perhaps—it couldn't be worse."

"Leo Narishkin's steward went to Moscow and got an order to search for useful men in the prisons and take them to his factory. And this is just the thing for me, so I got talking. They still remember me. Ah, my dear fellow, Kuzma Zhemov won't be forgotten so soon. They fed me, gave me cabbage soup with meat, and treated me well: no beating, though they spoke sternly. When they call you, just say you worked for me as a hammerman."

Tsigan and Zhemov were holding this conversation in the basement of the Tula prison. They had been there for nearly a month already. So far they had only been beaten once, when they were caught in the market-place with stolen clothes. Judas had managed to get away. They were expecting to be questioned and tortured. But the governor of Tula, with his clerks and scribes, had himself come under investigation. The prisoners were forgotten. Every morning the guard led them, with their feet shackled in wooden blocks, to beg alms in the market-place. In this way they fed themselves and also the guard. And then—out of the blue—they were to be sent to Leo Narishkin's munition factory instead of to Siberia. At least their nostrils would be safe.

Tsigan, when questioned, said what Zhemov had told him to say. From the prison they were taken, still in fetters, beyond the town to the river Upa. There on the bank stood low brick buildings surrounded by a palisade; in a stream, fed by the river, the wheels of water-mills creaked. It was chilly and thunderclouds trailed from the North. On the clay bank a crowd of convicts was unloading firewood, pig-iron and ore from boats. All round there were tree-stumps, bare bushes, lifeless fields. An autumn wind blew. Tsigan's single eye glowered with resentment as they approached the iron-studded gates guarded by watchmen with halberds. It wasn't enough that they had beaten him, chased him like a wild beast over the land, shaken the soul out of his body, that wasn't enough for them! He had to work for them, to work! They wouldn't even let him die.

They were led through the gates into a black yard, cluttered with iron. A rumbling clatter, the rasping of saws, the clang of hammers resounded. Through a smoke-blackened door they could see sparks flying from the forge; men, bare to the waist, swinging their hammers in a great arc were forging a bar; a sledge-hammer, weighing many hundreds of pounds and worked by the mill-wheel, fell on a pig and the scale pattered on to leather aprons. Along boards laid from the gates on to the roof of the squat furnace wheelbarrows trundled with coal, and flames and black smoke belched from the furnace. Zhemov kept nudging Tsigan:

"I'll show them who Kuzma Zhemov is!"

At some distance from the forges stood a neat brick house. A clean-shaven face, pink as though after a steam bath, and topped by a knitted cap, was looking out of a window. This was the manager of the factory, the German, Kleist. He knocked his pipe on the pane. The guard hastily led Tsigan and Zhemov to the window and explained who they were and where they had come from. Kleist raised the lower sash and poked his head out, pursing his lips. The tassel of his cap dangled over his fat face. Tsigan gazed at the tassel with fear and hostility. "Oh, the bloodsucker!" he thought to himself.

Behind Kleist he could see a clean table on which stood roast meat, crusty rolls and a gilt cup with coffee. The pleasant smoke of the pipe crept out of the window. Kleist's eyes, as unfeeling as ice, bored into the very souls of the Russians. Having looked his fill at the two convicts, he said slowly in broken Russian:

"Those who cheat come to a bad end. They send useless peasants, sons of pigs. They don't know how to do anything, the scoundrels. If you are a good smith, very well. But if you are deceiving me, I shall hang you." He rapped his pipe on the windowsill. "Yes, I can hang people too, the law allows it. Guard, take the fools and lock them up."

On the way the guard admonished them:

"Look, fellows, you've got to be careful with him. For the slightest fault—oversleeping or laziness—he shows no mercy."

"We haven't come to gape," Zhemov said. "We'll teach even your German something."

"What kind of men are you? I heard tell you were thieves and robbers. What did they get you for?"

"We, Christian soul, were making our way with this one-eyed fellow to the dissenters, for a holy life, but the devil led us into temptation."

"Oh, well, that's different," the guard replied, unlocking the padlock on a low door. "I'll tell you the way things are done here, so that you'll know. . . . Come on, I'll light a candle." They went down into a basement. The narrow beams of light shining through the holes in the iron lantern stole over bunks, plank tables, a smoke-blackened stove and ragged clothing hanging on lines. "This is the order of things: in the morning, at four o'clock I beat the drum—prayers, then off to work. At seven—drum—breakfast—half an hour. I've got the time on me, see." He pulled out a brass watch the size of a large turnip and showed it to the two men. "Then to work again. At noon—dinner and an hour's sleep. At seven supper—half an hour—and at ten knock off."

"And they don't overstrain themselves?" Tsigan asked.

"Of course it does happen. But, my good fellow, this is penal servitude. If you hadn't done any thieving, you'd be lying on the stove at home. We've got fifteen free men here, hired workers; they knock off at seven and sleep in separate quarters, and on feast days they go home."

"And what then?" Tsigan asked in a still hoarser voice, sitting on a bunk. "Is this to be our lot for ever?"

Zhemov, staring at the bright holes of the round lantern, broke into a shallow cough. The guard muttered something in his moustache. As he went he took the lantern with him.

22

His respectable beard, streaked with grey, was neatly combed, his hair greased with butter, a silk sash with the names of forty saints woven into it, was tied round his pink shirt under his nipples. But it was not at this, it was at Ivan Artemyich Brovkin's belly, round and well-fed to repleteness, that the peasants—his former kinsmen, associates and companions—stared. Former ones: that's what made all the difference. Ivan Brovkin sat on the bench with his hands tucked under him. His eyes were stern and unblinking; he wore trousers of fine cloth and boots patterned in leather of different colours, of Kazan workmanship, with curved toes. The peasants stood by the door on a new bast mat so as not to mark the clean floor with their birch-bark shoes.

"Well," said Brovkin, "I'm no enemy of yours. What I can do, I do, but what I can't you mustn't hold against me."

"We've nowhere to let so much as a chicken out, Ivan Artemyich."

"You can't reason with cattle; it strays and gets into your hayfield."

"We'll get the whole village to whip the shepherd, have no fear."

"Well and good," Brovkin said.

"Please, let the cattle go."

"We're so cramped, so cramped. . . ."

"I get little profit from you, peasants," Brovkin replied and, pulling his hands from under his seat, he folded them on his belly. "I like order, peasants. The amount of money I've distributed among you . . ."

"You have, Ivan Artemyich, we don't forget it."

"All out of kindness, because I'm a native of these parts, and my father died here. As God is my benefactor, so I am yours, the interest I take from you is trifling. Ten kopeks on a rouble a year, yes, yes, yes. It's not for gain, but for good order."

"Thank you, Ivan Artemyich."

"Soon I'll be leaving you altogether. I'm starting big business, big business. I'll be living in Moscow. Well, all right." He sighed and closed his eyes. "If I had to live only on what I get from you, I'd lead a miserable life. For old times' sake, for the sake of my soul, I act as your benefactor. But you? How do you show your gratitude? Your cattle stray into my hay-fields. And the pettifogging. Oh! Well, all right, I'll let you off this time. Three kopeks for each cow, half a kopek for each sheep. Take away your cattle."

"Thank you! May God grant you health, Ivan Artemyich!"

The peasants bowed and left. Today he felt kindly disposed and wanted to go on talking. Through his son Alioshka he had been able to reach Lieutenant Alexander Menshikov and make him a present of two hundred roubles. Menshikov arranged for him to meet Lefort. Brovkin had never yet moved in such high circles. He felt quite shy when he saw a small man with hair down to his waist, dressed in silk and velvet, with sparkling rings on his fingers. He looked severe, with his turned-up nose and eyes as sharp as needles. But when Lefort learnt that the man was Alioshka's father, and that he had a letter of introduction from Menshikov, he broke into a smile and tapped him on the shoulder. That was how Ivan Brovkin obtained an order to supply oats and hay to the army.

"Sanka," he called when the peasants had gone, "take the bast mat away. My kinsmen have muddied it."

Good-humoured wrinkles fanned out round his eyes. A rich man could afford to laugh: he had not had a chance to laugh from his childhood until now, when his beard had turned grey. Sanka came in, dressed in a grass-green silk gown with wide sleeves and buttons. Her ash-blond plait, as thick as her arm, reached down to her knees; she walked with her stomach slightly forward, ashamed that her breasts had grown so full. Her dark-blue eyes looked stupid.

"Pah, the mud they've brought in on their feet!" She turned her face away from the mat, picked it up gingerly by the corner and threw it out into the passage. Ivan Brovkin watched his daughter slyly. A girl like that was a fitting match for a king.

"I want to build a stone house in Moscow. We're going to be among the first hundred merchants. Listen, Sanka. You see what a good thing it was not to have been in a hurry about you. We're going to have fine relations. Why d'you turn away? Fool!"

"Yes, ah!" Sanka swished her plait and flashed her eyes at her father. "Don't you touch me."

"What d'you mean, not touch you? I'm the one to decide. If you anger me, I'll marry you off to a shepherd."

"I'd rather look after pigs than wither away because of your foolishness."

Brovkin threw a wooden salt-cellar at Sanka. He was too lazy to get up and give her a beating. Sanka began to wail tearlessly. At this moment there came such loud knocking on the gates that Ivan Brovkin gaped. The mastiffs set up a howl.

"Sanka, go and see what it is."

"I'm afraid. Go yourself."

"I'll show them how to knock!" Ivan Brovkin picked up a broom in the passage and went down into the courtyard. "I'll show you, you shameless fellows! Who's there? I'll let the dogs loose."

"Open!" came furious cries from outside the gates, and the timbers creaked.

Brovkin was frightened. He stumbled to the wicket-gate, his hands trembling. The minute he pulled the bar loose, the gates flew open and a group of horsemen rode in, richly dressed, carrying naked swords. Behind them came a gilt carriage drawn by four horses, with black dwarfs on the footboard behind it. The carriage was followed by a one-horse chaise in which sat the Tsar and Lefort, in three-cornered hats and coarse coats to shield them from the mud-splashes. There were stamping, laughter, shouting. . . .

Brovkin's legs gave way. While he remained on his knees, the horsemen dismounted and Zotov, the Prince-Pope, bloated, sleepy, dressed in foreign clothes, followed by a young boyar in a silver coat, got out of the carriage. Peter mounted the porch with Lefort and shouted in a deep voice:

"Where's the master of the house? Bring him here, dead or alive!"

Ivan Brovkin wetted his trousers. At this moment the others caught sight of him, rushed up to him—they were Menshikov and his own son Alioshka—lifted him up under his arms and dragged him to the porch. They kept holding him up so that he should not kneel again. Instead of a beating, or something even worse, Peter took off his hat and bowed low to him:

"Greetings, good friend! We've heard that you have some handsome goods. We've brought a merchant. We won't haggle over the price."

Brovkin opened his mouth but no sound came. Wild thoughts

crowded through his mind: had some trickery of his come to light? He must keep his mouth shut, say nothing. . . . The Tsar and Lefort burst into laughter, and the others also laughed until they choked. Alioshka managed to whisper to his father: "They've come to arrange a match for Sanka." Although Ivan guessed from the laughter that the company's arrival portended no evil, he continued to play the fool. He was a mighty clever fellow. So he accompanied his guests into the parlour as if driven out of his wits with fear. They seated him under the icons, with the Tsar on his right and Zotov on his left. From between his narrowed lids he stole glances to make out who was the suitor. And suddenly he became genuinely terrified: between the two groomsmen—Alioshka and Menshikov—there sat his former master, Vasily Volkov, dressed in a silver coat. Ivan Artemyich had long since paid off his bond-titles and today could have bought Volkov up with all his estates and serfs. But it was not in his mind that the fear was born, it was in his flogged behind.

"Don't you like the suitor?" Peter asked suddenly.

There was another burst of laughter. Volkov's lips twisted wryly under his turned-up moustache. Menshikov winked at Peter:

"Maybe he's remembered some old hurt?" He winked at Brovkin. "Maybe there was a time when the suitor pulled you by the hair? Or broke his whip handle on you? Forgive him as a good Christian! Make it up, you two."

What was there to reply? His arms and legs trembled. He looked at Volkov who sat pale and humbly resigned. And then he suddenly remembered how, in the yard at Preobrazhensk, Alioshka had come to his rescue and how Volkov had run over the snow after Menshikov, begging him, catching him by the sleeve, nearly crying.

"Oho!" Ivan Artemyich thought to himself. "It looks as though I'm not the biggest fool here." He glanced at Volkov and so great was his delight that he nearly spoilt the whole business. But he already knew what was expected of him: a dangerous game, crossing an abyss on a tight-rope. All right, then.

All eyes were fixed on him. Ivan Artemyich secretly made the sign of the cross over his navel under the table and bowed to Peter and to the Prince-Pope:

"Thank you for the honour, gentlemen matchmakers. Forgive me, a village fool, for the love of Christ, if unwittingly I have failed in something towards you. I am, of course, a tradesman, a rough peasant, unlearned in manners. I speak simply. The trouble is, my daughter's quite an old maid. I'd be glad to marry her off to the worst of drunkards." He stole a terrified glance at Peter, but all was well: the Tsar snorted with laughter like a spitting cat. "I can't understand why suitors pass my house by. She's a pretty girl, except that she's somewhat blind in one eye, but the other is all right. And then her face is a bit pock-marked, but she can cover it up with a handkerchief." Volkov fixed a sombre eye on Ivan Artemyich. "Then she drags her leg a little, and her head trembles and her hip is a bit crooked. But that's all. Take my dear child, kind matchmakers." Brovkin had entered into his part so well that he sniffed and wiped his eyes. "Alexandra, my child!" he called in a weak voice, "come out here! Alioshka, go, fetch your sister! Perhaps she's in the privy, her insides are ailing, I forgot to mention it, forgive me. Go, bring the girl!"

Volkov made a violent movement to leave the table, but Menshikov forced him back. Nobody laughed, only Peter's chin was trembling.

"Thank you, dear matchmakers," Brovkin said. "I like your suitor very much. I'll be a true father to him: treat him kindly when he's good and beat him when he's at fault. If I give you the taste of my whip or catch you by the hair, don't take it amiss, dear son-in-law; it's a peasant family you'll be marrying into."

Everyone at the table roared with laughter and held their sides. Volkov set his teeth; shame made his cheeks burn and brought tears into his eyes. Alioshka dragged in the resisting Sanka from the passage. She covered her face with her sleeve. Peter jumped up and pulled her hands away. The laughter ceased, so lovely did Sanka seem to them all: eyebrows like arrows, blue eyes, curling eyelashes, a tip-tilted nose; her childish lips were trembling, her even teeth chattered and her cheeks were as rosy as an apple. Peter kissed her on the lips, on her hot cheeks.

"Sanka, it's the Tsar himself. Let him!" Brovkin cried.

She lifted up her head and looked Peter in the face. He could feel her heart thumping. He put an arm round her shoulders, led her up to the table and pointed a finger at Vasily Volkov:

"Well, how do you like the suitor we've brought you?"

Sanka lost her head entirely. Instead of shrinking bashfully, as custom demanded, she stared like a wild thing at her suitor. Suddenly she sighed and whispered: "Oh, my goodness!" Peter caught hold of her again and started to kiss her.

"Eh, friend matchmaker, you shouldn't do that," the Prince-Pope said. "Let the girl go."

Sanka hid her face in her skirt, and Alioshka, laughing, took her away. Volkov was fingering his moustache, evidently much relieved in his mind. The Prince-Pope broke into a nasal chant:

"Being in our father Bacchus, brothers, let us love one another. We beg for wine and a snack."

Ivan Brovkin hastily recollected himself and began to bustle about. In the yard servants chased chickens. Alioshka, with an apologetic smile, laid the table. Sanka's voice, breaking with emotion, was heard calling: "Matrena, take the keys; in the parlour, under the Forty Martyrs." Peter shouted to Volkov: "Give thanks for the girl, Vaska!" And Volkov, with a bow, kissed his hand. Ivan Brovkin himself brought in a frying-pan with fried eggs. Peter said to him earnestly:

"Thanks for the entertainment; you gave us a good laugh. But, Vanka, know your place, don't presume."

"Sire, would I have dared if you hadn't wished it so? As it is, my heart's long been in my boots with fear."

"Well, well, I know you devils. And don't delay the wedding: the bridegroom will be off to the wars soon. Hire a girl from the Foreign Quarter to teach your daughter etiquette and dancing. When we get back from the campaign, I'll take Sanka to court."

chapter six

In February, 1695, Vinius, clerk of the boyars' council, announced from the Kremlin porch to all the courtiers, Tsar's attendants, lawyers, Moscow nobles and those of other towns that they were to foregather with their men-at-arms and bodyguards in the towns of Belgorod and Sevsk and report to the boyar Boris Petrovich Sheremetev for active service in the Crimea.

Sheremetev was an experienced and cautious general. Having assembled an army a hundred and twenty thousand strong and joined up with the Ukrainian Cossacks, he slowly moved to the lower reaches of the Dniepr. There stood the ancient fortress of Ochakov and the small fortified Turkish towns of Kizikerman, Arslan-Ordek and Shahkerman; and, on an island in the estuary of the Dniepr, a fort known as the Falcon castle, from which iron chains stretched to each bank to prevent access to the sea.

The enormous Moscow army, having come up to these towns, spent the whole summer attacking them. Money, arms and cannon were short and the correspondence with Moscow over every detail was slow. Nevertheless, in August, Kizikerman and two other small towns were taken by assault. To mark the occasion there was a great feast in Sheremetev's camp. With every toast drunk, guns fired in the trenches, driving fear into the Turks and Tatars. When the news of the victory reached Moscow, there was a sigh of relief: "At last! Even if it's only a small piece wrested from the Crimea, it's something."

That same spring, without any public announcement, twenty thousand of the best troops—the Preobrazhensky, Semenovsky and Lefort's regiments, streltsi, town militiamen and companies made up of clerks—embarked on barges, galleys and boats at the All-Saints' bridge on the Moskva river. The convoy extended over many miles, and it went off to the sound of music and gunfire towards the Oka and thence, by way of the Volga, to Tsaritsin.*

General Gordon, with twelve thousand men, moved across the steppe to Cherkassk.

Both armies were making for the Turkish fortress of Azov, on the Sea of Azov. Here the Turks held the key to all the trade-routes to the East and to the rich cornfields of the Kuban and Terek steppes. The diversion directed against Azov had been decided on at a War Council of the three commanders—Lefort, Gordon and Golovin—and Peter. To avoid publicity and over-much honour to the Turks Peter was known in the army as Bombardier Peter Alexeyev. Thus the humiliation would be less in case of failure. The Council discussed at length whom to leave in authority in Moscow. The people were restless. Brigandage was rife even near the capital, and travel was so perilous that the roads were overgrown with grass. That terrible adversary, Sophia, was in the Novodevichy convent, silent and inactive at the moment, but how long would she remain so?

There was only one man who could be relied on implicitly, a man who was wholeheartedly loyal and who alone could put fear into the people: Fedor Yurievich Romodanovsky, the ex-king of the mock wars and of the All-Fools' council. Moscow was put in his charge. And so that people should not laugh at him up their sleeves for bygone follies, it was ordered that he be given in full earnest the titles of Prince-Emperor and Majesty. The boyars recalled a similar case a hundred years ago, when Ivan the Terrible, having left for Alexandrovsky village, had set up over Moscow a half-jester, half-bogy—the Tatar Prince Simeon Bekbulayevich—as "Tsar of All Russia". They recalled it and submitted. As for the people, it was all one to them, whether it was the Prince-Emperor or the devil; they knew only that Romodanovsky was merciless and did not fear bloodshed.

Bombardier Peter Alexeyev sailed at the head of the flotilla in Lefort's many-oared galley. They had plenty of trouble on the way. The boats and tenders, built by merchants and government trading agents, leaked and sank. In the misty spring nights they lost their way on the flooded fields and shoals. In Nizhni-Novgorod the troops

* Now Stalingrad.

had to re-embark on Volga barges. Peter wrote to Romodanovsky:

"*Mein Herr König,* for your Royal Majesty we must shed our blood to the last drop, which is why we have been sent. About things here I inform you that your slaves, the generals Golovin and Lefort, with all the troops, are, thank the Lord, in good health. And tomorrow we intend to resume our voyage. The cause for the delay was that some of the boats took three days to get here. The boats built by the merchants are very bad, and some of them barely managed to make the journey. Of the men under arms only a small number have died. I herewith put myself under the protection of your generosity. Ever the slave of your serene Majesty, Bom Bar Dier Peter."

The expedition sailed without stopping past Kazan, its white walls lapped by the flooded waters; past Simbirsk on the steep bank of the river; past the small town of Samara, surrounded by a wooden palisade reinforced with earthen glacis to protect it from nomad tribes. Beyond Saratov the grassy banks were veiled in a sunlit haze, and the blue river flowed sluggishly; the hot breath of the steppe was like that of a furnace.

Peter, Lefort, Alexander and Zotov—who had been taken along for fun and drinking-bouts—spent their days smoking on the high poop of the galley. When they looked at the long flotilla of vessels, gleaming with the splashing of oars, it seemed like a continuation of the jolly days of mock wars. What kind of fortress was Azov? And how were they to take it? No one quite knew, but they would see when they got there. Zotov, drunk and maudlin, said, as he pulled the peeling skin off his purple nose:

"We've lived to see this at last, my son. . . . It seems not so long ago that I was teaching you arithmetic. Now we're going to the war. Oh, my fine lad!"

Lefort admired the beauty and majesty of the river that seemed limitless.

"Who cares about the King of France or the Emperor of Austria?" he said. "Oh, Peter, if only you had more money! If we could hire engineers in Europe, more officers, men with brains. What a great country, what a wild, empty land!"

The flotilla came to a halt at Tsaritsin. And here trouble began. Only five hundred horses were found. The soldiers, worn out at the oars, had to haul the cannon and the baggage-train. There was not enough bread, millet or oil. The tired, hungry troops marched three days over the steppe to the small town of Panshin on the Don where the main stores of provender were gathered. Many of them overstrained themselves and fell by the way. They had expected to rest in Panshin, but before they reached it a letter came from the boyar Tihon Streshnev, who was in charge of the provisioning of the entire army:

"Sir Bombardier! Terrible distress has been occasioned to us by the thieving contractors. The merchants Voronin, Ushakov and Gorezin had undertaken to deliver 15,000 buckets of mead, 45,000 buckets of vinegar and an equal amount of vodka, 20,000 salted sturgeon, and as many bream, pike and pike-perch, 360,000 pounds of ham, 180,000 pounds of oil and lard, and 29,000 pounds of salt. The contractors were given thirty-three thousand roubles. Half of this money they have stolen. There is not one pound of salt. The fish stinks so that one cannot enter the shed. All the wheat is stale. The only things that are good are the oats and the hay, which were delivered by the merchant Ivan Brovkin. This thieving is causing much distress to you, our gracious Sire, and privation to the soldiers. Now God alone can help you to avoid delays in your military undertaking."

Peter and Lefort, leaving the troops, galloped to Panshin. The small steppe village, on an island in the middle of the Don, was surrounded by raised waggon-shafts as by a fire-scorched forest. Everywhere big-horned oxen were lying and hobbled horses cropped the grass. But there was not a living soul anywhere: in the after-dinner hour everybody slept: sentries, watchmen, waggon drivers. The clatter of the hoofs of the riders' horses rang out, making a lonely sound over the Don. At Peter's furious shout a tousled head appeared out of the hemp, from behind a fence. Scratching himself, the peasant led them to the cottage where the boyar had his quarters. Peter tore the door open and was met by the buzz of disturbed flies. Streshnev was asleep on two benches pushed together, with a blanket pulled over his head. Peter wrenched the blanket away and seized the terrified boyar by his scanty hair. He was speechless with rage. He spat in the old man's face, pushed him down on the floor and kicked his flabby side with his jackboot.

Panting, Peter seated himself at the table and ordered the shutters to be opened. His eyes bulged and there were angry blotches under the tan of his thin face.

"Report! Get up!" he shouted at Streshnev. "Sit down! Have you hanged the contractors? No? Why?"

"Sire. . . ." Peter stamped his foot. "Sir Bombardier. . . ."

Streshnev was afraid to bow. "Let the contractors first deliver what they owe. How can we get anything from dead men?"

"No, you're wrong. You fool! Why doesn't Brovkin steal? My men don't steal, while all yours are thieves. All contracts are to be given to Brovkin. Ushakov and Voronin are to be sent in chains to Moscow, to Romodanovsky."

"That's right, *gut,*" Lefort approved.

"What else? Ships not ready?"

"Sir Bombardier, the ships are all ready. A short while ago the last were brought in from Voronezh."

"Let's go to the river."

Streshnev, in his soft morocco house boots and unbelted tunic, trotted feebly in the wake of the Tsar, who stalked along as though on stilts. On the mirror-calm bend of the Don innumerable vessels were riding at anchor in rows: tenders, barges, narrow Cossack boats with reed outriggers, long-prowed galleys, with oars only in the forepart, with a square sail and a cabin on the poop; all straight from the shipyard. They rocked gently on the current. Many were half swamped. The flags hung listlessly. In the heat of the sun the unpainted timber cracked and the tarred broadsides shone.

Lefort, with one foot in a yellow topboot planted forward, examined the flotilla through a telescope.

"*Sehr gut.* . . . There are enough ships."

"*Gut,*" Peter repeated abruptly. His grimy hands were shaking. And, as usual, Lefort voiced his thoughts:

"Here the war begins."

"Tihon Nikityevich, don't be angry," and Peter pecked Streshnev —who gave a low sob—on his beard. "The troops must embark straight away on to the boats. Without delay. We shall take Azov by storm."

On the sixth day, at dawn, wrapped in tobacco smoke in Streshnev's cottage, they wrote to Romodanovsky:

"*Mein Herr König,* your father, the Great Lord, the Most Holy Prince-Pope, Archbishop of Pressburg and Patriarch of all Yaouza and all Kukuy, as well as your slaves the generals Golovin and Lefort with their companions, are in good health and are leaving Panshin today. We ceaselessly labour in the service of Mars. And we drink your health in vodka, and even more in beer . . ." To this were appended the almost illegible signatures: "Franchishka Lefort. Olexashka Menshikov. Fetka Troyekurov. Petrushka Alexeyev. Artamoshka Golovin. Varenoy Madamkin."

For a whole week they sailed past small Cossack fortified towns on islets in the Don. They passed Goluboy, Zimoveysky, Tsymlyansky, Razdory, Manych. On the steep right bank they sighted the glacis, wattle-fences and oak walls of Cherkassk. Here they cast anchor and, for three days, waited for the tenders that had fallen behind to catch up.

Having re-assembled the convoy, they pushed on towards Azov. The night was warm, pitch dark, and there was a smell of rain and grasses. Crickets chirred. Nightbirds sent up weird cries. On Lefort's leading galley nobody slept, there was no smoking and no joking. The oars splashed in slow rhythm.

For the first time in his life Peter felt the dread of danger with every inch of his skin. Darkness and vague outlines moved close by along the bank. He peered, and his ear caught the sound of rustling leaves. At any moment in the darkness out there the string of a Tatar bow might twang. His toes curled. Far to the south a stormy light flashed in the clouds but the sound of the thunder did not reach him.

"In the morning we'll hear General Gordon's guns," said Lefort.

The sky cleared towards morning. The Cossack helmsman steered the galley down the river Koysoga and the rest of the convoy followed. They left the Don on their right. The hot sun rose, the river seemed to become fuller, the banks receded and the darkness melted away over the water-meadows. Ahead, the gleaming ribbon of the Don re-appeared beyond the sands. On the slopes they could see canvas tents, carts, horses. Flags fluttered. This was the main military camp set up by General Gordon—Mitishi Landing—nine miles from Azov.

Peter himself fired the gun on the prow, and the cannon-ball skittered along the water. The gunfire of muskets and cannon crashed from the whole flotilla. Peter cried in a breaking bass: "Row! Row!" The oars bent under the efforts of the soldiers, who rowed with bowed heads.

The troops disembarked at Mitishi Landing. The weary soldiers fell asleep on the sand and the non-commissioned officers roused them with their sticks. Soon white tents were put up and the smoke of camp-fires trailed towards the river. Peter, Lefort and Golovin, with three Cossack squadrons, galloped off beyond the hills to Gordon's fortified camp, half-way to Azov. The general's many-coloured tent, pitched on an ancient burial mound, was visible from afar.

Carcases of horses, pierced by arrows, and broken carts lay on the way. A small Tatar, bare to the waist, with blood on the nape of his neck, was lying with his face buried in the wormwood. Peter's mount whinnied and shied. The Cossacks said:

"As soon as our supply-trains leave Mitishi, the Tatars let fly clouds of arrows. This is the worst place. Look," they pointed with their whips, "there they are, moving beyond the hills. It's they. Look out, they'll be sending their arrows over at any moment now."

The riders pressed on towards the mound. Gordon stood by his tent. He was wearing a steel cuirass and a plumed helmet and held his telescope with one end resting on his hip. His wrinkled face was stern and proud. Horns sounded and cannon fired. From the mound they had a clear view of the bay lit up by the setting sun, of the slender minarets and grey-yellow walls of Azov, of the charred remains of the suburb which the Turks had burnt down at the approach of the Russians, and of the broken lines of the trenches and the pentagons of redoubts that stretched along the low hills in front of the fortress. In the far stretches of the calm bay tall ships with many guns were riding at anchor with slack sails. Gordon pointed to them:

"Last week the Turks brought in fifteen hundred janissaries by sea from Kafa. Today these ships also brought in troops. Yesterday we took a prisoner: I don't know whether he is lying or not, but he says they've got six thousand men in the fort and the Tatar cavalry in the steppe. They lack nothing: the sea is theirs. The fort can't be starved out."

"We'll take it by storm," Lefort said with a wave of his glove.

"We'll make short work of it. There's nothing to it," Golovin added with assurance.

Peter gazed enthralled at the expanse of the Azov Sea, at the walls, the tiny gleams of the crescents on the minarets, the ships, the splendour of the sunset. The favourite pictures of his childhood seemed to him to have come alive—here it was—tangible and real: the unknown land!

"Well, and what do you think, Gordon? Why don't you say anything? Shall we take Azov?"

"We must take it," Gordon replied, sternly wrinkling his lips.

A map was brought from the tent and spread on a drum. The generals bent over it. Peter marked with his nail the places where the troops were to be deployed: Gordon in the centre, about five hundred paces from the fort; Lefort on his left, Golovin on his right.

"Here, the siege-guns; there, the mortars. From here we'll start the approach works. Is that the way, Gordon?"

"We can do it like that; why not?" Gordon replied. "But the Tatar cavalry would be at our rear."

"We must crush it. We'll throw the Cossacks against them."

"Yes, we could crush it. What I mean is, it will be difficult to bring up supplies from Mitishi Landing. It's difficult to escort each supply-train with a large force."

"Listen, Generals, why shouldn't we bring up supplies by boat?"

The generals bent over the map, the curls of their wigs dangling.

"It's still more difficult by boat," Gordon said. "The Don is barred by chains. There are two watch-towers at the mouth with very powerful artillery."

"Then the watch-towers must be taken! How about it, Generals?"

"What an undertaking, two watch-towers!" Golovin laughed and, narrowing his fine, rather stupid eyes, looked towards the top of a round crenellated tower that showed above the hills to the West.

"Why not? We could take them."

"Well, then, with God's help, Gordon," and Peter took him by the cheeks and kissed him, "tomorrow we'll start from the approaches towards the fort. And we shall come up with the whole army, without delay. We'll pepper them with bombs for a day or two and then—to the assault!"

The winding of a horn carried faintly from the Turkish ships: they were sounding the retreat. Evening shadows spread over the bay. The tops of the minarets glowed red, but soon they too faded. The only sound was the dry chirring of the crickets. Peter went into the tent where two lighted candles stood on a lavishly-spread table. They seated themselves on drums. A steaming dish of mutton was brought in and Peter greedily plunged both his hands into it.

Lefort, who had taken off his cuirass to enjoy himself in greater ease, poured Hungarian wine into the pewter goblets. When the red-faced Golovin shouted lustily: "To the First Bombardier!" the call ran from the tent into the darkness below along the thin line of soldiers: "A toast! A toast!" The candles trembled with the booming of the guns.

"Wonderful!" Peter cried.

Lefort laughed, filling the goblets:

"It's a wonderful life, Peter."

"Any *vivandières* in your camp, General?" Golovin asked, also unbuckling his cuirass.

Lefort and Peter broke out laughing:

"Varenoy Madamkin is the great expert."

"Send a messenger on horseback to fetch Varenoy."

In the morning, reinforced by two regiments of streltsi, Gordon moved towards Azov. The vanguard of a few companies of Cossacks cantered up the brown height in front of the fortress, and immediately began to rein in. Several of them galloped back to the infantry, which was advancing in four columns, shouting: "The Tatars! On your guard! Bring up the guns!"

The Tatar cavalry, some ten thousand strong, was deployed in a semi-circle to the left of the height. As they advanced, their speed increased, and the clouds of dust rose thicker. Arrows flew. The Cossack squadrons broke their ranks in confusion. Single horsemen, bending low in their saddles, turned and fled. In vain did their colonels order the standards to be waved: the whole Cossack force galloped down the slope without drawing sword. But the Tatars were already outflanking them from the right, their small shaggy horses stretched out at full gallop, and their curved swords whirling over their heads. They yelled. Dust rose. Part of the Cossacks turned to fight. The antagonists mingled and clashed. Infantry rushed up and formed square. Streltsi dragged up the cannon with ropes. The Tatar crescent was closing. Scattered volleys rang out. Layers of smoke obscured the heights. A maddened horse rushed past. A Tatar rolled on the ground. A cannon ball whizzed past. Volleys thundered. People fired and shouted frenziedly. Officers rushed about. The roar of the siege guns submerged all other sounds. No one could tell who was gaining the upper hand.

Then something happened and suddenly the fighting eased. The smoke rolled away, neither Turk nor Tatar was in sight. Only fallen horses were struggling on the ground, and a great number of human bodies, still or twitching, were strewn over the brown earth. In the fore, on a mound, General Gordon was seated on his black horse. His steel-clad back glinted. He held his telescope with one end resting on his hip. His small grey head looked like a ball above his cuirass. He had lost his helmet. He waved his sword slowly and began to walk his horse down the slope towards Azov. Shouts were raised from the ranks: "Forward! Forward! Courage!"

Gordon's detachment began to dig itself into trenches opposite the fortress and to set up stockades. The Turks fired guns from the walls at the camp, spreading great fear. When a bomb fell, hissing and whirling, commanders, officers, equerries and courtiers flung themselves on their faces and covered themselves with their arms. These were no mock bombs filled with peas; they burst with terrific noise, raising columns of earth. The soldiers paled and crossed themselves, incapable of doing anything else. Only Gordon, stern and calm, strode about the camp, never turning at the angry hiss of the cannonballs and, from time to time, shouted to the soldiers not to bow before the Turkish shells:

"Those who bow will be punished. Cowardice is evil. *Schande! Schande!* Shame! And you a Russian soldier. . . ."

As he had foretold, the provisioning of the camp was difficult, especially with drinking water. The Tatars made fierce raids, destroying the provision trains moving up from Mitishi Landing. It was impossible to overcome the light Tatar cavalry; they refused action, showered the Russians with arrows and galloped off into the steppe. At last the camp was completed and the men found shelter from bombs in deep trenches. Lefort's and Golovin's forces came to take up their positions only on the fourth day, with bands playing, drums beating and colours flying.

Peter strode proudly at the head of the gunners' detachment where, among the rank and file, were Menshikov, Alioshka Brovkin, Volkov and the Dutchman Jacob Jansen, an able gunner recently enlisted. An enormous fellow, with a bear's nose and thick lips, pranced in front of Peter, clashing brass cymbals. This was a new booncompanion of the Tsar: a cymbalist nicknamed Varenoy Madamkin, a debauchee and a drunkard of the first order.

Peter, with a number of bombardiers, went straight to Gordon's camp. Lefort's troops on the left flank and Golovin's on the right were hurriedly digging themselves in. Redoubts, surrounded by fascines and sacks of earth, were carried forward some five hundred paces towards the stone walls of the fortress, from whose crenels the fezzes and sharp eyes of the Turkish riflemen showed. Steadying himself with a hand on Alexander's shoulder, Peter sprang on to the fascines. Gordon clutched at him hastily:

"*Achtung!* Take care!"

The long barrel of a musket in a crenel spat fire and the telescope was knocked out of Peter's hand. He jumped down into the trench and bent low. Men crowded round him. He bared his teeth in a dry-lipped smile:

"The devil! The dogs!" he said, speaking with difficulty. "Give me the match!"

The gunners wheeled up a small brass mortar with its muzzle raised skyward. Peter, glancing at the men, skilfully loaded in the cartouche of powder, tossed the twenty pound ball, fixed the fuse and rolled it into the mortar. Then, squatting, he took aim:

"With God's blessing, the first! Stand aside!"

The mortar belched a flaming cloud. The round bomb rose in a sharp curve and fell near the fortress wall. The Turks leaned out of the crenels and shouted something insulting. Peter's face flushed. A second mortar was wheeled up for him.

Under Azov's high walls they were ashamed to recall their recent bravado, when they had talked of taking Azov by storm. The investing army, having completed its redoubts and batteries, bombed the fortress for a fortnight. Fires broke out in the town. One of the watch-towers crumbled, and the occasion was marked by noisy festivity in Peter's dug-out. But twenty galleys again brought reinforcements to the Turks from the sea. The fires were extinguished. At night, janissaries with curved daggers crawled like snakes to the Russian trenches and murdered the sentries. And the walls remained standing, hopelessly impregnable. Worst of all was the shortage of provisions. At a council the generals took the decision to call for volunteers, promising them ten roubles each for taking the watch-towers. About two hundred Don Cossacks volunteered and were given a regiment of soldiers as reinforcements. In the night, having crept up to the watch-tower on the left bank, the Cossacks tried to blow up the gates and, when this did not succeed, breached the wall with crowbars and broke in. Of the thirty Turks who formed the garrison, four were killed and the others tied up. Fifteen guns were captured and turned on the other watch-tower across the Don, to such good effect that the Turks abandoned it too. This was a great achievement: the Don was free. Thanksgiving services were held in the camps, and Zotov arrived from Mitishi for the feast.

But suddenly a great calamity occurred. The days were sultry. Towards noon the men wandered about in the sweltering heat, in search of shade. They did not feel like fighting, there was no warlike temper. Mess-tins with cabbage soup and dried fish were taken round and tots of vodka distributed. The fringed sun poured out unbearable heat, crickets shrilled, flies pestered, excrement stank, and the walls and towers of Azov seemed to quiver in the heat-haze. Following time-honoured custom everybody in the camp lay down to rest after dinner—the whole army, from general to army cook— and snored. The sentries also nodded.

During one of these sleepy hours Jacob Jansen, the Dutch bombardier, disappeared. Peter was the first to miss him when, shortly after one o'clock, he crawled out of his dug-out, yawning and screwing up his eyes against the bright light. A short while ago they had made plans to bring down a minaret with three bombs. Jansen had boasted he would do it. Peter shouted:

"Has the devil carried him off?"

The whole camp was searched for the missing man. A soldier alleged that he had seen someone in a red coat, carrying a bag and other belongings, run towards the fort. In the heat of the moment Peter struck the soldier in the face. But, true enough, Jansen's effects were no longer in his dug-out. Had he gone over to the Turks? Orders were given for the accursed Dutchman to be anathematised at the morning service in all the regiments. Gordon, greatly perturbed by this treachery, demanded that a council be called and declared that, in Golovin's and Lefort's camps, the defence works were conducted carelessly and in slipshod fashion, that there were no communication trenches between the camps, so that if the Turks made a sortie it would end in disaster.

"War is no joke, Generals," Gordon said. "We are responsible for the lives of our men. Yet everybody here seems to be playing and joking."

Lefort's lips went white with wrath. Golovin, greatly offended, stared at Gordon like an ox. But the latter insisted that the defence line should immediately be put in order.

"At war, gentlemen, one should first of all fear the enemy."

"We—fear them?"

"We'll crush them like flies."

"Oh no, gentlemen! Azov is no fly."

The generals began to revile Gordon, calling him a cur and a coward and, had Peter not been present, they would have torn his wig off. And on the same day, at the hour when the whole army slept soundly after dinner, the Turks opened the fortress gates and noiselessly overran the unfinished trenches at the junction of the camps.

Half the streltsi were knifed to death in their sleep. The others, throwing down halberds and muskets, ran to the sixteen-gun battery which had also been only sketchily fortified. They did not even have time to fire the guns: the Turks overtook the running streltsi, clambered on to the redoubt with their curved daggers and, with shrill yells, heads lowered, threw themselves upon the tight group of gunners, where Gordon's son, Colonel Jacob Gordon, was laying about him with a ramrod.

Confusion reigned in the camp; shots were fired. Peter stood on the roof of a dug-out, clenching his fists and sobbing with excitement. It was quite useless to shout or give orders. The men, suddenly awakened, rushed to and fro in a frenzy. He saw Gordon climb over the earth wall of the camp with raised pistols, running at an old man's trot towards the redoubt to his son's rescue. A confused crowd of green, red and dark-blue coats rushed in his wake. On the earth wall of Lefort's camp someone was wildly waving the regimental colours; from there too numbers of men ran to the rescue. The whole field was covered with soldiers. The captured redoubt was shrouded in smoke; the Turks were firing to cover their retreat. They were taking the guns with them, wheeling them at the double down the slope towards the fort. They scuttled down the ramparts of the redoubt, hitting and firing back, with a flutter of red baggy trousers. The Russians, scattered over the field, were now drawing together into an uneven line which began to move swiftly, following the Turks towards the fort. From where Peter stood on the dug-out it looked like a game. We were getting the upper hand! The Turks, and the Russians after them, rolled down into the fortress moat.

"A horse!" Peter cried. "To the assault! Trumpeters!"

He stamped his feet. But no one listened to him. Alexander Menshikov, his eyes glassy, galloped past him. He slapped his horse with his sword and jumped over the moat. "Hur-rrrah!" roared his wide-open mouth. Drums rattled. Then suddenly something happened. The Turks had reached the walls. The gates opened. A crowd of janissaries swarmed out and, with them, someone on a white horse, in red with a big turban, who threw out his raised arms. Such a terrible howl sounded above the gunfire that Peter shuddered. The Russians were already running back pursued by Turks, mounted and on foot. They kept falling, falling; Peter clutched his temples. Once again he caught sight of Alexander: he was galloping towards the turbaned man in red, and they clashed. Clouds of gunpowder smoke rose, bombs exploded. Maddened horses rushed past. The men loomed larger as they ran up, their faces distorted with terror. They rolled over the breastworks into the trenches. They were beaten, beaten.

Five hundred men, a colonel, ten officers and the whole battery were lost in this affair. For several days Peter would not look towards the fort where the Turks showed their teeth in derisive grins. Alexander boasted to all and sundry of his bloody sword; yes, Alexander was a hero. The mood in the camps was despondent. That's what their nap had cost them! Lefort and Golovin kept out of sight, and now earth being flung up by spades was the most common sight in their camps.

Peter was astounded by the reverse. He went about gloomy and taciturn, as though he had matured in these few days. He had but one thought: Azov must be taken. With glory or without—even if the whole of Russia had to be driven to the point of exhaustion—Azov would be taken. In the evening, sitting under the stars by his dug-out and smoking, he would question Gordon about war, about luck, about famous generals.

"The lucky general," Gordon would say, "is the one who fights with a full mess-tin and a spade, the one who is stubborn and prudent. When a soldier trusts his general and when he's well fed, he fights bravely."

Peter did not amuse himself any more by firing guns at the fortress. He spent his days at the earthworks on the approaches, by means of which the army came step by step nearer to the fortress. There, having shed coat and wig, he dug and wove fascines, and there too he ate with the soldiers.

From the riverside Azov was on a slope. Gordon advised building an entrenchment with batteries on an island facing the fortress. Yakov Dolgoruky, a brave and obstinate man, volunteered for this dangerous enterprise. He was ready to risk his head for glory. During the night he occupied the island with two regiments and entrenched himself. In the morning the Turks realised the danger, and a strong contingent accompanied by Tatar cavalry began to cross to the right bank of the Don to drive the Russians off the island. Gordon sent a request for support for Dolgoruky to the other two generals and, without waiting for them, went at once with guns and cavalry to take up position below the island, protecting himself with stockades. The Turks took fright and halted. And so they stood: Gordon on the left bank, Dolgoruky in peril on the island, and the Turks, irresolute, on the right bank. Lefort and Golovin delayed, and finally decided not to move. Gordon stuck in their throats: let him manage alone.

Peter watched from the top of the redoubt and, like everyone else, could not understand what was happening. He was afraid to interfere. Then suddenly the Tatar cavalry took to the water and began to swim, the janissaries holding on to their horses' tails. The Tatars disappeared into the steppe and the Turks re-entered the fortress.

Gordon returned, with colours flying and bands playing. The engagement had been won without a shot.

Bombs from the island began flying across to Azov, which was clearly visible from there; they destroyed houses and started fires. The inhabitants could be seen running for safety to the walls. There was joy in the Russian camp, and people began talking again of storming Azov. But once more Gordon restrained them from so rash a step. He persuaded them to try a parley: perhaps the Turkish commander, Murtaza Pasha, would capitulate on good terms. After a fierce bombardment, when all Azov was smoking, they sent two Cossacks with a written offer to the Pasha.

What would be the outcome? The Cossacks went up to the walls, waving their caps and the document; they were admitted through the gates, but soon after were roughly thrown out. The Tsar's envoys! They brought back the document. On it, in the hand of Jacob Jansen, gross Russian words were written.

In Golovin's tent Gordon vainly insisted that, according to military science, they must first reach the walls by sapping, and make a breach, and only then attempt an assault. They would not listen to him. The generals sat drinking wine. Peter scratched the back of his head and stared at the candles: he could already hear the sound of victorious trumpets on the walls of Azov. Gordon rapped with his sword:

"The great marshal Condé always proceeded. . . ."

"Condé, Condé!" Golovin interrupted in a nasal drawl. "Go to the devil with your Condé! Because of you all we've done is to lose time and besmirch the Tsar's honour."

Lefort smiled insolently into Gordon's face. Peter stubbornly insisted on an immediate assault. It was fixed for the 5th of August.

Volunteers were called for. Officers were promised twenty-five, and privates ten roubles each for every gun captured. At mass the regimental priests spoke of the necessity for self-sacrifice. But not one of the streltsi or soldiers volunteered. They sullenly turned their backs: "We aren't fools to seek such danger."

But the Don Cossacks sent officers to Peter to say that two thousand five hundred of them, and if necessary more, were ready to storm the walls on condition that the town should be left to them to loot for at least twenty-four hours. Peter, and after him the generals, embraced the officers and promised them the run of the fortress for three days. Five thousand streltsi and soldiers were detailed to reinforce them.

The night before the assault Gordon came to the dug-out where Peter, by the light of a guttering candle-end, was poring over a military map sucking his pipe. "Have you talked to the soldiers? Well, General, so it's decided, with God's help."

Gordon sat down, holding his helmet on his knee. The old man was tired. His sunken cheeks were covered with grey stubble. He was breathing heavily, showing his large yellow teeth, of which two front ones were missing. With tender sadness he looked at the self-confident youngster. But perhaps it was right that youth should be reckless?

"This winter we'll build a big fleet in Voronezh," Peter said, raising his bloodshot eyes. "Tomorrow we must take Azov." With the stem of his pipe he pointed at a small bay to the West of the mouth of the Don. "See, here we'll build a second small fort. During the winter the Turks won't penetrate into the Azov Sea, and in spring we'll come back with a large fleet. Look, in the strait below Kerch we'll build a fort, and the whole sea will be ours. We'll build sea-going ships, and then for the Black Sea." The pipe flew over the map. "There we'll be out in the open. We shall conquer the Crimea from the sea. The Crimea is ours. Then the Bosphorus and the Dardanelles. By war or by treaty we'll make our way through to the Mediterranean. We'll flood the markets with silk and corn. Look at the countries there: Venice, Rome. . . . And here—look—here is Moscow: we'll take goods by water to Tsaritsin, and here, where we marched to Panshin over the portage, we'll cut a big canal to the Don. Straight from Moscow to Rome, eh? Then we'll be traders. . . ! Gordon, shall we take Azov?"

"I don't know for certain," Gordon replied after some thought. "I've seen the soldiers. Many are very stupid; they think they can scale the walls without ladders. Many seemed to regret their offer, they were dispirited. But I said: 'You made your choice, now you've got to stick to it. All those who volunteered will go; I'll have all cowards shot'. However, everything is ready: ladders, fascines, grenades. We will pray for God's aid."

Peter was restless. Soon after midnight he roused Menshikov and they galloped off to the Cossack camp. Everything was quiet there. The Cossacks were sleeping unconcernedly on their waggons. They were met by the ataman, a man with a shaven head, firm face and shifty eyes. He seated Peter on a saddle by the camp-fire and himself sat down crosslegged, Turkish fashion. Cossacks crowded round them. Vodka and dried fish were brought. They began talking—boldly and mockingly. Obviously the Cossacks feared nothing in the world. Elbowing their way to the fire that lit up black beards and reckless faces, they said with scoffing smiles:

"The Cossacks are the very strength, the very sap of the people. What do they know about us in Moscow? They regard us as bandits. Hah! They send us a governor, and he turns out a worse bandit. It's a good thing, Sire, that you've come to us. Take a good look at us. Do we look like evil men? The Cossacks are eagles! Ho-ho. . . . You must appreciate us."

When a green light spread over the East, orders given in low voices sped through the Cossack encampment. Hundreds of Cossacks started to crawl over the earth rampart and to disappear like cats in the dark steppe in the direction of the fortress walls facing the river. Others embarked in light boats, taking ropes with hooks attached and light ladders. The encampment emptied noiselessly.

In the vast sky the stars began to pale. The cocks in the baggage-train crowed. A chill, light wind blew, heralding the dawn. To the north a light gleamed briefly and a gun rumbled. General Gordon's Butyrsky and Tambovsky regiments had begun the attack.

Only these two regiments succeeded in scaling the walls. The streltsi who followed heard the furious hand-to-hand fighting and the clang of steel and lost heart: they dropped prone in the cherry orchards of the burnt outskirts. The Cossacks attacked furiously from the river, but their ladders proved too short, and the Turks rolled stones from the walls and poured down hot pitch. The Cossacks returned to camp without achieving anything. The assault had been repulsed.

When the sun rose masses of dead could be seen lying near the fortress. The Turks swung and flung the Russians from the walls, and the dead bodies rolled into the moat. Over fifteen hundred had perished. In the trenches the soldiers sighed:

"Yesterday we made fun of Vanushka; now there are birds pecking him over there."

"And why do we want to go for the Turks? What is there for us here?"

"Why should we fight? We'll all get killed."

"Only the generals will get back to Moscow."

The generals gathered round Peter in Golovin's tent. Gordon was sad and silent. Lefort wearily stifled his yawns and kept his eyes averted. Golovin, with drawn face, let his head droop from time to time. Only Menshikov, who had come with the Tsar, swaggered with his hands on his hips; a rag was tied round his head and there was again blood on his sword: he had been on the walls. He seemed to bear a charmed life, the devil!

Peter sat angrily bolt upright. The generals remained standing. "Well?" he asked. "What have you got to say, gentlemen?" Lefort furtively pressed Gordon's elbow. Golovin waved his hands hopelessly. "You've utterly disgraced yourselves. What then now? Are we to lift the siege?"

They made no answer. Peter tapped with his nails and his cheek twitched. Menshikov stepped up to the table, an insolent look in his eyes. He stretched out his hand:

"Peter Alexeyevich, allow me—though it's not for me to speak here. But as I myself have been on the wall. . . . I ran an aga through with my sword, after all. . . . I'll tell you their ways. You must count five of our soldiers to one Turk. It's because they're terribly fierce. I'd already stuck the aga through with my sword, and yet there he was, the accursed fellow, squealing with rage like a pig, and snapping at the steel with his teeth. Their weapons are also more convenient than ours: their daggers are like razors; while you lunge at him with a sword or a pike, he'll cut your head off three times. Until we breach the walls, we won't overcome the Turks. The walls must be breached. And the soldiers must be given grenades and Cossack swords instead of long arms."

Alexander, with a quirk of his eyebrows, drew back smartly into the shadows.

"The young man has given us an excellent explanation," Gordon said. "But one can only breach the walls with mines, and that means sapping must be done. And that is very dangerous and very lengthy work."

"As it is, we'll soon have no bread," Gordon said. "The stocks are running low."

"Hadn't we better put it off till next year?" Lefort said thoughtfully.

Peter, leaning back, looked with glassy eyes at his recent booncompanions:

"Damn you generals!" he barked, and his face flushed. "I'll take command of the siege myself. Myself! Tonight the saps must be started. Bread must be found. I'll hang the defaulters. Tomorrow war begins. Alexander, call the engineers."

Two men entered the tent: Franz Timmermann—much aged and grown fat and flabby—and a tall, bony young foreigner with an open and intelligent face: Adam Weide.

"Gentlemen," Peter said, smoothing the map with his palms and drawing the candle closer. "By September the walls must be blown up. Look, and think it over. I give you a month for completing the mining work."

He rose, lit his pipe at the candle and went out of the tent to look at the stars. Alexander was whispering something over his shoulder. The generals remained standing in the tent, perplexed by the unprecedented behaviour of the Bom Bar Dier.

The siege continued. Encouraged by the failure of the assault, the Turks gave the besiegers no peace day or night; they destroyed the saps and broke into the trenches. The Tatar horsemen galloped, in clouds of dust, at the very edge of the encampment and destroyed supply-trains. Many Cossacks were killed in encounters with them. The Russian army was melting away. There were constant shortages of one sort or another. Thunderclouds rolled up from the Black Sea: the Muscovites had never seen such storms. Lightning flashed in pillars of flame, the earth shook with the thunder; a deluge of rain swamped the trenches and the saps. After the storms the cold, murky days of autumn suddenly set in. No warm clothing had been provided for the army. Sickness broke out. The strelets regiments began to grumble. And day by day sails appeared on the cold stretch of the sea: reinforcements ceaselessly pouring in for the Turks.

More than once Lefort tried to persuade Peter to raise the siege. But Peter was adamant. He had grown stern and harsh. He had lost so much flesh that his green coat hung on him as on a pole. He no longer joked. When Zotov appeared drunk in the camp, he struck him with a spade handle.

No one thought it possible to work with such intensity as Peter demanded. But it turned out that they could. In the middle of September the engineer Weide reported that he had carried the sap under the bastion itself and the men working in it could hear noises: could the Turks be counter-mining? In that case all was lost. Peter crawled into the sap with a candle-end and heard the noises too. It was decided on the spot to wait no longer but to blow up at least this mine. Nearly a ton and a half of gunpowder was loaded. Orders were given to the troops to prepare for the assault. Workmen and soldiers were warned by three cannon-shots. Peter lit the fuse and ran to the far end of the camp, followed by Alexander and Madamkin. The Turks rushed from the walls to the protection of the inner fortifications. An extraordinary quiet fell. Only crows cawed as they winged their way over the Don. Suddenly the earth at the foot of the fortress wall rose in a hump, a dull roar sounded and, out of the bursting hump, an untidy column of fire, smoke, earth, stones and logs rose into the air and spread. The next moment it crashed down on to the Russian trenches. A hot whirlwind swirled. Burning logs flew, hissing, into the middle of the camp. Quite close to Peter, Madamkin fell with a shattered skull. A hundred and fifty soldiers and streltsi, two colonels and one lieutenant-colonel were killed and wounded. The troops were seized with indescribable terror. When the dust cleared they saw the walls standing intact and on them the Turks, laughing uproariously.

No one dared approach Peter. He wrote himself—crookedly, leaving out letters and sputtering the ink—the order for a general assault to be made by land and water not later than the end of the month. The two remaining undamaged mines were to be completed. The army was ordered to go to confession and to take Holy Communion. All prepared for death.

Peter was now constantly to be seen inspecting the camps, riding a small shaggy horse. The grass swished against his thin legs. His weatherstained, three-cornered felt hat was pulled down over his ears. He was invariably accompanied by Alexander Menshikov with pistols in his belt and Alioshka Brovkin with telescope and musket, who rode behind him. The men hid in the trenches. It wasn't only that you couldn't say a contrary word, but even if they noticed a gloomy face, those three devils would pounce, call a sergeant and start questioning. For the least thing, the whip. Several streltsi who had been talking among themselves about "Russians having been driven here to feed the Turkish ravens with Russian flesh", Peter struck in the face, and ordered them to be hanged on the upturned shafts of carts.

On the night of the 24th of August Peter crossed over to the island, to Dolgoruky, to watch the battle from there. No one slept in any of the camps. The regimental priests sat by the camp-fires, as they had been ordered to do. The sergeants' moustaches could be seen bristling. In the chilly dawn the regiments left the camps. Two explosions were heard. A grim flame for a moment lit up minarets, forts, low hills, the river and human faces with eyes staring in horror. The Russians began to attack.

The Butyrsky regiment broke in through the breach in the wall and fought on the inner palisades. Hand-grenades were showered on them. The Preobrazhensky and Semenovsky regiments rowed up in boats, got their ladders into position and swarmed up the walls. The Turks pierced them with arrows and thrust at them with pikes. Men by the hundred fell from the ladders. Mad with rage they climbed up, choking with savage oaths. They reached the top. Murtaza Pasha himself rushed into the *mêlée* with his fiercely yelling janissaries.

The other regiments reached the walls, shouting and rushing about, but they lacked the fury that would have sent them to face death. They did not attempt to climb up. The streltsi again went no farther than the earth wall. Then Gordon gave the order to beat the retreat. Only half the Butyrsky regiment got back through the breach alive. The play-army had been fighting for an hour, pressing Murtaza Pasha, breaking through into the narrow streets from whose burnt-out ruins arrows, stones and bombs rained on them. But no support came. Peter on the island was almost beside himself. He kept sending mounted messengers to turn the troops and throw them once more at the walls. Lefort, in a gold cuirass and plumed helmet, galloped among the confused regiments, carrying a captured Turkish banner. Golovin was beating the men right and left, like a blind man, with the broken shaft of his pike. Gordon stood alone on the ramparts among the flying arrows and bullets and shouted hoarsely. The soldiers would go as far as the moat and then draw back. Many, throwing down musket or pike, sat on the ground, covering their faces: kill us here, we won't go, we can't. . . . Again the drums beat the retreat.

All was silent in fortress and camp. Birds settled on the piles of dead bodies. On the third night the siege was raised. No lights were lit; noiselessly the guns were harnessed and they started along the left bank of the Don: the baggage-trains in front, then the remainder of the army and Gordon's two regiments bringing up the rear. In the fortified watch-towers they left three thousand soldiers and Cossacks.

In the morning a hurricane struck from the sea. The Don darkened and swelled. Many waggons and men were lost in an attempt to cross to the Crimean side. They continued the march along the same bank in full view of the Tatars. Gordon had constantly to beat off their attacks: guns were turned, the men formed square and fired volleys that drove off the attackers.

After Cherkassk the Tatars fell back. They were now marching over the uninhabited, naked steppe and eating the last of their dry bread. There was nothing to make a fire with, no shelter from the night's cold. Banks of autumn cloud covered the sky. A north wind brought hoar-frost and the earth grew ice-bound. Snow fell, and snow-storms raged. The soldiers, bare-footed, in summer coats, trudged over the desolate white plains. Those who fell did not rise again. Each morning many were left lying on the camp-site. Wolves followed the army, howling through the snowstorm.

After three weeks they reached Valuyki; only one-third of the army had survived. From here Peter, with his suite, rode ahead to Tula, to Leo Narishkin's arms factory. Two Turkish prisoners and a captured banner accompanied the Tsar.

On the way Peter wrote to Romodanovsky:

"*Mein Herr König,* on return from uncaptured Azov, the council of generals has directed me to build ships, galleys and other vessels for the future war. In these labours we are now going to be incessantly occupied. And as for our news, I inform you that your Majesty's father, the Most Holy Prince-Pope, archbishop of Pressburg and Patriarch of the whole of Yaouza and of the whole of Kukuy is, with his slaves, thank the Lord, in good health. Peter."

Thus ingloriously ended the first Azov campaign.

chapter seven

Two years passed. Those who used to shout now held their tongues, those who had laughed grew silent. Great and terrible things had happened during those two years. The western infection had irresistibly penetrated the drowsiness of Russian life. The cracks in it showed more clearly as the irreconcilable forces diverged still further.

The boyars and landed nobles, the clergy and the streltsi feared changes which meant new undertakings and new people; they hated the rapidity and harshness of the innovations. "It's no longer a decent world, it's a tavern; they smash everything, they disturb everyone. Low-born little merchants snatch at power. They don't live; they just hurry. The Tsar has delivered the country into the hands of corrupt lechers who have lost the fear of God. We are heading for the abyss."

But those others—the low-born, efficient men who wanted change, who stretched out their hands, entranced, towards Europe, to grasp even a grain of the golden dust that shrouded the lands of the Occident—those said that they had not been mistaken in the young Tsar: he had proved himself just the man they had expected. The disaster and humiliation of Azov had, at one stroke, made a man of the reveller of the Foreign Quarter; failure had curbed him with a violent bridle. Even his relatives did not recognise him; he was a changed man: fierce, obstinate and businesslike.

After the failure at Azov he made only a brief visit to Moscow—where everyone sneered: "This was something different from your

Kozhuhov sham battles"—and immediately went off to Voronezh. Artisans and craftsmen began to be driven there from all parts of the country. Waggon-trains stretched along the autumn roads. Age-old oaks on the Vorenezh river and on the Don rocked under the blows of axes. Wharves, warehouses and barracks were built. Two ships, twenty-three galleys and four fireships were laid down. The winter was a particularly cold one. There was a shortage of everything. Men died by the hundred. Such slavery had never even been dreamt of, and deserters were caught and brought back in irons. Blizzard winds swung the frozen corpses on the gallows. Desperate men set fire to the forests round Voronezh. The peasants bringing in the provision-waggons murdered the military escorts and, having looted what they could, made off to wherever chance led them. In the villages men maimed themselves, cut off their fingers to escape going to Voronezh. All Russia resisted; in very sooth the time of Antichrist had come: the old taxation and serfdom and forced labour were nothing to this new, incomprehensible labour now forced on them. The landowners swore as they paid ship-money and groaned as they looked at unsown fields and empty barns. The clergy—priests and monks—murmured in high disapproval: power was clearly slipping from their hands into those of foreigners and of their own low-born, upstart rabble.

The old century was closing in difficult conditions. And still, by spring, the fleet was built. Engineers and regimental commanders were enlisted from Holland. Vast stores were accumulated at Cherkassk and Panshin. The losses of the army were replaced. And in May, Peter, in his new galley *Principium,* appeared at the head of his fleet under the walls of Azov. The Turks, invested by land and sea, put up a desperate resistance, beating off every assault. But when all their bread and powder were exhausted, they capitulated unconditionally. Three thousand janissaries with the bey Hasan Arslanov left ruined Azov.

First and foremost this was a victory for Peter over his own people: the Foreign Quarter's victory over Moscow. Highflown despatches were immediately sent to the Emperor Leopold, to the Doge of Venice and the King of Prussia. By the efforts of Vinius a triumphal arch was erected at the end of the stone bridge over the Moskva river. The arch was surmounted by a double-headed eagle surrounded by banners and arms with the inscription underneath:

"God is with us, none is against us. A triumph unknown to history."

The roof of the arch was supported by gold effigies of Hercules and Mars, each twenty-seven feet high. Under them were painted wooden figures of the Pasha of Azov in chains and of a Tatar murza, also in chains, with the legend:

"Once we fought in the steppes, today we barely succeed in fleeing with our lives from the Muscovites."

The sides of the arch bore large paintings, one picturing the sea-god Neptune with the legend: "I too congratulate you on the taking of Azov and submit to you", the other showed the Russians defeating the Tatars with the legend: "Azov is lost to us, ah, it is disastrous".

At the end of September crowds thronged the river banks and the roofs: from beyond the river the Azov army marched over the bridge and through the arch, led by Zotov with sword and shield in a carriage drawn by six horses. Then came singers, pipers, dwarfs, clerks, boyars and troops. Following them came fourteen richly caparisoned horses belonging to Lefort. He himself, in armour, with a map of Azov in his hand, drove standing in a gilt royal sledge. Then came more boyars, clerks, soldiers, sailors and the newly appointed Vice-Admirals Lima and de Lozière. With great pomp, in a Greek chariot surrounded by drummers beating kettledrums, rode the Generalissimo, the boyar Shein, a squat, pompous man with a broad, fat face. This honour had been awarded him before the second Azov campaign in order to shut the mouths of the boyars. Behind his chariot sixteen Turkish banners were carried trailing along the ground and a captive was led: the Tatar Alatyk, noted for his prowess; his slanting eyes narrowed as he looked at the crowd and his teeth bared in a furious snarl. The people followed him with derisive hoots. Behind the Preobrazhensky regiment four horses dragged a cart with a gallows, under which stood the traitor Jacob Jansen, while two executioners on either side of him clicked pincers used for torture and joggled their whips. There were engineers, shipwrights, carpenters, smiths. After the streltsi came General Gordon on horseback, then Turkish prisoners clad in shrouds. Eight grey horses drew a golden chariot shaped like a ship. Peter walked in front of it in a naval coat and a three-cornered felt hat with an ostrich plume. People were amazed at his round face and long body—it was of more than human stature—and many, as they crossed themselves, recalled the terrible and mysterious rumours about this Tsar.

The troops passed through Moscow to Preobrazhensk. Shortly

after, the boyars received a summons to assemble there for a meeting of the council, at which, contrary to all custom, foreigners, generals, admirals and engineers were present. Peter addressed the boyars in manly accents:

"Since Fortune, who has never been so far to the South, is running through our midst, happy is he who seizes her by the hair. Therefore, boyars, let this be your decision: let ruined and burned Azov be restored and securely garrisoned, and let the fortress Taganrog, founded by me at no great distance from there, be completed and garrisoned too. And it is also necessary—since it is more convenient for us to make war on sea than on land—to build a fleet of forty or more ships. They must be complete in every detail, with guns and small arms in readiness for war. The way they are to be built is as follows: the Patriarch and monasteries shall give one ship for every eight thousand peasant families they own. Boyars and all crown servants shall give one ship for every ten thousand families of serfs. The merchants of all classes and grades shall give twelve large ships. And for this purpose boyars, clergy, men owing service to the Crown and those engaged in trade shall form companies, that is, associations, and of such companies there shall be thirty-five."

The boyars passed the decision asked for, though their eyes bulged and their fur coats were damp with sweat. It was ruled that the companies should be formed by December, under penalty of confiscation of houses and estates, whether inherited or granted by the Tsar. Each company, besides Russian carpenters and sawyers, was to engage at its own cost foreign craftsmen, interpreters, good smiths, one carver, one skilled cabinet-maker and one painter, as well as a doctor with a pharmacy.

Peter further ordered the creation of a special tax for cutting a canal from the Volga to the Don, work on which was to begin immediately. Although sorely perplexed, the boyars passed the tax without any argument. It was hard for them to make such rapid decisions, but they saw that argument was useless: Peter had decided everything in advance. Peter did not speak, he barked harshly from the throne, and his clean-shaven generals merely tossed the curls of their wigs. Oh, how sharp and sudden it was! The surroundings of Preobrazhensk had become a military camp: trumpets, drums, soldiers' songs. And so it turned out that the boyars' council was stewing here merely as a concession to ancient custom: at any moment the Tsar would dispense with it.

And, indeed, there soon occurred an event of great importance, not through the boyars' decision, but quite simply: the clerk to the Tsar's personal chancellery, Zotov, the Prince-Pope, wrote and sent by military messengers a Tsar's ukase to fifty of the highest Moscow nobles commanding them to prepare to go abroad to study mathematics, fortification, shipbuilding and other sciences (without which, God be praised, they had lived since the days of St. Vladimir). Consternation reigned in many Moscow families, but they did not dare to beg for the order to be rescinded or to feign ill health. The young men's effects were got together; their parents blessed them and took leave of them as though they were going to their death. An orderly was attached to each to serve him and to send reports, and in the spring they set out over the flooded roads for those far-away lands full of temptation.

One of them was Peter Andreyevich Tolstoy, Troyekurov's son-in-law, who was glad to wipe out at any price his participation in the strelets rising.

2

The taking of Azov had been an extremely foolhardy and dangerous enterprise: it brought Russia into full-scale war with the whole Turkish Empire. And Russia had only just enough strength to deal with a single small fortress, a fact that Peter and his generals had fully realised during the fighting at Azov. No trace of the former Kozhuhov bravado remained. There was no thought now of conquests, but merely of surviving if it pleased Turkey to attack Russia by land and sea.

It was imperative to find allies, to improve and arm both army and fleet with all speed, to reorganise the State machinery—which had rusted throughout—on the new European pattern, and to obtain money, money, money. . . .

Only Europe could supply all this. It was necessary to send men there, and to send them in such a way that Europe would give. It was a difficult problem, of pressing urgency. Peter and his advisers solved it with Asiatic cunning: they decided to send a large and luxuriously equipped mission, which Peter himself would accompany, masquerading as Peter Mihaylov, sergeant of the Preobrazhensky regiment. It amounted to saying: "You consider us ignorant barbarians, but, though we are Tsars and conquerors of the Turks at Azov, we are not proud, we are simple, easy-going people, and are perhaps less set in our ways than you are; we can sleep on the floor, and eat from the same bowl as peasants, and our one care is to shed our ignorance and stupidity and learn from you, gracious sirs!"

They had certainly reckoned correctly: not even a mermaid would have aroused as much wonder in Europe. People remembered that until quite recently Peter's brother had been revered almost as a deity; and now this giant, his handsome countenance distorted by a convulsive tic, snapped his fingers at regal grandeur out of his interest in trade and sciences. This was incredible and amazing.

The great ambassadors plenipotentiary were: Lefort, the governor-general of Siberia, Fedor Alexeyevich Golovin—a man of keen intelligence with a knowledge of foreign languages—and Prokofy Voznitsin, a clerk of the boyars' council. Their suite consisted of twenty Moscow nobles and thirty-five volunteers, among whom were Alexander Menshikov and Peter.

An unpleasant incident unexpectedly delayed their departure: a conspiracy among the Don Cossacks was discovered, headed by Colonel Tsikler, who had been the first to bring his strelets regiment over to Troitsa. Peter could never forget that Tsikler had been one of Sophia's most devoted adherents and obstinately refused to trust his obsequiousness. After the taking of Azov he had sent Tsikler to build the fortress at Taganrog which, for an ambitious man, was equivalent to exile. At Taganrog he had found the Cossacks in revolt against the forced labour; the Tsar's heavy hand was destroying their liberty in the steppe. Tsikler immediately turned traitor and told them:

"There is much disorder in the country because the Tsar is going overseas and using our enemy, the accursed foreigner Lefort, as his great ambassador, and he is taking vast treasure with him on this mission. The Tsar is obstinate and will listen to no one; he indulges in unseemly amusements and does grievous and deplorable things, expending the State treasure to no good purpose. He goes alone at night to the German woman; it would be easy to ambush him and knife him. And once you kill him nobody will interfere with you, you will do as Stenka Razin did. And if you do, you can choose a Tsar, me if you like: I stand for the Old Faith and I like simple, low-born folk."

The Cossacks shouted in answer: "Give us time, when the Tsar has gone abroad, we'll do as Stenka Razin did." A strelets officer, Yelizaryev, not sparing horses, hastened to Moscow and denounced this treachery. Enquiry disclosed that Tsikler was associated with the Moscow nobles Sokovsky and Pushkin, and that they were in communication with the Novodevichy convent.

Peter himself tortured Tsikler who, in desperate agony and under the shadow of death, told much that was new of the former deadly plans of Sophia and Ivan Miloslavsky, who had died three years ago. Once more Miloslavsky's ghost arose, bringing to life again the ever-smouldering horror of Peter's childhood.

The family vault of the Miloslavskys in the Don monastery was opened and the remains of Ivan Miloslavsky were put on a sledge; twelve hump-backed, long-snouted hogs, squealing under the whip, dragged the coffin over dung-heaps, through the Moscow streets to Preobrazhensk. The crowds that followed did not know whether to laugh or cry with fear.

In the open space in the soldiers' barracks in Preobrazhensk musketeers, formed in a square, stood at the present. Drums beat. In the middle there was a platform with a block. Tsikler was dragged up the steep steps of the platform. He was stripped and flung on to the block. Both arms and both legs were cut off before he was finally beheaded. His blood poured through the cracks into Miloslavsky's coffin.

3

The country was left in the care of the boyars, headed by Leo Narishkin, Streshnev, Apraxin, Troyekurov, Boris Golitsin and the council clerk Vinius, and Moscow, with all the offices concerned with Criminal Affairs, to Romodanovsky. In the middle of March the great mission, including Peter Mihaylov, left for Courland.

On the first of April Peter wrote, in invisible ink:

"*Mein Herr* Vinius, yesterday we arrived in Riga, God be thanked, in good health, and the ambassadors were received with great honours. When they entered, and also when they left the castle, a salute of 24 guns was fired. We found the Dvina still frozen and are therefore obliged to stay here for some time. Please convey my greetings to all my acquaintances. In future I shall continue to write in invisible ink—hold it over the fire, and then you will be able to read it. And for the sake of appearances I will write these words in black ink, whenever suitable: 'Please give my greetings to my master, the general, and beg him to be so kind as to take care of my family.' All the rest will be in invisible ink, for the people here are extremely inquisitive."

To this Vinius replied:

"On the occasion of the first mail having been received from the Great Ambassador and his companions, I joined such a goodly company and we drank so deeply to the health of the ambassadors and brave cavaliers, that Bacchus split his sides with laughter. The generals and colonels and all the commanders, the sergeants and the soldiers of Your Grace return your greetings. In the first company the drummer Luke has died. Hannibal, the Negro, is, thank goodness, behaving gently; his chains have been removed and he is learning Russian. All your families are well."

A week later a second letter arrived in Moscow:

"*Herr* Vinius, today I left this place for Mitau. We lived across the river which became ice-free on Easter day. We lived in slavish conditions and satisfied our hunger only with our eyes. The tradespeople here wear cloaks and seem to be extremely honest, but when our drivers started to sell their sledges, they haggled and cursed horribly over a kopek. They give ten kopeks for a horse and sledge. And they ask three times more than the proper price for whatever you want to buy from them. Please greet my master, the general, and ask him to take care of my family. (The rest in invisible ink.) When we were leaving Riga and drove through the town and castle, soldiers, of whom there were no fewer than two thousand, stood on the walls. The town is strongly fortified, but unfinished. They are very afraid here, and do not let anyone into the town or elsewhere even with an escort, and they are not at all agreeable. There is great hunger in the country due to a bad harvest."

And again three weeks later:

"Today we are leaving for Königsberg by sea. Here, in Mitau, I have seen a curiosity which at home we thought was a lie. At a certain apothecary's there is a salamander in a jar of spirits. I took it out and held it in my hand. It is exactly as they say: the salamander is an animal which lives in the fire. . . . Here we let all our drivers go. As for those drivers who have deserted: have them found and soundly flogged, leading them through the market-place, and make them restore the money so that others in future do not cheat."

4

A pleasant breeze filled the four great square sails on mainmast and foremast and the two at the end of the ship's long bowsprit. Slightly listing to port, the *St. George* glided over the grey, sunlit water of a spring day. Here and there floated brittle ice-floes ringed with foam. The Brandenburg flag fluttered from her poop, which rose cumbrously high, like a tower. The decks were clean and well-scrubbed and the polished brass glittered. Dancing waves flung themselves against the oak Neptune, and broke in rainbow spray under the bowsprit.

Peter, Alexander Menshikov, Alioshka Brovkin, Volkov and the priest Bitka, a sickly-looking man with a large head and a clipped beard—all dressed in Dutch clothes of grey cloth, in cotton stockings and shoes of Russian leather with iron buckles—had disposed themselves on coils of tarry rope, puffing pipes of good tobacco.

Peter, resting his elbows on his drawn-up knees, was gay and good-humoured. He said:

"Friedrich, Elector of Brandenburg, whom we are going to visit in Königsberg, is a man of our sort; you will see how he welcomes us. He has sore need of us. He lives in fear of the Swedes on one side and the Poles on the other. We have found this out already. He'll ask for a military alliance, you'll see, my lads."

"We'll think twice about that," Alexander said.

Peter spat into the sea and wiped the end of his pipe on his sleeve.

"That just it. Such an alliance is no use to us. Prussia won't fight the Turks. But, my lads, no nonsense in Königsberg; I'll tear your heads off. I don't want any ill fame spread about us."

Bitka, the priest, said in a voice hoarse from drinking:

"Our conduct is always respectable. No need for threats. But I've never heard of such a rank as Elector."

"Lower than a king and higher than a duke, and you get an Elector," Alexander answered. "But, of course, this one's country is ruined, he lives from hand to mouth."

Alioshka Brovkin listened with his light eyes and hairless lips wide open. Peter blew smoke into his mouth. Alioshka began to cough. The others laughed and poked his ribs.

"Now then, now then!" Alioshka said. "After all, it is startling: here we are all of a sudden visiting their country."

The old captain, a Finn, looked at them with amazement as they frolicked among the coiled ropes. It was hard to believe that one of these jolly youths was the Tsar of Muscovy. But the world was full of wonders.

To port, in the distance, sandy shores glided past. At rare intervals they caught sight of a sail. A large ship in full sail disappeared under the western horizon. This had been the sea of the Vikings, then of the Hanseatic merchants; now it was dominated by the Swedes. The sun was setting. Running before the wind, with topsails spread, the *St. George,* ploughing with a soft gurgle through the waves, made for the long sand-bar which cut off the closed bay of Frisches Haff from the sea. They could see a lighthouse and the low bastions of the fortress of Pillau, which guarded the entrance to the bay. They sailed up, fired a salute and dropped anchor. The captain invited the Muscovites to supper.

5

In the morning they went ashore. There was nothing very striking to be seen: sand, pines, a score of fishing vessels, nets pegged out to dry, and low, weatherbeaten huts, poor, but with white curtains behind glass-paned windows. Peter thought tenderly of Annchen. Housewives in linen caps were busy with their household tasks at their neatly-swept thresholds. The men wore leather sou'westers; they shaved their lips and wore their beards in a fringe under their chins. They moved more clumsily, perhaps, than the Russians, but it was evident that each was going about his business, and they were friendly, without shyness.

Peter asked for the tavern, where they sat down at clean oak tables, astonished at the cleanliness and the pleasant smell, and began to drink beer. Here Peter wrote a letter in Russian to the Elector Friedrich, asking for a meeting. Volkov, accompanied by a soldier from the fortress, set off with it to Königsberg.

The fishermen and their womenfolk stood in the doors and looked in at the windows. Peter winked merrily to these good people, asked their names and whether they had caught much fish, and finally invited them all to the table and offered them beer.

In the middle of the afternoon a gilt coach, surmounted by ostrich plumes, drove up to the tavern, and Kammerjunker von Prinz, powdered and attired in blue silk, jumped nimbly out, pushed the fisherfolk aside and, with an anxious face, made his way to the Muscovites who were clattering their pewter mugs. At three paces from the table he took off his broad-brimmed hat and swept the floor with its plumes, taking a step back, with one arm outstretched and knee slightly bent.

"His Grace, my master Friedrich, the Great Elector of Brandenburg, has pleasure in praying Your—" he hesitated and Peter shook a finger at him. "He prays the mighty and long-desired guest to leave this wretched hut and occupy the apartments befitting his rank which have been prepared for him."

Alexander stared at the blue cavalier and kicked Alioshka under the table:

"Now that's what I call real *politesse!* The way he stands on his toes is a picture! Look, his wig's short, while ours are down to the navel. Ah, the wretch!"

Peter got into the carriage with von Prinz; the others followed in a common cart. A merchant's house had been prepared for the guests in Kneiphoff, the best residential quarter of Königsberg. It was dusk when they entered the town; the wheels clattered noisily over the clean, cobbled streets. No fences, no palisades—extraordinary! The houses faced straight on to the street, their long windows with small panes coming down almost to the ground. Welcoming lights shone everywhere. Doors stood open. People were walking about fearlessly. They felt like asking: "How is it you aren't afraid of robbery? Haven't you got any thieves?"

Then again, in the merchant's house where they took up their quarters, nothing was hidden away; handsome things were lying about. Only a fool would not filch them. Looking round the dark oak dining-room, richly furnished, with pictures, porcelain and antlers, Peter said to Alexander in a low voice:

"Tell them all strictly, if anyone touches the slightest trifle, I'll hang him on the gates."

"Quite right, *mein Herz,* I was beginning to feel quite afraid. Till they get accustomed to it, I'll have all their pockets sewn up. Heaven forbid, if, in their cups. . . ."

Von Prinz came back again with the carriage and Peter accompanied him to the palace. They entered it through a hidden wicket-gate which gave access to a garden where a fountain played, and bushes—trimmed to the shapes of balls, birds and pyramids—showed dark against the lawns. Friedrich met his guest at the glass doors opening into the garden and offered him the tips of his fingers covered with lace cuffs. A silky wig framed his strikingly keen face, with its sharp nose and high forehead. Diamond stars sparkled on the blue ribbon across his chest.

"Ah, my brother, my young brother!" he said in French, and then repeated it in German.

Peter looked down on him like a stork, and did not know how to address him—brother? Too much honour. Uncle? Rather awkward. Your Highness or something like that? It wasn't safe to guess, he might take offence.

Without releasing his guest's hands, the Elector, stepping backwards, led him into a small, carpeted room. Peter's head reeled: it was like one of the pictures of his childhood come to life. On the marble mantelpiece over the fireplace, where a gay fire was burning, stood a clock of exquisite workmanship, adorned with a celestial sphere, stars and moon, its pendulum swinging. The soft light from three-branched sconces backed by mirrors lit up tapestries on the walls, delicate chairs and stools and a multitude of beautiful and diverting objects whose use it was hard to conjecture. Tall, narrow goblets of glass, fragile as a soap bubble, held sprays of apple and cherry blossom.

The Elector kept turning his snuff-box in his fingers; his keen eyes were half-closed with a good-humoured expression. He seated his guest by the fire on a gilt chair so frail that Peter kept his weight on his feet for fear of smashing the tiny thing. The Elector spoke in German interspersed with French words. Eventually he touched upon a military alliance. Here Peter began to follow, and he lost some of his shyness. He explained in his sailor's Dutch-German that he was here incognito and could not treat of affairs, but that in a week's time the great ambassadors would arrive and it was with them that talks should be held.

Friedrich clapped his hands. A mirrored door—which Peter had taken for a window—opened noiselessly and lackeys in scarlet liveries brought in a small table set with food and drink. Peter, who was faint with hunger, immediately became more cheerful. But there turned out to be pitifully little to eat: a few slices of sausage, a roast pigeon, a small pie and some salad. With an elegant gesture the Elector invited his guest to be seated and, unfolding a starched napkin which he tucked into his waistcoat, said with a shrewd smile:

"All Europe is watching with admiration Your Majesty's brilliant military success against the enemies of Christianity. Alas, I can but applaud, like a Roman in the amphitheatre. My unhappy country is surrounded by enemies—Poles and Swedes. So long as those robber Swedes are masters of the Baltic, of Saxony, Poland and Livonia, there can be no prosperity for the nations. My young friend, you will soon come to realise that our common enemy, sent by God for our sins, is not the Turk but the Swede. They take toll of every ship in the Baltic. We all toil: they live by brigandage, like wasps. Not only we, but the Dutch and English also suffer. And the Turks! The Turks! Their strength is due only to the support of France—that insatiable tyrant who stretches his usurper's hand to clutch the Spanish crown of the Hapsburgs. Dear friend, you will soon witness a great coalition against France. Louis XIV is old, his famous marshals are in their graves. France is ruined by unbearable taxation. She will not have the strength to help the Turkish Sultan. In the international game Turkey's card will be beaten. But Sweden—ah, Sweden is the most dangerous foe in Moscow's rear."

Resting his elbows lightly on the table, the Elector plucked at an apple-blossom. His watery eyes glinted. His shaven face looked devilishly clever in the candlelight.

Peter felt that the German would ensnare him. Drinking a large glass of wine he said: "I should like to learn artillery shooting from your engineers."

"The whole park is at Your Majesty's service."

"*Danke*. . . ."

"Taste this Moselle."

"*Danke*. It's a bit early for us to get mixed up in the European entanglements; the Turks are a great nuisance to us."

"Only don't count on Poland's help, my young friend. Poland dances to Sweden's tune."

"This Moselle is good."

"The Black Sea won't help in any way to develop your trade. Whereas a few ports on the Baltic coast would open up untold wealth for Russia."

The Elector nibbled apple-blossom petals and there was hidden mockery in his steely eyes as he glanced at the Muscovite's disconcerted face.

6

Peter spent the whole of the following week, until the arrival of the mission, outside the town, firing guns at targets. The chief artillery engineer, Steitner von Sternfeld, gave him the following testimonial:

"Herr Peter Mihaylov must be recognised and regarded as perfect in the firing of bombs, in the theory of the science and in its practice, and as a careful and able artist in firearms, and in respect of his excellent knowledge all possible assistance and kind favour should be rendered him."

The great ambassadors made their entrance into Königsberg with a pomp and magnificence that had never and nowhere yet been seen. Horses with rich saddle-cloths and horse-cloths were led in front of the train, followed by Prussian guardsmen, pages, cavaliers and knights. Russian trumpeters sounded deafening fanfares. Behind them came thirty volunteers in green coats laced with silver. The mounted retinue of the ambassadors was dressed in crimson coats with gold coats-of-arms on chest and back. In a roomy glass coach rode the three ambassadors: Lefort, Golovin and Voznitsin, attired in white satin coats lined with sables, with diamond double-headed eagles on their tall boyars' hats of beaver. They sat leaning back, motionless as graven images, the gems in their rings and in the tops of their staffs sparkling. Behind the coach came the Moscow nobles dressed in their richest apparel.

While receptions and negotiations with the Elector were going on, Peter went off sailing in a yacht on the Frisches Haff. There was no business to be done here: no matter how cunning the Elector might be, an alliance with Poland was much more necessary to Peter than an alliance with him. Unlike former times, the great ambassadors did not cavil at every word and letter and were conciliatory in their manner, save that they refused to kneel and kiss the hand of the Elector, saying that he was not a king yet. The alliance they proposed was not a military one, but merely one of friendship, and on this they stood firm. When the Elector tried to press them, they agreed to a military alliance on condition that war was made on those States which dropped out of the war against Turkey. This proposal was also not to the Elector's liking, and he went to join Peter on the yacht where he held him in conversation all through the night. But the lad only bit his dirty nails. In the end he said:

"Well, all right. Only we won't put it down on paper. If you are in need, Elector, we'll help you, here's the cross on it. Do you trust me?"

Having concluded the secret verbal agreement of alliance—which in the end they were obliged to confirm on paper—the great mission prepared to leave. They were detained, however, for three weeks in Pillau by news of the greatest importance: elections of a new king had begun in Poland. At the big and small Diets the nobles attacked each other with swords and fired pistols in defence of their candidates. Of these there turned out to be more than ten, but the two principal and genuine ones were August, the Elector of Saxony, and François-Louis, Prince de Conti.

A Frenchman on the Polish throne would mean the withdrawal of Poland from the alliance against the Turks and war against Muscovy. It was only here, on the European shore, that Peter came to realise the importance of the political game. From Pillau he sent a messenger to Vinius with the order to write a letter to the Poles, so worded as to drive the greatest possible fear into the partisans of the French prince. They composed a missive in Moscow addressed to the Cardinal Primate of Gniezdin in which it was said: ". . . If a Frenchman were to become King of the Polish State, then not only the alliance against the enemy of the Holy Cross, but also the perpetual peace with Poland would be gravely compromised. For this reason, Great Lord, inspired by our constant friendship for your Sovereigns, the Kings of Poland, as well as for the nobles, the Council and the Polish State, we do not desire a king adhering to the French and Turkish side." The document was accompanied by sables and gold. Gold was also sent from Paris. The frivolous Poles elected both August and Conti. Disorders broke out. The nobles armed their servants and peasants, destroyed each others' farms and burnt down small towns. Peter wrote in alarm to Moscow that troops should be moved to the Lithuanian frontier in support of August. But August himself appeared in Poland with an army of twelve thousand men to take possession of the throne. The French party was defeated. The great nobles dispersed to their castles, the lesser gentry to taverns. As for the Prince de Conti, it became known in Europe that, after coming no further than Boulogne, he had shrugged his shoulders and returned to his amusements. King August swore to the Russian Resident in Warsaw that he would side with Peter.

The great event ended happily. The ambassadors, together with Peter and the volunteers, left Pillau.

7

Peter travelled post in advance of the mission and passed through Berlin, Brandenburg and Halberstadt without stopping. He only turned aside to visit the famous iron works near Ilsenburg. Here he was shown iron poured from the smelting furnace, iron melted in crucibles, the forging of musket barrels from thin iron plates, and drilling and turning on lathes driven by water-wheels. Guild masters and apprentices worked in their own workshops and smithies. All that they produced was taken to Ilsenburg castle: muskets, pistols, swords, locks, horseshoes. Peter talked two good masters into going to Moscow, but the guild would not let them leave.

They travelled along roads lined with pear and apple trees, and none of the inhabitants stole the fruit. All round were oak groves, rectangular cornfields, gardens surrounded by stone fences and the tiled roofs of houses and dovecots showing through the trees. There were fine, well-fed cows. In the meadows, sparkling streams, ancient oaks, water-mills. There was a town every two or three miles: a brick church with a slender spire, a paved square with a stone well, the high roof of the Town Hall, neat, peaceful houses, a quaint signboard at the inn, a copper basin over the barber's door, and kindly, smiling men in knitted caps, short jackets and white stockings. This was the good, old Germany.

On a warm July evening Peter and Alexander, in the leading chaise, arrived at the small town of Koppenbrügge, near Hanover. Dogs barked; windows shed their light on the road. People were just sitting down to supper in their houses. A man in an apron appeared in the bright doorway of an inn showing the sign of the Golden Pig, and shouted something to the driver, who reined in the tired horses and turned to Peter.

"Your Grace, the innkeeper has killed a pig, and today he has stuffed sausage. We won't find better accommodation for the night."

Peter and Alexander got out of the carriage and stretched their legs.

"Well, Alexander, shall we ever bring this kind of life to our own country?"

"I don't know, *mein Herz*. Not soon, I imagine."

"It's a nice life. Just listen, even the dogs here bark without ferocity. It's paradise. When I think of Moscow, I'd like to burn it!"

"It's a pig-sty, that's a fact."

"They sit on all that's ancient till their behinds rot. In a thousand years they haven't learnt how to plough the land. Why? The Elector Friedrich is wise: we must push through to the Baltic, that's the thing, and build a new town there, a real paradise. Look! The stars here are brighter than ours."

"But our people, *mein Herz,* would have turned this place into a pig-sty."

"Just wait, Alexander. When I get back, I'll knock the breath out of Moscow!"

"That's the only way."

They went into the tavern. Hams and sausages hung from an oak beam on the ceiling and copper utensils gleamed in the light of brightly-burning brushwood. The innkeeper bowed low, beaming all over his red face. They ordered beer and were just seating themselves when a cavalier came in from the street. He was wearing a high, conical, broad-brimmed hat and a cloth cloak that swept his spurs.

He nodded a dismissal to the innkeeper, skipped forward, snatched off his hat and began to execute bows, raising his cloak with his sword and cavorting all over the kitchen. Peter and Alexander stared at him open-mouthed. The cavalier said in soft accents:

"Her Highness, the Kurfürstin Sophia of Hanover, with her daughter Sophia-Charlotte, Kurfürstin of Brandenburg and her son, Crown Prince George Ludwig, heir to the throne of England and Duke of Celle, as well as Her Highness's Court, have hastened from Hanover to meet Your Majesty with the sole object of finding compensation for the tiring journey and inconvenient quarters in making the acquaintance of the extraordinary and illustrious Tsar of Muscovy."

Koppenstein—that was his name—invited Peter to sup with the Kurfürstin and her daughter, who would not sit down to the table before their guest arrived. Peter understood only half of what he said and was so alarmed that he nearly bolted into the street.

"I can't," he stammered. "I am in a great hurry. Besides, it's very late. On my way back from Holland, perhaps. . . ."

Koppenstein's hat and cloak once more swept about the kitchen. He insisted, quite unabashed. Alexander whispered in Russian:

"You won't get rid of him. Better go for an hour, *mein Herz*; the Germans are very touchy."

In his vexation Peter pulled a button off his waistcoat. But he agreed, on condition that he and Alexander should be taken through a back entrance, where there were no people about, and that there should be only the Kurfürstin, with at most her daughter, at the supper table. He pulled down his dusty three-cornered hat over his eyes and glanced longingly at the sausages over the hearth.

A carriage awaited them outside.

8

The Kurfürstin Sophia and her daughter Sophia-Charlotte sat at the supper table in front of a fireplace draped with a piece of Chinese silk to hide its ugliness. Mother and daughter were stoutly putting up with all the inconveniences of the mediæval castle which had been put at their disposal by a local landowner. Some modern rugs and tapestries barely concealed the crumbling brick walls, and there were certainly owls high up in the vaulted ceiling. The few silk-covered armchairs, hastily procured, stood on the paved floor, scored by the boots of red-bearded knights and the hoofs of their horses. There was a general smell of mice and dust. The ladies shuddered at the thought of the coarse manners of those days, which, thanks be to the Lord, had gone for ever. Their eyes found comfort in a large picture hanging from a rusty nail intended to support shields and armour. The picture represented a board abundantly heaped with sea-fish and lobsters, bunches of dead birds, vegetables, fruit, and boars pierced by spears. The colours radiated a sunny light.

Both mother and daughter thought that the only things worthy of filling transient life were painting, music, poetry, and the play of wits exercised upon all that was exquisite and elegant. They were the most highly educated women in Germany. Both were in correspondence with Leibnitz, who said of them: "The minds of these women are so enquiring that one is sometimes obliged to capitulate before their searching questions." They were patrons of art and literature. Sophia-Charlotte had founded an Academy of Science in Berlin. A few days earlier, the Elector Friedrich had written them a good-humoured and witty letter describing his impressions of the Tsar of the barbarians who was travelling in the guise of a carpenter. "It seems that Muscovy is awaking from its Asiatic slumber. It is important that its first steps should be guided in a favourable direction." But neither mother nor daughter cared for politics; it was curiosity of the noblest kind that had brought them to Koppenbrügge.

Kurfürstin Sophia's lean fingers gripped the arms of her chair. She was listening, and thought that outside the window opening on to the dark garden she could hear, above the rustling of the leaves, the sound of wheels. The strings of pearls quivered on her white wig, which was built up on whalebone so high that, even if she raised her arms, she could not have touched the top. She was lean and very wrinkled, and the gap in her lower teeth was filled with wax. The lace on her low-cut lilac gown covered a bosom which could no longer charm. Only her large black eyes gleamed with sprightly animation.

Sophia-Charlotte's eyes were as dark as her mother's, but with a calmer glance; she was beautiful, majestic and fair-skinned. Her forehead, under the powdered wig, showed intelligence. She had thin lips and a strong chin, and her shoulders and bosom, uncovered almost to the nipples, were gleaming white. Her slightly tip-tilted nose invited a study of her face in search of hidden frivolity.

"At last!" Sophia-Charlotte said, rising from her chair. "They are here."

Her mother forestalled her. Both crossed the room with a rustle of silk and stood in the window-niche in the thick wall. A tall shadow, waving its arms, strode swiftly up the garden path, followed by another in a cloak and conical hat and, some distance behind, a third.

"It is he," the Kurfürstin said. "God, he's a giant!"

Koppenstein opened the door, announcing:

"His Majesty the Tsar!"

A clumsy foot in a dusty shoe appeared first: Peter came in sideways. When he saw the two ladies in the candlelight, he mumbled: *"Guten Abend."* Then he put his hand to his forehead as if to rub it, but completely lost his self-possession and covered his face with his palm.

The Kurfürstin advanced three steps, raised her skirts with the tips of her fingers and curtsied with a grace unusual for her years:

"Good evening, Your Majesty!"

Sophia-Charlotte then took her place and, with a swan-like movement, spread her beautiful arms, lifted her voluminous skirts and curtsied.

"Your Majesty will forgive the legitimate impatience with which we strove to see the young hero," she said, "the lord of countless peoples and the first of the Russians to break with the pernicious prejudices of his ancestors."

Removing his hand from his face with an effort, Peter bowed, bending like a pole; he felt that he looked so ridiculous that the ladies would burst into mocking laughter at any moment. In his extreme confusion he forgot his German.

"Ich kann nicht sprechen . . ." he mumbled in a stifled voice. But there was no need for him to speak. The Kurfürstin asked a hundred questions, without waiting for an answer: about the weather, his journey, Russia, the war and his impressions. She took him by the arm and led him to the table. The three sat down facing the gloomy hall with its dark vaults. The mother placed a small roast bird on his plate, the daughter poured wine into his glass. Both women were deliciously scented. The older woman talked and, in a gesture as affectionate as a mother's, put her dry, delicate fingers on Peter's fist which he clenched, ashamed of his nails against the snow-white tablecloth, the flowers and the cut glass. Sophia-Charlotte looked after him with charming hospitality, rising to reach a dish or a jug and turning to him with a bewitching smile:

"Try this, Your Majesty. It is really worth tasting."

Had she not been so beautiful and so naked, had not her scented gown rustled, she might have been his sister. And their voices were affectionate, like those of relations. Peter lost his self-consciousness and began to answer questions. The ladies spoke to him of celebrated Flemish and Dutch painters, of the great dramatists at the French court, of philosophy and beauty. There was a great deal about which he had not the slightest notion; he made them repeat what they said and expressed his wonder.

"Science and art in Moscow!" he said, shooting out his foot under the table. "I myself saw them here for the first time. They wouldn't have them at home, they were afraid of them. Our boyars and nobles are coarse peasants: all they do is sleep, stuff themselves and pray. Ours is a grim country. You would be afraid to live there a single day. As I sit here with you, it's terrible to look back. They say of me that I shed much blood; in anonymous tracts they say I torture people with my own hands. . . ."

His mouth twisted, his cheek twitched, and his prominent eyes became for a moment glassy as if they saw not the well-spread table but a windowless, blood-bespattered hut in Preobrazhensk. He jerked his neck and shoulder, sharply driving away the vision. The two women watched his changing expressions with awed curiosity.

"But you mustn't believe it. What I like best of all is building ships. The galley *Principium* was built with these hands from mast to keel." He unclenched his fists at last and showed his calloused palms. "I love the sea and I love to let off fireworks. I know fourteen trades, but not thoroughly, and that's why I have come here. And when they say I am cruel and like blood, they lie. I'm not cruel. But to live with our people in Moscow would drive anyone to a frenzy. In Russia everything must be smashed and built anew. And our people are so stubborn! They'll let themselves be whipped to the bone. . . ." He stopped, and looked into the women's eyes with an embarrassed smile. "It's an easy job to be a king here. While I, Mother"—he seized the Kurfürstin Sophia's hand—"I've got to begin by learning to be a carpenter."

The ladies were delighted. They forgave him his dirty nails, they forgave him for wiping his hands on the tablecloth and eating noisily, and for the way he told them about Moscow customs, using sailors' phrases, winking his round eye and emphasising his words by nudging Sophia-Charlotte with his elbow. Everything about him seemed terrifying but enchanting, from a certain impression of cruelty to his virginal ignorance of many aspects of culture. Like a powerful animal, Peter exuded a primeval freshness. The Kurfürstin wrote later in her diary: "He is a very good and also a very bad man. From the moral standpoint he is a perfect representative of his country."

The sparkling wine and the proximity of such clever and charming women made Peter's spirits rise. Sophia-Charlotte wished to present her uncle, her brother and their suite. Peter fumbled in his pocket for his pipe, smiling oddly with his small mouth, and nodded: "All right, as you wish." They entered: the Duke of Celle, a dried-up old man with a small beard of out-moded Spanish cut, and the twisted up moustache of a rake and duellist; the Crown Prince, a languid youth with a narrow face, dressed in black velvet; brightly and sumptuously attired ladies and cavaliers, and broad-shouldered, handsome Alexander, surrounded by maids of honour: that fellow made himself at home everywhere. The ambassadors Lefort and fat Golovin, the governor of Siberia, were also there for, having caught up with the Tsar's chaise in Koppenbrügge, and, learning Peter's whereabouts, they had hastened to the castle in great alarm, without eating or changing their clothes.

Peter embraced the Duke, picked up the future King of England and kissed him on the cheek, then, with a sweeping gesture of his arm, he bowed easily to the court. The ladies curtsied, and the men made flourishes with their hats.

"Alexander, shut the door!" Peter said in Russian. Then he filled a quart goblet with wine, beckoned the nearest cavalier to approach and said with another odd smile:

"It is the Russian custom that no one may refuse to drink the Tsar's cup. Let all drink to the dregs, ladies and cavaliers alike."

In short, they began to be as merry as in the Foreign Quarter. Italian singers came in with mandolines. Peter wanted to dance, but the Italian music was too soft and too slow, so he sent Alexander to the inn for his own musicians. The Preobrazhensk pipers and buglers, in crimson tunics, with hair cut in a fringe, stood like statues by the wall and beat wooden spoons and cymbals, and blew cowhorns, wooden whistles and brass pipes. Never had such diabolical music sounded under these mediæval vaults. Peter beat time with his foot and kept looking round.

"Alexander, let them have it!"

Alexander moved his shoulders, cocked his eyebrows, put on a solemn face and started off on heel and toe. Sophia wanted to see how Peter danced. He gingerly took the old lady's fingers and led her out in stately fashion. But when he had taken her back to her seat, he selected a plump young woman and began cavorting about.

Lefort took upon himself to order the dancing. Sophia-Charlotte invited the stout Golovin to dance. The volunteers who hastened in from the garden each took a partner and threw themselves into a Russian dance with all kinds of eccentric figures and wild Tatar yells. Skirts whirled, wigs slipped askew. They made the German ladies sweat. And many of the Russians wondered why the ladies had such hard ribs. Peter put the question to Sophia-Charlotte; at first she did not understand, and then she laughed until she cried: "It's not ribs, it's the bones of our corsets."

9

They separated in Koppenbrügge. The ambassadors went by a devious route to Amsterdam, while Peter with a few volunteers went straight on to the Rhine where, before reaching the town of Xanten, they embarked and sailed down the river. Holland, to which Peter had so long looked forward, began beyond Schenkenschantz. They took the right arm of the Rhine, and at the village of Fort passed through the lock into the canals.

Two broad-backed bay horses towed the flat-bottomed barge, sedately moving their heads up and down as they ambled along the sandy path of the grassy bank. The canal stretched out in a straight line across the plain, divided up, as on a map, into vegetable gardens, pastures and flower plantations, and intersected by a network of ditches and canals. It was a hot and slightly misty day. Wallflowers, hyacinths and narcissi were nearly over, and the few flowers left in the beds of rich earth were being cut and packed into baskets. But tulips—dark purple, flame red, variegated and golden—covered the earth with a velvet pall. Everywhere windmill sails were turning in the lazy wind; on all sides there were houses, cottages and farms with steep roofs and storks' nests, and rows of pollarded willows bordered the canals. The outlines of towns, cathedrals, towers, and windmills showed through the blue haze.

A boat laden with hay glided down a canal past vegetable gardens. A sail came out from behind the roof of a farm and moved slowly through the tulips. Dutchmen, in breeches as wide as barrels, tight jackets and wooden shoes, sat placidly smoking by the sluice, green with slime, waiting for the lock to open. Their boats, laden with vegetables, were close by on a canal which stretched away towards the sunlit haze in the distance.

Sometimes the barge floated above the level of the fields and buildings. Down below they could see fruit on trees trained against brick walls, clothes hung out on lines, and peacocks strutting about small, clean, sand-strewn courtyards. The Russians were astounded to see these birds alive. This country—conquered from the sea with infinite labour—seemed like a living dream. Every scrap of earth here was prized and carefully cultivated. How unlike the Russian wild steppe! Peter, smoking a clay pipe in the prow, said to the volunteers:

"Many a yard in Moscow is bigger, but no one dreams of taking a broom and sweeping it, or of planting fruit and vegetables, which would be both useful and pleasant. A building may be on the point of tumbling down, but none of you devils will climb off the stove to prop it up, I know you. You're too lazy to go to the proper place to relieve yourselves, you do it on the threshold. Why is that? We have untold land, yet we are paupers. It is lamentable. Look, here they have got their land from the bottom of the sea and every tree had to be brought and planted. And they have made a real paradise."

The barge passed through locks from the large canal into smaller ones. It was being punted with long poles, constantly meeting heavily-laden boats. The milky-grey surface of the Zuider Zee opened out to the East, and more and more sails showed, more and more people came in sight. Towards evening they neared Amsterdam. Ships, ships, on the rosy stretch of the sea. Masts, sails, the steep roofs of churches and buildings flamed in the glow of the sunset. Deep red clouds rose like mountains from the sea, then quickly paled and grew ashen. Lights came out all over the plain and glided along the canals.

They stopped for supper at a hospitably lighted inn, where they drank gin and English ale. From here Peter sent all the volunteers, with the interpreters and the baggage, to Amsterdam, while he himself, with Menshikov, Alioshka Brovkin and the priest Bitka, took a small boat and sailed on to Zaandam, avoiding the capital.

This was the place he wanted to see more than anything in the world; he had loved it since his childhood. His old friend, the blacksmith Herrit Kist, had told him about it when they were building the play-boats on lake Pereyaslav. Kist, having earned good money, had immediately gone home, but other blacksmiths and shipwrights had arrived from Zaandam, first for Archangel, and later for Voronezh. They told Peter: "Where they build good ships is in Zaandam: light, strong, fast—no other ships can touch them."

In the villages of Zaandam, Koog, Oost-Zaan, West Zaan and Zaandijk, half a dozen miles north of Amsterdam, there were no less than fifty shipyards. They worked day and night and with such speed that a ship was built in five or six weeks. The slips were surrounded by factories and workshops where machinery, worked by windmills, turned out everything that was needed: turned parts, nails, shackles, ropes, sails and implements. These private shipyards built whalers and medium-sized trading ships; warships and large merchantmen for trade with the colonies were built at Amsterdam on the two Admiralty stocks.

All night, as their boat sailed up the deep, narrow channel, they saw the shore lights, heard the strokes of axes, the creaking of beams and the clang of iron. By the light of a fire they could make out the ribs of a ship's frame, the poop of a ship on the stocks, the framework of a wooden crane which raised heavy beams and stacks of boards on blocks. Small boats with lanterns darted to and fro, and hoarse voices sounded. There was a smell of pine shavings, resin and river damp. The four sturdy Dutchmen rowing their boat with a creaking of oars puffed at their curved pipes.

In the middle of the night they stopped at an inn for a rest, and then the oarsmen were changed. The morning was damp and grey. Houses, windmills, barges, long sheds: all that had appeared so enormous in the night, seemed to crouch lower on the banks covered with grey dew. Weeping willows hung down to the misty water. Where was that famous Zaandam?

"There it is, that's Zaandam!" one of the oarsmen said, nodding towards a group of small, flat-fronted, steep-roofed houses of timber and weather-stained brick. Their boat moved past them on the dirty canal as if it were a street. The village was waking up; here and there fires were already burning. Women were washing the square windows—their small panes iridescent with age—and polishing the brass handles and latches on the sagging doors. A cock crowed on the turf-covered roof of an out-house. It was growing lighter and the water in the canal was smoking. Washing hung out to dry on lines stretched across the canal: enormously wide breeches, coarse linen shirts, woollen stockings. As their boat passed under them, they had to bend down.

They turned into a side canal past rotten piles, chicken-runs, barns with lean-to privies, hollow willows. The canal ended in a small backwater where a man in a knitted cap sat hunched up in a boat fishing for eels. Peter stared intently at him, and then jumped up and shouted:

"Herrit Kist, the blacksmith, is it you?"

The man drew in his line and only then looked up. In spite of his composure it was evident that he was surprised to see a young man dressed as a Dutch workman, in glazed hat, red coat and linen trousers, standing in the approaching boat. But there was no mistaking that face—imperious, frank and wild-eyed. Herrit Kist was startled: on this misty morning the Tsar of Moscow had rowed out of the canal in a common boat. He blinked his sandy lashes; yes, it really was the Tsar. He called out to him:

"Hey, is that you, Peter?"

"Good day!"

"Good day, Peter!"

Herrit Kist cautiously pressed Peter's hand with his horny fingers. Then he noticed Alexander:

"Oh, there you are, my lad! I said to myself, it must be them. It's splendid that you've come to Holland."

"For the whole winter, Kist, to work in a shipyard at carpentering. We'll buy the tools today."

"The widow of Jacob Ohm has good tools to sell, not too dear. I'll talk to her."

"Before I left Moscow I thought you would put me up."

"There isn't enough room, Peter; I'm a poor man. It's quite a ramshackle little house."

"But then I don't suppose they'll pay me much on the slips."

"Ah, I see you're still fond of a joke, Peter."

"No, we have no time for jokes now. In two years we must build a fleet and learn to be clever instead of fools, so that no one in our country will be left with white hands."

"It's a good idea, Peter."

The boats glided towards the grassy bank where there was a wooden house with two windows and a lean-to. Its tiled roof sagged. Smoke rose from its tall chimney and floated up to the branches of an old maple. By the crooked door with its latticed transom a clean mat was spread for people to leave their wooden shoes—for in Holland no one entered a house except in stockinged feet. A thin, elderly woman, with her hands folded under her clean apron, watched them from the doorstep. When Kist, dropping the oars on to the grass, shouted to her: "Hey, these people have come to us from Muscovy", she gravely nodded her cap with ear-pieces.

Peter liked the house very much and he rented a room with two windows, a small dark closet with a bed in it for himself and Alexander and an attic for Alioshka and Bitka, reached from the room by a ladder. That same day he bought good tools from the widow Ohm, and as he was bringing them back in a wheelbarrow, he met Rensen, a carpenter who had worked one winter in Voronezh. Fat, good-natured Rensen stopped short, opened his mouth and suddenly turned pale: this youth with his hard shiny hat pushed to the back of his head trundling a wheelbarrow reminded him of something so terrible that he felt sick at heart. His memory conjured up falling snow, a red glare and the bodies of Russian workmen swinging in the icy wind.

"How are you, Rensen?" Peter said, setting down the wheelbarrow. He wiped his sweating face with his sleeve, and held out his hand: "Yes, it is I. How are you getting on? You shouldn't have run away from Voronezh. As for me, I'm starting work at Lingst Rogge's wharf on Monday. But don't tell anyone, will you? Here I'm Peter Mihaylov." And the red glare of Voronezh shone again in his staring, prominent eyes.

10

"Mein Herr König, the navigators sent to study, according to your ukase, have all been placed. Ivan Golovin, Pleshcheyev, Krapotkin, Vasily Volkov, Vereshchagin, Alexander Menshikov, Alexey Brovkin, the permanently drunk priest Bitka and myself have been assigned to shipbuilding, some in Zaandam, others to the West-Indian shipyard; Alexander Kikin and Stepan Vasilyev, to mast-making; Yakim the painter and the Rolsk deacon Krivosyhin, to water-mills of every kind; Borisov and Uvarov, to boat-building; Lukin and Kobylin, to block-making; Konshin, Skvortsov, Petelin, Muhanov and Sinyavin have joined ships in different places as sailors; Archilov has gone to The Hague to learn gunnery. The equerries who were sent here ahead of us wanted to return to Moscow after having learnt about the compass, thinking that this was all. But their intentions have changed and we have ordered them to go as labourers to the Ostade shipyard: let them sweat a little.

"Jacob Bruce has been here and brought us Your Grace's letter. He showed us still unhealed wounds which he complained of having received from Your Grace at a feast. Brute! How much longer are you going to burn people? Your victims have even come here. Drop your acquaintance with Ivan Hmelnitsky,* or it will earn you a skinned nose. Peter."

* Personification of drunkenness.

"You say in your letter to me, my Master, that I am acquainted with Ivan Hmelnitsky, but this, my Master, is not true. Jacob came to you drunk straight from Moscow and said this in the confusion of his mind. I have no time for Ivan: there is constant trouble and quarrelling, and we constantly dabble in blood. It is for you to keep up acquaintance with Ivan at your leisure; we have no time for him. As I have already written to you, my Master, eight more men have been caught who belong to the same robber gang; these thieves are tradespeople from the town: butchers, drivers and boyars' men, Petrushka Selezen, Mitka Pichuga, Popugay, Kuska Zayka, and the nobleman's son Mishka Tirtov. Their hiding-place and cache of stolen clothing was outside the Tver gates. As for Bruce, or any others who came to complain about me, it is nothing but drunken lies. With greetings, Fedor Romodanovsky."

"*Mein Herr König,* I have received my State letter which speaks of the foreigner Thomas Pfadenbracht and asks how he is to trade in tobacco in future. There was a ukase about it already last winter: the first year he is to trade for himself, the second year for himself and to pay taxes, and the third year to hold an auction and sell it to the highest bidder. I am greatly astonished that your government boyars could not have thought this out for themselves, the more so as the matter is of no great importance. For your government service we have bought here 15,000 muskets and have placed orders for 10,000 more; and we have also ordered for your service 8 howitzers and 14 guns. I have spoken here many times about skilled iron-workers, but we have not been able to find any yet. The good ones will not move, and we do not want inferior ones. Please give my greetings to my master, the general, and beg him to take care of my family. (The rest in invisible ink.) The news here is the following: the French King is again preparing a fleet in Brest, but no one knows its destination. Yesterday news came from Vienna that the King of Spain had died. And what will happen after his death, Your Grace knows himself.*

"You also write about the great rains which you are having. And it makes us wonder how in such mansions in Moscow you can have such dirt. Here we live below water level and yet it is dry. Peter."

Vasily Volkov, who kept a diary on Peter's orders, noted:
"In Amsterdam I saw a female child, eighteen months old, all covered with hair and very fat, with a face ten inches across: she had

* The war for the Spanish succession. (*Author's note*)

been brought to the fair. There too I saw an elephant that played minuets, trumpeted in Turkish fashion, fired a musket and played with a dog which is its companion; most marvellous and extraordinary."

"I saw a human head made of wood that could speak! They wind it up like a clock, and whatever you say, this head repeats. I saw two wooden horses on a wheel: people sit on them and drive fast wherever they want along the streets. I saw a glass through which you can melt silver and lead; they burnt wood under water with it. There were about four finger-breadths of water, the water boiled and the wood was burnt.

"I saw a human body at a doctor's: all the insides had been taken apart—the heart, the lungs, the kidneys, and you could see how stones form in the kidneys. The nerve on which the lung lives is like an old rag. And nerves which live in the brain are like threads. Extremely wonderful.

"The town of Amsterdam stands by the sea on low ground; canals, large enough for ships to sail on them, have been dug in all the streets; on each side of the canals the streets are wide: in some places two carriages can drive abreast. On each bank of the canal there are great trees with lanterns between them. There are lanterns in all the streets, and each night everyone is obliged to light such a lamp in front of his house. On these streets there are great crowds taking their pleasure.

"The merchants here are so rich that in Europe they are considered above all others, and the trading people are very prosperous. They dress as nowhere else. The Bourse, which is built of white stone and decorated inside with carved alabaster, is very wonderful. The floor is laid out like a chess board, and each merchant stands on his own square. There are so many people in the public square every day that they can only move about with great difficulty. And the shouting there is tremendous. Certain people—poor men from among the Jews—mingle with the merchants and give them snuff when they want it in a hurry; in this way they make a living."

Jacob Nomen, a Dutchman of an enquiring turn of mind, wrote in his diary:

"The Tsar was unable to maintain his incognito for more than a week; some of the inhabitants who had been to Moscow recognised him. The rumour quickly spread all over our country. On the Amsterdam Bourse people laid heavy bets on whether it was the Tsar himself or one of his envoys. Herr Hautmann, who trades with Muscovy and has more than once had the Tsar as his guest in Moscow, came to Zaandam to pay his respects to the Tsar. He said to him:

" 'Your Anointed Majesty, is it you?'

"To which the Tsar replied rather curtly:

" 'As you see.'

"After that they had a long discussion on the difficulties of the northern sea-route to Muscovy and the advantages of Baltic ports. During the discussion Hautmann did not dare to look the Tsar straight in the face, knowing that this might anger him—he cannot bear anyone looking straight into his eyes. There was a case when a certain Alderston Blok looked straight into the Tsar's eyes in the street, very impudently, as if at something very surprising and amusing. For this the Tsar slapped his face so hard that Alderston Blok was hurt and hurried away in shame, while the passers-by laughed at him. 'Bravo, Alderston, you have received the accolade!'

"Another merchant wanted to see the Tsar at work and asked a master-craftsman in the shipyard to let him satisfy his curiosity. The master told him that the man to whom he said: 'Carpenter Peter, do this or that', would be the Tsar of Muscovy. The inquisitive merchant went to the wharf and saw some workers carrying a heavy beam. Then the master shouted: 'Carpenter Peter, why don't you lend them a hand?' At which one of the carpenters, a man nearly seven feet high, in tar-smeared clothes and curls clinging damply to his forehead, put his axe down and obediently ran across and put his shoulder under the beam and helped the others to carry it, much to the merchant's astonishment.

"On finishing work he visits a shabby eating-house near the docks, where he sits with a mug of beer, smokes his pipe and talks gaily with the commonest people, laughing at their jokes, not caring in the least on these occasions that no respect is shown to him. He frequently visits the wives of those who are serving at present in Muscovy, drinks gin with them, slaps them playfully and jokes. The following story exemplifies his odd behaviour: he bought some plums, put them in his hat and, holding the hat under his arm, ate them in the street as he passed over the dyke to Zuiddijk. A crowd of boys followed him. He liked the looks of some of them and he said: 'Little men, would you like some plums?' And he gave them a few. Then others came up and said: 'Give us some plums too, or something else.' But he only made a face at them and spat out a stone, greatly amused at teasing them. Some of the boys got so angry that they began to pelt him with rotten apples and pears, grass and other rubbish. He laughed and went on. One of the boys hit him in the back with a stone; this hurt him and made him angry. At last, near the lock, a clod of earth hit him on the head and he lost his temper and shouted at them: 'Have you no burgomaster here to keep order?' But even this did not frighten the boys in the least.

"On holidays he sails about the bay in a boat which he bought from Harmensen, the painter, for forty gulden and a pot of beer. One day, when he was sailing on the Kirkrak, a passenger-boat began to steer in close, and a number of people who were burning with curiosity to have a look at the Tsar crowded on deck. The boat came nearly alongside, and the Tsar, wanting to rid himself of their attentions, picked up two empty bottles and flung one after the other straight into the crowd of passengers, but luckily no one was hit.

"He has a very inquisitive turn of mind and is constantly asking: 'What is that?' and when he is told, he says: 'I want to have a look at it'. Then he examines it and asks questions until he understands it. He went to Utrecht with some of his companions to meet the Stadtholder of Holland, the English King William of Orange, and there he made them take him over orphanages, hospitals, and various factories and workshops. He was particularly interested in Professor Ruich's anatomical cabinet, and was so delighted with an embalmed child, smiling as if alive, that he kissed it. When Ruich lifted the sheet from another body which he had dismembered for anatomical research, the Tsar noticed that his Russian companions looked disgusted; he was so furious that he ordered them to tear away some of the muscles with their teeth.

"I have written all the foregoing from what various people have told me, but yesterday I succeeded in seeing him myself. He was leaving the widow Ohm's shop, walking rapidly and swinging his arms, a new axe-helve in each hand. He is very tall, well-built, vigorous, agile and graceful. His face is round, with a somewhat stern expression; his eyebrows are dark, and his hair is short, curly and rather dark. He was wearing a serge coat, a red shirt and a felt hat. Hundreds of people who gather in the streets have seen him like this, including my wife and daughter."

"Mein Herr König, yesterday the Imperial ambassadors sent a nobleman from Vienna to our ambassadors with the news that God has granted such a victory over the Turks to the Emperor Leopold's

armies that they could not hold out in three entrenchments, but were forced out and beaten and fled across the bridge, while the Emperor's men opened fire from their batteries. The Turks jumped into the water, while the others attacked them with swords from behind, till the Turks were utterly defeated and their baggage-train captured. In that battle 12,000 Turks were killed, among them the Grand Vizier, and they even allege that the Sultan has been killed too.

"The Commander-in-Chief of the Imperial troops was the brother of the Duke of Savoy, Eugene, a young man; they say he is twenty-seven and that this was his first battle.

"Having reported this, Sire, we congratulate you on this triumph and request that every manner of celebration be held, accompanied by gun and musket fire. From Amsterdam, on the 13th day of September, Peter."

11

In January Peter moved on to England and settled down four miles from London, at a shipyard in the small town of Deptford. There he found what he had vainly sought in Holland: the art of shipbuilding based on scientific laws, or the geometrical proportions of ships. For two and a half months he studied mathematics and ship-designing. In order to establish a school of navigation in Moscow he engaged Andrew Ferguson, a learned professor of mathematics; and he also arranged for Captain John Perry, a canal engineer, to supervise the cutting of the Volga-Don canal. But he did not succeed in engaging any English sailors: their demands were too high, and the envoys had little money. Sables and brocades, and even some articles from the Crown treasure—goblets, necklaces, Chinese porcelain—were constantly being sent from Moscow, but all this was not enough to cover the heavy orders and to engage men.

An amiable Englishman, Lord Peregrine, Marquess of Carmarthen, came to the rescue: he offered to buy the monopoly of the sale of tobacco throughout Muscovy, and paid in advance £20,000 sterling for the right to import into Muscovy three thousand casks of this nicotine weed, each weighing five hundred English pounds. At the same time they succeeded in engaging the celebrated Dutch captain Cornelius Kreis, a steadfast and headstrong man, and an able sailor with experience of long voyages. He was to receive nine thousand gulden, a house and full maintenance in Moscow, the title of Vice-Admiral and three per cent. of any prizes taken; and in the event of his being captured, he was to be ransomed at the expense of the treasury.

Foreign commanders, pilots, boatswains, doctors, sailors, ships' cooks and shipbuilding and artillery experts began to arrive in Moscow via Archangel and Novgorod. By the Tsar's orders they were quartered on nobles and merchants, and Moscow became very crowded. The boyars did not know what to do with such a swarm of foreigners.

Long trains of waggons brought arms, sail-cloth, tools for working wood and iron, whalebone, cartridge paper, cork, anchors, boxwood and ashwood, marble, cases containing infants and deformities preserved in spirit, dried crocodiles and stuffed birds. The people were half-starved, Moscow was full of beggars, even robbers were starving, and still these things kept coming. And those well-fed, impudent foreigners were flooding the country. Could the Tsar be in his right mind?

For some time the rumour had been going round the Moscow market-places that the Tsar had been drowned abroad; some said he had been nailed into a barrel and that Lefort had found a foreigner like him and was passing him off as Peter and would now rule in his name and oppress the people and uproot the Old Faith. Government agents seized these rumour-mongers and dragged them off to the Preobrazhensk administration, where Romodanovsky himself questioned them with the aid of whip and fire. But it was impossible to discover the source of these subversive rumours. The guards at the Novodevichy convent were strengthened to prevent any communication with Tsarevna Sophia.

Romodanovsky invited the boyars and great nobles to his palace and did not spare the wine. Musketeers were placed at the doors to prevent the guests leaving, and in this manner the feasting went on for days. Jesters and dwarfs crawled under the tables to listen to what was being said. A trained bear went round among the tipsy guests offering them a tankard of wine in his paws and, if anyone refused it, the bear threw down the tankard and clawed at him and hugged him, trying to bite his face. Romodanovsky, fat and weary, dozed half-drunk on a throne, though with ears pricked and eyes alert; but even in their cups the guests guarded their tongues, although he knew that many of them were only waiting for the time when the earth would start to rock under Peter and his companions.

Soon the enemy came out into the open. About a hundred and fifty streltsi who had deserted their regiments on the Lithuanian frontier arrived in Moscow. Four strelets regiments—those of Colonel Hundertmark, Chubarov, Kolzakov and Chermny—had been sent there to reinforce the governor Mihail Romodanovsky. These were the same regiments which, after the taking of Azov, had been left to build the fortifications at Azov and Taganrog and, during the previous autumn, had mutinied with the Cossacks, threatening to do as Stenka Razin had done. They were sick to death of the heavy work and wanted to return to Moscow, to their wives, to peaceful trade and handicrafts; but instead they had been sent to the Lithuanian swamps on short commons.

Apparently there were people in Moscow who had been expecting the streltsi. Their petition was taken at once by one of the palace maidservants to the women's quarters in the Kremlin, where Sophia's sister, Tsarevna Martha, lived under a none-too-strict surveillance. Through the same woman Martha soon gave an answer:

"We have trouble in high places: certain boyars who frequent the Foreign Quarter and hobnob with the foreigners, want to strangle Tsarevich Alexey. But we put a changeling in his place and this so angered them that they struck the young Tsaritsa in the face. We do not know what the future holds. No one knows whether the Tsar is alive or dead. Unless you hasten to Moscow, you streltsi will never see it again, for a ukase has already been issued against you."

The streltsi rushed with this letter to the public squares, and wherever appropriate, shouted: "In former days Tsarevna Sophia used to feed three hundred people eight times a year, and her sisters, the Tsarevnas, also gave the common people on flesh days cows' tongues and cow-heel jelly, smoked goose, fowls with buckwheat and meat and egg pies, and they also gave salt pork, salt fish, smelts, and plenty of vodka and double-strained mead. Such were the kind of Tsars we used to have. But today only foreigners eat well, and you can all die of hunger—the cost of your food is spent abroad on buying crocodiles."

They made an uproar in front of the strelets headquarters and were not afraid even of the boyar Troyekurov; and when several of the noisest of them were arrested and were being carried off to prison, the others beat off the guard and set them free.

Romodanovsky summoned Generals Gordon and Golovin, and it was decided to get the mutineers out of Moscow at once. Romodanovsky himself, greatly perturbed, went to inspect the Guards and other regiments, but there all was quiet and orderly. He selected a hundred men from the Semenovsky regiment and called for volunteers from the town tradespeople. In the night, they noiselessly entered the strelets suburb, broke open the doors and drove the men out one by one. But none of the streltsi offered any resistance: "Oh, it's you, the Semenovtsi? Why are you making so much noise? We'll be going anyway." The man would take up a bag of pies, his gun wrapped in a rag, and go off with a grin, as if he had accomplished his business in Moscow.

The streltsi took back with them to the Lithuanian frontier a letter from Tsarevna Sophia. On that day Martha had sent her dwarf to the Novodevichy convent with a pie for her sister which contained the petition from the streltsi. Sophia sent her answer back by the same dwarf:

"Streltsi! I am informed that a few men from your regiments have come to Moscow. All your four regiments must come to Moscow and set up their camp outside the Novodevichy convent, and petition me to return to Moscow and rule as before. And if the soldiers on guard at the convent refuse to let me go, you must deal with them and kill them, and then enter Moscow with me. And all those who oppose—with their retainers or soldiers—you must fight."

This was an order to take Moscow by force. When the deserters returned with the Tsarevna's letter to their regiments on the Lithuanian frontier, mutiny broke out.

12

Neither Peter nor the ambassadors understood much of European politics. For the Muscovites to make war meant to protect the steppes from the nomads, to put an end to the marauding incursions of the Crimean Tatars, to make safe the communications by land and water with the East and to break through to the seaboard.

European politics seemed to them a murky business. They firmly believed in written agreements and the oaths of kings. They knew that the French King was siding with the Turkish Sultan and that William of Orange, as King of England and Stadtholder of Holland, had promised Peter his help in the war with Turkey. And then suddenly, like a bolt from the blue, there came the incomprehensible news, brought from August, King of Poland, by a petty nobleman, that the Emperor of Austria, Leopold, had opened peace negotiations with the Turks, and that William of Orange was working hard for this peace, without consulting either the Russians or the Poles.

Then what of his recent assurances of zeal for the success of Christian arms against the foes of the Holy Sepulchre? What did it mean? He had presented Peter with a yacht, he had called him brother, they had feasted together. What was one to think now?

The Emperor Leopold's peace talks with the Turks were at least understandable: the war for the Spanish succession had begun between him and the French King, about—so the ambassadors thought —which of them should put his son on the throne in Madrid. A very important matter, but what had it to do with England and Holland?

It was difficult for either Peter or the ambassadors to grasp that the English and Dutch merchants and industrialists had long been concerned with the war for the destruction of France's mercantile and military supremacy in the Atlantic ocean and the Mediterranean, that the Spanish succession did not mean a throne for this or that king's son, not the precious crown of Charles the Great, but free routes for ships laden with cloth and iron, silk and spices, rich markets and open ports, and that it was more convenient for the Dutch and English not to fight themselves but invite others to do so.

And it seemed still more incomprehensible that the English and the Dutch in their desire to free the hands of the Austrian Emperor —for war with France—should be so insistent on the Russians continuing the war with the Sultan. This was the high and ambiguous European *politique*.

Peter returned to Amsterdam. The burgomasters, when asked about the unpleasant news from Vienna, gave evasive answers and turned the conversation to commercial matters. In the same way they evaded another business which was important for the Muscovites.

That year a master-smith, Demidov, had found magnetic iron-ore in the Urals. Vinius wrote to Peter:

"There can be no better ore, and there never has been in the world; it is so rich that a hundred pounds of ore yield forty pounds of pig-iron. Please urge the ambassadors to find good iron-workers who know how to make steel."

The English and Dutch listened attentively to talk of the magnetic ore in the Urals, but when it came to finding good craftsmen, they boggled and prevaricated, and said that the Russians would be unable to cope with such work, and that they would go and have a look on the spot and then perhaps would undertake the business themselves. So in the end they did not succeed in engaging skilled iron-workers either in England or in Holland.

To all these anxieties another was added by the news of the strelets mutiny in Moscow. A secret agent in Vienna informed the ambassadors that there too they already knew about the event: a Polish priest was going about the town spreading the rumour that there was a rising in Moscow, that Prince Vasily Golitsin had been brought back from exile, that Tsarevna Sophia had been set on the throne and the people had taken the oath of allegiance to her.

"*Mein Herr König,* in your official letter you inform me of the strelets mutiny and that it has been crushed by the efforts of your government and of the soldiers. We are very pleased. But I am much annoyed with you. Why did you make no enquiry into the matter and let the the culprits go back to the frontier? God will be your judge. It is not at all what we decided that time in the anteroom.

"In case you think we are dead, because the mails from here have been delayed, we have not lost a single man, thank God. We are all alive. I do not understand where you get these womanish fears. Please do not be angry: truly I write from the sorrow of my heart. This week we are leaving for Vienna. There all they can talk about is our disappearance. Peter."

13

Trinity Sunday was a clear, still day. The streets had been swept. Birch branches were fading at gates and wickets.* The only people to be seen were watchmen with cudgels or pikes outside heavily-padlocked shops. All Moscow was at mass. Hot, incense-laden air floated out of the low church doors decorated with little birches. Even the crowds of beggars on the church porches had grown languid on this azure day to the ringing of bells; the festive sun warmed their tousled heads and their bodies under their tattered clothing. There was a faint smell of alcohol in the air.

The peaceful quiet was suddenly broken by the clatter of wheels, and a good, iron-tyred light carriage rattled furiously over the log pavement. The well-fed horse was tearing along at a gallop, and a merchant, hatless, his blue cloth coat covered with dust, his eyes starting out of his head, bumped and jolted in the carriage, lashing the horse. Everyone recognised Ivan Brovkin. On reaching the Red Square he left his panting horse to the beggars who had run up, and

---

* Old Russian custom of decorating rooms and houses with a little birch or birch branches, on Trinity Sunday.

rushed headlong—hot and copper-red—into the Kazan cathedral, where the highest boyars were attending mass. Pushing aside people whom even in his thoughts he would have feared to touch, he saw Romodanovsky's broad, brocade-covered back. Romodanovsky was standing in front of all the others on a rug before the ancient altar-screen; his fat, sallow face was buried in his high, pearl-studded collar. Having pushed his way through to him, Brovkin gave him a hurried low bow and, looking boldly into his rather dim eyes made terrifying by their angrily puffed lids, said:

"My lord, I have been driving at full speed from Sychevka—that's my village near New Jerusalem. I bring terrible news."

"From Sychevka?" Romodanovsky could make nothing of it and glared at Ivan Artemyich. "What's the matter with you, are you drunk? Don't you know how to conduct yourself?" His neck swelled with anger and his drooping moustache quivered. Brovkin, unafraid, bent over his ear:

"Four strelets regiments are marching on Moscow. They are about two days' march from New Jerusalem. They are moving slowly, with baggage-trains. Forgive me, my lord, it's because of this news that I am troubling you."

Leaning his staff against him, Romodanovsky seized Ivan Artemyich's hand and squeezed it hard. His face flushed, and he turned and looked round at the richly-clad boyars staring at him inquisitively. All dropped their eyes under his glance. With a slow nod he signalled Boris Golitsin to approach:

"Come to me after mass. Tell the Archimandrite to hurry with the service. Tell Golovin and Vinius to join me at once."

And again, conscious of the boyars' whispers at his back, he half turned and looked at them calmly. They were so alarmed that they even forgot to cross themselves. There was no sound but the jingling of the censer and of a pigeon beating its wings against a dusty window in the vaulted roof.

14

The four regiments of Hundertmark, Chubarov, Kolzakov and Chermny camped on the marshy ground under the walls of the monastery of the Resurrection, known as New Jerusalem. A star twinkled in the green sunset sky behind the Babylonian belfry. The monastery was in darkness, and the gates were closed. It was dark too in the camp; the fires had been stamped out. Carts creaked and harsh voices sounded; the streltsi intended to cross the narrow Istra river that night and get on to the Moscow road.

They had been delayed at the monastery and at the village of Sychevka by their search for provender. The scouts returning from the vicinity of Moscow said that the town was in ferment, and that the boyars and great merchants were fleeing to their villages and estates. The townspeople were expecting the streltsi and, when they appeared, would kill the sentries at the gates and let the regiments into Moscow. The Commander-in-Chief Shein had collected about three thousand of the old play-soldiers from Lefort's and Gordon's regiments, and they would fight; but probably the whole people would help the streltsi, while the strelets women were already sharpening their pikes and axes and rushing round wildly, hoping to see their husbands, sons and brothers.

All day there had been arguments in the regiments; some wanted to push straight on to Moscow, others said they ought to avoid Moscow and entrench themselves in Serpuhov or Tula, whence they could send messengers to summon help from the Don Cossacks and the streltsi in the border towns.

"Why Serpuhov? Let's go home, to our quarters."

"We don't want to stand a siege. What's Shein to us? We'll raise the whole of Moscow!"

"Once before we didn't succeed in raising it. It's a dangerous business."

"They've got Gordon and Colonel Krage with their troops. That'll be no joke."

"We're tired. And we haven't got much gunpowder. Better dig ourselves in."

Ovsey Rzhov, who had been elected captain, climbed on to a cart. Already in Toropets, where the mutiny began, they had got rid of their colonels and officers. Tihon Hundertmark had just managed to save his life by riding away, and Kolzakov, with a broken head, barely succeeded in escaping across the river over the remnants of a bridge. Then and there they had called a general meeting and elected strelets leaders. Ovsey shouted, straining his voice to the utmost:

"Who has still got a shirt on his body? Mine has rotted away. Since last year I haven't combed my beard or been to the bath. Let those who have shirts go and entrench themselves. As for us, we have only one thought: to go home."

"Home! Home!" the streltsi caught up the shout, climbing on to waggons. "Have you forgotten what Sophia wrote to us? We must go and rescue her as soon as possible. Unless we hurry, we are lost: we shall have Lefort on our necks till the end of our days. We had better fight now and put Sophia on the throne. We'll have pay, food and liberty. We'll put back the pillar on the Red Square. We'll fling the boyars from the belfries, and pillage their houses and share out; the Tsaritsa will let us take everything. And as for the Foreign Quarter, no one will be able to remember where it stood."

The strelets ringleaders—Tuma, Proskuryakov, Zorin, Yorsh—jumped on to Ovsey's cart rattling their swords in their scabbards:

"Lads, start crossing the river!"

"Stick your pikes through anyone who doesn't want to go to Moscow!"

Many rushed to the carts, shouting wildly at the horses. The waggons and crowds of streltsi thronged towards the misty river. But on the far bank, in the dimly seen bushes, something which looked like a guidon was waved, and a hoarse voice shouted:

"Stop! Stop!"

Straining their eyes, they made out a man in armour and plumed helmet standing at the water's edge. They recognised Gordon. Silence fell.

"Streltsi!" they heard him shout. "I have with me four thousand troops who are loyal to their sovereign. We have occupied an excellent position for battle. But I do not want to shed the blood of brothers. Tell me what you want and whither you are going."

"To Moscow!" "Home!" "We are starved!" "We are in rags!" "Why did you send us to a forest swamp?" "Weren't there enough of us killed at Azov?" "Didn't we eat enough carrion on our way back from Azov?" "We are worn down with work on the forts." "Let us get back to Moscow. We'll have three days at home and then surrender."

When they had done shouting, Gordon put his hands to his mouth and shouted:

"Very well. But only fools cross rivers by night. Fools! The Istra is a deep river, you'll lose your waggons. Better wait on that side, and we will wait here, and tomorrow we will talk."

He mounted his big horse and galloped away into the darkness. The streltsi hesitated, shouted and argued, and then began to light fires and cook their food.

When the sun rose in the cloudless dawn, they saw the serried ranks of the Preobrazhensky regiment on the rising ground across the river and, above them, twelve bronze cannon on green gun-carriages. The fuses were smoking. Five hundred dragoons with their guidons were drawn up on the left flank. On the right flank, barring the road to Moscow, the rest of the troops were stationed behind palisades and chevaux-de-frise.

The streltsi raised a shout and hurriedly harnessed their waggons; then, Cossack fashion, they formed a square with the waggons. Gordon, with six dragoons, rode slowly down the hill to the river; his black horse sniffed the water and then, in a series of leaps, carried him over the ford. The streltsi surrounded the general.

"Listen," he said raising his hand in an iron gauntlet "you are good and sensible people. Why should we fight? Hand over the ringleaders, those scoundrels who went to Moscow."

Ovsey lunged towards the horse; his beard was matted and his eyes bloodshot:

"We have no scoundrels here. It is you, blackguards, who call Russian people scoundrels! We all have a cross round our necks. Is it perhaps Lefort who doesn't like the cross?"

They pressed closer with a buzz of voices. Gordon sat motionless with eyes half-closed:

"We won't let you into Moscow. Listen to an old soldier, stop this mutiny. It will only end badly for you."

The streltsi grew more and more excited and began to curse and use foul language. Tuma, tall, dark-haired and eagle-eyed, climbed on a cannon, waving a document.

"All our complaints are written here. Let us get across the river—if only three of us—and we will read our petition to the soldiers."

"Read it now! Listen, Gordon!"

Haltingly, sawing the air with his fist, Tuma read out:

". . . at Azov, in order to inflict heavy damage to Russian piety, the heretic Francis Lefort took the best Moscow streltsi up to the walls at an ill-timed moment and posted them in the most dangerous positions, thus causing the death of many. At his instigation a mine was laid, which killed three hundred and more of us. . . ."

Gordon touched his horse with his spurs and tried to seize the document. Tuma sprang back, and the streltsi shouted savagely. Tuma went on:

"And by his wish insults are showered on the people, beards are shaved off, and tobacco is smoked, and in every way our ancient piety is undermined. . . ."

Gordon lost all hope of making himself heard by the streltsi. He made his horse rear and, as the crowd scattered, he galloped to the river. They saw him dismount at the Commander-in-Chief's tent, and soon after the slanting rays of the sun caught the glint of the priests' vestments. Then the streltsi too demanded a litany before the battle. They spread a saddle-cloth over a gun-carriage and set on it a horse-pail with water for the blessing. They took off their caps. Barefooted, ragged priests fervently began the service: "Grant us victory, O Lord, over the Amalekites and Philistines and all heretic nations."

On the far side of the river, by Shein's tent, men were already going up to kiss the cross, while the streltsi still knelt and sang. Crossing themselves, they went to fetch their muskets, bit off the ends of their cartridges and loaded. The priests folded up their ragged stoles and went behind the carts. Then all twelve guns on the hill fired at once. The cannon-balls flew hissing over the carts and burst by the monastery walls, throwing up masses of earth.

Ovsey Rzhov, Tuma, Zorin and Yorsh brandished their swords: "Brothers, forward! Break through!"

"We'll take Moscow by force!"

"Form companies!"

"The guns, roll back the guns!"

The streltsi rushed forward in ragged lines, throwing their caps in the air and shouting wildly the watchword: "Sergiev! Sergiev!"

Colonel Krage ordered the guns to be aimed lower and the battery fired on the baggage-train. Splinters flew and horses fell kicking. The streltsi replied with musket fire and shells from their four cannon. The battery fired for the third time, right into the thick of the streltsi. Some of them tried to rush the barriers guarding the Moscow road, but they were met there by the regiments of Gordon and Lefort. The cannon thundered for the fourth time and the hill was wrapped in thick smoke. The strelets lines broke, turned this way and that, and fled. They ran in all directions, abandoning banners, arms, coats and caps. The dragoons crossed the river and gave chase, driving the fugitives back to their encampment as dogs drive sheep.

That same day Generalissimo Shein transferred his camp close to the monastery walls and began investigations. Not one of the streltsi betrayed Sophia or mentioned her letter. They wept, exhibited their wounds, shook out their rags and said that they had set out for Moscow in a moment of madness, but had now come to their senses and realised themselves that they were wrong.

Tuma hung on the rack with his flesh torn by the knout, but did not utter a word; he only looked at his tormentors with hatred in his eyes. Tuma, Proskuryakov and fifty-six of the most violent of the streltsi were hanged on the Moscow road. The rest were sent under escort to prisons and monasteries.

15

Never had the Russians met such evasive liars as the politicians at the Imperial court of Vienna. Peter was received with honours, but as a private individual. Leopold called him affably "Brother", but only when they were alone; he came to visit him incognito, at night, and masked. In discussions of peace with Turkey, the Chancellor agreed with everything, promised everything and denied nothing, but when it came to a decision, he wriggled like an eel. Peter said to him:

"The English and Dutch are making a fuss only because of their trade interests; you don't have to listen to them on everything. The Patriarch of Jerusalem has written, begging us to protect the Holy Sepulchre. Can the Holy Sepulchre be a matter of indifference to the Emperor?"

The Chancellor answered: "The Emperor fully shares your lofty ideals and worthy aims, but such huge sums have been spent in fifteen years of war that peace is the only thing possible at the present time."

"Peace? Peace?" Peter said. "But you are preparing for war with France—how is that?"

But for all reply the Chancellor's watery eyes only twinkled merrily as though he did not understand. Peter told him that he needed the Turkish fortress Kerch and asked that the Emperor demand Kerch for Moscow in the peace terms. The Chancellor replied that undoubtedly these claims were enthusiastically supported by the court of Vienna, but that he foresaw great difficulties in the matter of Kerch, for the Turks were not accustomed to giving up fortresses without a fight.

In short, no good came of the visit to Vienna. Even the envoys were not given a ceremonial audience for presenting their credentials and gifts. They were prepared to agree to cross the antechambers bareheaded and to make do with forty-eight ordinary citizens for carrying the gifts, but they stubbornly insisted that at the entrance to the audience hall the Oberkammerherr should loudly proclaim the Tsar's title, be it only the shortened version, and that the Tsar's presents should not be laid on the carpet at the Emperor's feet. "We are not Chuvashes * and are not tributaries of the Emperor, but a

* A primitive people in Eastern Russia.

nation equal in greatness." The Minister of the Court smiled and gestured deprecatingly: "It is quite impossible to satisfy such unheard-of pretensions."

Here, even more bitterly than in Holland, they learnt the true nature of European politics. To console themselves they went to the opera and marvelled. They visited the castles outside the town. They attended a great court masquerade. Peter was already preparing to start for Venice when letters arrived from Moscow, from Romodanovsky and Vinius, reporting the strelets mutiny at New Jerusalem.

"*Mein Herr König,* your letter, written on the 17th June, has reached me. In it Your Grace informs me that the seed of Ivan Miloslavsky multiplies. I beg you to be firm in this matter, for in no other way can the flames be extinguished. Although we regret leaving our present useful work, on account of these events we will be with you sooner than you expect. Peter."

16

During mass at the Cathedral of the Assumption, Romodanovsky, after kissing the cross, mounted the dais in front of the altar-screen, turned to the boyars and struck the stone flags with his staff:

"His Majesty Tsar Peter is on his way to Moscow."

Then he waddled through the crowd, got into his gilt carriage with two seven-foot lackeys at the back, and thundered through the Moscow streets.

The news came as a thunderbolt to the boyars. During the last eighteen months they had got used to peace and quiet. Now the young falcon was coming back! This meant good-bye to slumber and repose; they would have to masquerade again. And answer for the strelets mutiny? For the slackness in the war with the Tatars? For the empty treasury? For all those affairs which they were on the point of beginning to attend to, but somehow or other had not quite begun? Holy Saints, what a misfortune!

Now there was no question of rest or peace. The great boyars' council met twice a day. All the shopkeepers were ordered to close their shops and come to the Great Treasury to count the copper coin within three days. The chief clerks were summoned from the departments and asked, for the love of God, to put right somehow anything that might be found wrong, and not to let the clerks and scribes go home for the night during the next few days, but tie the refractory ones by their legs to the desks.

The boyars prepared for the Tsar's reception. Some pulled out of their coffers the hated foreign clothes and wigs, powdered with mint to keep out the moth. They ordered superfluous icons to be removed from the dining-halls and whatever mirrors and pictures could be found to be hung on the walls. Eudoxia hurriedly returned from Troitsa with the Tsarevich and Peter's favourite sister Natalia.

At dusk on the 4th of September two dusty carriages pulled up at the iron gates of Romodanovsky's house, and Peter, Lefort, Golovin and Alexander alighted. They knocked. Great watchdogs barked savagely in the courtyard. The soldier who opened the gates did not recognise Peter, who pushed him aside and, with his companions, crossed the untidy yard to a low porch with bulbous and twisted pillars covered by a lead roof. A tame bear was chained at the door. Romodanovsky raised a window sash and looked out, and his bloated face quivered with joy.

17

From Romodanovsky the Tsar drove to the Kremlin. Eudoxia already knew of his arrival and was waiting for him, dressed up and with flushed cheeks. Vorobyiha, in a handsome jacket, smiling and screwing up her eyes, kept a look-out from the Tsaritsa's side porch. Eudoxia kept looking out of her window at Vorobyiha, as she stood in the light falling through the crack in the door, waiting for her to signal with a wave of her handkerchief. Suddenly the woman ran into the room:

"He's come! But he went straight to Tsarevna Natalia's porch. I'll run and find out."

Eudoxia's head suddenly felt empty: a foreboding of evil seized her. Her strength oozed and she sank into a chair. She looked out; it was a starry autumn night. During his eighteen months' absence Peter had not written her a single letter. Now that he had come back he had gone straight to Natalia. She wrung her hands. "We were living in peace and happiness. Now he has swooped down on us to torment us!"

She sprang up. Where was Alioshenka? She must hurry with him to his father. In the doorway she collided with Vorobyiha. The woman began in a loud whisper:

"I saw with my own eyes. He went into Natalia's room, put his arms round her, and she burst into tears. His face was stern. His cheeks twitched. His moustache is curled upwards. He is wearing a grey coat of foreign make, there is a kerchief sticking out of his pocket, also a pipe. His boots are huge, not of our make. . . ."

"You fool, tell me what happened!"

"And he said to her: 'Dear sister, I wish to see my only son.' And she turned round and brought in Alioshenka."

"The viper, the viper, Natalia!" Eudoxia whispered with trembling lips.

"And he picked up Alioshenka, pressed him to his heart and kissed and caressed him. Then he put him down, put his foreign hat on his head and said: 'I'm going to sleep at Preobrazhensk'."

"And he went away?" Eudoxia clutched her head.

"He went away, dear Tsaritsa, my gentle angel, he went away; either to sleep at Preobrazhensk or to visit the Foreign Quarter."

18

At dawn next day carriages, coaches and horsemen began to take the road to Preobrazhensk. Boyars, generals, colonels, the landed gentry and clerks of the council hastened to pay their respects to their newly-returned master. As they pushed their way through the crowded antechambers, they asked anxiously: "Well, how is it? How is the Tsar?" Men answered smiling strangely: "The Tsar is in a gay mood."

He was giving audience in a large, newly-decorated room, by a long table covered with flasks, glasses, mugs and cold dishes. Tobacco smoke floated in opalescent clouds in the sunbeams. The Tsar did not look Russian: he was wearing a foreign coat of fine cloth, with lace round his neck, such as women wear; he had grown thinner, his short dark moustache was turned up, there was a small silky wig on his head, and he was sitting, as no Russian sat, with one leg in a worsted stocking tucked under his chair.

The courtiers, in their long robes, approached the Tsar, their beards pushed forward and their eyes bulging, and made obeisance according to their rank, some kneeling, some bowing low. And it was only then that they noticed Peter's two odious dwarfs, Tomosa and Seka, with sheep-shears in their hands.

After receiving the obeisance, Peter raised some and kissed them, and patted others on the shoulder; but to each of them he said gaily:

"Heavens, what a beard! My lord, in Europe they laugh at beards. Do lend me yours to mark the happy occasion."

The boyar, the prince, the general, young and old, all stood there perplexed, their arms dangling. Then Tomosa and Seka raised themselves on tiptoe and with their shears snipped off each well-combed, well-groomed beard. The ancient splendour fell to the Tsar's feet. The shorn boyar silently covered his face with his hands and trembled, but the Tsar offered him with his own hands a large glass of pepper vodka of treble strength:

"Drink to our health and long life! Samson too had his hair cut!" His shining eyes glanced round the courtiers and he raised a finger. "Why are beards cut off now? Because it pleases the women—that's the latest from Paris. Ha! Ha!" He laughed woodenly. "And if you regret your beard, have it put in your coffin, it will stick itself on again in the next world!"

Had he been harsh or wrathful, had he pulled them by these same beards, or threatened them with whatever he pleased, it would have been less terrifying. But he was incomprehensible, completely alien, a changeling, and his smile froze your heart.

A Polish barber was fussing about at the end of the table, lathering the shorn chins and shaving them. Then he would hold up a mirror so that the mutilated boyar might see his own naked, disgraced face with its crooked, childish mouth. The shaven ones who were drunk wept where they stood, at the table. Only by their clothes could they recognise Generalissimo Shein, the boyar Troyekurov, the Princes Dolgoruky, Beloselsky, Mstislavsky. The Tsar pinched their shaven cheeks and said:

"Now you needn't be ashamed to be seen even at the Emperor's court."

19

Peter went to dine with Lefort. His dear friend Francis had only just awakened towards noon and now he was sitting yawning in front of the mirror in his spacious, sunny bedchamber panelled in gilded leather. Servants were busy dressing, curling and powdering him. Two dwarfs whom he had brought from Hamburg were playing on the carpet. His steward, master of the stables, major domo and commander of his guard stood at a respectful distance. Peter came in, pressed Lefort's shoulders to prevent him from rising and, with his eyes on Lefort's face in the mirror, said:

"It wasn't an investigation they made, it was criminal laxity and foolishness. Shein has just told me, and the fool doesn't himself realise that he held the thread in his hands. When Falaleyev, a strelets, was being led off to the gallows, he shouted to the soldiers: 'You've eaten the pike, but left its teeth'."

Peter's wild eyes, staring at the mirror, darkened. Lefort turned round and ordered everyone to leave the room.

"Francis, the sting has not been torn out! Today when I was having the boyars shaved my blood was boiling. When I think of this bloodthirsty swarm of locusts! They know, they all know, but they say nothing, they lie low. It was no ordinary mutiny, it wasn't to their wives that they were going in Moscow. Terrible events were being prepared. The whole State is infected with gangrene. The rotting limbs must be struck off with the sword. And the boyars. the longbeards, must be bound by a blood pledge. The seed of Miloslavky! Francis, today the ukase must be issued: the streltsi must be sent from all the prisons and monasteries to Preobrazhensk."

20

During dinner he seemed to regain his good humour. Some of the guests noticed a new peculiarity in him: a dark, intent look. In the middle of a conversation or a joke he would suddenly fall silent and fix his eyes on someone in an unfathomable, searching, inhuman stare. Then his nostrils would quiver, and he would smile, drink, laugh woodenly.

The foreigners—soldiers, sailors, engineers—were enjoying themselves and breathing freely. But the Russians felt ill at ease. There was music; ladies were expected for the dance. Alexander Menshikov watched Peter's hands as they lay on the table: they were continually clenching and unclenching. Lefort was telling anecdotes about the French King's mistresses. Suddenly Peter sprang up with a shrill crowing noise and leant furiously across the table towards Shein:

"Villain! Villain!"

He threw his chair aside and rushed out of the room. The guests rose in consternation. Lefort hurried from one to the other trying to calm them. The orchestra in the gallery was playing loudly. The first ladies appeared in the anteroom, adjusting their wigs and gowns. All eyes were fixed on a stately, blue-eyed beauty with ash-blonde hair piled high on her head, her immensely wide silk skirts trimmed with gold lace, and her bare shoulders and arms unutterably white and seductive. She came into the hall without looking at anyone, curtsied slowly in the best approved manner and remained standing there gazing upwards with a rose in her hand.

The foreigners inquired eagerly: "Who is she?" It appeared that she was the daughter of a very wealthy merchant, Brokvin: Alexandra Ivanovna Volkova. Lefort kissed the tips of her fingers and invited her to dance. Couples began to advance, tripping and bowing. Then suddenly there was confusion again: Peter, his nostrils flaring, came back and, as his eyes found Shein, he swiftly drew out his sword and brought it down violently in front of the Generalissimo, who recoiled. Splinters of glass flew. Lefort rushed up, but Peter hit him in the face with his elbow and once again made a thrust at Shein.

"I'll cut your regiment to pieces, and all your colonels, you bandit, you low-born scoundrel, fool. . . ."

Alexander left his partner and walked boldly up to Peter. Taking no notice of the sword, he put his arms round him and whispered in his ear. The sword fell and Peter breathed into Alexander's wig:

"The scoundrels, oh, the scoundrels! He traded in colonel's posts."

"Never mind, *mein Herz*. It'll all come out right. Here, drink some Hungarian wine."

It blew over. Peter drank the wine, after which he shook an admonishing finger at Shein. Then he called Lefort and kissed him on his swollen nose:

"Where is Anna? Did you ask for news of her? Is she well?" Twisting his firmly-pressed lips he glanced at the orange sunset flooding the high windows. "Wait, I'll go and fetch her myself."

In the widow Mons' house there was a great running about with candles and banging of doors. The widow and the maids were worn out. A misfortune had occurred: Annchen was angry because her petticoats were badly starched, and they had to be starched and ironed all over again. Anna was sitting upstairs, in a powdered wig, but only half-dressed, in a powdering-gown, mending a stocking. That was how Peter found her when he ran upstairs past the terrified widow and her maids.

Annchen rose, threw back her head and gave a low cry. Peter greedily seized her, half-clothed, beloved. Her heart beat loudly in the low room.

21

Streltsi in irons were brought to Preobrazhensk from everywhere and put under guard in cottages and cellars. The investigation began at the end of September; it was carried out by Peter, Romodanovsky, Streshnev and Leo Narishkin. Campfires burned all night in the village in front of the houses where the prisoners were tortured. In fourteen different places streltsi were put on the rack, flogged, dragged out and held over burning straw, given vodka to bring them round, and then put on the rack again to extract the names of the ringleaders.

After a fortnight they began to get on the right track. Ovsey, unable to bear the pain of red-hot pincers breaking his ribs, told of Sophia's letter and that it was by her orders they had gone to the convent, to put her on the throne. Ovsey's brother, when blood was drawn a third time, said that the streltsi had trampled Sophia's letter into a manure-heap under the middle tower of New Jerusalem. Tsarevna Martha and the two dwarfs were implicated. But few spoke even under torture. The streltsi only admitted to an armed mutiny, but not to conspiracy. This obstinacy up to the point of death made Peter feel the full measure of their hatred for him.

He spent his nights in the torture-chambers and his days discussing business with foreign engineers and craftsmen, or reviewing troops. In the evening he dined with some ambassador or with Lefort. At ten o'clock, in the midst of the laughter and music, he would get up and, with his head erect, stride through the reception rooms to the dark courtyard, get into a small carriage and, covering his face to protect it from the icy wind, drive over the frost-bound roads towards Preobrazhensk, where the camp-fires were burning.

One of the secretaries of the Imperial embassy wrote down in his diary what he had seen and what he had been told during those days.

"The Danish Ambassador's suite," he wrote, "visited Preobrazhensk out of curiosity. They passed various places of detention and made for the spot where the most fearful cries indicated some terrible tragedy. Trembling with horror, they had already seen three huts whose floors were covered with blood that streamed out as far as the very porch, when even more terrible screams and groans of the most appalling agony made them wish to see the horrors taking place in a fourth hut.

"But no sooner had they entered than they rushed out again in terror, for they had come upon the Tsar and his boyars. The Tsar was standing in front of a naked man hanging from the ceiling. He turned round as they came in, obviously extremely displeased that foreigners should find him thus occupied. Narishkin rushed out after them and asked: 'Who are you? Why are you here?' And as they said nothing he ordered them to go at once to Prince Romodanovsky's house. But, feeling that they enjoyed immunity, they disregarded this rather impertinent order. Nevertheless, an officer galloped after them with the intention of overtaking and stopping their horses. Strength, however, was on their side. There were a number of them and they were brave. But, realising that the officer intended to take resolute measures, they made good their escape to a safe place. Later I learned the officer's name: Alexander; he is the Tsar's favourite and a very dangerous man. . . .

"A new money tax has been imposed: every clerk serving in a ministry has to pay in accordance with the position he fills.

"In the evenings, entertainments of royal magnificence are given at Lefort's mansion. The guests enjoy the display of fireworks. The Tsar, like a spirit of fire, rushes round the now leafless garden, lighting illuminations and fountains of sparks. The Tsarevich Alexey and his aunt, the Tsarevna Natalia, also look on, but from the windows. Everyone agrees that the most beautiful woman at the balls is Anna Mons who, they say, replaces the Tsar's wedded wife, whom he intends to send to a distant convent . . .

"On October 10th the executions began and the Tsar invited all foreign ambassadors to be present. There is a raised square in Preobrazhensk in front of a row of guardhouses. This is the place of execution; posts are permanently standing there and the heads of executed prisoners stuck on them. This square was surrounded by a fully-armed regiment of the Guards. Many people from Moscow had climbed on to the roofs and gates to see. Foreigners who came merely as sightseers were not allowed near the square.

"There blocks were already prepared. A cold wind was blowing and everyone's feet were frozen; they had to wait a long time. At last the Tsar drove up in a carriage with his favourite, Alexander, and got out and stood near one of the blocks. Meanwhile a crowd of condemned men came up, filling the square. A clerk stood on a stool which a soldier placed for him and read aloud the sentence on the rebels from several points in the square. The people were silent and the executioner began his work.

"The unfortunate men had to take their turns; their faces expressed neither sorrow nor horror at their approaching death. I do not consider such indifference to be due to courage or firmness of will, but to their memory of the tortures they had suffered: they no longer valued life, but hated it. One of the prisoners was accompanied by his wife and children who set up a most piercing wail; the man, however, calmly handed them his gauntlets and a coloured handkerchief, and laid his head on the block.

"Another, passing close to the Tsar, said in a loud voice: 'Make way, Tsar! I must kneel here!'

"I was told that on that day the Tsar complained to General Gordon of the streltsi's obstinacy and stubbornness: even under the axe they would not acknowledge their guilt. And in truth the Russians are extremely obstinate. . . .

"Thirty gallows were erected in a square in front of the Novodevichy convent and two hundred and thirty streltsi were hanged on them. Three of the ringleaders who had presented the petition to the Tsarevna Sophia were hanged on the convent walls just opposite her windows. . . .

"The Tsar was present at the execution of the priests who took part in the rising: the executioner broke the arms and legs of two of them with an iron bar and then, still living, they were put on the wheel. The third was beheaded. The two who were still alive were heard complaining that the third had got off with such a quick death. . . .

"Apparently with the object of proving that the walls of the town into which the streltsi tried to penetrate are sacred and inviolable, the Tsar has ordered beams to be pushed through the embrasures and two rebels hanged on each. Two hundred were executed in this way today. It is unlikely that any town ever had such a peculiar fence round it as the hanged streltsi formed round Moscow. . . .

"October 27th. The executions today were quite unlike the former ones. They were carried out in many different and almost incredible ways. Three hundred and thirty men stained the Red Square with their blood at the same time. This wholesale execution was only possible because all the boyars and senators of the Council of Clerks, by order of the Tsar, had to undertake the task of executioner. He is in the highest degree mistrustful and seems to suspect everyone of being in sympathy with the mutineers. He is determined to bind all the boyars by a bond of blood. All these highborn gentlemen arrived in the square already trembling at the ordeal before them. A condemned man was placed in front of each, and each had to read the sentence to the prisoner and then carry it out with his own hand by beheading him.

"The Tsar sat in a chair which had been brought from the palace and gazed dry-eyed at this horrible butchery. He is not well: both his cheeks are swollen with toothache. He was angry when he saw that the boyars were so unaccustomed to the work of headsmen that many of them had shaking hands.

"General Lefort was also invited to assume the duties of an executioner, but he excused himself, saying that in his country it was not done. Three hundred and thirty men, thrown almost simultaneously on the blocks, were beheaded, but some not altogether successfully. Boris Golitsin hit his victim not on the neck, but on the back; the man, almost cut in half, would have suffered unbearable agonies had not Alexander, with a deft stroke of his axe, managed to sever the unfortunate man's head. He boasted that he had cut off thirty heads that day. Prince Romodanovsky killed four with his own hands. Some of the boyars were so pale and weak that they had to be led away. . . ."

Tortures and executions continued all through the winter. In response to these, mutinies broke out in Archangel and Astrakhan, on the Don and in Azov. The prisons were filled and thousands of new corpses swayed with every snowstorm on the walls of Moscow. The whole country was seized with panic. The old order hid itself away in dark corners. Byzantine Russia was nearing its end. The March winds drove phantom trading ships along the Baltic coasts.

BOOK TWO

❊

chapter one

Cocks were crowing in the grey morning. The February dawn was reluctantly breaking. The night watchmen, their legs entangled in their long sheepskin coats, were removing the barriers from the streets. Smoke from ovens hung low over the ground; the smell of freshly baked bread began to fill the crooked alleys. Mounted patrols passed, asking the watchmen whether there had been any robberies in the night. "How could there be no robberies?" the men answered. "They're at it all round."

Moscow was unwillingly waking up. Bellringers climbed to the belfries, groaning with cold, and waited for the bell of Ivan the Great to strike. The Lenten peal floated slowly and sluggishly over the misty streets. Church doors creaked and opened. A verger, licking his fingers, snuffed the wicks of the sanctuary lamps that were always kept burning. Beggars, cripples and deformed creatures dragged themselves along to take up their places on church porches. They quarrelled in low voices, not having yet broken their fast. They crossed themselves, and swayed their bodies towards the dark inner porches where candles were glowing warmly.

A barefooted idiot came skipping along; he exuded a foul smell, his back was bare and last summer's burrs were sticking in his hair. There was a general startled gasp on the porch: the "man of God" held a great piece of raw meat in his hand. This meant that he would again say something which would set the whole of Moscow whispering. He seated himself right in front of the door with his pockmarked nostrils against his knees, waiting until there were more people about.

It grew lighter in the streets. Wicket-gates clattered. Traders appeared, with tightly drawn belts. They opened their shops without their former alertness. Crows flew overhead under the driving clouds. Throughout the winter the Tsar had kept the birds fed on raw flesh; innumerable flocks had come from nowhere and befouled all the cupolas. The beggar folk on the church porch said cautiously: "There'll be war and pestilence. This sham Tsardom will last, it is said, three and a half years."

In former years Kitay-gorod would have been full of noise and cries and crowds at this hour of the morning. Waggon-trains would have been bringing bread from across the Moskva river; the Yaroslav road would have been thronged with carts bringing poultry and firewood; and merchants on troikas would have been driving along the Mozhaysk road. But if you looked now, you could see only a couple of small carts from which they sold rotting meat. Half the shops were nailed up. And the suburbs and the far side of the Moskva river were deserted. Even the roofs had been torn off the strelets houses.

The churches too grew empty. There were many who turned away from them, saying that the Orthodox priests had been seduced by good living and were at one with those who had been beheading and hanging in Moscow that winter. In some churches the priest would not begin mass, but, sticking his beard in the air would shout to the bellringer: "Ring the big one, you idiot, ring louder!" Whether he rang or not, the people went by without stopping. They did not want to cross themselves with three fingers. The Old Believers told them: "The three fingers held together are a *fico* if you push your thumb between the two fingers. Everybody knows who it is who teaches people to cross themselves with a *fico*."

But all the same quite a few people were in the streets: the boyars' servants, hangers-on, all kinds of night rogues and tramps. Many crowded round the taverns, waiting for them to open; there was a smell of garlic, of meatless pies. Waggons loaded with gunpowder, iron cannon-balls, hemp and iron were coming in from across the Neglinnaya; lurching over the potholes they came down over the Moskva river to the Voronezh road. Mounted dragoons, in new short sheepskin coats, in foreign caps—with moustaches, as if they were not Russians—shouted obscene oaths, threatening the drivers with their whips. The people said: "The foreigners are again egging our Tsar on to make war. In Voronezh our Tsar has been eating food forbidden in Lent, with foreign men and women!"

The tavern opened, and the publican, a man they all knew, came out on to the porch. They were transfixed, and nobody laughed, for they realised that misfortune had overtaken him: his face was bare; the day before he had been shaved in the guardhouse in accordance with the Tsar's ukase. He pursed his lips as if he were crying, crossed himself at the five low church domes, and said with a scowl: "Come in."

Obliquely across the street, the idiot on the church porch began to jump about like a dog, worrying the lump of meat with his teeth. Men and women came running to stare at him. It brought good luck to a church when an idiot attached himself to it. But in these days it was also dangerous. At the Old Pimen church they had been feeding one such idiot, and he had got up on to the altar steps one day and, making horns with his fingers, had yelled: "Worship me, haven't you recognised *me?*" Soldiers had seized him, together with the priest and the deacon, and taken them to the Preobrazhensk administration, to the Prince-Emperor Romodanovsky.

Suddenly there was a shout: "Make way! Make way!" Hats with red feathers in them, wigs and bestial shaven faces bobbed up and down above the heads of the crowd. They belonged to outriders. The people rushed to the fences and up on the snowdrifts. A gilded covered sledge with glass windows dashed past. In it a painted woman was sitting bolt upright, like a lifeless puppet. A little felt hat covered with diamonds and ribbons perched on her piled-up hair and her arms were thrust up to the elbow into a sable bag. Everybody recognised the baggage, the Tsaritsa from the Foreign Quarter, Anna Mons. She drove up to the row of shops, where already the tradesmen were in high excitement, running out to meet her sledge carrying silks and velvets.

But the lawful Tsaritsa, Eudoxia Fedorovna, when the first snow fell in the autumn, had been taken in a common sledge to a convent in Suzdal, to weep for ever and ever.

2

"Brothers, good people, treat me to a drink. Truly, I'm faint. Yesterday I drank away my cross."

"Who are you then?"

"An icon-painter, from Palekh. We've been there from time immemorial. But as things are now, it's ruin."

"What's your name?"

"Andrey."

The man had neither cap nor shirt; there were only rags on him. His eyes were burning, his cheeks sunken; but he was well-mannered and had come up civilly to the table where they were drinking vodka. It was difficult to refuse a man of that sort.

"All right, sit down."

They poured out vodka for him and went on with their talk. An extremely crafty, dull-sighted peasant with a lean neck was saying:

"They executed the streltsi. Very well, that's the Tsar's affair." He raised a slightly crooked finger. "It's no concern of ours, but. . . ."

A sleek townsman in a strelets coat—there were many in those days wearing strelets coats and caps: the strelets women, wailing, would give their clothes away for almost nothing—tapped his nails on a pewter cup and said:

"That's just it—but. . . . There you are—that's just it!"

The crafty peasant wagged his finger at him and observed:

"We're sitting still. It's you, in Moscow, who riot and sound the tocsin on the slightest pretext. So there was good reason for hanging the streltsi from the walls and driving fear into the people. That's not what we are talking about, citizen. You, dear fellows, are wondering why no supplies are brought into Moscow. And you needn't expect any. Things will get worse. Today—it's both funny and sad—I brought in a barrel of salt fish. I salted it for myself but it went bad. I took it to the market. And I thought they would beat me for bringing such stinking stuff. But no: in an hour or two it was all sold. No, today Moscow is a hole of perdition."

"Ah, true enough!" the icon-painter said with a sad sniff.

The peasant glanced at him and went on in a matter-of-fact tone:

"There was a ukase: take the dead streltsi down from the walls by Shrovetide and cart them out of town. But there are some eight thousand of them. Very well, but where are the carts? That means again it's for the peasant to do the job. But what about the suburbs? Make the suburbs provide horse transport."

The townsman's flabby cheeks quivered, and he nodded reproachfully at the peasant:

"Ah, you ploughman! You should have walked past the walls this winter. When the snowstorms caught them, they began to swing. It's enough for us that we've had this horror."

"Of course, it would have been easier to have buried them straight away," said the peasant. "On Quadragesima Sunday we brought eighteen carts in, and we hadn't unpinned the covers when up ran soldiers: 'Empty the carts!' 'Why? What for?' 'Don't argue!' They threatened us with their swords and overturned the sledges. I had brought a barrel of small mushrooms—they upset it, the devils. 'Go,' they shouted, 'to the Varvarsky gates'. And at the Varvarsky gates we found three hundred streltsi in a heap. 'Load them up, you this and that!' So, without a bite or a sup, and without a feed for the horses, we carted those dead men till nightfall. When we got back to the village we were ashamed to look our own people in the face."

A stranger came up to the table, and set down a bottle with a clatter:

"Only fools carry water," he said. He sat down boldly and poured out drinks for all. Then he winked his roving eye and said: "Here's to your health!" Without wiping his moustache he began to nibble a clove of garlic. His face was tanned and fiery, and there were grey patches in his curly beard.

The dull-sighted peasant took the cup from him gingerly.

"The peasant is a fool, he's a fool, but you know, the peasant understands." He balanced the cup in his hand, drained it and grunted with satisfaction. "No, my dear fellows. . . ." He stretched out his hand for the garlic. "This morning—did you see the sledges going to Voronezh? They're fleecing the peasant to the bone. Pay quit-rent—pay service dues—give provisions for the boyar's table—pay the taxes to the treasury—pay bridge money—and if you go to market, pay again. . . ."

The man with the piebald beard opened his mouth wide and laughed, showing a lot of teeth. The peasant broke off, sniffed and went on:

"Very well. Now it's provide horses for the Tsar's waggons. They've even taken our dry bread. No, my dear fellows. Just count how many people are left in the villages. And where are the others? Try to find them! Nowadays nearly everyone is making ready for flight. The peasant's a fool so long as he's not hungry. But if you go on till you pull away what he's sitting on"—he took his bread in his hand and made a bow—"the peasant puts on his birch-bark shoes and goes wherever he pleases!"

"To the North, to the lakes, to the retreats!" said the icon-painter moving closer to the speaker, his dark eyes burning.

The peasant pushed him back: "You keep quiet!" The townsman took a look round and then, leaning his chest on the table, whispered:

"Lads, it's a fact, many are frightened and go to the lakes, to places beyond Belo-ozero, to Lake Vol, Lake Matka, Lake Vyg. . . . It's quiet there." His puffy cheeks quivered. "Only those who go will stay alive!"

The icon-painter's pupils dilated and he said, turning from one to the other of the group:

"What he says is true. We, in Palekh, painted six hundred icons for Lent. In former years this would have been too few. But this year we've not sold one in Moscow. There's woe in Palekh. And why? We use light colours and write the name of Jesus with two i's. His blessing hand is painted with two fingers and thumb gathered together. And we make the cross plain, four-pointed. All according to Orthodox rules. Is that clear? Those who buy icons from us are tradesmen. Korzinkin, Dyachkov, Vikulin say to us: 'Stop painting in this manner. These icons must be burnt, they are wicked.' They say there's a paw-mark on them. 'What paw?' " The icon-painter gave a short sniff. The townsman bent low over the table and his teeth chattered. " 'Why,' they say, 'there's the print of *his* paw. . . . Have you ever seen the print of a bird's claw on the ground—four lines? And there's the same on your icons.' 'Where?' 'Why, the four-pointed cross. . . . Do you understand? Don't bring these goods to Moscow', they say. 'Now the whole of Moscow knows where the smell of rotting comes from'."

The peasant blinked and it was difficult to tell whether he believed what he heard or not. The man with the piebald beard smiled as he nibbled his garlic. The townsman nodded agreement, and then suddenly, with a glance round, jutted his lips forward and whispered:

"And tobacco? In which Book is it written that a man must swallow smoke? Out of whose mouth does smoke issue? What? For forty-eight thousand roubles Siberia and all the towns have been leased to the Englishman to sell tobacco there. And there's a ukase: people must smoke this devil's weed. Who's responsible for this? And tea, and coffee. And potatoes—may they be damned! They're the lust of Antichrist, the potatoes. All this poison comes from abroad, and Lutherans and Catholics sell it here. The man who drinks tea falls into despair, and coffee, it's a trap for the soul! Pah, I'd sooner die than take such stuff into my shop."

"What do you trade in?" the man with the piebald beard asked.

"Well, what trade is there now? The foreigners trade, while we moan. Did you know Ovsey Rzhov and his brother Constantine? Streltsi of Hundertmark's regiment. My shop was just by their baths. There aren't any men like that today. Both were broken on the wheel. Ovsey said more than once: 'We're suffering now because long ago, in 'eighty-two, in the Kremlin, we didn't listen to the upholders of the Old Faith. We, streltsi, should have stood up for it as one man. There wouldn't have been a single foreigner left in Moscow, and the faith would have blazed out in glory, and the people would have been well-fed and happy. But now we don't even know how we're to save our souls!' That's the kind of righteous men that have been swinging on the walls all through the winter. But now there are no streltsi, they can do what they like with us. You'll see, they'll shave everybody's face, they'll make us all drink coffee!"

"As soon as we've eaten all our bread, in the spring, we'll scatter," the peasant said firmly.

"Brothers!" The icon-painter stared yearningly at the streaming window. "Brothers, in the North there are wonderful retreats, a peaceful refuge, a silent life. . . ."

It was growing noisier and hotter in the tavern, and the bast-covered door banged continually. Drunken men were quarrelling; at the counter a man stood swaying, naked to the waist and without a cross round his neck, begging for a drink on credit. Another was dragged out into the passage by his hair and beaten there—probably for some good reason—to the accompaniment of wild yells.

A beggar, bent nearly double, stopped at the table. Leaning on two crutches he beamed with kindly wrinkles. The man with the piebald beard glanced at him and knitted his brows. The bent man said:

"Where have you flown from, you falcon?"

"From farther than you can see. Go your way, what are you standing here for?"

"From the Don?" the crooked man asked rapidly in a low voice.

"Go away, go away; I'm here quite openly."

The cripple asked no more, but thrust out his wispy beard and went off with a tapping of crutches to the far end of the tavern.

"Who's that man?" the townsman asked in alarm.

"A lonely traveller on his way," the man with the piebald beard said curtly.

"In what language did he speak to you?"

"In the bird's language."

"He seemed to recognise you, my lad."

"Ask fewer questions, and you'll have more brains." He shook the crumbs off his beard and laid his large hands on the table. "Now listen. We are from the Don, on trading business."

The townsman quickly moved closer to him and blinked:

"What are you buying?"

"Gunpowder; we need ten barrels. About two thousand pounds of lead. Good cloth for coats. Iron for horseshoes, nails. We've got the money."

"Good cloth and iron, that can be got. Lead and gunpowder are harder: nowhere to get it outside government offices."

"That's just it: one must try to avoid the government offices."

"I know a clerk. Presents will be needed."

"Naturally."

The townsman, scratching the leather of his short sheepskin coat with the hooks as he hurriedly fastened it, said he would try. He would bring the clerk in a moment. With this he hurried away. The peasant wanted to join in the business deal. He wrinkled his forehead and coughed several times:

"Do you want lambs' wool for felt, or leather, friend? Now tell me: two thousand pounds of lead—are you Cossacks, preparing to fight?"

"To shoot quail."

The man with the piebald beard turned away. The bent man with the crutches was coming up again. Holding his cap with the alms he had collected, he sat down beside him and without looking at him said:

"How d'you do, Ivan."

"How d'you do, Ovdokim," the man with the piebald beard replied, also without looking.

"We haven't seen each other for a long time, chief."

"Begging, are you?"

"From infirmity. In the summer I played about in the forest a little; the years are telling. I'm tired of it all, it's time for me to die."

"Have patience."

"Why? Is there any good news?"

Ivan was looking with a smile through the steamy air at the drunken rabble. His eyes grew cold. He said very softly out of the corner of his mouth:

"We're raising the Don."

Ovdokim bent over his cap fingering the coppers:

"I don't know," he said, "I've heard the Don Cossacks have grown tame, settling down on farms, acquiring property."

"There are many newcomers, loose-footed fellows. They'll begin and the Cossacks will help. And if they don't help, they'll either have to go to Turkey or become serfs to Moscow for all time. Once they helped the Tsar at Azov, and now he has laid his hands on the whole of the Don. There are orders to surrender all newcomers. A lot of priests have been sent there from Moscow, the Old Faith is being uprooted. It's an end to the quiet Don."

"A big man is needed for such an enterprise," Ovdokim said. "Otherwise it might end as it did in Stepan Razin's time."

"We've got the man, he's not like Stepan who lost his head through his folly. He'll be a proper chief. All the men of the Old Faith will stand by him."

"You've disturbed my peace of mind, Ivan. The temptation is too strong, Ivan. And there was I already thinking of settling down peacefully."

"Come in the spring. We need old leaders. We'll have a jollier time than with Stepan."

"Hardly that, hardly that. . . . How many of us, of the old crowd are left? Only you and I, perhaps."

The townsman returned, out of breath, and winked. In his wake, stepping out importantly, came a bald-headed clerk dressed in a brown foreign coat with brass buttons and worn-out felt boots. A quill pen was stuck in a buttonhole on his chest. Not greeting anyone, he sat down at the table with an expression of distaste. He had a greedy face and dull and evil eyes, his nostrils were so wide that one could see up them. Without sitting down the townsman said in his ear over his shoulder:

"Kuzma Yegorich, that's the man who. . . ."

"Pancakes," the clerk said in a flat voice, without paying attention to him, "pancakes with salt fish."

3

Prince Roman Borisovich Buynosov sat clad only in his undergarments on the edge of his bed, grunting and scratching his chest and armpits. From old habit his hand moved up to his beard, but he drew it back quickly: his chin was shaven, prickly, repulsive. Ouah-ha-ha, he yawned and looked out of the small window. The day was breaking misty and dull.

At this time of day in former years Roman Borisovich would already have thrust his arms into the sleeves of his marten coat, proudly pulled his beaver cap down to his eyebrows and stepped out with his tall staff along the creaking passages to the porch. He had a hundred and fifty house serfs; some would have been by his covered sledge holding the horses, others would have been running to open the gates. They would have pulled off their caps cheerfully, bowed swiftly from the waist, and those nearest to him would have kissed his foot and, holding his arms and his sides, have helped him into the sledge. Every morning, whatever the weather, Roman Borisovich drove to the palace to wait for the Tsar's serene eyes—and later on the most serene eyes of the Tsarevna—to turn in his direction. And seldom did he wait in vain.

All that was past now. When he woke up—dear me! was it really past? It was strange even to recall that once there had been peace and honour. There, hanging on the wood-panelled wall—where nothing ought to hang—was a Dutch trollop with a hitched-up skirt, painted as a diabolical temptation. The Tsar had ordered it to be hung in his bedchamber either for fun or as a punishment. He had to put up with it.

Prince Roman Borisovich looked gloomily at the clothes which he had thrown on the bench the night before: woollen stockings with horizontal stripes, like a woman's, short breeches tight both back and front, a green braided coat which might have been made of tin. A black wig hung on a nail; even sticks couldn't beat the dust out of it. What was it all for?

"Mishka!" the boyar shouted crossly. A brisk lad in a long Russian shirt dashed into the room through the low door covered in red cloth. He bowed from the waist and tossed his hair back. "Mishka, water to wash my face." The lad took up a copper basin and poured out some water. "Hold the basin properly. Pour the water on my hands."

Roman Borisovich did more snorting into the palms of his hands than washing, so repulsive was it to feel his shaven, bristly skin. Growling he sat on the bed to put on his breeches. Mishka held out a saucer with chalk and a clean scrap of cloth.

"What's this now?" the Prince bellowed.

"To clean your teeth."

"I won't!"

"As you wish. Since the Tsar said teeth must be cleaned, the boyarinia has ordered me to bring you this every morning."

"I'll throw the saucer at your head! You talk too much."

"As you please."

When he had dressed, Roman Borisovich tried to move—his clothes irked him, and were tight and stiff. What was the point? But strict orders had been given that all nobles must present themselves for their duties wearing foreign clothing and wigs. He had to put up with it. He took the wig off the nail—heaven knew what woman's hair it was—and put it on with disgust. He struck away Mishka's hand when the lad tried to straighten the tightly curled ringlets. He went out into the passage where wood was crackling in the stove. From the kitchen down below, to which a steep staircase led, came a smell of something bitter and scorched.

"Mishka, what's that stench? Are they making coffee again?"

"The Tsar has ordered the boyars and their ladies to drink coffee in the morning, so they are making it."

"I know. Don't grin like that!"

"As you please."

Mishka opened the cloth-covered door into the house chapel. The Prince, crossing himself devoutly, went up to the lectern. A prayer-book, spotted with candle wax, lay open on the velvet. The Prince snuffed the taper and put on his round iron-framed spectacles. He licked his finger, turned a page and fell into a reverie, looking into the corner where the frames of the icons glimmered faintly: only one green light was burning before the image of St. Nicholas.

There was indeed food for thought. For if things went on like this it would mean the ruin of all the great families, the princes and the nobles, to say nothing of the dishonour and abuse. "How d'you like that? They've begun to exterminate the nobility! Just try! Under Ivan the Terrible they tried to ruin the princely families. The result was confusion and revolt. And now again there will be confusion. We are the mainstay of the State. Ruin us, and there's no State, no purpose to life. What then, Tsar, are you going to govern with serfs? Nonsense! You're still young, and haven't got much sense, and what little you had you've drunk away in the Foreign Quarter."

The Prince adjusted his spectacles and began to read in a nasal voice, according to custom. But his thoughts wandered past the lines.

"Fifty house serfs taken for the army. Five hundred roubles taken for the Voronezh fleet. From the Voronezh estate they've taken the grain into the government stores for a song—cleaned out all the barns. The wheat harvests of three years were there—waiting for the price to rise." His mouth tasted bitter with resentment. "Now it's said they're going to take the land from the monasteries, and all their revenues will go to the treasury. They've ordered me to prepare ten barrels of salt beef. Ah, dear me, what do they want the salt beef for?"

He read on. The morning looked green through the leaded mica window. Mishka was kneeling at the door and bowing with his forehead to the ground.

"At Shrovetide the great families were dishonoured. Some three hundred masqueraders descended on them at midnight or even later.

The terror of it! Faces blackened with soot. All drunk. And you couldn't tell which was the Tsar. They ate up everything, and drank and were sick all over the place, and pulled the skirts off the serving-women, bleating like goats, crowing like cocks, whistling like birds. . . ."

Roman Borisovich shifted his weight to the other foot; he remembered how on the last day they had made him drink until he was quite silly, had pulled down his trousers and seated him in a basket full of eggs. It wasn't at all funny. His wife had seen it, Mishka had seen it. "Oh, dear Lord! Why? For what purpose?"

The Prince made an effort to reason it out: what was the cause of this calamity? Was it because of their sins? In Moscow they were whispering that a Deceiver had come to the world: that Catholics and Lutherans were his servants, that foreign goods bore the stamp of Antichrist. That the end of the world was at hand.

Puckering his rubicund face as he glared into the candle flame the Prince pondered doubtfully: "It's inconceivable. The Lord will not allow the Russian nobility to perish. We must wait and be patient."

When he had fervently finished his prayers, he went to the window alcove and sat at a table covered with a rug. He opened a thick book in which everything was recorded: who had been given things on credit, from whom debts had been recovered, from what village money or grain or stores had been taken. He turned over the pages slowly, moving his shaven lips.

Senka, his chief steward—who had been selected from among his serfs for his cunning and the extreme malevolence he showed in his dealings with people—came into the room. He was a real watchdog: he squeezed out the last copper that was due to the boyar. He stole, of course, but moderately, not exorbitantly and, even if you were to cut him into pieces, he would never admit that he stole. Roman Borisovich had often gripped the thick beard on his fat chops and beaten his head against the wall, shouting: "You've stolen it, it's clear you've stolen it, confess!" Senka, without blinking his red-brown eyes, would look at his master as if he were God and only when he left off beating him would Senka turn back the tail of his coarse woollen coat, blow his soft nose and whine:

"It's not just, Roman Borisovich, to beat your servant like this. God forgive you, I am in no way guilty."

Senka sidled in through the half-open door, crossed himself at the icon of St. Nicholas, bowed to the boyar and went down on his knees.

"Well, Senka, what news have you got for me?"

"Everything is going well, Roman Borisovich."

Senka, still kneeling, raised his eyes to the ceiling and began to report, from memory, how much had been received and from whom, the day before, what had been brought, and whence, and who was still in debt. He had brought two peasants, Fedka and Koska, malicious defaulters, who, since the previous evening, had been kept in the yard for forced recovery of their debts.

Roman Borisovich was astonished, and his mouth fell open: were they really unwilling to pay? He consulted the book: Fedka had borrowed sixty roubles the year before; he had said it was to build himself a new hut, and buy harness, a ploughshare and seed. Koska had had thirty-seven roubles and fifty kopeks, and had also probably lied when he said it was for his farmstead.

"The rogues, the swindlers! Have you ordered them to be beaten with sticks?"

"They've been beating them since last evening," Senka replied. "I've put two men to each, to beat them mercilessly. But, master, don't worry about it: if Fedka and Koska don't pay, we hold personal servitude bonds against their debts, we'll take them both into servitude for ten years. We need serfs."

"I need money, not serfs!" Roman Borisovich said throwing down the quill on the table. "Slaves have to be fed—and the Tsar will take them again for the army."

"If you need money, do as Brovkin did: he has set up a canvas workshop in the Zamoskvorechye,* and supplies sail canvas to the treasury. His purse is bursting with money."

"Yes, I've heard that before. You're probably lying."

Brovkin's canvas workshop had long made Roman Borisovich uneasy. Almost every day Senka mentioned it; evidently he thought he could steal a lot from such a business. Then there was Leo Narishkin, the Tsar's uncle, who had done even better: he gave money to a Dutchman in the Foreign Quarter, who sent it to the Amsterdam Bourse to get interest, and every year Narishkin was getting six hundred roubles in interest alone from ten thousand roubles. "Six hundred roubles, just like that!"

"Our forefathers lived knowing no cares," the Prince said. "And the State was sounder then." He pushed his arms into the sleeves of a fleece-lined coat Senka held for him. "They sat with the Tsar and considered their counsel: that's what our cares used to be. But now there's no happiness even in waking up."

* District of Moscow beyond the Moskva river.

Roman Borisovich went up and down staircases and along chilly passages. On his way he opened a sagging door; a hot, sour-smelling vapour poured out and, in the depths of the room, barely visible in the light of a burning sliver of wood there were four men, barefooted and clad only in shirts, rolling felt from sheep's wool. "Well, well, work away, don't forget God!" Roman Borisovich said. The men made no reply. He went on and opened the door of the sewing-room. Twenty young women and girls stood up from their tables and embroidery-frames and bowed low. The boyar screwed up his nose: "Well, what a smell there is here! Work away, work away, girls, don't forget God!"

Roman Borisovich also looked into the tailoring workshop and the leather-room where hides were soaking in vats or being tanned. Sullen peasants were kneading the leather with their hands. Senka lighted a tallow candle in a round lantern with small holes and removed the heavy padlocks from the storerooms and closets where the provisions were kept. Everything was in order. Roman Borisovich went out into the spacious courtyard. It was already light, but cloudy. Sheep were being watered at the well. A line of hay-carts extended from the gates to the hay-loft. The peasants doffed their caps. Roman Borisovich shouted to them: "Hey, you men, the loads are none too big!"

The smoke, issuing from decrepit, chimneyless old huts and storerooms and beaten down by the wind, filled the courtyard. Heaps of ash and of manure lay everywhere. Frozen rags were flapping on clothes-lines. Near the stables two downcast, bareheaded peasants were standing with their faces to the wall, shifting their weight from one foot to the other. Some tall servants, seeing the boyar on the porch, rushed out of the stables and, hurriedly picking up some rods from the ground, began to belabour the peasants on their buttocks and thighs. "Oh, oh, Lord! What for?" Fedka and Koska groaned.

"That's it, serve them right, thrash them some more!" Roman Borisovich shouted approvingly from the porch.

Fedka, a tall, red-faced, pockmarked fellow, turned to him and said: "Gracious master, Roman Borisovich, we haven't got anything! God's our witness we'd eaten all our grain before Christmas. Take my cattle if you like; I can't stand this torture."

Senka said to the Prince:

"His cattle are small and lean, he's lying. But you could take his daughter for half the debt. And let him earn the rest."

Roman Borisovich frowned and said, turning away:

"I'll think it over. We'll talk about it this evening."

From beyond the smoke and the leafless trees came the sound of Lenten bells. Crows rose from the rusty cupolas. "Oh, grievous are our sins!" Roman Borisovich muttered, taking a last look at the yard, and then proceeded to the dining-hall—to drink coffee.

Princess Avdotya and the three young princesses were sitting on Dutch folding chairs at the end of the table. The brocaded tablecover was turned back at that end so that it should not get stained. The Princess was wearing a dark velvet, loose coat with wide sleeves and a foreign cap. The young princesses were in foreign gowns with trains: Natalia in peach-colour, Olga in green stripes and the eldest, Antonida, in a dress of a colour called "unforgettable sunset". All of them had their hair brushed up and sprinkled with flour. There were round spots of rouge on their cheeks, their eyebrows were blackened and their palms were red.

In former days, of course, neither Avdotya nor her daughters ever entered the dining-hall: they sat by the windows in their rooms doing needlework, or, in summer time, in swings in the garden. But one day the Tsar had come with his drunken companions and from the threshold he had looked round the room with terrible eyes: "Where are your daughters? Bring them to sit at the table." They were sent for hurriedly. There were terror, confusion, tears. They were brought in—three fools half out of their wits. The Tsar chucked each of them under the chin and asked: "Can you dance?" Dance indeed! Tears of shame poured from the girls' eyes. "They must learn. By Shrovetide they must be able to dance the minuet, the mazurka and country dances." He gripped Roman Borisovich by the coat and shook him, none too gently: "Introduce proper *politesse* into your house—don't forget!" The girls were placed at the table and made to drink wine. And, strange to relate, they drank, and showed no shame. And before long they were laughing, as though there were nothing extraordinary about it.

And so proper *politesse* had to be introduced into the house. The Princess Avdotya was so stupid that she could do nothing but marvel at everything; her daughters, however, quickly grew bold, pert and difficult to please. They wanted this and they wanted that. They did not want to embroider, but sat about in their fine clothes from early morning, enjoying themselves and drinking tea and coffee.

Roman Borisovich entered the room and glanced at his daughters. They only nodded to him. Avdotya got up and bowed: "Good morning, Roman Borisovich." Antonida hissed at her mother: "Sit down, *Mutter.*" Roman Borisovich would have liked to drink a glass of vodka and eat some garlic after coming in from the cold. He might get the vodka, but there was no chance of any garlic.

"Somehow I don't feel like coffee today," he said. "I must have got cold on the porch. Mother, give me something strong."

"You say the same thing every morning, *Vater*—vodka," Antonida said. "When will you get used. . . ."

"Hold your tongue, you great filly!" Roman Borisovich shouted. "Or I'll use my whip."

The princesses turned up their noses. Avdotya brought him a glass of spirits, bowing to him in the old-fashioned way, and whispered: "Help yourself to your heart's content, Roman Borisovich."

He drank and puffed out his breath. Then he chewed a cucumber, the brine dripping on his waistcoat. There was neither cabbage with cranberries on the table, nor minced salt mushrooms with onions. Munching a small pie, filled with goodness knew what, he asked about his son:

"Where's Mishka?"

"He's learning arithmetic. I don't know how his head will stand it all."

The slightly pockmarked Olga, the most punctilious student of foreign etiquette, pursed her lips and remarked:

"Mishka is always with the peasants. Yesterday he was in the stables again with his balalaika and playing vulgar card-games."

"He's still only a child," Avdotya murmured.

They were silent for a while. Then Natalia, the youngest, a lively girl, easily moved to laughter, bent towards the window—in which the mica had recently been replaced by glass—and cried:

"Oh, oh, girls! Visitors have come!"

The girls fluttered about, holding up their arms and shaking their hands to make them whiter. Serving-girls ran in to clear the table and replace the cover. The major-domo—formerly he had been called house-steward—a pious old servant, shaven and dressed up as for a Christmas Eve masquerade, struck his staff on the floor and announced that the wife of the boyar Volkov had arrived. Prince Roman Borisovich reluctantly heaved himself out from behind the table to play the gallant to the guest: to flourish his hat and kick up his legs. And for whose benefit had the Prince to perform these antics? Seven years ago this boyar Volkov's wife had been known as Sanka, who wiped her nose with the tattered hem of her skirt and lived in one of the poorest peasant homes. Her father, Ivash Brovkin, had been a serf, a backyard menial. She should have spent her life round a chimneyless stove. And now her arrival was announced by the major-domo! She had come in a gilt carriage! Her husband enjoyed the Tsar's favour: he was in fact the son of Prince Roman's first cousin. The devil had helped the girl's father: he had risen to be a big merchant and now, it was said, he was to do all the purveying for the army.

The major-domo opened the low, narrow, old-fashioned door, and a tea-rose-coloured gown rustled. Her naked shoulders drooping, the boyarinia Volkova entered the room, her beautiful impassive face tilted back and her eyelashes lowered. She halted in the middle of the room and, with a flash of rings, held her voluminous skirts, decorated with lace rosettes, put one foot forward—her satin shoe had a heel four inches high—and curtsied in the best French manner, not bending the knee of the leg stretched out in front. Her powdered head and the ostrich feathers in it bowed to right and to left. She then raised her dark blue eyes with a smile and opened her lips:

"Bonjour, princesses!"

The Prince's daughters in their turn bobbed down on their sterns and devoured the guest with their eyes. The Prince took up his hat and waved it, sticking out his arms and legs. The boyarinia was invited to sit at the table and drink coffee. They began to make mutual enquiries after the health of relations and households. The girls examined her gown and the way her hair was dressed.

"Ah, your hair is done up on whalebone of course."

"And ours is put up with twigs and rags."

Sanka replied: "It's terrible with the hairdresser—there's only one for the whole of Moscow. At Shrovetide ladies were waiting for a week, and those who had had their hair dressed in good time slept on chairs. I have asked my father to bring a hairdresser from Amsterdam."

"Please give my greetings to your respected father," said the Prince. "How is his canvas workshop doing? I'm always planning to go and see it. It's a new and interesting enterprise."

"My father is in Voronezh. And my husband is there too, with the Tsar."

"We've heard that, we've heard that, Alexandra Ivanovna."

"Vasya sent me a letter yesterday," Sanka inserted two fingers in her low-cut corsage—Roman Borisovich blinked: another minute and the woman would exhibit her nakedness!—and pulled out a pale-blue letter. "They may be sending him to Paris."

"What does he write?" The Prince asked, with a cough. "What does he say about the Tsar?"

Sanka took a long time to unfold the letter. She wrinkled her brow and a flush spread over her cheeks and neck. Then she said in a whisper: "It isn't long since I have learnt to read. Excuse me."

Running her finger along the lines, which were heavily blotted and thick with abbreviations and curlicues, she began to read aloud, pronouncing each word slowly:

"Sashenka, greetings, my love, may you long enjoy good health! This is how things are going with us in Voronezh. We shall soon be sending the fleet through to the Don, and then our stay here will come to an end. I do not want to alarm you, but I have heard privately that the Tsar wants to send me, with Andrey Artamonovich Matveyev, to The Hague and then on to Paris. I do not know what to think of it: it is far away and a bit frightening. We are all well, thanks be to God. Herr Peter sends you his compliments; we were talking about you at supper the other evening. He is at work every day. He works on the wharf like a common person. He himself forges nails and clamps, and caulks the ships. There is no time even to shave: he presses everybody very hard and wears people out. But the fleet has been built."

Roman Borisovich tapped his nails on the table:

"Yes, yes, of course, the fleet. He himself forges, he himself caulks —it means he doesn't know what to do with his energy."

Sanka finished reading the letter and wiped her lips gently. Then she folded the letter and put it back in her corsage.

"The Tsar will be back in Easter week. I shall throw myself at his feet—I want to go to Paris."

Antonida, Olga and Natalia threw up their hands: "Ah! Ah! Ah!" Princess Avdotya crossed herself: "You've frightened me, my dear. How dreadful, to go to Paris! It must be unholy there!"

Sanka's blue eyes darkened, and she pressed her rings to her breast:

"I am so bored in Moscow! I long to fly away abroad! There's a Frenchman at Tsaritsa Praskovya Fedorovna's * court who teaches etiquette—he teaches me too. The tales he tells!"—she gave a short sigh—"Every night I dream and see myself in a crimson dress dancing the minuet, dancing it better than anyone—then the cavaliers make way for someone, and King Louis comes up to me and hands me a rose. . . . It has got so dull in Moscow. Thank goodness, at least they have taken away the streltsi; I'm frightened to death of corpses."

The boyarinia Volkova had left. Roman Borisovich, having sat a while at the table, ordered the covered sledge to be harnessed to take him to his place of work, the chancellery of the Great Palace. Nowadays everyone was ordered to work. As if there weren't enough clerks

* Widow of Tsar Ivan, Peter's step-brother.

in Moscow, the nobles had been set to drive quills. And the Tsar himself, foul with tar and tobacco, spent all his time chopping away with an axe, drinking corn-brandy with peasants.

"Oh, things are in a bad way! Oh, I am so tired of it," Prince Roman Borisovich groaned as he climbed into his sledge.

4

In the deep moat by the Spassky gates, where rotting piles stuck up here and there from the ice, Roman Borisovich saw a score of sledges covered with bast matting. Lean horses stood with drooping heads. On the slope a peasant armed with a crowbar was lazily hacking free the corpse of a strelets that had frozen to the ground. The day was grey. The snow was grey. People in drab coats were trudging with heads bent through the Red Square over the snow worn into ridges and covered with dung. The clock on the tower wheezed and chimed hoarsely; there had been a time when it made a clear, ringing sound. Roman Borisovich felt miserable.

The covered sledge crossed the dilapidated bridge and passed through the Spassky gates. Men with their caps on walked about in the Kremlin, as though in a market-place. Common sledges were lined up at the tethering rails, champed by the horses. The Prince's heart sank. How empty this place had become! They were no longer there, the lustrous eyes that shone in the royal window, like a sacred lamp, to the glory of the Third Rome. Life had become wearisome indeed.

The sledge stopped at the porch of the chancellery. No one was about to help the prince out of the sledge. He got out by himself and, puffing and blowing, went up the covered staircase. The steps were foul with snow, brought in on people's boots, and spittle. Some common people in short sheepskin coats came running down and nearly collided with the prince. The one who came last—a fellow with a piebald beard—flashed an impudent roving glance at him. Roman Borisovich stopped half-way up the flight and rapped his cane indignantly:

"Your cap! You should take off your cap!"

But no one heeded him. Such were the manners that had now become current in the Kremlin.

The low rooms of the chancellery were full of fumes from the stoves; there was a terrible stench, and the floors were unswept. Clerks were scratching with their quills at long tables, elbow to elbow.

Now and then one or the other would straighten up and scratch his unkempt head or his armpits. Senior clerks, wise in the mysteries of red tape, and strongly redolent of Lenten pies, sat at small tables turning over pages and running their fingers down petitions. A dim light filtered through the grimy windows. The registrar, with spectacles on his pockmarked nose, walked up and down between the tables.

Roman Borisovich strode importantly from room to room, from one registry to another. There was a great deal of work in the chancellery of the Great Palace and the business was complicated: the chancellery was in charge of the Tsar's treasury, of the storerooms, of the gold and silver plate; it collected the customs duties and the Cossack money, as well as the strelets tax, the stage-post money and the quit-rent from the Palace villages and towns. Only the secretary and the senior registrars could find their way through this maze. The newly employed boyars sat all day in a small overheated room, suffering torments in their tight foreign clothes, and stared through the murky windows at the Tsar's deserted palace where, in times gone by, they had walked about the private porch, on the boyars' platform, wearing sable coats, flourishing their silk handkerchiefs and discussing matters of high importance.

Many terrible events had taken place in this square. From that decayed porch over there, now nailed up, Ivan the Terrible, as tradition had it, had gone from the Kremlin with his special guard to Alexandrovsky village to launch his rage and cruelty against the great boyar families. He cut off their heads, burnt them in frying-pans, impaled them. He took their estates from them. But God had not allowed the final destruction of the boyars. The great families had risen again.

From that high wooden building, with brass cocks on its onion-shaped roof, the accursed Grishka Otrepyev had thrown himself down: another destroyer of the glorious breed of Russian boyars. The land of Moscow had become a desert of burnt-out towns and villages with human bones whitening the roads; but God had not permitted it, and the great families had risen anew.

Today, once again, the storm had gathered—for their sins—and the boyars moaned dismally at the windows of the hot room. If they couldn't undermine them in one way they did it in another: they had shaved everybody's beards off, ordered everyone to serve, their sons had been sent to different regiments or abroad. . . . Ah, but God would not permit it this time either.

On entering the room Roman Borisovich saw that again today

something unpleasant had come from high quarters. Old Prince Martin Lykov's cheeks, as flabby as an aged woman's, were trembling. Ivan Yendogurov, a member of the boyars' council, and the equerry Lavrenty Svinyin were haltingly reading some document. They lifted their heads now and again only to say: "Oh! Oh!"

"Sit down and listen to this, Prince Roman," said Prince Martin, on the verge of tears. "What's going to happen now? Anybody will be able to abuse and insult us. We had one way open to us, and even this is now being taken from us."

Yendogurov and Svinyin again began to read out the Tsar's ukase syllable by syllable. It said that he, the Tsar, Grand Duke, etc., etc., was greatly importuned by princes, boyars and Moscow nobles and nobles of the council who presented complaints about the insults they had suffered. On such and such a day a petition had been presented to him, the Tsar, Grand Duke, etc., etc., by Prince Martin, son of Prince Grigory, Lykov by surname, alleging that he had been abused and insulted on the private porch by Alioshka Brovkin, lieutenant in His Majesty's Preobrazhensky regiment. That as he was crossing the porch Brovkin had shouted to Prince Martin: "Why are you looking at me *like a wild beast?* Today I am not your serf. You used to be a prince, now you are only a *myth.*"

"He's a puppy, a peasant's son, a clodhopper," Prince Martin said, his cheeks quivering. "I was too angry at the time to remember all his words, but he shouted even worse things at me."

"What was it he shouted at you, Prince Martin?" Roman Borisovich asked.

"What, what? He shouted, and many heard him: 'Monkey face! Bald-pate!' "

"Ah, yes, very annoying," Roman Borisovich remarked wagging his head. "By the way, isn't he the son of Ivan Artemyich, this Alioshka?"

"The devil knows whose son he is."

" 'The Tsar and Grand Duke, etc.',", Yendogurov and Svinyin read on, " 'in order not to be importuned at a time when things are difficult for the State, has ordered, in view of the vexation and nuisance caused to him, to exact ten roubles from the petitioner, Prince Martin, and to distribute this money to beggars, and henceforth to prohibit complaints of insults. . . .' "

When they had finished reading they wrinkled up their noses. Prince Martin again became agitated:

"A myth! Here, touch me! Am I a myth? Our family goes back

to Prince Lychko! In the thirteenth century Prince Lychko came from the Hungarian land with three thousand spearmen. And Lychko was the ancestor of the Princes Bruhaty, and Taratuhin, and Suponev, and the descendants of his youngest son were the Buynosovs. . . ."

"You lie! You're talking real nonsense, Prince Martin!" Roman Borisovich turned completely round on the bench, with beetling brows and flashing eyes; had it not been for his naked cheeks and slightly crooked bare mouth he would have been quite terrifying. "From time immemorial the Buynosovs took precedence over the Lykovs. We stem from the reigning Princes of Chernigov and can name every one of our ancestors. While you, Lykovs, made up a family tree for yourselves in the days of Ivan the Terrible. The devil saw him, this Prince Lychko when he came from the Hungarian land. . . ."

Prince Martin's eyes began to roll, the pouches under them trembled, and his whole face with its long upper lip quivered as if he were crying:

"The Buynosovs! Wasn't it in Tushino, at his camp, that the Tushin bandit granted you your estates?"

The two princes rose from the bench and began to measure each other with their eyes. And there would have been great vociferation and noise had not Yendogurov and Svinyin intervened and reasoned with them and quieted them. Wiping their foreheads and necks with their handkerchiefs the two princes seated themselves on different benches.

To relieve the tedium, Yendogurov, a noble of the council, started telling the others what the boyars in the council were babbling about: the poor fellows were quite at a loss; the only thing the Tsar and his advisers in Voronezh thought about was money and more money. He had gathered round him for counsel both Russian and foreign merchants, and other people of low birth—carpenters, blacksmiths, sailors and loafers who had narrowly escaped having their nostrils ripped by the executioner. And the Tsar listened to their thievish counsels: the real Council of State was sitting in Voronezh. Complaints flowed there from every town, from townsmen and tradesmen: they had found a sovereign after their own heart. And it was with that rabble that they were to vanquish the Sultan of Turkey! A fellow in Prokofy Voznitsin's embassy had written from Karlovitz to Moscow saying that the Turks were laughing at the Voronezh fleet, saying that it would go no farther than the mouth of the Don where all the ships would get stuck on the sandbanks.

"O Lord! We ought to stay quiet, why should we provoke the Turks?" said the gentle Lavrenty Svinyin. Three of his sons had been taken for the army and a fourth for the fleet. The old man was feeling his loneliness.

"What do you mean, quiet?" Roman Borisovich interjected, staring at him challengingly. "To begin with, Lavrenty, with your low rank you should not join in a conversation out of your turn." He slapped his thigh. "How can you talk of staying quiet in relation to the Turks and the Tatars? Why did we send Prince Vasily Golitsin twice to the Crimea?"

Prince Martin, looking at the stove, remarked:

"We haven't all got estates beyond Voronezh and Riazan."

Roman Borisovich sneered at him but disregarded his remark and went on:

"In Amsterdam they are paying a gulden for forty pounds of Polish wheat. And in France it is even dearer. The Polish lords are rolling in gold. Talk to Brovkin about it, he'll tell you where the money is. And I had to go begging the distillers to buy last year's grain for three and a half kopeks the forty pounds. What vexes me is that next door there's the Vorona river, and the Don, and my wheat could go by sea. It's a great enterprise; may God grant us victory over the Sultan! And you talk of peace! If we had only one little sea-port—Kerch, for instance. And then again, we are the Third Rome; are we to do nothing about the Holy Sepulchre? Have we already lost all conscience?"

"We shan't beat the Sultan, no. This blustering is vain," Prince Martin said comfortably. "And we've got as much grain as we want, God be praised. We shan't starve. If only we don't hurry to hang trains on our daughters and introduce gallantry into our homes."

After a short silence, Roman Borisovich, fixing his eyes between his spread knees on a knot in the floor, said:

"Well and good. But who is it that hangs trains on his daughters?"

"Of course no peasant can feed the kind of fools who buy coffee in the Foreign Quarter at fifty or seventy-five kopeks the pound," Prince Martin observed, looking at the stove and shaking his flabby chin, in an evident desire to provoke a quarrel.

The door was suddenly flung open. A ruddy, round-faced, snub-nosed officer rushed into the stuffy room from the frosty air outside. His wig was dishevelled and his small three-cornered hat was pressed down over his ears. His heavy topboots and green coat with wide red cuffs were plastered with snow. It was obvious that he had galloped full tilt across Moscow.

At the sight of the officer Prince Martin opened his mouth and gaped: this was the man who had insulted him, Alexey Brovkin, lieutenant in the Preobrazhensky regiment, one of the Tsar's favourites.

"Boyars, stop working!" Alioshka said hurriedly, holding on to the open door. "Francis Lefort is dying."

He tossed his wig, flashed his eyes insolently—as was usual with all Peter's low-born hangers-on—and rushed off with a clatter of spurs and heels along the rotten floors of the chancellery. The bald-headed senior clerks followed him with sour looks: "Not so much noise, young fellow, this isn't a stable!"

5

A week earlier Francis Lefort had been entertaining the Danish and Brandenburg envoys at his palace. A thaw had set in, and the roofs were dripping. It was very hot in the small hall. Lefort was sitting with his back to the flaming logs in the open fireplace and talking enthusiastically about the great projects. He got more and more animated, and raised a goblet of coconut shell and drank to the fraternal alliance of Tsar Peter with the King of Denmark and the Elector of Brandenburg. Every time the major-domo, standing at the window, signalled with his handkerchief, all the twelve guns on bright green gun-carriages standing in front of the house roared out a thunderous salute. Clouds of white gunpowder smoke veiled the sunny sky.

Lefort leant back in his gilded chair and opened his eyes wide; the curls of his wig clung to his pale cheeks:

"Forests of timber for masts move along our great rivers. We could feed every country in Christendom with our fish alone. We can sow thousands of our acres with flax and hemp. And the Wild Field, the southern steppes, where a man on horseback is hidden by the grass! When we have driven the Tatars out, we shall have as many cattle as there are stars in the sky. If we need iron—the ore is under our feet. In the Urals there are mountains of iron. What is it we admire in the western countries? The manufactures you have? We shall invite Englishmen and Dutchmen here and set up our own people. Before you have time to look round, we shall have all kinds of manufactures. We shall teach the townsmen science and the arts.

We shall raise the merchant and the manufacturer to heights undreamt of."

Thus spoke Lefort in his cups to the tipsy envoys. The wine and his discourse had reduced them to a state of stupefaction. It was close in the room. Lefort ordered the major-domo to open both windows and contentedly breathed in the cool damp air. He kept draining cup after cup to the great projects until the sun began to set. In the evening he went to the Polish embassy where he drank and danced until morning.

Next day Lefort felt an unusual fatigue. He put on a hareskin coat and wrapped a silk kerchief round his head, and gave instructions that no one was to be admitted. He began to write a letter to Peter, but could not finish even this and sat shivering and huddled up in his coat by the open fire. The Italian doctor Policolo was summoned. He smelt the urine and the phlegm, clicked his teeth and scratched his nose. Lefort was given a purgative and his blood was let. Nothing helped. During the night Francis Lefort developed a high fever and fell into a coma.

Pastor Strumpf, preceded by an acolyte ringing a small bell, and carrying the sacrament above his head, pushed his way with difficulty through the throng in the great hall. Lefort's mansion hummed with voices: the whole of Moscow was gathering there. Doors slammed, draughts whistled. The bewildered servants scurried about; some were already drunk. Lefort's wife, Elizaveta Franzevna, met the pastor at her husband's bedroom door. There were red blotches on her withered face and her drooping nose was swollen with crying. Her crimson gown had been laced up anyhow and thin strands of hair protruded from under her wig. She was almost frightened to death by the number of high personages who kept arriving. She knew hardly any Russian and had spent her whole life in the back rooms of the mansion. Poking her folded hands into the pastor's chest she whispered to him in German:

"What am I to do? So many visitors! Herr Pastor, tell me—ought I perhaps to offer them some slight refreshment? All the servants seem to have lost their wits: not one of them will pay any attention to what I say. The keys to the storerooms are under poor Franz's pillow." Tears gushed from the lady's pale-yellow eyes; she fumbled in her bodice, pulled out a damp handkerchief and pressed it to her face. "Herr Pastor, I'm afraid to go out into the hall, I always get so confused. What's going to happen, Herr Pastor, what's going to happen?"

Strumpf said some words of consolation in a tone suited to the occasion. Then he passed his hand over his blue-shaven face, brushing all worldly thoughts away, and entered the bedchamber.

Lefort was lying on a wide rumpled bed, with his back propped up against the pillows. Bristles had grown on his sunken cheeks and high skull. He was breathing fast, with a whistling sound, and his yellow collarbone moved as if he were still striving to slip into harness, into life. His open mouth was parched with fever. Only his eyes—black, motionless—were alive.

Doctor Policolo led the pastor aside, narrowing his eyes significantly and wrinkling his cheeks.

"The sinews," he said, "which, as our science knows, join the soul to the body, are in the case of the Admiral so clogged with dense mucus, that the channels through which the spirit flows into the body are narrowing every minute, and we must expect them shortly to be completely closed by the mucus."

Pastor Strumpf sat down quietly by the dying man's head. A short time earlier Lefort had come out of his delirium and coma, and was now evidently worrying about something. Hearing his name spoken, he turned his eyes with an effort to the pastor, and then again fixed them on a damp log smoking on the hearth. There, on volutes of stone, lay Neptune, god of the sea, with his trident; golden water flowed from a gilt vase under his elbow scattering in golden waves. In the centre, in a dark opening, the log was smoking.

Strumpf tried to draw Lefort's attention to the crucifix, and spoke of eternal salvation, which was open to every mortal. Lefort murmured something unintelligible. Strumpf bent closer to his purple lips and heard Lefort say, breathing fast:

"Make it short!"

Nevertheless, the pastor fulfilled his duty; he gave the dying man absolution and administered the sacrament. When he had gone, Lefort raised himself on his elbows. They understood that he was trying to summon his major-domo. They hurried out and found the old man weeping in the kitchen. He came, his face swollen with crying, and stood at the foot of the bed, with his staff and ostrich-plumed hat. Lefort said to him:

"Call the musicians—my friends—goblets."

The musicians came in on tiptoe, wearing whatever clothes they happened to be in. Goblets of wine were brought. The musicians stood round the bed, put the horns to their lips and then sixty horns —silver, brass and wood—played a stately minuet.

Lefort's shoulders sank into the pillows. He was deathly pale. His temples were sunken, like a horse's, but his eyes burnt with an unquenchable fire. A cup was presented to him, but he could no longer lift his hand and the wine spilled over his chest. While the music played he sank again into unconsciousness. His eyes ceased to see.

Lefort was dead. The people of Moscow were so overjoyed that they did not know what to do. Now the rule of the foreigners, of the Foreign Quarter, was at an end. Peter's accursed adviser was dead. They all knew, they had all seen, that he had made Peter drink a magic philtre, but no one was allowed to say anything. Now the streltsi's sufferings were avenged. Lefort's mansion—the nest of Antichrist—would be abandoned for ever.

It was said that on his deathbed Lefort had ordered his musicians to play, his clowns to caper and his dancers to dance, and that then he—already green in the face, like a corpse—had jumped out of bed and capered about. And that suddenly the powers of darkness had howled and whistled in the attics of the mansion.

For seven days boyars and officials of all kinds came to pay their last respects at Lefort's coffin. Concealing their joy and their apprehension, they entered the hall with its two tiers of windows, in the centre of which was a raised platform where the coffin stood, half covered with a black silk cloak. Four officers with drawn swords stood round the coffin, and another four below, round the platform. Lefort's widow, dressed in mourning, sat on a folding chair at the foot of the platform.

The boyars mounted the platform and, turning their mouths and noses aside—so as not to be polluted—touched the blue hand of the devil's admiral with their cheeks. Then they went up to the widow and bowed to her from the waist, touching the ground with their fingers, and withdrew.

On the eighth day Peter arrived; he had driven post-haste from Voronezh. His leather-covered sledge, drawn by six horses, dashed through Moscow straight to Lefort's mansion. The horses, unmatched in colour, panted with heaving ribs. A hand appeared from behind the apron fumbling to unhook the leather strap.

Alexandra Ivanovna Volkova was just coming out: she happened to be the only person on the porch. Sanka imagined it must be some low-born person who had arrived, judging by the horses. She was angry that the sledge had pulled up where it would hinder her carriage. "Take your crocks away, don't block the road!" she said to the Tsar's coachman.

The groping hand, not finding the strap fastening, ripped it open; then a man in a long-eared velvet cap, felt boots and a sheepskin coat covered with grey cloth, climbed out of the sledge. He stood up to his full height, and Sanka threw back her head as she looked at him. A round but haggard face, swollen eyes, a small dark turned-up moustache—goodness gracious, it was the Tsar!

Peter stretched one numbed leg and then the other and his brows knitted. Recognising the young woman whom, as a bride, he had sponsored, he gave her the ghost of a smile. Then he said in a hoarse voice:

"What a misfortune!"

And he went into the house with his coat-sleeves flapping. Sanka followed him.

The widow was stupefied when she saw the Tsar. She jumped up and made to throw herself at his feet. Peter put his arms round her, pressed her tightly and, over her head, looked at the coffin. Servants ran up and took his coat from him. Peter, in his felt boots, walked clumsily to the coffin to take his last farewell of his friend. He stood for a long time with his hand on the edge of the coffin. Then he bent over and kissed his dear friend's forehead and hands. His shoulders moved under his green coat and the back of his neck stiffened.

Sanka stood behind Peter and her eyes filled with tears. With her hand to her cheek, like a peasant woman, she wailed softly in a thin voice. She felt very sorry for something or somebody.

He came down from the platform, snuffling like a little boy, and stopped in front of Sanka. She nodded her head sadly.

"I shall never have such another friend," he said. He put his hand over his eyes and shook his dark curly hair, matted from the journey. "We shared our joys and we shared our cares. Our minds were one."

Suddenly he took his hand from his eyes and looked round. His tears had dried and he looked like a cat. Ten boyars were entering the hall, hurriedly crossing themselves.

According to their rank, they advanced solemnly towards Peter, went down on their knees and, supporting themselves with their palms on the floor, vigorously bumped their foreheads on the oak blocks.

Peter did not raise one of them from his knees, did not embrace them or even nod to them; he stood haughtily aloof. The nostrils of his short nose dilated.

"You are glad, I can see you are glad!" he said and went out of the house and got back into his sledge.

6

That autumn a brick house in the Dutch style, with eight windows facing the street, was built in the Foreign Quarter, beside the Lutheran church. It was built by the chancellery of the Great Palace, and built quickly—in two months. Anna Mons moved into this house with her mother and younger brother Willim.

The Tsar would come there openly and often stay the night. In the Foreign Quarter, and even in Moscow, this house was known as the Tsaritsa's palace. Anna Ivanovna ran the house in great style: a major-domo, liveried servants and, in the stables, two teams of six valuable Polish horses and carriages for all occasions.

It was no longer possible to drop in at the new Mons household, as it had been in the tavern, to drink a mug of beer. The foreigners laughed as they recalled: "It isn't long since blue-eyed Annchen, in a clean little apron, took the mugs round to the tables and blushed like a wild rose when some good-natured fellow slapped her little behind and said: 'Now then, my dear, sip off the froth: the flowers for you, and the beer for me'."

Now the only people from the Foreign Quarter who visited the Mons household were respectable traders and manufacturers, and then only when invited to dine on festive occasions. They had their jokes, of course, but with proper decorum. Pastor Strumpf always sat on Annchen's right hand. He liked to tell some amusing or instructive story from Roman history. The plethoric guests would pensively wave their mugs of beer and sigh comfortably over the transitoriness of things. Anna Ivanovna was particularly insistent on decorum in her home.

During these years she had become extremely beautiful: she walked with dignity and her eyes expressed calm, virtue and sorrow. After all, however low people might bow when her glass coach passed, the Tsar came only to sleep with her. And beyond that? The Chancellery of Estates had granted her some villages. At balls she could adorn herself with jewellery as good as others and on her breast she wore a likeness of Peter as big as a saucer, studded with diamonds. There was no lack of anything and her wishes were never refused. But there the matter ended.

Time passed. Peter spent more and more time in Voronezh or travelled post from the southern sea to the northern. Annchen sent him letters and, on every occasion, lemons and oranges by the half dozen, which were brought from Riga, sausages made with cardamom, and vodka infused with herbs. But could letters and parcels hold her lover for long? What if some other woman were to attach herself to him, worm her way into his heart? She spent sleepless nights tossing on her featherbed. Everything was precarious, uncertain, ambiguous. There were enemies, enemies all round, only waiting for the Mons woman to stumble.

Even her closest friend—Lefort—when Anna talked to him in a roundabout way, asking how long Peter was going to live his disordered bachelor life, would laugh vaguely, pinch her cheek tenderly and say: "Three years is not too long to wait for what is promised." Nobody understood: it was not even the throne she wanted, not power—power was uneasy and precarious—no, what she wanted was something stable, orderly and decent.

There was only one resource left: to try love-philtres, witchcraft. On her mother's advice Anna got out of the bed in which Peter lay fast asleep one night and sewed a small piece of cloth steeped in her own blood into the hem of his waistcoat. But he went off to Voronezh, leaving the waistcoat at Preobrazhensk, and from that day never wore it again. Anna's mother brought fortune-tellers into the back rooms of the house. But both mother and daughter were afraid to tell them exactly who was concerned. Romodanovsky put people on the rack for resorting to witchcraft.

It seemed to Anna Mons that if some ordinary fellow, with an adequate income, were to fall in love with her, she would gladly give up everything for a carefree life. Just a clean little house—even without a major-domo—and sunlight on the waxed floor; the pleasant smell of jasmine under the windowsill and the smell of roasting coffee in the kitchen; the sound of the church bell spreading tranquillity, and respectable people passing by and bowing respectfully to Anna Ivanovna as she sat at the window with her needlework.

Since Lefort's death a black cloud seemed to hang over Anna's head. She had wept so much during the seven days before Peter's arrival that her mother had sent for Doctor Policolo. He ordered an enema and a purge to rid her blood of excessive humours as a result of her grief.

Anna looked forward with terror to Peter's arrival: she herself did not know exactly why. She recalled his grey face, his cheek swollen with toothache on the day he had come to Lefort's after the most terrible of the streltsi executions. His dilated eyes seemed fixed in an expression of wrath. His hands, red with cold, lay beside his empty plate. He ate nothing and did not listen to their jokes—for they joked, though their teeth were chattering. Without looking at anyone he began to speak incomprehensibly:

"Not four regiments, but legions! As they laid their heads on the block they all crossed themselves with two fingers. For the old way of life, for beggary. To go about naked and act the idiot. Townspeople! It wasn't with Azov we should have begun, but with Moscow!"

To this day Anna shuddered when she remembered Peter at that time. She felt that he was cruelly pushing her away from her quiet window into a life of tormenting fears. For what purpose? Was he perhaps really Antichrist, as the Russians whispered? In her bed at night, by the soft light of wax candles, Anna wrung her hands and cried despairingly:

"Mother, Mother, what shall I do with myself? I don't love him. He will come to me impatiently, and I feel cold as death. Perhaps it would be better if I were lying in my coffin like poor Francis."

Suddenly, one morning, before she was dressed, when her eyelids were still heavy with sleep, she looked out of the window and saw the Tsar's sledge pull up in the rutted road beyond the fence. This time she did not fuss: let him find her as she was, in her nightcap and woollen shawl. As he came through the garden, Peter too saw her at the window, and nodded to her without a smile. In the anteroom he wiped his feet on the rug. He was sober and quiet.

"Good morning, Annushka," he said gently, kissing her on the forehead. "We have been orphaned." He sat down by the wall, near the clock which was slowly swinging the laughing brass face of its pendulum. Then he said in a low voice, as though astounded that death should have been so unreasonably careless: "Francis, Francis . . . He wasn't much of an admiral, but he was worth a whole fleet. It's a calamity, Annushka, a calamity. Do you remember when he first brought me to your house, when you were still a little girl: you were afraid I was going to break your musical-box? Death has taken the wrong man. Francis is no more! I can't realise it. . . ."

Anna listened and pulled the downy shawl up to her eyes. She had not been prepared for this; she did not know what to say. Tears trickled down under the shawl. There was a cautious clatter of plates outside the door. Sobbing, with her eyes full of tears, she murmured that Francis must now be happy with God. Peter looked strangely at her.

"Peter, you've had nothing to eat after your journey—please stay and eat something. As it happens, we've your favourite fried sausages today."

She saw with chagrin that even sausages did not tempt him. She sat by his side, took his hand which smelt of sheepskin and kissed it. His other hand caressed her hair under her nightcap.

"Tonight I'll come for an hour," he said. "Now that's enough, that's enough. You've made my hand all wet with tears. Go, bring me a sausage and a glass of vodka. . . . Go, go. . . . I've much work to do today."

7

Lefort was buried with great pomp. Three regiments marched with lowered standards and guns. The admiral's hat, sword and spurs were carried on cushions behind the bier, drawn by sixteen black horses tandem. A horseman in black armour and black plumes carried a torch reversed. Ambassadors and envoys walked in mourning attire. After them came the boyars and courtiers, nobles of the council and Moscow nobles: nearly a thousand of them. Military bugles sounded, drums beat slowly. Peter marched in front with the first company of the Preobrazhensky regiment.

Not seeing the Tsar anywhere near, some of the boyars mended their pace and gradually overtook the foreign envoys to be at the head of the procession. The envoys shrugged their shoulders and whispered to one another. Near the cemetery they were pushed into the background altogether. Prince Roman Borisovich Buynosov and the extremely stupid Prince Stepan Beloselsky trudged close to the very wheels, holding on to the bier. Many of the Russians were somewhat the worse for drink: they had gathered for the funeral at break of day and, feeling faint with hunger, had crowded round the tables, set with cold dishes for the meal after the ceremony, and had drunk and eaten.

When the coffin was laid on the frozen heap of earth dug out of the grave, Peter hurried up to it and, with a glance at the boyars' shaven, suddenly sobered faces, turned on them with so forbidding an expression that some of them tried to hide behind each other's backs. He summoned Leo Narishkin to him with a nod.

"Why have they pushed themselves in front of the foreign envoys?" he asked. "By whose orders?"

"I've already spoken severely to them," Leo Narishkin answered in a low voice, "but they pay no attention."

"Dogs!" Peter said, and then louder: "They're dogs, not human beings!" His neck twitched, he turned his head from side to side and his jackbooted leg kicked convulsively. The crowd of boyars parted and the ambassadors and envoys squeezed their way through to the grave where the Tsar, chilled through in his thin cloth coat, stood alone by the side of the open coffin. All watched him apprehensively, wondering what he would do next. Sticking his sword into the earth, he went down on his knees and pressed his face to all that remained of his wise friend, the adventurer and debauchee, the carouser and faithful comrade. Then he rose to his feet, wiping his eyes with an angry gesture.

"Close it! Lower it into the grave!"

Drums rolled and standards were lowered; guns boomed, emitting clouds of white smoke. One of the gunners, who was standing gaping and did not jump out of the way in time, had his head blown off. That day people in Moscow told each other:

"One devil's buried, but the other remains—evidently he hasn't destroyed enough people yet."

8

Worthy traders and manufacturers, leaving their sledges outside the gates and doffing their caps, walked up the long covered staircase that rose from almost the middle of the courtyard into the Preobrazhensky palace. Government trading agents, chosen from among the wealthier merchants, and members of the merchants' companies arrived in upholstered sledges drawn by three horses and walked in boldly in their coats of Hamburg cloth lined with fox fur. The dilapidated hall was badly heated. The merchants threw sharp glances at the cracks in the rotten ceiling and at the moth-eaten red cloth on the benches and doors, and said:

"What a state it's in! This is how the boyars look after things. It's a pity, a great pity."

The traders had been hurriedly gathered here by personal summons. Some of them had not come because they were afraid that they would be made to eat off the Tsar's crockery * and smoke tobacco.

* Unclean to the Old Believers.

They guessed why the Tsar had summoned them to the palace. Some days before, a clerk of the council had stood at the place of execution in the Red Square and, to the rolling of drums, had read out the Tsar's ukase: "It has become known to the Tsar that government trading agents and merchants' guilds, and all merchants, manufacturers and townspeople are *suffering great losses and ruin* as a result of the delays and procrastination caused by governors, and chancellery and other officials. The Tsar, in his mercy, orders that all matters concerning rights, litigation, petitions and trading affairs, and the collection of State taxes *shall be conducted by stewards and that they shall elect as stewards* every year the most worthy and upright men from amongst them, as they decide themselves. And one of these shall be their chief steward and shall sit for one month as president." In the towns, suburbs and large villages they were ordered to elect local stewards, for courts and enquiries and for the collection of taxes, from among the best and most upright men; and for the collection of customs dues and taxes on drink they were to elect customs and tavern stewards, whomsoever they pleased. The stewards were to sit in council and conduct trade and tax business in a special Stewards' Chamber, which would take all disputes and petitions, without referring to the chancelleries, direct to the Tsar himself.

A building of the old Tsar's palace in the Kremlin, near the church of St. John the Baptist, was assigned as the Stewards' Chamber, and the funds were to be kept in its cellars.

The merchants of Moscow spared no money for such a worthy purpose; not so long ago they had walked about in the Kremlin with their heads uncovered, and in fear; now they themselves were to sit there. They put a new roof on the palace, made to look like silver, painted it inside and out and put in windows, not of mica but of glass; and they set their own guards by the cellars.

For their liberation from the depredations of governors and the injustices of tax officials the merchants were now to pay double their former contributions. It was a clear profit for the treasury. They felt doubtful. Would the merchants stand to gain by it? They felt doubtful.

True, the governors and officials, big and small, had made life impossible: they were as greedy as wolves and, if you were not careful, they would tear your throat out; in Moscow they dragged you through the courts and stripped you, and in the towns and villages they wore you out by forced recoveries of debt in the governor's courtyard. All that was quite true.

But many—naturally the most cunning—were careful and did not do so badly: they made the governor a present of money, sent sugar, cloth or fish to the clerk, invited the registrar to come and take pot luck. With some of the rich men the devil himself—let alone the governor or chancellery official—would never find out how much they had in money and goods. Of course in the case of such big men as Mitrofan Shorin, head of the merchants' company, or Alexey Sveshnikov, everything was straight and above-board—even the Metropolitan went to their houses. They would have been glad to pay even three times their former taxes to the Stewards' Chamber: it brought honour and power and order. But how about, say, Vaska Revyakin Senior? There were hardly three altyns' worth of goods in his shop in the ironmongers' row, and he would sit there wiping his eyes with a rag. But people in the know said he had some three thousand peasant serfs. And it wasn't only peasants and townsmen: there was hardly a merchant who wasn't heavily in debt to him. And there was not a town or large village where Revyakin did not have a warehouse or a shop, though they were all registered in the name of some member of his family or of one of his clerks. There was no way of catching him; he was as naked and slippery as an eel. For him the Stewards' Chamber meant ruin: you can't hide things from your own kind.

While they waited for the Tsar to enter, the older merchants sat on the benches, while the lesser fry stood about. They understood that the Tsar, in whom their hopes lay, needed money and wanted a heart-to-heart talk with them. He should have had a heart-to-heart talk long ago. Those who were in the palace for the first time felt a certain fear as they looked at the door painted with lions and birds, by the side of the throne dais; there was no throne there now, only the canopy.

Peter entered unexpectedly from a side door; he was wearing Dutch clothes, and his face was red; apparently he had been drinking. "Good day, good day!" he said over and over again in a genial tone, shaking hands with some and clapping the backs of others or patting their heads. Several people came in with him: Mitrofan Shorin and Alexey Sveshnikov in Hungarian coats; the brothers Osip and Fedor Bazhenin, grave and stately, with turned-up moustaches and clothes of foreign cloth rather tight at the shoulders; short and dignified Ivan Artemyich Brovkin, the *parvenu,* clean-shaven and wearing a brown wig that reached his navel; Lubim Domnin, the stern-looking clerk of the council, and then a man no one knew, with a gipsy's beard and a high bald forehead, in the clothes of a plain townsman. It was obvious that he felt very nervous; he hung back behind the others.

Peter seated himself on a bench and rested his elbows on his spread knees. Then he said to the merchants who had moved towards him: "Sit down, sit down." They hesitated. He ordered them to sit down, and his head twitched. The senior merchants at once sat down. The clerk of the council remained standing; he took a rolled document out of his back pocket and mumbled his dry lips. The brothers Osip and Fedor Bazhenin immediately jumped up, holding their English hats against their stomachs, and lowered their eyes in a dignified way. Peter again nodded in their direction:

"We need more men like these. I wish to praise them in the presence of everyone. In England and Holland they confer honours for good trade activities and for good manufacturers. We must introduce the same custom. Am I right?" He turned right and left, and raised an eyebrow. "Why are you hesitating? Are you afraid I'm going to ask you for money? We've got to begin to live in a different way, merchants; that's what I want."

Momonov, a rich cloth merchant, bowed and asked:

"What does that mean, Sire—to live in a different way?"

"To drop our isolated way of living. My boyars live shut up in their mansions like badgers. You mustn't do that, you are trading people. You must learn to trade, not as each man for himself, but as companies. The East India Company in Holland is an excellent organisation: they build ships jointly, and they trade jointly. They earn great profits. We've got to learn from them. In Europe there are academies for this purpose. If you wish, we'll build a Bourse here as good as the one in Amsterdam. Set up your companies, introduce manufactures! But you people know only one maxim: unless you cheat you won't sell."

A young merchant who was looking admiringly at the Tsar, suddenly slapped his hand with his cap and said:

"That's true—that's what we're like."

Others began to pull him back into the crowd by his coat tails. But he went on, turning his head round and shrugging his shoulders:

"Why? Isn't it the truth? We live by swindling, and only by swindling: we give false weight, we give false measure. . . ."

Peter laughed, a deep mirthless laugh, rounding his parted lips. Those who were standing near him also laughed politely. Then he suddenly stopped laughing and said in a sharp tone:

"You've been trading for two hundred years, and you haven't learnt it yet. You pass wealth by. Always the same squalor and destitution. You trade and make a kopek and then take it to the tavern. Isn't that so?"

"It isn't so with everybody," Momonov said.

"Yes, it is!" Peter's nostrils dilated. "Go abroad and look at their merchants—they're kings! We've no time to wait for you to teach yourselves. There are some pigs whose snouts one has to force into the trough. Why do the foreigners give me no rest? They want me to lease them this and lease them that—timber, ore, manufactures. Why can't our own people do it? There was one fellow who came to Voronezh—the devil knows where he came from—but the noise he made, the schemes he put forward! You people, he said, have an immensely wealthy country, only you yourselves are poor. What's the reason? I said nothing. Now I ask you: are the people living in our country different from others?" He looked round at the merchants with bulging eyes. "God hasn't given us any others. We've got to manage with those we have, is that so or not? Sometimes you Russian people make my gorge rise, really make my gorge rise. . . ." His ears and the muscles in his neck were tense.

Then Ivan Artemyich Brovkin, who was sitting next to him, said in a mild, sing-song tone:

"The Russians have been thrashed a great deal, and thrashed without any reason, that's why they've become so warped."

"Fool!" Peter exclaimed. "Fool!" And he dug his ribs sharply with his elbow.

Brovkin rejoined in a still more deliberately stupid voice:

"You see, what did I say?"

For a moment Peter looked furiously into Brovkin's sleek face, screwed up in a silly grin, then he slapped him on the forehead with his palm:

"Vanka, I haven't yet made you court fool!"

But evidently Peter himself realised that it was unwise to flare up and lose his temper in front of the merchants. Merchants weren't boyars: the boyars couldn't escape, they couldn't take their estates away in their pockets. But the merchant was like a snail: at the slightest provocation he could draw in his horns and shut himself up with his capital. Indeed, there was already a certain aloofness, an ominous stillness, in the room. Brovkin glanced at Peter with a slyly narrowed eye.

"Read, Lubim," Peter said to the clerk.

The brothers Bazhenin again lowered their eyes modestly. The clerk began to read slowly and dryly in a high-pitched voice:

". . . these gracious letters-patent have been bestowed as a reward for zeal and great industry displayed in the building of vessels. Last year Osip and Fedor Bazhenin built in the village of Vovchug a water-driven saw-mill from a foreign model, *without foreign* craftsmen, entirely on their own, for the purpose of sawing timber into planks and selling these to foreign and Russian traders in Archangel. And they sawed the timber, and brought it to Archangel, and despatched it beyond the seas. And it is their intention to build at this same mill vessels and ships for the transport of planks and other Russian goods beyond the seas. And we, the Great Tsar, have rewarded them: we have given them orders to build vessels and ships in that village, and whatever materials are imported from overseas for the building of these ships will be allowed in customs free, and they will be permitted to hire foreign and Russian craftmen for wages, at their own expense. And when the said vessels are completed, they will be permitted to maintain guns and ammunition on them to protect them against pirates and other foreign trading ships. . . ."

The clerk read on and on. Then he rolled up the document with its dangling seal and, placing it on the palms of his hands, presented it to Osip and Fedor. The two brothers took it from him, then walked up to Peter and silently bowed to the ground before him, with proper ceremony and dignity. He raised them up by their shoulders and kissed them, not formally, touching cheek to cheek, as the Tsar usually did, but heartily on the lips.

"The important thing is that it is a start," he said to the merchants. Then his rapid glance caught the unknown townsman with the gipsy beard and bald forehead. "Demidich!" The man elbowed his way sharply through the crowd. "Demidich, make your bow to the merchants! Nikita Demidich Antufyev, Tula blacksmith. He makes pistols and muskets as good as the English ones. He casts pig-iron and seeks out ore. But he lacks the means to do better. Talk it over with him, merchants, think it over. And I am his friend. If need be, we will grant him land and villages. Demidich, make your bow, make your bow, I'll answer for you."

9

"Who are you? What have you come for? Whom do you want here?"

The stern, broad-shouldered woman looked distrustfully at Andrey Golikov, the icon-painter from Palekh. He was shivering and his skin had turned to gooseflesh under the tatters and patches of his rough brown coat. A damp March wind was blowing and whistled through the naked bushes on the crumbling walls of Beliy-gorod. Hungry crows, with ruffled feathers, cawed uneasily as they rose over the heaps of rubbish. The merchant Vasily Revyakin's high fences stretched along the Moscow walls which here formed an angle. It was a gloomy spot with narrow and deserted alleys.

"From the elder Abraham," Andrey whispered, pressing two fingers firmly to his forehead. Behind the woman, in the yard criss-crossed with ruts, by the ramshackle store-houses, lean watchdogs strained at their chains. Golikov was quite frozen, only his eyes gleamed hotly. The woman took her time over admitting him into the yard, then showed him the way along planks laid over the mud, towards a tall, long building without steps or porch. Shutters flapped over small mica windows high up under the roof.

They went down a dark passage smelling of damp vats. The woman nudged Golikov: "Wipe your feet on the straw, you're not in a pigsty." Then, after a pause, she said in the same unfriendly tone: "In the name of the Father, the Son and the Holy Ghost", and opened a low door into a room. It was hot here, and glowing embers in the stove lit up the dark panels of the icons in the corner. Golikov crossed himself over and over again at the terrible eyes of the saints' faces of ancient workmanship, and stayed timidly by the door. The woman sat down. From the other side of the wall came the muffled sound of many voices singing.

"What did the elder send you for?"

"For probation."

"What probation?"

"To go to the elder Nektary for three years."

"To Nektary!" the woman drawled.

"He sent me here to get directions how to reach him. I can't live in the world, my body is starving and my soul is full of dread. I am afraid. I am seeking a retreat, a saintly life." Golikov sniffed. "Have pity on me, good soul, don't drive me away."

"Elder Nektary will make a retreat for you," the woman said enigmatically. Her eyes, which he could see in the light of the embers, narrowed.

Golikov began to tell her about himself. For more than six months now he had been wandering about the town, suffering from hunger and cold. He had got involved with all sorts of people and they had tried to draw him into crime. "I can't, my soul recoils in horror." He told her how, that winter, during snowstorms, he had spent nights under the dilapidated roofs of the city walls. "I gathered a little straw and covered myself with bast matting. The wind howled, and the snow whirled; the dead streltsi danced on their ropes and rattled against the wall. On those nights I yearned for a quiet haven, a silent, saintly life."

Having questioned him closely about the elder Abraham, the woman got up with a sigh and said: "Follow me." She led Golikov again through the dark passage and down some steps. Ordering him to stay where the beggars were, she let him into the basement from which the sound of singing had come, and a hot wave of wax and incense met them. Thirty or more people were kneeling on the scrubbed floor. A crooked-shouldered man, wearing a black cassock and a skull cap, was reading at a lectern covered with velvet. When he turned the time-worn pages of the hand-written missal, he raised his ragged beard to the flames of the tapers. All along one wall, from the floor upwards, tapers were burning in front of large and small icons painted in the ancient Novgorod style.

They were holding a service according to the priestless rite.* The singing was mournful and rather nasal. On the elder's right, in front of the praying people, short, goat-bearded Vasily Revyakin knelt. Slipping his leather chaplet through his fingers, he lifted his eyes to the icons from time to time or, with a slight turn of his head, glanced out of the corner of his eyes at the people praying, and, under his glance, they bowed to the ground more fervently, even bruising their foreheads.

The crooked-shouldered elder shut the book and, raising it over his head, turned round: his beard had been torn out in patches, and his nose was broken. His face was not old. Fixing his dilated pupils as if on some terrible apparition, he opened his mouth, showing gaps in his teeth, and cried out:

"Let us recall the words of the blessed Hippolytus, Pope of Rome: 'In the time of the coming of Antichrist the Church of God will fall, and there will be no more bloodless sacrifice. Temptation will visit the towns and villages, the monasteries and hermitages. And none but a few will be saved. . . .'"

His voice was terrible. The worshippers fell on their faces and their shoulders heaved. The elder stood there with the book raised until everyone was wailing.

"Brothers, this is what I am going to tell you," the elder said, clutching at the wooden cross on his chest, when the service was over. "I was visited by God's grace. The Lord brought me to lake Vol, to elder Nektary's hermitage. I bowed to him and he asked me:

* An Old Believers' sect.

'What do you want: to save your soul or your flesh?' I said: 'My soul, my soul!' And the elder said: 'It is well, my son.' And he set to saving my soul and mortifying my flesh. In the hermitage instead of bread we ate fern, and woodsorrel, and acorns, and we stripped the bark off pine trees and pounded it with fish; this was our food. And God did not let us die. And what I endured at the hands of my spiritual master from the very first days! Twice every day I was beaten. And on Easter Sunday, too, I was beaten twice. And in all, during two years, reckoning two beatings each day, there were one thousand four hundred and thirty beatings. And I do not even count the wounds and blows received each day from his blessed hands. He mortified my flesh: with whatever he happened to have in his hands, he struck me, his orphan and his fledgling. He beat me with his staff, and with the pestle for pounding in a mortar, and with a poker, and with saucepans for cooking food, and with the stick for mixing dough. It was to bring light to my dark soul that my teacher mortified my flesh. With a yoke, for carrying pails of water, he struck the calf of my leg, so that my legs should be ready to obey. And it was not only with wood that he subdued my flesh, but also with iron, and stones, and bricks, and by tearing my hair. In those days my fingers were torn out of their sockets, and my ribs and bones broken. And the Lord did not let me die. Today my body is weak but my spirit is serene. Brothers, be not slothful with regard to your souls!"

"Be not slothful with regard to your souls!" the elder cried three times, his eyes boring unmercifully into those of his awe-stricken flock. They were all relatives, relations by marriage, or serfs of Vasily Revyakin: his clerks, warehouse employees and shopmen. They sighed heavily as they listened. Some were unable to stand the fanatical glare of the elder. Andrey Golikov was racked with sobs; he wept, clutching his cheeks, and saw through his tears the yellow beams of the candle-flames flutter all over the chapel like the wings of archangels.

The elder bowed low to his flock and stepped aside. His place was taken by Vasily Revyakin himself: short, grey-headed, with two slits for eyes in which his pupils shuttled to and fro. Fingering his chaplet he said in quiet, kindly tones:

"My dear, cherished friends, it is terrible! My beloved friends, it is terrible! The day was bright, and then a cloud rose and covered our whole life with its stench." He looked over his right shoulder, and then over his left, as if to see if someone was standing behind him. Then he took a step forward in his soft felt boots. "Antichrist is already here. Do you hear? He has enthroned himself on the domes of the Nikonian church. The three-fingered sign of the cross is his seal; there is no salvation for those who use it: they are already devoured. And there is no salvation for those who drink and eat in the company of those who cross themselves with three fingers. There is no salvation for those who accept sacrament from a priest: their consecrated bread is branded and their priesthood is an imposture. How are we to save ourselves? We have heard how people save themselves. I don't hold anyone back; go, go away, my dear friends, accept martyrdom, sanctify yourselves! You will be so many more intercessors for us who are sinful and weak. I may even go myself, close my store-houses and shops, and distribute my goods and chattels among the poor. The only salvation lies in the faith of our forbears, in obedience and fear." He shook his little beard bitterly and wiped his eyelashes with his sleeve. The flock had become very still, they neither moved nor breathed. "It is well for him who can embrace this, but he who cannot need not despair: the elders will save him with their prayers. Fear one thing more than death: that the Evil One should lead you into temptation. Today it is not as in former times; his invisible servants surround each man and only wait for him to succumb. If you sin, if you act against your conscience, if you keep back a kopek from your master—It seems a small thing to you, a kopek? No!—they will pounce on you and you will be lost, condemned to eternal torment. Fear only that the elders should cease praying for you." He took another step forward and hit his thigh with his chaplet. "Here's a temptation: the Stewards' Chamber! That's where hell is, true hell. From ancient times the merchants have paid their taxes to the treasury, and then it was my own private affair what I traded in and how I traded. God gives a man intelligence, so he becomes a merchant. But a fool will remain all his life in another man's service. Elect stewards! Then some fool will poke his nose into my warehouse, into my coffer. I'll have to tell him everything, show him everything. What for? Who needs it? The net of Antichrist is being cast over the merchants. And then again, the post! Why? I send a trustworthy man to Veliky Ustug, he gets there quicker than any post and says what is necessary, in private. But by post—how do I know what sort of fellow takes my letter? No, we don't need the post, we don't need stewards, we don't need to pay double taxes or smoke tobacco with foreigners and Nikonians." In spite of himself he gave way to anger. He plunged his trembling hand into his pocket, pulled out his handkerchief and wiped his face. Then he shook his head with his eyes on the tapers which were burning low, sighed heavily and said no more. "Let us go to supper."

All who were in the chapel went through the passage and the kitchen into the basement next door. There they sat down at a wooden table covered with a glossy, coloured linen cloth in the icon corner where Vasily Revyakin and his three old clerks—his first cousins—had their supper. They invited the elder to sit with them too under the icons, but he suddenly spat loudly and went to the door, to the beggars who sat on the floor. Golikov was among them.

A tallow candle was burning in the centre of the table. The stern-looking woman kept coming out of the darkness carrying full bowls. Occasionally a cockroach fell from the ceiling. They ate in silence, chewed slowly and laid down their spoons quietly. Golikov edged closer to the elder, who sat huddled up over the bowl on his knees, convulsively dipping in his spoon, dripping the broth on to his patchy beard, scalding himself and eating his bread in little pieces. When he had finished eating and said his prayers he folded his hands on his stomach. It was evident from the way his eyes had misted that his mood had mellowed.

Golikov said softly to him:

"Father, I want to go to elder Nektary. Please let me."

The elder breathed fast, but his eyes dimmed again.

"Later, when they lie down to sleep, come into the chapel. I will test you."

Golikov shuddered. A feeling of distress and of impending doom seized him, and he began to rub his head against the rough splinters of the log wall.

10

A warm wind was blowing from the southern steppe. Within a week the snows had thawed and the blue sky was reflected in the flood-waters which covered the plain. The tributary streams rose, and the ice broke on the Don. In one night the Voronezh river overflowed its banks and flooded the shipyards. Ships, brigantines, galleys, barges and boats rocked at their anchors all the way from Voronezh to the Don. Drops of still liquid tar dripped from their sides; gilded and silvered Neptune's heads gleamed. Sails that had been hoisted to dry flapped in the wind. The last ice-floes rasped and rustled as they dipped in the turgid waters. Over the walls of the fort—on the right bank of the river, opposite the town—puffs of gunpowder smoke rose in the air and were blown to shreds by the wind. The sound of the gunshots rolled over the water as if the earth itself were swelling and bursting in bubbles.

In the shipyards work went on day and night. The last touches were being given to the decoration of the forty-gun battleship *Reliance,* and its high carved poop and three masts swayed by the new piles of the pier. Barges laden with gunpowder, salt-meat and ship's bread were constantly crossing the river towards the ship and making fast to its black side. The current pulled the mooring ropes taut, the timbers creaked. Swarthy-faced Captain Pamburg stood on the quarter-deck, his great moustache bristling, his eyes like a furious ram's, his jackboots coated with mud. He was wearing a plain sheepskin coat over his uniform and a red silk kerchief bound round his head. Shouting in a voice that drowned the rumbling of barrels rolling along the decks and the screeching of blocks, he cursed in Russian and Portuguese: "Lubbers! Bastards! *Carraja!"* The sailors strained themselves to the utmost hauling on board sacks of ship's bread, barrels and crates, rolling them at a run to the hold where boatswains in high felt caps and brown balloon breeches snarled hoarsely like watchdogs.

On the hill above the river, wooden towers with pointed roofs leant crookedly and the small rusty domes of churches rose behind the crumbling walls. Mud-huts and boarded shacks where the workers lived were scattered over the slope of the hill in front of the old town. Closer to the river were the new log-houses of the recently-appointed Admiral Golovin, of Alexander Menshikov, of the chief of the Admiralty, Apraxin, and of Vice-admiral Cornelius Kreis.

The low bank on the far side of the river was scarred with wheeltracks and covered with wood-chips; there stood smoke-blackened smithies with earth roofs, and near them the ribs of unfinished vessels, half-submerged stacks of boards, rafts that had been dragged out of the water, barrels, cables, rusty anchors. Black smoke rose from cauldrons of pitch; thin wheels creaked as they twisted rope; the shoulders of sawyers on high sawing-blocks moved backwards and forwards; raftsmen ran barefooted through the mud with hooks to pull back logs carried away by the flood-waters.

The main work was done. The fleet had been launched. There remained only the battleship *Reliance,* which was being trimmed and decorated with special care. The admiral's flag was to be hoisted on her in three days' time.

The door kept opening, and more and more people came in. They did not take off their coats or wipe their boots, but just sat down on the benches, the more important ones seating themselves at the table. They ate and drank in the Tsar's house all day and all night. Candles stuck in empty bottles were kept burning. The log walls were hung with wigs: it was hot. Clouds of tobacco smoke from their pipes hung in the air.

Vice-admiral Cornelius Kreis slept at the table with his face in the gold-laced cuffs of his sleeves. Rear-admiral of the Russian fleet, the Dutchman Julius Riaz—a bold sea-rover, whose head had a price of two thousand pounds sterling on it for various deeds on distant seas—was drinking anisette, frowning with his one-eyed ferocious face at a candle. Shipwrights Joseph Nye and John Day, whose faces were overgrown with stubble in these feverish days, puffed at their pipes, and winked sardonically at the Russian shipwright, Fedosey Skliayev, who had just come in. He unwound his scarf and unbuttoned his warm coat, and began eating noodles with pork.

"Fedosey," Joseph Nye said to him, winking his sandy eyelashes, "tell us how you feasted in Moscow."

Fedosey did not reply and went on eating. He had had enough of this. Returning from abroad in February he should have gone on to Voronezh immediately, as Peter had told him to do in a letter. But the devil had led him astray. He had begun to make the rounds of his friends in Moscow and the fun had started. He spent three riotous days: pancakes, snacks, feasts and vodka galore. It all ended as could be expected: he landed up in the Preobrazhensky Office.

When the Tsar heard that his long-awaited favourite Fedosey had been put under arrest by Romodanovsky, he sent a special messenger to Moscow with a letter to the Prince-Emperor:

"*Mein Herr König*, why do you detain our comrades Fedosey Skliayev and others? I am much grieved. I was particularly awaiting Skliayev because he is the best man for shipbuilding, yet you have detained him. God will be your judge. Truly, I have no helper here. For the Lord's sake let him go and send him here. Peter."

Some ten days later Skliayev in person brought Romodanovsky's answer:

"This is what he has done: he was drunk and, driving with some friends, got into a fight with soldiers of the Preobrazhensky regiment at the barrier. The enquiry showed that both sides were at fault. And I, after looking into the business, have had Skliayev flogged for his foolishness, and have also flogged the soldiers with whom he quarrelled and who had come to complain. Do not be angry with me on this account; I am not accustomed to let foolishness go unpunished, no matter what the rank of the culprit."

Well and good. The matter might have ended there. When Peter met Skliayev, he embraced and caressed him, then he slapped his thighs and not only chuckled, but laughed till he cried. "You're not in Amsterdam now, Fedosey!" And at supper he read Romodanovsky's letter aloud.

Having finished his noodles, Fedosey pushed away his bowl and reached for Joseph Nye's tobacco:

"All right; enough, you devils, you've had your laugh," he said gruffly. "Did you go into the aftermost hold?"

"We did," Joseph Nye replied.

"No, you didn't."

John Day slowly removed his clay pipe and said in Russian through clenched teeth, the corners of his straight mouth drooping:

"Why do you ask as if we hadn't been in the hold, Skliayev?"

"Because. Instead of goggling at me, you'd better take a lantern and go and have a look."

"A leak?"

"That's just it—a leak. As soon as they began loading the barrels with salt-meat, the timbers gave and water is spouting from below."

"It can't be."

"Well, it is. What did I say? The ribs of the poop are weak."

Nye and Day exchanged looks, then they got up without haste, and pulled on their caps with ear-pieces. Fedosey irritably wound the scarf round his neck and picked up a lantern:

"Oh, you generals!"

Officers, sailors, craftsmen—all weary and covered with tar and splashed with mud—came to sit at the table. They swallowed a cupful of fiery vodka from the earthenware jug, then snatched something with their fingers from the dishes—roast meat, sucking-pig, brawn in vinegar—and as soon as they had eaten, many of them went out again, without crossing themselves, without saying a word of thanks.

By the wooden partition, his broad shoulder leaning heavily against the door-jamb, stood a sleepy-eyed sailor with a tall felt cap over one ear. Round his muscular neck hung a knotted and tarred rope, to the end of which he treated whoever needed it. He asked all who approached the door in a slow drawl:

"Where do you think you are going, you?"

Behind the partition, in the sleeping-quarters, men of State were at this moment holding a session: Admiral Fedor Alexeyevich Golovin, Leo Narishkin, Fedor Matveyevich Apraxin—Chief of the Admiralty —and Alexander Menshikov. After the death of Lefort, Menshikov had been raised immediately to the rank of major-general and made governor of Pskov. It was alleged that when Peter returned to Voronezh after the funeral, he had said: "I had two hands, now only one is left; although inclined to steal, it is a reliable one."

Alexander, in a wig, wearing a fine uniform coat of the Preobrazhensky regiment elegantly belted with a scarf, stood by the hot brick stove, his narrow chin buried in his lace cravat.

Apraxin and the obese Golovin sat on the unmade bed. Narishkin was sitting at the table, resting his forehead on the palm of his hand. They were listening to the council clerk and great ambassador Prokofy Voznitsin, who had just returned from Karlowitz on the Danube, where the Austrian, Polish, Venetian and Russian ambassadors had been discussing peace terms with the Turks.

He had not seen the Tsar yet. Peter had given orders for the ministers to assemble and confer, saying that he would come later. Voznitsin held note-books with coded entries on his knees and, with his spectacles resting on the tip of his thin nose, he was saying:

"I have arranged with the Turkish envoys, Rais-effendi Rami and the Privy Councillor Mavrocordato, for an armistice, that is, a temporary suspension of fighting. It was impossible to get more than that. Judge for yourselves, sirs: there is so much trouble brewing in Europe just now; it may involve nearly the whole world. The King of Spain is stricken in years, he may die any day and he is childless. The French King is anxious to set his grandson Philip on the Spanish throne and has already married him and is keeping him in Paris expecting to crown him any moment. On the other hand, the Emperor of Austria wants to set up his son Charles in Spain."

"We know, we know all that," Alexander interrupted him impatiently.

"Have patience, Alexander Danilovich, I speak in my own way." Over his spectacles Voznitsin turned his old eyes on the handsome young fellow in a heavy stare. "A great dispute between France and England is being decided. If Spain goes to the French King, the French and Spanish fleets will be paramount on the seas. If Spain goes to the Austrian Emperor, the English will· be able to deal with the French fleet by itself. It is the English who are stirring up the political situation in Europe. It is they who have brought the Austrians and the Turks together in Karlowitz. The Austrian Emperor must have his hands free to make war on the French King. And the Turks are extremely glad to make peace so as to have a respite and gather strength: Prince Eugene of Savoy has taken many lands and towns from them for the Austrian Emperor—in Hungary, in Transylvania and in Morea—and the Austrians have already got their eyes on Constantinople. The Turks' concern now is to retrieve their lost possessions. They do not even think about distant wars, either with the Poles or with us. Take Azov: to them it is not worth what they would lose fighting there."

"Is the Turkish Sultan really as weak as you want us to believe? I doubt it," Alexander said. Golovin and Apraxin smiled. Leo Narishkin, seeing them smile, also smiled and shook his head. Joggling his leg and making his spur ring, Alexander went on: "And if he is weak, why didn't you sign a permanent peace with him? Or did you forget to tell the Rais-effendi that we have forty thousand streltsi wintering in the Ukraine, Shein's large cavalry regiment gathered at Ahtyrka, and boats ready for crossing near Briansk? We did not send you empty-handed. An armistice!"

Prokofy Voznitsin slowly took off his spectacles. It was hard to get used to the new order of things when a puppy of low birth could speak like this to a great ambassador. He passed his dry palm over his face which was quivering with anger, in order to collect his thoughts. There was, of course, nothing to be gained by quarrelling.

"Here is why we arranged an armistice and not full peace, Alexander Danilovich. The Austrian envoys carried on negotiations with the Turks alone, in secret, without consulting us, or the Poles, or the Venetians. And the Poles came to an understanding secretly from us. We were left alone. After they had arranged matters to their satisfaction with the Austrians, the Turks at first did not want to talk with us at all, they were so puffed up. Had my old acquaintance Alexander Mavrocordato not been there, we wouldn't have obtained even an armistice. Here you sit, sirs, thinking that the whole of Europe is watching you. No, for them we are a minor political consideration, one could say no political consideration at all."

"That's still to be seen. . . ."

"Wait, don't get excited, Alexander Danilovich," Golovin gently stopped him.

"At the ambassadors' camp we were given the worst place. Guards were set to watch over us. We were forbidden to go anywhere, to see the Turks or even to communicate with them. While I was in Vienna I engaged a doctor, an experienced Pole. And I sent him to the

Turkish camp, to Mavrocordato. The first time I sent him Mavrocordato asked him to give me his greetings. I sent him a second time. Mavrocordato asked him to give me his greetings and say that it was very cold. I was pleased. I took my coat of crimson cloth lined with silver fox fur and sent it through the doctor, ordering him to ride round the ambassadors' camps, through the fields. Mavrocordato accepted the coat and, on the next day, sent me some tobacco, two handsome pipes, about a pound of coffee and some writing paper. Ah, I thought, he sends return presents. So I sent him a cartload: caviare, smoked sturgeon, five salted white sturgeon, big ones, and all kinds of fruit liqueurs. And then I went myself to the Turkish camp, alone, in simple clothes. On that very day the Turks had signed the peace with the Emperor."

"Oh! What a. . . !" Alexander stamped his spurred foot.

"Mavrocordato said to me: 'We'll hardly reach an agreement unless you return the Dniepr towns to us, so that we can close the Dniepr and finally bar your way to the Black Sea. And you'll have to give back Azov, and pay tribute to the Khan of Crimea, as in the old days'. That, Alexander Danilovich, is how the Turks began to bluster during the very first talk we had. And I was alone. Our allies had completed their business and had gone their way. I began to threaten the Turks with our Voronezh fleet, but they laughed: 'It's the first time we hear about ships being built six hundred miles from the sea; well, sail in them on the Don, but you won't be able to get out of the estuary'. I threatened them with the Ukrainian army, and they threatened me with the Tatars: 'Look out—now that the Tatars' hands are free, mind they don't do the same thing to you as in the days of Devlet-girey'.* If the Turks had had nothing to worry about, they would have declared war on us. I don't know, Alexander Danilovich, perhaps my poor understanding prevented me from achieving better results, nevertheless an armistice is not war."

There were still many small things to be done. There was a shortage of nails. Owing to the thaw, part of the sledge-train bringing iron from Tula had only arrived the day before. They worked all night in the smithies. Every day was precious, if they were to get the big ships down to the estuary of the Don while the river was still in flood.

All the forges were blazing. Blacksmiths in burnt-through aprons and shirts briny with sweat, tall hammermen naked to the waist and

---

* In 1584, when Ivan the Terrible was away fighting in the West, Devlet-girey with his Crimean Tatars burnt down Moscow and killed or carried off into captivity nearly half a million people. (*Author's note*)

with scorched skin, smoke-blackened boys at the bellows—they could all hardly stand on their feet or raise their arms. Those who were resting—the shift was changed several times during the night—did not leave: some munched dried fish at the open door, others slept on a heap of birch-wood charcoal.

The head foreman, Kuzma Zhemov, who had been sent there by Leo Narishkin from his Tula works, where he had been taken on from the Tula prison to labour for life, had injured a hand. Another foreman got poisoned by the charcoal fumes and was now lying groaning in the night wind on some damp planks outside the smithy. They were welding the flukes of the huge anchor for the *Reliance*. The anchor, suspended from a block attached to the beam overhead, was in the furnace. Brushing off their sweat and with wheezing lungs boys were working the levers of six bellows. Two hammermen stood ready with their long-handled hammers lowered. Zhemov stirred the charcoal with his one good hand—the other was wrapped in a rag —and kept saying over and over again:

"Don't dawdle, don't dawdle, give us some more. . . ."

Peter, in a dirty white shirt and canvas apron, smudges of soot on his haggard face, and his mouth tightly pursed, was carefully turning over the anchor fluke in the same furnace with long tongs. It was a skilled, responsible job, welding on such a large piece.

Zhemov turned to the men standing by the pulley-ropes and said: "Look out, stand by!" Then to Peter: "Now's the time, or it'll be overheated." Peter, without taking his staring eyes off the coals, nodded and moved the tongs. "Hoist sharply! Pull away!"

Quickly gripping the rope hand over hand, the men pulled. The block creaked. The anchor, half a ton in weight, rose from the furnace. Sparks flew all over the smithy like snow in a storm. The white-hot anchor-shank hung over the anvil, shedding flaming scale. Next it had to be lowered and put surely in position.

Zhemov—this time in a whisper—said:

"Lower away. . . . Lay it fast. . . ." The anchor came to rest. "Scrape off the scale." He began scraping it off with a flaming besom. "The fluke!" Turning to Peter he shouted furiously: "What are you about? Come on!"

"Ay, ay!"

Peter swung the forty-pound tongs out of the furnace and missed the anvil—the red-hot fluke almost dropped from the tongs. Crouching in the effort and baring his teeth he laid it on the anvil.

"Closer!" Zhemov shouted and merely glanced at the hammermen. Breathing hard, they began striking in turn, with lingering blows. Peter held the fluke, while Zhemov hammered with a small hammer: tack-tack-tack, tack-tack-tack. Flaming scale spurted off on to their aprons.

The welding was completed. The hammermen moved away, panting. Peter threw the tongs into a tub and wiped his face on his sleeve. His eyes narrowed merrily. He winked at Zhemov, whose whole face wrinkled:

"Well, such things do happen, Peter Alexeyevich. But another time don't swing the tongs like that—you might hit someone and you're bound to drop the metal past the anvil. I've been beaten too for that sort of thing."

Peter did not reply. He washed his hands in the tub, wiped them on his apron and put on his coat. Then he went out of the smithy. There was a sharp, damp smell of spring. Ice-floes rustled on the river, faintly grey under the large stars. The masthead light of the *Reliance* swayed gently. Sticking his hands in his pockets and whistling softly, Peter walked along the bank, by the very edge of the water.

When the sailor by the partition saw the Tsar coming, he thrust his head in at the door and warned the ministers. But Peter did not go straight in; he wrinkled up his nose with pleasure at the warmth and the tobacco smoke and, bending over the table, surveyed the dishes.

"I say," he said to a man with bright blue eyes in his small face, a round beard and arched eyebrows which gave him an astonished look—the famous ship's carpenter Aladushkin—"Mishka, pass me that, over there," and he pointed across the table to some roast meat surrounded by pickled apples. Lowering himself on to the bench opposite the sleeping vice-admiral, he drank a small glass of vodka slowly, as people drink when they are very tired. The liquor ran through his veins. He picked out an apple, firmer than the rest and, as he munched it, spat out a pip at Kreis's bald pate:

"Is he drunk or what?"

Then the vice-admiral raised his crumpled face and said in a hoarse voice:

"The wind is south to south-west, force one. Pamburg is standing commander's watch. I am resting." And he again buried his face in his gold-laced sleeves.

When he had eaten, Peter said:

"Well, why are you so gloomy in here?" and put his fists on the table. He waited a moment, then straightened his back and went through the partition. He sat down on the bed. The ministers deferentially remained standing. He stuffed some tangled Dutch tobacco into his pipe with his thumb and lit it from the candle which Alexander held out to him. "Well, how are you, illustrious envoy?"

Voznitsin's old legs in cloth stockings bent, the stiff tails of his French coat shot upwards as he bowed low, dangling the curls of his wig close to the Tsar's muddy shoes. He waited thus, expecting to be raised. Leaning an elbow on the pillow, Peter said:

"Alexander, raise the illustrious envoy. Don't take offence, Prokofy —I feel a bit tired."

Voznitsin refused Alexander's help and got up himself, feeling injured.

"I have read your letters," Peter went on. "You write asking me not to be angry with you. I'm not. You have honourably discharged your task—in the old way. I believe you. . . ." His lips curled angrily showing his teeth. "The Austrians! The English! Very well. It's the last time we go to pay our compliments to them like that. Sit down. Tell me all about it."

Voznitsin repeated his story of the insults and the great difficulties at the meeting of the envoys. Peter, who already knew it all from Voznitsin's letter, puffed absentmindedly at his pipe.

"Your servant, Sire, thought it out like this with his mean intelligence: if we don't provoke the Turks, we can drag out the armistice for a long time. We must send some clever, crafty envoy to the Turks. Let him negotiate, and spin out the time; he can promise a concession here and there: after all, Sire, it's no sin to deceive Mahometans, the Lord will forgive that."

Peter smiled. His face was half in shadow, but one round eye, lit up by the candle, looked stern.

"What else have you to say, boyars?" He took the pipe from his mouth and spat three yards away through his teeth.

The shadows of Apraxin's and Golovin's horned wigs swayed on the wall. It was certainly difficult to give a reply straight off like that. Peter did not like them to speak in the florid, roundabout way they used in the boyars' council. Alexander, rubbing his shoulder against the hot stove, made a wry face.

"Well?" Peter asked him.

"Well, Prokofy's suggestion belongs to a past age: just spin things out. This doesn't suit us today."

Leo Narishkin wheezed out passionately:

"God himself did not let us sign peace with the Turks. The Patriarch of Jerusalem writes to us with tears: protect the Holy Sepulchre. The rulers of Moldavia and Wallachia beg us on their knees to save them from the Turkish yoke. While we—ah, my God!"

Peter said jeeringly: "Don't you start weeping."

Leo Narishkin broke off, his mouth and eyes wide open. Then he went on: "Sire, we can't exist without the Black Sea! Praise be to God, we are strong now and the Turks are weak. We must not do as Vaska Golitsin did—advance through the Crimea—but must cross the Danube, march on Constantinople and raise the cross on St. Sophia."

The horned wigs quivered anxiously. Peter's eye held the same incomprehensible gleam as before, and his pipe wheezed faintly. The mild Apraxin said in a low voice:

"Peace is better than war. War is costly, Narishkin. If we could make peace with the Turks for, say, twenty-five, even ten years without surrendering Azov or the Dniepr towns, it would be to the good. . . ." He glanced at Peter and sighed.

Peter rose, but there was no room to stride up and down, so he perched himself on the table:

"Must I always look to you, boyars, landowners! As for the militia of the nobles! The sleek devils mount their horses and don't know in which hand to hold their swords. Good-for-nothings, real good-for-nothings! You ought to have a talk with the merchants! Archangel! All we have is this one hole on the edge of the earth, with Englishmen and Dutchmen offering whatever price they please, buying things for a song. Mitrofan Shorin told me he had six hundred tons of hemp rotting in his warehouses for three summers, waiting for a proper price. Those rascals walked by and just laughed. And timber! They need timber abroad—we've got all the timber, and yet we bow low and beg them to buy it. Linen! Ivan Brovkin says: 'I'd rather burn it together with the warehouse in Archangel, than let it go at such a price'. No! It's not the Black Sea that we must worry about. It's on the Baltic that we need our own ships."

He had said the word. Tall, covered with grime, he sat on the table and stared at his ministers. They knitted their brows. It was bad enough to make war on the Tatars, or even on the Turks; they had got used to it. But to fight for the Baltic? Fight the Livonians, the Poles? The Swedes? Get caught up in the European entanglement? Leo Narishkin's plump hand groped along the stiff tails of his coat, he pulled out a brown silk handkerchief and wiped his head.

Voznitsin shook his withered face. Peter went on, pulling his tobacco-pouch out of his trouser pocket:

"We shall now seek peace with the Turks, not in Voznitsin's way, but in a new way. We'll come with more than a coat lined with silver fox."

"That's it!" Alexander said suddenly and his eyes flashed.

11

The fleet sailed down the turbid, swollen Don, with a warm wind filling its striped sails. There were eighteen two-decker ships of the line and, preceding and following them, twenty galliots and twenty brigantines, scout-boats, sloops and galleys: eighty-six war vessels and five hundred barges filled with Cossacks stretched far along the winding river.

From the high decks they could see the steppes, just turning green, and the ripples on the lakes formed by the flood-waters. Flocks of birds were flying north. From time to time chalk ridges gleamed white in the distance. A south-easterly wind was blowing, which was at first against them, and it was only with great difficulty that they reached the point where the Don turned west: the sails flapped, the ships drifted, the captains bellowed furiously through their brass trumpets. The order was issued to the fleet:

"No one is to dare lag behind the flagship, but all to follow closely in its wake. Whoever falls behind by as much as three hours will lose three months' pay, by six hours, two thirds of the year's pay, and for twelve hours a year's pay."

After the turn to the south-west sailing became easy. The sunsets that spread in misty splendour above the steppes were brief. A gun thundered from the flagship. Ship's bells sounded the hours. Lights crept up to the mastheads. Sails were furled and anchors dropped with a splash. Camp-fires were lighted on the dark river-banks and Cossack voices rang out in long-drawn cries.

From the dark hull of the *Apostle Peter,* in which the Tsar held the post of commander, a rocket with a witch's tail soared up into the starry sky, startling the quail. The officers gathered in the ward-room for supper. Admirals, captains and intimate boyars came from the ships nearby to join these feasts which were merry enough without them.

Near the Divnogorsky monastery the fleet was joined by six ships built by the company of Prince Boris Golitsin. To mark the occasion the fleet anchored by the chalky bank and, during two days, feasting went on in the open air of the monastery garden. They upset the monks by blowing horns and making ribald jokes, and frightened them with gunfire from eight hundred ships' cannons.

Then again sails billowed out all along the river. They sailed past high banks, past small towns, surrounded by wattle-fences and earth ramparts. Past new boyars' and monastery estates, and fisheries. Near the town of Panshin they saw, on the left bank, crowds of mounted Kalmuks with long spears and, on the right, Cossacks with two guns inside a square formed by the baggage-waggons. The Kalmuks and Cossacks had come together to fight it out, having quarrelled over the sharing of horse-droves and sturgeon-fishing areas.

General Shein was rowed to the Kalmuks and Boris Golitsin to the Cossacks. They succeeded in bringing about a reconciliation and, to mark the occasion, they feasted on the grassy banks under slow-sailing clouds and strung-out lines of migrating cranes. Cornelius Kreis, suffering from the after-effects of drinking, had a lot of turtles caught and himself made them into soup. Peter also ordered some and treated the boyars to a strange dish; when they had eaten it he showed them the turtle heads. General Shein was sick. There was a good deal of laughter.

At noon on the 24th of May the bastions of Azov loomed out of the sea mists to the south. At that point the Don widened out, but it was still too shallow for forty-gun ships to pass through the estuary.

While the vice-admiral was sounding an arm of the Don—the Kuturma—and Peter went in a sloop to inspect the forts at Azov and Taganrog, the Khan's envoys arrived from Bahchisaray,* mounted on handsome horses and accompanied by a pack-train. They pitched rug-tents and set up their standard on a hill: a horse's tail with a crescent on a long spear. Then an interpreter was sent to ask whether the Tsar would receive the Khan's greetings and presents. The reply was given that the Tsar was in Moscow, but his viceroy Admiral Golovin was here with the boyars. The standard fluttered over the hill for three days. The Tatars galloped about on their fiery steeds right in front of the Russian guns. On the fourth day the envoys came to the admiral's ship. They spread a white Anatolian carpet and on it laid their gifts—a hammered saddle-bow, a small sword, pistols, a knife and harness ornamented with silver and set with cheap gems—none of them too good in quality. Golovin sat with dignity in a folding chair and the Tatars sat on the carpet with their legs

* Capital of the Tatar Crimea.

crossed. They talked of the truce that Voznitsin had signed and of one thing and another, pinching their thin two-pointed beards; their eyes, quick-darting like a seal's, looked about everywhere and they clicked their teeth:

"The Muscovites are fine, the fleet is fine. Only your hope is vain: you won't get down the Kuturma with big vessels; not long ago the Sultan's fleet tried to get into the Don, but it had to go back to Kerch."

Everything showed that they had only come to spy. In the morning standard, tents and horsemen had vanished from the hill.

The soundings showed that the Kuturma was too shallow. Each day the flood-waters of the Don were subsiding. The only hope was that a strong south-westerly wind might drive the sea-water into the estuary.

Peter returned from Taganrog and his face clouded when he heard of the low water. A lazy wind was blowing from the south, and the days grew hot. Tar began to drip from the ships' sides. The timbers, poorly seasoned that winter, started to shrink. Water was pumped out of the holds. With furled sails, the ships lay motionless in the sultry haze.

Orders were given to jettison the ballast. Barrels of gunpowder and salt-meat were hoisted out of the holds and loaded on barges which took them to Taganrog. The ships were lightened, but the waters of the Kuturma went on subsiding.

At dinner time on the 22nd of June, Admiral Julius Riaz, ruddy and corpulent, came out of the ward-room, which was as hot as a Turkish bath, to make water over the ship's side. Looking round his eye caught a swiftly-spreading grey cloud in the south-west. When he had relieved himself, he looked once more at the cloud, returned to the ward-room and, taking up his hat and sword, said in a loud voice: "A storm is brewing."

Peter, the admirals and the captains rushed out. Ragged clouds were rushing overhead and darkness was spreading from beyond the white expanse of water. The sun shed a hot metallic light on drooping flags, pennants and sailors' clothes hung out to dry on the shrouds. On every ship the boatswains piped all hands on deck. The sails were secured and storm anchors lowered.

The thundercloud half covered the sky and the water grew dark. Sheet lightning flashed on the horizon. The wind whistled in the rigging more and more fiercely, more and more alarmingly. The pennants cracked. The gale hit the ships with full force among the swirling, tattered fragments of cloud. The masts creaked, underpants were torn off the shrouds and carried away. The wind lashed the water and tore at the rigging. Sailors on the yard-arms clung desperately to the ropes. Captains stamped and tried to make themselves heard above the rising storm. Foam-topped waves beat against the ships' hulls. The sky was rent asunder with peals and ear-splitting claps of thunder, that merged into a continuous roar, while lightning flashed in pillars of fire.

Peter, bareheaded, with the tails of his coat flying, stood gripping the handrail on the rising and falling poop. Deafened and blinded, he opened his mouth like a fish. Lightning seemed to fall all round the ship, striking the crests of the waves. Julius Riaz shouted in his ear:

"This is nothing. The real storm's coming now!"

The storm passed leaving much damage behind. Two sailors had been killed by lightning on the bank. Anchor-cables had been broken and some masts snapped; a number of smaller vessels had been driven ashore and swamped. But a strong south-westerly wind was blowing steadily: that was what was needed.

The water rose rapidly in the Kuturma and, at dawn, the ships began to move. The *Reliance* went first, towed by fifty rowing barges on long hawsers. She passed from pole to pole marking the channel, her keel not once scraping the bottom, along the Kuturma into the Sea of Azov; there she fired a salute and hoisted Captain Pamburg's personal flag.

That same day the other ships that drew most water were brought out—the *Apostle Peter, Voronezh, Azov, Gut Dragers* and *Vein Dragers*—and by the 27th of June the whole fleet dropped anchor under the bastions of Taganrog.

There, in the lee of the mole, the ships were re-caulked and painted, the rigging repaired and ballast taken on again. Peter spent whole days in a cradle over the side of the *Reliance* whistling and hammering on the caulking oakum. Sometimes he would climb the ratlines, his bony behind sticking out in dirty canvas trousers, to secure a new spar on the mast; or else he would go down into the hold where Fedosey Skliayev—who had quarrelled violently with John Day and Joseph Nye—was working on a cunning contrivance to brace the stern timbers.

"Peter Alexeyich, for God's sake, don't get in my way," Fedosey would say gruffly. "If the bracing doesn't turn out well—you can cut my head off, if you like. Only don't get in my way."

"All right, all right; I only want to help."

"Go and help Aladushkin. You and I will only quarrel."

The work went on all through July. Julius Riaz was continuously training the crews, who had been selected from the soldiers of the Preobrazhensky and Semenovsky regiments. Among them were many noblemen's sons who had never seen the sea. Julius Riaz, a true sailor both in ferocity and courage, drove the zeal for seamanship into the men with rope-ends. He made them stand on yard-arms eighty feet above the water, or dive fully clothed from the ship's side: "He who drowns is no sailor!" Standing with legs straddled on the captain's bridge, his hands holding his cane behind his back, with a jaw like a mastiff, the pirate noticed everything with one eye: who dawdled over unhitching a knot, who belayed a rope the wrong way. "Hey, there, on the fore-top-mast back-stays, you dirty cow, what do you think you're doing with the halyard?" He stamped his foot: "Everybody on the quarter-deck. Begin all over again!"

The newly-appointed envoy Yemelian Ukraintsev, the most experienced official in the Ambassadors' Department, arrived with the clerk Cheredeyev and the interpreters Lavretsky and Botvinkin. They brought with them sables, walrus-tusks and sixty pounds of tea as gifts for the Sultan and his pashas.

On the 14th of August the *Reliance* hoisted sail and, followed by the entire fleet, made for the open sea, running west-south-west before a strong north-easterly wind. On the 17th the slender minarets of Taman came into sight on the port bow. The fleet passed through the strait and, with a salute that wrapped the ships in smoke, dropped anchor in full view of Kerch. The walls of the town were very old and here and there the tall square towers had crumbled. There were neither forts, nor bastions. Four ships were lying close inshore. The Turks were evidently alarmed: they had not expected nor even dreamed that they would see the whole bay filled with sails and gunpowder smoke.

Murtaza Pasha, the sleek and lazy governor of Kerch, felt alarm as he looked at the fleet through an embrasure in one of the towers. He sent his officials to the Muscovite flagship to enquire why had such a vast flotilla come? A month earlier the Khan's Tatars had reported that the Tsar's fleet was not up to much and carried no guns and that it would never get past the Azov shallows.

With many sighs Murtaza Pasha bent back the branch of a shrub to get a better view. He began counting the ships, but gave it up. "Who believed the Khan's scouts?" he shouted to his officials who stood behind him on the square platform of the tower, fouled by birds. "Who believed the Tatar dogs?"

He stamped his slippered foot. His officials, who had grown fat and lazy in this peaceful backwater, laid their hands on their hearts and shook their fezzes and turbans ruefully. They realised that Murtaza Pasha would have to write an unpleasant report to the Sultan, and no one could say how that would end: although the Sultan was the Most Serene Viceroy of the Prophet, he was hot-tempered and there had been cases when even more exalted pashas had ended groaning, impaled on the stake.

The slanting sail of the felucca with the Turkish officials left the flagship. Murtaza Pasha sent one of his men to the shore to hurry them back, and he himself again began counting the ships. His envoys—two Greeks—arrived, eyes rolling, shoulders shrugging and tongues clicking. Murtaza Pasha savagely turned his bloated face towards them, and they reported:

"The Muscovite admiral sends greetings and says that they have brought an envoy to the Sultan. We told the admiral that you could not let the envoy go by sea, and that he must travel as all do, through the Crimea to Baba. The admiral replied: 'If you don't want to let him go by sea, then we'll escort him to Constantinople with the entire fleet'."

Next day Murtaza Pasha sent his chief beys to the admiral, and they said to him:

"We are sorry for you, Muscovites, you do not know our Black Sea: there are times when, on its waters, men's hearts become black, that is why it is called Black. Hearken to our advice, and travel by land to Baba."

Admiral Golovin only puffed out his chest: "How you frighten us!" A tall man standing by him—with flashing eyes and dressed in Dutch clothes—laughed, and the other Russians laughed too.

What was to be done? How could Murtaza Pasha stop them when the Moscow ships hoisted their sails in the morning breeze and, lined up in correct naval fashion, sailed up and down the bay firing at canvas screens on floats? Refuse passage to such insolent fellows? Putting his trust in Allah alone, Murtaza Pasha dragged out the negotiations.

A boat drew alongside the Turkish flagship, and Cornelius Kreis and two oarsmen in Dutch sailors' clothes—Peter and Alexander —came on board. On the quarter-deck the Turkish crew saluted the Muscovite vice-admiral. Admiral Hassan Pasha emerged with an air of importance from the stern cabin; he was clad in a white silk robe and a turban with a diamond crescent. He put his fingers to his chest and lips in a dignified gesture, while Cornelius Kreis took off his hat, stepped backwards and bowed with a wave of his plumed hat.

Two chairs were brought, and the admirals seated themselves under a canvas awning. The cook—a short, fat eunuch—brought a salver with a dish of sweetmeats, a coffee-pot and cups hardly bigger than thimbles. The admirals began polite conversation. Hassan Pasha asked after the Tsar's health; Cornelius Kreis replied that the Tsar was well, and himself enquired whether His Majesty the Sultan was in good health. Hassan Pasha bowed low and replied: "Allah protects the life of His Majesty the Sultan." Then, looking past Cornelius Kreis with melancholy eyes, he went on:

"We do not keep a large fleet in Kerch. Here we have nothing to fear. But in the Sea of Marmora we have huge ships. Their guns are so immense that they can fire stone cannon-balls weighing a hundred and twenty pounds."

Sipping his coffee Cornelius Kreis replied:

"Our ships do not use stone cannon-balls. We fire iron balls eighteen to thirty pounds in weight. They go right through both sides of an enemy ship."

Hassan Pasha slightly raised his finely shaped eyebrows:

"We were not a little surprised to see that English and Dutch sailors—the best friends of Turkey—are assiduously serving in the Tsar's fleet."

"Ah, Hassan Pasha," Cornelius Kreis replied with a bland smile, "people serve the one who pays them most." Hassan Pasha inclined his head with dignity, and Kreis went on: "The Dutch and English are carrying on a very profitable trade with the Muscovites. It pays better to live at peace with the Tsar than to fight him. Muscovy is richer than any other country in the world."

"Vice-admiral," Hassan Pasha asked thoughtfully, "how did the Tsar get so many ships?"

"The Muscovites built them themselves in two years."

"Ai-ai-ai!" Hassan Pasha exclaimed wagging his turban.

While the admirals were talking, Peter and Alexander treated the Turkish sailors to tobacco and cracked jokes with them. Hassan Pasha threw occasional glances at these immensely tall fellows: they were altogether too inquisitive. One climbed up the mast into the crow's nest. The other looked keenly at an English quick-firing gun.

But out of politeness Hassan Pasha said nothing, even when his sailors took the Muscovites with them on to the lower deck. Cornelius Kreis asked permission to go ashore to buy fruit, sweets and coffee. Hassan Pasha, after some reflection, said that perhaps he himself could sell the vice-admiral some coffee.

"Do you want much coffee?"

"To the value of seventy gold pieces."

"Abdullah!" Hassan Pasha called, stamping the heel of his foot. The eunuch-cook waddled up and, having received his orders, returned with some scales, followed by sailors dragging bags of coffee. Hassan Pasha drew his chair up close and examined the scales; then he pulled out of the bosom of his coat his amber beads on which to count off the measures. He ordered the bag to be untied and, running his well-kept fingers through the grains, half closed his eyes:

"This coffee is the best grown in Java. You will thank me for it, Vice-admiral. I see that you are a good man." He bent close to his ear. "I wish you no evil: dissuade the Muscovites from sailing this sea; there are many submerged rocks and dangerous sandbanks along the coasts. We ourselves fear these spots."

"Why should we sail along the coasts?" Cornelius Kreis answered. "With a favourable wind, our course will lie straight across the sea."

He counted out seventy gold pieces. Farewells were said. As he approached the ladder, he shouted sternly: "Hi, Peter Alexeyev!" A voice hurriedly answered: "Here!"

Peter, followed by Alexander, sprang out of the hatchway; both were wearing red fezzes. The vice-admiral waved his hat and took his seat at the rudder; the boat went swiftly towards the shore. Peter and Alexander, pulling at the bending oars, grinned merrily.

A breaker ran the boat up the shingly beach. Officials and the same beys who had been to see the admiral came hurrying out of the fortress gates and down past rotting boats and slimy-green piles to tell them that they should not enter the town on any account, but that if they needed anything merchants would bring all kinds of goods to the boat. Peter's eyes flashed and his cheeks reddened with anger. Alexander, holding his oar upright, said:

"*Mein Herz,* tell them. We'll bring the whole fleet within gunshot. After all . . ."

"They have the right not to let us enter the town: it's a fortress," Cornelius Kreis said. "We'll take a stroll along the beach near the walls; we shall see all we need."

12

Murtaza Pasha could not think of any more excuses: "Go ahead," he said, "and Allah be with you."

Peter returned with the fleet to Taganrog. On the 28th of August the *Reliance,* having taken the envoy, the clerk and the interpreters on board, accompanied by four Turkish warships, rounded the headland of Kerch and sailed along the southern shores of the Crimea with a gentle breeze filling her sails.

The Turkish ships followed close in her wake; a police inspector was on the leading ship. Hassan Pasha remained in Kerch. At the last moment he had begged them to give him some kind of written deposition that the Tsar's envoy was making the voyage on his own initiative, and that he, Hassan, had advised him not to do so. But even this had been refused.

When they came in sight of Balaclava, the inspector got into a boat and pulled level with the *Reliance*; then he asked them to call at Balaclava to take on fresh water. He waved the sleeve of his robe vigorously towards the red-brown hills: "It's a fine city, let us call there, please." Captain Pamburg, with his elbows on the rail, shouted down in his deep voice:

"Do you think we don't understand that the inspector wants to call at Balaclava to get some good backsheesh from the inhabitants out of provisioning the envoy? Our water-casks are full."

The inspector's suggestion was turned down. The wind was freshening. Pamburg looked at the sky and ordered more sail. The heavy Turkish ships began to fall noticeably astern. The leading one signalled: "Shorten sail!" Pamburg stared through his telescope and swore in Portuguese. He ran down to the ward-room, which was richly panelled in walnut. There Yemelian Ukraintsev, the envoy, was sitting on a polished bench at the table feeling very seasick, with closed eyes and with his wig, which he had taken off, clutched in his hand. Pamburg said to him furiously:

"Those devils have ordered me to shorten sail. I'm paying no attention. I shall sail for the open sea."

Ukraintsev only waved his wig feebly at him:

"Go where you please!"

Pamburg climbed to the captain's bridge on the poop. He curled his moustache up and shouted:

"All hands on deck! Set the fore-royal! The mainsail and mizzen-top-gallant! The fore-top-mast stay-sail, the fore stay-sail! On the port tack! Keep her so!"

The *Reliance* swung round, heeling over and, her timbers creaking, caught the wind with her full sails, leaving the Turkish ships behind as if they were at anchor, and sailed straight across the Euxine deeps towards Constantinople.

Heeling over to the north-east wind that lashed the sea, the *Reliance* sped on across the dark-blue water. The waves seemed to raise their foamy crests to see how much farther they would have to roll over the wastes before they reached the sun-scorched coast. The sixteen men of the crew—Dutchmen, Swedes and Danes—all sea vagrants, looked at the waves and smoked their pipes: it was an easy and pleasant job to sail like this. But half the soldiers and gunners lay in the hold among the water-casks and barrels of salt-meat. Pamburg ordered vodka to be issued three times a day to the seasick men: "One's got to get used to the sea!"

They sailed for a day and a night and, on the second day, they took in a reef: the ship was plunging heavily and shipping water that swept her decks in foamy sheets. Pamburg blew the drops of water from his moustache.

The envoy Ukraintsev and his clerk Cheredeyev were very seasick. Lying in the small, freshly-painted cabin at the stern, they raised their heads from their pillows and looked towards the small square port-hole. There it went slowly sinking into the depths, the green water hissed, rose to the four small panes and, with a heavy splash, light was shut out of the cabin. The partitions creaked, the low ceiling reeled. The envoy and his clerk groaned and shut their eyes.

In the clear morning of the 2nd of September the boy in the crow's nest on the top-mast, a Kalmuk, shouted: "Land!" The blue, hilly outline of the Bosphorus coast drew closer. Slanting sails were seen in the distance. Seagulls flew out and circled round the high carved poop. Pamburg ordered all hands to be piped on deck: "Wash yourselves. Brush your coats. Put on your wigs."

At noon the *Reliance,* under full sail, swept past the ancient watch-towers into the Bosphorus. Signals were hoisted on the fortress wall: "Whose ship are you?"

Pamburg gave orders to signal in reply: "You ought to know the flag of Muscovy." From the shore came: "Take on a pilot." Pamburg replied: "We are going on without a pilot."

Ukraintsev put on his gold-laced crimson coat and his plumed hat; the clerk Cheredeyev, bony, thin-nosed, like a martyr on an icon of the Suzdal school, put on his silver-laced green coat and also a hat with plumes. The gunners stood by the guns, the soldiers drew up on the quarter-deck with their muskets.

The ship glided across the mirror-like gulf. On the left, among parched hills, there were still unreaped fields of maize, water-pumps, sheep on the slopes, and fishermen's stone huts covered with maize straw. On the right bank were magnificent gardens, white walls, tiled roofs, and flights of steps leading down to the water. There were green cypresses, like tall spindles, and the ruins of a castle, overgrown with bushes. A round cupola and a minaret rose above the trees. As they drew closer to the shore, they saw wonderful fruit on the branches. The smell of olives and roses drifted to them across the water. The Russians marvelled at the richness of the Turkish soil:

"Everybody calls them 'shaven-headed infidels', but look how they live!"

In the far distance, as if at the very end of the world, the sun set in a blaze of gold. The gold changed swiftly to scarlet and then faded, turning the waters of the Bosphorus blood-red. They anchored three miles from Constantinople. Huge stars, such as were not seen in Moscow, spangled the dark sky. The Milky Way was reflected in the water like a mist.

No one in the ship wanted to sleep. They gazed at the shores, now quiet but for the creaking of wells and the shrill chirrup of cicadas. Even the dogs here barked in a special way. Strange gleaming fish were swept along by the current in the depths. The soldiers, sitting quietly on the guns, said to each other: "It's a rich country, and life must be easy here."

Thoughtfully gazing into the candle-flame, whose light dimmed the large stars in the black port-hole of the stern cabin, Yemelian Ukraintsev carefully dipped his quill, looked to see whether there was no hair on it (if there was, he wiped it on his wig) and wrote in a leisurely way a coded letter to Peter:

"We have been at anchor here for twenty-four hours. On the 3rd the Turkish ships which we had left behind arrived. The inspector, with tears in his eyes, reproached us for hurrying ahead; the Sultan, he said, would have his head cut off for it. He begged us to wait here while he himself informed the Sultan of our arrival. We insisted that the Sultan must receive us in state. In the evening the inspector returned from Constantinople and informed us that the Sultan would receive us in state and would send caiques for us—the boats they use here. We replied that we would go in our own ship. We argued about it and then agreed to go in their boats, but with the *Reliance* leading us.

"Next day they sent three of the Sultan's caiques spread with rugs. We got into them, and the *Reliance* led the way. Soon we came in sight of Constantinople—a really marvellous city. The walls and towers are ancient, but immensely strong. All the roofs are tiled, the mosques are of white stone—really wonderful and magnificent—and St. Sophia is of sandstone. From the water you can see Stamboul and the suburb of Pera as on the palm of your hand. A salute was fired from the shore and Captain Pamburg replied with a return salute from all the guns. We stopped opposite the Sultan's seraglio; the Sultan was on the wall looking at us, a fan was held over him and they were fanning him.

"On the beach we were met by a hundred mounted chaoushes and two hundred janissaries with bamboo staves. Richly caparisoned horses were brought for me and the clerk. When we left the boat the chief of the chaoushes enquired after our health. We mounted the horses and went through many narrow, winding streets to an inn. People ran along on each side of us.

"Your ship has aroused great wonder here: they ask who built it and how it got over the shallows and out of the Don. They ask whether you have many ships and of what size. I replied that you have many, and that they are not flat-bottomed as it is falsely alleged here, but that they can sail the open sea. Thousands of Turks, Greeks, Armenians and Jews come to look at the *Reliance*; in fact the Sultan himself came in a boat and was rowed three times round the ship. They particularly praise the strength of the sails and ropes and the timber of the spars. But some say she is not strongly built. Forgive me for stating my opinion: we encountered only a moderately strong wind, but the *Reliance* was certainly straining and heeling over excessively and shipping water. I imagine that Joseph Nye and John Day made some profit out of building her. A ship is not a trifle, it is worth a good-sized town. Here they come and look at her, but do not bargain for her; no buyer has offered. Forgive me, but I write what is in my mind.

"Turkish ships are very carefully and strongly built, the timbers are very closely joined, they are lower than ours but do not ship water.

"A Greek said to me: 'The Turks fear the Tsar might close the

Black Sea, and then Constantinople would starve because grain, oil, timber and firewood are brought here from the Danube towns'. There is a rumour here that you have already been with your fleet to Trebizond and Sinope. I was asked about it, and I replied that I did not know, that you did not go while I was with the fleet. . . ."

Pamburg went with his officers to Pera to visit some of the European ambassadors. The Dutch and French ambassadors received the Russians very affably, thanked them and drank the health of the Tsar in wine. Their third visit was to the English embassy. They dismounted at the porch and knocked. A footman, red-bearded and seven feet tall, came out and, holding the door, asked them what they wanted.

Pamburg, whose eyes had begun to smoulder, told him who they were and why they had come. The footman slammed the door and returned after quite a long while—although the Muscovites were waiting in the street—to say with a sneer:

"The ambassador has sat down to dinner and has ordered me to say that he sees no reason to meet Captain Pamburg."

"Go and tell the ambassador he can choke on a bone!" Pamburg shouted. He sprang furiously on his horse and sent it clattering over the broad, shallow brick steps of the streets, past street vendors, naked children and dogs, down into Galata, where a little earlier he had seen some old friends of his in the eating and coffee houses and at the doors of brothels.

Here Pamburg and his officers got as drunk as lords on Greek wine, became very noisy and challenged English sailors to a fight. Here, too, Pamburg was joined by his friends: master mariners, famous freebooters, all manner of odd characters, who had found shelter in the low haunts of Galata. Pamburg invited all of them to a feast on board the *Reliance*.

Next day the *Reliance* was visited by seamen of many nations brought by caiques. There were Swedes, Dutchmen, Frenchmen, Portuguese, Moors, some wearing wigs, silk stockings and swords, others with red kerchiefs bound tightly round their heads, slippers on their bare feet and pistols in their wide sashes; still others were clad in leather coats and sou'westers reeking of salt fish.

They sat down to feast on the open deck under the mild September sun. In full view of them rose the Sultan's gloomy palace behind its walls, its windows guarded by close grilles; on the far bank of the Bosphorus stretched the luxuriant groves and gardens of Scutari. Preobrazhensky and Semenovsky soldiers played on horns and spoons, sang dancing songs and whistled "Spring" in various birds' voices.

Heated with wine, Pamburg, in a silver-powdered wig and scarlet coat trimmed with lace and ribbons, with a goblet in one hand and a handkerchief in the other, was telling his guests:

"If we feel the need of a thousand ships, we'll build a thousand. Eighty-gun, one-hundred-gun ships have been laid down. Next year you can expect us in the Mediterranean, you can expect us in the Baltic. We'll take into our service all the famous seamen. We'll come out into the ocean. . . ."

"Hurrah!" cried the sailor guests, who were by now very red in the face. "Hurrah for Captain Pamburg!"

They sang sea shanties. They stamped. The smoke from their pipes hung over the deck in the still air. They did not notice the sun set and the Attic stars begin to shed their light on this extraordinary feast. At midnight, when half the sea-wolves were snoring, some under the table, others with their heads—turned grey in the course of their stormy lives—laid among the dishes, Pamburg rushed on to the captain's bridge:

"Listen to the command! Bombardiers, gunners, to your guns! Load! Light the fuses! Now: from both broadsides—volley! Fi-i-ire!"

Forty-six heavy guns simultaneously belched flames. The sky seemed to have been brought down by the thunderous explosion over sleeping Constantinople. The *Reliance,* wrapped in smoke, thundered out a second volley.

Yemelian Ukraintsev wrote in code:

". . . great fear seized the Sultan himself and the whole people: Captain Pamburg drank all day on board his ship with sailors and got very drunk and fired all guns at midnight several times. This firing caused an outcry in the whole of Constantinople and a rumour spread according to which he, the captain, was signalling to your fleet, Sire, which is sailing in the Black Sea, for it to enter the straits.

"His Majesty the Sultan was frightened that night and ran out of his bedchamber in his night-clothes; ministers and pashas were terrified, and two pregnant sultanas of the upper seraglio had miscarriages on account of the captain's extraordinary salvoes. As a result His Majesty the Sultan was very angry with Pamburg and gave orders to tell us to take the captain off his ship and cut off his head. I replied to the Sultan that I did not know for what reason the captain had fired, and that I would ask him about it, and if this firing had incommoded

His Majesty the Sultan, I would instruct the captain not to fire in future and make my orders very strict, but that there was no need for me to take him off his ship. With this the matter ended.

"The Sultan is to receive us on Tuesday. The Turks are expecting the arrival of Medzomort Pasha, a former Algerian pirate, to discuss whether to make peace with you or war. . . ."

chapter two

The September sun hung low over the wooded bank. Day after day, as they advanced farther north, the country round them became wilder. Flocks of birds rose suddenly from the quiet river. Trees felled by the wind; marshes; not a living soul in sight. At rare intervals they would see a fisherman's mud hut and a small boat pulled up on to the bank. There was still another week's journey to lake Belo.

Fourteen men hauled with a rope the heavy grain-laden barge. With bent heads and dangling arms they leaned their chests against the broad straps. They had come all the way from Yaroslav. The sun, as it set behind the black crests of the firs, lingered for a long time in a sullen, fiery glow. A cry would come from the barge: "Hi, make fast!"

The boatmen would hammer a post into the ground or wind the tow-rope round a tree. A camp-fire would be lit. On the swampy bank the fir forest slowly veiled itself in a milky mist. Ducks flew across the sunset like long-necked shadows. Elks, tall as horses, came to the river with a crashing of wind-fallen branches. The forest was full of wild animals, unafraid because they had never been hunted.

Oars splashed on the river and the elder, Andrey Denisov, the owner, came ashore from the barge. He brought his workmen dry bread, millet and sometimes fish and, on meat-days, salted meat. He would inspect the mooring-rope to make sure that it had been made fast. With his hands thrust in his leather belt, he would stop at the camp-fire, a fresh-faced man in a cassock and cloth skull-cap, with clear eyes and curly beard.

"Brothers, are you all alive?" he would ask. "Exert yourselves! God loves labour. Be merry! It will all go to your credit. You are lucky as it is to have escaped from the Nikonian stench. And when we come to lake Onega, there's a country for you! A real paradise."

Pulling his hands out of his belt, he would squat by the fire. The weary men listened to him in silence.

"In those parts, an elder lived on the Vyga river. Like you, he had fled the temptations of Antichrist. Before that he had been a wealthy merchant; he had a house and shops and warehouses. He had a vision: he saw flames and, in the flames, a man, and heard a voice crying: 'I have succumbed to temptation and I am doomed for ever!' He gave all his property to his wife and sons and went away. He built himself a log hut. There he began to live, and his only sacrament was his fiery yearning. He ploughed with a poker and sowed two capfuls of barley. He dressed himself in a fresh goatskin; it dried on him, and he went about in it winter and summer. His only possessions were a wooden bowl, a spoon and a prayer-book in the old writing. And soon he acquired such power over the evil spirits that they were no more to him than flies. People began to come to him. He heard them in confession and for communion gave them a leaf or a berry. He taught them that it was better to perish alive in the flames than to incur eternal torment. A year or two went by and people began to settle down near him. They burnt clearings in the forest and ploughed them. They hunted, fished, gathered berries and mushrooms. They did everything in common, and their barns and cellars were common property. And he divided them up: the women by themselves, and the men by themselves."

"That's good!" a stern voice said. "When one lives with a woman, one doesn't amass wealth."

Denisov threw a laughing glance into the darkness at the man who had spoken.

"Thanks to the elder's prayers, game was plentiful, and sometimes they landed such fish it was a marvel! Mushrooms and berries grew plentifully. He showed them the way, and they found iron and copper ore and set up smithies. Truly it became a saintly refuge, a peaceful life."

Andrey Golikov rose from behind some dead wood and, squatting down by Denisov, fixed his eyes on his face. Golikov had joined the boatmen in fulfilment of a vow. That day, in Revyakin's house, the elder had heard his confession, beaten him with his chaplet and ordered him to go to Yaroslav to wait there for Denisov's grain barge. Out of the fourteen boatmen nine had come, like him, either in fulfilment of a vow or to perform a penance.

Denisov went on:

"In his dying hour the elder blessed us two brothers, Semyon and me, Andrey, and appointed us to be the heads of the Vyga retreat. He gave us communion and we started off. His cell stood alone, in a dell. When we had gone a little way, we looked back and saw a light. The cell was surrounded by fire, as by a burning bush. I started to run. Semyon grasped me by the hand: Stay! And then we heard sweet-voiced singing coming out of the flames. And above, in the smoke, devils were whirling, like soot, and screaming. Can you believe it? My brother and I fell on our knees and also began to sing. In the morning we went to that spot, and there was a clear spring bubbling from under the ashes. We built a well-head of logs over the spring and set up a little penthouse for an icon. The trouble is we can't find an icon-painter: we would so much like to have an icon made."

Golikov gave a sob. Denisov passed his hand lightly over his unkempt, shaggy hair:

"Our one worry, brothers, is that every third year our harvest fails. Last summer rains rotted everything, we could not even gather straw. So we have to bring grain from afar. But this is a holy cause, my children. You are not labouring in vain."

Denisov spoke a little longer, then he recited a common prayer. After that he got into his boat and went off to the barge across the dull strip of the afterglow mirrored in the river. The nights were cool, and it was chilly sleeping in threadbare clothing.

At the first light Denisov came ashore again and roused the men. They coughed and scratched themselves. Then they said their prayers and started cooking their porridge. When the opalescent sun was suspended in the mist, like a dim bubble, the boatmen harnessed themselves in the straps and began to trudge in their birch-bark shoes along the wet bank. They tramped mile after mile, day after day. Banks of dark clouds spread slowly from the north, and a sharp wind rose. The Sheksna overflowed its banks.

Now the dark clouds were rushing low over the agitated waters of lake Belo. The men turned to the west, towards Belozersk. The waves ran up the empty beach, knocking the boatmen off their feet. It grew difficult to steer the barge. During the dinner hour they dried themselves in a fisherman's hut. Here two of the hired men quarrelled with Denisov over the food, took their earnings—seventy-five kopeks each—and went off, no one knew where.

The barge rode at anchor opposite the town, on the breakers. The wind freshened, cutting the men to the bone. They were seized with despair. Only think: to go north, harnessed to the tow-rope! All the hired men quarrelled with Denisov and scattered among the fishermen's settlements. The others too did not stay: one came across a friend, another would grow restive for a while and then disappear.

Among the wet stones on the shore, on an overturned boat sat Andrey Golikov, Ilya Dehtyarev, a fugitive peasant from Kashiry, and Fedka, nicknamed Mudwash, a round-shouldered man—once a monastery serf, now a vagrant—who had been much beaten and tortured. They looked about them.

Everything here was grim: the turbid stretch of lake, snowy with white horses, the dark banks of cloud that drifted slowly from the north, the flat plain beyond the ridge of the shore, and on it the decrepit wooden town, almost hidden by the clouds: broken roofs on the towers, rusty, onion-shaped church cupolas, tall log-houses with sagging roofs. On the beach, the wind shook the poles used for spreading fishing-nets. There was hardly a living soul in sight. A bell tolled dismally.

"Denisov is clever at feeding you with words. By the time you reach his paradise it's likely nothing but your souls will remain," Mudwash said, picking a callous on his palm with his nail.

"You must believe him!" Golikov turned angrily on him. "You must believe him!" He looked wistfully at the white waves. It was cheerless, lonely, cold. "Here too it must be far from God."

Dehtyarev, a wide-mouthed muscular fellow with merry eyes, went on talking quietly and slowly:

". . . and so I asked him, this man: why is it so empty in your town, half the houses are nailed up? The reason why it's empty, he said, is that the monks are making trouble. We have sent more than one petition to Moscow, but there, it seems, they have no time for us. What they did in Easter week—it was more than flesh and blood can stand. The monks drove out with holy icons in ten sledges, some went into the town, others into the suburbs or the villages. They went into the houses and pushed the cross into people's faces: 'Cross yourself with three fingers!' 'Kiss the criss-cross!' And they asked for bread and cream and eggs and fish. They swept everything clean, as if with a broom. And they asked for money too. 'You,' they would say, 'are a dissenter, a priestless sectarian. Where are your Old Believers' books?' And they would take the man to their monastery, chain him up and torture him."

Mudwash suddenly threw back his head and laughed loudly and hoarsely:

"How they eat! How they drink! Ah, the monks, there's no holding them."

Dehtyarev poked him with his knee. A monk with a gipsy's beard, a skull-cap pulled low over his eyes, was coming towards the boat, struggling against the wind and holding his cassock which was blown about. He looked with terrible eyes at the barge creaking on the waves, and then at the three men.

"Where does this barge come from?" he asked.

"From Yaroslav, father," Dehtyarev answered in lazy, friendly tones.

"What's it loaded with?"

"We weren't told."

"Grain?"

"Well, yes. . . ."

"Where are you taking it?"

"Who knows? Where we're told."

"Don't lie, don't lie, don't lie!" The monk began hastily rolling up his right sleeve. "It's Denisov's barge. You are going to Povenets, you are taking grain to the dissenters' retreats, you infidels!"

With a sudden lunge he seized Dehtyarev by the front of his coat, shook the frightened man and, turning towards the town, yelled at the top of his voice:

"Guards!"

Golikov jumped off the boat and ran at the edge of the waves to the fishermen's huts.

"Guards!" the monk yelled once again and suddenly broke off. Mudwash seized him by the hair, tore him away from Dehtyarev, knocked him off his feet and began to circle, looking for a stone. The monk sprang up briskly and rushed at him sideways, but Fedka had gone hard with anger and did not budge; he again laid hold of the monk, bent him down and struck him on the neck. The monk groaned. Four men armed with poles were running out of a side street towards the bank.

Golikov watched in terror from behind the corner of a fisherman's hut. Mudwash was fighting all five men: he had torn a pole out of the hands of one of them, and was lunging at them with wild cries; Golikov had never in all his life seen such fury in a man. "A devil, a veritable devil!" Then Dehtyarev stepped into the fray: he got in a blow at the monk's ear, and the monk went sprawling for the third time. The monk's helpers began to give ground. Here and there townsmen came out of their gates and grunted approvingly: "That's it! That's it! That's it!"

Dehtyarev and Fedka got the upper hand and started to chase their opponents, but soon returned and, after blowing their noses to get rid of the blood, went straight to the hut where Golikov was trembling.

"To tell the truth, you ought to get a thrashing too," Mudwash said to him. "You're a fool, and yet you plan to get into paradise."

Out of the door of the mud-hut, which opened away from the sea, there appeared an unkempt head and a smoky beard that started under the man's very eyes. After blinking a little he came out; he was stocky, barefooted and dark from soot. He looked towards the town, but there was no longer anyone in sight.

"Come in," he said and went back into the low hut. Its only light came from the slit over the door. There was a smell of stale fish and half the space inside was taken up with fishing gear. Ilya, Andrey and Fedka crossed themselves with two fingers as they entered.

"Sit down," the fisherman said to them. "Do you know whom you've just been beating?"

"They've been beating me all my life and never asked who I was," said Fedka.

"You've been beating Feodosy, the sacristan of the Krestovozdvizhensk monastery. A bandit, oh what a bandit! A real devil! Rabid!"

Seeing that the men were of his own kind, the fisherman sat down with them on the bench, tucked his hands under his armpits and, swaying backwards and forwards, began to tell them:

"These parts are as rich as can be in fish. You could live well, but I'm leaving. It's become quite impossible; this devil has got hold of the whole lake. We used to give the monks a quarter of our catch of smelts, and we give them something every fishing season. That's not enough for him. When he sees a sail, he runs to the shore and leaves you only enough fish for a meal. If you don't give it him, he pounces on you: 'How do you cross yourself?' Well, of course, you sin and cross yourself with three fingers. 'No,' he says. 'You're pretending! Come with me!' But to go with him means to go to the monastery cellar and be chained up. And how many nets of ours he has torn, how many boats he has spoilt! We complained to the governor. But the governor is only on the look-out to grab something himself. You know, at the monastery they've got the Metropolitan's special order:

to uproot the Old Believers. You fellows must get away from here as soon as you can."

"Oh, no, we are with Denisov," Golikov said, glancing timidly at the other two.

"Denisov will buy himself off, he's a powerful man. Nothing can harm him. When he comes from the north—with furs, walrus tooth, copper—he buys himself off. When he comes back the other way, he buys himself off. He's done it more than once. He's got his own men everywhere, my lad."

"A fine talker!" Mudwash said with a sneer. "All the way he fed us on dry bread, but to listen to him you'd think we were eating chicken."

Golikov grimaced painfully while the others discussed the Vyga elder in very plain terms. He recalled how Denisov passed his hand over his head with a soberly affectionate gesture: "Well, my boy, is your soul alive? That's good." He recalled the wonderful way in which Denisov spoke round the camp-fire, how he went off in his boat, his pointed skull-cap showing black against the water tinted by the sunset glow. He, Andrey, used to paint such holy men in a boat on the old icons. He was ready at this moment to be burnt alive in straw for this man's sake.

They sat on the bench and deliberated: what to do? Where to flee? Should they, after all, go north? The fisherman did not advise this; to go on foot without a boat to lake Vyg meant two months in the forest. They would certainly perish.

"You ought to go to some easy country, to the Don, for instance."

"I've been on the Don," Mudwash said hoarsely. "There's none of the old freedom left there. In the Cossack villages they surrender men who come by themselves. I've been chained and taken to Voronezh twice, to the Tsar's works."

They could not make up their minds and finally told Andrey to go and find Denisov; what would he say?

Andrey came in for a thorough scare. No sooner had he reached the ancient town gates when he heard cries: "Stop! Stop!" Ragged, barefooted men were running; some of them climbed over the fence. Two soldiers in green coats were chasing them, holding on to their hats. Panting heavily they disappeared down a crooked alley. A small, respectable-looking old man at a wicket-gate said: "It's the second day that they're rounding them up." Golikov asked him whether he knew the wealthy merchant Denisov and whether he had seen him. The old man pondered a while and then said:

"Go to the market-place and look for Denisov at the governor's house."

In the small market-place, littered with dungheaps, the rows of shops were nailed up, the pillars leant crookedly, the roofs sagged. Only two or three shops trading in fancy rolls and leather mittens were open. The walls of the ancient cathedral were crumbling and there was no fence round it. On the grass, by its low enclosed porch, beggar-women wrapped in rags were sleeping, and an idiot, with three pokers lying at his side, wagged his head and yawned till tears came into his eyes. Apparently life moved slowly here.

A guard, armed with a pike, stood shifting his weight from foot to foot in the middle of the place, by the execution pillar. Golikov went up to him in some trepidation. A foxy tradesman stuck his head out of a weatherboarded shop and said wheedlingly:

"Oh, what lovely fancy rolls with poppy-seed!"

Golikov bowed humbly to the guard and asked him where the governor's house was. The short-legged guard, clad in a patched strelets coat, turned away with a frown. A sheet of tin, bearing a ukase stamped with an eagle, was nailed to the pillar. "Go away!" the guard shouted. Andrey stepped back and looked round at the rotten fences, the crooked log-houses. The dark clouds seemed to catch on the church crosses. A man in a low-belted coat and felt boots was coming towards him, his thick, peeling lips greedily thrust out. The guard at the pillar and the tradesmen in the shops watched to see what would happen.

"Where have you come from? Whom do you belong to? Are you a tramp?" The man breathed in his face with a reek of stale garlic. All Golikov could do was to hiccup and babble. The man seized him by the collar.

"He's a Denisov man," someone shouted from a shop.

"He's taking nine of them to be burnt," a thin voice said from another shop.

The man shook Andrey:

"Have you read the Tsar's ukase on the pillar? Come with me, you whore's son."

And he dragged him—although Andrey did not resist—to the far end of the place, to the governor's house.

Denisov, smartly dressed and with his hair neatly combed, sat holding his marten-fur cap on his knee in the governor's parlour. The governor, Maxim Lupandin, a down-at-heel equerry, was looking dejectedly at the merchant's boots of fine kid leather and his mouse-grey coat lined with scarlet silk, of Hamburg or perhaps even of English cloth. The governor himself was dressed in a worn-out squirrel coat; he was by no means fat and was bald and pimply. Under the late Tsar Fedor Alexeyevich he had been an equerry, but under Peter Alexeyevich he had barely managed to get this post in Belozersk.

They were talking about nothing in particular: Denisov did not press the governor, nor did the governor press Denisov.

"What a coat he's got!" the governor thought. "What if he were to give it to me?" He had secretly sent a servant to the Krestovozdvizhensky monastery to fetch Father Feodosy, but Denisov too had something up his sleeve.

"The weather doesn't matter much," Denisov was saying. "If the wind turns, we'll cross the lake under sail. If it doesn't, we'll manage somehow along the shore. The main thing is to reach Kovzha, there we'll find men who'll take us all the way to Povenets."

"Of course your business is easy to understand," the governor replied evasively, eying the coat.

"Maxim Maximich, do me the favour, don't delay my barge and my men."

"If it weren't for the ukase, there'd be no question." The governor pulled out of his pocket the Tsar's ukase rolled up in a scroll and, holding it close to his eyes, so that his straggly little beard brushed against it, began to read:

" 'By order of the Grand Duke and Tsar of all. . . . It is said. . . . Tramps and beggars who are fed by the monasteries, and all kinds of monastery lay-dependants are to be conscripted into the army. . . .' "

"Monasteries don't concern us, ours is a trading business."

"Wait a minute! '. . . and also to be conscripted are boyars' grooms and servants and all tramps, beggars and runaway serfs'. I don't know what to do in your case, Andrey. If it had been some clerk who'd brought the ukase. . . . But it was brought by a lieutenant of the Preobrazhensky regiment, Alexey Brovkin, accompanied by soldiers. You know what it means today to have to deal with lieutenants."

Denisov turned back the skirt of his coat and jingled the silver coins in his pocket. The governor, fearing that he might not set the price high enough, glanced at the door to see whether Feodosy was coming. The one to enter was the thick-lipped myrmidon of the law, pushing Golikov in front of him. He whipped off his cap and bowed low.

"Maxim Maximich, I've caught another one," he said.

"On your knees!" the governor cried wrathfully. Golikov's captor pushed his shoulders and he went down on his bony knees with a thump. "Whose son are you?" the governor went on. "Whose serf? Where did you run away from?" Then turning to his underling: "Vanka, give me the ink and a pen."

"Let him be, Maxim Maximich," Denisov said in a low voice. "He's my employee."

The governor's eyes gleamed. He forced open the lid of the brass inkstand and began to fish out a fly with the quill, wheezing with the exertion. "Oh, why doesn't the sacristan come?" he kept thinking. At that moment the boards in the passage creaked. Vanka opened the door and the monk with the gipsy beard whom Golikov had seen not so long ago strode in angrily. One of his eyes was swollen shut as a result of the fight.

"His men beat me and manhandled me, they nearly killed me," he said in a loud voice. "And you, Maxim, have seated him by your side! Whom, whom, I ask you? An accursed dissenter! Surrender him to me, surrender him, governor, I tell you!"

With his hands crossed on his tall staff, the monk fixed alternately on Denisov and the governor the wild gaze of his one good eye. Golikov, nearly bereft of his senses, crawled away into a corner. Vanka avidly awaited the signal to hurl himself upon his victim and tie his arms behind his back. "The coat is mine," the governor thought.

"Who you are, monk, to come here abusing people, I don't know and don't want to know," Denisov said and got up. Feodosy's hands clutching the staff turned blue. Denisov unbuttoned his shirt and took a small bag from the eight-pointed brass cross he wore round his neck. "I want to deal honestly with you, Maxim Maximich, and make you a gift out of my poor profits. But it seems that our talk has been to no purpose."

He took a folded paper out of the bag and carefully opened it.

"The present document has been issued by the Stewards' Chamber to us, Andrey and Semyon Denisov, to allow us to trade wherever we wish and in order that no one should dare inflict losses or ruin on us, Andrey and Semyon. The document is signed by the President Mitrofan Shorin in his own hand."

"What's Mitrofan to me!" Feodosy cried tearing one hand away from his staff. "Here's a *fico* for your Mitrofan!"

"Oh!" the governor moaned feebly.

Denisov's cheeks reddened:

"You dare show a *fico* to the President, one of the best men among the merchants of Moscow? That's a crime!"

"Choke on it, choke on it, curse you!" Feodosy repeated furiously, pushing his beard into Denisov's face. He seized Denisov by his Old Believer's cross. "And for this, you Priestless fellow, I'll burn you alive. . . . I've got a powerful document against your trashy one."

"Oh, do make peace, you two!" the governor wailed. "Andrey, give the monk twenty roubles, then he'll leave you alone."

But neither Denisov nor the monk listened to him as they stood snorting at one another. The guard started to approach them crabwise. Then Denisov, wresting his cross from the sacristan, rushed to the window, raised the sash and shouted outside:

"Lieutenant, I claim the Tsar's word!"

Silence immediately fell in the room, and the men ceased snorting. Spurs jingled in the passage. Alioshka Brovkin entered, in jackboots, white scarf and sword. His youthful cheeks were ruddy, and his three-cornered hat was set low over his eyebrows.

"What's the quarrel about?"

"Lieutenant, the sacristan Feodosy and the governor are shamefully abusing the President's document, and making *ficos,* and tearing at my coat, and threatening to burn me."

Alioshka's eyes grew round and bulged sternly: exactly like Tsar Peter's. He gave a look at the monk, then at the governor, who was pressing his hands on the bench to rise, then he rapped his cane and said to a soldier who immediately appeared: "Arrest both of them."

2

The people of the Foreign Quarter said of Anna Mons: "It's extraordinary! Where did this young girl get so much common sense? Any other girl would have lost her head long ago. Annchen is just like her late father!"

Peter was very generous when he returned from the Black Sea. "My dear heart," Annchen said to him more than once with tender reproachfulness, "you are accustoming me to waste money on silly finery. It would be much more sensible if you would allow me to write to Reval: I have heard that cows yielding two pails of milk a day can be bought there at a reasonable price. Then you could sometimes and have lunch at my nice, clean little dairy farm and eat whipped cream."

Her farm had been built in a birch-copse on a small piece of land she had been given; the plot was wedge-shaped and ran from her back gates past the Kukuy stream down to the Yaouza river. The farm consisted of a small house, painted to look like a brick building from the distance, cattle sheds, roofed with tiles, a threshing-shed and barns. The slopes by the river pastured fat piebald cows—each named after some Greek goddess—sheep with fine fleece, English pigs and many varieties of fowl. Foreign vegetables and potatoes grew in the kitchen-garden.

At dawn Annchen would come out in a fleecy shawl and plain warm coat and walk down the sanded path to the dairy. She would superintend the milking and the feeding of the fowl, and count the eggs, and she herself would gather the lettuce for breakfast. She was strict with the servants and particularly severe on any slovenliness. The time had come for chopping cabbage. Such heads had never been seen even in Pastor Strumpf's kitchen-garden. The Germans came to admire them: such a cabbage-head or such turnips could be sent to the museum in Hamburg. They said jokingly that Annchen must know some charm that made the fruits of the earth flourish on what not long before had been a waste.

Russian girls sang as they chopped the cabbages in a new lime-wood trough. Annchen had taken the healthiest and jolliest girls from the villages belonging to Menshikov and Admiral Golovin, whose new mansions rose not far from the Foreign Quarter. The choppers tapped, the red-cheeked girls smelt of fresh cabbage-stalk. The hoar-frost still lay on the grass in the long shadow of the barn; snow-white geese waddled haughtily across it from the poultry-yard to the artificial pond. Smoke rose above the pointed roof of the dairy into the intensely blue autumn sky. Two neat bakehouse men carried a basket with freshly-baked fancy loaves across the well-swept courtyard.

Annchen was happy: stamping her half-frozen feet, she beamed at all this prosperity. Alas, her happiness would end as soon as she got home: she never had a day's peace; always some whim of Peter's was to be expected. One day it would be half-tipsy Russians who came along, to leave dirty marks with their boots, fill the place with tobacco smoke, smash wine-glasses and empty their pipes into the flower-pots; or else, whether she liked it or not, she would have to dress herself up and drive to some assembly to dance.

Banquets and dances were all very well once in a while, on dark autumn evenings or during the winter holidays. But the Russian lords gorged themselves and danced every day. What annoyed Annchen most, however, was Peter's own scatterbrained behaviour. He never told her when he would be coming to dinner or supper or how many guests he would bring. Sometimes a whole cavalcade of gluttons would drive up to the house at night. She had to have mountains of good things boiled and baked in case they might be needed: it nearly broke her heart; and often it all had to be thrown to the pigs.

Annchen once cautiously begged Peter: "My angel, I would have less needless expense if you were so good as to warn me every time of your coming." Peter gave her a surprised look, frowned and said nothing, and all went on as before.

The sun rose over the birches which were shedding their yellow leaves. The serving-girls went into the kitchen. Anna looked into the shed where geese were hanging in canvas sacks with their heads protruding: a fortnight before they were killed they were fattened on nuts. Annchen herself stuffed a nut in its shell down the gullet of each goose, torpid with fat. Then she went to see the feather-legged hens have their legs washed—it had to be done every morning. In the sheep-pen she picked up the little lambs and kissed their curly foreheads. Then she went back reluctantly to the house. Yes, there was a carriage at the door. The major-domo met her on the back porch and announced in a whisper:

"The Ambassador of Saxony, Herr Königseck."

Well, that wasn't too bad. Annchen smiled and, picking up her skirts, ran up the narrow staircase to change her gown.

Königseck sat with one foot under his chair, his snuffbox in his left hand and his right free for elegant gestures while, interspersing his German speech with French words, he chattered of one thing and another: of diverting adventures, women, politics, his sovereign, August, Elector of Saxony and King of Poland. His wig, scented with musk, was almost wider than his shoulders. His hat and gloves lay on the carpet. His snub nose wrinkled amusingly when he joked and his bold, colourless eyes rested caressingly on Annchen. She sat facing him by the fireplace where logs were burning, upright in her stiff corsage, with her arms curved and her hands, palm upwards, lying in her lap. She listened with downcast eyes, roguishly turning up the corners of her mouth as civility demanded.

The Ambassador said:

"It's impossible not to worship him. He is handsome, courteous and brave. King August is a god in human form. He is indefatigable in his passions and his amusements. When he gets bored with Warsaw, he rushes off to Cracow, and on the way hunts wild boars, feasts magnificently in the lords' castles or bestows the kiss of Phoebus on a bemused country wench in a hayloft. He has a passport made out for himself in the name of Cavalier Winter and, in the guise of a soldier of fortune, crosses Europe and turns up in Paris. This sword of mine has often warded off blows aimed at his breast in night brawls at street crossings in Paris. We galloped to Versailles one night, with King August in officer's uniform. Ah, Versailles! Oh, Fräulein Mons, you must see that earthly paradise some day! The immense windows are lit by millions of candles, and flaming lampions shimmer on the façade. Ladies and cavaliers stroll beside the shrub borders on the terrace. Chinese lanterns hang on the trees, like fruit of paradise. Rockets soar into the sky across the lake, and their sparks fall into the water, where musicians in boats are playing harps and viols. Fountains splash and night-moths flutter. The marble statues, seen through the foliage, look like gods come to life. The Most Christian King Louis sits in an armchair. His fat face is shaded by his wig, but all the same I managed to catch a glimpse of his haughty profile, with its protruding lower lip and narrow line of moustache, familiar to the whole world. A lady in a black domino, with the hood down over her eyes, was leaning on his chair—it was Madame de Maintenon. On his right hand, in a chair, sat Philippe d'Anjou, the future king of Spain, his grandson, a prey to melancholy. . . . Everything around—the thousands of faces in masks, the palace, the whole park—seemed bathed in a golden blaze of glory."

Annchen's slender fingers fluttered, and the curves of her breasts rose above her tight corsage:

"Ah, it's impossible to believe that it's not a dream. . . . But who is this Madame de Maintenon who stood behind the king's chair?"

"The king's mistress. The woman before whom ministers and ambassadors tremble. My sovereign, King August, walked several times past Madame de Maintenon and attracted her attention."

"Tell me, Ambassador, why does King Louis not marry Madame de Maintenon?"

Königseck was slightly taken aback and for a moment his expressive hand hung limp between his knees. Annchen's head drooped lower and a little wrinkle showed at the corner of her mouth.

"Ah, Fräulein Mons. . . . Can a queen's importance be compared with a favourite's power? A queen is only the victim of dynastic interests. Men bend their knees before the queen and hurry on to the favourite, because life is politics, and politics is gold and fame. At night the king draws the curtains not of the queen's bed, but of his favourite's. Between their embraces, on the hot pillow. . . ." A faint flush suffused Annchen's cheeks. The ambassador leant his scented wig closer. "On the hot pillow the most secret thoughts are imparted. The woman who holds the king in her arms hears the beating of his heart. She belongs to history."

"Sir," Annchen said raising her moist blue eyes, "the most precious thing of all is to know that happiness is lasting. What are these pretty clothes, these handsome mirrors to me if I have no certainty. . . . Better have less fame, but let God alone dispose of my small share of happiness. I am afloat in a luxurious but very frail boat."

She slowly pulled a little lace handkerchief from her corsage, shook it out weakly and pressed it to her face. Under the lace her lips began to tremble like a child's.

"What you need is a loyal friend, my charming child." Königseck took her by the elbow and pressed it tenderly. "You have no one in whom you can confide your secrets. Trust me with them. I put myself at your service with delight. . . . All my experience. . . . Europe has its eyes on you. My gracious monarch asks in every letter about the 'nymph of the Kukuy stream'."

"In what sense do you offer me your service? I don't understand."

Annchen removed her handkerchief and drew back from the too dangerous proximity of the ambassador. She suddenly felt afraid that he might throw himself at her feet. She rose impulsively and almost tripped over her dress. "I don't know whether I ought even to listen to you," she said.

Covered with confusion, she went across to the window. The bright sky of the morning was now clouded over and the rising wind was driving dust along the street. In a gilded cage on the windowsill, among pots of geranium, a trained quail—a present from Peter—was ruffling its feathers at the darkening day. Annchen tried to collect her thoughts, but—was it because Königseck was sitting motionless, looking at her back?—her heart beat anxiously. "What nonsense! Why should it?" she was afraid to turn round. And it was as well that she did not: Königseck's eyes were gleaming as if he had only just discovered this girl: her slender waist above the billowing skirts, the creamy softness of her shoulders, her fair hair piled high on her head, and her delicate nape made for kisses.

But all the same he did not lose his head: "With just a shade more keenness of wit and ambition in the nymph—history might be made with her."

Annchen suddenly stepped back from the window and her flickering glance rested in confusion on Königseck:

"The Tsar!"

The ambassador picked up his hat and gloves and smoothed his lace cravat. A chaise pulled up outside the front garden and Peter, screwing up his eyes against the dust, got out. A heavy, closed leather coach pulled up in its turn. Peter shouted something in its direction and started towards the house. Two men climbed out of the coach and, sheltering themselves from the flying dust with their cloaks, hurried through the front garden. The chaise and the coach drove off at once.

Annchen had not seen these two men before. They bowed with dignity, and Peter himself took their hats. He put his hands on the shoulders of the taller one—a man with a sullen, arrogant face—gave him a shake and a slap and said:

"Here you are in my house, Herr Johann Patkul. We'll have dinner now."

Peter was sober and in high good humour. He pulled a wig out of his red cuff and said to Annchen:

"Take a comb and comb it out, Annchen. At table I shall be wearing hair, as you wish me to. I sent a soldier specially to fetch it." And, turning to the second guest, General Karlowicz—a man with fat purple cheeks—he went on: "No matter what wig I wear, I am no match for King August; he's very splendid and magnificent, whereas I spend my time in the smithy and the stables."

His jackboots were thick with dust and his coat reeked of horsesweat. As he went off to wash he winked at Königseck:

"Look out, Mr. Ambassador, your visits to my young woman seem to have become rather frequent of late."

"Your Majesty," Königseck replied with a sweep of his hat, backing and bending his knee, "no mortal can be condemned for bringing flowers and doves to the altar of Venus."

While Peter washed and cleaned himself up, Annchen played the hostess: she took glasses of caraway vodka from a salver, offered them to the guests, asked after the health of each, how long they had been in Moscow and whether there was anything they lacked. Remembering what Königseck had said, she pushed the blunt toe of her slipper out from under her skirt, which she spread out on both sides of her chair, and said:

"People who come from Europe find it dull here at first. But soon, with God's help, we shall make peace with the Turks, and then we shall order everybody to wear Hungarian and German clothes, we shall pave our streets with stone and do away with the robbers in Moscow."

Johann Patkul replied in icy tones, hardly opening his thin lips. He had come to Moscow from Riga about a week ago. He was not staying at the embassy but at the house of Vice-admiral Cornelius Kreis, together with General Karlowicz, who had come a few days earlier from Warsaw, from King August. For the moment they did not lack anything. It was quite true that Moscow was unpaved and dusty, and the people were poorly dressed.

"I have already had time to observe," Patkul said with a sneering glance at Karlowicz, who was wheezing slightly with full-bloodedness and the tightness of his uniform coat, belted round his vast paunch with a wide sash, "I have observed a peculiar method which the local rabble has of getting a few kopeks to buy vodka. Whenever you buy anything from anyone and ask for change, he deliberately miscounts in his favour and asks you to check it. You count the change and tell him that it is not correct. He swears that it is you who have made the mistake, begins to count again and assures you, crossing himself at all the church domes, that the change is right. You count it over again two and three times, and he disputes your figure and again counts it himself. And so it goes on, ten times in succession, until you get tired of it and go away, abandoning your loss."

"You should order your servant to seize the fellow and drag him to the guardhouse; they'd give him a good beating," Annchen said firmly.

Patkul shrugged his shoulders disdainfully.

Peter came in, wearing a small, well-combed wig. Annchen hastened to offer him some caraway vodka. He drank, then put out his lips and kissed her on the cheek with a smack. The major-domo opened the door and struck the floor with his staff. They passed into the dining-room, on the vaulted ceiling of which cupids frolicked among little clouds; the stucco walls were covered with Flemish tapestries, and over the glazed fireplace hung a picture of dead birds and fruit by Snyders.

Peter sat with his back to the flaming logs, with Patkul on his right and Karlowicz and Königseck on his left, and Annchen, very much preoccupied, facing him. Crystal goblets on the brightly-coloured linen tablecloth were already filled with Hungarian wine, and a dish in the centre of the table was heaped with sausages: blood, pork and liver. The cold dishes smelt of spices. Outside the wind swept the prickly dust and whipped the bare branches. But in the room it was warm. The handsomely set table, the guests' contented faces and the flames from the open fire were genially reflected in the mirrors backing the sconces on the walls.

Peter raised his goblet for a toast to his dear friend August, King of Poland. The guests pushed the curls of their wigs back over their shoulders and began to eat.

"Sire," said Johann Patkul after the fourth course, which consisted of young geese with walnuts, "we ask for a private talk because the business is very secret."

"All right," Peter nodded. He pushed aside the pewter dishes with his elbows, and his face wrinkled in a smile as he looked at Annchen's cheeks flushed with wine. All through the meal he had been jokingly twitting her for her stingy housekeeping, saying, with a wink at Königseck: "Is the fricassée we have here by any chance made of the doves which he brings to your altar of Venus?" It was impossible to tell whether he really wanted to listen to the extremely important communications which had brought Johann Patkul and Karlowicz so urgently to Moscow.

Up to now they had seen him only once at the vice-admiral's. Peter had been affable, but had avoided any serious conversation. Today he had himself invited them to a private dinner at his mistress's home. Patkul watched this Asian with a cold, though deferential gaze. The talk with the Tsar did not brook delay. The envoy sent by the young Swedish king, Charles XII, had been in Moscow for some time, negotiating with Leo Narishkin and the boyars for a permanent peace with Sweden; the Swedes too had not seen the Tsar yet, but were expecting an audience at the Kremlin to present their credentials within the next few days.

"General Karlowicz and Herr Königseck will confirm that what I say is in complete accord with the heartfelt desires of His Majesty King August. My words come from a heart burdened with grief. All the Livonian knights and the notable merchants of Riga implore you, Sire, to lend us your ear."

Patkul wrinkled his high forehead and said slowly, at times restraining his anger:

"Unhappy Livonia seeks quiet and peace. There was a time when we formed part of the Polish State. We kept our liberties and the city of Riga was renowned throughout the Baltic. But men's hearts are black with envy. Poland stretched out her hand to grasp our wealth, the Jesuits began to persecute our faith, our language and our customs. The Lord clouded our minds in that ill-omened year. The knighthood of Livonia voluntarily placed itself under the protection of the Swedish monarch. Out of the Polish eagle's talons they threw themselves into the mouth of the Swedish lion."

"This was imprudent," Peter said. "The rapacity of the Swede is known the world over." He pulled a short pipe out of his pocket.

Königseck hastily rose and struck a flint. Then he handed Peter the smoking tinder on a plate. Johann Patkul waited politely until the Tsar had lighted his pipe.

"Sire, you doubtless know of the law passed by the Swedish Senate and confirmed by their late king, Charles XI: the Reduction Law. Twenty years have passed since then. I do not know what potion the Swedish senators—burghers, malicious hucksters—gave the king to induce him to such unparalleled villainy: to take from the nobles all the lands granted to them by former kings. The earls and barons were compelled to abandon their castles, and the hinds began to plough the lands of the nobility. We, Livonian knights, were given a sacred promise that the reduction would not touch us. But eight years later the king nevertheless ordered the Reduction Commission to confiscate for the treasury the lands which had been given us by former sovereigns. Knights, Grand Masters of the Order * and bishops had to prove by ancient documents their title to lands held for centuries, and if no documents could be produced the land was forfeit. Since the days of Ivan the Terrible and Stefan Batory Livonia has been devastated by wars, our documents have been lost and we cannot prove our ancient rights. I wrote a petition against the evil work of the Reduction Commission and presented it to the Swedish king in the name of all the Livonian knights. But the only result was that the Senate condemned me to have my right hand cut off, the hand that had written the petition, and to be beheaded." Patkul raised his voice and his thin lips paled. "To be beheaded," he went on, "because I was unwilling to bow my head humbly before wrong. Sire, the Livonian knights are ruined. But our merchants do not fare any better." From that moment Peter began to listen with great attention. "The Swedes have imposed heavy duties on all that enters or leaves the port of Riga. Their greed and corruption threaten ruin not only to us but to them too. Foreign ships now sail past Riga to Königsberg and all Poland's grain goes to the Elector of Brandenburg. Our fields are overgrown with weeds. The port is empty, the town is like a graveyard. And in Reval the Swedes have done even worse. The only choice left us is either final ruin or war. It is now or never, Sire. All our knights will ride. King August has sworn to bring us under the sovereign hand of Poland."

Patkul looked firmly at General Karlowicz, then turned his yellowish eyes on Königseck. Both of them gravely inclined their wigs. Peter, biting the stem of his pipe, replied:

"Mind you don't once again jump out of the frying-pan into the

* Of Livonian Knights.

fire. King August has a light hand, but the Polish *Pans* have tenacious claws. You are giving them a great lump—Riga and Reval."

"Poland today is not what it was in the days of Stefan Batory. Poland does not seek our ruin," said Patkul. "We have a common enemy on land and sea. Poland will not attack our faith and our liberties."

"God grant it! But the Diet will decide one thing today, and another tomorrow—whatever comes into the nobles' heads. If King August had sole power, you could rely on him. But the *Pans!*" Peter was arguing good-humouredly, puffing out smoke. The bones of Patkul's face stood out under his skin, so intently did he fix his eyes on the Tsar. "And besides, will the *Pans* be willing to fight?"

"Sire, King August has ordered the Saxon army, which is under his sole command, to take up winter quarters in the districts of Szavli and Birzen, near the Livonian border."

"How large is the army?"

"Twelve thousand picked Germans."

"It seems rather small for such an enterprise."

"An equal number of Livonian knights will gather near Riga. The Swedish garrison is not large. We shall take Riga by storm. And once the war has begun the *Pans* will draw their swords of their own accord. Another ally of this coalition is the king of Denmark, Christian. Sire, you know the hatred he bears to the Swedes and the Duke.* The Danish fleet will protect us from the sea."

Patkul had reached a difficult point. The Tsar, his hand dangling, tapped the table with his nails. His round face expressed neither encouragement nor opposition. Twilight was falling; the wind outside gained force and made the shutters creak. Annchen was going to light the candles, but Peter said through his teeth: "Don't."

"Sire, there could be no more opportune time for you to get a strong foothold in the Baltic and to take back from the Swedes your ancient provinces, Ingria and Karelia. After routing the Swedes and establishing yourself on the coast you will achieve world fame, you will trade with Holland, England, Spain and Portugal, with all the northern, western and southern countries. And you will do what no other monarch of Europe has been able to do: open a trade-route through Moscow between East and West. You will enter into relations with all the Christian monarchs and have your say in the affairs of Europe. When you put a powerful fleet on the Baltic, you will become the third sea-power. And you will gain far more in the

* Duke of Holstein whose sister was married to Charles X of Sweden.

world by this policy than by conquering the Turks and the Tatars. It is now or never!"

Patkul raised his hand as if calling God to witness. Königseck repeated in a whisper: "Now or never!" General Karlowicz wheezed meaningly.

"Why now? Is the roof on fire? It's a great understaking to fight the Swedes," Peter said, gnawing his pipe. The firelight gleamed in the visitors' watchful eyes. "Twelve thousand Saxons is a considerable force. The Danish fleet. . . . hm. . . . The knights and the *Pans?* That's all guesswork. The Swedes. . . . They've got the best army in Europe. It's difficult to give you any advice."

He started tapping his nails again. Patkul said with repressed fury:

"Today the Swedes could be routed without striking a blow. Charles XII is young and foolish. A fine sort of king! He decks himself out like a girl, and the only things he knows are feasting and chasing hares through the forest. He has emptied the treasury on masquerades. A lion without teeth. No wonder that the Swedish envoy has been in Moscow since the spring asking for a lasting peace. It's ridiculous to call them envoys. All Europe knows that not one of them has silk stockings. They've squandered everything and live on peas. Last year, Sire, General Karlowicz was in Stockholm and saw enough of the king. General, tell us what you saw."

Karlowicz eased his neck in his collar and began:

"I was there, that's so. The town is not large, but inaccessible both from land and sea—a real lion's den. I left the ship in civilian clothes and under an assumed name. I went to the market-place and was surprised; it was as if some enemy had entered the town: they were closing the shutters of shops and houses and women were clutching their children. I asked a passer-by what it meant; he waved his hand and started to run away: 'The King!' I have seen a good deal in my campaigns and in many towns where I was quartered; but I had never seen such a thing as a people fleeing headlong from its own king as from the plague. I looked and saw not less than a hundred hunters riding down from the wooded hills, with horns slung on their backs and hounds on the leash. They raced over the stone bridge into the town. The square was already deserted. On a black stallion at their head was a youth of some seventeen years, in soldier's jackboots, and coatless, in his shirt. He was galloping with loose reins: King Charles XII! The lion-cub! Behind him came the hunters, whistling and laughing. They galloped across the market-place like demons. It was lucky no one was hurt, but sometimes people get ridden down. Being of an inquisitive turn of mind I persuaded a man I knew to take me to the palace in the guise of a merchant trading in Arabian spices. It was early in the morning, but already they were feasting in the palace. The king was amusing himself. The walls of the dining-hall were splashed with blood up to the height of a man, and blood was streaming over the floor. There was a terrible stench and drunken men were lying about. The king and those who could still stand on their feet were cutting off the heads of sheep and calves with a single slash of the sword for a wager of ten Swedish crowns. I could not but admire the king's skill: grooms would push a calf towards him, and the king would run forward, swing his sword in a circle and cut off the calf's head, turning aside nimbly so that the blood should not spurt over his boots.

"I bowed respectfully. The king threw his sword down on the table and held out his grimy hand for me to kiss. On hearing that I was a merchant, he said: 'By the way, can you lend me five hundred Dutch guilders?' They seated me at the table and made me drink to excess. One of the courtiers whispered to me: 'Don't cross the king, he's been drunk for three days now. Yesterday a respectable merchant was stripped here and covered with honey and feathers.' To avoid any such ignominy I promised the king the five hundred guilders which I did not possess and spent the whole day under the table pretending to be drunk. The courtiers would wake up, eat, drink, shout songs, throw dishes at the servants' heads and then roll to the floor again.

"When night came, the king went out with a crowd of his hangers-on, smashing windows and frightening the sleeping citizens. I took advantage of the darkness and made off. The whole town is groaning at the king's folly. I myself heard preachers in three churches tell the people: 'Woe to the land where a young king rules!' The citizens send their best representatives to the palace to beseech the king to abandon his profligacy and apply himself to affairs of State. The petitioners are thrown out. The earls and barons whom the late king ruined hate the ruling dynasty. The Senate still supports the king but already they are tightening up the purse-strings. But much does he care, the madman!

"Not long ago he came to the Senate and demanded two hundred thousand crowns unconditionally. The Senate unanimously refused. The king was furious and broke his cane in two, saying: 'So it will be with all who oppose me!' And the following day he and his huntsmen burst into the Senate hall; they released half a dozen hares from a sack and set the hounds after them—" Peter suddenly threw back his head and gave a gay laugh. "The senators climbed on to the windowsills; some of them had their coats torn by the hounds. That's what the king is—a rapscallion. Not so terrible, this lion-cub!"

General Karlowicz pulled a silk handkerchief from his cuff and wiped his face and neck under his wig. Peter, with his elbows on the table, went on laughing. To everyone's surprise Annchen said with contempt:

"A king indeed! Why, our Preobrazhensky regiment could capture him by itself."

All turned their heads towards her. Königseck put his handkerchief to his mouth. Peter said in a low voice: "This is a matter above your understanding, Annchen. Better go and tell them to light the candles."

The candles in the sconces, with their mirror reflectors, were lighted. The crystal goblets were filled with wine. Even Johann Patkul's face was softened in the warm candlelight. Annchen brought in a small musical box, wound it up, opened the lid and put it on the mantelpiece. The box played a German air with reedy voices singing about everything being happy in this world, with food on the table and candles burning, and blue eyes smiling, though the wind might bluster outside. Peter smiled and nodded his head and tapped his shoe in rhythm. He did not say another word about politics that evening.

3

Every Sunday Ivan Brovkin's daughter Alexandra and her husband dined with him at his new brick mansion on the Ilyinka. Ivan was now a widower. His eldest son, Aliosha, was at present recruiting men for the regiments. A recent ukase had ordered thirty regiments to be mustered: three divisions. A new Department had been set up for supply, under a quartermaster-general. Naturally the quartermaster-general could not produce oats or hay or biscuits and other provisions from his departmental records. So Brovkin still remained the main purveyor, though without position or title. His business was rapidly expanding and many important merchants were in partnership with him or acted as his agents. One of his other sons, Yakov, was serving with the fleet in Voronezh and another, Gavrila, was in Holland learning the trade in the dockyards. Only the youngest, Artamon, then in his twenty-first year, stayed with his father to write letters, keep accounts and read various books. He was quite fluent in German and translated for his father treatises on commerce and, for entertainment, Puffendorf's *History*. As he listened Ivan Artemyich would sigh: "And we live here, dear Lord, at the edge of the world, no better than pigs."

All his children—they had been born at intervals of a year—were clever, and this one was pure gold. Their mother must have given her blood drop by drop, torn her soul to shreds striving for her children's happiness. Through the winter storms she would sit in the smoky hut, her spindle flying, and her eyes, terrible as an abyss, fastened on the burning pine-splinter in the cresset. The little ones would be sleeping on the stove, cockroaches would stir in the chinks and the storm would seem to rage against the cruelty of life as it swept over the thatched roof. "Why should the little ones suffer for no fault of their own?" She did not live to see the good fortune that came. In those days Ivan Artemyich had not pitied her—there was no time for it—but now, in his old age, he constantly thought of his wife. When she lay dying she begged him: "Don't take a stepmother for the children." And so he never married again.

Brovkin's house was arranged in foreign style: in addition to the usual three rooms—bedroom, prayer-room and dining-room—there was a fourth, the drawing-room, where guests were kept till dinner-time, and not on benches along the walls, to yawn into their sleeves with boredom, but on Dutch chairs round the table in the middle of the room, and the table was covered with stamped velvet. On it lay diverting engravings, a calendar with forecasts, a musical box, chessmen, pipes and tobacco for their entertainment. Against the walls, instead of chests and coffers with all kinds of goods and chattels, such as were in the houses of the nobles who still lived in the old-fashioned way, stood dressers and cupboards whose doors were opened when visitors came, to display the costly china on their shelves.

All this was Alexandra's doing. She also saw that her father dressed properly, shaved himself frequently and changed his wig. Ivan Brovkin realised that he had to obey his daughter in such matters. But to tell the truth he found the life rather boring. There was hardly anyone now in whose presence he could plume himself—he shook hands with the Tsar himself. Sometimes he felt he would like to go and sit in a tavern on the Varvarka, among the shopkeepers, listen to spicy talk and wag his tongue himself. But he couldn't go there; it was not seemly. He must just bear it and be bored.

He stood at the window. There was Sveshnikov's head clerk running along the street in a great hurry, the whore's son! A brainy chap. You're too late, my good fellow, we bought the flax there this morning! And there's Revyakin in new felt boots, turning his phiz away from the window: he must be coming from the Law Office. What did I tell you, my friend? Don't go to court against Brovkin.

In the evenings, when Sanka was out, Brovkin would take off his wig and his Spanish velvet coat, and go downstairs to the kitchen to sup with the clerks and peasants. He would eat cabbage soup and jest with them. He particularly liked it when someone from his own village arrived, someone who remembered Ivash Brovkin, the most insignificant man in the village. The peasant would come into the kitchen and, at the sight of Ivan, would behave as if almost frightened to death, not knowing whether to go down on his knees or how to greet him, and refusing out of shyness to sit down at the table. Of course, bit by bit, he would start talking, leading up in a roundabout way to the business that had brought him.

"Ah, Ivan Artemyich, I wouldn't know you if it wasn't for your voice. And yet you are all we talk about down in the village: the peasants come together on the bench at the gates and start talking; we remember the days when you yourself had only one horse and were up to your eyes in debt, but even then you were an eagle!"

"I got my start in life with three roubles, three roubles. That's how it was, Constantine."

The man opened his eyes solemnly and wagged his head:

"It means that God sees a man and marks him out. Yes." And he would add softly, ingratiatingly: "Ivan Artemyich, it's Constantine Shutov you're thinking of, not me. I'm not Constantine. He lived opposite you; I was a little to the side, on the left. A tumbledown hut."

"I've forgotten, I've forgotten."

"The hut is no good," the man would now say with tears in his throaty voice. "It will fall down any minute. The other day the cowshed collapsed, a heifer was killed. I don't know what's to be done."

Ivan Artemyich understood what was to be done, but he did not immediately say: "Go tomorrow to my clerk. I'll give you till Intercession Day." Until yawns overcame him, he would ask how people were getting on, and who had died, and who had grandchildren. And he would joke: "Expect me, I'll be coming down after Easter to find a bride for myself."

The peasant would stay in the kitchen for the night. Ivan Artemyich went upstairs to his overheated bedroom. Two liveried servants, long since asleep on a felt mat by his door, jumped up and undressed his short, stout person. Bowing to the ground the prescribed number of times before the icons, and having scratched his sides and his stomach, Brovkin thrust his feet into low-cut felt boots and went to the cold privy. The day was over. As he laid himself on his featherbed Brovkin sighed deeply every night and said to himself: "Another day is gone." There were not so many days left. A pity, just when life had become good. He would begin to think about his children, about his business, until sleep ravelled his thoughts.

That day he was expecting important guests after mass. The first to arrive were Sanka and her husband. Vasily Volkov did not bow, but kissed his father-in-law and seated himself moodily at the table. Sanka, brushing her father's cheek with her lips, hurried to the mirror and began to twist her shoulders and swing her billowing skirts of crushed strawberry colour, examining her new gown.

"Father, I must have a word with you—a very serious talk." She raised her bare arms and straightened the silk flowers in her powdered hair. She could not tear herself away from the mirror: blue-eyed, sensuous, with a rosebud mouth. "A very serious talk. . . ." And she looked at the mirror again and curtsied, waving an open feather fan.

Volkov said sourly:

"She's gone quite mad. She's got Paris on her brain. Paris! Paris! She thinks they can't do without her there. We sleep apart now."

Brovkin, sitting by the Dutch stove, laughed:

"Ai-ai-ai. You ought to beat her."

"Just try! She screams the house down. At the slightest thing she threatens to complain to the Tsar. I don't want to take her to Europe; she'll lose her head completely."

Sanka left the mirror, narrowed her eyes and lifted a finger:

"You shall take me. Peter Alexeyevich himself ordered me to go. And you are rude."

"Father-in-law, do you see? What is this?"

"Ai-ai-ai!"

"Father," Sanka said and sat down by him, spreading her skirts. "Yesterday I had a talk with Natalia, Prince Roman's youngest daughter. The girl's in great distress. They haven't married the eldest sister yet, so when will Natasha's turn come? She's at the best age, and a beauty. She understands etiquette and court gallantry as well as I do."

"What's that? Are Prince Roman's affairs in a bad way?" Brovkin asked, scratching his soft nose. "That's probably why he keeps talking about a canvas factory."

"They're bad, very bad. Princess Avdotya has been complaining about it. And he himself goes about as black as thunder."

"He was foolish enough to go in for army contracts; our people gave him a rough time."

"It's a great family, Father, the Buynosovs. It's no small honour to take such a princess into the family. If we don't insist too much on the dowry, they will give her. I'm thinking of our youngest boy, Artamosha." Brovkin was about to scratch the back of his head but his wig was in the way. "The main thing," Sanka went on, "is to get Artamon and Natalia married before I leave for Paris. The girl is simply pining. I've spoken to the Tsar about it too."

"You have?" Brovkin stopped kneading his nose. "Well, and what did he say?"

"He says it's a good idea. I was dancing with him at Menshikov's last night. He tickled my cheek with his moustache and said: 'Have the wedding as soon as possible'."

"Why as soon as possible?" Brovkin got up and looked intently at his daughter. She was taller than he.

"A war, or something. I didn't ask him, I had other things on my mind. Last night everybody was saying there would be war."

"With whom?"

Sanka only pouted. Brovkin put his short arms behind his back and waddled up and down in his white stockings and square-toed shoes with large bows and red heels.

A carriage rumbled up to the porch: the guests were arriving.

According to the visitor's rank, Brovkin either greeted him at the door, sticking out his paunch under his silk waistcoat, or else went out on to the porch. He met Prince Roman, who had just arrived in a carriage with grooms on the footboard, half-way down the stairs and shook hands with him affably. Antonida, Olga and Natalia held up their skirts and came running up the iron steps after the prince. Brovkin, having let Natalia pass, ran his eye over her: the girl was quite ripe for marriage.

The Buynosov girls noisily seated themselves at the table in the middle of the drawing-room, and began to twitter all kinds of nonsense, catching at Sanka's bare elbows. The guests of honour—the President of the Stewards' Chamber, Mitrofan Shorin, Sveshnikov, Mononov—in order not to tread on the girls' trains, retreated to the stove and from there glanced from under their eyebrows at the young people: "Of course it's all very well, it's the Tsar's wish that we should follow the example of Europe, but one can't expect much good to come from taking girls about visiting."

Sanka was showing some pictures which had just been brought from Hamburg: engravings by famous Dutch masters. The girls put their handkerchiefs up to their noses as they examined the naked gods and goddesses. "Who's this?" "And what's this he's got?" "What's she doing?" "Ai!"

Sanka explained impatiently:

"This man with legs like a cow is a satyr. There's no need for you to make a wry face, Olga—he's wearing a fig-leaf; that's how they're always drawn. Cupid is trying to pierce her with his arrow. She, poor thing, is weeping; her heart is broken. Her lover made love to her and sailed away—see, there's the sail. It's called 'Ariadne forsaken'. You ought to learn about all this. Nowadays gentlemen are always asking about the Greek gods. This isn't last year. But unless you know it, don't even try to dance with foreigners."

"We would have learnt, but we have no books," Antonida said. "We can't get as much as half a kopek from our father for any sensible purpose."

The slightly pockmarked Olga bit the lace on her sleeve in vexation. Sanka suddenly put her arm around Natalia's shoulder and whispered something. Natalia's round face flushed up to the roots of her fair hair.

Then Artamon, in brown clothes of foreign make, came into the room quietly and deferentially. He was thin and rather like Sanka, but with darker eyebrows and cloud-grey eyes; there was down on his upper lip. Sanka pinched Natalia to make her look at her brother. Natalia was so covered with confusion that she bent her head low and stuck out her elbows, refusing to look round.

Artamon made a low bow to the older guests and came across to his sister. Sanka, with prim lips, dropped him a short curtsey and said quickly:

"Let me present my youngest brother Artamon."

The girls languidly nodded their high, powdered heads. Artamon stepped back, according to the best manner, tapped his foot and flourished his hand as if he were rinsing linen. Sanka presented the girls: "Princess Antonida, Princess Olga, Princess Natalia." Each rose and curtsied, and to each Artamon replied with a flourish of his hand. He gingerly took a seat at the table and pressed his hands between his knees. Red patches flared up on his cheekbones and he raised his eyes unhappily to his sister's. Sanka drew her brows together threateningly.

"How often do you go out for pleasure?" he asked haltingly, addressing Natalia.

She whispered something inarticulate, but Olga answered boldly: "The day before yesterday we danced at the Narishkins. We changed our gowns three times. It was a great success and terribly hot. But why have we never met you?"

"I'm still too young."

"Father's afraid he might become too dissipated," Sanka said. "When we get him married—then he'll be able to. But he's a prodigiously good dancer. Don't mind his shyness. He speaks French so that you don't know where to look!"

The older guests were throwing curious glances at the young people. "Well, well, that's what the children are like today!"

"Where did you train your son?" Mitrofan Shorin asked his host.

"Tutors come to teach him. We can't do otherwise, Mitrofan Ilyich: we're in the public eye. We can't shine by our descent, so we must shine by something else."

"True, true. One has to creep out of one's hole."

"And the Tsar takes it badly too: how's this, he says, if you rake in money with a shovel, you've got to give of your best."

"Naturally. These outlays will pay for themselves."

"Sanka alone costs me a tidy sum. But the wench has quite a position."

"She's a sprightly young woman. Only, Ivan Artemyich, you'll have to look out, or else. . . ."

"Of course, one could drive her back with a whip to sit at an embroidery frame upstairs in the women's quarters," Brovkin replied thoughtfully after a short silence. "But would that be a great advantage? Just to reassure her husband? Pah! I realise that she's fluttering round sinful temptation. God knows, that's true. There's sin flashing out of her eyes. But, Mitrofan Ilyich, times have changed. In England—have you heard?—Marlborough's wife is directing the affairs of all Europe. You'd look a fool standing with a whip over her skirts."

Alexey Sveshnikov—a stern-faced, bushy-browed, wealthy merchant, in a loose, frogged Hungarian coat, with no wig on his hair, which was black and curly and streaked with grey—twisted his fingers behind his back, waiting till Shorin and Brovkin stopped talking about trifles.

"Mitrofan Ilyich," he said in his deep bass, "I'm raising that question again: we must hurry up with that affair of ours. There's a rumour that someone may get in first."

The president's sharp-nosed, well-scrubbed, foxy face wreathed itself in honeyed smiles.

"It's for our kind host to decide," he said. "It's he you must ask, Alexey Ivanovich."

Brovkin also began to twiddle his fingers rapidly behind his back; he set his short legs far apart and looked up at the two eagles, Shorin and Sveshnikov. He immediately realised: they're in a hurry, the villains; they must have discovered something special. Brovkin had spent the previous day in the grain sheds and had seen no one of importance. He did not reply, but puffing himself up, speculated what it could be. He drew his hands from behind his back and scratched his nose.

"Well," he said, "there's a rumour that cloth will rise in price. We might discuss that."

Sveshnikov immediately rolled his gipsy eyes:

"So you, too, Ivan Artemyich, know about what took place yesterday?"

"I know one or two things. My business is to know and hold my tongue." Brovkin clutched his chin and thought: "What the devil! What is it they've found out?"

Glancing at the other guests he backed away behind the tiled stove, followed by Shorin and Sveshnikov. There, standing close together, they began to talk cautiously round and about the subject.

"Ivan Artemyich, all Moscow is chattering about it."

"Yes, there's a lot of chatter."

"But with whom? Can it really be with the Swedes?"

"That's the Tsar's affair."

"Well, but all the same. Is it to be soon?" Sveshnikov dug his nails into his wiry beard. "This would be the right moment for us to put up a factory. The Tsar doesn't care that it's cheaper than Hamburg cloth, what he wants is his own cloth. The frontiers may be closed—but he'd have his own cloth. It's a gold mine. The number of people who are already sniffing round it! That Martisen, for one. . . ."

"So that's what they've smelt out!" Brovkin told himself, hiding his smile with his hand. Only a few days before, this Martisen, a foreigner, had come to Brovkin with an interpreter and offered to open a cloth factory: the Tsar and Brovkin would provide the money, while he, Martisen, was to have a third of the profits, for which he was to bring in weaving looms and skilled workmen from England and manage the whole business. Sveshnikov and Shorin, for their part, had long ago suggested that Brovkin should become a partner in a company to start a cloth factory. But up to now the matter had gone no further than talk. Apparently something had happened the day before; most probably Martisen had himself approached the Tsar.

"Is it possible to let a business of such importance go to foreigners?" Sveshnikov said, his eyes burning.

Shorin half closed his eyes and sighed:

"And here are we ready to lay down our lives, give our last kopek...."

"Tomorrow; we'll go into it tomorrow," Brovkin said hurrying from the stove to the door. A short, clean-shaven, plump man with a wide-bridged aquiline nose had entered the room; he was dressed in a black cloth suit and his shoes were covered with dust. No one had come forward to greet him. His dark eyes restlessly scanned the faces of the guests. Catching sight of Brovkin, he held out his short arms in an un-Russian gesture and said with a crooked smile: "Most esteemed Ivan Artemyevich!" pronouncing every letter of the name in a singsong voice, and began to embrace his host, kissing him three times—the odd creature—as if it were Easter. Then, with nods of his fiery-red wig this way and that, he whispered: "For the moment nothing decided with Martisen. Alexander Danilovich will be here soon."

"Glad to see you, Peter Pavlovich; be welcome."

This was the interpreter from the Ambassadors' Office, Shafirov, a Jew. He had accompanied the Tsar abroad, but until this autumn had been relegated to the background. Now, however, he was attached to the Swedish embassy and saw Peter every day, and was already regarded as one of the mighty.

"Tomorrow, Ivan Artemyevich, please come to the Kremlin, to the palace. The Tsar has ordered ten representatives of the Stewards' Chamber to attend. The Swedes are going to present their credentials."

"Have they reached an agreement?"

"No, Ivan Artemyevich. The Tsar won't kiss the Gospel for the Swedish king."

At these words Brovkin drew a deep breath and hurriedly crossed himself over his navel.

"Then, Peter Pavlovich, these rumours are true?"

"We'll see, Ivan Artemyevich. These are grave matters, grave matters . . ." and he turned towards the Buynosov girls, kissing their fingers in the foreign fashion.

Prince Roman was moodily sitting on a chair against the wall. It was not much of an honour to visit a house like this. He glanced dully at his daughters: "Magpies, fools! Who'll take them? Lord, what cruel times these are! Money, money! It's as if the wind blew it out of one's pocket. . . . From early morning one keeps racking one's brains how to make ends meet, how to go on with it. Everything has been squeezed out of the villages, but that isn't enough. Why? It used to be enough. Ah, in the old days you could sit by the window; eat an apple if you felt like it, and if you didn't, just sit and listen to the church bells. Everlasting peace. . . . Then the whirlwind struck and people have started running about like ants from an ant-heap when boiling water is poured over it. It's incomprehensible. And always money, money, money! And all these factories and companies."

Evstrat Momonov, an elderly merchant—one of the most influential members of the merchants' guild—who was sitting next to the prince, said in a low voice:

"Things can't go on this way, Prince Roman Borisovich. We merchants look at it like this: it's become too cramped, quite impossible, the foreigners outdo us at every turn. They won't buy our goods; they first send a letter to Hamburg: it takes eighteen days to get there, and after another eighteen days there's an answer, giving the price on the Hamburg Exchange. While our silly people stick to the same price for a year, and even two, though it's ages since that price disappeared from the world. The foreigners have long ago cut themselves a trade-route out of our land, while we keep sitting in the same hole. No, Prince, war can't be avoided. If we could only get one town even: Narva, say, an ancient fief of the Tsars."

"You're bursting with money, but it's never enough for you merchants!" Prince Roman replied with disgust. "War! War's a State affair—it's not for you low-born merchants to stick your noses in such matters."

"True, true, Prince," Momonov immediately agreed. "I'm only talking out of foolishness. . . ."

Prince Roman looked at him out of the corner of his bloodshot eyes: just think, he was plainly dressed, his face was ordinary, yet he had pots of gold buried in his cellar.

"Have you many sons?"

"Six, Prince Roman Borisovich."

"Unmarried?"

"Married, Prince, all of them married."

A carriage rumbled over the long pavement outside. Ivan Artemyich rushed to the steps and some of the guests hurried to the windows. The chatter stopped. The jingle of spurs on the iron steps could be heard. Alexander Menshikov—major-general, governor of Pskov—came in, followed by Brovkin. He was wearing a coat with red cuffs which looked as if he had dipped his sleeves in blood up to the elbow. His deep blue eyes glanced round the guests with a cold official stare as he crossed the threshold. He took off his hat and made a sweeping bow to the princesses. Then, cocking his handsome left eyebrow, he went up to Sanka with a lazy smile, kissed her on the forehead, touched the tips of her fingers lightly, and then, turning round, nodded briefly to the guests.

The doors leading to the dining-room were opened. Alexander Danilovich, clapping Brovkin on the shoulder, bent over his ear:

"Drop the talks with Shorin and Sveshnikov, it's no good. We won't give anything to Martisen. We must take it on ourselves. Have a word with Shafirov."

4

In fourteen carriages, each drawn by four horses, the Swedish envoys left the Ambassadors' Yard. Infantry clad in three-cornered hats, short coats and white stockings stood at attention, lining the route all along the Ilyinka across the square right up to the Kremlin walls. Standards and guidons on pikes fluttered in the October wind. The Swedes looked grave as they surveyed this new army through their carriage windows.

When they passed through the Spassky gates they saw piles of cannon-balls, plastered on one side with snow, and brass mortars with their mouths raised to the sky; by each stood four tall, moustached gunners holding ramroads and smoking fuses. In front of the Red Porch old General Gordon sat on a fiery-red Don stallion. His red cloak billowed in the wind, and icy sleet drummed on his helmet and armour. When the carriages pulled up, the general raised his hand; the guns roared and smoke shrouded the dull windows of the offices and the cupolas of the churches.

On the porch the envoys surrendered their swords at the demand of the equerries.

A hundred men of the Semenovsky regiment, carrying the Swedish king's gifts—silver bowls, goblets, jugs—took up their positions on the porch and in the ante-chamber and held up a full-length portrait of the youthful King Charles XII himself in an elaborate wooden frame. The envoys walked with measured tread into the dining-hall, taking off their hats at the door.

Boyars, Moscow nobles and merchants and the most important tradesmen sat on benches round the four walls. All were simply dressed in cloth suits, many of foreign fashion. At the far end of the hall, where the square vault of the ceiling was covered, like the walls, with paintings of knights, beasts and birds, on a throne of ivory and silver, sat Peter without hat or wig, in a grey cloth coat lined with lynx-fur. He sat motionless, like an idol, his eyes staring. On his left hand stood Svinyin holding a golden basin, and on his right Volkov, with a towel on his outstretched hands.

The envoys approached and bent their knees on the carpet in front of the throne steps. Svinyin presented the basin and Peter, looking straight in front of him, dipped his fingers into the water; Volkov wiped them, and the envoys kissed Peter's rough hand. After this Peter rose—his head nearly touching the canopy—and, his throat swelling, said in Russian according to ancient ritual:

"Is Charles, King of the Swedes, in good health?"

The ambassador, laying his hand on his breast and inclining his great horned wig sideways, replied that by the grace of God the King was well and enquired after the health of the Tsar of All the Russias. The interpreter Shafirov, dressed like the Swedes in a short cloak and silk knee-breeches with ribbons and slashes on the thighs, translated the ambassador's answer in a loud voice. The boyars half-opened their mouths attentively, raised their eyebrows and pricked up their ears to hear whether any syllable of the reply was in any way insulting. Peter nodded: "I am well, thank you." The ambassador, taking a scroll—the credentials—from a velvet cushion carried by the secretary, knelt and presented it to Peter. The Tsar accepted the document and, without looking at it, pushed it towards the Chief Minister, Leo Narishkin. In contrast to all the others, Narishkin was dressed with great magnificence in white satin sparkling with gems. Without unrolling the scroll he announced in a loud voice that the audience was over.

The envoys walked backwards to the door, bowing as they went.

The envoys had apparently expected that they would be able, at the audience itself, to raise the main question for which they had been languishing six months in Moscow: Peter's confirmation—by an oath sealed by the kissing of the Gospel—of a peace treaty with Sweden. But a week passed before the Muscovite ministers invited the envoys to a conference at the Foreign Affairs Department. At this conference Prokofy Voznitsin replied to the Swedes that Tsar Peter confirmed the former peace treaties with Sweden *with his soul* and would not kiss the Gospel a second time, as he had already taken an oath to the present king's father. But that, on the other hand, it was necessary for young King Charles to kiss the Gospel, as he had not taken the oath to Tsar Peter. Such was the Tsar's will, and it was announced to the envoys and would not be altered.

The envoys grew excited and began to argue, but their speeches merely rebounded from the haughtily puffed-up Muscovites as peas rebound from a wall. The envoys said that without their king's sanction they could not accept such a final treaty of perpetual peace and that they would write to Stockholm. Voznitsin replied with an ironic gleam in his old eyes:

"You know the road to Stockholm: you will not receive a reply even in four months' time, and you will have to spend this time vainly in Moscow, at your own expense."

At the second and third conferences it was the same. The Ambassadors' Department stopped supplying even hay for their horses. The envoys sold some of their belongings—wigs, stockings, buttons —in order to provide themselves with food. And at last they gave in. In the Kremlin, Tsar Peter, sitting on the throne in his lynx-fur coat, handed the final document, unkissed, to the rather wasted envoys.

One misty November morning a leather-covered coach, splashed with mud, drove up to the back porch of the Preobrazhensky palace. The fantastic roofs of the palace were shrouded in a damp mist. Alexander Menshikov was on the porch, impatiently stamping his feet in top-boots. When he saw a serving-girl making her way somewhere with a coat thrown over her head, he shouted at her: "Away from here, carrion!" The girl fled headlong, her bare feet slipping awkwardly over the wet leaves.

The Polish general, Karlowicz, and the Livonian knight, Patkul, emerged from the carriage. "Well, here you are, God be praised!" Menshikov said, shaking hands with them. They went along deserted passages and up stairways that smelt of mice. Menshikov knocked lightly at a low door.

Peter opened the door and silently inclined his head. He led his visitors into a small, smoke-filled bedroom with one mica window which hardly let in the misty light. "Well, I'm glad to see you, very glad," he muttered, returning to the window. Here sheets of paper, books and quill pens were scattered on the small bare table, the windowsill and the floor.

"Menshikov!" Peter sucked his ink-stained finger. "Menshikov, I'll have that clerk's nostrils split—you tell him so! His only work is to trim the pens, and the devil sleeps all day. Oh, these people, these people!" As Patkul and Karlowicz remained standing expectantly, Peter suddenly recalled himself. "Menshikov, bring some chairs for the guests, take their hats. Here. . . ." He tapped his nails on the small sheets of paper covered with crooked, slanting writing. "We have to begin with the A B C. In Moscow boobies of this kind grow up—seven feet tall. You've got to take a cudgel to them to make them study. Oh, these people, these people! Tell me, Herr Patkul, are those Englishmen, Ferguson and Grant, eminent scholars?"

"I heard about them when I was in London," Patkul replied. "They are not very famous men, they are not philosophers; they follow practical science rather."

"That's just it. Thanks to theology we're devoured by lice. Navigation, mathematics, mining, medicine! That's what we need." He took up the papers and again threw them on the table. "The trouble is, it has all to be done in a hurry."

He sat down crossing his legs and, his elbows on the table, began to smoke. Karlowicz, bursting with good health, wheezed and blinked at the Tsar. Patkul looked morosely at his feet. Menshikov coughed discreetly. The hand in which Peter held his pipe began to tremble:

"Well, have you written it? Have you brought it?"

"We have written out a secret treaty and have brought it," Patkul said firmly, raising his face that had grown pale. "Ask Karlowicz to read it."

"Read it out."

Menshikov tiptoed close to them. Karlowicz pulled out a small sheet of pale blue paper and, holding it far from his eyes, began to read, swelling with the effort:

"In order to aid the Russian Tsar to reconquer from Sweden the territories which it has unjustly wrested and to secure Russian dominion on the Baltic Sea, the King of Poland will begin war with the King of Sweden by the invasion of Livonia and Esthonia by Saxon troops, promising to persuade the Polish State to join in the hostilities. The Tsar, for his part, will begin military operations in Ingria and Karelia immediately on conclusion of peace with Turkey, not later than April in the year 1700 and, in the meantime, if necessary, will send a supporting army to the King of Poland in the guise of mercenary troops. The Allies agree not to enter into separate negotiations with the enemy and not to abandon each other. This Treaty is to be maintained in inviolable secrecy."

Moistening his dry lips Peter asked:
"Is that all?"
"That's all, Your Majesty."
Patkul said: "After receiving Your Majesty's approval, tomorrow I shall leave for Warsaw, and hope by the middle of December to bring you King August's authentic signature."

Peter stared with a strange expression—so fixedly that tears came to his eyes—into Patkul's yellowish, hard eyes. A smile stretched his mouth crookedly:

"It's a great undertaking. Well then. . . . Go to Warsaw, Johann Patkul."

5

Twelve o'clock struck resoundingly from the cathedral tower. Self-respecting citizens were preparing for their midday meal. Senators left their chairs in the session hall. Tradesmen closed their shop doors. The master craftsman put down his tools and said to his apprentices: "Wash your hands, my sons, and to prayer!" The aristocrat took off his spectacles and, rubbing his sad eyes, solemnly proceeded to the dining-hall, dark with the smoke of bygone glory. Merry groups of soldiers and sailors made for the taverns over whose doors hung appetising bunches of sausages or smoked hams.

There was probably only one man in the town who did not listen to the voice of common-sense: King Charles XII. On a small table by his bed a cup of chocolate was growing cold among bottles of golden Rhine wine. The purple curtains on the tall windows had been drawn back. In the garden snow was falling on the bushes, still green, cut in the shape of globes, pyramids and rectangles. The mirror over the mantelpiece reflected the snowy light; it also reflected two candelabra from which wax stalactites were hanging from burnt-out candles. Pine logs crackled on the hearth. The king's trousers were hanging over the head of a golden Cupid at the foot of the bed. Silk skirts and a woman's underclothes were scattered on chairs.

With his elbow resting on the pillow, Charles was reading aloud from Racine. Between the verses he stretched out his hand towards a goblet of aromatic wine. By his side, with the quilted coverlet pulled up to the tip of her nose, a black-haired woman was dozing; her curls were dishevelled, the rouge on her cheeks was rubbed off, and her face looked yellow, almost the same colour as the wine in the goblet.

This was the frivolous Athalie, Countess Desmont, notorious for her escapades. The course of her life was as erratic as the flight of a bat. She could wear with the same elegance a court dress, an actress's costume or the uniform of an officer of the Guards. She could let herself down on a rope-ladder from a window to escape the unwelcome attentions of the Imperial or the Royal Police. She had sung in the opera in Vienna, but had lost her voice in mysterious circumstances. She had danced in the presence of Louis XIV in a fairy-play staged by Molière. Disguised as a musketeer, she had accompanied Marshal Luxemburg to the siege of the Flemish towns, and it was said that, after the capture of Namur, her haversack was packed full of jewellery. She went to London, apparently on the insistence of the French court, and impressed the English with her fine saddle horses and her gowns. Several peers of England surrendered to her charms and, finally, the handsome hero, the Duke of Marlborough. But the Duchess of Marlborough sent her a warning to leave London by the first ship. And now the wind of adventure had blown her into the Swedish king's bed.

"Love, love," Charles said, stretching his hand towards the bottle, "and once again love! In the long run it gets boring. Racine wearies me. Pyrrhus, the King of the Myrmidons, was probably not a bad soldier, but he talks wretched nonsense all through the five acts of the play. I prefer Plutarch or Cæsar's commentaries. Do you want some wine?"

"Leave me alone, Your Majesty," the countess answered, without opening her eyes. "My head is splitting; I doubt if I shall live through the day."

Charles laughed and drank from the glass. There was a scratching at the door. Absorbed in Racine Charles said languidly: "Come in." Baron Berkenhelm, a gentleman of the bedchamber, came in smiling with a rustle of silk. His tip-tilted nose, with a small wen, seemed to express his eagerness to impart the very latest news.

With a bow to the king's trousers, he began, in pleasing language, to recount various unimportant happenings at the palace. Nothing could escape his inquisitive mind, even such a trifle as a suspicious noise during the night in the bedchamber of the virtuous lady-in-waiting Anna Bostrem. Athalie groaned, turning over on her right side.

"My God, my God, what nonsense!"

The baron was not disconcerted; evidently he had something more vital to report. "Today," he said, "at nine in the morning, the shop-keepers presented a new petition to the Senate asking for a review of the civil list." Charles snorted. "There is no limit to these burghers' greed," the baron went on, "I have just seen the French ambassador —he was riding with some magnificent English harriers to hunt in the snow; and what a stallion he's got! It's the one he won at cards from Rehnsköld—I told him of the petition, and he shrugged his shoulders. 'Evidently a Huguenot intrigue'—those were his words—'those shop-keepers and tradesmen are dispersed all over Europe. They took sixty million livres out of France with them. These heretics are stubborn, and they're undermining the very principle of monarchy wherever they can. They are all in secret touch with one another: in Switzerland, England, Holland and France. They use every opportunity to instil hatred of the nobility and of the king among the burghers'."

"What else have you learnt?" Charles asked gloomily.

"Of course I went to the Senate. Today's petition was only a pretext among others. I had a word or two with some of the senators in the corridors. They are preparing a law to restrict the king's right to declare war."

Charles angrily closed Racine's *Andromache* and flung it aside. He sat up, tucking the bedclothes round him and said:

"I want to know what you've heard today." Berkenhelm looked pointedly at the countess's head. "Rubbish! There are no ears here that should not hear; tell me what you know."

"Yesterday a nobleman arrived from Riga in a merchant ship. I have not managed to see him yet. He says—if he can be believed— that Patkul has suddenly turned up in Moscow."

The countess lifted her head slightly from the pillow. Charles bit his lip and said: "Go and send Count Piper to me."

Berkenhelm flapped his hands in their lace cuffs like wings, and skimmed over the carpet out of the room. Charles looked through the window at the falling snow. His narrow face with its high forehead, long nose and girlish mouth was as colourless as a winter's day. He did not notice the countess's eye looking at him with an ironical gleam through a lock of hair. As he watched the snowflakes, he was aware of the new sensations within himself: rising anger and prudent calculation.

When he heard heavy footsteps outside the door, he picked up a pillow and threw it over the countess's head. "Cover yourself up, I must be alone!"

He pulled his shirt straight and picked up the cup of chocolate which had long grown cold: following the custom of the French court, chocolate was always brought to the king in bed.

"Come in."

Privy Councillor Karl Piper, whom Charles had recently made a count, entered the room. He was tall, with thick legs, meticulously but not well dressed; his crumpled, guarded face was that of an experienced official.

Charles looked him up and down coldly and said:

"I have to learn the news from the court gossips."

"Sire, they hear it from me." Piper never smiled and never lost his equanimity; his burgher's legs could stand any pitching and rolling. "But they hear only what I deem necessary to give out for court gossip."

"Is Patkul in Moscow?"

Piper remained silent.

Charles raised his voice: "If the king pretends that he is alone, this means he is alone—for earth and sky, the devil take it!"

"Yes, Sire, Patkul is in Moscow, and with him is the well-known adventurer General Karlowicz."

"What are they doing there?"

"One can conjecture. But so far I have no precise information."

"But our envoys are in Moscow."

"Envoys sent at the instance of the Senate. The senators want peace in the East at any price; well, let them try for peace with the means at their disposal. In any case, we did not sacrifice a farthing from your treasury for this purpose."

"I wish I could scrape up that farthing in my treasury!" Charles said. "Have you heard of the new petition? Have you heard what the senators are planning to present me with?" Piper shrugged his shoulders. Charles hastily set the cup on the table. "Are you aware that I no longer wish to play the part of the docile jackass? It was for the sake of these tedious skinflints that my father ruined the nobility. Now these 'Huguenots' want to turn me into a dumb puppet! They are making a mistake!" He nodded his narrow head at Piper. "Yes, yes, they're making a mistake. I know all you can tell me, Count Piper: I'm scatterbrained, my purse is empty and my reputation unsavoury. Cæsar conquered Rome through his victories in Transalpine Gaul. Cæsar was no less fond of women, wine and follies than I am. Set your mind at rest: I have no intention of storming our most respected Senate with a cavalry charge. There is plenty of scope for glory in Europe." He bit his lip. "If Karlowicz is in Moscow, this means that we have to deal with King August?"

"It seems to me that he will not be the only one."

"You mean?"

"If I'm not mistaken, there is a coalition against us."

"So much the better. Who are they?"

"I am collecting information."

"Excellent. Let the Senate carry on its own deliberations and we shall carry on ours. You have nothing further to report? Thank you, I will not detain you any longer."

Piper bowed clumsily and withdrew, somewhat perplexed: the unexpected twists of the king's thoughts were enough to bewilder anyone. Piper was cautiously preparing for a struggle with the Senate, which feared war expenditure more than anything else on earth. After a brief interval, there was the pungent smell of war again, from the Rhine to the Baltic lands. War was the only road to power. Charles realised this, but he was too ardently and prematurely longing to rush into battle: his ardour alone was not enough.

In the passage, at the door of the bedchamber, Piper took Berkenhelm by the elbow and said anxiously:

"Try to distract the king's attention; arrange a great hunt, get him out of Stockholm for a few days. I will provide the money."

Charles continued to sit in his bed; his pupils were dilated, like those of a man who contemplates imagined events. Athalie angrily threw the pillow off her head and, holding up her nightdress with her teeth, began to straighten her hair. She had beautiful arms and her shoulders were the colour of old ivory. The smell of musk at last attracted the king's attention.

"Have you met King August?" he asked. Athalie's dark, round eyes rested on him in a vacant gaze. "They say he is the most dashing cavalier in Europe, fortune's favourite. He spends as much as four hundred thousand zlotys on masquerades and firework displays. Piper swears that August once said of me that I had fallen into my father's jackboots and that it would be a good thing to pull me out and give me a whipping."

Athalie let the lace of her nightdress drop from her teeth and broke into gay, husky laughter. One of Charles's eyelids flickered.

"Didn't I say that August is witty and brilliant? He has his own army of ten thousand Saxon infantry and has large schemes. Naturally, with such a king in his father's jackboots, Sweden is as helpless as a sheep. All the same, I want to give myself the pleasure of reminding August of that story when my dragoons bring him to my tent with his arms bound behind his back."

"Bravo, boy!" Athalie said. "To the success of all your enterprises!" She drained a goblet of Rhenish wine at a gulp and wiped her lips with the lace of the sheet.

Charles jumped out from under the bedclothes and, barefooted, in his nightshirt that reached to his heels, ran to his desk. Out of a secret drawer he took a jewel-case in which lay a diamond tiara. Sitting on the side of the bed, he put the tiara against Athalie's dark curls and said:

"Will you be faithful to me?"

"In all probability, Your Majesty. You are nearly half my age; sometimes I feel almost maternal towards you." She kissed his nose, as it was the first object that met her lips, and turned the tiara round in her fingers with a tender smile.

"Athalie, I want you to go to Warsaw. The *Olaf* will be sailing in a few days' time; she's a fine ship. You will land in Riga. Horses, a covered sledge, men and money—everything will be in readiness. You will write to me by every post."

Athalie looked with curious attention at his youthful eyes: they were clear, hard and—the devil take these northern watery-grey eyes!—somewhere they concealed an insane will. There was promise in the lad. From force of habit, acquired in the course of her campaigns with Marshal Luxemburg, she gave a low whistle.

"Is it Your Majesty's wish that I should find my way into King August's bed?"

Charles immediately went over to the fireplace, put his hands on his hips and half-closed his eyelids as though in languor:

"I will forgive you any betrayal," he said. "But if that happens, by the Holy Gospel, I will find you wherever you may hide and kill you."

6

In Kitay-gorod people talked of nothing but the Brovkins. Peter, as suddenly as usual, was intent on marrying off the youngest of the Buynosov princesses—a descendant of Rurik—to Artamon Brovkin. He abandoned all serious affairs. Ministers and boyars visited the palace in vain; the only reply they got was: "No one knows where the Tsar is."

One evening, when the street-barriers were already being put up, he drove to Brovkin's house. Ivan Artemyich was in the kitchen with the peasants, playing cards by the light of a tallow candle; he liked to amuse himself in the old way. Suddenly a head in a three-cornered hat appeared, bending forward in the low door. At first they thought it was some soldier guarding the stores who had come in to warm himself. Suddenly they froze. Peter laughed, looking the host up and down: he didn't look very dignified in his worn-out hareskin jacket, his grey head hunched between his shoulders in fear.

Peter asked for some kvass and seated himself on a bench. In the presence of the peasants and clerks he said:

"Ivan, once I was a matchmaker for you. I want to be one again. Make your bow."

Brovkin, his skin all at once greasy, flopped down on to the earthen floor without a word and bowed to Peter's feet.

"Ivan," Peter said, "go and fetch your son."

Artamon was already there, behind the stove. Peter placed him between his knees and looked at him searchingly:

"How is it, Ivan, that you've been keeping this fine fellow hidden from me? I'm giving myself the devil's own trouble, while here they are. . . ." He turned to Artamon: "Can you read?"

Artamon only paled slightly and then, without hesitation, rattled off in French:

"I know French and German, and I can read and write quite well."

Peter gaped: "Holy Mother! Say some more!"

Artamon said the same to him in German. Then, screwing up his eyes at the candle, he said it in Dutch, only stumbling a little.

Peter kissed him, slapped him with his palm, pushed him away and pulled him back to him and shook him.

"Well, what do you say? You fine fellow! Ah! Well, Ivan, thank you for the gift! You'll have to say goodbye to the lad now. But you won't regret it. Just wait; I'll soon reward those who show intelligence with counts' titles."

He ordered supper to be served. Brovkin implored him to go upstairs, into the living-rooms—this was no place for him! Behind the stove he hurriedly put on his wig and pulled on his waistcoat. He sent a servant secretly to fetch Sanka. The major-domo appeared in the door holding his silver-knobbed staff. Peter only laughed:

"I won't go upstairs. It's warmer here. Cook, set on the table whatever you've got in the oven!"

He made Artamon sit by him and talked to him in German. He jested and poured out wine for the clerks and peasants, and made them sing songs. Elderly peasants, standing closely packed at the door, began to sing in growling voices, like bears. Suddenly Sanka—powdered, half-naked, dressed in silk—burst into the kitchen. Peter seized her by the hands and seated her on his other side. Unabashed, she added her sweet, drawling voice to the peasants' chorus. She moved the candle closer to her face and threw sly, limpid glances at Peter. The feasting went on till after midnight.

In the morning Peter and the groomsmen drove to Prince Roman's house to ask for Natalia's hand in marriage to Artamon. And so he went on, visiting Brovkin and Prince Roman in turn, settling the terms, with some fifty people trailing in his wake. They dressed up and they feasted at the girl's and the young man's farewell parties, and the marriage was noisily celebrated on the Feast of Intercession. The wedding cost Brovkin a pretty penny.

A fortnight later Sanka and her husband left for Paris.

They travelled slowly, joining up with sledge-trains. There were long waits at the posting-stations to feed the horses. Plenty of snow had fallen, the days were clear and travelling was easy.

At the inn in Viazma Alexandra quarrelled with her husband. He had intended to stay overnight, take a bath and, on that next day, after mass, dine with the governor, who was a distant relative of his; and also to re-shoe the horses, and other things.

"I want to travel quickly. This road has worn me out," Alexandra said to her husband. "We'll rest in Riga."

"Sanka! I've already told you, there are robbers beyond Viazma. Trains of five hundred sledges are put together to cross those parts in safety."

"I know nothing about that."

They were sitting at supper upstairs, in a small clean room, lit by icon-lamps. Vasily was in an unfastened travelling sheepskin coat,

Alexandra in an acorn-coloured velvet gown with long sleeves and a downy shawl; her fair hair was wound in a plait round her head. She ate nothing and only crumbled her bread. Her face was drawn and there were shadows under her eyes—due to her impatience. Lord, what a woman!

Volkov, chewing salt ham without pleasure, said:

"Tell me, what kind of person are you? It's a real curse. You know no rest, no peace—you neither sleep, nor eat—and you won't even talk like a human being. Why do you want to go off to the ends of the earth? To dance minuets with kings? But will they want to?"

"It's only because this is an inn that I listen to you."

Vasily lowered his fork with a piece of ham on it and looked for a long time at his wife's forehead, her eyebrows wistfully raised, her dark blue eyes lost in the devil knew what visions.

"Oh, Alexandra, I am quiet and patient."

"Shout, if you like; what do I care?"

Vasily shook his head reproachfully. He loved his wife, though it humiliated him, for she did not seem to deserve it. When disputes arose and she started to shower him with stinging abuse, he was completely at a loss. And so it was now: he knew that he would give way, though only a rash fool would decide to travel through the forests from Viazma to Smolensk. Terrible stories were told about these places. Travellers were set upon by the robber chief Yesmen Sokol; you would be travelling, say, in daylight; suddenly on the road you would see a tall fellow in a high cap, in birch-bark shoes, with a knife in his belt, a mouth from ear to ear, large teeth. He would whistle, and the horses would fall on their knees, and then there was nothing to be done but recite the prayer for the dying.

"If I was afraid of robbers, I might as well have stayed in Moscow," Alexandra said. "We have good horses, they'll get us past. It would be even better if it happened, there'd be something to talk about. I don't want to talk to people about the way you snored at the inns."

She pushed away her plate and called her Kalmuk maid, ordering her to bring her the book and make the bed. The manuscript book had been written out by her brother Artamon; it was a translation from Puffendorf's *History,* the chapter dealing with the Gauls. She put it on her knees and, bending over it, began to read.

Volkov, with his cheek resting on his hand, looked at Sanka's lovely head, at her neck with the little tendrils of hair. A fairy princess. Yet not so long ago she had mowed grass with a scythe and driven a cart filled with horse-dung. And now she was not afraid to travel to

Paris and even to talk all sorts of nonsense to the king. Ah, Sanka, Sanka, if only you would settle down and bear me a child, if only we could live together quietly at home!

Sanka was reading, moving her lips:

" 'And, besides, the French are people with gay minds, quick in everything they do, ready and graceful, especially in their outer adornment and the movements of their bodies, and natural beauty is apparent in them. Many of them glorify themselves in the lust of Venus and the embraces of beautiful persons of the female sex, and perform all this with the greatest boasting. When other nations try to resemble them and imitate them, they dishonour themselves and make laughing-stocks of themselves. . . .' "

"Instead of sitting there like that—" She raised her head, and Volkov, who was just preparing to yawn, started. "You had better practice your swordsmanship on the way."

"What's that for?"

"When you get to Paris you'll see what for!"

"Really, you're too much!" Volkov said angrily. He rose from the table, put on his cap and went out into the yard to take a look at the horses. A misty moon hung high above the snow-covered roofs of the sheds. There was not a star in the sky: only tiny needles of ice gleamed as they fell. The still air froze the hairs in his nostrils. The horses were munching in the dark shadow under a penthouse. The watchman near the little church nearby drowsily clacked his rattle.

A dog came up to Vasily, smelt his high speckled felt boot and, raising its muzzle with its marked eyebrows, looked at him as if surprised and expectant. Vasily suddenly felt a great repugnance to the idea of leaving this native quiet and journeying to Paris. Scrunching his felt boots on the snow he turned round regretfully. A mild light showed through the little mica window in the timbered room upstairs: Sanka was reading Puffendorf. There was nothing to be done; it was his fate.

The crimson sunset, flaming with a wild light, glowed over the tree-tops of the forest. Tree-trunks and ragged roots flew past; heavy, purple branches grazed the top of the sledge and scattered snow over it. Volkov, leaning forward to his waist over the unfastened leather apron of the sledge, held the reins and shouted in a frenzied voice. The coachman had been knocked off his seat and was lying far back beyond the bend. The stout horses, harnessed tandem—the black one, covered with hoarfrost, in the shafts, a chestnut one in front, and a vicious grey mare in the lead—snorted as they galloped along. The sledge was flung this way and that over the holes in the road. Behind them the robbers were running in a straggling line. The whole forest resounded with their yells.

Some five minutes earlier, over there, before the bend, where a cart-track crossed the main road, ten tall men armed with axes and staves had come out from behind last year's hay-rick. The frightened driver foolishly reined in. Four of the men rushed to the horses with terrible shouts of "Halt! Halt!" Others, sinking deep in the snow, ran to the sledge. The driver dropped the reins and waved his mittened hands at the robbers. They hit him on the head with a cudgel.

It all happened in a flash. It was the leading mare that saved them: it reared, pulling the two men who were hanging on to the bridle off their feet, and began to kick and bite. Sanka unfastened the apron and shouted: "Catch the reins!" Then she pulled the pistol from the breast of her husband's sheepskin coat and fired into a bearded face. The men jumped back at the shot, but mainly because the sight of a woman surprised them. The horses plunged forward. Volkov snatched up the reins and away they went. Sanka kept hammering her husband's back with the butt of the pistol, shouting: "Drive on! Drive on!"

The chase ended. Steam rose from the horses. In front they could see the tail of a long train of sledges. Volkov let the horses walk. He looked round, searching for his cap in the sledge. He saw Sanka's round eyes and dilated nostrils and said:

"Well, are you satisfied? You wouldn't believe in the robber-chief Yesmen Sokol. Oh, you silly fool! You've got the brains of a hen. What are we going to do without a driver? And the pity of it—he was a good fellow. And all because of your woman's folly, you she-devil."

Sanka did not even notice that he was swearing at her. Ah, this was life! Not slumber and boredom!

7

Every day long trains of sledges entered Moscow through every gate, bringing men for the regular army; some were tied up like robbers, but many came voluntarily, because of their poverty. Decrees written on sheets of tin were nailed to posts in the public squares of Moscow, calling for volunteers for the regular army. A soldier was promised eleven roubles a year, bread and other food and a ration of vodka. Serfs and bonded servants, who lived in semi-starvation in the crowded mansions of the boyars, having quarrelled with the house-steward, or even thrown their caps at the feet of the boyar himself, went off to Preobrazhensk. Up to a thousand men were brought together there every day.

Sometimes the men had to wait in the cold till dusk before officers on the porch finished calling out the names from the register. Then they were taken to the basement of the palace. Moustached men of the Preobrazhensky regiment sternly ordered them to strip. A man felt shy as he unwound the linen bands round his legs and stripped naked; then, covering his private parts with his hand, he would go into the upper room. Here, between lighted candles, sat long-haired officers in felt hats; they looked like hawks at the man as he came in: "Name? Surname? How old are you?" But they never enquired what he was: he might even be a fugitive serf or a robber. They measured his height, pulled back his lips to see his teeth and made him show his private parts. "Fit. To such-and-such a regiment."

Newly built soldiers' quarters stretched into the snow-covered fields behind the palace courtyard. The men accepted as fit were taken to the log-houses in crowds; the houses were tightly packed. In each, a junior non-commissioned officer with a cane was in command. To the new arrivals he said: "Obey my orders as you would obey God: I shan't give an order twice, I'll flay the hide off your back. For you I am God, and Tsar, and father." They were well fed, but were not allowed any freedom: not like the old days in the strelets regiments. This was soldiering! A drum awakened them. Before they had eaten they were driven into a well-trampled field and made to form fours. The first thing they were taught was to distinguish the right hand and the left. Many a peasant had never in his life stopped to think what sort of hands he had. The cane impressed it on his memory. An officer would then appear, generally not a Russian, and often half-drunk. Facing the line, he would stare with bleary eyes at the rough peasant coats, the sheepskin jackets, the birch-bark shoes, the felt and sheep-skin caps. Puffing out his cheeks he would begin to bawl in a foreign tongue. He insisted that they understand him and threatened them with his cane. Under the smart they gradually began to understand: "Marschieren"—march; "Halt"—stop; "Schwein" or "Russisch Schwein"—meant he was abusing them. After breakfast they were out in the field again. When they had had their dinner they went out for a third time to march with sticks or muskets. They were taught to form solid ranks, as in Eugene of Savoy's army, to march in step, to fire volleys and to attack with fixed bayonets. Men who did the wrong thing were brought out on the spot in front of the line, made to drop their trousers in the snow and flogged unmercifully.

The military exercises were difficult: "Load your musket!" You had to remember it all in order: "Open the priming-pan. Put the powder on the pan. Close the pan. Take out the cartridge. Bite on the cartridge. Put it in the barrel. Take out the ramrod. Ram down the charge. Cock the musket. Take aim. . . ." They fired in platoons: one rank loading as they knelt on one knee, another, standing up, fired; they also fired in *Niederfall,* when all ranks, except one, fell flat in turn.

The drilling was directed by an Austrian Brigadier Adam Ivanovich Weide, who, together with General Artamon Mihaylovich Golovin and Prince Anikita Ivanovich Repnin, had orders to organise three divisions, each consisting of nine regiments.

Lieutenant Alexey * Brovkin collected in the North five hundred men fit for service and handed them over, at some places to the governors, at others to *Landrats* (district chiefs in the old nomenclature) to be sent to Moscow. Now he was on his way beyond Povenets, into the dense forests, where he had been told there were many fugitive serfs and tramps round the hermitages. People who knew these parts tried to dissuade him from adventuring so far:

"Rumours have got to the hermitages and the dissenters are on their guard. There are many of them, while there are only ten of you on three sledges. You'll all disappear without leaving a trace."

The people in those parts were rough fellows, hunters and woodmen. They lived in huge solid houses built of logs, with the cattle-yard and threshing barn all under one roof. The villages were called parishes. From one habitation to another was several days' journey through trackless forests. Alexey realised that the enterprise was no easy one. But you could not go through life without fear. Now, if you were to report to Peter Alexeyevich that you had reached the North and then taken fright, he would look down at you like a crane from his height, with a devouring glance, twitch his shoulder and turn away: that indeed meant fear, and an end to your good fortune, no matter how hard you tried. Alexey was young, eager and obstinate. Even in his sleep he did not forget how he had come to Moscow long ago with a quarter of a kopek in his cheek; he had wrested his white officer's scarf from fate by sheer grit.

* Alioshka.

In the Povenets market Alexey met a hunter called Yakim Krivopalov and engaged him as a guide. Yakim had been working for twenty years supplying the merchant Revyakin, hunting silver foxes, martens, squirrels and, in former days, sables too, but these were no longer to be found in those parts. He would bring his pelts to Povenets, hand them over to the agent and go on a spree till he had drunk away everything but the cross round his neck. Revyakin's agent would again furnish him with clothes, arquebus and ammunition. That autumn, hunting had been bad, and the records showed that not only was there nothing coming to him, but that for at least two winters he would be in debt. He quarrelled with the agent and drank away all he had. Alexey Brovkin picked him up by the tavern, lying naked and badly beaten in the snow. Yakim proved worth his weight in gold, so long as he knew there was a bottle of spirits in the sledge, under the driver's seat.

Yakim ran on his short snowshoes ahead of the sledges, showing the way. The forests were wonderful and terrifying. Between the trunks of the trees they could see enormous rounded outcroppings of rock grown with trees. When they drove out on to the shore of some deserted lake, the smooth, snowy surface made their eyes ache. Sometimes they would hear the deep roar of falling water. Yakim would come and perch himself on the side of the sledge:

"People here," he said, "have never been counted. There are such devil's thickets, only I know how to find the way. But the people here are fierce; it will be hard to take them."

For the night, they would turn off to a wintering hut or a clearing on the bank of some little stream, where felled timber lay under the snow ready for spring burning. The horses would be unharnessed by the crooked hut. The soldiers cut down fir branches and dragged them inside. They made a fire on the earthen floor, and the smoke rolled softly out of the chinks under the roof and rose into the grey sky over the forest. Yakim bustled about until he got his cup of vodka. Then he would settle down quietly on the branches close to the fire—a real wood-goblin himself, with his broad beard, thick lips, wide nostrils and round eyes, like those of a forest creature—and start his tales:

"You see, I've been everywhere; all over the Vyga, lived for weeks in the Vyga hermitage. I know retreats that can be reached only by one path that you follow with fear. I can't find out where the elder Nektary is hiding. They conceal him and won't tell. If you so much as mention him to any dissenter, he'll fall silent and won't speak even if you carved him to pieces. Yet it would be useful for your business to see him; he might let some two hundred young fellows go with you. Oh, he's a power!"

"What is he among them?" Alexey asked. "Is it something like a Patriarch?"

"He's an elder. The Archpriest Avvakum blessed him in Pustozersk before his execution. Some twelve years ago he burnt two and a half thousand dissenters in the Paleostrov monastery. They came up to the monastery at night over the ice, broke down the gates, locked up the monks and the superior in the cellar, and broke open the storerooms. He gave everyone plenty of food and drink. They took the treasure. Then they washed the icons in the church with holy water, lit the candles and held a service after their own manner. There weren't so many men with them, but lots of women and children. The governor came with streltsi over the ice from Povenets. 'Surrender!' For three days the peasants threatened to fight, but the streltsi had a cannon. So they dragged a lot of straw, tar and saltpetre into the church and in the night—it happened to be Christmas Eve—they burnt themselves to death. But Nektary got out, and some of the men with him. Three years later he burnt fifteen hundred people in Pudozhesk parish. Quite recently again there was burning in the woods near Lake Vol. They say it was he who did it. Now there are rumours of war, of recruiting for the army; there'll be a big immolation soon, believe me. The people are rallying to him in great numbers."

Alexey and the soldiers listened to him with wonder:

"To burn oneself to death voluntarily! Where do such people come from?"

"It's very simple," Yakim said. "Serfs and peasants paying quitrent, and bondsmen, flee to him from Novgorod and Tver, from Moscow and Vologda abandoning their homes and stock. These forests are strewn with human bones. Thousands come to the hermitages; how to feed them all? There's no grain here. They begin to moan and waver. So, to put a stop to their needless sinning, Nektary sends them straight to heaven."

"You're joking!"

"Alexey Ivanich, I never tell lies. There are even people who let themselves be buried alive. Over there, towards the White Sea, there's a little old man who administers raisins as Holy Communion: when he puts a raisin into someone's mouth, it means that he has given that person his blessing to lie down alive in a coffin."

"Get along with your stories! And at night time too!"

Alexey wrapped himself up in his sheepskin coat on the branches by the fire. A little later he said: "Yakim, we must get hold of this Nektary."

Two men on snowshoes came out of the forest into the moonlit clearing. A faint tang of smoke drifted from the hut. Horses covered with matting stood with drooping heads by the sledges, and the soldier on sentry duty slept, slumped over the front of a sledge, his musket held between the sleeves of his sheepskin coat.

The two men on snowshoes soundlessly made the round of the hut. Then they stood still and listened, leaning on their bear-spears. There was a pale halo round the moon and the forest, covered with hoar-frost, was silent. Inside the hut someone muttered in a low voice. A horse by the sledge sighed with the whole of its belly. The sentry lay with his moustached face bathed in moonlight, like a man frozen to death.

One of the men on snowshoes said:

"Shall we tie him up? He's fast asleep. Afterwards we could throw him into the fire with a prayer."

The other peered with his beard thrust out.

"It would make a noise," he said, "he might shout. There are ten of them in there."

"Then what shall we do?"

"Give him a jab with a bear-spear. Then we can prop the door fast from outside."

"Oh, Petrusha, Petrusha!" the first man said shaking his head in its cap with big ear-pieces. "What makes you speak like that? We're all of one blood: he's a man, not a wild beast. It is said that man receives baptism in fire. In fire. But you want to use your spear! You'd damn your soul."

"I'll take the sin upon myself."

"Don't dare to think of it! Don't tempt me, for the love of Christ!"

"But it would be easy; quick and silent."

"I wonder what Father Nektary would say to you for having such thoughts."

"I only want to do what's best."

They fell silent, thinking what to do. The shadow of an owl glided unevenly over the bluish snow: the owl had sensed a prey and was circling, curse it! The door of the hut creaked suddenly, and Yakim's wood-goblin's head appeared in the opening; he was evidently going out to relieve himself. Catching sight of the two he gasped, sprang back and raised the alarm. The two glided behind the snow-laden branches and ran. They heard the thunder of a shot that shattered the silence of the forest.

They ran for a long time, purposely making innumerable turns to confuse their tracks. When they pushed their way through a fir thicket to the bed of a brook, daybreak was already near, the moon rode high. From somewhere quite close came the slow mournful clanging of an iron sheet being struck.

Andrey Golikov was ringing for early mass. He was wearing a much-worn fox-fur coat, with the fur inside, but was barefooted. Stamping his blue feet bitten by the snow, he repeated in a chant the words of Avvakum: "Join the martyrs' rank! Join the army of the apostles! Join the choir of the saints!" and—bang!—struck with an iron stick the sheet of iron that hung in the place of a bell on a gabled post opposite the hermitage gates. This was the punishment imposed on him by the elder because the day before, which was a fast-day, he had grown thirsty and drunk some kvass.

The community assembled at the sound of the clanging. The inhabitants of the hermitage came out of their cells, men and women separately. The hermitage, surrounded by a log wall, was not large. Many of the people lived outside, on the banks of the stream or on the edge of the marshy island. They came from there by forest paths, and those who lived farthest hurried, fearing to be late; the elder was very strict.

In the centre of the hermitage, among straw-ricks set close together, stood the prayer-house: a low log structure with a broad, square, sloping roof, and a single cupola set on a small octagonal tower.

The people, as they entered the gates, stepped fearfully, with bowed heads and hands pressed to their breasts: men, still young or middle-aged, and women in coarse linen shrouds on top of their warm coats and shawls pulled down over their faces. Dull and cracked, full of the sorrow of earthly existence, the iron sheet rang out in the moonlit mist, and the only other sound was the creaking of birch-bark shoes on the snow.

The people crossed themselves with two fingers at the door and then humbly stepped into the prayer-house. Its logs walls were covered with rime; one-kopek tapers burned in front of icons painted in the ancient style. This was like a miracle: a taper in the wild forests.

The people went down on their knees, the men on the right, the women on the left, and a curtain of patchwork was drawn between them on a bast cord.

Panting heavily, the two men on snowshoes ran through the hermitage gates and shouted to Andrey:

"Stop ringing! A calamity has happened!"

"Hurry, tell the elder to come out to us!"

Andrey's soul was drawn as taut as a string, from fasting, from sleepless watching, from constant terror. He dropped his iron stick in alarm and began to tremble and pant. But not in vain had Nektary taught him how to overcome evil spirits (and they are innumerable: as many demons as there are thoughts). He hastily sent up a silent cry: "Satan, my enemy, get thee gone!" and, picking up the stick, struck the sheet of iron under the penthouse, at the same time shaking his head: don't get in my way, go away.

"Andrey, we're telling you: that officer with the soldiers is only three miles from here."

"At least don't gong so loud, they'll hear it. Yakim is with them, he'll bring them straight here by the sound."

Through his chattering teeth Andrey replied:

"The elder is still in his cell. Go straight to him."

They discarded their snowshoes and went off. Both of them, Stepan Barmin and Peter Kozhevnikov, were from Povenets and lived by hunting and fishing. Because of their Old Believers' ways the governor of Povenets had more than once seized their property and had them beaten, and had driven off their cattle. They grew tired of it and, for two years now, their wives and children had been living in the Vyga hermitage, while they themselves lived here and there, wherever it was farthest from human habitation and best suited to their trade. When the rumour had gone round that an officer with soldiers (shaven, meat-eaters, reeking a mile off of tobacco, the "devil's weed",) was coming to the hermitages, Nektary had ordered Stepan and Peter to watch them, lead them astray and, if possible, without committing a sin, to do away with the servants of Antichrist altogether.

People were not easily admitted into Nektary's presence. A lay-brother came out into the cold passage; the elder had two of them: Andrey and this one, the lame Porfiry, a weedy youth with turned-up eyes. They told him their tale in whispers. Porfiry put his head on one side and breathed: "Come in." The woodmen pulled off their caps and tried to make themselves small as they stepped out of the passage into the cell: they were inordinately healthy and rough. The elder regarded robust flesh with disfavour.

Standing at his lectern Nektary gave a sidelong glance at the two men. He was small, bent, and dressed in a black cloak of homespun material and ancient cut. His narrow, wedge-shaped beard hung nearly to his knees; his eyes, under their black eyebrows, were like coals. The taper, stuck to the worm-eaten book-cover, was crackling softly, probably forecasting hard frost. The stove, built of lake-side boulders, radiated heat. The log walls were scraped clean and bunches of herbs hung from the ceiling on bits of bast.

Icicles began to slide off Stepan's and Peter's moustaches, but they dared not wipe themselves or make any movement until the elder had finished. He was reading in a terrible voice. From a dark corner a man was looking at him, lying on his side. He was supposed to be possessed and was chained by his waist to an iron staple in the wall. In a trough by the stove, dough was rising, covered with an old cassock.

"Well, what is it?" Nektary asked, turning towards the men and thrusting his grey beard towards them. They did not fear bears and tackled an elk single-handed, but in his presence they felt completely cowed. Stepan began to give a muddled account of what had happened. Peter diffidently confirmed his story.

"So," Nektary said softly, "so you, Petrusha, wanted to kill that soldier with your bear-spear, while you Stephan, were afraid of committing a sin?"

Stepan replied eagerly:

"Father, we have been dogging them for a fortnight. Yakim—curse him!—knows these parts well, he's leading them straight here. They're careful, otherwise it would be easy: block the door of the hut and set fire to it. So with a prayer, we'd have baptised them. It would have been good for them and good for us. But, you see, it couldn't be done. And to kill, as robbers do—Jesus preserve us! This time it was just the devil tempting us."

"Did I give you a blessing to do this burning?" the elder asked. The men looked at him in astonishment but did not answer. "Your prayer must have been a very hot one, Stepan—yes, indeed!—to baptise ten men by fire. Oh, oh! Who has given you such power?"

Stepan frowned. Peter blinked at the elder not quite understanding what he meant.

"Porfiry, my dear boy, put a coal in the censer, blow on it, with a prayer," the elder said. The lame Porfiry took the censer off its peg, hobbled to the stove, put a live coal on the cedar resin and blew on it; then he presented it to the elder, kissing his hand. His long arm almost scraping the floor with the jingling censer, Nektary began to send the smoke into the men's faces, then from the sides, and at last went round them from the back, whispering and bowing. After that he handed the censer to Porfiry, pulled his plaited chaplet from his leather belt and slashed Stepan painfully across the face. Then he did the same to Peter. The men dropped to their knees, while he, whispering with lips that had gone blue: "Pride, accursed pride!" beat them on their cheeks with growing frenzy. The possessed man suddenly neighed loudly with laughter and began to tear at his chain, straining at it like a watchdog:

"Beat them, beat them, old man! Beat the devil out of them!"

The elder grew weary, his frenzy left him, and he panted heavily.

"You'll understand later on what this was for," he said coughing a little. "Go with Jesus!"

The men stepped cautiously out of the cell. The moonlight had dimmed; beyond the prayer-house, beyond the black forest, day was breaking. It was freezing hard. The men gesticulated in bewilderment: wherein lay their fault? Why? What were they to do now?

"We have walked much but eaten little," Peter said in a low voice.

"How can we ask him now?"

"Perhaps he'll give us some bread?"

"Better not show ourselves to him. Let's go as we are, to those others again. We'll kill a squirrel and eat it."

Andrey Golikov climbed on to the stove trembling in every limb. On his way to the prayer-house the elder had ordered him to stop ringing; he did not allow him to attend mass: "Go, put the loaves into the oven." Andrey's frozen feet ached on the hot stones; hunger made him dizzy. He lay on his stomach, gnawing the coverlet under him with his teeth. To stop himself from screaming he kept repeating to himself a quotation from Avvakum: "Man is pus and excrement. It is good for me to live with dogs and pigs; they stink in the same way as my soul stinks, with a foul stench. I stink because of my sins, like a dead dog."

The possessed peasant, moving about on his chain in the corner, said:

"Last night the old man guzzled honey again."

This time Andrey did not shout at him: "Don't lie!" but only clenched his teeth harder on the coverlet. He no longer had the strength to suppress the terrible devil of doubt in himself. This devil had entered him after an incident of no great importance. The three of them—Nektary and his two lay-brothers—were fasting for forty days, touching no food and drinking nothing but water, and that only a small mouthful at a time. In order that Andrey and Porfiry should not waver as they read the rules, he ordered them to wet their lips with kvass and dampen their chests with hot water. As for himself he said: "I do not need it: an angel freshens my lips with the dew of paradise." And it was really astounding: Andrey and Porfiry could hardly murmur from weakness; only their eyes were still alive, while he remained quite fresh.

Then one night Andrey saw the elder climb softly from the stove, scoop up a spoonful of honey from the pot and eat it with a piece of unconsecrated church bread. Andrey's limbs went cold: it seemed to him that he would rather have seen a man's throat cut before his eyes than this. And he did not know whether to keep to himself what he had seen or to speak of it. In the morning, however, he confessed it with tears. Nektary nearly choked:

"You cur! You fool! That was the devil, not I. And you were pleased. That's what accursed flesh does to you. You would sell the kingdom of heaven for a spoonful of honey."

He started to belabour Andrey with the forked pole used for putting pots into the oven and chased him out of the cell on to the snow, clad only in his shirt. After this Andrey's thoughts left him in peace for a time. But when there happened to be no one else in the cell, the possessed peasant—who had been chained here since the autumn, mercifully in the warmth—said to him:

"Look, the spoon is sticky with honey, yet it was washed last evening. Lick it."

Andrey swore at him. The next night the elder again ate honey secretly, rapidly smacking his lips, like a hare. At dawn, when all the others were still asleep, Andrey examined the spoon: it was sticky with honey! And a grey hair was stuck to it.

His soul was rent with a great doubt. Who was lying? Were his eyes deceiving him—the honey on the spoon, the grey hair from a moustache (it couldn't be the devil's hair, after all). Or was the elder lying? Whom to believe? There was a moment when he nearly went out of his mind: all was confusion, all was despair! Nektary constantly repeated: "Antichrist has come to the gates of the world and everything under the sky is full of his creatures. And in our land there is a great devil, whose measure is the deepest hell." And if it was so, how to be sure that he himself, Nektary, was not the devil? To beat you on the back with a forked pole was something the devil could do too. Everything was unclear, unsure as a moss-covered swamp. The only thing left was not to think about anything, to hang his head like a beaten cur and believe: believe with his belly. But what if he could not believe? If he could not help thinking? You could not crush thoughts, put them out like a candle; they flickered like summer lightning. Then did this, too, come from Antichrist? Were thoughts the lightning of Antichrist? Then suddenly everything inside Andrey swooned: whither was he going, whither was he rolling? He was small, poor, stupid. If only he could fall to the elder's feet and say: teach me, save me! But he could not: he kept seeing the moustache smeared with honey. He had come to the hermitage to seek a peaceful life, and had found doubt.

But later, physical weakness wore him down and his thoughts became blunted and less agitated. He endured the daily beatings as he would tickling. The elder treated him day after day with greater cruelty. With the other one it was: "Porfiry, my dear boy," but with Andrey—even horses weren't beaten like that. If only he could go away. But where? It was true that Denisov had said to Andrey in late December, when they had brought grain in sledges to the Vyga hermitage: "Come and live with us; give of your labours in adorning the church. When the ice breaks, I'll send you with wares to Moscow. I trust you." Andrey had refused: it was not what he wanted, which was quiet and serenity. He could see it in his mind: a cell in the forest, a little, old elder in a skull-cap, on a boulder by the stream, speaking of the heavenly light to his beloved lay-brother and to the beasts, who had come out of the forest to listen to him, and to the birds, who had come to perch on the boughs, and to the northern sun, shining palely on the calm smoothness of the solitary little stream. And this was the peace he had found! Never had there been such a tempest in his soul, not even when, in the nights of winter snowstorms, he had shivered in the crack of the Kitay-gorod wall, listening to the frozen bodies of the streltsi banging against each other and to the creaking of gallows.

The possessed peasant would begin to speak, glancing at the stove where Andrey lay prone:

"You won't last long here, you're too sickly. The old man will beat you into the grave; you stick in his throat. Oh, he's a tyrannical old man, and proud! The saints won't let him sleep. He reads the lives of the saints, and then he starts doing all sorts of strange things. He'd spend ten years in a pine-tree if it weren't for the fierce winters. And he burns people for the same reason, because he loves power. The forest king! I see through him, I, my friend, am cleverer than he is, I tell you. I'm cleverer than the whole lot of you. It's true that I'm possessed by three devils. The first devil is epilepsy, it's quite a strong devil. The second devil is laziness. If it weren't that, would I stay here chained up? The third devil is that I'm too clever, it's terrible! Just before epilepsy starts tormenting me, why, I understand everything. And I get so angry, everything disgusts me. I know about everyone —where he comes from and what a fool he is and what he expects. And I talk nonsense on purpose, for fun. I bite my chain and roll about; it's funny how they believe it. The elder, he stares too. He, my good fellow, is afraid of me. In spring I'll go away from him again. But you, Andrey, he'll beat your insides loose with his pole, you'll waste away. And more likely still—at his next burning you'll be the first to burn."

"Oh, hold your tongue, will you!"

Andrey climbed down from the stove, washed his hands, rolled up his sleeves and uncovered the trough with the dough. In the other cells the dough was made of one-third of flour and two-thirds of dried, crushed bark; but here the dough was made with flour alone and it had risen very high. The possessed peasant stretched up to look. Then he wrenched at the chain and pulled it out of the wall together with the staple. Andrey was alarmed, but the man said, rolling up his sleeves:

"That's nothing. I often do it. When the elder comes back, I'll stick the staple in again and stay there."

He also washed his hands and began to help Andrey to shape the loaves and put them into the oven.

"All the same, it's dull here, Andrey. Now if we could have a woman."

"Be quiet! Pah!" Andrey wanted to make a sign of the cross to protect himself against such words, but his fingers were sticky with dough. "Honestly, I'll complain to the elder."

"I'll teach you to complain! You silly fool, d'you think it's the wind makes the women in the hermitages pregnant? In the Vyga hermitage there are some thirty of them going about like cows in calf. And yet it's very strict there."

"That's all lies!"

"It looks to me as if you'd never tasted of this sweetness, Andrey."

"I won't pollute myself, not as long as I live."

"If only we could call in a nice, smooth woman and make her wash the floor! While she washes, you sit on a bench and your blood begins to run hotter and hotter. It's stronger than wine."

Andrey hastily rubbed the dough off his fingers and went out of the cell into the frost outside, just to stand there for a while. The dawn had spread broadly beyond the forest; the sun would rise at any minute now. The footprints in the snow were filled with a warm shade, now sugar-like snowdrifts lay against the huts and the tops of the great firs looked very green. The sound of plaintive singing came through the half-open door of the prayer-house. Stepan and Peter ran past Andrey again and shouted:

"They're coming! Shut the gates!"

Alexey Brovkin sent Yakim to have a talk with the dissenters and ask them who they were and how many in number, and why they refused to open the gates to an officer of the Tsar? He left the horses on the road in the wood and went up to the hermitage with the soldiers, who were ordered to load their muskets. Behind the high fence the snow-capped roofs sparkled and the eight-pointed cross on the prayer-house gleamed blue; plaintive singing still sounded from there, although the time for mass was long past.

Yakim knocked for a long time at the wicket-gate. Then he climbed up on the fence, looked round to see whether there were any dogs, and jumped down into the courtyard. To make himself look more formidable Alexey had put on his three-cornered hat and had strapped his sword-belt over his short sheepskin coat; he might get hold of some men if he drove fear into them. It wasn't likely that government clerks or agents of the Stewards' Chamber ever came into these fastnesses to collect double taxes from the dissenters. Time was passing. The soldiers kept looking at the sun hanging low in the sky; they had not eaten anything since morning. Alexey coughed angrily into his woollen mitten.

At last Yakim dropped over from inside the fence.

"Alexey Ivanovich," he said, "we're in luck—Nektary is here."

"Then why doesn't this devil's cousin open the gates? My men will get frostbitten."

"Alexey Ivanovich, the people have locked themselves in the prayer-house. You see, I met a man I know—a Novgorod peasant —they keep him chained up here. He told me there are two hundred in the flock, and some of them are suitable for soldiers; but it'll be difficult to get them; the elder wants to burn them."

Alexey stared sternly and incredulously at Yakim:

"How do you mean, burn them? Who gave him permission? We won't let him. The people aren't his; they're the Tsar's."

"That's just it: in their forests he's their Tsar."

"Stop talking nonsense!" Alexey frowned and called the soldiers. They came up rather unwillingly, realising that something unusual was afoot. "We won't argue long. Lads, break open the gate."

"Alexey Ivanovich, you had better be careful. There are straw-stacks all round the prayer-house, and inside it there's straw, tar and a barrel of gunpowder. It would be better if I could get the elder outside somehow. He must know himself that it's no laughing matter to induce two hundred people to do a thing like that. Show him some respect, Alexey Ivanovich—he's a masterful old man—and then you'll be able to settle the matter amicably."

Alexey pushed the talkative fellow out of the way and, going to the gate, tried to see how strong it was.

"Lads, bring a beam."

Yakim moved aside and stood blinking and looking on, curious to see what would happen next. The soldiers swung the beam and then drove it against the frozen timbers of the gate. After the third blow the distant singing of the dissenters stopped.

"Go into the prayer-house."

"I've told you I won't; leave me alone!" the possessed peasant repeated sullenly.

Nektary had come in out of breath, long drops of wax in his beard. The pupils of his eyes were narrowed to pin-points: either he was trying to inspire fear, or, more probably, he was beside himself. In a strangled voice he cried:

"Yevdokim, Yevdokim, Judgment Day has come! Save your soul! Only one hour remains before eternal torment! Oh, horror! The devils in you are rejoicing! Save yourself!"

"Go and drown yourself in the swamp!" Yevdokim shouted, angrily shaking his head. "What devils? There never were any in me. Go and play-act before fools!"

Nektary raised his chaplet. The possessed peasant crouched and gave him such a look from under his brows that the elder sank on to the bench, momentarily deprived of all strength. There was silence.

"Where's Andrey?"

"The devil knows where he is, your Andrey."

"There's no salvation for you, none, you accursed fellow!"

"All right, don't start whining."

The elder jumped up to see whether Andrey had not hidden himself behind the stove in fear of his life. At that moment a loud thump and crash sounded from the yard.

"They're breaking down the gate," the peasant said with a grin. Nektary stumbled before he reached the stove and began to tremble violently. His cloak billowed out like a sail as he hurried into the yard. He left the door wide open.

"Andrey," the peasant called, "close the door, it's cold."

No one answered. He pulled the staple out of the wall and, cursing, went to slam the door.

"Nothing good to be expected here. It's time to get out."

He took a look behind the stove. There, in the narrow gap between the wall and the stove, stood Andrey Golikov, white as a sheet and apparently dazed. He was hiccuping faintly. Yevdokim pulled him by the hand:

"You don't feel you want to die, is that it? If you don't, there's no need to; you can do without the fire. Find the key, d'you hear? Where did the old man hide the key? I want to take off the chain. Andrey! Wake up!"

All were on their knees. The women were weeping silently, holding their children close. Some of the men buried their faces in their calloused hands, their hair hanging down, others stared vacantly at the flames of the tapers. The elder had left the prayer-house for a short time. They were resting: these long hours had exhausted them; it was not enough for him that they were all as submissive as little children. He had shouted in a terrible voice from the altar steps:

"He who is lukewarm I shall spit from my mouth! I want one who is burning hot! It is not sheep I am driving into Paradise, but burning bushes!"

It was hard to do what he demanded: kindle their souls. All the people here were broken men who had left the unending toil of their villages where they did not allow a peasant to improve his condition, but fleeced him bare like a sheep. They had come here seeking peace. It did not matter that the marsh-damp swelled their bodies, that they had to eat bread mixed with ground bark: in the forest and in the fields they were at least their own masters. But evidently no one gave peace freely. Nektary was a fierce shepherd of their souls. He never ceased trying to rouse in them hatred for

Antichrist, the ruler of the world. He punished those who were slow to hate; sometimes he even drove them out altogether. The peasant had long been accustomed to obeying any command. If they ordered your soul to flame, there was no help for it: it had to flame.

Today the elder had tormented them more than usual, and seemed to have worn himself out too. Porfiry, in the choir, was reading in a high-pitched, remote voice. Vapour from the people's breath hung under the boards of the cupola. Drops fell from the ceiling.

The elder returned in an unexpectedly short time. "Do you hear?" he clamoured from the threshold. "Do you hear the servants of Antichrist?" They all heard the heavy blows on the gate. He strode swiftly through the prayer-house, brushing their heads with the hem of his cloak. Raising his beard he bowed three times in a sweeping motion to the blackened faces of the icons. Then he turned towards his flock with such fierceness that the children began to cry loudly. He was holding an iron hammer and nails in his hand.

"My soul, my soul, rise up, why do you slumber?" he cried. "It has come, the end is near. The only place left to us in this world is within these four walls. Let us fly upwards, children! In a flame of fire! Over the temple, so help me God, I have just seen a vast hole in the sky! Angels are descending to us, children, they are rejoicing, my dear ones."

The women raised their eyes and wept. Some of the men too began to snuffle heavily.

"When will there be another such time? The heavenly kingdom is falling into our very laps. Brothers! Sisters! Hearken! They are breaking down the gates. The devilish host has surrounded this island of salvation. Beyond these walls there is only darkness and a stinking whirlwind!"

Raising the hammer and nails he strode to the door where three planks were standing in readiness. Ordering the men to help him he himself began to nail the planks across the door. His breath came wheezingly. The people watched him with horror. One young woman in a white shroud gasped loudly:

"What are you doing? Good people, dear people, don't do it!"

"It must be done!" Nektary shouted and returned to the altar steps. "How can a Christian not want to enter the flames? We shall be consumed, but we shall have eternal life." He paused and struck the young woman on the cheek. "You fool! Well, you have a husband, and a house, and a coffer full of good things. But what comes after that? Is it not the grave? We used to pity you, foolish people. Now it is no longer possible. The enemy is at the doors. Antichrist, drunk with blood, is outside the door seated on his scarlet beast. He is raging and holds in his hand a cup filled with abomination and excrement. He offers it to you as the Sacrament! Horror!"

The woman sank down with her face between her knees, trembling and screaming more and more piercingly and hysterically. The others put their fingers in their ears and clutched at their throats to stop themselves from screaming too.

"Go, go outside the door!" Again there were sounds of thumping and rending. "Hearken! Tsar Peter is Antichrist in the flesh! His servants are breaking into our souls. Hell! Do you know what hell is? It is in the empty universe above the earth. Unfathomable pit, darkness and the depths of hell! The planets circle round it, and the cold is fierce and unbearable. Worms and brimstone! Burning pitch! The kingdom of Antichrist! Is it there you want to go?"

He began to light tapers, seizing them in handfuls off the tray and running about nimbly, sticking them on to the icons anywhere. Their yellow light spread warmly through the prayer-house.

"Brothers! We are setting sail—into the kingdom of heaven! The children, bring the children closer—it will be better here—the smoke will put them to sleep. Brothers, sisters, rejoice! Give us rest with the saints . . ."* he began to chant, making his cloak billow with his elbows.

The men, their beards raised and their eyes fixed on him, moved on their knees closer to the pulpit, joining their voices to his in the singing. The women crept up too, covering the children's heads with their shawls.

The walls of the prayer-house trembled: something struck the door, nailed up with the planks and braced by a thick pole. The elder mounted a stool and pressed his face against the narrow transom over the door:

"Go back!" he shouted. "We shall not surrender ourselves alive!"

"Are you the elder Nektary?" Alexey Brovkin asked. They had broken in the gate and were now forcing the door of the prayer-house. The white face of an old man was staring at him sideways from the long window. Alexey said to him angrily:

"Are you all mad in there?"

The old man's hand struggled out of the window and, with two fingers, made the sign of the cross at the Tsar's officer. A hundred voices on the other side of the wall chanted loudly: "Let God arise!"

* Sung during the Orthodox funeral service.

"Don't wave your fingers at me," Alexey said, angrier than ever. "I'm not the devil, and you are no priest for me. Come out, all of you, or I'll break down the door."

"And who are you?" the old man asked in a strange, mocking voice. "Why have you come to such a wild place in the forests?"

"We are men with the Tsar's ukase—that's who we are," Alexey answered. "If you don't obey, we'll tie you all up and take you to Povenets."

The old man's head disappeared without a word. What was to be done? Yakim whispered despairingly: "Alexey Ivanovich, believe me, they'll burn themselves!"

The chanting went on inside: ". . . peace with the saints."

Alexey paced in front of the door, sniffing with annoyance. What if he were to go away? The news would spread to all the hermitages that an officer had been driven off. He took off his mittens and, jumping up, caught hold of the edge of the narrow window and pulled himself up. He saw, by the hot light of innumerable tapers, bearded faces looking at him with horror, crossing themselves and hissing: "Holy, holy, holy!" Alexey jumped down.

"Ram the door again!"

The soldiers struck once. Then they waited. Then three men, among whom Yakim recognised Stepan Barmin and Peter Kozhevnikov, climbed out of a dormer window. Two of them were holding hunting bows, with a spare arrow stuck in their belts, and the third man was armed with an arquebus. They climbed out on to the roof and looked at the soldiers. The man with the arquebus said grimly:

"Get back, or we shall fire. There are many of us."

This boldness disconcerted Alexey. Had they been townspeople, he would have lost no time arguing with them. But these were peasants born and bred, he knew how stubborn they were. The man with the arquebus was the spit of his own late godfather: thick-legged, belted low, with a shaggy beard and eyes like a bear's. After all, a man couldn't fire at his own kind. Alexey only made a threatening gesture. Yakim took a hand:

"What's your name?"

"Well, they call me Osip," the man with the arquebus answered reluctantly.

"Now, Osip, can't you see that the officer here is himself under orders? Why don't you have a friendly talk with him and settle things quietly?"

"What does he want?" Osip asked.

"Give him ten or fifteen men for the army, and let our soldiers warm themselves a little. We'll leave in the night."

Peter and Stepan squatted on their heels at the edge of the roof as they listened. Osip pondered for a long time, and then answered:

"No, we won't give them."

"Why not?"

"You'll send us all back to our old villages, into servitude. We won't give ourselves up alive. We want to die for the old prayers, for the two-fingered sign of the cross. That's all we've got to say."

He raised the arquebus, blew on the priming-pan, poured some powder on it from his horn and stood squarely over the door. What was there to do? Yakim advised that they should give the whole thing up: Nektary was not a man to be subdued.

"He's obstinate, but I too am obstinate," Alexey replied. "I won't leave here without some men. We'll take them by siege."

He sent two soldiers to unharness and feed the horses, and four others to warm themselves in the cell. The rest were to mount guard, to see that no water or food was taken into the prayer-house. The day was drawing to a close, and the frost was growing more severe. The dissenters were singing funereal hymns. Peter and Stepan, after sitting for some time on the roof whispering to each other, realised that it was going to be a long-drawn-out affair.

"We want to relieve ourselves," they called. "It's sinful to do it on the roof, let us jump down."

Alexey said: "Jump, we won't touch you."

Osip suddenly shook his great beard menacingly at them, but all the same, after hesitating a little, they went behind the cupola and jumped down into the straw.

Evidently Nektary also realised that a siege had begun in earnest. Twice he put his face up to the little transom over the door and strained his eyes peering into the twilight. Alexey tried to talk to him, but he only spat. Then once more his hoarse voice was heard from the prayer-house covering the singing, the supplications, the crying of children. Something evil was going on in there.

When the sunset had completely faded, ten peasants climbed out on to the roof. They were bareheaded. Waving their arms and throwing themselves about like madmen, they screamed:

"Get back! Get back!"

Then they all began hurriedly taking off their clothes—their coats, their felt boots, their shirts, their trousers.

"Take them!"—they picked up the clothing and threw it down to the soldiers—"Take them, persecutors! Cast lots for them. Naked we came into the world, naked we shall leave it."

Naked and blue with cold, they flung themselves down on the roof, rubbed their faces in the snow, sobbed and screamed; then they jumped up, raising their hands to heaven and, their beards thick with snow, climbed back through the dormer window. Osip alone remained on the roof. He aimed the arquebus at the soldiers and would not let them come near the door. The naked men made Alexey feel greatly alarmed. Yakim plaintively called out towards the window over the door: "Have pity on the children at least! Brothers! Have pity on the women!"

A wailing started in the chapel; it was not loud but of a kind to make one want to stop one's ears. The soldiers began to move closer. They all looked grave:

"Lieutenant," they said, "it's not turning out well. Let Osip fire at us, we'll break open the door."

"Break it open!" Alexey cried, clenching his teeth.

The soldiers quickly laid down their muskets and picked up the beam again. Suddenly the cupola with its cross, barely visible in the twilight, tottered. The ground shook violently, there was the roar of an explosion and a rush of air struck their chests. Smoke began to pour out of the cracks under the roof; it grew thicker and turned to flame. Tongues of fire flickered between the timbers.

When the door gave way under the blows, a man with a blackened head and all in flames rushed out and began to writhe in the snow like a worm. Inside the chapel smoky flames whirled and human figures on fire were jumping and throwing themselves about. Flames were darting from under the floor. The straw heaped all round was already smoking.

The soldiers staggered back from the unbearable heat. It was impossible to save anyone. They took off their hats and crossed themselves; the faces of some were wet with tears. Alexey went away, out of the broken gate, in order not to see anything, not to hear the savage wails. His knees were trembling and nausea rose in his throat. He leaned against a tree and sat down. He took off his hat, cooled his head and put snow in his mouth. There was nowhere to escape from the smell of roasting flesh.

Suddenly he saw three men quite close, their feet sinking deep in the red-tinted snow. One of them lagged behind and seemed to be wringing his hands as he watched the great tongues of flame whirl out of the billowing smoke over the hermitage, high above the forest, and the hurricane of sparks rush upwards. The other man, in a raging fury, was dragging by the arm a small, long-bearded old man in a plain sheepskin coat over his cloak.

"He was getting away, the whore's son!" the raging man shouted, as he dragged the old man towards the Tsar's officer. "He ought to be torn to pieces! He crept out of the fire through a hole in the cellar. He wanted to burn Andrey and me, the accursed devil.

8

It was ordered by the Tsar's ukase: "Following the example of all Christian nations the years will be counted, not from the Creation, but from the birth of Christ, eight days after it, and the New Year will begin, not on the 1st of September, but on the 1st of January of this year 1700. And as a sign of this good beginning and of the new century all must congratulate one another on the New Year. By the gates and houses along the main streets and thoroughfares decorations of pine, fir and juniper trees and boughs are to be arranged on the model of those set up at the lower end of the trading rows near the chemist's. People of small means must set up at least a tree or a bough over their gates. In the courtyards of serving, military and trading people, small cannon or muskets are to be fired, and rockets let off, as many as they have, and lampions lighted. For smaller houses, five or six households must combine and make bonfires of old tar-barrels filled with straw or firewood. In front of the Guildhall the merchants will arrange for salutes and illuminations as they see fit."

Such a ringing of bells had not been heard for a long time in Moscow. People said that the Patriarch Adrian, not daring to cross the Tsar in anything, had given the sextons a thousand roubles and fifty barrels of the strong patriarchal small-beer for the ringing. In the bell-towers and belfries the bell-ringers literally danced with their efforts. The frosty snow squeaked shrilly under the sledge-runners. The trees bent under their load of hoar-frost. The taverns, open day and night, were wrapped in clouds of vapour. The sun rose red and fantastic from behind the smoke and gleamed on the broad halberds of the watchmen by the fires.

Through the peal of bells all Moscow could hear the crack of shots and the deep bark of cannon. Dozens of sledges galloped past, full of drunken people and masqueraders, their faces blackened with soot and wearing fur coats turned inside out. They kicked up their legs, waved bottles, yelled, threw themselves about and, when the sledges skidded, fell out in a heap at the feet of the common people stupefied by the bell-ringing and the smoke.

For a whole week, until Epiphany, Moscow was in an uproar of merry-making. Fires broke out. Fortunately there was no wind. Many bandits from the neighbouring forests had hurried into Moscow. As soon as smoke showed somewhere above the snow-covered roofs, evil men in dried sheeps' snouts and fools' caps would gallop up in sledges, break open the gates and rush into the burning house, pillaging and smashing everything in it. Some were caught, others were trampled to death by the crowd. There was a rumour that the robber chief Yesmen Sokol in person was having his fun in Moscow.

The Tsar with his close associates, with the Prince-Pope—the old reprobate Nikita Zotov—and the All-Fools' archbishops, in an archdeacon's vestments adorned with cats' tails, made the round of notables' mansions. Drunk and stuffed with food though they were, they still descended on a house like a swarm of locusts, not so much to eat as to waste food, and bawl hymns and relieve themselves under the tables. They made their hosts drink themselves silly and then they went off to the next house. To save themselves the trouble of gathering the following day from all parts of the town, they would spend the night sleeping in a heap in any house where they happened to be. They made merry all over Moscow, from end to end, greeting everyone for the New Year and the opening of the new century.

The quiet and God-fearing townspeople endured those days in anguish; they were afraid to go out of doors. They could not understand the reason for all this frenzy. Was it the devil who was inciting the Tsar to stir up the people, to break the old customs—the cornerstone of their lives? Though their lives were frugal, yet they lived honourably, counted their kopeks and knew what was right and what was wrong. Now it turned out that everything was wrong; nothing suited him.

Those who did not recognise the four-pointed cross and the sign of the cross made with three fingers gathered in cellars for evening services. Once again the whisper spread that they need only endure till Shrovetide: that on the night between Saturday and Sunday the Trump of Doom would sound. In the Bronna suburb a man appeared who gathered people together in a bath-house; he spun round, slapping his face with his palms and crying out that he was the Lord of Sabaoth, with hands and feet, and finally fell to the ground frothing at the mouth. Another man, naked, shaggy and terrible, came before the people holding three pokers in his hand, and made obscure prophecies about calamities to come.

A second ukase of the Tsar was nailed up at the Kitay-gorod and Beliy-gorod gates: "Boyars, courtiers, service men, clerks and tradespeople must henceforth without exception wear Hungarian attire, and in the spring, when the frosts lessen, they must wear Saxon coats."

These coats and hats were hung out on hooks. The soldiers guarding them said that soon all merchants' wives, soldiers' wives, townswomen, priests' and deacons' wives would be ordered to go about bareheaded, in short foreign skirts and wear whalebone ribs round their sides under their dresses. Crowds stood about by the gates, dismayed and filled with vague apprehension. They told each other in whispers that the unknown man with the three pokers had thrown dung at one of these coats on a hook and shouted: "Soon you won't be allowed to speak Russian, you wait! Roman and Lutheran priests will come and re-baptise the whole nation. The townspeople will be handed over to the foreigners in perpetual bondage. Moscow will be given a new name: Deviltown. The old books have revealed that Peter is a Jew of the tribe of Dan."

How was it possible not to believe such rumours when, on the eve of Epiphany, the merchant Revyakin's clerks suddenly began to report—running along the rows of shops—the great and terrible sacrifice for the redemption of the world from Antichrist that had just taken place? Near Lake Vyg several hundred dissenters had burned themselves alive. The sky had opened above the conflagration and made visible the glassy firmament and a throne supported by four beasts, and on the throne the Lord was seated. On His left and on His right hand there were twice twelve elders and around Him cherubim were "flying with two wings, covering their eyes with two other wings and their legs with another two." A dove flew down from the throne, the fire died out and a sweet fragrance arose on the site of the burning.

In the Mails Department some man, of ordinary stature and appearance, dropped a letter on the floor as he was leaving. They called after him: "Hey, you've dropped something!" but he took flight, ran away and disappeared. The sealed letter bore the inscription: "To be presented to the Tsar without opening". The head clerk, Pavel

Vasilyevich Suslov, hardly managed to get his trembling arms into the sleeves of his greatcoat. He galloped off to Preobrazhensk, threatening to flay the postilion's back.

The officer on guard in the palace anteroom looked the clerk over with contempt from his bald spot to his morocco-leather fur-lined boots: "You cannot see the Tsar." Suslov, weak with anxiety, sat down on a bench. The place was crowded with people: insolent military men—the Russians all tall, broad-shouldered, strong as bulls; the foreigners built on a smaller scale but with pleasant faces (many of the poor fellows were being of late dismissed from service for stupidity and drunkenness)—astute dealers, tradesmen and merchants from Vladimir, Yaroslav and Orel; two high-born boyars sitting side by side, one with his head bound up, the other with a black eye; a foreigner with a gentle, hungry face, wearing spectacles and a cotton wig, and dressed in a short brown coat, pacing up and down without looking at anyone: a mathematician and chemist, inventor of the *perpetuum mobile*—a perpetual water-wheel—and of a brass man—an automaton who played draughts and relieved himself of wine or beer in the natural manner. The mathematician was offering the Tsar over one hundred patents which could enrich the Russian kingdom.

Nikita Zotov, drunk and accompanied by a man of extraordinary girth, stumbled into the anteroom from outside. "Don't be afraid," he was saying, "he likes deformities, he'll give you a lot of money." The Prince-Pope was dragging the fat fellow towards the Tsar's apartments. Suslov, afire with zeal, went up to the officer on guard and said into his face in a strangled voice: "I claim the Tsar's word." Immediately silence fell in the anteroom. The officer drew himself up; taking a short breath he unsheathed his sword: "Come with me."

Peter, who had a headache, received the clerk with an impatient frown. The letter, which Suslov put into his hands and which was opened on the spot, was signed by Alexey Kurbatov, a house serf of Prince Peter Pavlovich Sheremetev. Glancing over it rapidly, Peter stroked his chin: "Hm!" Then he read it a second time, threw back his head: "Ha!" and, forgetting Suslov, strode swiftly into the dining-hall where his close advisers were languishing in expectation of dinner.

"Ministers!"—Peter's eyes had even cleared—"I feed you, and give you plenty to drink, but how much profit is there from you? Here!" He waved the letter. "A poor fellow, a serf, has had a wonderful idea! Enriching the treasury. Fedor Yurievich," he turned to Romodanovsky who was gently snoring, "give orders for Kurbatov to be found and brought here immediately. We won't sit down to dinner without him. This is the thing, my dear Ministers: we must sell stamped paper, for all deeds, for petitions, paper with a stamp, from one kopek to ten roubles. Is that clear to you? You think there's no money for war? Well, there it is, the money!"

chapter three

It was still dark, but already doors were slamming and stairs creaking all over the house; the serving-girls were dragging hampers, bundles and travelling-coffers out into the courtyard. Prince Roman Borisovich was breakfasting at a makeshift table, by the light of a tallow candle. Between mouthfuls of cabbage soup he turned round peevishly:

"Avdotya! Antonida! Olga! Oh Lord!"

He heaved his great paunch up slightly and reached for the bottle. The major-domo had disappeared like the others. There! Someone was tumbling downstairs head over heels.

"Quiet there, you devils! Oh Lord!"

Antonida ran in distractedly, dishevelled and wearing her mother's old fur coat.

"Sit down, Antonida, eat something."

"Oh, Daddy!"

She caught up a woollen shawl and ran out into the hall. Roman Borisovich looked round for something more to eat. Overhead they were dragging a heavy object across the floor, then they dropped it and a shower of dust fell from the rafters. What on earth were they doing? Breaking up the house? Shaking his head he helped himself to some sturgeon.

Princess Avdotya came floating in through the door, swathed in shawls over a fur coat. She flopped down on a Venetian chair by the wall. Her face was drawn with anxiety. She had only been out of Moscow twice in her life: to the Troitsa monastery and to New Jerusalem. And now such a long journey, all of a sudden!

"Why have you wrapped yourself up in shawls so soon? Come, take them off and eat a little. Eating on the road is nothing but trouble."

"Roman Borisovich, are we going far?"

"To Voronezh, Mother."

"Dear God!"

She gave a dry sob. From upstairs came Olga's shrill voice: "Mama, where did you put the wigs?" Princess Avdotya was wafted off her chair, and out of the room, as lightly as a leaf in the wind.

Roman Borisovich's one consolation was that the same turmoil was going on all over Moscow. The day before yesterday Romodanovsky, the administrator and bugbear of the capital, had proclaimed the Tsar's ukase: officials with their wives and children, important merchants and notables from the Foreign Quarter were to travel to Voronezh for the launching of the *Predestination,* a ship of such size that even abroad there were few to match it. The orders were to hurry while the snow still held, because of the imminence of spring which would make the roads impassable.

Roman Borisovich was already beginning to understand something of politics, even though it cost him no small effort. In January, after the noisy celebrations, letters had come from the great ambassador Yemelian Ukraintsev in Constantinople: the Turks were on the point of agreeing to permanent peace, only asking for some small concessions which would mollify irritated feelings, and Ukraintsev had even made them accept the idea that the Russians stood firm by the principle established at the Karlowitz congress: "whoever holds something, let him retain possession of it." But then something had happened in Constantinople, some enemy had interfered in the negotiations and the Turks began to make even more presumptuous demands than previously: they asked for the return of Azov and the town of Kizikerma, together with the Dniepr towns and the resumption of payment by Moscow of tribute to the Khan of the Crimea. As for the Holy Sepulchre, they would not even have it mentioned.

This news made Peter rush off to Voronezh. Alexander Menshikov, after ridding himself in the steam-baths of the last effects of the celebrations, made the round of the wealthy merchants in a magnificent carriage. He told them feelingly: "You must help us out. Unless, by the spring, we succeed in intimidating the Turks with a great fleet, there will be no peace. The whole undertaking will go to wrack and ruin."

Leo Narishkin, in his turn, said to the high officials in the Kremlin with tears in his eyes: "Can we brook dishonour? Can we, as of old, pay tribute to the Khan of the Crimea and accept the incursion of the Tatar hordes into our most fertile lands every spring? Can we put up any longer with the desecration of the Holy Sepulchre by Turks and Catholics? As in the days of Minin and Pozharsky * we must give our all for the building of the great Voronezh fleet."

The shipbuilding companies were again obliged to loosen their purse-strings. Sinister rumours of an early war began to spread through Moscow: nearly the whole world, they said, was rising in arms. Foreigners, who scuttled in and out of Moscow like mice, carried their tales all over Europe, saying that Moscow was not the quiet haven of true Christianity it had once been, but was full of soldiers and guns, that the Tsar was arrogant in his pride and his advisers over-bold. According to them, Moscow was asking for trouble.

Recently in the Kremlin Roman Borisovich had got carried away and had promised to supply a year's provisions for the ship *Predestination* which had been laid down. Swelling with purple rage he had shouted into Leo Narishkin's face: "I shall myself take to horse if need be, but there shall be no dishonour for the Tsar." And even during the night, when he had gone down to the secret cellar with a candle, dug up a pot out of the damp earth and was counting out, kopek by kopek, one hundred and fifty roubles for the company— his share—even then, alone in the cellar, feeling with his fingers every kopek in the feeble light, he did not allow himself any rebellious thoughts. Prince Buynosov was a changed man: they had civilised him.

He had crushed the rebellious thoughts in his heart and locked them up safely. It was with thoughts of that kind that Prince Lykov was now living in exile in his village. The stupid Prince Stepan Beloselsky had got drunk at a feast at Romodanovsky's and shouted: "What, you want to forbid me to think in my own way even in my sleep? They've shaved my cheeks, I wear French breeches, but as for my soul . . . !" and he had made a contemptuous gesture. Romodanovsky had only smiled grimly. On the morrow Prince Stepan received the order to leave for Pustozersk as governor.

Roman Borisovich had some intelligence. But it was difficult to

* National heroes who rallied the Russian people during the Times of Trouble (1598–1613).

know what kind of intelligence was needed to keep pace with Tsar Peter's fantasies. It was as though even at night he itched with the desire to disturb other people's peace. All Moscow had to rush headlong to Voronezh. What for? To lie on benches in overcrowded tumbledown huts without enough to eat? To drink vodka with the sailors? And why, above all, had one to drag the women there? Oh Lord!

Roman Borisovich drank an extra glass of vodka to stifle his confused thoughts. Dawn showed through the window. Rooks came to perch on the leafless trees under it. No matter how the Tsar disturbed a man's peace, the green morning light was the same as in the time of his grandsires, and the same clouds blushed rosily behind the church domes. Roman Borisovich groaned from the very depths of his belly, without opening his lips. He could hear sledge-bells tinkle in the yard and the grooms shout at the horses as they harnessed them.

The family drove off in two covered sledges. Three others were loaded with household gear and victuals. The harness-bells tinkled mournfully. The road to Kolomna was worn smooth but full of potholes. Red posts marked each verst, and between them grew recently-planted birches. Antonida and Olga counted the posts and the trees. There was nothing else to do to while away the time; there was only the ice-crust on the snow shining in the March sun and the brown copses in the distance. With the crows on the trees lining the roads as omens, the girls told their fortunes concerning possible love affairs. In the second sledge Roman Borisovich snored, leaning his shoulder heavily against his wife and moving his lips when the sledge bumped over a hole. The drive was uneventful.

They were to stop at the village of Ulyanino, thirty miles from Moscow, to feed the horses. Before the thatched roofs showed in the hollow, a high leather-covered sledge drawn by six bays with two outriders galloped past them. A languid beauty, wrapped in black sables, glanced indifferently out of the glass window at the girls who were fidgeting with curiosity.

"The Mons woman, the Mons woman!" Antonida cried, craning her neck out of her mother's fur coat. "Look, Olga, there's a gentleman with her!"

And, indeed, there was a glimpse of a shaven face and gold lace on a hat in the back of the sledge as it galloped past.

"That's Königseck, or may my eyes drop out!"

Antonida threw up her mittened hands:

"You don't say so! Oh, the shameless hussy!"

"Why so surprised? She's a bitch, a German woman. All Moscow whispers about Königseck, the Tsar alone is blind."

"She ought to be flogged in the market-place."

"That's how she is sure to end."

Trains of sledges were drawn up in nearly every yard in the village; boyars' covered sledges could be seen through the open gates. Village women ran over the dung-covered snowdrifts catching fowls. Roman Borisovich grumbled at his wife:

"That's what you've done with your silly preparations! We should have started before dawn! Now we won't be able to find a house to stop at."

He gave orders to drive to the Tsar's house. Such posting-stations —with four windows and a flight of five steps leading up to a front porch—had been built that year at every stage-point between Moscow and Voronezh. The custodians of these houses had instructions to keep supplies of food and drink and, above all, to keep the place clear of cockroaches because the Tsar was afraid of such domestic pests.

The custodian, with wig and sword, rushed out on to the porch and waved the newcomers on: "Full up! Full up! You can't stop here!" Roman Borisovich pushed the man importantly aside and entered the hall, followed by the princess and the girls. The custodian hissed desperately behind them. And, indeed, both rooms—to the right and left of the hall—were so crowded that it was impossible to get in. Fur coats, felt boots, hats and swords were piled in heaps on the floor. Serving-girls scurried about, and there was a smell of cabbage soup.

"Daddy, this is for the higher quality," Olga whispered. He himself realised that they ought to withdraw quietly. But suddenly, from the room on the right, where bewigged courtiers were laughing, a German voice said in Russian:

"Princess Olga! Princess Antonida! Please come and share our table!"

The wigs made way, and there was Anna Mons, in a red gown and travelling-bonnet, sitting at a table laden with food. She raised a tall wine-glass, turned and smiled at the girls, inviting them to join her. Königseck, the Saxon ambassador, with Karl Kniperkron, nephew of the Swedish resident in Moscow, and a Frenchman whom the girls did not know, sprang forward to help the princesses out of their coats. "Oh, we can manage ourselves"—and the girls hastily pulled off their mother's old coats and dropped them on a heap of other fur coats. "Just you wait, Mama, we won't forget the shame you put us to!" They entered on their cavaliers' arms and curtsied with their hearts in their mouths.

A dark-haired, large-eyed little boy, with his mouth slightly open, sat on a bench with his back to the sweating window. His delicate head drooped sideways as he looked with tired eyes at the tall, red-cheeked, well-fed grown-ups with their deafening chatter and laughter. He was wearing the bright green tunic of the Preobrazhensky regiment and a little sword hung from his belt; his legs, encased in white boots of combed felt, did not reach the floor.

Roman Borisovich, with a preliminary sob at the threshold, solemnly approached the little ten-year-old boy, fell on his knees, touching the floorboards with his forehead and, breathing heavily, begged permission of his Royal Highness, the heir to the throne, Alexey Petrovich, to kiss his hand.

"Give him your hand, Alioshenka, give it to him," his aunt, the rosy-cheeked Tsarevna Natalia, said gaily in her musical voice. Since the Tsaritsa Eudoxia had been taken away to Suzdal she stood in his mother's stead.

Alexey slowly lifted his eyes to her face and obediently held out his fingers half-covered by his lace cuff. Roman Borisovich pressed his thick lips to the hand. The Tsarevich tried to draw it back—Olga and Antonida spread their skirts before him according to the rules of etiquette and the tall cavaliers shook their wigs and stamped their feet, joining in the homage of the Buynosov family—and his dark eyes filled with tears.

"Come, come to me, Alioshenka! This crowd is too much for you," and Natalia, high-bosomed, fair-haired, with a round face like her brother's, and a humorous dimple in her chin, drew the child to her and covered him with a corner of her fleecy shawl.

"Never mind, just wait till you grow up, and then you'll frighten other people, won't you, Alioshenka?" The Tsarevna kissed his forehead, took a rich honey-cake from the plate, bit off a piece with her beautiful teeth and gave it to the Tsarevich. "Now, Princesses, you must sit down and eat. And you, Prince Roman, stand with the gentlemen, you will be served when we have finished."

A tall young woman with a clever, sallow face and eyelashes and eyebrows of the same colour as her skin sat at the table with Natalia and Anna Mons. Her flaxen hair was twisted into a tight knot on the top of her head. She had already finished eating and, having pushed aside her plate and half-emptied wine-glass, was rapidly crocheting something in coloured wool. This was Amalia Kniperkron, the Swedish resident's daughter and a friend of the Tsar's.

"Alexey Petrovich, please, your sweet little face," she said gently in Russian and put her crochet-work against the boy's neck. "You will soon be wearing this scarf."

Without smiling the little boy rubbed his cheek against her hand, which was nearly as large as a man's. Anna Mons, who was sitting bolt upright, lifted the corners of her lips sweetly and said, also in Russian:

"The Tsarevich got sick in the sledge. But we are all sure that he is a brave soldier. He wears his little sword so gallantly."

From under his aunt's elbow and her woollen shawl the boy scowled at the white-faced German woman. The gentlemen, who stood behind the chairs, began to assert that the Tsarevich gave every sign of bravery.

"Dear Tsarevich, our protector and master," Roman Borisovich suddenly cried and, half-squatting, peered close into the boy's face. "Mount your good steed, draw your sharp sword and smite the untold hosts of our enemies. Defend our Orthodox Russia: she is alone in the world, dear Tsarevich!"

He wanted to kiss the boy's head but, his courage failing, kissed him on the shoulder instead and stood up, rubbing his back, well pleased with himself. For some reason Natalia looked at him with fear in her face. Anna Mons shrugged her shoulders and said, with a condescending smile:

"Prince Roman, who has so roused your wrath? It seems to me that we have no foes except the Turks—and even with them we are seeking peace. There is no prospect of any war . . ." She glanced diplomatically at Amalia Kniperkron.

"What are you saying, my dear Anna Ivanovna! Why, as soon as the roads are dry we shall start on a great campaign. It is not for nothing that we are levying troops and equipping them with Liège muskets. It is not for fun."

Amalia Kniperkron lowered her crochet-work; her eyes opened wide, her mouth dropped and her whole face grew long with astonishment. The men exchanged glances as they listened to Prince Roman who, carried away by his own boastfulness, described the military preparations that were being made. Königseck, aghast, pulled his snuffbox out of his waistcoat and offered it to Roman Borisovich, but the prince impatiently pushed it aside.

"No, no, no, my dear Anna Ivanovna, all Moscow is talking of it. We are preparing. We shall stand up valiantly for our ancient Livonian provinces."

At this Königseck trod on Prince Roman's foot. Natalia, flushed with anger, shouted at him:

"Stop talking nonsense! You must have dreamt all this about war. You have probably not sobered up since last night."

Holding Alexey by the shoulders, she went off with him behind a striped linen curtain, where logs were crackling in the stove. Anna Mons glided after her, followed by Olga and Antonida and, after a while, by Amalia Kniperkron, whose face still showed amazement. The gentlemen sat down at the table. Nobody looked at Roman Borisovich; they completely ignored his presence. He realised that he had displeased them. But how? Had one no longer the right to stand up for Orthodox Russia? Must a Russian hold his tongue in the presence of foreigners? He frowned and looked at the table. Food was being served. There was only one place vacant, at the foot of the table. It was bad enough that he had waited like a fool to be invited. To the devil with you! Prince Roman turned round and went into the hall. There Princess Avdotya was sitting quietly on a chair by the stack of coats.

"Why are you waiting here like a woman of no account?"

"They didn't invite me into the parlour."

"They didn't invite you! You simpleton! You've forgotten your station. Come into the other parlour."

Having eaten and drunk his fill, Roman Borisovich calmed down. Perhaps he had really talked too much in the presence of the Tsarevich and the Tsarevna. People of high rank were sensitive, especially in front of foreigners. Well, never mind, they wouldn't hold it against an old man.

In the afternoon he got into the sledge, heavy and sleepy, yawned, shifted about to find a soft place, and fell blissfully asleep, fanned by the light March winds. His conscience might have been uneasy, but no, it did not disturb him. How could he foresee what unpleasant and extraordinary consequences would result for him from this apparently trifling incident at the Tsar's posting-station?

Nevertheless they had plenty of trouble before they reached Voronezh. Were it not for a cold wind that brought on a snowstorm, they would probably have been drowned somewhere at a river crossing. In their haste they abandoned their horses and hired post-horses. The nearer they approached the Don, the more intractable they found the peasants, who looked at them sullenly, like beasts, and took off their caps only after they had been shouted at. Roman Borisovich grew hoarse with arguing at every posting-station as he demanded horses. He himself went into the peasants' houses and, seizing the man by the coat, shook him and said: "Don't you know whom you are talking to, you whore's son? I'll ruin you!"

The peasant clenched his teeth angrily as his head wagged to and fro; the eyes of the children on the stove glinted like those of wolf-cubs; the broad-boned peasant's wife looked malevolent as she held a poker or an oven-fork in her hand: "You can't ruin us, boyar; we're already ruined. We have no horses, go your way."

In one village of about ten houses, badly battered by the stormy weather, the Buynosovs were obliged to spend a night and a day. There were no men, and no horses, only women in this village, which stood on a slope above a small river. The Buynosovs slept in a chimneyless hut, the upper half of which was lost in smoke. The young princesses moaned as they lay under sheepskin coats on benches that had been set close together. The smoke made their eyes smart. The wind howled like a lost soul.

Roman Borisovich woke up in the night and heard the sound of voices outside; apparently someone had driven up to the gates. Groaning, he crawled out reluctantly from under his fur coat. In the yard everything was white; stars shone in the sky between flying clouds. Having relieved himself, Roman Borisovich went to the gates. Outside men were talking in subdued voices:

". . . the Zhukov peasants will all run away in the spring, Ivan Vasilyevich. . . ."

"We lived quite well before all this mud work started. That Azmus, or whatever his name is—the Antichrist—came and then it began. They made a lot of scoops, and began to ladle up mud out of the marsh and make bricks, and dry them in the threshing-barns. Our peasants cart this mud from morning till night; the threshing-barns are stuffed full of it. The horses are all crippled. We can neither plough nor sow."

"The Tsar came here. He said it wasn't enough. He ordered a mill to be built with scoops, to haul the mud up from the bottom. They fired the mud in his presence; took it from the threshing-barns. No, we can't stand this servitude. We must run away and never look back."

"We hide in the ravines, Ivan Vasilyevich. We only go home at night to get a piece of bread. Is that a way to live?"

"Is the revolt going to start soon, chief?"

Unconscious of the wind chilling him under the coat that he had thrown over his head, Roman Borisovich peered through a chink in the gates. In the dim starlight he discerned several peasants standing dejectedly by a sledge with a carpet-covered back and, in it, holding the reins, a broad man in a warm coat and Cossack cap, with a piebald beard that looked as though it had been splashed with whitewash. "Ah, I've seen that rascal somewhere," Roman Borisovich thought to himself and was seized with fear.

One of the peasants bent over the back of the sledge and asked:

"What news from the Don, chief?"

The man with the piebald beard fingered the reins and replied importantly:

"Expect it before the summer."

"God grant it!"

"If only it would end soon, one way or another."

"It will end, it will end," said the man with the piebald beard and there was menace in his deep voice. "We've got teeth." He turned abruptly in the sledge and asked: "Where shall I put up my horse, lads?"

"You might have left it at my place, Ivan Vasilyevich, but yesterday the devil brought a boyar with his women. The insolent way they behave! They've scattered the hay and the straw; I had hidden my oats, but they found them. You won't believe me: they give a whole pailful to each of the horses. And what do I get for it? He won't give me a kopek."

The man with the piebald beard opened his mouth wide.

"Ha!" he laughed. "Ha-ha! I've got a knife in a sack under the seat—take it! Get yourself a kopek. That's how things are, you bonded peasants." He tightened the reins. "Well, to whom do I go?"

One of the men sprang away from the sledge:

"To my place, Ivan Vasilyevich, there's plenty of room."

Only then did Roman Borisovich suddenly feel the cold. With chattering teeth he hurried back into the dark hut.

"Avdotya," he said, shaking the princess, dazed with sleep. "Where did you put my pistols? Get up, Olga, Antonida! Light the fire! Where have you put the flint and the tinder? Mishka, Vanka, get up! harness the horses!"

The Tsar's palace—a newly-built, log structure—stood across the river from the town on the peninsula between the old and the new river-beds. Peter used it little—he would sleep wherever the night overtook him. Tsarevna Natalia with the small Tsarevich stayed there, as well as the widowed Tsaritsa Praskovya with her three daughters: Ekaterina, Anna and Praskovya. Boyars' wives and daughters, who had arrived for the celebrations, were also crowded in there. There was nowhere to go outside the palace, nothing but streams and swamp all round. All that could be seen from the windows were the plank roofs of the wharfs, the bright yellow skeletons of ships on the stocks along the bank of old Voronezh, ravines full of dirty snow and low hills bristling with the stumps of trees.

The Buynosov girls languished at the window as they waited for the balls and fireworks to begin. Really, they couldn't have found a worse place! No grove to stroll in, no nice river-banks to sit on, nothing but slime, rubbish, wood-chips. Shouts and the clatter of hammers drifted across from the yellow ships on the bank. Crowds of gentlemen often came there on horseback, but the girls could only cry out in distant admiration of the elegant horsemen. No one knew when the entertainments would begin. Now bonfires were lit near the ships and work went on all night. The girls hung their skirts over the windows so that the fearsome reflections of the flames should not waken them.

When the mud in the yard, surrounded by log walls, dried a little, they would come out on to the porch where the sun was hot and while away the time in boredom. Of course they could have found some relief from the dullness in the company of the girls who sat on other porches: with Princess Lykova, a terrible fool, as broad as she was high, even her eyes were sunk in fat; or with Princess Dolgorukova, a swarthy, haughty creature (no matter how well she tried to conceal it, all Moscow knew she had hairy legs); or with the eight Princesses Shahovskoy, a pernicious brood, who did nothing but whisper tittle-tattle together. Olga and Antonida cared nothing for feminine company.

One day peasants were brought into the yard and, in one morning, erected swings and a roundabout with horses and boats. But it was impossible to get near them: either the Tsarevich wanted to have a go, pushing away the nurses who tried to hold him by his belt, or else it would be the small princesses, who were accompanied by their tutor, Johann Ostermann, a German with a large, very stupid face, frowning with self-importance and wearing round spectacles; in one pocket of his snuff-coloured coat he carried a silk handkerchief for wiping his nose, and in the other a bunch of twigs—the birch. He would seat the princesses in the boats, and himself mount a brightly-painted horse, saying to the peasants who turned the roundabout: "Begin, *aber langsam, langsam.*" With his eyes closed behind the spectacles and the soles of his great shoes scraping the ground, he turned round and round until he grew giddy.

Sometimes a motley crowd would pour down the steps of the main porch: jesters in coats turned inside out, Ethiopians, black as soot, two old fools dressed up as women, broad-bottomed waiting-women, and then Tsaritsa Praskovya, dressed in an ample gown of black velvet, would float down the steps, helped by her women who supported her elbows. A chair and cushions would be brought out for her, and she would seat herself, with her rouged face as round as a melon turned away from the sun. She had a handsome head of dark hair and did not wear a wig. The dwarfs, fools and jesters, blowing out their cheeks, would sit at her feet, while the attendant women stood behind her chair simpering fondly.

"Sit down, sit down!" the Tsaritsa would say languidly to the boyars' daughters, so that they should stop bowing and stay seated on the porches. She would watch the swings and the roundabout, and then begin to moan softly with her head drooping sideways. The women would move up anxiously:

"Where does it hurt, dear Tsaritsa, light of our eyes, where does it hurt?"

"It's nothing. Leave me alone." The Tsaritsa, with her flaccid body, always had a pain somewhere. "Hey, you, Johann! That's enough whirling, the princesses will get dizzy. Heaven help me, what a fool of a German! Such a tall fellow and with spectacles, but all he likes to do is to go round and round."

Johann Ostermann would lead the little girls up to their mother. Ekaterina, the eldest, eight years old, was pockmarked and had a squint, which made the Tsaritsa pity her. She loved the youngest best —chubby, merry Praskovya; she would draw her between her knees to her stout body, stroke her curly hair and kiss her forehead. The middle sister, Anna Ivanovna,* a slightly sallow, sulky little girl with pale lips, approached her mother timidly, always a few paces behind her sisters.

"Why do you keep looking at your toes? Your mother won't eat you," the Tsaritsa would say. She would take some sweetmeat from a plate presented by an old jester and give it to her favourite, Praskovya, then give one to Ekaterina and, finally, with a: "here's a

* The future Empress Anna (1730–1740).

honey-cake for you", push one into Anna's hand. With a sigh she would look the tutor up and down, from his brown cloth stockings to his neat wig. "Oh, I entrusted the children to him too early; I ought to have let them be coddled a little longer by their nurses."

The broad-bottomed women shook their skirts behind her chair: "It is too early, dear Tsaritsa, they are too young to study."

"Be quiet, don't hiss in my ear," the Tsaritsa would say with a grimace. Then she would beckon to Ostermann. "Well, you German, did you read to them today? Have you been teaching them German? And arithmetic?"

Johann Ostermann, with one foot planted forward, adjusted his spectacles and reported at length without much substance. The Tsaritsa nodded slowly, not understanding a word he said. One thing she had grasped: that the old life was no longer possible nowadays. She had to adapt herself to the new ways, although it was hard. She remembered only too well the year 1698 when all those who had held the highest positions in the Kremlin had been driven out for clinging to the old ways; when Tsarevna Sophia and her sisters had narrowly escaped the knout; and Tsaritsa Eudoxia was now, with a living husband, a grey nun shedding tears in Suzdal.

Tsaritsa Praskovya was not a Saltykov for nothing: although flabby in body, she had a shrewd mind, and so too had her brother, Vasily, her adviser, bailiff and house-steward. They realised that Tsar Peter could not do without a proper royal court in Moscow: the ambassadors and foreigners of rank were particular; it was not everyone who could be taken to the Foreign Quarter, to the Mons woman. So Tsaritsa Praskovya introduced foreign etiquette into her house and entertained ambassadors, travellers and distinguished merchants from abroad. Her beloved old customs were kept up in the back rooms of the house and whisked out of sight when the need arose. For all this Peter liked and respected her.

When she wearied of this dull sitting in the sunshine, Tsaritsa Praskovya would go in again with her daughters and attendants. The Buynosov girls would then get on to the roundabout and order the men to turn it as fast as they could. They let out faint squeals as they revolved. In the distance they could hear the booming of guns and the shouts of the workmen raising a mast on one of the ships.

Then it would be time for dinner, and after dinner they would doze in the hot bedrooms smelling of resin. Once or twice a messenger came from town to fetch clean linen for Roman Borisovich. The messenger said that the Prince was living in very crowded quarters—four in one small room at Apraxin's house—and that no one knew when this sitting and waiting in Voronezh would come to an end.

But one day at noon Peter rode into the yard. He was lean and his sunburnt cheeks were freshly shaved. He threw an amused glance at the roundabout and looked up at the windows where the sleepy womenfolk were startled into agitation. He jumped from his horse, straightened his belt on his tight-fitting coat, and ran upstairs to Tsaritsa Praskovya's apartments.

Before a minute had passed the whole palace knew that the ship would be launched the following morning and the celebrations would begin.

The two-decker fifty-gun *Predestination* was on the stocks on the gently sloping bank of the river. Her high poop, with its three tiers of square port-holes, was handsomely ornamented with carved oak. Two white bands were painted along her black sides and the gun-hatches were thrown open on their brass hinges. Her sails of unbleached canvas were furled along the yard-arms. On the rounded bows, which were much lower than the stern, a naked naiad supported with her powerful arms, as broad as beams, a long bowsprit which carried, unlike the older ships, only fore-and-aft sails. The vessel had been built to Peter's designs, under his supervision and that of Fedosey Skliayev and Aladushkin.

The sun rose behind the tender green hills and the ancient towers of Voronezh. It was a cool, cloudless blue day. A pleasant breeze lightly rippled the water, tempting one to hoist sail and set off to follow the swollen river into the vernal distance.

On a wooden platform near the ship stood tables loaded with food and drink. The wind sported with the corners of the red tablecloths, the plumes on the ladies' hats, the curls of wigs and the tassels of the officers' sword-belts. Round the tables sat Tsaritsa Praskovya with Tsarevna Natalia and the children, ambassadors and envoys, Dutch and English merchants, Poles, Germans, a Jesuit from Paris, Amalia Kniperkron, the Saxon military engineer Hallart and the Imperial Duke Charles Eugene de Crouy, who had just arrived with a letter from August, King of Saxony and Poland. The other guests, who, though of the best blood, were at the moment less important, stood on the platform behind the tables. Sailors took round vodka in wooden buckets.

The Duke de Crouy sat in a negligent attitude between the Tsaritsa and the Tsarevna, his elbows on the table; he kept twirling his fair moustache and fixed an unseeing gaze over the heads of the people. His nose was long and slightly crooked, his face listless, with pouches under the eyes; his smooth wig came down to his eyebrows. Under his lilac coat he wore the ribbon of some Order; there was a golden chain round his neck and diamond stars at the sides. Even the Tsaritsa and the Tsarevna were overawed by this Duke of the Holy Roman Empire, this conquering hero, who had taken part in fifteen famous battles. Yet apparently—the Muscovites thought, though they did not show it—the Duke's pocket must be empty, otherwise he would never have come to Voronezh. Shafirov, the interpreter, stood behind his chair.

The Duke said, narrowing his slightly reddened eyelids:

"Russia is a splendid country, the Russians are an industrious and God-fearing people, and the women in Russia are ravishing. In Europe we are somewhat surprised by the persistent efforts of the Russians to adopt our customs and our dress. It has been ordained by God Himself that the Russians should turn their eyes towards Asia. It would be an excellent thing, to the advantage of all Christianity, if the countless multitudes of the Asian peoples were rallied round the throne of the Tsar and a free route opened into Persia and China."

The Duke did not conclude his reflections: there was a buzz and a shuffling of feet among the guests. The Tsar was striding rapidly up from the ship, in Dutch velvet knee-breeches and a linen shirt with rolled-up sleeves and a round oilskin hat on the back of his head. He stopped in front of the platform and respectfully doffed his hat to fat Admiral Golovin who sat in his enormous wig drinking Hungarian wine.

"Good day, Admiral!"

"Good day, shipwright Peter Alexeyevich," Golovin answered with dignity.

"Admiral, the ship is ready for launching. Shall we knock out the props?"

"With God's help, you may begin."

The Duke stopped twirling his moustache and stared with amazement when the Tsar, like any ordinary carpenter, like a man of low birth, bowed to the admiral, put on his hat and quickly strode over the chip-strewn ground. "Ready!" he shouted to the workmen, and they got busy under the ship's steep keel. On the way he had picked up a hammer: "To the props! All together! Strike home!" The hammers rang on the beams that supported the bows of the great ship. The trumpets sounded a prolonged flourish. The guests stood up and raised their glasses. One could see Peter's shoulder-blades move as he wielded his hammer. The masts quivered, the ship subsided slightly on the slips and, after a slight pause, began to move on the greased incline. "She's off! She's off!" the guests on the platform shouted.

The ship gathered momentum as she slid down to the river, and the grease began to smoke. The bows touched the water. The gilded naiad went in to her waist. In a swift rush the ship swept out on to the water, throwing out two waves on either side, and turned and swung to. Pennants ran up to her mastheads and the wind tugged at the narrow silk tongues. Flames spurted from her broadsides as her guns boomed.

Feasting was going on for the second day at Menshikov's quarters, on the town side, by the bridge. Some of the guests did not sleep at all, others lay under the tables on hay, which had been renewed several times already. The ladies, having taken a short rest, and rouged and powdered themselves and changed their gowns, drove up again at a gallop in their rumbling carriages. There had been fireworks the day before, today there was to be a great ball.

The foreigners were well pleased with the celebrations. Shafirov, without sparing himself, filled them with the best Hungarian and Champagne wines; the Russians were given inferior sorts. The cunning interpreter had succeeded in inducing several envoys to write to tell their friends in Constantinople what they had seen in Voronezh: that after the *Predestination* five more big ships and fourteen galleys had been launched within the week, and that more ships were being hurriedly completed. Their frames could be seen right down to Chizhovka village. If all these ships reinforced the Azov fleet, the Sultan, who jealously guarded the Black Sea, would not be able to bluster at the peace negotiations.

Antonida, in a gown of soft blue, and Olga, in a bright yellow one, were dining in a hastily-erected wooden hall with two tiers of windows. A hundred and fifty guests were sitting on the outer side of the tables, which were arranged in a horseshoe. Within the horseshoe jesters performed, playing at leap-frog, fighting each other with bladders in which peas rattled, barking, mewing and raising so much dust that it flew on to the guests' plates. Nobody was watching them any more. Zotov, the Prince-Pope, was sitting under a canopy in a tin mitre; the old man was weary from waving his handkerchief to the gunners after every toast. The walls shook with the salvoes. The old jester, Yakov Turgenev, had made everyone laugh when he rode in on a dirty hump-backed pig, dressed in a turban, a Tatar gown and Turkish slippers. Shaking the false beard tied to his drink-sodden face he shouted:

"Approach, approach and kiss the heel of His Majesty the Sultan!" Now he was lying under the table, drunk as a lord.

The sailor-choristers had grown hoarse and the musicians were playing goodness knows what on their wind instruments. All were waiting for the dancing to begin. Olga's neighbour at the table was Leopoldus Mirbach, an ensign of the Preobrazhensky regiment, and next to them sat Antonida with Bartholomew Brahm, a naval lieutenant. Olga's partner had a smattering of Russian and kept squeezing his face with his hands to sober himself up; but the Dane Brahm, as red as raw meat, did nothing but drink and leer at Antonida, who was completely unstrung. Oh, what need for conversation and, in any case, what about? It was all so paltry. Just give the tips of your fingers to your partner, lift up the front of your skirts and, to the tune of the fiddles, go curtseying and gliding over the waxed floor. The girls were a-quiver like a forest lake in a thunderstorm.

Roman Borisovich was sitting with his wife at the other end of the table. The prince was very upset at being so far from the Tsar. Peter was surrounded by foreigners. Amalia Kniperkron was on one side of him and, on the other, the Duke de Crouy, so drunk that he could only jerk his head like a horse tormented by flies. Peter was in a merry mood, joking and enjoying himself. Then something happened—the guests only saw Menshikov whisper in his ear—and the laughter faded from his eyes. He was visibly making an effort to control himself. When the next course was served his hands holding the knife and fork jerked spasmodically so that he missed the plate or jabbed himself in the face. Amalia Kniperkron laid her hand on his cuff with tender solicitude:

"Herr Peter, you must calm yourself."

Peter threw down his knife and fork and laughed with a grimace:

"My hands are my enemies," he said and hid them under the table. "Why do you stare at me like that, you wise girl? We shall have such dancing tonight that our heels will fly off."

She frowned and said with quiet reproach in her voice:

"Herr Peter, am I no longer worthy of your confidence?"

His eyes flickered and the nostrils of his short nose quivered:

"Nonsense, nonsense!"

"Herr Peter, I have serious misgivings."

"Has some old woman been predicting bad luck?"

He turned away. Amalia's lips trembled:

"My father too is extremely anxious. Today I received a letter. . . ."

"A letter?" He stared with round eyes, like a bird of prey, at the girl's troubled face. "And what does Kniperkron write?"

"Herr Peter, we should be glad not to see what we can no longer fail to notice. We should be glad not to hear. . . . But it is being openly discussed already." There was some word that Amalia feared to pronounce; her nose began to redden. "It is against all reason. It would be perfidy." Her eyes filled with tears. "A word from you, Herr Peter. . . ." She half opened her mouth as though to take a deep breath.

Vasily Volkov came up quickly and grimly behind Peter's chair. His face, whipped raw by the wind, was unshaven, the creases in his coat showed that he had just taken it out of his travelling bag, and the corner of a letter protruded from his cuff. Amalia turned very pale and her eyes kept shifting rapidly from the Tsar to Volkov. She knew that Vasily and his wife had gone abroad. It was obvious that he had come galloping here with bad news.

Peter pointed to a chair beside him: "Sit down." Menshikov, in a magnificent wig, came up with a crooked smile. Peter held out his hand and Volkov hurriedly gave him the letter.

"From King August," said Peter without looking at Amalia. "Bad news. Unrest in Livonia." He turned the letter over in his hands, then resolutely pushed it into the breast of his coat. "Still, Livonia is far away. It won't stop us from making merry." He turned to Volkov: "Tell me by word of mouth."

Volkov started to rise but Menshikov pressed him back and himself stood leaning on the back of his chair.

"King August's Saxon army has invaded Livonia without a declaration of war," Volkov said, his voice faltering. "They advanced to within a short distance of Riga, but could take only a small fortress, Koberschantz. They were afraid to attack the town because of the furious fire of the defending Swedes. After this unsuccessful diversion General Karlowicz marched to the sea and took the fortress of Dünamünde by storm. Towards the end of the attack he was killed outright by a musket shot."

"It's a pity, a great pity about Karlowicz," Peter said. "Well, is that all your news?" He laid his cold hand on Amalia's. She was breathing fast. Peter squeezed her hand till it hurt. Volkov was silent. Menshikov said carelessly, passing the curls of his wig through his beringed fingers:

"I questioned him. That is all he knows. He was in Warsaw when the news came from Riga. King August sent him here the same day. The Saxons have not taken Riga and are not going to—the Swedes have strong teeth. It was a foolish enterprise."

With her hand still in Peter's, Amalia hung her head, her face distorted with emotion.

"This means war, this means war, Herr Peter," she whispered. "Don't hide it from me. I realised it already when we were on the way here. Oh, what a misfortune!"

Peter was silent for a moment. Then he asked in a harsh voice:

"What was it you realised? Was anything said? Who said it?"

She told him somewhat incoherently about Prince Roman's utterances at the posting-station which had so much astonished her.

"Buynosov babbled this nonsense to you?" Peter asked in a threatening tone. "What, that fool?" Amalia nodded, shaking the tears off her cheeks. "You believed that dolt? You, whom we all regard as a wise girl! Take a handkerchief and wipe your tears." He felt that Amalia was involuntarily heeding him and regaining her composure. "Write to your father and say that I shall never consent to start an unjust war. I shall not break the permanent peace made with King Charles. Even should the Polish King take Riga, he will not keep it, I will tear it from his grasp, I swear before God."

Peter's round eyes looked sincere. Menshikov nodded in confirmation; but he put his fingers over his mouth, for any kind of smile would have been out of place.

Amalia dabbed her cheeks with her handkerchief and smiled uncertainly. She believed Peter and felt repentant. Peter leant back in his leather chair and called out gaily:

"Prince Roman, come here!"

Roman Borisovich did not distinguish the Tsar's voice at once because of the din raised by the jesters who had started squealing and romping round a dish of lampreys, rolling about and tearing the fish out of each other's mouths. He was laughing until it made him hiccup. Antonida and Olga indicated with frowning glances that the Tsar was calling him. Princess Avdotya plucked his trousers: "Go for the Tsar's favour, go. It has come to us at last."

Prince Roman went off at a trot to answer the summons, and

bowed, his sword raising his coat tails: "Here I am, Sire, yours body and soul." Peter did not even turn in his direction, but said to Amalia:

"This man is a splendid and daring politician. I don't quite know whether to make him Commander-in-Chief, I fear he might shed a lot of blood. Or I might use him at home."

And he turned so abruptly to Roman Borisovich that the prince's sight was suddenly clouded by a red mist.

"I hear you are preparing for war, to take back our ancient Livonian lands? Is that so, I ask you?"

Roman Borisovich blinked and nausea slid from his belly to his knees.

"We need brave generals. For your great daring I appoint you Commander-in-Chief of the whole jesters' army."

Peter jumped up and dragged Roman Borisovich by the hand to the platform where Zotov, the Prince-Pope, his arms dangling and his bloated face frowning, was growling in his sleep as though he were dying. Peter started to shake him. "Go to the devil!" Zotov mumbled. The guests, sensing some new piece of fun, crowded round the platform. The jesters crawled between their legs and seated themselves on the steps. They put a cross made of two pipes tied together and an egg into Zotov's hands. Roman Borisovich was made to kneel. Zotov, now shaken awake, wiped his drooling mouth.

"Confirm his appointment?" he asked. "All right, drat him!"

And he tapped Roman Borisovich on the crown of his head with the egg, so that the yolk dripped down his wig. Then he pushed the pipes into his face and gave him a shove with his foot. The jesters began to crow. Then they seated Roman Borisovich astride a chair, put a bare ham-bone into his hand and dragged him into the centre between the tables. Roman Borisovich was completely paralysed, clutching the bone and gaping. The guests pointed at him and swayed with laughter. Amalia Kniperkron also laughed loudly; all her fears and heartache had ended in a joke.

Antonida and Olga only fully realised the misfortune when, looking round, they missed their partners. Mirbach and Brahm were at the door of the ballroom, bowing low with drunken insistence before the detestable Princesses Shahovskoy. The eight princesses, curving their arms and turning their powdered wigs this way and that, curtsied endlessly, throwing provocative glances at the Buynosov girls the while.

2

The Volkovs never reached Riga that winter. The broad sledge-track led from Smolensk through Orsha to Kreuzburg. Beyond the Polish frontier things were very different from Muscovy, where a day's journey through dense forests separated village from village. In Poland there were villages at short intervals, and on a hill there would be a monastery, or a church and a mansion, or in some places even a walled and moated castle. In Russia only petty landowners, owing service to the Crown, lived in their country houses, or else some boyar in disgrace would be gloomily entrenched, like a badger, behind his high log walls. The Polish landed gentry lived gaily and entertained lavishly.

Alexandra Ivanovna was dying to turn off the road towards one of these wonderful castles, whose pointed slate roofs and enormous windows showed between age-old lime-trees. Volkov replied angrily: "We are on the Tsar's service, we are carrying credentials. It is not fitting for us to invite ourselves. Do try to understand."

They did not have to invite themselves after all. One day, late in the evening, they drove into a large village which seemed dead—even the dogs did not bark. They drew up before an inn. While the innkeeper, a tall, stooping Jew in a fox-fur cap, was struggling to open the gates, Alexandra Ivanovna got out of the sledge to stretch her legs. She looked up at the half-moon; its melancholy light had not eclipsed the stars. She felt a strange, wistful yearning as she walked slowly along the village street. The small log-houses were nearly all ramshackle, many were without roofs and the bare rafters showed black against the moonlit sky. Under a weeping willow, white with hoar-frost, she saw a small chapel. At the closed door a woman, in a white coat, lay prone with her hands pressed over her face. She did not turn round at the crunching of the snow. Sanka stood for a while, then sighed and walked away. It seemed to her all the time that she could hear music playing in the distance.

Volkov called her, and they went together into the inn through a long passage cluttered with small vats and barrels. The innkeeper lit their way with a tallow candle. His thick beard stuck out from his small face and his eyes were old and morose. "There are no bed-bugs, you'll sleep well," he said in Byelorussian. "If only Pan Malahovski doesn't take it into his head to come to the inn. Oh, God, God!"

It was hot inside the inn and there was a sour smell. A child in a cradle hanging from the ceiling was crying behind a ragged curtain. Sanka took off her fur coat and lay down on the cushions brought in from the cold; she too felt like crying. She half-closed her eyes, feeling an unbearable uneasiness somewhere near her heart—in the seat of the soul. She could not tell whether she felt pity for someone, or was yearning for love.

The door of the inn kept slamming all the time: the innkeeper and other people constantly went out and came in. The child was crying forlornly. "No sleep again tonight." Her husband called: "Sanka, are you going to have supper?" She pretended to be asleep. She kept seeing the waning moon shedding its dim light on the back of the woman in the white coat by the chapel. She tried to drive the image away, but could not. A vision of long ago rose before her: her mother's terrible eyes as she lay dying. The cresset burning, her small brothers in wetted shirts hanging their heads from the stove, listening to their mother's groans and looking at the shadow of the spinning-wheel on the log wall: like an old man with a thin neck and a goat's beard. "Sanka, Sanka," her mother murmured in a voice as weak as a sigh, "Sanka, it's for them I'm sorry."

Volkov was unhurriedly eating soup. The door banged again and someone came in and sighed cautiously. Sanka was swallowing her tears: "That's how one can miss one's happiness." Her husband said again: "Sanka, do have some milk at least."

A woman's voice said at the door: "Kind gentleman—may the Holy Mother preserve you!—we haven't eaten for three days. Spare us some bread of your kindness." Sanka sat up on the bench feeling as though she had been stabbed through her heart. At the door a woman knelt, a pitiful child's face showing in the breast of her white coat. Sanka sprang up and seized a dish of roast goose. "Here, take it!" she said giving it to the woman and involuntarily nodded to her in peasant fashion. "Now go, go!"

The woman went away. Sanka sat down at the table; her heart was beating so violently that she could not even swallow the milk. Volkov turned to the Jewish innkeeper:

"What is it? Did you have a bad harvest?"

"No, God has not let that happen yet. Pan Malahovski took the good harvest and has already sent it to Königsberg."

"Fancy that!" Volkov said with astonishment, and laid down his spoon. "They sell in Königsberg. And do they get a good price?"

"Oh, the prices, the prices!" the innkeeper croaked, wagging his matted beard. He set the candlestick on the bench but did not dare to sit down. "Nowadays the Königsberg merchants know only too well that there is no one else to whom you can take the wheat; you can't take it to Riga, for who would want to pay custom duties to the Swedes? And so they offer a guilder."

"A guilder! For thirty-six pounds?" Volkov opened wide, incredulous blue eyes. "You must be lying!"

"Believe me, I'm not lying, why should I lie to the noble *Pan*? When I was young, the wheat used to be taken to Riga, and there they gave one and a half and even two guilders. The noble *Pan* will not be angry if I sit down? Oh, God, God! It's all Pan Malahovski's little joke. He hacked the Jew, Alter, to death with his sword in Pan Badovski's village. And Pan Badovski is such a man that for no more than a hen he's prepared to muster all the small nobles dependent on him. Alter was his bailiff. And so Pan Badovski, together with his noble followers, attacked Pan Malahovski. The pistol shots that were fired! Oh, God, God! After that Pan Malahovski with his noble followers attacked Pan Badovski. The amount of gunpowder they used! And all because of one Jew who had been killed. Then they made it up and drank fifty barrels of beer. Pan Malahovski's noble followers galloped into our village, seized me, seized five other of our Jews, threw us into a cart, fastened us down with poles, and drove us to Pan Badovski's yard. Pan Malahovski held his belly with his hands, he laughed so much. 'There you are, Pan Badovski,' he said. 'Six Jews in the place of one'. Yankel Kagan had a rib broken while he was lying in the cart, Moses Levid's liver was damaged, and my legs have started to shrivel since that time."

"Then, if you're not lying," Volkov said pouring milk into an earthenware saucer, "why is your village so poor?"

"How are the peasants to fatten?"

"Who said fatten? One can't let a peasant grow too fat. Still, the huts should have their roofs mended. The way things are here, I can see, the cattle live better. You don't seem to have any quit-rent peasants."

"All our peasants work on the landowner's land."

"How many days a week?"

"They work all six days for the landlord."

Volkov was again astonished. "With us the Tsar's treasury wouldn't allow it: you couldn't get half a kopek out of such a peasant," he thought to himself and said:

"Who then pays the taxes to the State treasury here? Is it the *Pans*?"

"No, the *Pans* don't pay any taxes. We pay the *Pans*."

"A strange kind of State." Volkov smiled and shook his head. "Sanka, this is indeed freedom for the *Pans*. . . ."

But Sanka was not listening. The pupils of her wide-open eyes were fixed. Then she turned to the window and pressed her face to the damp glass. The sound of music, of tinkling harness-bells and of voices came louder and louder from outside. The innkeeper grew uneasy; he picked up the candle and, stooping, shuffled to the door:

"Didn't I tell you? Pan Malahovski won't let you sleep."

A dozen sledges had drawn up before the inn. Jews were scraping fiddles and blowing reedy clarinets. The Polish gentry reclining on rugs kicked up their legs, roared with laughter and shouted encouragements. One of them, with a huge moustache, dressed in a short fur-trimmed jacket, was dancing on the well-trodden snow: now prancing haughtily, gently stroking his moustache, now whirling furiously, with his sword flying round him.

Horsemen carrying torches galloped up and sprang off their mounts. Out of the darkness emerged four tall horses with peacock feathers on their proudly raised heads. In the open sledge ladies were seated. Sanka remained glued to the windowpane staring at the foreign ladies: all were dressed in tight velvet coats trimmed with fur and tiny hats on the sides of their heads. The ladies, lit up by the torches, were laughing. A thickset *Pan* climbed off the footboard of the sledge and walked, swaying, towards the inn. When he caught sight of Sanka's face behind the dim glass, he waved his arm to the attendant gentry: "Come on!" The *Pan*, followed by the company, some in plain fur jackets, others quite ragged, but all armed with swords and pistols, broke noisily into the inn. The *Pan*, with a face as red as a copper kettle, stood straddling and stroked his moustache, which was so magnificent that his hand could not contain it. His coat, lined with silver fox-fur, was covered with snow; he had evidently fallen more than once off the footboard. Rattling his sword and fixing his glittering eyes on Sanka he said pompously, in a voice hoarse with prolonged drinking:

"Gracious Princess, the accursed innkeeper was late in reporting your arrival to me. How can it be that such a beautiful high-born lady should spend the night in a nasty village inn? We shan't allow it. Gentlemen, throw yourselves at the lady's feet, beg the Princess to come to the castle!"

His followers, some of whom were grey-haired, and had faces slashed with sword scars, had filled the room with the reek of alcohol.

Now they began to fall down on one knee before Sanka and, whipping off their caps, struck their chests with the palms of their hands:

"Gracious lady Princess, I shall die, and not rise from your ravishing feet, until you accept Pan Malahovski's invitation."

Sanka had jumped up from the table pulling her travelling shawl off her shoulders and now she stood before the kneeling gentry, pale, with raised eyebrows, her nostrils quivering. As he gazed at this beautiful woman, Pan Malahovski pushed aside one of the gentlemen, then another and, going up to her himself, fell heavily on one knee:

"I implore you!"

Sanka still retained enough sense to look round at her husband. Vasily was greatly alarmed. With a trembling hand he was unbuttoning the collar of his shirt to get at the little bag he wore on his chest which contained the document certifying the inviolability of his person. Sanka's voice faltered slightly but she managed to say sweetly:

"I shall be happy to make your acquaintance."

Pan Malahovski had been carousing for over a week and making the whole of the Orsha province resound with it. Pani Augusta, his wife, was so fond of entertainments and balls that she danced her partners off their feet. If one of them, completely worn out, hid in a closet, they would wake him up and drag him, half asleep, into the pillared hall where, in the gallery, gaunt musicians in patched coats were exerting themselves to the utmost. From the Venetian chandeliers, under the richly decorated ceiling, candle-wax dripped on to sweaty wigs and flying skirts; in the neighbouring rooms the petty gentry drank and shouted enthusiastically.

Suddenly, in the middle of the night, Pani Augusta—small, curly-haired, with dimpled cheeks—would think of some new amusement and clap her hands: "Let's be off!" They piled into sledges and, lighted by torches, rushed off to some neighbour, where there would again be barrels of Hungarian wine, sheep roasted whole for the high-born guests and great tureens of tripe with garlic for the lesser fry. Toasts were drunk to the beautiful ladies, to Polish honour, to the great freedom of the Polish State. Or else Pani Augusta would take it into her head to dress up her guests as Turks, Greeks and Hindus, while the less important ones had their faces blackened with soot. After spending a gay night, they drove in their fancy-dress to the neighbouring monastery, whose bell tinkled hospitably on a low hill behind the bare trees. They attended mass and afterwards went to the white dining-hall, warmed by logs flaming on the hearth, and there drank century-old mead and joked with monks wearing scented robes and spurred, in readiness to play the gallant.

Sanka threw herself into this gaiety with all the fire of her being. She just changed her gowns and damp chemises, rubbed herself down with scented vodka and once more, tall and looking thinner, steeped in music, proudly curtsied in a minuet or whirled in a mazurka.

At the start Vasily behaved with discretion, until two great eaters and drinkers, famous through Poland for their size and prowess—Pan Hodkovski and Pan Domoratski—were attached to him. These two gentlemen could empty at one draught a tankard holding four quarts of beer, devour a whole goose with plums followed by a tureen of cheese dumplings and wash down the lot with five bottles of Hungarian wine. Vasily spent day and night with them exchanging maudlin embraces. During lucid intervals, he sought out his wife unhappily: "Sanka, dear heart, we must be going; it's enough." But Sanka did not even look round at him. Pan Hodkovski would then put his arm round his shoulder and the two would totter off to more feasting.

Vasily made inarticulate sounds, burrowing his head into the pillow; someone was shaking him by the shoulder. He was sleeping fully dressed except for his coat and boots. His head felt like lead; he could not lift it. Whoever it was went on shaking persistently, and he felt the nails dig into his flesh. "Oh, what now?"

"Come and dance with me! Come, come on now!" Sanka repeated in so strange a voice that Vasily raised himself on his elbow. Sanka stood by the bed nodding her powdered head at him and her eyes were tragic, as though the house were on fire or some calamity had happened.

"You don't want to dance with me?"

"You're crazy, my girl. It's already morning."

Sanka's altered face and bare shoulders looked blue in the light of the dawn that came through the large, clear window. "That's what she has driven herself to—as pale as a ghost," he thought to himself.

"You'd better go to bed," he said.

"You don't want to, you don't want to! Ah, Vasily!"

She dropped on a high chair and let her arms hang loose. She smelt of sweet French scent, of something alien. She gazed at her husband without blinking and a lump rose in her throat.

"Vasya, do you love me?"

If only she had put her question gently, in her ordinary voice; but no, it seemed to hold a threat. Vasily thumped the pillow with his fist in vexation:

"Let me at least live in peace."

She again swallowed the lump in her throat:

"Tell me, how much do you love me?"

What could he say to that? Woman's foolishness! If his head had not been splitting, Vasily would certainly have sworn. But he had neither the strength nor the desire to do so, and he was silent, looking at his wife with a reproachful smile. Sanka flung up her hands softly:

"You won't keep me safe. . . . It'll be your fault."

She got up, kicked back the long train of her gown and went out.

"Sanka, you might at least close the door!"

After that Vasily could not get to sleep; he kept sighing, turning over in the bed and listening to the distant sound of music in the halls downstairs. In spite of himself the thought nagged him: "It's bad, it's wrong." He sat up in bed holding his head in his hands. "This is no way to live." He dressed and went out by the back door to the service quarters to see whether their sledge was in proper shape. When, near the coach-house, he saw the coachman Antip—whom he had bought for sixty roubles from the governor of Smolensk to replace the one they had lost near Vyazma—the sight of a man of his own filled him with pleasure:

"Well, Antip, we'll be leaving tomorrow."

"Oh, Vasily Vasilyevich, it's a good thing; I'm sick of this place."

"Go to the innkeeper tonight and inquire about the horses."

Vasily walked slowly back through the park. The clean snow was blown along by the wind, and the trees, with their rooks' nests, soughed solemnly. A number of peasant men and women were working on the pond: apparently the whole village had been rounded up to clear away the snow and put up poles with flags of some kind that snapped in the wind. "Nothing but trifling and amusements. . . ." Vasily stopped suddenly as though someone had seized him by the shoulders. His heart thumped. Light broke upon him: this was the man! How many times he had seen it through his drunken haze, but only at this moment did he realise it: this was the man—Pan Wladislaw Tyklinski—a tall handsome fellow in a Paris coat of orange velvet. Alexandra was always with him: she danced the minuet with him, the country dance, the mazurka; always with him.

Vasily looked at the ground. Snow plastered his cheek, his neck. But the acute perception was only momentary and was again lost in the drunken haze. He took no decision. In the meantime people had started looking for him to take him to breakfast. It was the custom here to have an early breakfast after a gay night and then sleep till dinner-time. His friends, of whom he had by now become heartily sick—Hodkovski and Domoratski, paunchy braggarts and liars—seized him by the elbows with roars of laughter: "What a lovely hash they have served, Pan Vasily. . . ." Alexandra was not at the table, nor was the other one. Vasily swallowed some potent old vodka, but it had no effect on him.

He got up from the table and went into the ballroom; there was no one there. In the gallery a tall, bony Jew was sleeping, sprawled across the big drum. Vasily softly opened the double doors leading into the mirror-gallery: there, on the waxed parquet floor, strewn with scraps of coloured paper, Alexandra was walking by the windows with Pan Wladislaw, his sword impudently cocking up the tails of his coat. He was telling her something with great warmth, with an impatient jerking of his wig. She listened to him with bent head. There was something girlish and defenceless in the curve of her neck: they had taken an inexperienced little fool to a foreign land and left her alone and, if somebody hurt her, she would only swallow her tears.

Vasily ought to have acted wrathfully, demanded satisfaction from the proud Pole, but all he did was to look through the half-opened door and suffer pangs of pity. "Ah, you're a poor sort of protector, Vasily!" Meanwhile Pan Wladislaw made a graceful gesture towards a side door, at which Sanka's shoulders lifted slightly and she gently shook her head. They turned round and went out into the winter-garden. Vasily involuntarily stretched out his arm to roll up his sleeve. It wasn't a sleeve—nothing but lace. And he had left his sword upstairs. Damn!

He flung back one leaf of the doors with a bang, but was assailed from behind by the noisy, fat Hodkovski and Domoratski.

"Come, Pan Vasily, you must taste the hot cheese dumplings with cream."

And again he was sitting at table in great confusion of mind. He felt both shame and anger. There was evidently some collusion here. These gluttons were purposely making him drink too much. Should he run and fetch his sword and fight? A fine Tsar's envoy, fighting on a woman's account like a peasant in the village square! No matter; better put an end to it here and now.

Pushing away the glass he was being offered he strode hastily out of the dining-room. Upstairs, clenching his teeth, he looked for his sword. He found it at last under a pile of Sanka's skirts. He put on his sword-belt and drew it as tight as he could. Then he ran down the stone staircase. Everyone in the castle had already laid themselves down to sleep. He made a round of the winter-garden but found it deserted. A serving-girl he met curtsied low and squeaked:

"The Pani Princess, Pani Malahovska and Pan Tylinski have gone out for a drive and left word not to expect them till the evening."

Vasily returned upstairs and sat by the window watching the road until twilight fell. His thoughts even drove him to compose a remorseful letter to the Tsar. But he could find neither paper nor pen.

Later it turned out that Sanka had returned a long time ago and was resting in Pani Augusta's room. After supper there was to be a carnival and fireworks on the pond. Vasily made a trip to the coachhouse and gave orders to Antip to prepare the horses on the quiet and carry some of their luggage into the sledge. He started moodily back to the castle. Fire-pans were being lit along the cornices and the wind fluttered the little flames. The snow-clouds had blown away and the night was pale blue with a gibbous moon.

Near a small pavilion with stone statues, half-covered with snow, Volkov suddenly heard hoarse shouts, loud panting and the clash of sword blades. He felt no curiosity and was about to pass on. Round the corner, at the foot of a Cupid armed with an arrow, a woman stood holding together at her neck the fur coat thrown over her shoulders; her head in its white wig was thrown back. He peered at her and recognised Alexandra. He ran up to her. Close by, behind the corner in the moonlight, Pan Wladislaw and Pan Malahovski were fighting with swords. They leaped about on legs planted wide apart, with knees slightly bent, lunging at each other, stamping, panting with noisy fury and clashing sword against sword.

Sanka threw herself at Vasily, put her arms round him and clung to him. Throwing back her head and shutting her eyes she said, through clenched teeth:

"Take me away, take me away!"

The moustached Malahovski gave a loud cry as he caught sight of Vasily. Pan Wladislaw ran at him shouting: "She's not yours; we won't let you!" Their followers came running through the park with drawn swords to separate the duellists.

Vasily recovered his composure when they had put about thirty miles between themselves and Pan Malahovski. He did not utter a single word of reproach nor did he ask Sanka anything, but he was grave. She sat very quiet in the sledge, her eyes shut. When they came to rich estates, they drove past them, taking by-ways.

Once the guide who sat with the coachman, his fingers thrust in the narrow sleeves of his sheepskin coat, turned round pointing from the rising ground at the tiled roof of a chapel by the road. Antip thrust his head inside the sledge:

"Vasily Vasilyevich, we won't be able to help stopping here."

It appeared that this chapel, dedicated to St. Jan Nepomuk, had been built by the famous Pan Boreyko, whose obesity, gluttony and hospitality had become proverbial. The *Pan's* house stood far off the road, beyond a small dark wood. In order to facilitate the mustering of boon-companions he had built the chapel on the high-road. One building contained a kitchen and a cellar, in another was a dining-room. Here a fat and merry friar lived permanently. He held divine service, and whiled away the tedious hours playing cards with the *Pan.* Together they lay in wait for travellers.

Whoever happened to be passing—whether an important *Pan,* a carefree petty nobleman, who had drunk away his last cap, or a tradesman from some small town—the servants stretched a rope across the road and Pan Boreyko, waddling and wheezing, offered him a goblet of wine, while the servants quickly unharnessed the horses. The alarmed traveller was then dragged into the chapel, the friar said grace and feasting began. Pan Boreyko did no harm to anyone, but no one left him sober; some were carried back to their sledges in a state of unconsciousness, but there were some who passed away without recovering their senses and were given absolution by the friar.

"What are we going to do, Vasily Vasilyevich?" Antip asked.

"Turn off and drive as fast as you can across the fields."

Apparently the *Pans* had but one thought: to amuse themselves. The whole of the Polish State seemed to be light-heartedly carousing. In the boroughs and small towns every house of any consequence had its gates wide open, with tipsy gentry roistering on the porch. But the streets in the towns were clean, there were many good shops and markets. Over the shops and barbers' shops and over guild enterprises there were painted signs at right angles to the street: a lady in a carriage, or a gentleman on horseback, or else a barber's copper basin. In a doorway a German with a china pipe would be standing, smiling affably, or a Jew in a good greatcoat, politely inviting those who walked or rode past, to come in and have a look round. Unlike

Moscow—where a petty tradesman dragged the customer by the skirts of his coat into a poor shop where shabby wares were sold at high prices—here, in whatever shop you set foot, your eyes were dazzled. And if you had no money, they let you have the things on credit.

The nearer they came to the Livonian frontier, the more little townships they passed. Windmill sails turned on the hills and, in the villages, manure was already being carted out to the fields. There was a promise of spring in the lowering sky. Sanka's eyes were again shining. They were approaching Kreuzburg when something unexpected happened.

Peter Andreyevich Tolstoy, a chamberlain, returning from abroad to Moscow, was resting at the inn behind a partition. Hearing Russian voices he came out, with a short sheepskin coat thrown over his shoulders and a silk kerchief tied round his bald head.

"Pardon an old man," he said with a courteous bow to Alexandra Ivanovna. "This pleasant meeting affords me great happiness."

While Sanka was taking off her things, he watched her with a steady and warm gaze from under his eyebrows, as black as ermine tails. He was about fifty years old, short and lean, but sinewy. Tolstoy was not popular in Moscow, and the Tsar could not forgive him the past, when he and Hovansky had rallied the streltsi in support of Sophia. But Tolstoy knew how to wait. He undertook difficult missions abroad and acquitted himself with great credit. He knew languages and literature, could buy, at a suitable price, a fine picture (for Menshikov's palace), or a useful book, and engage an efficient man for the service. He did not push himself forward. Many were beginning to fear him a little.

"Are you going to Riga?" he asked Alexandra Ivanovna, while her Kalmuk maid was pulling off her felt boots.

"We are going to Paris," she replied with feigned nonchalance.

Tolstoy groped for his horn snuffbox, tapped it with his middle finger and plunged his big nose into the snuff:

"You'll have no end of trouble; better go through Warsaw."

Volkov, rubbing his face, reddened by the cold and the wind, asked: "Why?"

"Because there is war in Livonia, Vasily Vasilyevich; Riga is besieged."

Sanka's hands flew to her cheeks. Volkov blinked with alarm:

"Has it begun? How? King August alone, then. . . ?"

He choked on his words under Tolstoy's glance of cold warning.

Tolstoy raised his tobacco-stained nose and sneezed. The ends of his silk kerchief flapped like ears:

"I advise you, my dear Vasily Vasilyevich, to turn immediately towards Mitau. King August is there. He will be glad to see you and especially your charming wife."

Tolstoy told them something about the war which had just begun. Already in the autumn King August's Saxon battalions had begun to assemble near the Livonian frontier, in Janiszki and Mitau. Dalberg, the governor of Riga, who, three years ago, had insulted Peter and the great Muscovite mission, either shut his eyes or attached little importance to this movement of troops. Riga could have been taken by a surprise attack. But priceless time had been lost in love-making and unreasonable frivolity: the Saxon commander-in-chief, young General Fleming, fell in love with the niece of Pan Sapieha and spent the whole winter carousing in his castle. The soldiers caroused in their turn and plundered the Kurland villages. The peasants sought refuge in Livonia, and finally in Riga they realised the danger. The governor fortified the town.

"When General Karlowicz arrived, military operations were, thank God, properly started," Tolstoy went on, wrinkling his shaven lips, as if savouring his words. "But alas! Venus and Bacchus disdain the whistling of bullets: General Fleming seeks more arduous battles. Instead of attacking the Swedes, he boldly lays siege to the fortress of the beautiful Polish lady, whom he has already taken to Dresden, where the wedding will soon take place."

From this whole story Volkov realised that King August's affairs were going none too well. He decided that, to avoid some blunder for which he might have to answer to the Tsar, he had better go to Mitau.

"Where are your knights, sir? Where are your ten thousand cuirasses? Your sworn promises, sir? You have lied to the king!"

August wrathfully banged down the lighted candelabrum among the powder-puffs, gloves and scent-bottles in front of his mirror. One candle fell down and went out. He began to stride to and fro on the silvery carpet of his bedchamber. His tightly stockinged strong calves twitched angrily. Johann Patkul stood in front of him, pale and grim, clutching his hat in his hands.

He had done everything within human power. All through the winter he had been writing rousing letters and sending them out secretly to the knights in Riga and on their Livonian estates. Braving the penalties of Swedish law he had crossed the frontier, disguised as a merchant, and visited von Benckendorf, von Sievers and von Pahlen in their castles. The knights read his letters and wept as they recalled the former power of their Order. They complained of the corn duties, and those who had lost part of their lands through the Reduction Law swore that they would not spare their lives. But when at last the Saxon army invaded Livonia and King August issued a proclamation on the overthrow of Swedish bondage, not one of the knights dared to mount his horse; worse than that, many of them joined the burghers in fortifying and defending Riga from the king's mercenaries, who were thirsting to sack the town.

That very day Patkul had brought his unwelcome news to Mitau. The king left his dinner, snatched up a candelabrum, seized Patkul by the hand and hurried him to his bedchamber.

"You pushed me into this war, sir; you! I drew my sword relying on your plighted word. And now, you dare announce that the Livonian knights—those drunkards and liver-sausage guzzlers—are still hesitating."

August, enormous and magnificent in his white military coat, advanced on Patkul with clenched fists, shook his lace cuffs furiously and, in his rage, shouted many things that would have been better left unsaid.

"Where are the Danish auxiliaries? You promised them to me. Where are Tsar Peter's fifty regiments? Where are your two hundred thousand gold pieces? The Poles, damn it, are waiting for this money! The Poles are waiting for my victory to draw their swords, or for my defeat to start a terrible civil war."

Foam trickled from his full, shapely lips and his handsome face quivered. Patkul turned his eyes away, controlling the rage that was rising in his throat. He answered:

"Sire, the knights would like a guarantee that if they overthrow Swedish rule they won't be invaded by the Moscow barbarians. In my opinion this is the reason for their hesitation."

"Nonsense! Those are idle fears. Tsar Peter has sworn on the crucifix that he will not go beyond Yamburg. The Russians want Ingria and Karelia. They will not attempt to seize even Narva."

"Sire, I fear treachery. I know that spies have been sent from Moscow to Narva and Reval, ostensibly to purchase goods, but they have orders to draw plans of these fortresses."

August drew back. His large hand with its tinted nails fell on the hilt of his sword and his round chin rose haughtily:

"Herr von Patkul, I give you my royal word that neither Narva, nor

Reval, and still less Riga, will see the Russians. Whatever happens, I will snatch these cities from Tsar Peter's clutches."

The king was terribly bored in the ducal palace of Mitau. His presence near the army did nothing to advance matters. The only success was the fall of the fortress of Koberschanz. Riga was bombarded twice without result. The Livonian knights were still making up their minds whether they should mount and ride. The Polish magnates were guardedly waiting and apparently preparing to question the king at the next session of the Diet on why he was drawing Poland into this dangerous war.

The weather in Mitau was bad. There was little money. The Kurland squires were clods, their wives more like cows about to calve than members of the bewitching sex. The young Duke of Kurland, Friedrich Wilhelm, was a conceited braggart and an intolerable bore. Only the efforts of August's new friend, Athalie Desmont, who had left gay Warsaw with him, saved the high-spirited king from falling a victim to melancholy.

Athalie Desmont arranged dances and hunts, brought Italian actors from Warsaw, and squandered money with such incomprehensible generosity that even August sometimes snorted as he instructed the Lord Chamberlain to find so many gold dubloons for the countess. The harsh climate made the Italian artists cough and sneeze. At the elegantly devised balls the local nobility, unacquainted with refined pleasures, only goggled at all this luxury, mentally calculating how much it must have cost the king.

One day the king was having dinner. According to his custom he ate alone, sitting at a small table with his back to the fire. The ladies sat opposite to him, in a semi-circle, on little gilt chairs. The king was wearing a small elegant wig, a light coat with a floral design and a lawn shirt with a lace frill that fell to his waist. The royal cup-bearer, a parchment-faced old man with dyed whiskers, kept refilling the king's glass with mulled wine. That day six local baronesses with beetroot-coloured cheeks were present at the audience, and six stout barons stood self-consciously behind the floured wigs. Two chairs were unoccupied.

August, chewing stuffed hare, looked dully at the ladies. The logs in the fireplace crackled. The barons and baronesses did not stir, obviously afraid of making unseemly noises, such as sniffing. The silence grew oppressive. August put his elbow on the table, wiped his lips and dropped the napkin on the table.

"*Mesdames et messieurs,* I shall never tire of repeating how glad I am to be the guest of your delightful city." He emphasised his words with a slight gesture of his hand. "The high moral qualities of the Kurland nobility should serve as an example to all: it felicitously combines sober common-sense with a noble outlook."

The barons bowed their horsehair wigs with dignity, and the baronesses, after a pause (for they did not understand French very well), raised their ample behinds and curtsied.

"*Mesdames et messieurs,* alas, in our practical age even kings, in their concern for their subjects' welfare, are sometimes obliged to descend to earth. Alas, not everyone understands this truth." He sighed and turned his eyes to heaven. "What else but bitterness can one feel at the shortsighted and frivolous extravagance of the Polish lord who, swollen with pride, squanders his gold on feasting and hunting, on the keep of drunkards and idlers, while his king, like any simple soldier, draws his sword to storm the enemy's strongholds?"

August took a sip of wine. The barons listened with strained attention.

"It is not customary to question kings. But kings read the emotions of their subjects in their eyes. *Messieurs,* I began this war alone, with ten thousand of my guards. *Messieurs,* I began it in the name of a great principle. Poland is torn by internal strife. The Elector of Brandenburg, that savage wolf, is gnawing at our liver. The Swedes are masters of the Baltic. King Charles is no longer a boy, he is audacious. Had I not forestalled him in Livonia, tomorrow the Swedes would be here, imposing a fivefold duty on Kurland grain and extending the Reduction Law to your estates."

His light eyes opened wide. The barons began to breathe heavily, the ladies stiffened.

"The Lord has entrusted me with a mission: to establish peace and prosperity in a great united State stretching from the Elbe to the Dniepr, from Pomerania to the Finnish coast. Someone must eat the broth that has been brewed. Swedish, Brandenburgian and Amsterdam merchants are stretching out their spoons towards it. *Messieurs,* I am a nobleman. I desire that this broth should be eaten in peace by yourselves." He raised his eyes to the ceiling as though measuring the distance from which he must descend. "Yesterday I had two foragers hanged for robbing several farms on Baron Yxkul's estate. But, *messieurs,* my soldiers are shedding their blood, they desire nothing but glory. The horses, however, need oats and hay, the devil take them! I am compelled to appeal to the farsightedness of those for whom we are shedding our blood."

The barons' faces grew purple as they at last realised what the king was driving at. August, in growing irritation at their silence, began to spice his phrases with barrack-yard expressions. Then Athalie entered the room; her lowered eyelids gave a passionate expression to her pale-olive face. With exquisite nonchalance she dropped a curtsey to the king, waved her mother-of-pearl fan—the baronesses looked askance at this amazing Parisian novelty—and said with a bow:

"Sire, grant me the pleasure of presenting to you the Venus from Moscow."

She walked to the door, dragging her enormous train behind her, and led in Alexandra Volkova by the hand. Of all her devices this was, perhaps, the shrewdest. Having been the first to learn about the Volkovs' arrival, she called on them at their inn and was quick to size up Alexandra's qualities. She took her to her own apartments in the palace, looked over all her clothes and strictly forbade her to wear any of her Moscow garments: "My dear, these are clothes for Samoyeds!" she said even of Alexandra's best dresses that had each cost a hundred gold pieces. "Wigs! But they were worn last century! After the Nymphs' festival in Versailles no one wears wigs, my child." Athalie ordered the maid to throw all the wigs into the fire. Alexandra was so overawed that she only blinked and agreed with everything. Athalie opened her chests and dressed up Alexandra as a *"femme de qualité* in evening attire".

August gazed at the Moscow Venus with pleased surprise. He saw two ash-blonde waves on her bent head, with a curling tress falling over the low-cut bosom of her dress, and a few flowers in her hair and on her dress. The dress was simple, without panniers, cut straight like a Greek tunic, with a mantle of gold brocade thrown over her shoulder and trailing on the ground.

August took the tips of her fingers and, bending down, kissed them. Alexandra had only a brief glimpse of the flushed faces of the baronesses. This was the long-awaited hour. The king was like a fairytale king, like a king out of a pack of cards: big, splendid, gracious, with a red mouth and high well-shaped eyebrows. Sanka looked as if bewitched into his confidently gleaming eyes. "I am lost," she thought to herself.

Volkov had been waiting at the inn for little short of a week.

Alexandra had been taken away and he was forgotten. He drove to the palace to enquire, and the king's adjutant amiably assured him each time that the king would not fail to receive him tomorrow. To while away the time Volkov wandered through the crooked little streets of the town. The tall, narrow houses, with their plain roofs and iron doors, seemed to be deserted; only now and then he would see an angry face, topped by a nightcap, peering through some high window. In the market-places nearly all the shops were closed. At times guns, drawn by four gaunt horses, thundered over the great cobblestones. Sullen horsemen wrapped themselves in their woollen cloaks to shield themselves from the searching wind. Only beggars —peasants, women with tear-stained faces and children in rags— wandered in groups through the town and looked up at the windows, cap in hand.

In the evenings, after supper, Volkov would sit by the light of a candle, his cheek propped up in his hand, thinking of his wife, of Moscow, of the difficulties of his service. To be humble, God-fearing and respectful to your elders, as father and grandfather had taught you to be, did not take you very far nowadays. Those who had teeth and claws were the ones who succeeded. Alexander Menshikov was bold, impudent—until quite recently merely an orderly—and now he was a governor, a courtier, and only waiting for an opportunity to rise two heads above everyone else. Alioshka Brovkin had been promoted captain of the guard for recruiting troops. Yashka Brovkin, a clumsy, surly brute of a peasant, was in command of a ship. And Sanka! Ah, Sanka, dear God, dear God! Another husband would have covered her back with weals from his whip. It meant then that there was something else that he ought to understand. Those who kept quiet were not in favour. Whether you wanted to or not, you had to climb. He looked wistfully at the flame of the candle. How he longed for the peace of mind of those days when he had sat in his quiet mansion, listening to the howling of the storm over the snow-covered roof! The stove, the crickets and the unhurried, pleasant thoughts. Ought he to start reading Puffendorf? Engage in commerce, like Alexander Menshikov or Shafirov? It was difficult, he had never been used to it. If only war would start soon. The Volkovs were quiet men, but once they mounted their horses, it remained to be seen who would come out on top: would it be the Brovkins, Yashka and Alioshka?

On one such pensive evening the royal adjutant put in an appearance at the inn and, with exquisite politeness and many apologies, invited Volkov to come to the palace at once. Volkov was agitated and dressed hurriedly. They drove off in a coach. August received him in his bedchamber. He stretched out his hand in welcome, would not allow him to kneel, embraced him and made him sit down at his side.

"I am at a loss to understand it, my young friend. All I can do is to offer you my apologies for the lack of order at my court. It was only at dinner that I learnt of your arrival. Countess Athalie, that most frivolous of women, was charmed by your wife, dragged her from the arms of her husband and for a whole week now has been enjoying her friendship alone, hiding her from all eyes."

Volkov attempted to rise but before he could bow in reply August held him down with a hand on his shoulder. He spoke loudly, laughing the while, but soon he ceased laughing:

"You are on your way to Paris, I know. I want to ask you, my friend, to carry confidential letters to my brother the Tsar. Alexandra Ivanovna will wait for you in complete safety under Countess Athalie's roof. Are you informed of the latest events?"

It was as if the laughter had been wiped off his face; angry lines formed at the corners of his lips.

"The situation at Riga is bad. The Livonian knights have betrayed me. My best general, Karlowicz, died the death of a hero three days ago."

He covered his face with his hand, devoting a moment's silence to the memory of the unfortunate Karlowicz.

"Tomorrow I am leaving for Warsaw to attend the Diet, to prevent terrible confusion arising in people's minds. In Warsaw I will give you the letters and papers. You will spare no effort, you will convince the Tsar of the necessity for the Russian army to take the field immediately."

During the night Athalie would wake up her maid. Candles would be lighted, the fire lit and a small table would be brought in, laden with fruit, pies, game and wine. Athalie and Sanka would get out of bed and sit down to supper, clad only in their nightgowns and lace caps. Sanka was dying to sleep, which was not surprising after a whole day without a minute's rest, or a word simply spoken: everything so complicated, and always having to be on the alert. But she would rub her swollen eyes and bravely sip wine from a glass as iridescent as a soap-bubble, and smile, raising the corners of her lips.

She had come abroad, not to sleep, but to learn refinement. This refinement, as Athalie had explained it to her, was not always understood even at royal courts: at Versailles itself there was plenty of rudeness and swinishness.

"Imagine, my dear, that on a damp evening one cannot open one's window, there is such a stench all round the palace, from the shrubbery and even from the balconies. The courtiers live in crowded quarters, they sleep anyhow, in slovenly beds; they drench themselves in scent to smother the smell of dirty underclothes. Ah, you and I must go to Italy. It would be a delightful dream. It's the land of every sort of refinement. Poetry, music, the play of passions, the exquisite pleasures of the mind—everything is at your disposal."

Athalie was peeling an apple with a silver knife. With her legs crossed, she swung her small slipper and sipped wine with half closed eyes:

"Refined people are the true kings of life. Listen, it has been said thus: 'The good husbandman follows his plough, the diligent weaver works at his loom, the bold trader hoists the sail of his ship, risking his life. . . . Why do men toil? For the gods are dead. . . . No, it is other deities that I see on Mount Olympus among the blushing clouds'."

Sanka listened to her like a hypnotised rabbit. Little creases formed on Athalie's forehead. Stretching out her empty glass she would say: "Fill it, please", and go on:

"I still cannot understand, my friend, why you fear to accept August's love—he is suffering. Virtue is only a sign of lack of intelligence. A woman uses virtue to conceal her moral ugliness in the same way as the Spanish Queen covers her flabby breasts with a high-necked gown. But you—you're clever, you're brilliant. You are in love with your husband. No one prevents you from showing him your passionate feeling, but don't do it openly. Don't make yourself ridiculous, my friend. A good townsman goes out walking on a Sunday with his wife, holding her round the waist so that no one should dare to take this treasure from him. But we are refined women, and that lays obligations on us."

The lace of her cap hid Sanka's lowered face. What was she to do? She was capable of dancing twenty-four hours without a rest, playing the part of any kind of Greek goddess, reading a book through in a night, learning poetry by heart. But there was something in her which she could not overcome: she would have died of shame, been filled with torment, if she had let herself be persuaded by Athalie to yield in womanly compassion to the king. ("All this will come, of course, but not now.") How explain it? She could not, after all, confess that she had not been born on Parnassus, but had herded cows; that she was quite prepared to abandon virtue, but had not yet the strength to tear something out of herself—as if her mother's terrible eyes were watching over this sacred something, some core of her being.

Athalie did not insist. Pinching Sanka's cheek she would change the subject:

"It is my cherished dream to see Tsar Peter. Oh, with what reverence I would kiss the hand that can wield the hammer and the sword! Tsar Peter reminds me of Hercules and his twelve labours: he fights the hydra, he cleans the stables of Augeas, he raises the terrestrial globe on his shoulders. Isn't it like a fairy-tale, my friend, that in a few years Tsar Peter has created a powerful fleet and an invincible army? I would like to know the names of all the marshals, all the generals. Your Tsar is a worthy opponent of King Charles. Europe is waiting for the day when the Moscow eagle plunges its talons at last into the Swedish lion's mane. You must satisfy my curiosity."

Athalie always brought the conversation round to the affairs of Moscow. Sanka replied as best she could. She did not understand why the cautiously insinuating voice of her new friend began to strike her unpleasantly. Later, in bed, with the coverlet pulled up to her nose, she could not go to sleep for a long time, too disturbed by these nocturnal conversations. Oh, how difficult was this refinement!

3

". . . And finally this whole coalition is nothing more than a scrap of paper which may frighten the respectable senators but not your impetuous courage. The Danes will not dare to break the peace —trust a woman's discernment. Tsar Peter is held back by the peace negotiations; he will not take the field until the Turks untie his hands. But this will not take place. Ukraintsev, the envoy, has distributed all his sable-lined coats to the viziers and has no further arguments. Tsar Peter tried to intimidate the Turks by launching his new Voronezh fleet, but instead he has put the English and the Dutch very much on their guard. Their ambassadors in Constantinople will not hear of Russian ships in the Black Sea. The most uncompromising of them is Leczynski, the Polish ambassador, a deadly enemy of

King August. He implored the Sultan in the name of the Polish State to help the Poles to take the Ukraine with Kiev and Poltava from the Russians.

"These are the latest items of news, or gossip, as you prefer. Warsaw is full of it. August and I are spending a lot of money on balls and amusements and, alas, the king's popularity is still declining. He is furious and is making himself ridiculous by running after a Russian ninny.

"And so the favourable wind of history is filling your sails and whistling in the shrouds of your coming fame. Now or never! Your devoted Athalie."

This letter reached Charles in the Kungsör forest. He read it leaning against a tree. The pines rustled and low clouds drifted in the March sky. Down below, in the mist-filled gorge, hounds were giving tongue; their excited baying showed that they had started big game. An old huntsman, trampling the snow between the stones, took several steps down and turned expectantly. The king read and re-read the letter. The messenger who had brought it was holding his horse by the bridle; the horse was straining a violet eye in the direction of the hounds' voices.

A stag emerged from the gorge and bounded powerfully up the slope. Charles did not raise his musket. The stag, throwing back its branching antlers, sped away between the trees. Some fifty yards away a shot rang out from the spot where the French ambassador was posted. Charles did not turn round; the letter fluttered in his reddened hand. The huntsman, burying the wrinkles of his chin in his leather collar, returned to his former position behind this youth with the small head and narrow face, thin as a lath, in an elk-skin long-backed coat.

"Who gave you this letter?" Charles asked.

The officer came a step nearer, without letting go of his horse's bridle.

"Count Piper. He also instructed me to convey by word of mouth to Your Majesty some most important news still unknown to the Senate."

The red-cheeked, round-faced officer's grey eyes were inquisitive and bold.

Charles turned away. These gentlemen of the nobility all looked at him like that, with expectation—all the Guards were like a pack of hungry harriers.

"What was it you were to convey to me?"

"The Danish army—fifteen or twenty battalions—has crossed the Holstein frontier."

Charles slowly crushed Athalie's letter in his hand. The baying of the hounds came nearer. The roar of a bear rose from the wooded gorge. Charles took up his musket, which was propped against a tree, and said to the officer over his shoulder:

"Change your horse and go back to Stockholm. Tell Count Piper that we are enjoying ourselves here as never before. We have got three old bears surrounded. I invite Count Piper, General Rehnsköld, General Löwenhaupt and General Schlippenbach to the *battue*. Go. Hurry!"

Red patches showed on his usually pale face. With an unsteady finger he cocked his musket. He strode resolutely towards the lip of the gorge, his frozen boot-tops slapping against each other. The officer looked with a smile at his boyish, stooping back and his proudly stiff neck; then he sprang into the saddle, and galloping off through the deep snow, disappeared in the forest.

Fourteen bears had been killed or snared. Charles laughed like a boy at the desperate roars of the snared bear-cubs, which were bound with rawhide thongs to be sent to Stockholm. Piper, Rehnsköld, Löwenhaupt and Schlippenbach, who had arrived at dawn (in leather coats and hats adorned with woodcock feathers), had each speared a bear. Guiscard, the French ambassador, had shot a monster seven feet high.

The tired hunters returned to the log hunting-lodge above the waterfall, which roared over the ice at the bottom of the gorge. It was hot in the dining-room with the pine branches flaming on the hearth. The glass eyes of the stuffed heads of stags and elks gleamed from the walls. Guiscard, a little man, flushed with wine, curled his moustache and waved his short arms as he recounted enthusiastically how the bear had sprung out of its lair in a hurricane of snow, all ready to devour him: "I already felt his foul breath on my face! But I succeeded in jumping back. I took aim. Misfire! In an instant the whole of my life passed before my eyes. . . . I grasped the second musket. . . ."

The taciturn Swedes listened, drank and smiled. Charles did not drink even a sip of beer during the meal. When the French ambassador, with some difficulty, had been taken away to bed, Charles ordered a sentry to be posted at the door and sat down by the fire. Piper and the generals drew close up to his chair.

"I wish to hear your opinion, gentlemen," he said and pressed his lips firmly together. His boyish nose, reddened by the wind, glowed in the heat of the fire.

The generals inclined their heads. All matters, but especially such a matter, needed careful thought. Piper slowly rubbed his square chin:

"The Senate fears war and does not want it. The day before we left there was a special meeting. The rumours of the invasion of Livonia by the Polish king, and especially of the opening of hostilities by the Danes, caused alarm in Stockholm. The shipowners and timber and grain merchants sent a deputation to the Senate. They were given an attentive hearing, and not a single voice was raised among the senators in favour of war. It has been decided to send envoys to Warsaw and Copenhagen to settle the matter peacefully at all costs."

"And what of their king's opinion in this matter?" Charles asked.

"The Senate apparently thinks that Your Majesty's ambition is adequately satisfied by bear-hunting."

"Excellent!" Charles turned his narrow face swiftly, like a lynx, towards Rehnsköld. The general drew a deep breath through the large nostrils of his snub nose.

"I believe," he said with a look of sincerity in his round, pale eyes, "I believe that in the army there are many young nobles who find Sweden too small. There will be enough volunteers who wish to win glory by the sword. If the King leads us to the ends of the earth, we will go to the ends of the earth. It will not be the first time for us Swedes."

His straight mouth smiled good-humouredly. The generals nodded assent: "It would not be the first time that we leave our native rocks for foreign shores to win gold and glory." When the heads ceased nodding, Piper said:

"The Senate won't give a farthing for war. The treasury is empty. This must be considered."

The generals were silent. Charles bit his lip. The soles of his jackboots, propped against the fender, were steaming.

"We need money only for the first few days, to embark our troops and take them to Denmark. The French ambassador will give me this money. He will give it to me, because otherwise I would take it from the English. Our further military operations must be paid for by the Danish king. He will pay."

The generals drew close up to the king's chair agreeing: "That's so, that's so." Piper raised and lowered his eyebrows several times; he was once again amazed by this youth.

"Even if we ourselves did not decide to wage this war, the other powers would force it on us," Charles said. "So let us take the better course and be the first to attack. The magnificent August is dreaming of a great empire. Like myself, he has no money: he begs ducats from Tsar Peter and spends them on drink with his wenches. August might have made quite a good strolling player. Still less do I fear the Muscovite Tsar: he will lose his allies before he has taught his peasant regiments to fire a musket. Gentlemen, I wish to submit a plan for your consideration."

The same evening, bending over a map spread on Charles's knees, the three generals drew up a plan. Welling, the governor of Narva, was to assume command of the Swedish troops in Livonia and Esthonia and go to the relief of Riga; Löwenhaupt and Schlippenbach were to assemble the Guards and the army at Landskrona, the naval port on the Sound, as if for manœuvres; Piper was to do everything necessary to divert the attention of the Senate from these preparations.

They threw pine roots on the fire and removed the sentry from the door. The table was laid for supper. Monsieur Guiscard, who had had a good nap, came into the dining-room rubbing his hands. Charles invited him to a seat by the fire and said, clearing his throat as if he had difficulty in getting the words out:

"My dear friend, you may rest assured of my warm and devoted affection for my brother King, your sovereign." Guiscard slowly rubbed his palms together; he was on his guard. "Sweden will remain a faithful guardian of French interests in the northern seas. In the dispute for the Spanish succession my sword belongs to Louis." Guiscard bowed low, spreading out his short arms. "But I will not conceal from you that the English are doing their best to win Sweden over to their side. In Sweden, besides the king, there is also the Senate, and I cannot read their thoughts. Alas! the world today is full of contradictions. I have learnt today that the Engish fleet has appeared in the Sound. In order to avoid a fatal mistake, I need tangible proof of your friendship, Monsieur Guiscard."

The roaring bear-cubs were driven in a cart through the streets of Stockholm. Behind them rode Charles, the members of the shooting-party and the huntsmen. Brass trumpets blared and the packs bayed. The honest citizens came to their windows and shook their heads, saying: "The king has chosen none too suitable a time for his amusements."

Disturbing rumours alarmed the city, accustomed to many years of peace. The English and Dutch fleets had appeared in the Sound: for what purpose? Was it not to join the Danes and put an end to Swedish power in the northern seas? Poland, that enormous country, was threatening to sweep the Swedish garrisons from the shores of the Baltic. In the East the thousand miles of the Muscovite frontier were practically undefended, but for the little fort of Nienschanz near the estuary of the Neva and the fortress of Noteburg at the outlet of Lake Ladoga.

It was terrible to think of fighting almost the whole of eastern Europe with only a small army of twenty thousand men and a crazy king. Peace, peace, of course: better to yield a little in order to save the essential.

Charles appeared in the Senate without changing his hunting-coat. He listened with haughty inattention to paternal speeches about God's hand now raised over Sweden and about prudence and virtue. Playing with the bone handle of his dagger he replied that he was busy with the arrangements of the spring carnival in Kungsör castle and would not give his opinion on foreign affairs until after the festivities. The senior senator rose to his feet and, bowing low, expressed in well-chosen words the hope that no cares would cloud the king's pleasures.

The king shrugged his shoulders and went out. A few days later he left for Kungsör. From there, having changed horses, he galloped to Landskrona, accompanied by Rehnsköld and a dozen officers of the Guards. He spared neither men nor beasts on the way, travelling almost without rest. He seemed to be a different man: a single thought dominated his passions and his will.

One cloudless spring morning the Swedish fleet, with fifteen thousand picked men on board, sailed out into the Sound. Towards noon they saw the dark outlines of warships, brigs and galleys above the sunlit waves as if suspended in mid-air between the horizon and clear sky. Hundreds of pennants fluttered in the wind. This was the Anglo-Dutch fleet lying to.

When the leading Swedish frigate ran up the royal standard, little clouds of smoke began to detach themselves from the ships' sides, and the boom of guns rolled across the water. The pall of smoke was carried away to the south. The English and Dutch admirals, glittering with gold lace, started in their barges for the leading Swedish frigate.

Charles was awaiting them on the quarter-deck, in a grey-green cloth coat closely buttoned up to his black neckcloth and blacked jackboots very wide at the top, well adapted to any kind of emergency. His wig, under a small hat with the brim turned up at both sides, was plaited in a pigtail and encased in a leather sheath. His hand rested on a long sword as on a staff. That was how he set out on the long road of the conquest of Europe.

The admirals who had heard much gossip about this debauched young man were surprised by his extraordinary resolution and self-control. He spoke of the intolerable insults inflicted upon him by the Danish and Polish kings and generously agreed to accept the aid of the English and Dutch fleets in punishing the Danes for their treachery.

The same day the three united fleets laid their course towards Copenhagen, covering the sea with their sails.

4

The rain stopped and the clouds were swept away. The evening was warm and smelt of grass and smoke. The distant tinkling of a church bell came from the Foreign Quarter.

Peter was sitting at the open sash-window—the candles had not yet been lit—reading petitions. At the far end of the bedroom, by the door, Nikita Demidov, the smith from Tula, stood motionless, his bald head gleaming white.

"Truly, Sire, the people are growing slacker in the discharge of their obligations and any relaxation makes them think that everything will again be as of old." This petition was from the tax-collector, Alexey Kurbatov. "The merchant Matvey Shustrov presented a list of his deals and property and stated therein that his goods and chattels amounted to no more than two thousand roubles and that he was completely ruined. But I know that Matvey has buried in his house in Zariadye, under the floor of the privy, which you are ashamed to enter, forty thousand gold pieces of his grandfather's money. And he, the said Matvey, is an unreliable man; he squanders his wealth on drink instead of increasing it, and if he be not restrained he will waste it all. Give orders, Sire, that a bailiff with twenty soldiers be sent to Matvey's house in Zariadye and he will unearth those gold pieces. . . ."

Peter shook his head and laid the document on the windowsill, to his left hand—to be acted upon. The next petition was from the judge, Mihail Beklemishev, written in such a wavering hand that all he could make out was: ". . . served your father and brother in many capacities and was appointed judge in the Moscow Department of Justice. And to this day I am honestly discharging my duties. From such disinterested service I have fallen into debt and am greatly impoverished. Take pity, Sire, and, in reward for my disinterested service, send me as governor, to, for instance, Poltava. . . ."

Peter yawned and threw the petition on to a heap of papers to his right. There were also reports from Belgorod and Sevsk that townsmen and service men of all ranks, as well as serfs and peasants, detailed to regiments, did not want to enter the Tsar's service, nor work in shipbuilding or on timber cutting, and were running away everywhere to the Donets Cossack settlements. Peter wrote on a corner of the report: "Summon the Belgorod and Sevsk governors and question them severely."

There was a petition from State serfs with piteous complaints about the Kungur governor, Suhotin, who, it said, had begun to levy eight altyns on each house for his own use, over and above all taxes, and ordered the doors of houses and bath-houses to be sealed, no matter how cold it was, and many women gave birth to their babies in cattle-sheds, and the infants died untimely deaths and in the courtroom the governor seized some of the women by their breasts and squeezed their nipples till the blood came and tormented and mutilated them in other ways.

Peter scratched the back of his head. A storm of complaints rose from all over the country: if one governor was displaced, the next one behaved still worse. Where was he to find men? They were all thieves. He started to write with a spluttering quill pen: "Send to Kungur. . . ."

"Nikita," he said, turning round. "If you were made governor, would you steal?"

Without moving from the door Nikita Demidov sighed discreetly: "Like everybody else, Peter Alexeyevich—it goes with the office."

"There are no men, then?"

Nikita shrugged as if to say: true enough, there are no men. . . .

"Put them on the rack, or give them large salaries—they steal all the same," Peter said. He dipped his pen and wrote, although it was quite dark. "They have no conscience, no honour. I've turned them into fools and jesters. Why?" He turned round.

"The well-fed man steals more, Peter Alexeyevich, he's bolder."

"Now, now, you're pretty bold."

"I feel like weeping, Peter Alexeyevich. You're worried because there are no men. And eleven of my best smiths have been taken away from urgent work to serve as soldiers."

"Who took them?"

"The boyar Chemodanov—he came to Tula with the clerks for the registering. . . ." Nikita hesitated, peering at Peter whose face he could not distinguish, for he had turned away from the window. "Why should I hide it from you? Such doings as went on in Tula! All those who could pay bought themselves off. The boyar sent a clerk to my factory too. If I had been in Tula at the time I wouldn't have grudged paying five hundred roubles for my skilled workers. Be merciful, help somehow. After all, they are all gunsmiths, as good as the English ones."

"Submit a petition," Peter said through his teeth.

"Very well, Sire. But, Peter Alexeyevich, of course men can be found."

"All right. Now tell me your business."

Nikita approached cautiously. The matter was tremendously important. During the winter he had been to the Urals with his son Akinfy and three knowledgeable dissenter peasants from the Daniel hermitage, who earned their living working ores. They had prospected in the Ural ranges from Nevyansk to the towns on the Chosovaya river. They had found mountains of iron, they had found copper, silver ore and asbestos. Riches were lying there unused, in the midst of a desert. The only iron foundry on the Neyva river, built two years ago at Peter's command, produced less than a ton of iron, and even this small quantity could be shipped only with the greatest difficulty, owing to the lack of roads. The manager, the boyar's son Dashkov, had taken to drink out of boredom, and the same had happened to the Nevyansk governor Protasyev. Those of the workers who were sound had run away and only the weaklings were left. The shafts were crumbling. All around was virgin forest, and in the ponds and streams you could scoop up the gravel with a dipper and wash out the gold on a sheepskin. This was quite different from conditions in Tula, at Nikita's factory, where the ore was poor, the timber scanty (since last year it was forbidden to cut down oak, ash and maple trees for charcoal), and every pettifogging clerk plagued you. In the Urals there was space—mighty and free. But it was difficult to get at: much money was needed. The region was uninhabited.

"Peter Alexeyevich, we can't do anything about it. I have seen Sveshnikov and Brovkin and a few others, they are not keen to become partners in such a difficult enterprise. And I wouldn't like to take orders from them. Just think of the amount of labour it will take to open up the Urals."

Peter suddenly stamped his foot.

"What is it you want?" he asked. "Money? Men? Sit down!" Nikita seated himself hastily on the edge of a chair and fixed his sunken eyes on Peter. "This summer I shall need three thousand tons of iron cannon-balls and fifteen hundred tons of iron. I cannot wait till you fellows talk and turn things over in your minds. Take the Nevyansk foundry, take the whole of the Urals! This is an order!" Nikita thrust forward his gipsy beard and Peter moved closer to him. "I have no money, but for this venture I will give you money. I will attach several districts to go with the foundry. I will order you to buy men from the boyars' estates. But mind . . . !" Peter lifted a long finger and shook it warningly. "I pay the Swedes one rouble for thirty-six pounds of iron, you must supply me at thirty kopeks."

"Not a fair price," Nikita said quickly. "It can't be done. Fifty kopeks. . . ."

And he looked at Peter with the bluish whites of his eyes bulging. Peter gazed at him for a minute in fury. Then he said:

"All right. We'll see about it later. And another thing: I can see through you, you thief. You will pay it all back to me in pig-iron and iron within three years. By God, you are bold! But remember, if you don't keep your promise, I'll break you on the wheel."

Nikita cleared his throat gently and said in a hoarse whisper:

"I'll return the money earlier, believe me."

It was one of those evenings when Peter did not know what to do with himself. He thought of ordering someone to light the candle, but after a glance at the unread documents, he leant over the window-sill and looked out of the window.

Night had already fallen, but it seemed warmer than ever. Water dripped from the leaves and a light mist rose from the grass. Peter breathed in the warm, damp air through his nostrils; it smelt of rising sap. A drop fell on the back of his neck and a shiver ran over his body. He slowly rubbed the moisture on his neck.

Everything was sleeping guardedly in the spring stillness. There was not a light anywhere, and the only sound was the distant long-drawn call of a sentry: "Ha-a-arken!" in the soldiers' quarters. His body felt as languid as if every part of it were bound fast. He could hear the quick beating of his heart against the windowsill. There was nothing for it but to wait—to wait with clenched teeth. Wait, wait. . . . Like some wench in the quiet night, lifting up her head from the hot pillow to listen to the imagined tread of footsteps.

All that day he had been unable to get on with his work. Menshikov had invited him to supper, but he had not gone. They must be feasting there! Things had never been so difficult for him as now. His strength lay in waiting—in being able to wait. King August had started the war in haste, without biding his time, and had got stuck at Riga. Christian of Denmark had not waited long enough; he had only himself to blame.

"Only himself to blame, only himself to blame," Peter muttered, staring at the dark lilac bushes, heavy with the recent rain. Someone was scuffling there; probably an orderly with some girl. Colonel Langen had come that day from King August with alarming news: the Swedish lion-cub had unexpectedly shown his teeth. He had appeared before the forts of Copenhagen with an enormous fleet and demanded the surrender of the town. Christian, intimidated, had begun negotiations without risking battle. In the meantime Charles had landed fifteen thousand infantrymen in the rear of the Danish army which was besieging a Holstein fortress. The Swedes had burst on Denmark like a thunderstorm. Neither his own people nor his enemies abroad could have imagined that this rake, this spoilt youngster, could in so short a time have displayed the wisdom and daring of a real military leader.

Langen also conveyed King August's request for money: he said that Poland could be drawn into the war if the Primate and the Crown Hetman could be given twenty thousand ducats for distribution among the nobility. Langen begged Peter with tears in his eyes not to wait until peace was concluded with the Turks, but to take the field at once.

Such reports made Peter itch all over. But it could not be done. He could not be involved in a war as long as the Crimean Khan was sitting on his tail. He had to wait, to bide his time. Ivan Brovkin had been in a short while ago and said that there had been a great uproar in the Stewards' Chamber. Sveshnikov and Shorin had begun to buy up grain in secret and send it to Novgorod and Pskov by water and by land. Wheat at once jumped up three kopeks. Revyakin had shouted at them: "Are you mad? Ingria is not ours yet, and when will it be ours? Your grain will rot uselessly in Novgorod and Pskov." But they had answered him: "Ingria will be ours in the autumn; as soon as the roads are dry enough we will take the grain to Narva."

The wet bushes suddenly shook and drops pattered from the leaves. Two shadows moved swiftly. "Oh, don't, my dear, don't, don't . . . !" The shorter of the two shadows backed and began to run lightly, on bare feet. The other, a long one—that of Mishka, the orderly—followed with a stamping of jackboots. They stopped together under a lime-tree, and again there came: "Oh, no, my dear . . . !"

Peter leant out of the window almost to his waist. A great moon, veiled in mist, was rising beyond the grey willows on the low ground. Hay-ricks, groups of trees and the milky streak of the stream became visible in the plain. It all seemed ageless, immovable, unalterable, and fraught with alarm. And those two hurriedly whispering shadows under the dark lime-tree were only concerned about one thing.

"Stop that!" Peter shouted in a deep voice. "Mishka! I'll flay the skin off your back!"

The girl slipped behind the trunk of the tree. In less than a minute the orderly flew up the creaking stairs on tiptoe and scratched at the door.

"A candle," Peter said. "My pipe."

He smoked and paced the room. From time to time he took up a paper from the table, brought it close to the candle, and threw it down again. It seemed impossible even to think of going to bed. The smoke from his pipe drifted towards the window, where it curled round the window-frame, and was carried out into the cool night.

"Mishka!" The orderly again popped in at the door. He had round cheeks and a snub nose and his eyes held a dazed expression. "Mind what you're at with the girls! What d'you mean by it?" Peter moved towards him, but it was clear that he was too stupefied to care even if he was beaten. "Run, tell them to bring round my carriage. You're coming with me."

The moon rose over the plain; drops glistened on the bluish grass. The horse snorted, eying the dim outlines of the bushes. Peter slapped it with the reins. Mud flew from the wheels as they splashed through the mirror-smooth water filling the ruts. The carriage dashed through the sleeping streets of the Foreign Quarter, where the tobacco-plants behind the hedges exhaled their stifling sweetness, as they had done many years before. Light shone through the heart-shaped openings in the shutters of Annchen's house, surrounded by poplars that had grown and thickened magnificently.

Anna Mons, Pastor Strumpf, Königseck and de Crouy were peacefully playing cards by the light of two candles. From time to time Pastor Strumpf filled his nose with snuff, pulled out a checked handkerchief and sneezed with enjoyment, while his humid eyes glanced merrily at his partners. De Crouy inspected his cards, blinking his lashless eyelids with concentration, his drooping moustache, which had been through fifteen famous battles, pressed upwards to his nostrils. Anna Mons, in a pale blue house-gown, with her arms, that had now grown plump, bare to the elbow, with diamond pendants in her ears and on her velvet neck-ribbon, was slightly wrinkling her forehead as she sized up her cards. Königseck, trim, well-groomed and powdered, smiled tenderly at her or soundlessly moved his lips in an effort to help without being observed.

No doubt all storms passed by this peaceful room, which smelt pleasantly of vanilla and cardamoms, used for spicing buns, and where the armchairs and sofas were already in their summer linen covers, and the clock on the wall ticked slowly. "We modestly say—clubs," Pastor Strumpf sighed, raising his eyes to the ceiling. "Spades," said the Duke de Crouy, sounding as though he were pulling a rusty sword half way out of its scabbard; Königseck, raising himself to take a look at Anna's cards over her shoulder, said sweetly: "We again say hearts."

Peter came in through the back entrance and suddenly opened the door. Anna Mons dropped her cards. The men rose hastily. In spite of her self-control, Anna Mons gave a little cry of pleasure and, with a beaming smile, dropped a curtsey, then kissed Peter's hand and pressed it to her bosom, half-covered by her kerchief; but for all that Peter fancied that he saw a fleeting glint of fear in her clear blue eyes. He turned to the sofa, stooping his shoulders and said:

"Go on playing. I'll sit here and smoke."

But Anna Mons, running to the table on her high heels, had already shuffled the cards together.

"We were only playing to while away the time. Ah, Peter, how nice it is—you always bring joy and gaiety into this house." She clapped her hands like a child. "We'll have supper now."

"I'm not hungry," Peter growled. He chewed his pipe. For some reason he could not tell he felt his gorge rising. He squinted at the chair-covers, at the embroidery frame with its balls of wool. A heavy little crease showed on Annchen's smooth forehead; he had never noticed it before.

"Oh, Peter, then let us invent some amusing game." And again there was something pitiful in her eyes.

Peter said nothing. Pastor Strumpf looked at the clock and then at his watch: "Dear me," he said, "it's already past two o'clock." He picked up his prayer-book from the windowsill. The Duke de Crouy and Königseck also found their hats. Annchen twisted her fingers and cried in a voice that held more regret than politeness demanded:

"Oh, don't go yet!"

Peter began to breathe heavily; sparks flew from his pipe. He drew back his feet, then jumped up and went out, striding purposefully and slamming the door behind him. Annchen's breath came faster and faster and she covered her face with her handkerchief. Königseck hurried out on tiptoe to fetch a glass of water. Pastor Strumpf discreetly shook his head. The Duke de Crouy idly picked up and threw down the cards on the table.

Steam rose from the wooden roofs, from the drying street; the puddles were bottomless wells of blue. Bells were ringing: it was Sunday, the first Sunday after Easter. Street vendors selling pies and hot mead cried their wares. Idle people wandered about, mostly drunk. On the peeling town wall, standing in the embrasures, youths in new shirts waved poles with bunches of bast to drive up the pigeons. The white birds fluttered in the azure height, wheeled, spun and dropped. Everywhere—behind tall fences, under the limes washed by the night and the grey willows—swings rose and fell: girls with plaits tossing flew up among the branches, or a bald old man amused himself by swinging a fat woman who sat shrieking on the swing.

Peter drove along the street at walking pace. His eyes were sunken, his face drawn. The sun was hot on his back. Mishka, the orderly, who had waited for him all night in the carriage, kept jerking his head in the effort to keep awake. People made way for the horse; only a few recognised the Tsar and, tearing off their caps, bowed low to his back.

From Anna Mons Peter had gone to Menshikov's that night. But he only glanced up at the great curtained windows, through which came the sounds of music and drunken shouts. "To the devil with them!" He shook the reins and driving out of the courtyard turned straight towards Moscow, to the strelets suburb, first at a smart trot, then at a gallop.

In the suburb they shopped at a simple house, where a pole with a bundle of hay tied to it was planted over the gate. Peter threw the reins to Mishka and knocked at the wicket-gate. In his impatience he stamped round in the squelching dung, and then battered the gate with his fists. A woman opened the wicket. Mishka managed to see that she was tall, had a round face and was dressed in a dark sarafan. She gasped and put her hands to her cheeks. Peter stooped, strode into the yard and slammed the wicket.

Standing up in the open carriage Mishka saw a light appear behind the gate in two high windows in the log-house. Then the woman hurried out on to the porch and called:

"Luka, hi, Luka!"

"Ye-e-s?"

"Luka, don't let anyone in, do you hear?"

"But if they try to break in?"

"Aren't you a man?"

"All right, I'll take a pitchfork to them."

"Everything's clear," Mishka thought to himself.

A short time later three men in strelets caps came out of an alley, glanced up and down the empty street bathed in moonlight, and made straight for the gates. Mishka said sternly:

"Be on your way."

The streltsi came up threateningly to the carriage:

"Who are you? Why are you in our suburb at such an hour?"

"Be off with you, fellows, and make haste about it," Mishka answered in a low and menacing tone.

"Why?" one of the men, more drunk than his companions, cried angrily. "Why are you trying to frighten us? We know where you come from. . . ." The other two grasped him by the shoulders and whispered to him. "Your head's only held on by a thread too. Wait a bit, wait a bit—" His companions were already pulling him away, not allowing him to roll up his sleeves. "Not all of us have been hanged yet. We still have teeth. He may yet get stuck on a pole." The others hit him in the neck, knocking his cap off, and dragged him away into the alley.

The light in the windows soon went out. But Peter did not come. Inside the gate every now and then Luka sleepily struck his watchman's board. Soon the silence was complete. Even the tired horse hung its head. As he dozed Mishka heard the cocks crow. The moonlight grew colder. At the end of the street the dawn showed yellow, then pink. For the second time Mishka woke with the sound of whispering; the carriage was surrounded by small boys, some without trousers. But the moment he opened his eyes they ran off, with a flapping of sleeves and a twinkling of dirty, bare heels.

The sun was standing high when Peter came out through the wicket-gate, his hat pulled over his eyes. He coughed deeply as he took the reins. "Well, that is one thing off my shoulders," he said in his deep voice and started off the horse at a trot.

When they had driven out of Moscow into the green fields, with the sharp roofs of the Foreign Quarter in the distance, and beyond them snowy clouds rising from below the horizon, Peter said:

"That's how to deal with you orderlies. And if you go on playing round at night, I'll lock you up in a dark closet." And he laughed, pushing his hat to the back of his head.

They overtook a half-company of soldiers in grey-brown ill-fitting coats. Each man had a bunch of hay tied on one foot and a bunch of straw on the other. They were marching in ragged files, with their bayonets knocking against each other. The sergeant shouted desperately: "Attention!" Peter got out of the carriage, took first one man by the shoulder, then another, turned them round and felt the shoddy cloth.

"Trash!" he shouted, staring wrathfully at the pimply-faced sergeant. "Who supplied these coats?"

"Sir Bombardier, the coats were issued by the Suharev workshops."

"Off with your coat!" Peter said, catching hold of a third man, a lean, sharp-nosed soldier who seemed to choke with terror as he looked up into the round face and small bristling moustache towering over him. His mates nearest him jerked the musket out of his hands, unclasped his belt and pulled the coat off his shoulders. Peter snatched the coat, threw it into the carriage and, without another word, jumped in and drove away at full speed towards Menshikov's mansion.

The coatless soldier, trembling in every limb, followed the carriage bowling away along the grass-grown road with a fascinated gaze. The sergeant poked him with his cane:

"Golikov, leave the ranks and tramp back. Attention!" He opened his mouth wide, threw back his head and yelled so that he could be heard all over the field: "The left foot is hay, the right foot is straw.

Remember what I said. . . . March! Hay, straw—hay—straw. . . ."

The cloth for the Suharev workshops had been supplied by Ivan Brovkin's new factory, built on the Neglinnaya river by the Kuznetsky bridge, in which both Menshikov and Shafirov had shares. One hundred thousand roubles had been paid in advance by the Preobrazhensky commissariat for this uniform cloth. Menshikov had boasted to Peter that they would supply cloth as good as was made in Hamburg. But what they had provided was shoddy mixed with cotton. Alexander Menshikov was born a thief, bred a thief and had remained a thief. "Just you wait!" Peter thought, and jerked impatiently at the reins.

Alexander Menshikov was sitting on his bed drinking cucumber brine to pull him round; they had caroused till past six in the morning. His deep blue eyes were clouded and his eyelids swollen. His house-chaplain, a deacon nicknamed Pedrila, held the bowl before him. He was an uncouth looking man with a stentorian voice, nearly seven feet high and with a girth like a barrel. He said pityingly, fishing in the bowl with his fingers:

"Have a cucumber, here's one. . . ."

"Go to the devil!"

Shafirov was sitting near the luxurious bed with his open snuffbox held ready in his hand. His clever face had grown bland and fat, like a pancake. He advised Menshikov to have himself bled—half a glassful—or put leeches on the back of his neck:

"Alexander Danilovich, my dear fellow, you are ruining your health by your immoderate use of strong drinks."

"Go to the devil!"

The deacon was the first to catch sight of Peter from the window: "It looks as though he's in an angry mood." Before they could collect their thoughts, Peter strode into the room and, without any greeting, went straight up to Menshikov and pushed the soldier's coat under his nose:

"Is this better than Hamburg cloth? Hold your tongue, you thief, hold your tongue—there's no excuse for you!"

He seized Menshikov by the breast of his lace-fronted shirt and dragged him to the wall; when Menshikov, with mouth agape, was pressed against it, he began to hit him, first right, then left, so that his head rolled from side to side. Then he let go, snatched up a cane that was standing against the fireplace and broke it on him in his rage. Leaving Menshikov, Peter turned to Shafirov, who was humbly kneeling beside his armchair. Peter only snorted at him. "Get up!"

Shafirov jumped up. "You will sell all this rotten cloth to King August at the price I paid you. I give you a week. If you don't sell it, you'll be beaten with the knout, on a whipping block, with your shirt off. Is that clear?"

"Oh, I'll sell it, I'll sell it in much less time than that, Your Majesty."

"And you will supply me and Brovkin with good cloth instead."

"Mein Herz," Menshikov said, wiping the tears and blood off his face, "good God, how can you think that we ever cheated you? What happened with this cloth was . . ."

"It's all right," Peter said. "Order breakfast now."

chapter four

It was very hot. Not a breath of wind. The tiled roofs of Constantinople were bleached. Over the town the air quivered with the heat. There was no shade even in the sun-scorched, dusty gardens of the Sultan's palace. Ragged people slept on the stones by the glassy water at the foot of the fortress walls. The town was very quiet. Only from the tall minarets long-drawn voices would begin to sound their calls as a sorrowful reminder. And at night the dogs howled at the great stars.

A year had passed since Peter's envoy, Yemelian Ukraintsev, and his clerk Cheredeyev had arrived at the hostelry in Pera. Twenty-three conferences had been held, but neither side would make any concessions. A few days earlier a messenger had arrived from Peter with instructions to conclude the peace forthwith, to concede everything possible, except Azov, to the Turks and that it would be better not to mention the Holy Sepulchre at all, so as not to antagonise the Catholics; but, once having made these concessions, to take a firm stand.

At the twenty-third conference Ukraintsev had said: "This is our last word: we shall remain in Constantinople another fortnight. If there is no peace, you will have only yourselves to blame: the Tsar's fleet is very different from what it was last year. You must have heard about it."

To drive the threat home the ambassador and his suite moved from the hostelry to the ship. The *Reliance* had been lying at anchor so long that its sides were overgrown with mould, and cockroaches and bugs had appeared in the cabins; Captain Pamburg had grown quite bloated with boredom.

Ukraintsev and Cheredeyev would wake before dawn, and groan and scratch themselves in the stuffy cabin. They put on Tatar gowns over their underwear and went on deck. They felt depressed. A cloudless dawn fraught with the coming heat spread gradually over the dark Bosphorus and the scorched hills. They sat down to eat. How nice it would be to have some kvass, cold from the cellar! Vain desire! They ate stinking fish and drank water and vinegar without appetite. Captain Pamburg, having broken his fast with a glass of something strong, paced the warped deck, clad only in his underclothes. The orange-coloured sun rose into the sky. Soon it became unbearable to look at the flowing water, at the boats loaded with melons and water-melons, lazily rocking near the shore, at the chalk-white domes of the mosques and the dazzling crescents against the blue sky. The hum of voices, shouts and the sound of street-vendors' bells reached their ears from the narrow streets of Galata.

"Yemelian Ignatyevich, what use am I to you?" the clerk Cheredeyev would say. "Let me go. I'll go on foot."

"We'll soon be going home, have patience, Ivan Ivanovich," Ukraintsev would reply, closing his eyes to shut out the sight of the town, of which he was weary to death.

"Yemelian Ignatyevich, there is just one thing I would like to do: to lie for a little in the cool of the grass in my garden." Cheredeyev's long face with its narrow beard had grown emaciated with heat and homesickness, and his eyes were sunken. "I've got a small house in Suzdal. In the garden there are two old birches; I see them in my dreams. You get up in the morning and go and look at the cattle, and you find they have been turned out into the meadow already. You go to the bee-garden—the grass comes up to your waist. On the little river peasants are dragging a net. Peasant-women are beating their washing with clappers. It's all so friendly."

"Ah, yes! ah, yes! ah, yes!" The envoy nodded his wrinkled face.

"For dinner there'd be a sheat-fish pie."

Ukraintsev, swaying to and fro, answered without opening his eyes:

"Sheat-fish is a little too rich, Ivan Ivanovich. In summer cold fish and vegetable soup are better. And mint kvass."

"Fish soup made with ruff is good, Yemelian Ignatyevich."

"And the ruff oughtn't to be cleaned, it should be cooked slimy, just as it is. And when it's cooked, you throw it out and put a sterlet into the broth."

"What a country, dear God! But here, Yemelian Ignatyevich? They are real heathens. Just a kind of mirage. And the Greek women here are truly vessels of corruption."

"Now that is something you ought to avoid, Ivan Ivanovich."

Little drops of sweat like millet seeds stood out on Cheredeyev's large nose. His eyes seemed to sink deeper into his head. A six-oared barge, covered with a carpet, left the shore for the ship. Captain Pamburg suddenly gave a hoarse shout:

"Boatswain, pipe all hands on deck! Lower the ladder."

The barge came alongside, and Solomon, one of the Grand Vizier's officials, climbed the ladder with a rapid flapping of slippers. He had high cheekbones and a flat nose, and was nimble both in body and mind. His eyes quickly took in the ship; his hand quickly touched his heart, his lips and his forehead. He said in Russian:

"The Grand Vizier begs to enquire after your health, Yemelian Ignatyevich. He fears that your quarters on board are somewhat cramped. What made you angry with us?"

"Good morning, Solomon," Ukraintsev replied with the greatest deliberation. "Tell me whether the health of the Grand Vizier is good. Is everything well with you?" At these words he opened wider one sharp eye. "As for us, we are quite happy here. But we are longing for home. Our home here is nothing but the fifty feet we stand on."

"Yemelian Ignatyevich, can I have a word with you in private?"

"Why not? Let's have it in private." He coughed and turned to Cheredeyev and Pamburg: "Step aside, will you?" and he himself retreated into the shade of a sail.

Solomon smiled, showing his misshapen gums.

"Yemelian Ignatyevich, I am your sincere friend and I can tell all your enemies on my fingers," he said rapidly ticking off his fingers under Ukraintsev's nose. The latter only said: "Yes, yes."

"I laugh at their intrigues," Solomon continued. "Were it not for me, the Divan would have broken off negotiations. I have succeeded in giving the matter a favourable turn and the Grand Vizier is ready to sign the peace tomorrow. . . . Some baksheesh will have to be given to a few people."

"Is that so?" Ukraintsev said. He saw it all now. A Greek in his pay had reported the day before that the French ambassador was back in Constantinople from Paris; that there had been a consultation of the Divan—the Sultan's ministers—and that they had received important gifts. All through the night the Russian envoy, tormented by the heat and the cockroaches, had wondered: "What can this mean? It must be that they are inciting the Turks to make war on the Austrian Emperor again. Therefore the Turks have to settle things with Moscow."

"Well, baksheesh is of no importance. You tell the Grand Vizier this: we are only waiting for a favourable wind. If peace is concluded, well and good; if not, it's still better for us. And the peace must be like this. . . ." He looked firmly at Solomon from under his grey eyebrows. "We shall raze the small fortified towns on the Dniepr, as agreed. But in exchange for this the territory round Azov, as far as can be covered by ten days' riding, will be Russian. This is definite."

Solomon was afraid he might lose his baksheesh altogether. These Russians appeared to know more than they ought. He caught hold of Ukraintsev's sleeve and began to argue with him. They went into the cabin. Pamburg, aware that many eyes were watching the *Reliance* through telescopes, sent sailors up the rigging as if to make ready to sail. Ukraintsev looked out of the cabin and said to his clerk: "Get dressed, we are going ashore."

Soon he himself came out wearing wig and sword. Solomon assisted him down the ladder and into the barge.

In the afternoon, for the first time in many days, the narrow pennant at the masthead gave a lazy flutter. A colourless mist began to veil the distant hills. The azure seemed to grow dust-laden, and the town to disappear in a haze. The wind from the desert had risen.

Next day the peace was signed.

2

The great bell of Ivan Veliky boomed over Moscow. Twenty-four stalwart men from the merchants' quarter swung its brass clapper. Prayers were being offered for the victory of Russian arms over the enemy. That day, after mass, Voznitsin, clerk of the council, dressed according to ancient custom in fur-lined coat, tall fur cap and morocco-leather boots, had appeared on the Tsar's private porch (now overgrown with nettles and burdock) and, with careful articulation, had read out the Tsar's ukase to the great crowd that had gathered: all those inscribed for military service were ordered to muster for war on the Swedes. All equerries, men of law, Moscow nobles and those in attendance at the palace, and men of all ranks registered for training in the military art were to ride.

This had long been expected, but nevertheless Moscow was shaken to its very depths. Since morning, regiments and baggage-trains had been passing, filling the streets with clouds of dust. Soldiers' wives ran alongside, desperately waving their wide sleeves. The citizens pressed themselves against the fences as the guns lurched and jolted along the log-paved streets. The thunderous voices of deacons praying for victory streamed out through the open doors of small, ancient churches. The gates of the boyars' houses were flung open and riders came galloping out, some in old-fashioned cuirasses and cloaks. They spurred their horses and cut into the crowd, hitting out at peoples' heads with their whips. Carts collided, axles creaked, and horses bit and screamed.

In the Uspensky cathedral, blazing with the light of innumerable candles, the frail Patriarch Adrian, wrapped in a cloud of incense, wept with his hands raised high. The boyars and, behind them, a serried crowd of wealthy merchants and the more notable tradespeople, were on their knees. All wept looking at the tears that streamed down the Patriarch's face lifted up to the high vault. The archdeacon, his mouth wide open and the veins swelling on his temples, gave voice, calling for victory in tones like the sound of the Last Trump, drowning the singing of the Patriarch's choir. The Patriarch's surplice was black, and black were the faces of the saints in their gold settings; the cathedral shone with gold and glory.

It was the first time that the merchants had been admitted in such numbers to the Uspensky cathedral—that boyars' stronghold. The Stewards' Chamber had donated nine hundred pounds of wax candles for the occasion, and many wealthy merchants had personally offered candles, some weighing eighteen pounds, others as much as thirty-six pounds. The deacons had been asked not to spare the incense.

Ivan Artemyich Brovkin, sniffling with tears, repeated: "Glory, glory. . . !" On one side of him Mitrofan Shorin, in an ecstasy of emotion, joined his voice to those of the choir; on the other, Alexey Sveshnikov stared so fervently with his gipsy eyes at the gold of the altar-screen, of the surrounds and haloes of the icons, that all this wealth might have been the work of his hands. "Grant us victo-o-o-ry!" the magnificently-robed archdeacon thundered, shaking the vaults, and the red roses woven in the pattern of his vestment were veiled in clouds of incense.

The congregation moved up to kiss the cross. The first to do so was the corpulent, grey-haired Prince-Emperor, Fedor Romodanovsky; he kissed the cross for fully a minute and his old shoulders heaved. After him came, in turn, the princes and boyars, one older than the other, for the younger ones were all by this time serving or in the field. The merchants came up solemnly, throwing gold coins, rings and strings of pearls on to the tray held by the churchwarden. They came out of the cathedral with heads held high. Crossing themselves again at the great icon over the door, they shook their hair back, put on caps or hats, and went across the square patchily overgrown with tender grass, to the Stewards' Chamber, with a quick tapping of heels and businesslike looks at the crowds of common people and the windows of the government offices.

Dozens of black, misshapen hands seized Ivan Brovkin by the tails of his velvet coat as he came out of the cathedral: "Prince, Prince! A kopek. . . . A li-i-i-tle something!" wailed the shaggy, toothless, naked, pus-covered beggars. They crawled, stretched towards him, shook their rags: "Prince, Prince!" Ivan Artemyich looked round in horror: "What are you saying, you fools, I'm no prince!" He turned out his pockets, distributing coppers. A bald idiot rattled pokers and howled in a voice that did not sound human: "I want hot coals!"

Vasily Revyakin was standing nearby, smiling through his slits of eyes and plucking at his thin beard. Having at last shaken himself free, Brovkin said to him:

"Is this your army, merchant? You'd do better to cross yourself on such a day."

"We are with the community, Ivan Artemyich," Revyakin said and bowed with hands folded over his stomach. "We humble ourselves with the community. Poor is the world, and we are with God."

"Pah! Dog of a dissenter! A real dog!" Ivan Artemyich walked off and the idiot bleated after him, like a goat.

3

The soldiers were obliged every now and then to join their efforts and pull waggons and cannon out of the mud. The wind had been blowing for many days from the west whither the troops of the Generals Weide and Artamon Golovin were slowly moving in a column that stretched over sixty miles. Repnin's division had still been unable to start from Moscow. Forty-five thousand infantrymen and cavalrymen and some ten thousand waggons were on the move.

Chilly mists drifted across the tree-tops in the forest. The rain beat down the last leaves from the birches and aspens. In the bluish mud of the trampled and rutted roads wheels sank to their hubs and horses broke their legs. All along the route their swollen, stiff-legged carcasses lay. Men would sit down silently at the edge of ditches: even the threat of death could not move them on. The foreign officers proved particularly delicate: they had long since got out of their saddles and sat shivering in their wet cloaks and wigs among the impedimenta under the bast covers of the waggons.

The troops left Moscow in full dress, with plumed hats, green coats and green stockings. When they reached the Swedish frontier they were barefooted, plastered to the neck with mud and marching in disorder. As they were working their way round lake Ilmen the swollen waters flooded the low grassy shore and many waggons of the baggage-train were lost.

In the general confusion the waggons lagged behind and lost their way. The rain from above and the swamp below prevented the lighting of fires at the halts. The mounted squadrons of the noblemen's militia were worse than the fiercest enemy; like locusts they seized all the food in the surrounding villages. When they rode past the infantry, they shouted: "Out of the way, you clodhoppers!" Alexey Brovkin— captain in von Schweden's regiment of the vanguard—quarrelled with and more than once used his cane on the mounted landowners. There was much hardship and toil and little order.

The van of the army only emerged from the mud on reaching the river Luga, near the frontier. Here they made camp and waited for the baggage-train. They put up tents and dried themselves as best they could. The soldiers recalled the Azov campaigns; some of them remembered Golitsin's campaigns in Crimea. There was no comparison with those marches over the open steppe towards the warm south. They could remember singing as they marched. But this? What a land! Dismal swamps, clouds and wind. They would have to go through much suffering to conquer this desolate land.

Acrid smoke rose from the fires between the tents. The soldiers were mending their clothes or going down the slippery, steep bank to the river to wash their things. The footwear issued to them had fallen to pieces; the lucky ones had got hold of birch-bark shoes and legcloths; the others wrapped their feet in rags. At this rate even without any fighting half the men would be dead before November. The horsemen sometimes brought in a captured Finn at the end of a rope. The men would surround him and ask in Russian and Tatar how people lived here. They were stupid folk, these Finns; they only blinked their cow-like eyelashes. They were taken to Alexey Brovkin's tent for questioning. Such captives were seldom released. Usually they were bound and sent to the baggage-train, where they were sold for seventy-five kopeks—the sturdier ones for more—to the sutlers, who resold them in Novgorod, where the agents of the army contractors had their offices.

Alexey Brovkin kept strict order in all regimental affairs. His soldiers were well fed; he did not punish them unjustly and ate out of the same pot with them. But he tolerated no slackness, no infringement of discipline: every day by his tent some man would scream, with his naked buttocks under the rods. At night Alexey would wake up and himself inspect the sentinels. One night as he soundlessly approached the outskirts of the wood he stopped to listen: it might have been a tree creaking or some animal squealing. He called out in a low voice. Vaguely he could see a soldier sitting on a tree-stump, hugging his rifle and pressing his cheek to the iron.

"Who's on guard?" Alexey asked.

"I," the soldier replied barely audibly as he jumped up.

"Who's on guard?" Alexey shouted.

"Golikov, Andrey."

"Were you snivelling?"

"I don't know," the soldier replied looking him in the face with a strange look.

" 'I don't know!' Oh, you Lenten bigots!"

Of course he ought to be given a beating. Alexey's memory brought back to him the flames eddying higher than the forest above the gutted prayer-house, over those who had been burnt alive and, on the flame-lit snow, this man, wringing his hands. At the time Alexey had ordered him to be taken, together with the possessed peasant and the elder Nektary. On the way Nektary had escaped in the night —the devil knew how—when they were camping under the firs; Andrey Golikov lay in the sledge insensible; he would neither eat nor speak. At Povenets, in the guardhouse, when during his questioning they threatened him with the knout, he suddenly let himself go: "Why do you torment me? I've been tormented enough already. There have never been such torments . . ." and he began to tell the whole of his story so that the clerk had hardly time to dip his pen. He tore off his cassock and showed the wounds from the beatings he had received. Seeing that this was an uncommon man, and a literate one besides, Alexey gave orders to have his hair cut and to wash him in the bath-house. After which he was enrolled as a soldier.

"A soldier shouldn't snivel. Are you sick or what?"

Golikov stood at attention, in the proper manner, but remained silent. Alexey made a threatening gesture with his cane and turned to go. Golikov called out desperately:

"Captain!"

This voice coming out of the darkness made Alexey wince: he himself had been like that long ago. He stopped and said sternly:

"Well? What do you want?"

"I'm frightened in the dark, Captain. I'm afraid of the emptiness of the night. This heartache is worse than death. Why have we been brought here?"

Alexey was so astonished that he again went up close to the man.

"How can you reason so, you tramp? You know what you get for such talk?"

"Kill me at once, Alexey Ivanovich! I am my own worst enemy. To live like I do—why, a beast would have died long ago. The world won't accept me. I've tried everything; death too won't have me. There's no sense in it all. Take my musket, stab me with the bayonet!"

For all reply Alexey, clenching his teeth, boxed his ears. Golikov's head wobbled, but he did not utter a sound.

"Pick up your hat! Put it on! I'm telling you for the last time in kindness, you priestless fellow. You learnt from the elders! They've taught you wisdom! You are a soldier. When you are told to march—march! When they tell you to die—die! Why? Because it's necessary. Stay here till dawn! If you start snivelling again, I'll hear you; look out!"

Alexey went without once looking back. He lay down on the hay in his tent. Dawn was still a long way off. It was cold and damp, but there was neither rain nor wind. He pulled the horse-blanket over his head and sighed. "Of course, every one of them keeps silent, but they are thinking. . . . Oh, the men!"

The round-shouldered soldier, Fedka Mudwash, was gloomily pouring water from a dipper into Alexey's hands. Alexey snorted into the cold water and a shudder went over the skin of his whole body. The morning was cold, and grey hoar-frost covered the flattened grass. The clinging mud crunched under his jack-boots. Smoke from the camp-fires rose high between the tents. The sleepy ensign Leopoldus Mirbach, a sheepskin coat thrown over his braided jacket, was shouting something to two frightened soldiers who stood with their heads thrown back.

"You'll be flogged! You'll be flogged!" he kept repeating in a hoarse voice. *"Pfui! Schwein!"* He put his hand over the face of one of the men, squeezed it and pushed him away. Pulling the sheepskin up over his shoulders, he went towards Alexey's tent. His long, unshaven face was bloated and his eyes swollen. He said in broken Russian:

"No hot water. No food. This is not war. When it's a proper war the officer is content. I am not content. Your soldiers are rotten soldiers."

Alexey did not reply and went on rubbing his cheeks fiercely with the towel. With a grunt he presented his back clad in a dirty shirt to Fedka: "Now then!" The other began to slap him with his palms. "Harder!"

At this moment a heavy waggon with a canvas hood stretched on hoops, drawn by six steaming horses of different colours, drove out of the forest. Behind it rode a dozen mud-splashed horsemen. The waggon lurched as it rolled over the trampled field of stubble and approached the camp at walking pace. Alexey caught up his coat, missing the sleeves in his haste and, snatching his sword, ran towards the tents:

"Drummers, sound the alarm!"

The waggon came to a halt and Peter, in a fur cap with earpieces, clambered out of it. He was followed by Menshikov, whose star-shaped spurs kept catching in his broad crimson cloak lined with sables. The horsemen dismounted. Peter stuck his red hands into the pockets of his fur-trimmed jacket and looked at the camp with a frown. The blare of trumpets and the roll of drums sounded in the limpid air. The soldiers jumped off the carts, ran out of the tents, buttoning themselves up, buckling on their belts, and formed a square. Ensigns went down the line at a trot, prodding the men with their canes and swearing in German. Alexey Brovkin, his left hand on his sword and his hat in his right hand, stopped in front of Peter. In his haste he had not found his wig.

Peter said, looking over his tousled head:

"Put on your hat. You don't take your hat off in the field, you fool! Where are your powder-carts?"

"Left behind at Lake Ilmen. All the powder got wet, Sir Bombardier."

Peter turned his eyes towards Menshikov, whose well-shaven face grimaced languidly.

"Kindly tell us," Menshikov said, also looking over Brovkin's head, "where the other companies of the regiment are? Where is Colonel von Schweden?"

"They are scattered farther down the river, General."

Menshikov shook his head with a slight sneer. Peter only scowled. Then both—seven foot tall—walked along the prickly stubble to where the square stood in formation. Without taking his hands out of his pockets, Peter looked with apparent inattention at the grey, haggard faces of the soldiers, at their weather-beaten hats of poor felt, at their shabby coats and the rags on their feet. Only the foreign ensigns stood smartly at attention.

They stood for a long time in front of the ranks. Then Peter raised his head with a jerk and shouted:

"Good health to you, lads!"

The officers turned furiously to the men, and from the ranks came a disjointed:

"We wish you good health, Bombardier!"

"Any complaints?" Peter asked, coming nearer.

The soldiers were silent. The officers, standing with one hand on their canes and one jackbooted foot forward, kept their eyes on the Tsar. Peter repeated sharply:

"Whoever has any complaint, step forward, without fear!"

Someone suddenly sighed deeply, with a sob. Alexey saw Golikov: his musket was wavering in his hands, but he controlled himself and remained silent.

"Tomorrow we shall advance on Narva. There will be much hard work, lads. Charles, the Swedish King, is coming himself to meet us. We must beat him. We cannot give up our land. Here are Yamgorod, Ivangorod, Narva—the whole land up to the sea was once our fatherland. We shall beat him quickly and shall soon rest in winter quarters. Is that clear, lads?"

His eyes protruded sternly. The soldiers looked at him in silence. It could not be more clear. One gloomy voice from the ranks croaked: "We'll beat them, we have enough men for that." Menshikov stepped forward at once to see who had spoken. Brovkin's heart sank: the speaker was Fedka Mudwash, the most unreliable of his soldiers.

"Captain!" Peter said. Brovkin sprang forward. "I thank you for the good order of the company. For the rest you are not responsible. Please issue a triple ration of vodka to the men."

Peter went towards the waggon, with head bent. Menshikov winked at Brovkin—on this occasion he deigned to recognise his old friend—

put his well-kept hand out from under his cloak, patted Alioshka and whispered in his ear:

"Peter Alexeyevich is well pleased. Yours is much better than the rest. Distinguish yourself at Narva and you move up to colonel. I saw your father in Novgorod. He asked me to give you his greetings."

"Thank you, Alexander Danilovich."

"Good luck!" Menshikov caught up the front of his cloak and ran after Peter. They got into the waggon and drove along the bank to where the river, reflecting the cold sky, wound round behind the fir forest.

A little over a mile below Narva a pontoon bridge was thrown over the two arms of the Narova, which encircled the long marshy island of Kamperholm. The cavalry regiments of Sheremetev crossed over and moved on to the Reval road to harry the enemy. Parts of Trubetskoy's division followed them to the left bank and took cover behind their baggage-train half a mile from the stone bastions of Narva. The Narva garrison did not resist the crossing; they evidently felt too weak to risk battle in the open field.

On the 23rd of September the whole of the vanguard turned off the Yamgorod road and came out on to the hilly plain. In full view of the squat, grass-grown towers of Ivangorod—once a stronghold of Ivan the Terrible—and of the pointed spires and tiled roofs of Narva, showing misty blue across the river, they approached the island of Kamperholm and began to cross the swaying bridges over the swiftly-running, turbid river.

The day was calm. The sunshine was fitful and pale. The bells from the brick churches of Narva and Ivangorod jangled, sounding the tocsin.

The soldiers were crowding to the bridges by a broad roadway trodden in the sand, without keeping to any formation. There were streltsi in the high caps bordered with fox-fur so hateful to Peter; broken carts, held together somehow with ropes, carrying barrels, sacks, boxes and mouldy loaves of bread; peasant carters, whose clothes had fallen into rags on the march, whipped up their scraggy horses that strained as hard as they could at their bast collars; a furled standard would drift past, or a pennon on a pike, or a ramrod shouldered by some gunner who had strayed from his battery; a mounted officer, with his cloak flung over his shoulder, would clear a way for himself by rapping heads with his cane; a young boyar, showing his grandfather's mail-armour under his open fur coat, would gallop past with a shout, followed by his ill-mounted retainers carrying Tatar bows and quivers on their backs, looking like barrels in their padded felt coats. As they passed, they all turned towards a bare hummock at the side of the road, where the Tsar, wearing an iron cuirass, was sitting on a grey horse, looking through a telescope. Menshikov, hand on hip, was on a black horse close at his side; he threw gay looks about him, and the wind played with the plumes on his gilded helmet.

The army was disposed in a semi-circle, a cannon-shot's distance from the fortress, the two flanks resting on the Narova river; the units of Weide's divisions were posted above the town; Golovin's division occupied the centre, at the foot of the wooded hill Hermannsberg; and on the left flank, by the bridge over the island of Kamperholm, were the Semenovsky and Preobrazhensky regiments and Trubetskoy's streltsi. Here also stood de Crouy's tent: he was attached to the army as chief adviser. Peter and Menshikov took up their quarters in a fisherman's hut on the island itself.

Along the whole line the Russians began to dig a deep trench with lunettes, redans and bastions facing outward, in case the Swedes advanced along the Reval road. Redoubts were constructed for the siege guns, facing the Narva bastions. The siege works were organised by the engineer Hallart. Puffs of smoke rose from the turrets of the fortress, and the guns barked fiercely in the damp air; bombs rose in high, smoking curves and fell and burst near the carts, the tents, or in the trenches, out of which the soldiers hurriedly jumped. A few farmhouses among the gardens and orchards were set on fire by the bombs. The smoke from the burning houses and the innumerable campfires drifted in a grey cloud towards the town, from where flashed the flaming tongues of gunfire. The military commander of Narva was an experienced and valorous soldier, Colonel Horn.

Taking cover behind gardens and houses, Peter and Hallart rode out to inspect the bastions: Thomas, Gloria, Christeval and Triumph. Sometimes they had to come so close that they could see the grim faces of the Swedish gunners through the loopholes. Smartly, and without fuss, the Swedes loaded and aimed their guns and waited. "Fire!" The cannon-ball, pitilessly rending the air, flew whistling over their heads. Peter opened his eyes wide and the muscles stood out on his cheekbones, but he did not flinch. Hallart, the engineer, experienced, efficient, calm and phlegmatic, spurred his horse at the right moment and rode out of the way. The resplendent Menshikov—they took him as their target every time—shook the plumes of his helmet and shouted arrogantly to the gunners: "A poor shot, comrades!" and patted the neck of his prancing stallion. Fifty tall and moustached dragoons waited motionless to see who would be struck by the black cannon-ball.

The walls of the fortress were high. The bastions, protruding in semi-circles, were built of boulder stone, so hard that an iron ball cracked like a nut on hitting it. Heavy guns thrust their muzzles out of the loopholes and embrasures in the turrets. There were no less than three hundred of them in the fortress. The garrison consisted of two thousand men, infantry, cavalry and armed burghers. The scouts had lied when they said that Narva could be taken by storm.

Peter dismounted, sat down on a drum and spread a sheet of paper on his knees. Mishka, the orderly, held the inkpot. Hallart squatted on his heels near the Tsar and measured the distance with his eyes. Peter's large hand holding the goose-quill, carefully traced shaky lines. Menshikov strode backwards and forwards in front of the semi-circle of dragoons sitting their horses.

"Fifteen siege-guns to each bastion; altogether for the breakthrough we need sixty brass forty-eight-pounders," Hallart said in his even, dull voice. "One hundred and twenty thousand cannon-balls, at least."

"That's a lot!" Peter said.

"At least forty mortars with a thousand bombs each will be needed to start fires in the town before we storm it."

"So that's how they reckon in Europe!" Peter said, writing down the figures.

"Ten large casks of vinegar to cool the guns. Only ceaseless fire, a veritable hell of all batteries, breaks the resistance of the besieged, according to Marshal Luxemburg. We need fifteen thousand handgrenades. A thousand thirty-foot siege ladders, light enough for two men to carry at a run. Five thousand sacks of wool."

"What's that for?"

"To protect the soldiers from musket bullets. At the siege of Dunkirk, Marshal Vauban, under cover of such sacks, succeeded in getting close to the gates despite furious fire, because a bullet easily gets caught in the wool."

"All right," Peter said, unconvinced, making a note of it. "Menshikov, we shall need five thousand sacks of wool."

Menshikov bent over the paper that fluttered in the wind, with his knees apart and his hands resting on his knees. He pursed his lips:

"That's just waste, *mein Herz*. Besides there's no wool at all to be had." He turned to Hallart: "At Azov the men climbed the walls with nothing but their swords and took the town."

Behind them, among the dragoons, a horse began to struggle and a man cried out hoarsely. They turned round. A grey horse was kicking and blindly jerking its head: a stream of dark blood was gushing from a wound above its nostrils. The moustached dragoons threw anxious glances towards the bushes about a hundred paces away, from which little puffs of smoke were belching. Peter sat quite still on the drum, the hand that was holding the pen still raised.

Unheard, because of the thunder of the cannon, a detachment of jaegers had sallied out from the gates of the fort tower—screened from sight by the Gloria bastion—and stolen along behind the hedges of the gardens. They were swiftly followed by half a squadron of troopers in iron cuirasses and deep helmets. With swords drawn they were galloping in a long line over the heather to encircle from the left.

For one second, no more, Menshikov stared with wide eyes at this diversion created by the enemy. Then he rushed to his black stallion, unclasped and drew off his cloak and leapt into the saddle.

"Draw swords!" he yelled, the blood rushing to his face. He whipped out his sword, drove home his spurs and, bending forward on the neck of his rearing stallion, sent him off at full gallop. "Dragoons, follow me!" and the whole troop dashed round Peter, who stood by the drum, to intercept the Swedish horsemen, who were already reining in and turning.

Hallart pressed his thin lips together with concern and leading up Peter's restless, black-maned grey mare, said:

"I beg you to get out of the field of fire, Your Majesty."

Peter hopped on one leg as he mounted—he was watching the dragoons and Swedish troopers drawing together. The Russians rode in a serried group. The plumes on Menshikov's glittering helmet rose and fell at their head. The Swedes were spread out over the heather, and now the men on the flanks wheeled sharply, spurring their horses and beating them with their swords. But they were not given time to form a line. Peter saw Menshikov's black stallion collide with a sorrel horse; the Swedish rider clutched at the mane and fell. The red plumes tossed among iron helmets. But already the dragoons were hurling themselves at them in a compact body and, without a pause, continued to gallop, waving their swords as if in play. Behind them men were left lying on the field: one kept shaking his bowed head as he tried to rise, another lay with his bent knees twitching. Several frightened, riderless horses galloped over the field.

Hallart was insistently pulling at the rein. "Your Majesty, it is dangerous here!" The grey mare was dancing and plunging. Peter struck her with his heels. Even when they had covered some distance, he kept turning round. The Swedish troopers were now in full flight from the Russians: on the right, barring their way to the town, a motley crowd of horsemen, mounted on horses of different colours, were galloping over the brown strips of a harvested field, waving their curved swords with Tatar fierceness: several hundred men of the noblemen's irregular troops. Musket fire, aimed at them, cracked from under a wooden awning on the fortress wall.

When they reached a birch-copse Peter drew a deep breath. He pulled up his mare to a walk. "Yes, it won't be easy," he told himself in answer to his thoughts. Hallart said:

"I can congratulate Your Majesty. Your cavalry is excellent."

"What good is that? That's only half the job. Working yourself up into a fury, galloping, slashing—that alone won't take a fortress."

He rode up on to a hillock, reined in and looked for a long time, frowning, at the line of troops and baggage-trains stretched over some four miles. Everywhere lumps of earth were being sluggishly thrown up out of the trenches. There was shouting and cursing. There were men by the camp-fires and carts doing nothing. He saw hobbled, scraggy horses. Rags were spread on the bushes. It seemed as if this immense body of troops was moving and living clumsily, with great reluctance.

"Before November nothing can be done," Peter said. "We cannot bring up the siege-guns until the frost is hard enough. It's one thing on paper and another in reality."

And again, setting off at a walking pace, he began to question Hallart about the campaigns and sieges of the famous marshals Vauban and Luxemburg, the founders of military science. He asked about the arms and cannon factories of France. His thin neck, tightly bound in a linen neckcloth, twitched as he said:

"Naturally. There everything is organised, everything is to hand. Take their roads and our roads. . . ."

Menshikov galloped up, jumping the trenches. He was still flushed, with teeth bared in a happy grin and wild eyes. Only one plume was left on his helmet and his cuirass showed the traces of blows. He reined back his winded horse.

"Bombardier," he said, "the enemy has been thrown back with heavy losses. Hardly one half of the Swedes have got away." In his enthusiasm he was, of course, exaggerating. "We have two killed and some lightly wounded."

Peter wrinkled up his nose with pleasure at the sight of Menshikov. "Good," he said. "Well done!"

That evening the generals assembled in de Crouy's tent. There was pompous, extremely severe Artamon Golovin, the original creator of the play-soldiers; there was Prince Trubetskoy, the idol of the streltsi regiments, a portly, rich boyar; there was Buturlin, commander of the Guards, famed for his stentorian voice and heavy fists; and there was bald-headed Weide, very ill and shivering in his sheepskin coat. When Peter, Menshikov and Hallart arrived, the Duke invited them to sup on his camp fare. Then rare and even unknown food was served—it had been brought by special messenger from Reval—and French and Rhenish wines poured out in abundance.

The Duke was in his element. He ordered many candles to be lit. Gesticulating with his bony hands, he told stories of famous battles, when, standing on an eminence overlooking the bloody battlefield, with his foot on a shattered cannon, he had ordered his cuirassiers to break a square, and his jaegers to overrun the enemy's flank. He had drowned whole divisions in a river, burnt cities to the ground.

The Russians sat with moodily lowered eyes, eating asparagus and Strasburg pie. Peter stared absent-mindedly at de Crouy's long nose and wet moustache. He kept drumming his fingers on the table and wriggling his shoulderblades as if they were itching. This absent-minded look had been noticed in Peter since the beginning of the campaign.

"Narva!" the Duke exclaimed holding out his empty goblet to his orderly. "Narva! One day's proper bombardment and a short assault on the southern bastions, and the keys of Narva would be presented to you, Sire, on a silver platter. Then leave a small garrison here and, deploying the cavalry on the flanks, throw all forces against King Charles. We shall celebrate Christmas Eve in Reval, on my word of honour!"

Peter left the table, paced up and down, bending his head not to touch the roof of the tent, picked up a straw from the floor and lay down on the Duke's bed, which came from the nearest farmhouse. He picked his teeth with the straw.

"Hallart has given me a list," he said, at which all the others stopped eating and turned to him. "If we had everything that is down on that list, we would take Narva. We need sixty siege-guns." He sat up, pulled a piece of crumpled paper out of his pocket and threw it down on the table in front of Golovin. "Read it. At the moment we haven't a single good gun on the redoubts. Repnin is struggling with the siege-guns in the mud near Tver. Our mortars, I learned today, got stuck in the Valday. The powder-carts are still at Lake Ilmen. How does this strike you, Generals?"

The generals drew the candles closer and bent their heads over the list. Only Menshikov sat apart, with a sneer on his face and a full cup in front of him.

"This isn't a military camp, it's a gipsy camp," Peter resumed after a pause, slowly and grimly as before. "We prepared for this for two years, yet nothing is ready. It is worse than at Azov. Worse than in Vaska Golitsin's army." Menshikov jingled a spur and grinned from ear to ear. "Call this a camp! The soldiers prowl about among the baggage-carts. And the baggage-train is full of Finnish women. Commotion! Disorder! They work lazily. It makes one sick to watch them. The bread is mouldy. Some regiments have only two days' rations of salt-meat left. Where is all the salt-meat? In Novgorod? Why not here? The rains are coming soon. Where are the huts for the soldiers?"

The only sound in the tent was the sputtering of the candles. The Duke, understanding little of what was being said, looked curiously from Peter to the generals.

"Two months we have been marching from Moscow and aren't there yet. Call this a campaign! Do you know that King Charles has forced Christian to accept a shameful peace and to pay a contribution of two hundred thousand gold doubloons? Now Charles has landed at Pernau with his whole army and is marching on Riga. If he defeats King August at Riga, we can expect him here in November. How are we going to meet him?"

Artamon Golovin, as the senior officer, stood up and bowed. Then, with beetling brows, he said:

"Peter Alexeyevich, with the help of God . . ."

"It's guns we need!" Peter interrupted and a vein swelled on his forehead. "Bombs! One hundred and twenty thousand cannon-balls for siege-guns! Salt-meat! You old fool!"

It had been raining again for a fortnight. Dense fogs drifted in from the sea. The soldiers' dug-outs were flooded, the tents leaked, and there was nowhere to take shelter from the damp, cold nights. The whole camp was waist deep in a bog. The men began to sicken with dysentery and fever, and every night dozens of carts transported dead men away from the camp.

The besieged kept the besiegers under constant fire from their guns and muskets. They sallied out, mostly at dawn, overpowered the sentries, crept up to the dug-outs and threw hand-grenades at the sleepers. Every day Peter rode round the whole line of fortifications. Taciturn and grim, he emerged on his grey mare from the curtain of rain in his wet cloak and bedraggled hat, stopped, stared with glassy eyes and rode off at a walking pace over the rough field into the fog.

The supply-trains were slow in coming up. Reports came in from the road that the real trouble was the haulage: all horses and carts had been taken from the peasants, and they had now to turn to the landowners and monasteries. The horses were sorry animals, the grazing-grounds had been cropped bare, and every day heavy rain and bad roads made things more difficult. There was a rumour that, in his fisherman's hut, Peter had with his own hands beaten the general in charge of the commissariat insensible and had ordered the general's assistant to be hanged. The food seemed to improve a little. There was better order in the camp. The officers were a poor lot: the Russians were slow, used to old ways, garrulous and inefficient, while the foreigners did nothing but drink vodka against the damp and beat the soldiers with good reason, or for no reason at all.

It was certain knowledge now that King Charles had landed at Pernau and turned towards Riga; that his mere appearance had subdued the Livonian knights and that he had driven King August's troops into Kurland. August himself was in Warsaw, among the Polish nobility torn by internecine feuds, and was sending one messenger after another to Peter asking for money, Cossacks, guns, infantry. The besiegers of Narva knew that they must expect the Swedes with the first frosts.

Sheremetev, who had been sent with four regiments of irregular cavalry to harry the enemy, had got as far as Wesenberg and had successfully overcome the Swedish protecting detachment, but then had suddenly retreated to the coastal defiles of Pigaioki, some twenty-five miles from Narva. From there he wrote to Peter:

". . . I have retreated, not out of fear, but for greater security. Near Wesenberg there are endless marshes and great forests. All the grazing-grounds both here and in the neighbourhood have been cropped bare. But more than this I feared that we might be outflanked on the way to Narva. As for your anger at my burning down villages and scattering the Finns, do believe me: only a few villages have been burnt down and those only to prevent the enemy finding shelter. And now I have given orders that the land should not be devastated without special instructions. Where I have taken up position at Pigaioki the enemy will not be able to pass unnoticed. I shall not retreat any farther, and you may rest assured that we shall stand here to the death."

Finally, for good or evil, the wind turned north. In a day it blew away the wet mist, and the sun, hanging low in the sky, shed a scanty light on the mud-logged camp and lit up a golden cockerel on the church spire in the town. The earth was frost-bound. Supply-trains with ammunition began to come in. Two famous culverins, called "Lion" and "Bear"—cast a hundred years ago in Novgorod by Andrey Chohov and Semion Dubinka, and weighing five tons each—were brought in, each drawn by ten pairs of oxen. Howitzers crawled like tortoises on low, broad wheels, short mortars firing bombs a hundred pounds in weight. The whole army stood under arms, the cavalry with horses saddled and swords drawn in case the Swedes attempted a sally.

Ropes were tied to the "Lion" and the "Bear" and two hundred men hauled them on to the central redoubt facing the southern bastions of the fortress. Throughout the night howitzers and mortars were placed on the batteries. In the fortress no one slept either, preparing for the assault; the lights of lanterns crept along the walls and the voices of sentries could be heard calling to one another.

On the 5th of November at dawn Peter, with the Duke and the generals, rode out to the Hermannsberg hill. A keen wind was blowing. The camp still lay in shadow; the red gleam of the sun touched only the steep roofs of the town and the battlements of the towers. Tongues of fire darted from the plain, the earth shook, the guns roared and thundered and bombs flew in fiery curves into the town. The camp and the walls were wrapped in smoke. Peter lowered his telescope and, with distended nostrils, nodded to Hallart. Hallart rode up and clicked his tongue discontentedly:

"It's bad. The bombs fall short. The gunpowder is no good."

"What should be done? Immediately. . . ."

"Increase the charge—if the guns can stand it."

Peter rode down the hill and galloped over the drawbridge and through the log gates behind the palisade and the chevaux-de-frise. At the central battery the gunners were cooling the long barrels of the "Lion" and the "Bear" with vinegar and water. The battery commander, the Dutchman Jacob Winterschwerk, a short, old seaman, with a beard like a frill round his chin, came up to Peter and said calmly:

"This is no good. This powder is only fit to shoot sparrows with—all smoke and soot."

Peter threw off his cloak and coat, rolled up his sleeves, took a ramrod from a gunner and, with a vigorous movement, cleared the sooty barrel.

"Charge!"

Packages of powder done up in grey paper were passed along from hand to hand from the battery dump. Peter tore open a package, poured out some powder on his palm and snorted angrily, like a cat. He rammed six packages into the barrel.

"That's dangerous," said Jacob Winterschwerk.

"Hold your tongue! Ball!"

Peter tossed up the round ball, weighing thirty-six pounds, rolled it into the barrel and rammed it home. He crouched down behind the sights and turned the screw.

"Match! Everyone stand back from the gun."

The "Bear" belched flame with an ear-splitting roar, jerked heavily back on its iron wheels, and sank its tail into the ground. The ball flew up, growing smaller in the distance. Stones spurted from the Gloria bastion and a tooth broke from the edge of the tower.

"Oh, that's not bad!" the Dutch gunner said.

"Keep on firing like this," Peter said. Putting on his coat he galloped away to the howitzer battery. The order was given to all batteries that the charges were to be increased by one half. Again the earth trembled with the thunder of a hundred and thirty guns. A terrible flame leapt from the upturned mortars. When the clouds of smoke dispersed they saw two houses burning in the town. The second volley was successful. But it soon became known that two howitzers of the western battery had burst. They had been recently cast in Narishkin's Tula factory. The axles of several gun-carriages cracked. Peter said: "We will deal with that later. We'll find out who's to blame. Keep on firing like this."

That was how the bombardment of Narva began; it continued without intermission until the 15th of November.

Felten, the Tsar's cook, muttered under his breath as he fried eggs over kindlings on the hearth. A dozen eggs had been found with difficulty—the cook's underling had ridden nearly as far as Yamburg—and they had all proved rotten.

"What are you muttering about? Put more pepper on them, Felten."

"Yes, Your Majesty, I'll pepper them."

Peter was sitting by the hot stove. This was the only warm place: in the closet behind the partition, where he and Menshikov slept, draughts came through the walls. Now, at midnight, he could hear the howling of the wind and the creaking of the windmill sails by the hut on the island. The birch kindling crackled pleasantly. The short, irate Felten had spread out the provisions on the hearth and kept smelling them. The flames flickered in angry reflections on his fleshy nose.

"What if the Swedes were to take you prisoner, Felten? What then?"

"I hear you, Your Majesty."

" 'Aha!' they'll say, 'the Tsar's cook!' And they'll hang you by the feet."

"And what if they do? I know my duty."

He spread a clean towel over the rickety plank table. He put a flat earthenware bottle on it with pepper vodka and cut the black, dry bread in thin slices. Peter, gently puffing at his pipe, watched Felten move—deft, soft and capable—in his felt boots and quilted jacket with an apron tied round his waist.

"I'm not joking about the Swedes. You'd better collect your paraphernalia."

Felten gave Peter a sidelong glance and realised that he was indeed not joking. He set the skillet with the fried eggs on the table and poured out some vodka into a small tin cup.

"Please to come to the table, Your Majesty."

The whole ramshackle building shook with the wind. The candle wobbled. Menshikov came in noisily from outside.

"What weather!"

He grimaced, struggling with the knot in his scarf. Then he went to warm his hands over the fire.

"He'll be here at once."

"Sober?" Peter asked.

"He was asleep. I just got him out of bed."

Alexander sat down opposite Peter. He tried whether the table stood firmly, then poured out some vodka, drank it and shook his head. For some time they ate in silence. Then Peter said in a low voice:

"It's too late. Nothing can be put right now."

Alexander replied, swallowing with difficulty:

"If he's within sixty miles and Sheremetev doesn't delay him, he'll be here the day after tomorrow. If we come out into the open field, is it not possible to beat him, with our cavalry?" He unfastened his collar and turned to Felten: "Have you any cabbage soup left?" He poured himself out some more vodka. "All he has is ten thousand men; prisoners swear to this on the Gospel. Are we really such clods? It's mortifying!"

"It is," Peter agreed. "You can't sharpen men's wits in two days' time. If things go against us at Narva, we shall try to stop him at Pskov and Novgorod."

"*Mein Herz,* it's wrong even to think of it."

"All right, all right."

They fell silent. Felten, squatting down, blew on the charcoal; he was heating beer in a copper kettle.

Things were not going well at Narva. For two weeks the Russians had bombarded the city, blown up mines and run saps, but they neither made breaches in the walls nor set fire to the town. The generals dared not attempt an assault. Of one hundred and thirty guns half had burst or been damaged. The day before, they had gone over the gunpowder and balls in the ammunition dumps and found that there was just enough for one more day of such firing—and the powder-carts were still dragging themselves along near Novgorod.

The Swedish army was approaching by forced marches along the Reval road and was perhaps at this moment fighting Sheremetev in the Pigaioki defiles. The Russians were caught in a vice between the guns of the fortress and King Charles's advancing army.

"We've made a lot of noise. In that we are efficient," Peter said throwing down his spoon. "We haven't learnt to fight yet. We started at the wrong end. All this is no good. If we want a gun to fire here, we must load it in Moscow. Do you understand?"

Menshikov said:

"On my way here I heard soldiers of the first company talking round the camp-fire. They're expecting the Swedes, the whole camp is buzzing. The way they abuse the generals—my word! I heard one of them say: 'The first bullet for our officer'."

"The generals!" Peter's eyes glinted. "All they are good for is to walk round the walls in procession with church-banners! Generals! Dotards. . . ."

Menshikov said cautiously, with a sidelong look:

"Peter Alexeyevich, let me have the control of the troops for these three days. Seriously. Will you?"

Peter fumbled in his pocket for his tobacco-pouch as if he had not heard him. Breathing heavily through his nose, he rammed in the crumbs of tobacco with his fingers.

"From tomorrow de Crouy will be Commander-in-Chief," he said. "He's pretty much of a fool, but he knows European ways in military matters, and he's a good soldier. Our foreigners will pluck up heart under him. Get ready before dawn, see? We'll be leaving."

Still breathing heavily, he pulled the candle towards him and drew at his pipe. Menshikov asked in a low voice:

"Peter Alexeyevich, where are we going?"

"Novgorod."

Peter looked at last into Alexander's clear blue eyes now wide with surprise. Suddenly his face was darkly suffused with blood and a vein swelled on his sweating forehead.

"That boy has nothing to lose," he said controlling his anger, "but I have. Do you think that Narva is the beginning and the end? The war has only just begun. We must win. But with this army we cannot win. Do you understand? We must start with the rear, with the baggage-waggons. Galloping about with a sword is the last thing. You fool, do you want to be braver than Charles? Lower your eyes!" His face was for a moment convulsed with fury. "I forbid you to look at me!"

Alexander did not obey; he did not lower his eyes now filled with tears of burning shame; a drop rolled down his tense cheek. Peter stared at him with narrowed eyes. Both held their breath. Then Peter suddenly gave a short laugh and, leaning back against the wall, stuck his hands deep into his pockets.

"Mein Herz," he mimicked Menshikov's voice. "Friend of my heart! So you are ashamed of me? Wait, there is more to come and they will all turn their faces from me. I was scared by Charles. I abandoned my army. I ran off to Novgorod, as once I did long ago to Troitsa. All right! Wipe your pretty face. Go and meet the generals, they've just arrived."

Sentries challenged. There was a clatter of hoofs on the frozen earth. The light of torches showed outside the window. De Crouy and the generals came in clanking their spurs. Their faces, reddened by the wind, were alarmed: what could have happened at such a late hour? Peter nodded to them and, going up to de Crouy, embraced him. He made a sign to Menshikov to take up the candle and went behind the wooden partition into the closet.

Here Menshikov put the candle on a small table littered with papers and strewn with tobacco. Everyone was standing. Peter sat down, picked up a sheet of paper sprinkled with cinders and sternly read the lines—crossed out here and there—over to himself, moving his lips. Then he coughed and, without looking at anyone, began to read out in a dry firm voice:

"*In Gottsnam,* in the name of God: inasmuch as His Majesty is leaving the army on important business, for this reason we entrust the army to His Grace the Duke de Crouy under the following articles." The Duke's thigh, as he stood quite close to the table, began to twitch. Peter looked at the lean thigh in white buckskin, then at the dry hands that grasped the gold hilt of his sword. "Article one: His Grace is to be Commander-in-Chief. Article two: all generals, officers and soldiers are to be under his orders as if he were His Majesty the Tsar himself. Article three"—Peter raised his voice—"take Narva and Ivangorod immediately by any means. Article four: for insubordination he is to discipline generals, officers and soldiers as if they were his own subjects, even to death."

He looked past the Duke at the generals: Weide was nodding in agreement, Prince Trubetskoy's sweating face was swelling, Buturlin's low forehead creased under his cropped grey hair, Artamon Golovin's head hung as if humiliation and misfortune were already weighing him down.

"His Grace is also to keep himself well informed about the Swedish relief force. When he receives reliable news of the approach of King Charles and if the king's army is very strong, His Grace must strongly guard against the king's entry into the town of Narva, and is to seek to defeat him with the help of God. But he would do better to wait, if possible, for reinforcements." Peter lowered the paper and said to de Crouy: "Repnin and the Hetman with the Cossacks and ammunition trains are within a few days' march from here." Then he turned to Golovin: "Sit down and make a fair copy."

There was a knock at the outside door. Menshikov anxiously elbowed his way through to the kitchen. Someone came in, and the distant shouting of many voices came through the open door with the noise of the wind. Peter pushed someone out of his way and strode into the kitchen.

"What's happened?" he cried in a terrible voice.

In front of him stood a very young man: his face, as rosy as a girl's, was drawn; he had a snub nose, bold eyes, and his fair hair above one ear was clotted with blood.

"Paul Yaguzhinsky, lieutenant attached to Boris Petrovich Sheremetev," Menshikov interposed quickly.

"Well?"

The youngster's face quivered. He raised his face to Peter and pulled himself together:

"Boris Petrovich has sent me, Sire, to ask where he should quarter his troops."

Peter said nothing. The generals were crowding anxiously in the doors of the closet.

Menshikov said, hurriedly pulling at his short warm coat:

"To their shame they've run all the way from Pigaioki. They even left their caps behind. Noblemen!"

When, on the morning of the 17th of November the irregular regiments of the nobles' militia heard from the outposts that Swedish patrols had slipped into the rear past the defiles along the seashore and gained the Reval road during the night, they broke ranks and, disregarding Sheremetev's commands, began to retreat from Pigaioki for fear of being cut off from the main army. Sheremetev rode out to the disordered squadrons, caught hold of bridles, shouted, struck horses and men with his riding-whip, but those behind pressed on those in front and his horse twisted and turned in the torrent of fugitives. All he could do was to gather a few squadrons to cover the rear and save part of the baggage-train from the Swedes, who, in iron cuirasses and ribbed helmets, appeared at sunrise on all the surrounding heights. The Swedes did not pursue the regiments of the nobility, which fled at a gallop and, during the night, reached the palisades of the camp at Narva. In the darkness the sentries on the ramparts took them for enemy forces and opened fire. The horsemen shouted desperately: "Friends! Friends!" The whole camp woke up and hummed with excitement.

Lieutenant Paul Yaguzhinsky was allowed inside the palisade and galloped to see the Tsar. An icy wind was blowing in strong gusts. The noblemen's militia dismounted and waited on the other side of the trench, by the raised bridges. From the palisades men shouted at them: "Landowners, why did you come running so fast? Do you want to take cover, you poor fellows?"

Drums began to beat throughout the camp, lights floated about and riders galloped round with lanterns. The regiments and squadrons were listening, under their colours, to the Tsar's ukase transferring the command of the army to the famous and invincible Duke of the Empire, de Crouy. The troops were silent, overcome with surprise and fear. Soon the rumour flew from mouth to mouth that the

Tsar was no longer in camp and that the entire Swedish force was only three miles away.

No one slept. Fires were lit, but the wind scattered them. Towards morning Sheremetev's cavalry was shifted to the right flank. They did not shelter behind the palisades, but took up their position on the very edge of the water, at a spot above the town where the Narova roared furiously over the rapids between small islands. Dawn came, but no Swedes were to be seen. The patrols sent to reconnoitre could not discover the enemy anywhere near, although Sheremetev's men swore that the Swedes had been on their tail all the way from Pigaioki.

To the harsh blare of trumpets the Duke, wearing a resplendent mantle and holding his marshal's baton resting against his hip, and followed at half a horse's length by the generals Golovin, Trubetskoy, Buturlin, the Royal Prince of Imeretia and Prince Yakov Dolgoruky, rode round the encampment. The Duke, brushing up his drooping moustache with the side of his glove, shouted to the soldiers in broken Russian: "Good health, fine lads! Let us die for our father the Tsar!" Drums rolled and this order was read aloud to all the regiments:

"During the night one half of the troops are to remain under arms. Before dawn twenty-four charges and bullets will be distributed to each man. At sunrise the whole army will be lined up and when three guns are fired the bands will play, the drums will beat and all standards will be raised on the entrenchments. No shot is to be fired until the enemy is within thirty paces."

During the night the wind shifted to the west, blowing landward from the sea. It grew warmer. Under cover of darkness the Swedish major-general Ribing and two troopers, their horses' hoofs wrapped in felt, secretly rode up to the palisades and measured the depth of the trench and the height of the parapet.

Alexey Brovkin, hungry as a wolf, pierced by the wind, was pacing the rampart by the company's pennant—three paces one way, three paces the other. The rampart stretched for four miles, and soldiers were stationed at long intervals. The horns had sounded, the drums had rattled; guns and muskets were loaded, fuses were smoking. The wind fluttered the standards on the entrenchments. It was eleven o'clock in the morning.

Alexey tightened his belt as far as it would go. The new Commander-in-Chief had thought of everything except feeding the troops. For some days now the soldiers and the officers with them ate mouldy biscuit and the crumbs they shook out of their haversacks. The night before no biscuit had been issued. The soldiers on the ramparts stood out like scarecrows: in Brovkin's company only eighty fit men remained. There had been a time when Alexey was eager to fight, to lead the company in the smoke of guns, to seize the shaft of an enemy standard ("Thank you, Alexey, I promote you to colonel . . ."), but all he yearned for today was to creep into the warm stench of a dug-out and eat thin porridge out of a mess-tin, scalding his throat.

Screwing up his eyes against the wind, Alexey shouted at the nearest soldier, who was Golikov:

"What are you gaping at? Hold yourself up!"

The man did not hear him. Ragged shoulders hunched, he stood with his sharp-nosed face tense, as if he were seeing death. The other soldiers too were looking, like bristling dogs, in the direction of the Hermannsberg hill. Above it the sun appeared and disappeared among racing clouds. Heavily loaded men were moving between the tree-stumps and the bare, swaying birches. More and more of them came out of the wood. They threw sacks and pack-loads off their shoulders, ran forward and formed wide serried columns. Guns, pulled by six horses, drove out; some went down and straight ahead towards the central redoubt, others crossed the stream at a trot towards Weide's fortifications, while a third lot galloped to the right along the plain. Six infantry columns were drawn up on the Hermannsberg hill. The cavalry rode out of the wood in double file, with a dull glint of iron.

Alexey shouted wildly:

"Drummers, sound the battle alarm!"

Moustached non-commissioned officers clambered up the rampart, pulling down their three-cornered hats to prevent them being blown away by the wind. The drums began to beat. Leopoldus Mirbach, sounding unaccountably pleased, pointed and shouted to Alexey: "Look, the one on the horse, that's King Charles!" The Swedish columns, terrifying in their order and discipline—as if they were not human but immortal and without feeling—poured slowly down the hill in undulating blue-black lines. Over there, on the height, half a dozen horsemen sat their mounts, and one slender man, in advance of the others, waved his hand: other horsemen rode swiftly up to him and then galloped down to the columns.

The wind bent the shafts of the standards and pennants on the rampart, and the drums rolled poignantly. A leaden, snow-laden cloud was rising from the sea and rapidly overspreading the sky. Four gun-teams galloped up to a spot two hundred paces from the trench, opposite the position occupied by Brovkin's company; they turned before halting and unlimbered; then green caissons were drawn up at a gallop, and also turned. Strongly-built men in dark-blue uniforms jumped down and took up their positions by the guns. An infantry column came up at a run, without losing its regular formation, and several men with white lapels hurried to the front. At the flourish of glinting swords the ranks of the Swedes doubled, deployed along the sides of the battery and dropped down; clods of earth began to fly.

Alexey, cupping his mouth with his hands, shouted to make himself heard in the wind: "Officers! Pass on the word to the non-commissioned officers—pass on to the soldiers—no shooting until the order is given, under pain of death!" Leopoldus Mirbach ran in his long jackboots along the rampart, yelling in German and threatening with his cane. Fedka Mudwash, bearded, dirty, a frightened figure, bared his teeth viciously. Mirbach aimed a blow at his head. The wind tore at coat-tails, and somebody's hat was whirled into the air.

Alexey kept turning to the Russian battery: "Come on! Hurry up!" At last a heavy blast crashed against his ear-drums. "The devils, they don't know how to shoot!" In reply the four Swedish guns jerked back and spat fire. Half a mile away the "Lion" and the "Bear" thundered out impressively. The four gun-teams galloped up again, hitched the guns and brought them closer up to the rampart. The gunners came up running, cleaned the guns, loaded them and jumped back—two to the wheels, the third squatting down with the match. A man with white lapels raised his sword. A volley burst. Four cannon-balls crashed into the pine logs of the palisade; there was a sudden scream of iron and pieces of wood flew in all directions. Alexey backed and fell. He sprang up and, in a glimpse, but with terrible clarity, so that he remembered it till the end of his days, caught sight of a galloping white horse coming over the uneven field, close alongside the trench, and on it a youth, as slim as a finger, in a small three-cornered hat, and under it a narrow leather bag beating against the back of his neck, his legs stretched out and forward, in an un-Russian way, with his feet thrust into the stirrups up to the heels, his face mockingly turned to the men shooting from the palisade and, behind him, a score of regular, double lines of cuirassiers on very bony horses, galloping neck-and-neck. "God help me!" came Golikov's desperate cry.

The low cloud was spreading over the whole sky. The day was rapidly darkening. A curtain of snow veiled the camp, the lines of galloping cuirassiers, the moving Swedish columns. The howling of the wind was torn by the bark of the guns and their flames burst in misty haloes. The palisade was cracking and bursting. Cannon-balls hissed furiously overhead. The snowstorm began to whirl, and the slanting, prickly snow stung and blinded the men. They could see nothing that was going on in front on the far side of the trench, nor were they aware of what had been happening during the last quarter of an hour in the camp. A desperately running soldier, bent low, crashed into Alexey; the man did not belong to his company: Alexey seized him by the sides. The soldier yelled wildly: "We've been sold!" tore himself away and disappeared in the snowstorm. It was only then that Alexey noticed that out of the whirling snow something like bundles of dry branches had began to fall into the trench. Driving the snow from his face he shouted:

"Fire! Fire!"

Agile men were already busy in the trench.

The Swedish grenadiers, who had the wind in their backs, had run up and begun to fill the trench with fascines, over which, without ladders, they started to climb up the palisade.

Alexey saw Golikov shoot and then back, poking his bayonet in front of him. A big snow-covered man threw his legs over the palisade and seized the bayonet with his hands. Golikov pulled the musket towards himself, the other man tugged at it. Alexey screamed shrilly, sticking him, like a pig, with his sword. More and more men came tumbling over, as though the snowstorm were driving them. Alexey thrust his sword into the empty air and into something soft. Pain shot through his eyes; his skull, his whole face seemed to flatten out with the blow.

Golikov did not remember how he rolled into the trench. He crawled on all fours in animal terror. Somebody ran past waving his arms and, behind him, two Swedes, broad and filled with fury, with pointing bayonets. Golikov crouched down and lay flat like a beetle. "Oh, what men!" He lifted up his head and snow filled his mouth. He jumped up, swaying on his feet, and immediately came upon two men struggling. Fedka Mudwash sprawled over Leopoldus Mirbach, groping for his throat. Mirbach was tearing at Fedka's beard. "No, you don't, you devil!" Fedka was muttering hoarsely, and he pressed down with his shoulders. Golikov broke into a run. "Oh, what men!"

The central column of the Swedes—four thousand grenadiers—hurled itself furiously at Golovin's division. The battle on the palisades lasted a quarter of an hour. The Russians, blinded by the snowstorm, weakened by hunger, mistrustful of their commanders and not understanding why they must die in this snowy inferno, fell back from the ramparts. "We've been sold, lads! Kill the officers!" Shooting confusedly, they rushed about the camp and trampled each other in the snow-filled trenches and on the gabions of the batteries. They broke up and carried along with them Trubetskoy's regiments. In their thousands they fled to the bridges, to the crossings.

The Swedes did not pursue them far, fearing to get lost themselves in the snowstorm in the midst of such a vast encampment. Trumpets imperiously summoned them back on to the ramparts. But a section of the grenadiers blundered into the chevaux-de-frise protecting the baggage-train. *"Mit Gotts Hilf!"* they shouted and took the baggage-train by storm. Here, under snow-covered matting they found barrels of rotten salted meat and kegs of vodka. Over a thousand grenadiers stayed by the kegs till the end of the battle. Those Russians who were running about among the waggons they either killed or simply drove away.

The infantry was followed by the cavalry which broke into the camp through the smashed gates. It went straight for the main redoubt. The culverins "Lion" and "Bear" were overrun, the gun-crews cut down, and the commander, Jacob Winterschwerk, wounded in the head, surrendered his sword. The culverins were turned and began to fire at Weide's fortifications. Here the Swedes met with stubborn resistance: Weide placed the entire division on the parapet in four close rows, and he himself, armed with an officer's lance, repelled the Swedes who were clambering up the palisade. The soldiers behind loaded the muskets and those in front kept up a running fire. The whole trench was filled with dead and wounded. When balls fired from the main redoubt began to reach them, and they recognised the voices of the "Lion" and the "Bear", Weide mounted his horse and galloped along the rampart: "Boys, stand firm!" A bomb exploded under his horse and, through the flying snow and the smoke, the men saw the horse rear and crash on its back.

Sheremetev's cavalry regiments were caught with their backs to the river, between Weide's palisades and the forest. Snowy whirlwinds hit their faces, and behind them the Narova roared. The noise of the forest was terrifying. They stood seeing nothing, understanding nothing. To their right, from afar, the sound of guns came more and more frequently. Quite close, on the palisades, musket fire broke out, and shouting, and death-cries so appalling that the hair on the heads of the boyars' sons stirred under their caps.

Sheremetev was on a hillock in the midst of his troops. He had put his telescope into his pocket for he could hardly make out the ears of his horse. He could not understand what was happening in the Russian camp. As he vainly waited for the Commander-in-Chief's orders, he thought that the noblemen's cavalry must have been forgotten, or could not be found, or else that some disaster must have occurred.

The sound of firing came now from the left, probably from the forest. Sheremetev listened, standing up in his stirrups. He called to the young Prince Rostovsky:

"Here, take four squadrons with you and clear the enemy out of the forest. God be with you!"

The Prince, frozen stiff in his coat-of-mail and iron helmet, mumbled something in reply and rode down the hillock. Then from the forest too a cannon barked. A voice cried out in mortal agony. And immediately—from the right, from the left and from the front—musket fire began to rattle. Sheremetev looked round to give the command: "Draw swords! Forward, with God's help!" But there was no one to give orders to: horses' cruppers were retreating up the hillock. "We're done for! We're done for! Get away across the river!" thousands of voices shouted. All that remained for Sheremetev to do was to turn his own mount so as not to be ridden down. He frowned and his eyes filled with tears as he tore at the bridle.

There were roars and wild yells; a tossing torrent of rearing horses' heads, of shaggy manes and backs covered with snow rushed towards the river. The bank was steep, the horses slithered down on their hindquarters, balked, and those behind crashed into them full-tilt and leapt over those that fell. Horses' heads and drowning human faces swirled in the yellow water under the veil of the snowstorm; arms convulsively clutching the air showed for a moment out of the eddies. More and more hundreds of horsemen threw themselves into the Narova, swimming, struggling in the current, drowning.

Sheremetev's good steed scrambled on to an islet in the middle of the river, stood for a while with heaving flanks, then cautiously stepped again into the water and, with bared teeth, started to swim and carried its rider on to the far bank.

The snowstorm that veiled the battlefield was perhaps more dangerous to the Swedes than to the Russians. Communications between the advancing columns were disrupted; messengers vainly rushed about in the snow blizzard in search of the generals and of the king. The bold plan to overrun the enemy's flanks in a headlong attack, to surround him and pin him to the fortress under the fire of the bastions did not succeed. The Russian centre was broken through at the outset, Artamon Golovin's troops retreating in disorder and disappearing in the snowstorm; but the flanks defended themselves with unexpected stubbornness, especially the right flank, where the best regiments—the Semenovsky and Preobrazhensky—were placed.

It was already after three o'clock, but the firing did not die down. Snow was falling and whirling. The battle had to be brought to a victorious end before darkness fell, otherwise the four Swedish battalions that had penetrated into the camp in the centre—tired and battered as they were—might, in their turn, be surrounded and annihilated if the Russians were to venture to come out from behind their palisades at last: at a conservative estimate they still had some fifteen thousand fresh troops on the flanks.

At the beginning of the engagement Charles, with three squadrons of cuirassiers, remained between the columns of Stenbock and Maidel, to watch simultaneously the attacks of the centre and of the right flank. It was here that the snowstorm struck him. The advancing columns disappeared behind the veil of driving snow and even the flames of the firing cannon could no longer be distinguished. Charles, with head lifted and teeth clenched, listened to the entrancing sounds of battle. An adjutant of General Rehnsköld galloped up and reported that the grenadiers had broken through in the centre and were driving the Russians into the interior of the encampment. Charles gripped the officer's shoulder and shouted in his ear:

"Tell the general that the king's orders are to stop the pursuit, to occupy the central redoubt, to prepare for defence and await further orders."

He sent one messenger after another to the right flank, where Schlippenbach was unsuccessfully assaulting Weide's line of fortifications. "Tell the general that the king is surprised." He ordered him to be sent two companies from the reserve as reinforcements, but these could not be found and did not go. The Swedes furiously attacked the half-destroyed palisade. General Weide had been wounded by a bomb splinter, and the Russians continued to defend themselves with whatever they could lay their hands on.

Every minute the danger grew greater. The previous day, at the council of war, all the generals had declared themselves against the foolhardy operation at Narva, attacking with ten thousand hungry, weary soldiers, loaded with heavy packs (the baggage-trains had had to be abandoned during the forced march) an army of fifty thousand, protected by strong fortifications. They thought it too risky, but Charles had said: "It is the attacker who wins; danger multiplies one's strength. Tomorrow you will bring Tsar Peter to my tent." He acquainted the generals with his disposition: it foresaw and took into account everything except the snowstorm.

With his head raised, stretching up in his saddle, he listened to the sounds of battle. Danger intoxicated him. Even bear-hunting in the Kungsör forest could not stand comparison with this sport. The wind brought particularly loudly the sound of firing on the left flank, where General Löwenhaupt's two battalions of grenadiers were storming the positions of the Semenovsky and Preobrazhensky regiments. Was it possible that they had still not succeeded in that most vital sector of the battle?

Turning round, Charles seized the bridle of somebody's horse—neither the horse nor its rider was visible in the whirling snow—and shouted that four companies from the reserve were to be sent to Löwenhaupt's aid. These companies, too, could not be found and sent. The firing on the left waxed more and more desperate. A rider, completely covered with snow, loomed suddenly out of the clouds of snow:

"Your Majesty, General Löwenhaupt asks for reinforcements."

"I have sent him four companies. I'm surprised."

"Your Majesty, the palisades are destroyed, the trenches are filled with fascines and corpses. But the Russians have retreated behind the chevaux-de-frise. They have gone mad with fear and blood. They shout curses and hurl themselves against the bayonets. General Löwenhaupt has been wounded several times and goes on fighting on foot at the head of his soldiers."

"Show me the way!"

Charles urged on his horse and, bending low against the wind and snow, rode swiftly, stirrup to stirrup with the officer, towards the firing on the left flank. The wind that pierced his body seemed to sing in his heart. As he revelled in the wind, the snow, the thunder of the firing, he yearned to feel the resistance of his blade penetrating a live body. The officer shouted something and pointed ahead, where a yellow patch had spread in the snow. This was the snow-covered bed of a stream. Charles pressed home his spurs. His horse leaped heavily over the yellow snow and stuck in the morass. As it struggled its cruppers sunk deeper and its nostrils snorted in the icy wind. Charles jumped out of the saddle and his left leg plunged up to the crotch in the sticky mud. He jerked violently and pulled his leg out of the jackboot; then, on all fours, having lost his hat and his sword, he crawled to the far bank where the officer, who had dismounted, was standing and stretching out a hand to him.

So, with only one boot and hatless, Charles climbed on to the officer's lean horse, which was shivering and covered with an icy crust. Pricking it with his spur he galloped towards the firing and the wild shouts, which now sounded quite close. The horse began to jump over snowy hummocks: the bodies of the killed and wounded. In front of him, vague shadows were running. A gun flamed and thundered. Suddenly he saw a disordered crowd of his grenadiers quite close. They were standing, leaning on their muskets and looking towards where—beyond the trampled, blood-stained snow, and the huddled bodies of the killed—the sharp, slanting stakes of the chevaux-de-frise bristled. Behind them, the Russians stood like an animated wall, shouting and threatening with their fists and muskets. It was evident that an attack had just been beaten off.

Charles rode his horse into the midst of the grenadiers. "A sword!" he cried, and his cry came like an explosion. The men turned towards him and recognised him. He bent from the saddle, stretched out his arm and spread out his fingers: "A sword!" Someone pushed the hilt of a sword into his hand.

"Soldiers!" he cried. "The honour of your king is here, on these defences! They must be taken! You will throw these dirty barbarians into the river." He raised his sword and immediately a trumpet sounded its long-drawn call, then another and still others, invisible in the snowstorm. "Soldiers! God and your king are with you! I shall lead you! Follow me!"

He set off at a gallop over the blood-bespattered snow. Behind him stern throats roared: "In the name of God!" Occasional shots came from behind the chevaux-de-frise. Charles marked out a Russian, a giant, who was standing with lowered head in a breach between the stakes shattered by the cannon-balls. Charles smiled and reared up his horse on its hind legs. The Russian, with a ferocious look on his face, plunged his bayonet, like a pitchfork, into the horse's chest. Charles threw himself flat on its back and, as he slid off, stretched out with all his might and thrust his sword into the giant's breast. But, as he leapt from his horse, he tottered. All around him were yelling mouths, the clang of iron, the crunch of blows. Someone pushed him and he fell. A heavy boot trod on his back pressing him into the snow. He was immediately caught up, lifted and carried away. He fainted. He came to himself on a gun-carriage, covered with an ill-smelling soldier's coat. The trumpets were sounding the retreat. He threw off the coat and sat up.

"Bring me somebody's boots," he said. "I am barefooted. Boots, and a horse!"

Golovin's and Trubetskoy's regiments, mingling in confusion, rushed to the bank in their fear of being cut off from the river-crossing, and swarmed so thickly on to the bridge that the pontoons subsided; the yellow waters of the Narova, swollen by the westerly wind, began to splash over the rail. There, in the foamy water, under the curtain of falling snow, they could see the floating bodies of the men and horses of Sheremetev's cavalry, drowned during the crossing three miles upstream. The corpses of the horses fetched up against the water-logged bridge and piled up there. Yelling men kept pressing on from the bank. The shaky bridge sank deeper along its right edge, the water poured over the boards, the rail cracked, the hempen ropes began to give; the pontoons in the centre of the bridge were completely submerged and tore loose. Those who were on the bridge fell into the roaring torrent, among the swirling bodies of men and horses. A great shout went up, but those behind continued to press on, and hundreds of soldiers were thrown into the Narova, until at last the severed half of the bridge was washed against the marshy bank.

There, close to the river, stood the tent of the Duke de Crouy, in the rear of the positions of the Preobrazhensky and Semenovsky regiments. The desperate battle on the defences of the southern and western sides of the camp had lasted for over two hours. It was impossible to give directions or orders in this snowy hell. In the tent, at a table, the fat Preobrazhensky Colonel Blumberg was sitting with his head in his hands, puffing heavily from time to time. Facing him, the phlegmatic Hallart blinked his eyes at the candle, waiting calmly for the moment when he would have to surrender his sword—hilt first, with a bow—to some Swedish officer.

The Duke entered the tent. The deerskin coat which he wore over his cuirass was covered with snow. His visor was raised, icicles hung in his moustache and his lips were trembling.

"Let the devil lead these Russian swine into battle!" cried the Duke. "Major Cunningham and Major Gast have been strangled in their dug-outs. Captain Wahlbrecht is lying a dozen paces from this tent with his throat cut. The Tsar knew what he was foisting on me—call that an army! A mob of blackguards!"

Hallart rose hastily and threw aside a rug; a whirlwind of snow burst into the tent. The roar of a crowd of many thousands of men rose louder than the sound of firing. The Duke rushed out of the tent. Down below he could see the outline of the bridge which was being borne towards the bank; on the bridge men were shouting. To the right, where the palisade of the camp abutted on the river, a numberless crowd was in violent commotion.

"The Swedes have broken through in the centre," Hallart said. "Those are Golovin's troops."

The soldiers were climbing over the palisade and separate groups were running towards the tent.

"The devil!" the Duke cried. "On your horses, gentlemen!" He started to pull off his deerskin coat, but his armour impeded his movements. "Help me, can't you? Ah, the devil!"

The Duke, Hallart and Blumberg mounted their horses, rode down to the water's edge and galloped heavily over the marshy bank to the west, towards the Swedish gunfire. They were going to surrender themselves in order to save their lives from the enraged soldiers.

Night fell. The wind was dying down and soft snow was falling. At rare intervals there came the sound of a single shot. In the Russian camp all was quiet, as in a graveyard, and not a light showed. Only in the centre, in the captured baggage-train, drunken Swedish grenadiers were singing hoarsely. The flame of burning barrels lit up the veil of snow that fell over the dead-drunk and the dead.

Golovin, Trubetskoy, Buturlin, the Prince of Imeretia, Yakov Dolgoruky, ten colonels (among them the son of the famous General Gordon and the son of Francis Lefort), lieutenant-colonels, majors, captains, lieutenants—eighty officers—had gathered, mounted and on foot, round the dug-out where the generals were conferring. Prince Kozlovsky and Major Peel had just been sent to parley with King Charles, but they had stumbled upon their own soldiers and were recognised and killed.

In the dug-out lit by a burning wood splinter Golovin was speaking:

"The defences have been broken, the Commander-in-Chief has fled, the bridges are destroyed and the powder-carts are in the hands of the Swedes. Tomorrow we shall be unable to resume the battle, but in the night the Swedes cannot see our disaster, and we can get generous conditions from the king, retain our arms and our troops. You, Ivan Ivanovich," he bowed to Buturlin, "go, my friend, go yourself to the king and tell him that, as we do not wish to spill Christian blood, we want to break off: we will go home and let him too go back to his country."

"What about the guns? Are we to give them up?" Buturlin asked hoarsely.

No one answered him. The generals lowered their eyes. Golovin's proud face was distorted by a tearful frown. Thick-lipped, black-haired Yakov Dolgoruky said, drawing his brows together:

"What's the use of this idle prattle? We shall have our fill of shame. We are surrendering to the enemy's mercy."

Buturlin snapped the flints of two pistols, thrust them into his belt, pulled his hat over his eyes and left the dug-out.

"A trumpeter!"

The officers surrounded him:

"Well, Ivan Ivanovich? Are we surrendering?"

"We're ready to die, Ivan Ivanovich. But it's our own men who will kill us."

Charles and his generals received Buturlin at a farm half a mile from the Russian camp. The Swedes, like the Russians, were fearing the morrow. After making some difficulties for honour's sake, they agreed to let the whole Russian army cross the Narova, with its arms and colours, but without its guns and baggage-trains. They demanded that all the Russian generals and officers should be brought as hostages to the farm, and then the army could go home peacefully.

Buturlin tried to argue, but Charles said with a sarcastic smile:

"Out of affection for my brother, Tsar Peter, I am saving his generals from the fury of the soldiers. You will have more peace and will be better fed in Narva than with your troops."

Buturlin could do nothing but accept the conditions. A squadron of cuirassiers galloped off to bring in the hostages. The Swedish sappers lit bonfires on the river bank and began to throw a bridge across, to get rid of the Russians as soon as possible. The first to leave the camp were the Preobrazhensky and Semenovsky regiments: with their arms and their colours they crossed the bridges to the beating of drums. All the soldiers were tall, moustached, sombre. The wounded were carried on their comrades' shoulders. When Weide's division began to cross, the Swedish cuirassiers moved up threateningly and demanded that they give up their arms. The soldiers swore and threw down their muskets. The other regiments were driven over simply by gunfire.

At daybreak, the remnants of the Russian army of forty-five thousand men, barefooted, hungry, without its officers and in confusion, began its retreat. The bastions of Ivangorod fired a few bombs after them.

4

The news of the disaster at Narva overtook Peter on the day he reached Novgorod as he was driving into the governor's courtyard. Paul Yaguzhinsky galloped through the open gate in the wake of the Tsar's carriage, sprang from his staggering horse and looked at the Tsar with gleaming eyes.

"Where do you come from?" Peter asked with a frown.

"From over there, Bombardier."

"How are things there?"

"Disaster, Bombardier."

Peter's head sank. Menshikov came up, stretching his legs, and saw at once what had been asked and answered. The governor, Ladyzhensky, a little old man with protruding eyes, gaped as he stood on the lowest step of the porch. The searching wind lifted his thin hair.

"Well, come along and tell me about it," Peter said, setting his foot on the first step; then suddenly he turned to the governor, and looked at him as if in the greatest astonishment.

"Have you got everything ready for the defence?" he asked.

"Sire, I do not sleep at night: all the time I am thinking how to please you." The governor went down on his knees, with an imploring, dog-like expression fluttering his eyelids. "How can it be defended? The town is poor, the moats have fallen in, the bridge across the Volhov is quite rotten. And we can't get the peasants out of the villages, all the horses have been taken for the waggons. Be merciful!"

The governor was whining rather than speaking, and he clutched at the Tsar's feet. Peter kicked him aside and ran into the hall, which was filled with monks, priests, nuns and elders in skull-caps. They all jumped up at his entrance and one of them, with clanking chains on his naked body, crawled under a bench.

"Who are these people?"

The black-robed monks and priests bowed low, and a stern, corpulent priest-monk began to speak, turning up his eyes:

"Let not the monasteries and the temples of God be turned into wildernesses, great Tsar! By your ukase each monastery is commanded to supply ten or more carts and horses, and as many men as possible with iron spades, and also the food required for them. And, again, every parish is to supply vehicles and men. In sooth, great Tsar, this is beyond the power of man. We live only on the gifts of charity."

Peter stood listening with his hand on the door-latch. His bulging eyes surveyed the bowing forms.

"Are there petitioners here from all the monasteries?"

"From all," the monks answered briskly in unison. "From all, from all," the nuns chanted in chorus.

"Menshikov, let no one out. Put a sentry on the door." He went through to the dining-room and ordered Yaguzhinsky to report on the disaster to the army. He strode up and down the low-ceilinged, overheated room. Now and again he picked up a salt cucumber from the table and chewed it as he asked questions. Yaguzhinsky told him how all the artillery had been lost; how a thousand horsemen of Sheremetev's cavalry had been drowned in the Narova; how five thousand soldiers perished when the bridge collapsed, and more than that in battle; how seventy-nine generals and officers (among them the wounded Weide) had surrendered. He told of the miserable retreat of the army without officers or supplies—only subalterns and non-commissioned officers had remained with it, and those for the most part in the Guards regiments only.

"So the Duke was the first to surrender? The Austrian, the hero, the whore's son! And Blumberg with him? Alexander, can you understand this? Blumberg, who was like a brother to me, to run away to the Swedes! The rogue, the rogue!" Cucumber pips squirted out of Peter's mouth. "Seventy-nine traitors! Golovin, Dolgoruky, Vanka Buturlin—I knew he was a fool, but a rogue too! Trubetskoy, the sleek swine! How did they surrender?"

"Captain Wrangel with his cuirassiers rode up to their hut and our people gave up their swords."

"And not one—not a single one. . . ."

"Some of them wept."

"They wept! The heroes! And what? Are they hoping that after this disgraceful business I shall sue for peace?"

"To sue for peace now would be like death," Menshikov said in a low voice.

Peter came to a stop before the mica-paned window at the far end of the vaulted room and stood with his legs apart, clasping and unclasping his fingers behind his back.

"This defeat is a good lesson. We are not seeking glory. They'll beat us another ten times, and in the end we shall win. Alexander! I put you in charge of the town. You will start work today, dig trenches, put up palisades. We must not let the Swedes advance beyond Novgorod, even if we all have to die to stop them. Give instructions to find Brovkin and Sveshnikov and tell them to come here at once. Let the leading Novgorod merchants come too. The governor is to be removed." As an afterthought he added, to Menshikov's retreating back: "Have him thrown out of the house." Menshikov went out hurriedly. Turning to Yaguzhinsky, Peter said: "Go and find about three hundred carts, load them with bread and take them out before nightfall to meet the army. Do you understand?"

"It will be done, Bombardier."

"Call the monks!"

Peter sat down on a bench facing the door; his face was grim—the very image of Antichrist. The clerics came in. It had been stuffy enough before, but now the room was stifling.

"Now, God's defenders," Peter said to them, "go back to your monasteries and parishes: everyone is to come out today to dig trenches." The priest-monk raised his thick eyebrows below his cowl. "Silence, father!" Peter said to him threateningly, and went on: "All are to come out with iron spades and with horses—not only the novices and lay-brothers, but all the monks up to the highest rank, and all the nuns and all the priests and deacons with their wives. Do some work for the glory of God! Be silent, priest, I tell you! I will do the praying for us all: the Patriarch of Constantinople has anointed me for such a purpose. I will send a lieutenant to the monasteries and churches, and anyone whom he finds idle he will take to the whipping-post in the market-place and give him fifty strokes. I will take this sin also on my conscience. Until the trenches are dug and the palisades put up, there will be no divine service in any church except the Cathedral of St. Sophia. Go now!"

He gripped the edge of the bench and stretched out his neck. His round cheeks were covered with stubble, his moustache bristled. Oh,

he was terrible to behold! The frightened clerics, crowding each other, squeezed through the door. Peter shouted:
"Hey, you out there, remove the guard!"
He poured out a cup of vodka and resumed his pacing up and down. In a short while the street door banged and there were low voices in the anteroom:
"Where is he? Is he angry? Oh dear, oh dear!"
Brovkin, Sveshnikov and five Novgorod merchants came in, the latter kneading their caps and blinking apprehensively. Peter did not let them kiss his hand, but put his hands gaily round their shoulders and kissed them on the forehead and Brovkin on the lips.
"Good morning, Ivan Artemyich, good morning, Alexey Ivanovich!" He turned to the Novgorod men: "Good morning, my respected friends. Sit down. You see, there is food and wine on the table, but I've had the host thrown out. Ah, how the governor has annoyed me! I thought that trenches and insurmountable palisades were all ready here, and not a spade has even been stuck into the ground."
He poured out vodka for all. The Novgorod men jumped to their feet with their cups. Peter drank first, gave a satisfied grunt and tapped on the table with his empty cup.
"We have drunk to the beginning!" he said with a laugh. "Well, merchants, have you heard? The Swedish king has given us a little drubbing. Good enough for a start. A beaten man is worth two unbeaten ones, isn't he?"
The merchants said nothing. Ivan Artemyich looked at the table with his lips pursed. Sveshnikov, his terrible eyebrows knitted, also looked away. The Novgorod merchants sighed softly.
"We must expect the Swedes here this week. If we lose Novgorod, we lose Moscow—and then we shall all be lost."
"Oho-ho," Brovkin sighed deeply. Sveshnikov's black-bearded face grew as yellow as tallow.
"If we can hold up the Swedes at Novgorod, before summer we can gather and train a stronger army than the one we had before. We will cast twice as many guns. Our guns at Narva! They are welcome to them: they were just trash. We won't cast any more such guns. The generals are prisoners of war; I am glad of that. The old men were like leaden weights on my feet. We must have young, fresh men for generals. We will rouse the whole country. We have suffered a defeat—all right! This war is only just beginning. If you give me

one rouble for this war, Ivan Artemyich, and you, Alexey Ivanovich —I will return you ten in two years."

He threw himself back and hit the table with his fists:

"Isn't that so, merchants?"

"Peter Alexeyevich," Sveshnikov said, "where are we to get that one rouble? It isn't money we've got in our coffers. It's mice."

"True, very true," the Novgorod merchants muttered.

Peter threw them a glance and they cowered. Letting his hand rest heavily on Ivan Brovkin's short back, he asked:

"And you, what do you say?"

"God has bound us to you, Peter Alexeyevich, where you go, we go too," Brovkin answered, a serene and honest expression on his fat face.

Sveshnikov was aghast: they had only just agreed to go slow with the money, and now suddenly Ivan, the artful fellow, had come forward of his own accord.

Peter put his arms round Brovkin's shoulders and pressed the merchant's sweating face to the brass buttons on his chest.

"I expected no other answer from you, Ivan Artemyich. You are clever and bold, and you will be well recompensed for this. Merchants, the money is needed immediately. In a week's time we must have fortified Novgorod and garrisoned it with Nikita Repnin's division."

5

The officer on duty in the porch of Preobrazhensky palace said to all comers:

"Orders are not to let anyone enter. Pass on."

Many covered sledges and carriages were waiting in the courtyard. The December wind filled the black ruts with hard pellets of snow. The frozen trees swished and the vanes on the weather-beaten roofs of the palace creaked. Ministers and boyars had been waiting all day in their covered sledges and carriages since the morning. Menshikov drove up in a gilded coach drawn by six horses, but even he was turned away.

Soon after ten at night Romodanovsky arrived. The officer on duty trembled when he saw the prince in his bearskin coat waddling up the worn brick steps. If he let him enter, he would be disobeying the Tsar's orders, and if he did not, the prince might on his own authority, without asking the Tsar, have him severely flogged.

Romodanovsky entered the palace. The guards standing at every door hid themselves when they heard his heavy step approaching. He sat down to rest three times before he reached the Tsar's bedchamber. He knocked with his nail on the door, went in and made obeisance according to ancient custom.

"Why have you come here, Uncle?" Peter asked; he was pacing the room, pipe in mouth, wrapped in a cloud of smoke, and turned round with displeasure, not returning the old man's greeting. "I gave orders that no one was to be admitted."

"No one is being admitted, Peter Alexeyevich. As for me, your father used to let me come in without being announced." Peter shrugged his shoulders and continued walking up and down, chewing at the mouthpiece of his pipe. "What is it, Peter Alexeyevich, that has occupied your thoughts all day? Your father and your mother enjoined you to listen to my advice. Let us take counsel together. Perhaps we'll think of something."

"Stop this empty chatter. You know well enough what I'm thinking about."

Romodanovsky did not answer at once. He sat down and threw open his coat—the old man found it difficult to breathe in that stuffy room—and wiped his face with a coloured kerchief.

"Perhaps what I've come to say isn't empty chatter. How can you tell? How can you tell?"

Peter, unconsciously raising his voice, suddenly began to roar so loudly that the sentry in the dark throne-room on the other side of the wall dropped his musket in fright:

"The money-bags began to argue in the Stewards' Chamber; they said that at Narva we have proved that we were no match for the Swedes and that we must make peace. They will not look me in the face. I talked to them like this"—Peter seized Romodanovsky by the breast of his coat and shook him—"but they weep and say: 'Though you send us to the block, great Tsar, we have no money, we are completely ruined!' What's occupying my thoughts? I need money! For twenty-four hours I've been racking my brains where to get it!" He released his hold of Romodanovsky. "Well, Uncle?"

"I am listening, Peter Alexeyevich. My turn to speak will come presently."

Peter narrowed his eyes: "Hm!" He went on pacing up and down for a while and then said, in an easier voice:

"We need copper. Superfluous bells are just so many empty peals, people can do without them. We'll take down these bells and recast them. Demidov writes to me from the Urals that he will have eight hundred tons of pig-iron ready by spring. But money! Press the townsmen and peasants again? But can I get much from them? They are sucked dry as it is and, besides, the levy could not be collected before next year. And yet there is both gold and silver; it's there, lying unused." Peter Alexeyevich had not finished speaking but already Romodanovsky's eye were bulging like a lobster's. "I know what you're going to say, Uncle. That's why I didn't send for you. But I shall take this money."

"You mustn't touch the monastery treasure just now, Peter Alexeyevich."

"Why not?" Peter cried in a high voice, like a cock's crow.

"This is the wrong time. It would be dangerous at present. I won't tell you what sort of people are being dragged before me almost every day." Romodanovsky's thick fingers lying on his knees moved uneasily. "The merchants of Moscow are your faithful servants for the time being. What if they got frightened by Narva? Anyone would be frightened. They'll talk and get over it: the war brings them profits. And they'll provide money, only don't be impatient. But if now you were to touch the monasteries—their citadels—the next day idiots would be shouting in every public place what the other day Grishka Talitsky * shouted from the house-tops in the market-place. Do you remember? Well then! The treasure of the monasteries must be taken by degrees, without noise."

"You're being very crafty, Uncle."

"I'm an old man; why should I be crafty?"

"I must have the money at once, even if I have to get it by highway robbery."

"Is it much you want?"

Romodanovsky asked the question with a barely perceptible smile. Peter said. "Hm!" took another turn up and down the small bedchamber, lit his pipe at the candle, blew out a cloud of smoke and said firmly:

"Two millions."

"You couldn't do with less?"

Peter dropped down on his haunches before the old man and gripping his knees began to shake them:

"Enough of this teasing! Let's make a deal—I won't touch the monasteries for the time being. Done? Have you got the money? How much?"

* Grigory Talitsky—Dissenter, author of writings in which Peter was called "Antichrist". Executed in 1700. (*Author's note*)

"Tomorrow we shall see."

"No, at once. Let us go."

Romodanovsky took his cap and struggled to his feet.

"Have it your own way then," he said. "If you want it so badly." He shuffled to the door like a bear. "Only don't bring anyone with you. We'll go alone."

The clock on the Spassky tower struck one when Romodanovsky's leather-covered coach drove into the Kremlin, wound in and out through the narrow alleys between the old houses of the government offices and came to a stop in front of a low brick building. A lantern stood on a step of the shallow porch, and a man in a sheepskin coat was snoring, huddled against the iron door. Romodanovsky got out of the coach after the Tsar, picked up the lantern, inside which the tallow candle was smoking, and kicked the birch-bark shoe which was sticking out from under the sheepskin coat. The man muttered sleepily: "What do you want?" raised himself, turned down the edge of his sheepskin collar, recognised the visitors and jumped to his feet.

Romodanovsky pushed him away from the door and unlocked it with his own key. He let Peter enter first and then followed, locking the door after him. Holding the lantern high he waddled through the cold outer hall, then through a heated anteroom into a low, vaulted hall with peeling walls. This was the Office of Secret Affairs which had been established by Tsar Alexey. It smelt of dust, dry-rot and mice. And the two latticed windows were covered with cobwebs. A door opened a little and the frightened face of the trusted old keeper showed in the crack.

"Who's there? Who are you?"

"Bring a candle, Mitrich," Romodanovsky said to him.

Along the far wall stood low oak cupboards with forged iron padlocks. To express curiosity about the files these cupboards contained, let alone touch them, was prohibited under pain of death. The keeper brought a candle in an iron candlestick.

Romodanovsky pointed to the middle cupboard and said:

"Pull it away from the wall!" The keeper shook his head. "I order you to do it. I make myself responsible."

The keeper put the candlestick on the floor and set his frail shoulder to the cupboard, but it would not budge. Peter impatiently threw off his short coat and cap and heaved. His neck grew red, but he moved the cupboard. A mouse ran out from under it. In the wall behind was a small iron door, thick with dusty cobwebs. Romodanovsky took out a huge key and, breathing heavily, said: "Mitrich, hold the light, I can't see", as he poked the key clumsily at the key-hole. In thirty years the lock had rusted and it would not open. "We'll have to use a crowbar—go and fetch one, Mitrich."

Peter had picked up the candle and was examining the door.

"What's in there?"

"You shall see, my son. According to the palace register, secret documents are kept there. When Prince Golitsin was campaigning in the Crimea your sister Sophia came here one night. But it was just as it is now—I couldn't unlock it." Romodanovsky gave a ghost of a smile under his Tatar moustache. "She stood here and went away, did Sophia."

The keeper brought a crowbar and an axe. Peter set to work on the lock. He broke the handle of the axe and tore the skin on his finger. He began to beat the edge of the door with the heavy crowbar. The blows resounded through the empty building, and Romodanovsky, feeling uneasy, went up to the window. At last Peter managed to get the point of the crowbar into the crack of the door and, heaving with all his weight, broke the lock. The iron door opened with a groan. Peter impatiently seized the candle and entered the vaulted, windowless chamber ahead of the others.

Everything was covered with cobwebs and dust. On the shelves along the walls stood delicately chased beakers of the time of Ivan the Terrible and Boris Godunov; Italian goblets on high stems; silver basins for washing the hands of the Tsar on ceremonial occasions; two silver lions with golden manes and ivory fangs; piles of golden platters; broken silver church-lustres; a large peacock of solid gold with emerald eyes—one of the two peacocks which used to flank the throne of the Byzantine emperors in times long past. Its mechanism no longer worked. On the lower shelves lay leather bags. Through the rotted seams of some of them Dutch gold pieces had slipped out. Under the shelves lay heaps of sable pelts and other furs, and velvets and silks, all moth-eaten and rotten.

Peter took up some of the things; he wetted his finger and rubbed them: "Gold! Silver!" He counted the bags with the Dutch pieces; there were forty-five of them, or more. He picked up the sables and fox-tails and shook them:

"Uncle, this is all rotten."

"Rotten but not lost, my son."

"Why did you not tell me of this before?"

"I had given my word. Your father, Alexey Mihaylovich, rode

away to the wars several times and entrusted all his spare money and treasures to me for safe keeping. When he was on his deathbed, your father sent for me and commanded me not to give up the treasure to any of his heirs unless the country was in great distress in time of war."

Peter slapped his thighs and said:

"You've saved me; truly you've saved me. There's enough for me here. The monks will thank you. That peacock! Enough to shoe, clothe and arm a regiment and give Charles the beating he deserves. But as for the bells, Uncle, you mustn't be angry, I'll pull down the bells."

chapter five

Europe laughed at and soon forgot the Tsar of the barbarians who had come so near to frightening the nations of the Baltic coast, but whose louse-infected hordes had melted away like phantoms. King Charles, who had thrown them back after Narva into their savage Muscovy, where they were rightly destined to vegetate for ever in their traditional ignorance—the base and dishonest nature of the Russian people being well known through the tales of famous travellers—became for a short time the hero of the capital cities of Europe. In Amsterdam the town hall and the Bourse were decorated with flags in honour of the victory of Narva; in Paris the booksellers exhibited two bronze medals, one bearing the figure of Glory crowning the youthful Swedish king and the inscription: "Right triumphs at last", and the other showing Tsar Peter in flight, losing his Kalmuk cap in his hurry; in Vienna the former Austrian ambassador to Moscow, Ignace Guarient, published the diary of his secretary Johann Georg Korb, very vividly describing the ridiculous and unenlightened customs of the Muscovites and the bloody executions of the streltsi in 1698. At the court of Vienna there was much talk of a new defeat of the Russians at Pskov, of Tsar Peter's flight with a few followers, of a rising in Moscow and the liberation from her convent of Tsarevna Sophia who had again taken over the reins of government.

But these insignificant events were overshadowed all at once by the outbreak of the long-expected war. The king of Spain died, and both France and Austria made a bid for the succession. England

and Holland intervened. Brilliant generals, such as John Churchill, Duke of Marlborough, Prince Eugene of Savoy and the Duke of Vendôme, began to ravage the countryside and burn the cities. In Italy, in Bavaria, in lovely Flanders, the roads were teeming with armed vagabonds who committed acts of violence against the peaceful population and devoured all stocks of food and wine. Rebellions broke out in Hungary and in the Cévennes. The fate of great countries hung in the balance; the question at issue was whose navy would rule the seas. Affairs in eastern Europe had to be left to take care of themselves.

In the flush of the Narva victory, Charles was all for pursuing Peter into the depths of Muscovy, but his generals implored him not to risk a second challenge to fate. The weary and battered army was sent to winter quarters at Laisa, near Dorpat. From there the king wrote a haughty letter to the Senate demanding reinforcements and money. In Stockholm, those who were opposed to the war were now silent. The Senate imposed new taxes and in the spring sent twenty thousand infantry and cavalry to Laisa. A book was published in Latin on *The Causes of the War of Sweden against the Tsar of Muscovy,* which was read with satisfaction at all the courts of Europe.

Charles now had one of the strongest armies in Europe. He had to decide where to direct the blow: towards the east, towards desert Moscow, where a few poverty-stricken towns promised little loot or glory, or towards the south-west, against the treacherous King August, into the depths of Poland, into Saxony, towards the heart of Europe, where the guns of the great marshals were already thundering. Charles's head was dizzy with the prospect of the glory of a new Caesar. His Guardsmen, descendants of sea-robbers, dreamt of the rich silks of Florence, of the gold in the cellars of the Escorial, of the flaxen-haired women of Flanders and the taverns at the crossroads of Bavarian highways.

When the roads grew passable in summer, Charles formed a corps of eight thousand men commanded by Schlippenbach and sent them to the Russian frontier. He himself with his whole army advanced through Livonia by forced marches, crossed the Dvina in barges in full view of the enemy, a mile and a half above Riga, and completely routed King August's Saxon army. One of those wounded in this battle was Johann Patkul, who barely managed to flee from the Swedish cuirassiers and, for the moment, to escape capture and execution.

The army routed at Riga was an army not of lousy Russians, but of Saxon soldiers of European fame. Glory seemed to be unfolding its wings over Charles. "He thinks of nothing else but war," General Steinbock wrote about him to Stockholm. "He will no longer listen to counsels of prudence. He talks as though his projects were directly due to divine inspiration. He is filled with conceit and folly. I think that were he to be left with one thousand men, he would lead them to attack an entire army. He does not even want to know how his soldiers are fed. When any of our men are killed he is not in the least concerned."

From Riga, Charles threw himself in pursuit of King August. In Poland a bloody civil war broke out among the Polish nobles. Some of them stood for King August and against the Swedes, others maintained that only the Swedes would bring order and help to win back the Ukraine and Kiev. They urged that Poland needed a new king, Stanislaw Lesczinski. King August fled from Warsaw and Charles entered the city without encountering any resistance. August was hurriedly forming a new army in Cracow.

A strange chase began: king hunting king. Again the courts of Europe applauded the youthful hero, and his name was quoted on an equal with those of Prince Eugene and Marlborough. It was said that Charles let no woman approach him, that he even slept in his jackboots, that at the beginning of a battle he would appear in front of his troops on horseback, hatless, his grey-green coat buttoned up to the neck and, with the name of God on his lips, rush headlong at the enemy, carrying his troops forward with him. He had left it to Schlippenback to deal with Tsar Peter in the gloomy East.

Peter spent all that winter between Moscow, Novgorod and Voronezh, where the work of building ships for the Black Sea fleet was proceeding apace. Fifteen hundred tons of bell metal had been brought to Moscow. The old clerk of the council, Vinius, an expert in mining, was appointed to supervise the casting of the new guns. He established a school at the foundry in Moscow where two hundred and fifty young men—young nobles and townsmen, as well as youths of low birth but of good promise—learnt casting, mathematics, fortification and history. There was not enough red copper to alloy the bell metal, and Peter sent Vinius to Siberia to look for ore. Fifteen thousand muskets of the latest pattern, quick-firing guns, telescopes and ostrich feathers for officers' hats were bought in Liège by Andrey Artamonovich Matveyev, the son of the boyar Matveyev who had been killed on the Red Porch. Five cloth and canvas factories were operating in Moscow, and craftsmen were recruited for good money throughout Europe. The training of soldiers proceeded from sunrise to sunset. The greatest difficulty was to groom a corps of officers who had to train themselves while training the soldiers; when a man was promoted to higher rank he was either intoxicated with his new power, or took to idleness and drink.

A fortnight after the reverse at Narva, Peter had written to Boris Petrovich Sheremetev, who was in Novgorod gathering what remained of the cavalry regiments—some of whom had no horses, or no swords, while others were stripped of everything.

"It is a bad thing when misfortune occurs to give up everything. Therefore I order you to carry on with the task which you have undertaken and begun; that is, organising the cavalry to guard the home territory in the future and to advance farther abroad, the better to inflict damage on the enemy. There can be no excuses: there are enough men and the rivers and marshes are frozen over. I warn you once again: do not make any excuses, not even of illness. Many of the fugitives are ill, and one of them, Major Lobanov, has been hanged for such illness. . . ."

But the irregular cavalry of the nobility was unreliable, and in its stead a force of ten dragoon regiments was recruited from among men of all walks of life, peasants and bondsmen, who enlisted freely for a pay of eleven roubles a year and their keep. There were so many who sought relief from bondage and peasant serfdom by taking cavalry service that only the strongest and best-looking were accepted. When their training was ended the dragoon squadrons were sent to Novgorod, where General Repnin was re-forming and training the divisions that had been at Narva.

By the New Year Novgorod, Pskov and the Pechersk monastery had been fortified. In the North, Holmogory and Archangel were being fortified; ten miles from Archangel, on the Berezovsk estuary, a stone fort, Novo-Dvinka, was being hurriedly built. In the summer many merchant ships came to Archangel from England and Holland for the June Fair. That year the government monopolised a number of new articles for trade with the foreigners in addition to those which it had formerly controlled, such as marine animals, fish-glue, tar, potash and wax. The Tsar's agents took up everything for the treasury, leaving little else for the private merchants to trade in but leather goods and carved ivory. On the 20th of June a Swedish war fleet penetrated into the estuary of the Northern Dvina. Unable to ignore the newly-built fort and proceed towards Archangel, it opened fire on the forts of Novo-Dvinka from all its broadsides.

During this diversion one of the four Swedish frigates ran aground in front of the fortress, and the same happened to a yacht. The Russians jumped into their boats and, after a fight, seized the two vessels. The rest of the fleet sailed back ingloriously into the White Sea.

Skirmishes between the advanced detachments of the Swedes under Schlippenbach and of the Russians under Sheremetev continued all through the summer. The Swedes advanced up to the Pechersk monastery, but only burnt the surrounding villages without taking the stronghold. Schlippenbach wrote in alarm to King Charles asking for another eight thousand men, as the Russians were growing bolder from month to month, having obviously recovered from the disaster at Narva much more quickly than expected. They had even made great progress in military science and equipment, and it was no longer easy to beat the Russians with a force of only two brigades. At that time Charles had taken Cracow and was driving August back into Saxony, and he turned a deaf ear to the voice of common-sense.

Such was the course of affairs until December 1701.

In mid-winter Sheremetev learnt from a captured enemy soldier that General Schlippenbach had taken up winter quarters at the Erestfär farm near Dorpat. This information gave him an idea so audacious, that it actually frightened him; why not penetrate suddenly into the enemy's territory and take him by surprise in his quarters? It was an exceptional opportunity. In former times, of course, Sheremetev would have thought it wiser not to tempt fickle fortune, but this year Peter Alexeyevich was making things very hard; he gave no one a moment's peace or quiet and blamed people, not so much for what they had done, as for what they might have done but failed to do.

The risk had to be taken. Sheremetev put ten thousand of the newly-trained recruits into sheepskin jackets and felt boots, and loaded fifteen field-guns on to sledges. Rapidly, but with the greatest caution, he moved with an advance guard of Circassian, Kalmuk and Tatar light horse and reached Erestfär in a three days' march. When the Swedes saw the tall-capped horsemen, armed with bows and spears adorned with horses' tails, appear on the high, snow-covered bank of the small river Aya, it was already too late. Lieutenant-Colonel Lieven came down to the river with two companies and a gun. On the far side the slant-eyed barbarians raised their curved bows and shot a volley of arrows. A gradually swelling howl, like that of a pack of wolves, rent the air and, down the snowdrifts and over the river, striped Tatars with curved swords and blue-coated Circassians with pikes and lariats, rushed forward in a whirl of snow, outflanking the Swedes on the right and left, while howling Kalmuks attacked them from the front. Lieven's three hundred Esthonian riflemen and the lieutenant-colonel himself were cut down or run through and stripped to the very skin.

The whole Swedish camp was now in an uproar. A fresh force, with six guns, drove the mounted raiders back from the river. Schlippenbach galloped about the camp with his trumpeters; the Swedes sprang out of their cottages and mud-huts in whatever clothes they happened to be wearing, and ran through the deep snow to join their units. The whole army formed up in front of the farm and met the approaching Russian force with artillery fire. Sheremetev himself, wearing only his cloth coat with a tricolour sash across his shoulder, was riding in the centre of the square.

The Swedish gunfire threw into confusion the leading squadrons of the dragoons, men who had never yet been under fire. The Swedes surged forward. But the Russians brought up fifteen light guns on sledges at the gallop, and these opened such a rapid fire with small-shot that the surprised Swedes stopped in disorder. Meanwhile the dragoon regiments of Kropotov, Zybin and Gulitsa had rallied and were swiftly closing in on them from the flanks. "Brothers!" Sheremetev shouted in a strained voice from the centre of the square. "Brothers! Strike hard at the Swedes!" The Russians advanced with fixed bayonets. Darkness was falling swiftly, lit up by the flashes of gunfire. Schlippenbach gave orders to retreat to the cover of the farm buildings. But no sooner had the mournful trumpets sounded the retreat than dragoons, Tatars, Kalmuks and Circassians, rushed with renewed fury from every side at the retreating Swedish squares, to break and scatter them. A massacre began. General Schlippenbach himself, with three of his staff, barely succeeded in escaping under cover of darkness and made for Reval.

In Moscow this first victory was celebrated with bonfires and illuminations. Barrels of vodka and beer were set out in the Red Square, whole sheep were roasted before the fires and white fancy loaves were distributed to the crowd. The Swedish standards were hung from the Spassky tower. Menshikov hastened to Novgorod to present Sheremetev with a diamond-studded portrait of the Tsar and the hitherto unprecedented title of General-Field-Marshal. Every soldier who had fought in the battle was given a silver rouble, newly struck at the Moscow mint to replace the old coins.

Sheremetev wept when he tried to express his gratitude, and he sent back a letter with Menshikov asking Peter for leave to go to Moscow on urgent business. "My wife is even now still living in a strange house. I must find her a home, be it of the meanest, where she can lay her head." Peter replied: "There is no need for you, General-Field-Marshal, to come to Moscow. But that is a matter for your discretion. If, however, you decide to come, let it be during Passion Week, so that you will be able to return in Holy Week."

Six months later Sheremetev again met General Schlippenbach near Hummelshof. In this bloody battle the Swedes lost five thousand five hundred dead out of seven thousand. There was no one left to defend Livonia and the road to the seaports was open. Sheremetev set out to ravage the countryside, the towns, the farms and the ancient castles of the knights. In the autumn he wrote to Peter:

"God the Almighty and the Holy Mother of God have fulfilled your desires: there is nothing more left to ravage in this enemy country, everything has been sacked and devastated, except only Marienburg, Narva, Reval and Riga, which remain untouched. I am greatly troubled what to do with the prisoners. The camps and prisons and all other places are filled with Finns. There is also danger because the people are so hostile. Give orders that it be decreed: to pick among the Finns the best men, those who can use an axe or who are craftsmen, and send them to Voronezh or Azov to labour there."

2

For twelve days bombs had fallen on the ancient fortress of Marienburg. It was impossible to assault it from any side, for it stood on an island in Lake Poyp and its stone walls rose straight from the water. The wooden bridge, seven hundred feet long, protected at the bridgehead by a bastion, had been destroyed by the Swedes themselves.

There were large stocks of rye in the fortress and the Russians, who were feeling the pinch of hunger in the devastated countryside, would have been glad of them. Sheremetev called for volunteers and went out to them and said:

"There is wine in that fortress—and women. Do your best, lads, and I shall give you twenty-four hours to enjoy yourselves."

The soldiers quickly tore apart a few log-huts in a village by the lake, and made rafts of them. About a thousand volunteers, punting themselves along with poles, approached the walls of the fortress. The Swedish bombs fell and exploded among the rafts.

Sheremetev was standing on the porch of his hut, looking through a telescope. The Swedes were furious and desperate—could they beat back the attack? To take them by siege—oh, how he disliked the idea!—would keep him till the late autumn. Suddenly he saw a great flame shoot up from the earth near the gates of the fortress and the log superstructure on the tower tottered. Part of the wall collapsed. The rafts were already gathering near the breach. At that moment a broad strip of white cloth was pushed through one of the fortress windows and hung there. Sheremetev closed his telescope, took off his hat and made the sign of the cross.

The inhabitants of the fortress began to make their way to the shore over the piles of the dismantled bridge. They carried children in their arms, and bundles and baskets. The women wept as they looked back at their abandoned homes and glanced with terror at the Russians who were eyeing possible loot. But no sooner had the last fugitives left the fortress than the iron-bound gates shut with a clash and puffs of smoke shot out of the narrow embrasures. The first casualty was a lieutenant who had approached in a boat to raise the Russian flag on the fortress. Mortars fired from the shore in reply. The people on the bridge rushed in panic, dropping their bundles and baskets. A huge flame hurled the roofs of the castle into the air; the explosion shook the lake and falling stones began to drop on the people. The fortress and store-houses broke into flames. It was learnt that the ensign Wulf and the cadet Gotschlich had, in their helpless rage, hurried down into the powder-magazine and set fire to a fuse. Wulf did not have time to escape before the explosion. As for the cadet, he appeared scorched and covered with blood in the breach of the wall and tumbled into the water, where he was picked up by a boat.

The commander of the fortress, together with his officers, entered the hut where General-Field-Marshal Sheremetev was sitting solemnly at the table laid for dinner, with his back to the window. The commander took off his hat, bowed courteously and tendered his sword. The officers followed his example. Sheremetev threw the swords on a bench and began to shout furiously at the Swedes: why had they not surrendered sooner, why had they caused so much unbearable suffering and death to the people and treacherously blown up the fortress? The sun-burnt, unshaven, dare-devil cavalry commanders who were standing about in the hut threw angry glances at the Swedes. Nevertheless the commander courageously replied:

"There are many women and children among our people. There

is the much respected pastor Glück with his wife and daughters. I ask you to give them a free-pass and not let the soldiers molest them. The women and children will not bring you any glory."

"I don't want to hear a word!" Sheremetev shouted.

His shaven, kindly face, more suited to peaceful family life, was sweating with wrath. Pulling in his belly he got up from behind the table.

"Put the commander and officers under arrest!"

He straightened his tricolour sash, threw his short cloak of crimson cloth over his shoulders with a martial air, and went out to his troops, accompanied by the colonels.

Black smoke billowed from the fortress, veiling the sun. Some three hundred Swedish prisoners stood with drooping heads on the bank. The Russian soldiers, uncertain of what was to be the captives' fate, merely walked round the angry Livonian peasants who had fled a fortnight ago to Marienburg to shelter from the invasion, and tried to talk to the woebegone women, who sat on their bundles with their heads resting on their knees. A trumpet sounded, and the General-Field-Marshal passed by with an air of importance, jingling his great star-shaped spurs.

From behind a group of dismounted dragoons he noticed two eyes looking at him: they were like little flames that stung his heart. In time of war a woman's eyes are sometimes sharper than the blade of a sword. Sheremetev cleared his throat with a dignified "Hm!" and turned round. A blue skirt showed behind the dusty coats of the soldiers. He frowned, set his jaw and saw those eyes again: dark, glistening with tears, full of supplication and youth. A young girl of about seventeen, standing on tiptoe, was looking at the field-marshal from behind the soldiers' backs. A heavily moustached dragoon had thrown a crumpled soldier's cloak over her thin frock—the August day was cool—and was now trying to interpose his shoulder between her and the field-marshal. She silently craned her neck; her fresh face, drawn with terror, attempted to smile and her lips creased. "Hm!" Sheremetev grunted once again and went to look at the prisoners.

After his dinner and a nap, Sheremetev was sitting on a bench and sighing in the twilight. Only Yaguzhinsky was with him in the hut, scratching away with his pen on the corner of the table.

"Take care, you'll spoil your eyes," Sheremetev said in a low voice.

"I'm nearly finished, sir."

"Well, if you've nearly finished, get on with it." Then he added, speaking now to himself: "That's how it happens to us fellows. . . . Well, well. . . . Ah, dear me, dear me. . . ."

He drummed lightly on the table with his hand and looked out of the dim little window. On the lake the fortress was still burning. Yaguzhinsky glanced quizzically at the field-marshal: fancy, how it's taken him! His neck is all swollen and his face has quite a lost look.

"Take the order to the colonel," Sheremetev said. "And look in on the second regiment of dragoons. See if you can find that sergeant, what's his name, Osip Demin. He has a little woman there in the baggage-train. A pity that she should perish—the dragoons would be the death of her. You go and bring her here. Wait a minute. Here is a rouble for Osip, say it's a gift from me."

"Your orders will be carried out, Field-Marshal."

Left alone in the hut Sheremetev sighed and shook his head. It could not be helped: try as you might, you could not live without sin. In '97, when he was in Naples, a little black-haired girl had crept into his heart. It was searing. . . . He climbed Vesuvius and looked down into the flames of hell; he scaled the terrible rocks on the island of Capri; he looked at the temples of the heathen Roman gods and assiduously visited the Catholic monasteries, where he saw and touched with his hand the board on which the Lord had sat when He washed His disciples' feet; he saw a slice of the bread eaten at the Last Supper and a wooden cross in which was embedded a fragment of Christ's navel and foreskin, and one of Christ's shoes—quite worn out—and the head of the prophet Zachariah, father of St. John the Baptist, and many other marvellous and miraculous things. But still bright-eyed Julia, who danced with a tambourine and sang, crowded everything else out for him. He had wanted to take her with him to Moscow, he had grovelled at her feet. Ah, dear me, dear me!

Yaguzhinsky, as usual, was soon back. He gently pushed the girl, whom Sheremetev had seen a while ago, into the hut. She was in a blue dress with spotless white stockings and a shawl tied crosswise over her bosom. But there were wisps of straw in her dark, curly hair—obviously the dragoons had already set about her under the baggage-carts. At the threshold she went down on her knees and bowed her head, an image of humility and supplication.

Yaguzhinsky chuckled and went out. Sheremetev surveyed the girl for a little while. She was well-proportioned; one could see that her movements would be deft; her neck and hands were white and delicate. Most attractive. Sheremetev addressed her in German:

"What's your name?"
The girl gave a light, short sigh and replied:
"Elena Ekaterina."
"Katerina. Good. Who is your father?"
"I am an orphan. I was in service at Pastor Ernst Glück's."
"In service, eh? Very good. Can you launder?"
"I can launder. I can do many things. I can look after children."
"Indeed? Well, there is no one here to launder my linen. Are you unmarried?"
Katerina gave a little sob and answered without raising her head:
"No. I was married not long ago."
"Ah. And to whom?"
"To the king's cuirassier, Johann Rabe."
Sheremetev frowned and asked drily what had happened to the cuirassier: was he among the prisoners? Had he perhaps been killed?
"I saw Johann start to swim across the lake with two other soldiers. I have not seen him since."
"Don't cry, Katerina. You are still young. You'll find another. Are you hungry?"
"Very," she replied in a small voice; she raised her pinched face and smiled again, humbly and trustingly. Sheremetev went up to her, took her by the shoulders, lifted her to her feet and kissed her fine warm hair. Her shoulders too were warm and delicate.
"Come to the table and sit down. We'll find you something to eat. We won't hurt you. Do you drink wine?"
"I don't know."
"That means you do."
Sheremetev called his orderly and in a strict tone—lest the fellow might think something unseemly and, God forbid, even grin—ordered him to lay the table for supper. At supper he himself did not so much eat as watch Katerina; she certainly was hungry! She ate daintily and deftly, glancing at Sheremetev with swimming eyes and showing her little white teeth in a grateful smile. Her cheeks grew rosy with the wine and the food.
"I suppose all your clothes have been lost in the fire?"
"I've lost everything," she answered lightly.
"Never mind, we'll get you others. We'll be going to Novgorod some time this week, you'll be more comfortable there. Tonight we'll sleep on the stove, in war-time fashion."
Katerina glanced darkly under her eyelashes at him, blushed, turned her face away and covered it with her hand.

"What a woman you are! Katerina, my dear. . . ." Sheremetev was enchanted with this little chambermaid. He reached out across the table and took her hand. She was still covering her face, but an eye gleamed entrancingly through her fingers.

"Well, well, don't worry, we won't turn you into a serf. You will live in the house. I have long been wanting a housekeeper."

3

When the troops defeated at Narva were returning to Novgorod, many soldiers deserted; some went to the North, to the dissenters' villages, others to the great rivers, to the Don, to the lands beyond the Volga, to the lower reaches of the Dniepr. Fedka Mudwash, a sullen peasant with a long and bitter experience, went off too. In any case, his life was already forfeit for the murder of Lieutenant Mirbach. He persuaded Andrey Golikov to desert together with him; after all, there was a time when they had pulled together at the tow-line and had long eaten out of the same pot. After the horrors of Narva it was all one to Golikov where he went, so long as it was not to shoulder a musket again.

In the night they left the camp, taking with them the regimental broken-down nag. They sold the animal to a monastery for fifty kopeks, shared the money and tied it up in rags. They made their way, avoiding the high-road, going from village to village, begging and, at times, even stealing: they stole a chicken out of a priest's yard, in Ostashkovo they took a silver ornamented bridle and pillion from the village bailiff's yard, which they sold to a tavern-keeper. Twice they succeeded in tearing down church collecting boxes, but one of them proved empty and in the other there was only one kopek.

They managed to spend the winter in the Valday hills in chimneyless huts, buried in snow, with children dizzy from the smoke and babies screaming in their hanging cradles to the howling of the night wind. Golikov often waked in the night and would then sit up, holding his bare feet in his hands. Close to him, on a bed of foul straw, a calf would be chewing. A peasant snored on the bench. On the floor by the hearth, his wife slept with her knees drawn up. The children on the stove muttered in their sleep. Cockroaches nipped the baby's fingers and cheeks. The baby in his cradle cried: oo-ah, oo-ah. Why had he been born, why were the cockroaches biting him?

"Why aren't you asleep?" Fedka asks. He too is not sleeping but thinking his own thoughts.

"Let's go away, Fedka."

"Where can we go, you fool, at night, in a snowstorm?"

"I can't stand it, Fedka."

"It stinks here, you can hardly breathe. They live worse than animals. Listen to the man snoring! He'll snore his fill, then he'll drink a dipperful of water and go off to work, like a horse, for the whole day. I asked them yesterday: the entire village works for the landowner. The young landowner has gone off with the army, but the old one is living here, in the village. He's got a good house on the other side of the ravine. He's a skinflint and heavy-handed. He takes everything from the peasants, leaves them only pigweed. All his peasants are stupid. When there's one a bit cleverer and bolder than the rest, he puts him at once on a cart and takes him to Valday. And there, in the market, he himself sells the peasant straight off the cart. He's done away with all the clever ones: makes it easier for him. Even the children here are born stupid."

Golikov sits, clutching his bare, cold feet and swaying his body to and fro. All he has endured in the twenty-four years of his life would be enough to fill ten men's lives to the brim. But he's hard to kill. And it is not even his frail body that makes him cling to life, but his unquenchable desire to come out of the darkness. It is as if he were pushing his way, torn and hungry, through thickets, through terrible places—year after year, mile after mile—in the belief that somewhere there is a happy land which he's bound to reach when he has pushed his way through life. Where is it, this land; what is it like?

And just now, hardly listening to what Fedka is saying—on the straw by his side—Golikov peers into the darkness with wide-open eyes. It may be a memory, or it may be a dream: a green hillock, a birch with all its branches, all its leaves quivering in the warm breeze. . . . Oh, what joy! And then it is no longer there. . . . A face is floating, a face never seen before, it comes nearer, it floats close up to him, opens its eyes and looks at him—more real than any living one. If only he had a board, brushes and paints, he could paint it. . . . It smiles and floats away. . . . In a blue haze he seems to see a city. A wonderful, marvellous city! Where is he to seek this city, this birch with quivering leaves, this lovely smiling face?

"In the morning we'll go straight to the mansion, tell the boyar as many lies as will please him, and then he might let us eat with the servants," Fedka says hoarsely.

In rich houses he always told stories about the Narva disaster, lying about things that had happened or had never been; he drew tears from his listeners, above all—and the landowner himself would sometimes come into the servants' quarters and sit dejectedly with his cheek on his hand—by describing how King Charles, after killing numberless thousands of Orthodox soldiers, rode over the battlefield.

". . . His face is fair, in his left hand he holds the orb and in his right a sharp sword. He is clad in gold and silver, and his horse is white and mettlesome, splashed up to the belly with human blood. Two brave generals lead the horse by the bridle. The king rides up to me. I am lying on the ground, of course, for there's a bullet in my breast. All around me dead Swedes are lying, like sacks. The king rides up to me and asks his generals: 'Who is this man lying there?' The generals reply: 'That's a brave Russian soldier, he killed twelve of our grenadiers with his own hand.' The king says to them: 'It's a brave man's death.' 'No,' say the generals, 'he isn't dead, there's a bullet in his chest.' And they lift me up and I get up and take up my musket and present arms according to all the rules for a king. And he says: 'Brave fellow!' and takes a gold coin out of his pocket. 'Here you are, brave Russian soldier,' he says, 'go in peace to your country and tell the Russians: do not struggle against God, do not go to law against the rich, do not fight against the Swedes. . . .'"

After such a story Fedka, and Golikov with him, were unfailingly fed and allowed to spend the night in the servants' quarters. But it was not easy to get inside a rich house. People had become mistrustful. Each year more men ran away from the recruiting, from the military and local taxes, and hid in the forests, robbing singly or in bands. There were some small towns where only the old men and women and small children remained. No matter whom you asked about, it was: he's been taken into the dragoons; he's at the earthworks or has been taken away to the Urals; and somebody else, who not so long ago kept a shop in the market-place and was God-fearing and respectable, has abandoned his wife and his small children, and is sitting with a cudgel whistling in a ravine by the highway.

More than once Fedka toyed with the idea of joining some robber-band. For what were they to do? They could not go on forever tramping from village to village, they would get tired of it in the end. But Golikov would not hear of it. He went on saying: "Let's go to the South, to the end of the world." Fedka would reply: "Well, you'll get there, and there'll be people there too, they won't feed you for nothing, you'll have to hire yourself out to the Cossacks, or sell yourself in bondage to a landowner and break your back with work. Now, if we played on the highways, we'd have a hundred roubles to sew inside our caps. With money like that you can be a merchant. Then no dragoon, no clerk, no landowner, would be able to molest you; you'd be your own master."

One day—it happened in summer—they were sitting at sundown in a field. The dung fire was smoking gently, and a breeze was rustling and ruffling the grass. Golikov gazed at the fading sunset; only a pale streak remained at the edge of the earth.

"You know, Fedka, what I'm going to say. There's power in me, so much power—greater than any man's. As I listen to the wind whistling in the grass I understand it, I understand everything, until I feel my breast is bursting. As I look at the sunset, at the twilight, I understand everything; there is such gladness and sorrow in me that I could spread myself all over the sky with the sunset."

"There was an idiot in our village, he herded the geese," Fedka said, digging the crumbling embers with a dry twig. "He also used to talk like that. You couldn't make any sense of what he said. He played the reed-pipes very well, the whole village used to go and listen to him. In those days they were looking for musicians for the late Francis Lefort. And what do you think? They took him."

"At Narva one of Sheremetev's serfs was telling me about the Italian country. About the painters, how they live and how they paint. I won't rest, I'm ready to become the least of such a painter's slaves to crush the paints for him. I know how to do it, Fedka. You take a board, an oak board, rub it with oil, prime it. You crush the colours in little pots, some with oil, others with egg. You take brushes. . . ." Golikov was speaking so softly that his voice did not rise above the stirring of the breeze. "You know, Fedka, the day dawns and dies, but on my board daylight burns forever. If there's a tree standing—a birch or a pine—what is there in it? But if you look at my tree on my board, you'll understand everything, and you'll weep."

"Where is it, this country?"

"I don't know, Fedka. We'll ask and people will tell us."

"Well, we might go there. It's all one to me."

4

In the spring of the year 1702 there arrived in Archangel ten experts in lock-building engaged by Andrey Matveyev in Holland at high salaries: seventeen roubles and twenty kopeks a month each and their keep. Half of them were sent to the neighbourhood of Tula, to lake Ivanovskoye where they were to build, in accordance with plans made the previous year, thirty-one locks between the Don and the Oka by way of the Upa and the Shat. The other five went to Vyshny Volochok to build a lock between the Tveritsa and the Msta.

The lock of Vyshny Volochok would link up the Caspian Sea with Lake Ladoga, while the locks of Ivanovskoye would connect Lake Ladoga and the basin of the Volga with the Black Sea.

Peter was in Archangel, where the mouth of the Dvina was being fortified and frigates were being built for the White Sea fleet. The local traders told him that since time immemorial a route was known from the White Sea to Lake Ladoga, through Lake Vyg and Lake Onega and the river Svir. The journey was a difficult one because of the many portages and rapids, but if canals were dug and locks built up to lake Onega, the whole of the White Sea coast could bring its wares directly by water to Ladoga.

There, at lake Ladoga, all three great waterways from three seas converged along the Volga, the Don and the Svir. From the fourth sea—the Baltic—lake Ladoga was separated by the short channel, the Neva, guarded by two fortresses—Noteburg and Nienschanz. The Dutch engineer, Isaac Abraham, said to Peter, pointing to the map: "By digging canals with locks you will bring life to dead seas, and hundreds of your rivers, the waters of the entire country, will flow into the great stream of the Neva and carry your ships into the open ocean."

And so it was that, from the autumn of the year 1702, all efforts were directed to gaining control of the Neva. Apraxin—the son of the admiral—spent the summer devastating Ingria. He penetrated as far as Izhora and, on the banks of this swift stream which meanders over the desolate plain near the sea, he defeated the Swedish general Krongjort and threw him back beyond the Duderhof hills; from there the Swedish general retreated in disorder beyond the Neva into the small fortress of Nienschanz on the Ohta river.

Apraxin led his troops to lake Ladoga and took up his position on the river Naziya. Sheremetev was also moving towards Ladoga from Novgorod, with powerful artillery and baggage-trains. Peter, with five battalions of the Semenovsky and Preobrazhensky regiments, arrived by water at the Gulf of Onega and landed on the low shore near the fishing village of Nuhcha. From here he sent Captain Alexey Brovkin to Soroka, a dissenters' village at the mouth of the Vyg. That summer Ivan Artemyich Brovkin had succeeded in obtaining the exchange of his son for a captive Swedish lieutenant-colonel; he himself had made the journey to Narva and had paid, in addition, three hundred silver roubles. Alexey was given the task of travelling by boat along the whole course of the Vyg to ascertain whether the river was suitable for the building of locks.

From Nuhcha the troops passed across Lake Pul and the dissenters' village Vozhmosalma to Povenets, through forest cuttings and over brushwood roads and log bridges. This road had been built in three months by peasants and lay-brothers from Kem, the Sumsk settlement and dissenters' villages and retreats, collected and driven there by Sergeant Shchepotev. The soldiers dragged along two fully-rigged sailing-boats on rollers. Their way lay over marshes where trees rotted and mosquitoes pinged, and where great boulders were covered with moss as with a fur coat. They came in sight of the wonderful Lake Vyg with its innumerable wooded islets, whose bristling humps rose like monsters out of the sunlit waters. There was not a cloud in the pale sky; the lake and its shores were deserted, as though every living thing had hidden itself in the thickets.

At the Vygoretsky Daniel hermitage, six miles from the military road, services were held day and night, as during Passion Week. Men and women in linen shrouds prayed on their knees and kept tapers burning day and night. All four gates were shut and barred, and in the gate-lodges and round the prayer-houses stocks of straw and pitch had been prepared. Now the elder Nektary came out of his solitary retirement. After the holocaust of his flock and his escape, he had taken up his quarters in the hermitage, having nowhere else to employ his energies. But Andrey Denisov had no liking for him and would not let him near the people. To mark his resentment Nektary retired into an earth-hole where he remained in perpetual silence for two years. If anyone approached his retreat, which was a large hole covered with laths and turf, the elder threw excrement at him. Today he appeared before the people of his own accord: his narrow beard reached his knees, his cloak was worm-eaten and his yellow ribs showed through the holes. Raising his shrivelled arms he cried: "Andrey Denisov has sold Christ for a mushroom-pie. Where are your eyes? Antichrist in person has honoured us with his visit, he's brought two ships on runners. They'll pack you into them like pigs, and take you away to the nethermost hell. Save yourselves! Don't listen to Andrey Denisov! See his bloated phiz in the window. Tsar Peter has sent him a pie with a nice filling!"

Andrey Denisov, realising that things were becoming dangerous and that there might be people who would really try to burn themselves alive, began to upbraid the elder and shouted at him from the cell-window: "You must have lost your senses in your hole, Nektary! All you think of is burning people: you would like to burn the whole world. The Tsar does not interfere with us; let him go his way in peace, and we can mind our own business. As for the pie with which you reproach me—why, you in your lifetime have eaten more pies than I have. We know who brings you chickens at night to your earth-hole, there's not a chicken left in the settlement and your hole is full of chicken-bones."

At this several people rushed to the earth-hole and, sure enough, in a corner they found a lot of chicken-bones buried in the earth. Great confusion ensued. Denisov secretly left the settlement and, mounted on a good horse, rode across the river to the army which he found by the glare of the camp-fires, the neighing of horses and the sounding of brass trumpets at sundown.

Peter received Denisov in a canvas tent where he was sitting with his officers at a camp-table; they were all smoking pipes to keep away the mosquitoes. At the sight of the fresh-faced man in cassock and skull-cap Peter smiled:

"Welcome, Andrey Denisov! What good things have you to tell me? Do you still protect yourselves against me with two fingers?"

Denisov, in obedience to a sign, sat down by the table; he did not wrinkle his nose at the tobacco-smoke, but merely waved it away from his face. He said, meeting Peter's eyes with an honest and open look:

"Gracious Sire, Peter Alexeyevich, we started our business in wild country. Ignorant people came here, all kinds of people. Some we brought to obedience by kindness, others by driving fear into them. We used you to frighten them; forgive me, things were like that. In a large undertaking one is bound to make some mistakes. All sorts of things happened, and some of them are best forgotten."

"And what's going on now?" Peter asked.

"Now, gracious Sire, our business is on a firm footing. Over thirteen hundred acres of land have been cleared for ploughing, and there is as much meadow land. We have a herd of one hundred and twenty cows. Fisheries and curing-sheds, tanneries and felting-shops. We've got our own mining works. We have ore experts and smiths better than those in Tula."

Peter now began to question him, no longer with a scoffing smile, about what kind of ore was worked and where. When he learnt that there was iron-ore on the shores of lake Onega, and that near

Povenets there was a place where eighteen pounds of iron were smelted out of thirty-six pounds of ore, he wreathed himself in smoke and said:

"Then what do you, priestless folk, want of me?"

Denisov replied, after some reflection:

"You, gracious Sire, need iron for your army. Give us directions and we shall set up smelting furnaces and smithies where it will be most convenient. Our iron is better than the Tula kind, and it will cost you less. Akinfy Demidov reckons it at fifty kopeks. . . ."

"You're wrong there. At thirty-five kopeks."

"Very well, we'll also reckon it at thirty-five. But the Urals are far away, while we are close at hand. There's copper here too. In the forests near Povenets, in the Bear Hills, there's mast timber over ninety-feet high, and strong—it rings. When the Neva is yours, we'll send rafts of timber to Holland. The one thing we're afraid of is priests and clerks. We don't need them. Forgive me for speaking in my own way. Allow us to live according to our customs. The people are terrified. In the hermitage for three days now they have stopped all work; they've dressed themselves in shrouds and sing psalms. The cattle is neither fed nor watered and is lowing in the sheds. If you send us a priest with his four-pointed cross and communion, everyone will run away without looking back. You couldn't hold them. They have all known torture and oppression. They'll go off into the wilderness and the business will fall into decay."

"It sounds strange to me," Peter said. "And have you got many people in the hermitage?"

"Five thousand workers, men and women, and old people who do not work any more, and children."

"And all of them free?"

"They escaped from bondage."

"Well, what am I to do with you? All right, take off your shrouds. Cross yourselves with two fingers, or with one, if you like, and pay double taxes on the whole of your business."

"We agree with all our hearts!"

"Send craftsmen to Povenets; good shipbuilders. I need large and small rowing-boats—about five hundred of them."

"With all our hearts!"

"Well, drink to my health, Andrey Denisov!" Peter poured out a full cup from a pewter flagon and offered it with a bow of his head. Denisov grew pale. His light eyes flickered. But he stood up with dignity and made a broad sign of the cross slowly, with two fingers.

He emptied the cup to the last drop and taking off his skull-cap, wiped his red lips with it.

"Thank you for your favour."

"Have a smoke to chase it down."

Peter stretched out his pipe towards him with the chewed stem foremost. Denisov's eyes now held an ironic gleam. Without flinching he took hold of the pipe, but Peter moved it away.

"And you must measure the places," he went on as though nothing had taken place in the interval, "the places where you find ore, and as much land round as you need, and drive in stakes. Write about this to Moscow, to Vinius. I will tell him not to exact taxes on the industries and smelting furnaces for the next ten years." Denisov raised his eyebrows. "Isn't that enough? Then we won't take any taxes for fifteen years. We'll settle the price of the iron later. Start work at once. If you need more men or anything else, write to Vinius. Don't ask for money. Have another cup, saintly man."

At the end of September, in very bad weather, three armies converged on the banks of the Naziya and advanced towards Noteburg. That ancient fortress stood on an island in the middle of the Neva where the river issues from lake Ladoga. Ships could enter the river through both channels past the fortress only by passing within seventy feet of the bastions, right under the mouths of the guns.

The troops came out on to the headland opposite Noteburg. Through lowering rain-clouds they could see the stone towers and weathervanes on the cone-shaped roofs. The walls were so high and strong that the Russian soldiers sighed as they dug approaches and redoubts for the batteries on the headland. It was not for nothing that the men of Novgorod who had built the fortress had nicknamed it the Nut—it was hard to crack. The Swedes seemed to take a long time to make up their minds. Not a soul could be seen on the ramparts. The lead roofs were hidden in low-flying clouds. Then suddenly, on the round tower of the citadel, the royal standard with the lion crept up the flagstaff and fluttered in the wind. A heavy gun roared brazenly and a cannon-ball fell hissing in the mud on the headland in front of the approaches. The Swedes had accepted the battle.

The right bank of the Neva, on the far side of the fortress, was strongly fortified, and it was difficult to reach it from the lake because of the marshy ground. On the left bank a clearing had been cut through the forest from the lake across the headland to the Neva before the whole army had come up to Noteburg. Now several thousand soldiers with ropes were pulling boats from the lake, dragging them along the clearing and launching them in the Neva below the fortress. About fifty men hauled at the ropes, while others held up the gunwales to keep the boats on an even keel as they slid over the log run.

"And again! And again! All together!" Peter shouted. He had thrown off his coat, his shirt was wringing wet, and the veins stood out on his long neck with a twisted cravat tied tightly round it. His ankles were bruised from slipping into the chinks between the logs. He would catch hold of a rope and shout, with his eyes bulging: "All together now! Pull hard!"

The men had not eaten since the day before and their hands were raw and bleeding. But the devil gave them no respite; he shouted, he swore, he struck the men and pulled with them. By nightfall fifty heavy boats, fitted with platforms for the musketeers at bow and stern, had been dragged to the other side and launched on the Neva. The men were too tired to eat and went to sleep dropping where they stood on the damp moss or on hummocks.

The drums began to beat before daybreak. The ensigns shook their men and pulled them to their feet. The orders were to load the muskets and to put two charges into the breasts of their coats—to protect them from the rain—and two bullets into their cheeks. Covering the locks of their muskets with their coattails the soldiers scrambled on to the platforms of the swaying boats. The water was rough. They rowed in the dark across the swiftly-flowing river to the opposite bank, where the forest rustled. They sprang out into the reeds. The officers swore under their breath as they rallied their companies.

They waited. A windy dawn began to break: red streaks showed through the flying mist. A rowing-boat crossed the leaden river, and Peter, Menshikov and Königseck jumped on land. The Saxon ambassador had volunteered to accompany the army and had been attached to the Tsar. "Ready!" The long-drawn order ran down the ranks. Peter scrambled up the steep bank, pulling himself up by the bushes. The wind flapped the tails of his short coat. He strode along, a dimly-perceived, long shadow, and the soldiers hurried after him. Menshikov was on his left, carrying a brace of pistols, and Königseck on his right.

Suddenly they came to a halt. The leading rank of the soldiers, still moving, overtook them. Peter gave the order: "Muskets at the ready! Raise cocks! Fire by platoons!" Flints clicked harshly along the line. The second rank came forward, passing Peter. "Eyes front!" Peter shouted in a savage voice. "First platoon: Fire!" Flashes of musket fire lit up the scattered little pines swaying in the wind and the low parapet of the Swedish entrenchment on the plain beyond the tree-stumps. The fire was returned from there, but only haltingly. "Second platoon: Fire!" The second rank, like the first, fired and dropped to one knee. "Third . . . Third!" shouted the strained voice. "Bayonets! At the double!"

Peter ran across the uneven field. The soldiers broke ranks and, in an excited crowd, a thousand strong, with shouts that grew in volume and fierceness, rushed the earthworks with their bayonets at the ready. The raised hands of the surrendering defenders were already showing over the parapet. Some of the Swedes fled in the direction of the forest.

The trenches on the right bank had been captured. As soon as it was light, mortars were taken across the river, and that same day the Russians began to bombard Noteburg from both banks of the Neva.

After two weeks of fierce bombardment a great fire broke out in the fortress, causing some of the powder vaults to explode, as a result of which the eastern section of the wall collapsed. Then the Russians saw a small boat, with a white flag at the stern, being hurriedly rowed towards the trenches on the headland. A tall, pale officer with a bloodstained kerchief tied round his head landed from the boat. He looked round him uncertainly. Alexey Brovkin jumped over a trench and went up to him. With an insolent look at the Swede, Alexey asked him: "What brings you here?" The officer began to talk fast in Swedish, gesturing towards the great billows of smoke rising from the fortress into the windless sky.

"Talk Russian: are you surrendering or not?" Alexey interrupted him angrily.

Königseck, well-dressed and smiling, came up to help. He politely uncovered himself and bowed to the officer and, having made him repeat what he had first said, translated: the commander's wife, and the wives of the other officers, asked for permission to leave the fortress where it was impossible to stay because of the great smoke and fire. The officer carried a letter to this effect addressed to Sheremetev. Alexey took it from him and turned it over in his hands. Suddenly his face was distorted with anger and he threw the letter into the mud at the officer's feet.

"I won't repeat this to the field-marshal!" he cried. "What does it mean? If we let the women out of the fortress, we'll be losing our men in assaults for another fortnight. Capitulate at once; that's all."

Königseck was more polite. He picked up the letter, wiped it on his coat and returned it to the officer, explaining that the request could not be granted. The Swede shrugged his shoulders and went back indignantly to his boat. No sooner was the boat on its way than all forty-two mortars of Goshka's, Hinter's and Peter's batteries barked together.

The fire blazed all night. The lead roofs of the towers melted and the burning rafters collapsed, sending up great tongues of flame. The glare lit up the river, the Russian camps on both banks and, farther downstream, a hundred moored boats, crowded with volunteers and storm-ladders laid across their sides. The cannonade ceased after midnight, when the only sound was the roaring of the flames.

Two hours before dawn a gun was fired from the Tsar's battery. The drums beat a rousing tattoo. Rowing-boats approached the fortress, lit up more strongly by the glare as they came closer. The flotilla was commanded by three young officers: Mihail Golitsin, Karpov and Alexander Menshikov. The day before Alexander had begged Peter with tears in his eyes: "*Mein Herz*, Sheremetev has been made a field-marshal. People are laughing at me: major-general, governor of Pskov! But when it comes down to it—I was an orderly and I've remained one. Let me go and fight to win military rank."

Peter was standing by the battery on the headland with the field-marshal and the regimental commanders, watching through telescopes. The boats rapidly approached the breach in the eastern wall. They were met with red-hot cannon-balls. The first boat ran into the bank, the soldiers poured out like peas, dragged their ladders forward and started to climb. But the ladders were too short: they did not even reach the top of the breach. The men climbed on each other's backs and scrambled up the projecting stones. From above, boulders came hurtling down and molten lead was poured on the attackers. Wounded men fell from a height of twenty feet. Several boats were set on fire by the cannon-balls and drifted downstream in flames.

Peter watched eagerly through his telescope. When powder-smoke screened the fight, he pushed the telescope under his arm and began to twist the buttons on his coat—some of them he had already torn off. His face was ashen, his lips black and his eyes sunken. "Now how's this? It's all wrong!" he repeated tonelessly, and his neck twitched. He turned to Sheremetev, who only sighed placidly: he had seen worse sights in the last two years. "They've again grudged the ammunition. . . . Taking the place with bare hands! It can't be done like that!"

Sheremetev closed his eyes and replied: "God is merciful, we'll take it anyway." Peter straddled his legs and again raised the telescope to his left eye.

Many dead and wounded were lying under the walls. The sun was already high and veiled by wisps of cloud. Smoke from the fortress towers rose to meet the clouds, but the fire itself was apparently subsiding. A fresh company of volunteers, having approached in boats from the west, rushed to the ladders. They all had lighted fuses between their teeth; they quickly snatched grenades from their haversacks, bit off the heads, lighted and threw them. A few men succeeded in getting a foothold on the breach of the wall but, once there, they had to keep their heads down. The Swedes put up a stubborn resistance. Cannon-fire, the explosion of grenades, shouts that carried faintly across the river, now weakened, now swelled again. This went on for an hour, two hours. . . .

All Peter's hopes, the whole future of all his difficult enterprises, seemed to be concentrated now on the stubborn will of the tiny figures that moved rapidly up the ladders, rested for a moment under the projections of the walls and fired, taking cover from the Swedish grapeshot behind heaps of stones. Nothing could be done to help them. The batteries were compelled to inaction. Had more boats been available another two thousand men could have been brought up to help. But there were no spare boats, nor were there any more ladders, and there were not enough grenades.

"Sire, why don't you go to your tent and eat and rest? What's the use of fretting in vain?" Sheremetev said, sighing like an old woman.

Peter snarled impatiently, without lowering his telescope. There on the wall a tall, grey-bearded old man in an iron cuirass and an old-fashioned helmet was pointing down at the Russians and opening his mouth wide, obviously shouting. The Swedes gathered closely round him and also shouted, apparently arguing about something. The old man pushed one of them away, hit another with his pistol and, with some difficulty, climbed down the jutting stones into the breach, followed by some fifty men. At the breach Swedes and Russians mingled in one furiously fighting cluster. Human bodies dropped off the wall like sacks. Peter gave a long-drawn-out groan.

"That old man is the commander, Erik Schlippenbach, elder

brother of General Schlippenbach whom I beat," Sheremetev said.

The Swedes rapidly took possession of the breach and opened fire with their muskets. They ran down the ladders and threw themselves at the Russians, armed only with their swords. The tall old man in armour stood in the breach, stamping his feet and waving his arms like a cock flapping its wings.

"When a Swede's blood is up, he fears nothing—not even death," Sheremetev remarked.

The Russian survivors were retreating towards the water, to their boats. One man, his face bandaged with a rag, rushed to and fro, driving the soldiers from the boats. He jumped up and down and struck the men to prevent them from getting in, then, hurling himself at the bows of a boat, pushed it away from the bank empty. He ran to another and pushed that out too.

"That's Mishka Golitsin," Sheremetev said. "His blood's up also."

Hand-to-hand fighting was now raging round the boats.

Twelve large boats full of volunteers raced against the current to the fortress, their oars bending with the effort. These were the last reserves—Menshikov's men. Menshikov himself, coatless and hatless, in a pink silk shirt, with sword and pistol, was the first to leap ashore.

"Showing off, the braggart!" Peter muttered.

When the Swedes saw the fresh enemy force, they ran to the walls, but only some of them succeeded in climbing to safety; the rest were killed. Again stones and logs came hurtling down and a gun belched grapeshot. Again the Russians climbed the ladders. Peter followed the pink shirt through his telescope. Menshikov was fearlessly fighting to win glory and military rank. He clambered up into the breach and sprang at old Schlippenbach; he dodged a bullet from his pistol and the two began fighting with their swords. Schlippenbach's men only just rescued him and dragged him back. The Swedes were weakening under this fresh onslaught.

"Look at that devil!" Peter cried, stamping his foot. Menshikov's pink shirt was already flashing between the battlements, at the very top of the wall.

Peter could not see clearly through his telescope. The vast red glow of the northern sunset spread behind the fortress.

"Peter Alexeyevich, they seem to have hoisted the white flag!" Sheremetev said. "Well, it was time, we've been fighting thirteen hours."

That night great bonfires burned on the banks of the Neva. No one in the camp slept. Broth simmered in copper kettles and whole sheep were roasted on spits. Corporals with long moustaches stood before barrels sawn in half and gave each man as much vodka as he wanted, as much as his soul thirsted for.

The volunteers, who had not yet cooled down after their thirteen-hour battle, and nearly all of whom were bandaged with bloodstained rags, sat on tree-stumps or fir-branches round the fires telling pitiful stories of combat, of wounds and of their comrades' deaths. The soldiers who had not been in the fight stood, open-mouthed, in a circle behind the narrators. As they listened, they glanced over their shoulders at the blackened towers dimly visible on the river. There, under the walls of the deserted fortress, lay corpses in heaps.

More than five hundred of the volunteers had been killed, and about a thousand wounded were groaning in the tents and on the carts of the baggage-train.

The soldiers repeated with a sigh: "There's the Nut for you—we've cracked it."

Shouts and the music of horns sounded from the Tsar's illuminated tent, pitched on rising ground beyond a brook. No discharge of guns accompanied the toasts: they had had their fill of shooting that day.

From time to time drunken officers lurched out of the tent to relieve themselves. One of these, a colonel, stared for a long time at the soldiers' camp-fires on the other side as he came to the brook and then bellowed:

"Well done, lads!"

Some of the soldiers raised their heads and muttered: "What are you yelling for? Go back to your drinking, you fire-eater."

Peter came reeling out of the tent, also to relieve himself. As he did so, he swayed. The camp-fires swam before his eyes: he rarely got drunk, but today the wine had gone to his head. Menshikov and Königseck came out after him.

"Shall I bring you a candle, *mein Herz*? You're taking a long time about it," Alexander said in a drunken voice.

Königseck broke into laughter: "Ha, ha!" and began to hop about like a hen, lifting up his coat-tails.

"Königseck!" Peter said.

"I'm here, Your Majesty."

"What were you boasting about at table?"

"I wasn't boasting, Your Majesty."

"Don't lie, I heard you. What were you babbling to Sheremetev?

'This trinket is dearer to me than the salvation of my soul'. What is this precious trinket of yours?"

"Sheremetev was boasting about a slave-girl of his, a Livonian. But I don't remember that I . . ."

Königseck broke off, as if he had suddenly grown sober. Peter looked down, like a crane, into his frightened face. His teeth were bared in a mirthless grin.

"Ah, Your Majesty, I must have meant a snuffbox I've got. Of French make. It's in my luggage. I'll go and fetch it. . . ."

He set off at an unsteady trot towards the brook, nervously unbuttoning his waistcoat. "My God, my God, how did he find out? I must hide it, throw it away at once. . . ." His fingers caught in the lace; when they found the locket, he tried to wrench it off, but the silk cord cut painfully into his neck. Peter was standing on the hillock following him with his eyes. Königseck nodded to him reassuringly, as if to say: "I'm bringing it at once." A log had been thrown from bank to bank across the deep brook that splashed noisily over granite boulders. Königseck started to cross, but his shoes were slippery with clay. He went on tugging at the silk cord. Suddenly he lost his footing, waved his arms wildly and fell backwards into the brook.

"The drunken fool!" Peter said.

They waited a little. Menshikov frowned and, slightly alarmed, started towards the brook.

"Peter Alexeyevich, I'm afraid it's a bad business. We'll have to get some men."

Königseck was not found at once, although the brook was only six feet deep. In his fall the back of his head had apparently hit a boulder and he had immediately gone to the bottom. The soldiers carried him to the tent and laid him by the fire. Peter began to raise and lower his torso, stretch out his arms and blow into his mouth.

It was an inglorious end for the Saxon Ambassador. As he unbuttoned Königseck's shirt, Peter found on his chest, against the skin, a locket the size of a child's palm. He searched the pockets and pulled out a packet of letters. He went back at once with Menshikov to his tent.

"Gentlemen," Menshikov said to the officers, "the feasting is over. The Tsar wishes to sleep."

The guests hurriedly left the tent. Some of them had to be dragged out supported under their arms, their spurs trailing along the ground. Here, among the unfinished dishes and half-burnt candles, Peter laid out the sodden letters. He prised open the locket with his nails. It was a portrait of Anna Mons of exquisite workmanship. Annchen's innocent blue eyes and even little teeth were smiling from it as if the portrait were alive. A strand of the fair hair which Peter had so often kissed lay round the portrait under the glass. On the inside of the lid the words "Love and Fidelity" had been scratched with a needle-point in German.

Peter picked out the glass too, felt the strand of hair and threw the locket into a little pool of wine on the table. He began to read the letters. They were all from Anna to Königseck, the silly, maudlin letters of a lovesick woman.

"So," Peter said, resting his elbows on the table and staring at the candle. "Fancy that!" He smiled and shook his head. "She was false to me. I don't understand. She lied to me, Alexander, how she lied! All her life, perhaps from the first? I can't understand it. 'Love and Fidelity'!"

"Trash, *mein Herz*, a bitch, a tavern wench . . . I wanted to tell you long ago. . . ."

"Hold your tongue! How dare you? Get out!"

Peter filled his pipe, rested his elbows again on the table and smoked. He looked at the miniature lying in the pool of wine. "I climbed over the fence to reach you; how often your name was on my lips; I trusted you, I went to sleep on your warm shoulder. What a fool you are! You're only fit to mind hens. Very well—that's over." With a gesture as if dismissing the whole affair, Peter got up and, throwing down his pipe, lay down on his creaking camp-bed and covered himself with his sheepskin coat.

5

The fortress of Noteburg was renamed Schlüsselburg—"key-town". The breach was filled and wooden roofs built over the fire-gutted towers. A garrison was left in the fortress, and the army went off to winter quarters. Peter returned to Moscow.

At the Miasnitsky gates he was greeted by peals of bells and by the great merchants and traders carrying church banners. The Miasnitskaya was carpeted with red cloth over a stretch of seven hundred feet. The merchants threw up their caps and shouted "Vivat!" in the foreign fashion. Peter drove, standing upright in a gilded chariot; behind him Swedish standards trailed in the dust and prisoners walked with bowed heads. On a high cart, sitting astride a wooden lion, drove Zotov, in a tin mitre and red fustian mantle, a sword in one hand and a flagon of vodka in the other.

Moscow feasted for two weeks, as befitted the occasion. Many respectable people grew ill and died from over-eating. In the Red Square pies were baked and distributed to the citizens. A rumour spread that the Tsar had ordered the distribution of decorated Viazma honey-cakes and kerchiefs, but that the boyars had swindled the people: peasants from distant villages came to Moscow for these cakes. Each night rockets soared from the Kremlin towers and fiery catherine-wheels turned on the walls. The feasting and fireworks ended in a great fire on the Day of Intercession. It started in the Kremlin and spread to Kitay-gorod; the strong wind carried burning embers across the Moskva river. The flames spread in waves over the whole city. The people fled to the gates. They saw Peter galloping along in the fire and smoke on a Dutch fire-engine. Nothing could be saved. The Kremlin was completely gutted, save for the Zhitny building and the Kokoshkin palace; the old palace was burnt down, and Tsarevna Natalia and Tsarevich Alexey, the heir to the throne, were nearly lost with it; all the office buildings, the monasteries, the ammunition stores were destroyed by the fire; on Ivan the Great, the bells crashed to the ground, and the largest of all, weighing a hundred and twenty-eight tons, was cracked.

Later, among the burnt ruins, people said: "Reign a little longer, and you'll see worse things."

The whole Brovkin family assembled at Ivan Brovkin's house round the table, after midday mass, to celebrate the return of his son Gavrila from Holland. Alexey, recently promoted to the rank of lieutenant-colonel, was there; Yakov, the navigation officer from Voronezh, sombre, rough-spoken, reeking of tobacco; Artamon with his wife Natalia—he was now working under Shafirov as interpreter in the Ambassadors' Office. Natalia, pregnant for the third time, had grown beautiful, indolent and broader in body: Ivan Artemyich never tired of looking at her. Prince Roman and his two other daughters were also there. Antonida had been successfully married off that autumn to a Lieutenant Belkin, of low birth, but in favour with Peter and now away in Ingria. Olga was still languishing in spinsterhood.

Roman Borisovich had aged a good deal in the last few years, mainly because he was obliged to drink so much. He had barely slept off the effects of one feast when there was a soldier who had been waiting in the kitchen since morning with an order for him to be somewhere or other that day. Prince Roman took a pair of moustaches made of bast—an invention of his own—and a wooden sword with him and drove off on the Tsar's service.

There were six such boyars whose task was to entertain the Tsar at table. They were all of high birth and had been turned into buffoons either because of their stupidity or owing to malicious intrigues. At their head was Prince Shahovsky, a dry, ill-natured little old man, a drunkard and a tale-bearer. The service was not very onerous: usually after the fifth course, when much had already been drunk, Peter Alexeyevich would lay his hands on the table, stretch out his neck, look round and say loudly: "I see that the powers of intoxication are pressing hard on us. There is a danger of our being defeated." Then Prince Roman would leave the table, tie on his false moustache and get on to a low wooden horse on castors. A goblet of wine was presented to him, which he had to drink briskly, holding up his sword. After that he had to say: "We die, but do not surrender!" Then dwarfs, fools and buffoons rushed up to him, yapping, and dragged him on his horse round the table. This constituted all his duties, unless Peter Alexeyevich invented some new diverting trick.

Ivan Artemyich was in excellent humour that day. The family was gathered round him, business was prospering and even the fire had spared the Brovkin mansion. Only Alexandra, his favourite, was missing. It was about her that Gavrila—a self-possessed young man who had just graduated at the Amsterdam school of navigation—was now telling his father.

Alexandra and her husband were at The Hague with Matveyev, the Tsar's ambassador, but they were not staying at the embassy and had taken a house of their own. She kept thoroughbreds, carriages and even a yacht. "Oh, oh!" Ivan Artemyich exclaimed, pretending to be surprised, although, without letting Peter know, he was sending Alexandra large sums for these horses and yachts. The Volkovs had left Warsaw over a year before, when King August had fled before the advancing Swedes. They had been to Berlin, but did not stay long; Alexandra did not like the Prussian royal court: the king was mean, the Prussians led a dull life and were parsimonious, keeping count of every mouthful.

"At The Hague her house is always full of guests," Gavrila told them. "Of course, few of them are of great importance. Mostly they are people of small account: adventurers, painters, musicians, and

Indian conjurors. She goes sailing with them on the canal, sitting on deck and playing the harp."

"She's learnt to play the harp?" Ivan Artemyich said throwing up his hands and looking round the family circle.

"When she goes out walking in the street, all bow to her and she only nods in reply, like this. She does not always let Vasily come out to the guests, but he's only too pleased. He's grown very quiet and thoughtful: always with some book, and he even reads Latin and visits the shipyards, the museums and the Bourse, taking note of everything."

Just before Gavrila left, Alexandra had told him that in spite of everything she was bored with The Hague: the Dutchmen talked of nothing but business and money, they had no real manners with women and trod on her toes when they danced. She wanted to go to Paris.

"She's set on dancing the minuet with the French king! The minx!" Ivan Artemyich exclaimed and screwed up his eyes with satisfaction. "And when does she intend to come home? Tell me that."

"At times she gets tired of the adventurers and says to me: 'Gashka, you know what I would like—gooseberries, our own, from our garden. And I would like to rock on the swings in the garden above the Moskva river'."

"It shows that one can't forget what's bred in the bone."

Ivan Artemyich could have listened all day to stories about his daughter Alexandra. In the middle of dinner Peter arrived with Menshikov. He was a frequent guest now in Brovkin's house. He nodded to the family and said to Prince Roman who had become quite agitated: "Sit still, no service today." He went to the window and gazed for some time at the gutted ruins; where there had been streets full of life and bustle, there were now only chimneys sticking out from the heaps of ashes and charred churches without cupolas. A chilling wind drove clouds of ash before it.

"A God-forsaken place," he said clearly. "In foreign countries cities stand a thousand years, but this—I can't remember when it was not being burnt to the ground. Moscow!"

He sat down at the table and ate a large meal, but sombrely, in silence. Then he beckoned Gavrila and began to question him closely about his studies in Holland and the books he had read. He called for a pen and paper to sketch ships' hulls, sails, plans of sea fortifications. Once he contradicted Gavrila, but the young man stood fast by his opinion. Peter patted him on the head: "You haven't been wasting your father's money I see." Ivan Artemyich sniffed deeply with happy tears.

Lighting his pipe Peter again went to the window.

"Artemyich," he said, "we must build a new city."

"It will be rebuilt, Peter Alexeyevich. In a year's time they'll have quite recovered."

"But not here."

"Where else, Peter Alexeyevich? This is an ancient site, this Moscow of our ancestors." He spoke with his head thrown back—short, thickset—and blinked rapidly. "I have already given thought to the matter, Peter Alexeyevich. Five thousand peasants have been hired to cut timber. We'll shape the logs on the Sheksna, the Shelon, and float them down the rivers ready to put together. A house with gates and wicket-gate would cost five roubles. What could be better? Menshikov is going shares with me in the business."

"Not here," Peter repeated, looking out of the window. "The city must be built on Ladoga, on the Neva. It is there that you must send your wood-cutters."

Ivan Artemyich ached to put his short arms behind his back and twiddle his thumbs.

"It can be done," he said in a small voice.

"Mein Herz, that old Mons woman has been to see me again. She weeps and asks to be allowed at least to go to church for the service," Menshikov said cautiously as they were driving home from Brovkin's in the evening, past the gutted ruins. The wind whipped the ashes against the leather side of the carriage. Peter leant back in the far corner and seemed not to hear what Menshikov said.

After Schlüsselburg he had mentioned Anna Mons only once, in Moscow, when he had ordered Menshikov to see her and take from her his—Peter's—locket portrait studded with diamonds. She was to keep all other jewellery and moneys and was to go on living where she was, unless she wanted to go away into the country, but she was not to go out and not to show herself anywhere.

He had painfully torn that woman out of his heart as he might have torn out a weed, by the roots. He had forgotten her. And now, in the carriage, not a muscle of his face moved. Anna had written to him, but had had no reply. She sent her mother to Menshikov with gifts, imploring permission to throw herself at the feet of His

Majesty, the only man she had loved in her life. The locket, she said, Königseck had stolen from her; she did not know that her letters had been found on him.

Menshikov saw that *mein Herz* was much in need of a woman's tenderness. The Tsar's orderlies—they were all in Menshikov's pay—reported that Peter Alexeyevich was sleeping badly, groaning and banging his knees against the wall. He needed, not simply a woman, but a gentle companion. Menshikov had mentioned Anna Mons only to see how Peter would take it. But Peter had shown no response at all. They left the log-paved road and drove along a soft track. Menshikov suddenly burst out laughing and shook his head. Peter said to him coldly:

"I wonder how I put up with you at all. I don't know why."

"What have I done? I swear . . ."

"Whatever you do there's some dishonesty about it. And now you are up to something—I can see it."

Menshikov sniffed. They drove in silence for a while. Then Menshikov began again, with a little laugh:

"I've had a quarrel with Sheremetev. He'll be complaining to you presently. He was always boasting of his housekeeper. He says he bought her from a dragoon for a rouble. 'But I wouldn't let her go for ten thousand,' he says. 'She's so lively and gay, like fire. And there's nothing she can't do'. So I started to get round him. We'd been drinking a bit, and then I said: 'Let me see her'. He hedged: 'I don't know where she is.' But I insisted. The old man was in a fix, he made excuses, but finally called her in. I was taken with her from the start. Not that she's one of those real beauties, but she's pleasant, with a clear voice, lively eyes, curly hair. I said: 'According to ancient custom the guest is offered a cup with a kiss'. Sheremetev gave me a black look, but the girl laughed. She filled a goblet and presented it to me with a bow. I drank it and kissed her on the lips. *Mein Herz,* that kiss burnt me, I couldn't think of anything else, my blood raced in my veins. 'Boris Petrovich,' I said, 'let me have this girl. I'll give you my palace, my last shirt. You can't manage a girl like that. She needs a young fellow to make love to her. You only stir her up to no purpose. And besides, you have a wife and children, it's sinful of you. And there's no knowing too how Peter Alexeyevich will take your lechery when he hears of it'. I had him in a corner there. The old man began to wheeze. 'Alexander Danilovich,' he said, 'you are trying to take my last joy from me'. He waved his hand helplessly and began to weep. It was really quite funny.

Then he went out and shut himself up alone in his bedroom. It didn't take me long to settle things with that housekeeper of his. I sent for a coach, loaded her on it with all her bundles and took her to my hostelry. Next day I brought her to Moscow. She cried a little for a week, but I think it was just for show. Now she's as happy as a bird in my house."

There was no telling whether Peter was listening or not. But when Menshikov came to the end of his story, Peter coughed and Menshikov, who knew all his coughs by heart, understood that he had been listening intently.

6

Brovkin, Sveshnikov, the trader Zatrapezny and the government agents Dubrovsky, Shchegolin and Yevreinov were setting up cloth, linen and silk factories, paper-mills and rope-works on the Yaouza and the Moskva rivers. A number of villages were attached to these factories in permanent bondage from those belonging to the Department of Estates, which absorbed the granted estates that had belonged to landowners killed in the war or disgraced.

The merchants were stirring out of their inertia. When they assembled on the roomy porch of the Stewards' Chamber, which had been quickly rebuilt after the fire, they talked of nothing but newly-conquered Ingria, where they ought to establish themselves firmly on the seaboard this coming summer. They unearthed in their cellars their grandfathers' pots of gold coins and thalers, and sent their employees to the market-places and taverns to enlist working men for bond-service.

During that winter Brovkin had greatly extended his operations. Through Menshikov he had obtained the right to take convicts from Romodanovsky's prisons under bond-writs, and set them to work— some chained, others free—in his cloth and linen factories, whose water-wheels turned noisily on the Yaouza. For seven hundred roubles he bought off the famous craftsman-smith Zhemov from the Office of Criminal Affairs and brought him in a troika from Voronezh, and now, in Brovkin's new sawmill in Sokolniki, Zhemov was setting up a wonderful fire machine that worked from a boiler.

Everywhere there was a dearth of workers. Many men from the villages, bonded to the works, ran away from the new slavery to distant wildernesses. Working for the landlord was hard enough, and many a horse had a lighter job of it than the peasant; but the slavery in these factories seemed even more hopeless: worse than prison for convict and free labourer alike. A high palisade surrounded them, and the guards at the gates were fiercer than dogs. In the dark workshops, bending over the rattling looms, a man could not even sing; the foreign foreman would lash him over the shoulders with his stick and threaten him with the dungeon. In the village the peasant could at least sleep his fill on the stove during the winter, but here, winter and summer, day and night, he had to ply the shuttle. His pay and his clothes had long since been exchanged for drink—in advance. It was slavery. But most terrible of all were the rumours about the Ural factories and mines of Akinfy Demidov. People from the districts attached to his works ran away to wherever they could out of sheer terror.

Demidov's recruiting agents went round the market-places and taverns, treated all and sundry generously and described in glowing colours the easy life in the Urals. There, they said, was land in plenty; work for a year—sew your money in your cap—and leave in peace: nobody would hold you. If you wanted, you could go gold-prospecting; gold was like dirt under your feet there.

When such an agent had got a suitable man drunk, with the tavern-keeper for witness, he would lay a bond-writ before him. "Make a cross in ink, my dear fellow, just here." And the man was lost. They put him on a cart and, if he was violent, they chained him up. Then they took him hundreds of miles away, beyond the Volga, beyond the grassy Kirgiz steppes, beyond the high wooded mountains to the Nevyansk works, to the mines. Few returned from there. The men were chained to the anvils, to the smelting furnaces. The refractory ones were flogged. There was no running away: mounted Cossacks with ropes guarded all the roads and forest paths. As for those who tried to revolt, they were thrown into deep mine-shafts or drowned in the ponds.

After Christmas, new recruiting for the army started. The Tsar's recruiting-agents enlisted carpenters, stonemasons and labourers in all the towns. Between Moscow and Novgorod everyone, without exception, was enlisted for waggon driving.

7

"Why don't you show me this Katerina of yours?"

"She is shy, *mein Herz*. She has grown so fond of me, so attached to me that she won't look at anyone else. It's enough to make me want to marry her."

"Then why don't you?"

"Well, after all . . ."

Menshikov squatted on the waxed floor by the fireplace and, turning away his face, poked the burning logs. The wind howled in the chimney and rattled the sheet-iron roof. Snow was whirling against the panes of the high window. The flames of two wax candles on the table were flickering. Peter was smoking, drinking wine and wiping his red face and damp hair with a table-napkin. He had just returned from Tula, from a visit to the factories, and had driven straight to Menshikov's house to have a bath. He steamed himself for three hours. Wearing Menshikov's scented linen and silk coat, with his neck and chest bare, Peter sat down to supper, after giving orders that no one should come into the little dining-room, not even the servants. He questioned Menshikov about all sorts of trifling matters, laughed —and suddenly enquired about Katerina. This was the first time he had mentioned her since the conversation in the carriage.

"For me, Peter Alexeyevich, with my low birth, to marry a captive . . . I don't know. . . ." He dug the poker into the fire, making the sparks fly. "I've been approached about Eudoxia Arsenyeva. It's a very old family, from the Golden Horde. After all, she would help to make people forget I ever sold pies. Foreigners are always coming to visit me and the first thing they want to know is who is my wife and what is my title. Our fat-arsed, high-born nobles are only too glad to whisper to them that you took me from the streets."

"Quite right," Peter said, wiping his face with the napkin. His eyes were gleaming.

"If only I had some title, say a count's," Menshikov said, throwing down the poker. He set a brass-meshed fire-guard before the fire and came back to the table. "The snowstorm is terrible. You mustn't think of going home, *mein Herz*."

"I wasn't intending to."

Menshikov took up a wine-glass. It trembled in his hand He sat without raising his eyes.

"It was you, not I, who started this talk," Peter said. "Go and call her."

Mensihikov grew pale. With a violent movement he got up and left the room. Peter sat swinging his leg. The house was quiet save for the howling of the wind in the vast attics. Peter listened with eyebrows raised. His leg kept swinging like clockwork. Then came the sound of rapid, angry steps. Menshikov, returning, stopped in the doorway, bit his lip and said:

"She's coming at once."

Peter's ears flattened as he heard light feminine feet that seemed to be flying gaily and lightheartedly on tapping heels through the silence of the house.

"Come in, don't be afraid," Menshikov said, letting Katerina pass through the door. She narrowed her eyes a little at the light of the candles after the darkness of the passage. Then she looked questioningly at Menshikov. She reached only to his shoulder; she had black hair and mobile eyebrows. With the same light step and without timidity she went up to Peter, made a low curtsey, picked up his large hand where it lay on the table, as if it were an inanimate object, and kissed it. He felt the warmth of her lips and the cool touch of her even white teeth. Folding her hands under her small white apron, she stood before Peter's armchair. Her feet, which had brought her here so lightly, were set slightly apart under her skirts. She looked frankly and merrily into Peter's eyes.

"Sit down, Katerina."

She replied in broken Russian but in such a pleasant voice that Peter immediately felt warm and safe from the howling of the storm outside; his ears lost their tenseness and he stopped swinging his foot.

"I will sit down, thank you," she said and at once sat on the edge of a chair, still keeping her hands folded on her stomach under the apron.

"Do you drink wine?"

"Yes, thank you."

"You don't find life hard in captivity?"

"Not hard, thank you."

Menshikov came up to the table moodily and poured out wine for all three.

"Can't you find anything else to say except 'thank you, thank you'?" he said to her. "Tell us something."

"How can I talk to him—he's not an ordinary man."

She disengaged a hand from under her apron, took a wineglass and smiled at Peter with a quick flash of her eye:

"He knows what he wants to talk about."

Peter laughed. He had not laughed so heartily for a long time. He began to question Katerina: where she came from, where she had lived and how she had been taken prisoner. As she answered him she settled in the chair and rested her bare elbows on the tablecloth. Her dark eyes sparkled and her black curls shone like silk as they lay in two clusters over her softly gleaming bosom. It seemed to Peter that she must have tripped through all the storms of her short life with the same light grace as when she had run up the stairs a short while ago.

Menshikov kept refilling the glasses. He put more logs on the fire. The snowstorm howled eerily. Peter stretched, wrinkled his short nose, looked at Katerina and said:

"Well, time for bed, I suppose. I'm going. Katusha, take a candle and light the way."

The sullen peasant, Fedka Mudwash, with a fresh purple brand on his forehead and straddling bare legs chained together, was driving in a pile with a wooden mallet. He was a stalwart fellow. The other men had set down their wheelbarrows, or stood waist-deep in the water with their faces raised, or had thrown the log off their backs—all watching the pile sink deeper into the swampy bank with every blow.

The first pile was being driven in for the shore embankment of the little island which the Finns called Yanni-saari—Rabbit Island. Three weeks before, the Russians had stormed the earthworks of Nienschanz, a little over a mile up the Neva river. The Swedes, abandoning the banks of the Neva, had retreated beyond the Sestra river. The Swedish fleet, afraid of the shallows, kept well out in the bay, its sails showing dark against the rippling waters that shimmered in the sun. Two small ships had ventured up the estuary of the Neva as far as the island of Hirvi, where a Russian battery lay concealed among the trees; they were surrounded by galleys, boarded and taken.

At the cost of much blood and effort, the passage from lake Ladoga to the open sea had been cleared. Countless trains of waggons and hordes of workers and convicts trailed in from the east. Peter wrote to Romodanovsky: "Men are greatly needed; give orders to all towns, offices and town-councils to collect criminals and send them here." Thousands of men, brought from thousands of miles away, were carried on rafts and in boats to the right bank of the Neva, and the island of Koibu. There mud-huts and wattle-huts were put up, fires smoked, axes rang and saws rasped. Here, at the ends of the earth, working men kept coming and coming, and none returned. In front of Koibu-saari, on the marshy island of Yanni, a fortress with six bastions was being built to guard the dearly-bought outlet of all the trade routes of the Russian land. ". . . They are to be built by six commanders: the first bastion will be built by Bombardier Peter Alexeyev, the second by Menshikov, the third by Prince Trubetskoy, the fourth by the Prince-Pope Zotov. . . ." When the foundations were laid there was a great drinking-bout in Peter's hut and, amid toasts and gun salutes, the decision was taken to call the fortress Petersburg.

The open sea, where the wind covered the water with merry ripples, was only a stone's-throw from the fortress. To the West, beyond the sails of the Swedish fleet, great sea-clouds hung in the sky, like smoke rising from some other world. Only the sentinels on the barren island of Kotlin watched those un-Russian clouds, those wastes of water and the terrible glow of the sunset. There was a shortage of bread. None could be brought from ravaged Ingria, where plague had broken out. Men ate roots and ground tree-bark. Peter wrote to Romodanovsky asking him to send more men, for: "there is much sickness here, and many have died." More and more trains of waggons came, more peasants, more convicts. . . .

Fedka Mudwash, his hair falling on to his hot, damp forehead, went on hammering at the pile with his oak mallet.

BOOK THREE

❊

chapter one

Life had become very dull in Moscow. At noontide, in the July heat, only stray dogs, with tails hanging, slunk about the crooked streets, sniffing at the refuse and rubbish that people threw outside their gates. There was none of the former bustle and shouting in the public squares, when a respectable man ran the risk of having his coat-tails torn off by traders pulling him towards their booths, or having his pockets turned inside-out before he had had time to buy anything in the hurly-burly. Formerly, before daybreak, carts used to come driving in from all the suburbs—the Arbat, the Suharev and those beyond the Moskva river—piled with hardware, textile and leather wares, with pots, bowls, platters, fancy bread, bast sieves full of berries, and all kinds of vegetables; street-sellers came carrying poles hung with birch-bark shoes or trays with pies; the carts were hurriedly placed in position and the booths set up in the squares. Today the strelets suburbs were deserted, the roofs had fallen in, the yards were thickly overgrown with nettles. Many of the people were now working side by side with convicts and bondsmen in the newly established factories, from which linen and cloth were taken straight to the Preobrazhensky Office. All the Moscow smithies were busy forging swords, spears, stirrups and spurs. Not an inch of hemp string was to be bought in Moscow; all the hemp had been commandeered by the treasury.

Nor was there any of the former bell-ringing from dawn till dawn: in many of the churches the great bells had been taken down and carted to the foundry yard, where they were melted down and turned into guns. When dragoons, reeking of foul tobacco, had dragged the great bell from the belfry of Old Pimen, the sexton got drunk and tried to hang himself from the beams. Later, lying trussed up on a chest, he screamed frenziedly that: "Moscow was once famous for its mellow chimes, but now Moscow was in for anxious times."

Formerly, before the gates of every boyar's mansion, there had been insolent house-serfs, their caps set at a jaunty angle, grinning and joking among themselves, playing at pitch-and-toss and shove-ha'penny, or simply annoying every passer-by, mounted or on foot; there had been laughter, pawing, horse-play. Today the gates were fast shut and quiet reigned in the spacious yards. The men had been taken away to the war, the boyars' sons and their sons-in-law were either serving as non-commissioned officers in the regiments or had been sent abroad, while the younger sons had been sent to school to learn navigation, mathematics and fortification. The boyar himself sat idly at the open window, grateful for even a short respite while Tsar Peter was away from Moscow and not forcing him to smoke tobacco, scrape off his beard, and skip and caper in white knee-length stockings with a wig of woman's hair on his head reaching down to his navel.

Joyless and dreary were the boyar's thoughts as he sat at the window. "All the same, my Mishka can't be taught mathematics. Moscow was built without any mathematics, and people have lived —God be praised—five hundred years without mathematics, and lived better than today. There's nothing to be expected from this war except final ruin, no matter how many unholy Neptunes and Venuses are carted round Moscow in gilt waggons in honour of the glorious victory on the Neva. The Swedes are sure to defeat our army, and then the Turks, who have long been waiting for this, will pour in hordes out of the Crimea and make their way over the Oka. Oh-ho-ho!"

The boyar stretched a fat finger towards a plate of raspberries —the damned wasps were swarming all over the plate and the windowsill. Lazily fingering his beads of olive-stones—from Mount

Athos—the boyar gazed out on the yard. Desolation! What with the Tsar's whims and amusements there had been no time for him, these many years, to think about his own house. The store-houses were leaning askew, the turf roofs of the cellars were sagging, dank weeds were thick everywhere. "And, look, the hens seem to be all legs, and ducks today come small, and the hunchbacked piglets trailing behind the sow are dirty and thin. Oh-ho-ho!" The boyar knew that he ought to summon the woman in charge of the pigs and the poultry-maid and have them birched on the spot with their skirts trussed up, but the effort of shouting and losing his temper in this heat was too much for him.

The boyar raised his eyes to look beyond the fence, beyond the lime-trees smothered in pale yellow blossom and droning bees. In the near distance rose the weatherbeaten Kremlin walls with bushes growing in the crenels of the battlements. It would have been funny were it not sad: that's what Tsar Peter's reign had brought things to! From the very Troitsky gates, where heaps of refuse were piled up, the moat was now nothing but a muddy puddle that a hen could cross. And the stench of it! The Neglinnaya river had become quite shallow: on its right bank was the Rag Market, where thieves openly sold stolen goods, while on the left bank, under the wall, boys in dirty shirts sat with fishing rods, and nobody drove them off.

In the shopping rows in the Red Square the merchants were locking up their shops before going off to their dinner and hanging huge heavy padlocks on their doors, for trade was slack. The sexton too had shut the doors of the church, shaken his goat's beard at the beggars and shuffled off home to eat his kvass with onions and salt-fish, and then to snore gently in the shade of an elder-bush. And the beggars too, the cripples, all the deformed creatures had crawled off the church porch and gone, each his own way, in the noontide heat.

And indeed it was about time dinner was served, for torpor was quite overcoming the boyar from the unutterable dullness. Suddenly he started, stretched out his neck and lips and even rose slightly from his stool, shielding his eyes with his hand: over the brick bridge that spanned the Neglinnaya from the Troitsky gate to the Rag Market a glass coach was driving, flashing in the sunlight. It was drawn by four horses harnessed tandem with a crimson-liveried servant astride the leader. This was the coach of Tsarevna Natalia, Peter's favourite sister, endowed with as restless a nature as her brother, off on some expedition. Where could she be going now?

The boyar leant out of the window, crossly flapping his handkerchief to drive away the wasps.

"Grishutka!" he called out to a small lad in a long tunic of coarse linen with red gussets under the arms, who was cooling his bare feet in the puddle by the well. "Run as fast as you can, or else you'll get it from me! When you see a gilt coach in the Tverskaya, run after it, don't let it get away from you. Then run back and tell me where's she's gone to."

2

The four greys, with red plumes over their ears and brass ornaments and bells on their harness, bore the coach at a heavy gallop across the broad meadow and came to a halt in front of the old Izmaylovsky palace. This palace had been built by Tsar Alexey Mihaylovich who had liked to indulge his fancy on his estate in the small village of Izmaylovo. There, to this day, bears were kept in pits and peacocks strutted about the poultry-yard, perching at night on the trees in summer. It would have been impossible to count how many coloured and tinned roofs there were over the rooms, passages and porches of the palace built of logs grown dark with time: some steep-pitched with a comb like a ruff's, others barrel-shaped or curved and pointed like a woman's headdress. Above them, impetuous swifts cut through the air in the midday silence. All the windows of the palace were shut. On the porch an old cock dozed standing on one leg. When the coach drew up, it started, screeched and fled; at this, hens began to cackle under all the porches, as though the house were on fire. A small, low door opened on the ground floor and the custodian, old too, peered out. Seeing the coach, he went down unhurriedly on his knees and bowed, touching the ground with his forehead.

Tsarevna Natalia put her head out of the coach and asked impatiently:

"Where are the young ladies, grandfather?"

The old man got up, thrusting forward his grey beard and his lips.

"Welcome, Mistress, welcome beautiful Tsarevna Natalia Alexeyevna," he said looking affectionately at her from under his overhanging eyebrows. "Ah, our God-sent, ah, our beloved Tsarevna! You want to know where the young ladies are? I don't know where they are, I haven't seen them."

Natalia jumped out of the coach, pulled the heavy, pointed, pearl-embroidered headdress off her head and threw her brocaded, wide-sleeved coat off her shoulders: she wore the old Moscow dress only when driving out. Vasilisa Miasnaya, her lady-in-waiting, caught up the things and put them in the carriage. Natalia, tall, slim, quick in her movements, dressed in a light Dutch frock, started off across the meadow towards a grove. There, in the cool of the shade, she half-closed her eyes, so strong and sweet was the scent of the blossoming lime-trees.

"Ah-oo!" Natalia shouted.

A lazy woman's voice replied from close by, where the sun sparkled blindingly on the water through the branches. A many-hued tent stood by a pond on the sand near a small, plank jetty. In its shade four young women were lying on cushions, oppressed by the heat. They scrambled up at Natalia's approach, languid, with loosened plaits. One of them, older than the others—the small, long-nosed Anisya Tolstaya—was the first to run to her. She threw up her hands and cried, rolling her sharp eyes:

"Our darling Nataliushka, our Tsarevna! Ah, ah, a foreign dress! Ah, ah, you divine creature!"

Two of the others half opened their full lips and stared with a wide-eyed, limpid gaze at the Tsarevna. They were Martha and Anna, Alexander Menshikov's young sisters, both equally buxom and still somewhat awkward, for it was not long since they had been brought, by Peter's order, from their father's house to the Ismaylovsky palace, there to acquire polish and learn reading and writing under the supervision of Anisya Tolstaya. Natalia's Dutch dress consisted of a wide skirt of fine red wool, with three rows of gold braid round the hem, and an unusually tight bodice that left bare her neck, shoulders and arms up to the elbows. Natalia realised herself that she could only be compared to a goddess, to Diana, for instance; her oval, slightly rounded face, with its short, tip-tilted nose—like her brother's—and small ears and mouth, was serene, youthful and haughty.

"The dress was brought yesterday. Sanka—Alexandra Ivanovna Volkova—sent it to me from The Hague. It's pretty and comfortable. Of course it's not for State occasions, but for wearing in a grove, in a meadow, to play."

Natalia kept turning round to let the others have a good look. The fourth young woman stood a little apart, her arms slack and her hands modestly folded in front of her; her roguish mouth, as fresh as a cherry, was smiling and her eyes, too, were like cherries, quick to light up, very feminine. The heat had brought a high colour to her round cheeks and her dark, curly hair was damp. Natalia, as she turned round to the exclamations and applause of the others, glanced at her several times and pouted irritably. She did not know herself yet whether she liked or disliked this Marienburg captive, taken in a soldier's coat from under a cart into Field-Marshal Sheremetev's tent, bargained for by Menshikov and then, one night over a glass of wine by the fire, humbly given by him to Peter Alexeyevich.

Natalia was a virgin, unlike her half-sisters, Katka and Mashka, the sisters of the Regent Sophia—now shut up in a convent—who were the laughing-stock of all Moscow. Natalia was hot-tempered and uncompromising. Many a time she had called them strumpets and cows to their faces and slapped their cheeks in the heat of anger. In her own palace she had done away with the old customs of the women's quarters and the hot, lewd whisperings of female dependants and hangers-on. She had even chided her brother, Peter Alexeyevich, when, after he had sent away the shameless favourite Anna Mons forever, he had at one time become too loose and promiscuous with women. At first Natalia had thought that this woman—a soldier's captive—would, like the others, keep him only for a short while; that he would shake himself free and forget her. But no. Peter had not forgotten that evening at Menshikov's, when the storm was raging outside and Katerina had taken up the candle and lighted him to his bedchamber. Orders had been given to buy a small house in the Arbat for Menshikov's former housekeeper, and Menshikov himself had brought there her bedding, bundles and baskets. Shortly afterwards she had been taken from there to the Izmaylovsky palace and put under Anisya Tolstaya's supervision.

Here Katerina lived without a care, always gay, simple-hearted and blooming, even though there had been a time when she had lain under a soldier's cart. Peter often sent her short, amusing letters —by somebody who happened to be travelling that way—from the river Svir—where he had begun to build the fleet for the Baltic —from the new city of Petersburg, or from Voronezh. He missed her; while she, as she laboriously spelt out his notes, only blossomed out the more. Natalia's curiosity was whetted: what was there in her that had so bewitched him?

"Would you like me to get the same kind of frock made for you when the Tsar cames back?" Natalia asked looking severely at Katerina.

Katerina curtsied in confusion and murmured:

"I'd like it very much. Thank you."

"You make her shy, Natalia, my dear," Anisya Tolstaya whispered. "Don't look at her so fiercely, be kinder to her. I keep telling her in one way or another of your kindness, but she sticks to her notion: 'The Tsarevna is virtuous, I'm a sinner', she says; 'that the Tsar should have come to love me is like a bolt from the blue. I can't get over it'. And these two silly girls here keep pestering her with questions: what happened to her and how? I've strictly forbidden them to think or speak about it. 'Here are Greek gods and Cupids for you', I tell them, 'think and talk about their doings'. But no, their rustic vulgarity is still too strong for them, they prefer to chatter about everything common. From morning till night I keep telling them: 'you were slaves, now you've become goddesses'."

The crickets in the hot, mown grass set up such a chirring that it made one's ears feel dry. Far away, across the pond, the tree-tops of the black pine wood seemed to melt in the heat-haze. Dragon-flies clung to the reeds, water-spiders rested motionless on the pale water. Natalia went into the shade of the tent, threw off her bodice, wound her dark plaits round her head, unfastened and let down her skirt and her fine chemise. Then, exactly as in the Dutch engravings which, together with books, were sent from time to time from the palace Office, unashamed of her nakedness, she walked on to the jetty.

"All of you, come and bathe!" Natalia called, turning to the tent and continuing to tighten her wound plaits.

Martha and Anna lingered coyly over their undressing until Anisya Tolstaya snapped at them: "What are you bobbing about for, you fat creatures? No one's going to steal your charms." Katerina was also embarrassed, noticing the Tsarevna's intent gaze fixed upon her. When Katerina, with curly head slightly bent, stepped gingerly over the mown grass, the heat throwing a golden light on her rounded shoulders and firm thighs, on the whole of her healthy, strong body, it crossed Natalia's mind that it was natural for her brother to long for this woman, up there in the North where he was building his ships; he must visualise her, through the clouds of tobacco smoke, lifting a child to her high bosom in her beautiful arms. Natalia expelled a deep breath and, closing her eyes, threw herself into the chilly water. At this place cold springs rose from the bottom of the pond.

Katerina climbed down sedately from the jetty and, dipping more and more boldly, broke out into happy laughter. At that moment Natalia knew at last that she was prepared to love her. She swam up to her and laid her hands on her tawny shoulders.

"You're beautiful, Katerina. I'm glad my brother loves you."

"Thank you, Tsarevna."

"You may call me Natasha."

She kissed Katerina's cool, round, damp cheek and looked into her cherry-coloured eyes.

"Be clever, Katerina, and I'll be your friend."

Martha and Anna, dipping first one foot, then the other, were still lingering fearfully on the jetty and giving vent to little squeals. Anisya Tolstaya, losing patience, pushed the two plump girls into the water. All the little spiders fled, all the dragon-flies rose from the reeds and skimmed over the bathing goddesses.

3

In the shade of the tent, with her wet hair twisted up, Natalia was drinking fruit-juice, pear-mead and slightly acid kvass that had just been brought from the cellar. She said, as she put a small piece of sugar cake into her mouth:

"It's a shame to see our ignorance. We are, thank God, no stupider than other nations, our girls are better-built and more beautiful than any others—all the foreigners say so—and they are capable of acquiring learning and polish. Year after year my brother has been doing his best, dragging people by force out of their women's quarters, out of their mustiness. They resist, and it isn't the girls, it's the fathers and mothers. When he was leaving for the war my brother pleaded with me: 'Natasha, please don't give them any peace, those longbeards who cling to ancient customs. Plague them if they won't listen to kindness! Otherwise this swamp will suck us in'. I do my best, but I'm alone. I'm grateful to Tsaritsa Praskovya, she's been helping me lately. Though it's hard for her to break with old habits, she introduced new ways for her daughters: on Sundays, after mass, they entertain visitors in French clothes, they drink coffee, listen to the musical box and talk about worldly matters. Now, this autumn, I'm going to have something in the Kremlin that will really be a novelty."

"And what is this novelty, light of our eyes?" Anisya Tolstaya asked, wiping the syrup off her lips.

"Something quite out of the ordinary. A theatre. Of course it won't be anything like the one at the French court. There, in Versailles, they've got world-famous actors, dancers, artists, musicians. Here I'm alone. It's I who've got to translate the plays from the French into Russian, it's I who've got to make up what they lack, it's I who've got to take all the trouble over the actors."

At the word "theatre" the two Menshikov girls, Anisya Tolstaya and Katerina, who was listening without taking her dark eyes off Natalia, looked at one another and threw up their hands.

"For a start, not to scare people too much, we'll show the *Drama of the Burning Furnace,* with the singing of verses. And for the New Year, when the Tsar comes for the festivities and people come from Petersburg, we'll show *The Morality of the Depraved Rake Don Juan,* or *Swallowed by the Earth.* I'll order everybody to come to the theatre and, if they stay away, I'll send dragoons to fetch the spectators. It's a pity Alexandra Volkova is not in Moscow. She'd have been a great help. Now take her. She comes from an ignorant peasant family, her father used bast for a belt, she herself learnt to read and write only after she was married. Yet now she speaks three languages fluently, she composes verses. At present she is at The Hague, at Andrey Matveyev's embassy. Cavaliers fight duels with swords over her, and some have even got themselves killed. And she plans to go to Paris, to the court of Louis XIV to shine there. Do you see the advantages of learning now?"

At these words Anisya Tolstaya dug her fingers hard into Martha's and Anna's sides.

"You've asked for this! Now when the Tsar comes back, if he happens to introduce to you some gallant cavalier, he'll stay to listen to you covering yourselves with shame."

"Leave them alone, Anisya, it's too hot!" Natalia said. "Well, goodbye. I've still to go to the Foreign Quarter. There have been complaints again about my sisters. I'm afraid it might reach the Tsar's ears. I'm going to give them a proper talking to."

4

The Tsarevnas Ekaterina and Maria had long been moved out of the Kremlin—ever since Sophia had been shut up in the Novodevichy convent—and had been given quarters in the Pokrovka district, to be well out of sight. The palace Office provided for their upkeep and all kinds of luxuries and paid the wages of their musicians, grooms and all other servants, but they were not given any money to handle; firstly, because there was no need for it and, secondly, because it would even have been dangerous in view of their notorious foolishness.

Katka was nearly forty and Mashka a year younger. It was common knowledge in Moscow that the life they led in their house in the Pokrovka was unseemly and dissolute. They got up late and spent half the day sitting unkempt by the windows, yawning their heads off. Then, as soon as it was dark, musicians with pipes and stringed instruments would come into their room. The Tsarevnas, dressed up, with cheeks painted as red as apples and eyebrows thickened with soot, listened to the singing, drank sweet fruit-liqueurs and danced and skipped till late into the night, so that the old log-house shook. It was said that the Tsarevnas misbehaved themselves with the musicians and bore them children, whom they sent away to the town of Kimry to be brought up.

These musicians were so pampered that, even on weekdays, they went about in crimson silk tunics, tall marten-fur caps and morocco-leather boots; they constantly extorted money from the Tsarevnas and spent it on drink at the tavern near the Pokrovsky gate. To find the money, the Tsarevnas sent a Kimry woman, Domna Vahrameyeva, who lived in their house in a closet under the stairs, to the Rag Market where she sold their old clothes. But this money did not suffice them and Tsarevna Ekaterina kept hoping to find hidden treasure; for this purpose she ordered Domna to have dreams about hidden treasure. Domna had such dreams and the Tsarevna lived in hopes of having money some day.

Natalia had been intending for a long time to give her sisters a good talking to, but she could never find the time: either there was a deluge of rain and a thunderstorm, or something else would put her off. The day before, she had been informed about some new misbehaviour on their part: they had started to make frequent visits to the Foreign Quarter. They had driven in an open carriage to the house of the Dutch envoy; while he, much surprised, was donning his wig, coat and sword, Katka and Mashka sat in his parlour, whispering and laughing. When he began to bow to them in the manner proper before persons of high rank, they had not known how to respond and had only lifted their behinds off their chairs and flopped down again. Then they immediately enquired: "Where does the German confectioner who sells sugar and sweets live?" This, they said, had been the reason for their visit to him.

The Dutch envoy courteously accompanied the Tsarevnas to the confectioner's shop. Once there, they started picking up all sorts of things and finally chose nine roubles' worth of sugar, sweets, patties, marzipan apples and eggs. Maria said:

"Take this quickly to our carriage."

"I won't until I'm paid," the woman replied.

The Tsarevnas consulted each other in angry whispers and then said to her:

"Wrap it all up and seal the parcel. We'll send for it later."

From the confectioner's they drove on, having lost all shame, to the former favourite, Anna Mons, who still lived in the house that had been built for her by Tsar Peter. They were not admitted at once, but had to knock for a long time while the watchdogs howled. The former favourite received them lying in bed: she had probably purposely undressed and got into bed. They said to her:

"We wish you health for many years to come, dear Anna Ivanovna. We know you lend money at interest. Give us, say, one hundred roubles, though we would really like two hundred."

The Mons woman replied very harshly:

"I won't give the money without surety."

Ekaterina actually burst into tears:

"What bad luck! We have no surety. We hoped to get the money for the asking."

And the Tsarevnas left the favourite's house.

By now they were beginning to feel hungry, so they ordered the driver to stop at a house where, through the open windows, they could see guests merrymaking. It was a christening party given by the wife of Sergeant Danila Yudin—absent at the war in Livonia—who had given birth to twins. The Tsarevnas went into the house and invited themselves to the table, and were received with honours.

Some three hours later, as they were driving away from the Yudins' house, an English merchant, William Peel, recognised them in their carriage. They stopped and asked him whether he would not like to give them dinner. William Peel threw his hat into the air and said gaily: "With the greatest of pleasure!" The Tsarevnas drove to his house where they ate and drank English spirits and beer. And an hour before nightfall, having left Peel, they began to drive about the Foreign Quarter looking into lighted windows. Ekaterina wanted them to invite themselves to yet some other house for supper, but Maria dissuaded her. In this way they amused themselves till dark.

5

Natalia's coach was driving post-haste through the Foreign Quarter, past small wooden houses skilfully painted to look like brick, past long warehouses with iron-bound gates, past amusingly clipped little trees in front gardens. Everywhere painted signs hung at right angles to the street and the doors of the shops stood wide open, hung with all kinds of wares. Natalia sat with pursed lips, without looking at anyone, like a doll in her pointed headdress and her coat thrown over her shoulders. Fat men in braces and knitted caps bowed to her; sedate women in straw hats pointed out her carriage to their children; a dandy in a coat with wide skirts would jump off the road, shielding himself from the dust with his hat. Natalia nearly wept with shame, realising only too well that Katka and Mashka must have made the whole Foreign Quarter laugh at their expense and that all the women—Dutch, Swiss, English and German—must be telling each other what barbarians and hungry spongers Peter's sisters were.

She caught sight of her sisters' open carriage in a crooked lane by the striped red and yellow gates of the house of Kaiserling, the Prussian envoy. It was said of him that he wanted to marry Anna Mons but kept hesitating for fear of the Tsar. Natalia rapped with her rings on the glass front of the carriage. The coachman turned his pitch-black beard and yelled in a stentorian voice: "Whoa, my pigeons!" The greys came to a halt with heaving flanks. Natalia turned to her attendant:

"Go, Vasilisa Miasnaya, and tell the German envoy that I must urgently see Ekaterina Alexeyevna and Maria Alexeyevna. And don't let them swallow a single mouthful, but bring them away by force if need be!"

Vasilisa climbed out of the coach, groaning softly. Natalia leant back and waited, cracking her finger-joints. Within a short while the envoy Kaiserling came running down the steps of the porch. He was short and thin, with eyelashes like a calf's. Pressing his hastily snatched-up hat and cane to his chest, he bowed at every step, turning out his legs in red hose. Beseechingly he raised his sharp little nose and implored the Tsarevna to do him the honour of stepping into his house and partaking of some cool beer.

"I haven't got the time," Natalia replied curtly. "And I wouldn't drink beer in your house. You're doing shameful things, my good man." Without letting him put in a word she continued: "Go, go, and send the Tsarevnas to me without delay."

Ekaterina Alexeyevna and Maria Alexeyevna at last came out of the house, as clumsy as haystacks in their wide gowns with looped and ruffled skirts. Their round, rouged faces looked stupid and frightened; instead of their own hair they were wearing jet-black wigs twisted and piled up high and decorated with strings of beads. Natalia positively growled through her clenched teeth. The Tsarevnas blinked at the sun, their eyes buried in fat, while behind them the lady-in-waiting Miasnaya hissed: "Don't shame yourselves any more, get into her carriage quickly." Kaiserling opened the carriage door with many bows. The Tsarevnas, forgetting to say goodbye to him, got in and squeezed themselves into the seat facing Natalia. The carriage started off at a gallop across the waste ground towards the Pokrovka, swaying from side to side and raising the dust under its red wheels.

Natalia kept silent all the way, while the Tsarevnas fanned themselves with their handkerchiefs, greatly perplexed. Only when they had all gone upstairs to their room and after she had ordered the door to be shut did Natalia let herself go:

"Are you, shameless creatures, quite bereft of your senses or are you anxious to be shut up in a monastery? Is the sorry reputation you've got in Moscow not enough for you? Now you've started to cover yourselves with shame in the eyes of the whole world! Who gave you the idea of calling upon foreign envoys? Take a look at yourselves in the mirror: your cheeks are bursting with fat, yet you're greedy for Dutch and German dainties! What put it into your heads to go begging for two hundred roubles from that nasty trollop, Anna Mons? She's well pleased to have turned you out, you spongers! Kaiserling is sure to write about it to the Prussian king, and the king will spread it all over Europe! You wanted to swindle that confectioner—you did, don't try to deny it! It's a good thing she was clever enough not to let you have anything without money. Dear God, what will the Tsar say now? What is he to do with you, you fat bitches? Cut off your hair and send you to the Pechora river, to Pustozersk?"

Without taking off her headdress and coat, Natalia paced the room, clenching her hands in her agitation and throwing furious glances at Katka and Mashka. At first they had remained standing, but their legs gave way and they sat down. Their noses reddened, their fat cheeks quivered and swelled with suppressed wails, but they were too frightened to give voice.

"The Tsar is straining to the utmost to pull us out of the abyss," Natalia went on. "He robs himself of sleep and food; with his own hands he saws planks and drives in nails, he risks his life under bullets and cannon-balls—all to make human beings of us. His enemies are only waiting for this, to defame him and bring ruin upon him. And you! Why, his worst enemy would not have thought of the things you have done. I'll never believe it—I'll find out who put it into your heads to go to the Foreign Quarter. You're old, sluggish creatures. . . ."

At this Katka's and Mashka's puffed-out lips dropped open and twisted and they burst into tears.

"Nobody put it into our heads," Katka blubbered. "May we sink through the earth. . . ."

"You're lying!" Natalia shouted at her. "Who told you about the confectioner woman? Who told you that the Mons hussy lent money at interest?"

Maria howled in her turn:

"It's the Kimry woman, Domna Vahrameyeva, who told us about it. She saw this confectioner woman in a dream. We believed her, we wanted some marzipan."

Natalia ran to the door and flung it open. A little old man—a buffoon dressed in woman's clothes—leapt back and with him a crowd of waiting-women, hunchbacks and fools with burrs in their hair. Natalia seized a neat soft woman in a black shawl by the hand.

"Are you the woman from Kimry?"

The woman silently and rapidly bowed low with her whole body.

"Tsarevna," she said, "quite right, I come from Kimry. I am the humble widow Domna Vahrameyeva."

"Was it you who persuaded the Tsarevnas to go to the Foreign Quarter?"

Domna's white face quivered and her long lips twisted.

"I have an evil spell on me, Tsarevna," she said. "When I'm out of my mind I say all kinds of nonsense. The Tsarevnas, my benefactresses, laugh at my silly words and it makes me happy. At night I have the most wonderful dreams. Whether the Tsarevnas believe my dreams or not, I don't know. I've never been to the Foreign Quarter in my life and I've never set eyes on any confectioner." With another low bow to Natalia, Domna stood still, her hands folded on her stomach under her shawl, as though she had been turned to stone; torture by fire would not have moved her.

Natalia threw a sombre glance at her sisters: Katka and Mashka were merely moaning softly, overcome by the heat. The little old buffoon stuck his head through the door. He had no nose, only nostrils, his moustache and beard were tousled, his lips were thrust out in a hideous pout.

"Do you want us to make you laugh?" he asked.

Maria impatiently waved her handkerchief at him. But already a dozen hands were clutching at the door from outside, and women-jesters, misshapen creatures in rags, bareheaded, some dressed in comic sarafans with birch-bark headdresses, pushed the old buffoon forward and tumbled into the room. Nimble and shameless, they began to skip, squeal, to fight among themselves, pulling each other's hair and slapping each other's faces. The old buffoon jumped astride a hunchback, stuck his birch-bark shoes out from behind her patched skirt and cried in a nasal voice: "Here's the foreigner off on his foreign woman to go and drink beer!" In the anteroom the musicians, who had hurried in, broke into a dancing song accompanied by whistling. Domna Vahrameyeva walked away and stood behind the stove, pulling her shawl down to her eyebrows.

Annoyed and angry, Natalia stamped her foot. "Be off with you!" she shouted at the leaping and tumbling rabble. "Be off with you!" But the fools and buffoons only screeched the louder. What could she alone do with this devilish swarm? The whole of Moscow was full of them; in every boyar's house, round every church-porch these dark forces were whirling. She picked up her skirts in disgust, realising that this was the end of her talk with her sisters. But to go away at once would be foolish, for Katka and Mashka would hang out of the windows and laugh their fill as her carriage drove away.

Suddenly, through the noise and hubbub, there came the sound of horses' hoofs and the rattle of wheels in the courtyard. The singers in the anteroom fell silent. The old buffoon bared his teeth and cried: "Disperse!" The fools and jesters scuttled like rats to the door. In an instant all life seemed to have left the house. The wooden staircase creaked under a heavy footfall.

A very stout man, with his cap and silver-mounted staff in his hands, entered the room, panting and blowing. He was dressed in the old Moscow fashion in a long, loose, dark-red coat that reached the ground. His broad, dark-skinned face was shaven, his black moustache was turned up in the Polish way, and his light, moist eyes

629

protruded like a lobster's. He bowed silently to Natalia, touching the floor with his cap; then he turned with an effort in the same way to the Tsarevnas Ekaterina and Maria, who were quite breathless with fear. This done, he sat down on a bench, laying his staff and cap beside him.

"Oof!" he said. "Well, here I am." He drew a large, coloured handkerchief out of the bosom of his coat and wiped his face, neck and the damp hair combed down over his forehead. This was the most feared man in Moscow: Prince Fedor Yurievich Romodanovsky.

"We've been hearing, we've been hearing about the mischievous doings that have been going on here. Ay-ay-ay!" The prince thrust the handkerchief back into his coat and rolled his eyes at the Tsarevnas Ekaterina and Maria. "You had a sudden longing for marzipan? Well, well, well! You know, foolishness is worse than dishonesty. It's made a lot of noise." He turned his broad face towards Natalia. "They were sent to the Foreign Quarter to get some money, that's what it was, and that means someone needs money. Don't be angry with me, but I'll have to set a guard on your sisters' house. They've got a woman from Kimry living in a closet here. She secretly takes food in a pot to the waste plot beyond the garden, into an abandoned bath-house. A fugitive, the unfrocked priest Grishka, is living in that bath-house." At these words Ekaterina and Maria went pale and clapped their hands to their cheeks. "This ex-priest Grishka is supposed to be distilling love-potions there and drugs to prevent conception and bring on miscarriages. Very well. But we know that besides all this the ex-priest Grishka writes criminal anonymous letters and by night visits the houses of some of the envoys in the Foreign Quarter. He also visits a lay-sister who frequents the Novodevichy convent and washes the floors there. And she washes the floor in the cell of the former Regent Sophia Alexeyevna." The Prince spoke slowly, in a low voice, and everybody in the room held their breath. "So I shall remain here for a short spell, my dear Natalia Alexeyevna. As for you, you'd better not soil your hands by mixing in these affairs. Go home in the cool of the evening."

chapter two

The three Brovkin brothers—Alexey, Yakov and Gavrila—were sitting at the table. It was a rare occasion, as times were, to be able to meet like this and have a heart-to-heart talk over a cup of wine. Nowadays there was nothing but hurry, there was no time for anything. You were here today and tomorrow you were driving posthaste in a sledge, buried in the hay under a sheepskin, on your way to some place a thousand miles away. It seemed that there were too few people, not nearly enough people.

Yakov had come from Voronezh, Gavrila from Moscow. They both had orders to build warehouses on the left bank of the Neva, above the mouth of the Fontanka, and jetties by the water, and booms on the water, and to reinforce the whole bank with piles in expectation of the first ships of the Baltic fleet, which was being built with all haste near the Lodeynoye Pole on the river Svir. The year before, Alexander Menshikov had visited the place and given orders to fell mast-timber; during Easter week he had laid the foundations of the first shipyard there. Famous carpenters from the Olonetsk district and smiths from Ustuzhina Zheleznopolskaya had been brought there. Young master-navigators, who had acquired their knowledge in Amsterdam, old craftsmen from Voronezh and Archangel and famous craftsmen from Holland and England were building on the Svir twenty-gun frigates, snows, galliots, brigantines, sloops, galleys and smacks. Peter had hurried to join them while the roads were still open to sledges, and now he was expected here, in Petersburg.

Alexey, coatless, in a shirt of Dutch linen—a fresh one, this being Sunday—had tucked up his lace ruffles and, armed with a knife, was cutting up salt beef on a board. The brothers had before them an earthenware bowl with hot cabbage soup, a flagon of vodka, three small pewter mugs and in front of each lay a slice of stale rye-bread.

"In Moscow, cabbage soup with salt beef is common enough," Alexey was saying to his brothers. His ruddy cheeks were clean-shaven, his light moustache was curled up and his hair cropped; his wig was hanging on a peg on the wall. "Here we break our fast with salt beef only on feast days. As for sour cabbage, Menshikov has got some in his cellar, Bruce has some and so have I—and that's all. And we only have it because we thought of it in the summer and planted cabbages in the garden. We're living hard, very hard. And everything is both expensive and scarce."

Alexey swept the sliced salt beef off the board into the cabbage soup and filled the mugs. The brothers bowed to each other, sighed, drank and began sedately to eat their soup.

"People are afraid to come here. There are practically no women, we might be living in a hermitage, upon my word. It's not so bad in winter—the blizzards are terrible, it's dark, and besides, last winter there was plenty to do. But when, like today, there's a spring breeze blowing, all sorts of unreasonable things come into your head. And here, you know, you're held very strictly to your responsibilities."

"Yes, it's pretty grim country you've got here," Yakov said crunching a piece of gristle.

In contrast with his brothers, Yakov was very ill-groomed. His brown coat was covered with stains, buttons were missing, his black necktie was greasy round his hairy neck and he reeked of *kanuper* tobacco. He wore no wig and his shoulder-long hair was unkempt.

"Now that's where you're wrong, brother," Alexey replied. "The countryside round here is actually very gay—farther down along the coast, in the direction of the Duderhof farm. The grass grows waist-high, the birches in the woods are so tall you've got to put your head back to see their tops, and rye and all kinds of vegetables grow there, and berries too. Round the estuary of the Neva itself, of course, it's all marshy and wild. But for some reason the Tsar has set his heart on building the town just here. From the military point of view, it's a suitable place. The one trouble is that the Swedes won't leave us in peace. Last year they pressed us so hard from the Sestra river, and with their fleet from the sea, that our hearts were in our boots. But we drove them off. Now they won't dare attack us from the sea. In January we sank barges with stones under the ice near Kotlin island, and all the winter we carted and piled up stones. Before the ice on the river breaks, a circular bastion with fifty guns will be ready. Peter Alexeyevich sent plans for it from Voronezh and a model he had made himself, and he gave orders to name the bastion Kronshlot."

"I know all about it," Yakov said. "We had an argument with Peter Alexeyevich over this model. I told him the bastion was too low; in rough weather the waves would swamp the guns. I said it should be raised by another three and a half feet. So he gave me a taste of his stick. In the morning he sent for me. 'You're right, Yakov,' he said, 'and I'm wrong'. And he offered me a glass of vodka and a cake. We made it up. He gave me this pipe."

From his pocket, filled with all kinds of odds and ends, Yakov fished out a small, charred pipe with a cherrywood stem and well-chewed mouthpiece. He filled it and, pulling hard, struck a spark on the tinder. Gavrila, the youngest—taller than his brothers and of sturdier build, with fresh cheeks, a small, dark moustache and large eyes, in looks very much like his sister Sanka—suddenly shook his spoon filled with cabbage soup and said, irrelevantly:

"Alioshka, I've caught a cockroach!"

"What do you mean, you silly fellow, it's a bit of charcoal." And Alexey picked the little black piece out of his spoon and threw it on the table. Gavrila threw back his head and laughed, showing all his sugar-white teeth.

"Just like our late mama," he said. "Father would throw down his spoon. 'It's disgusting!' he'd say, 'here's a cockroach'. And mama would reply: 'My dear man, it's a bit of charcoal!' Funny, but sad too. You, Alioshka, were older, but Yakov remembers how we lived all the winter on the stove without trousers. Sanka used to tell us frightening stories. Yes, that's how it was. . . ."

The brothers laid down their spoons, put their elbows on the table and were lost in thought, as if each of them had felt the touch of a distant sorrow. Alexey refilled the mugs and the leisurely conversation was resumed. Alexey began to complain: he was in charge of the works in the fortress where they were sawing planks for the cathedral of SS. Peter and Paul, there were not enough saws and axes, it was getting more difficult all the time to find bread, millet and salt for the workers; horses, that were used during the winter to draw sledges with stone and timber from the Finnish coast, were dying for lack of fodder. Now, when sledges could no longer run, carts were needed, but there were no wheels.

Having once more refilled their mugs the brothers passed on to a review of European politics. They expressed both surprise and disapproval. One would have thought that these enlightened States could work and carry on honest trade. But no. The French king was fighting on land and sea against the English, the Dutch and the Austrian emperor, and there was no end to this war in sight; the Turks were squabbling with Venice and Spain over the Mediterranean, and they all kept burning each other's fleets; only Frederick, the king of Prussia, was keeping quiet for the time being, on the look-out for something he could grab without too much trouble; Saxony, Schleswig and Poland with Lithuania were ablaze from end to end with war and feuds. Two months ago, King Charles had ordered the Poles to elect a new king, and now Poland had two: August of Saxony and Stanislaw Lesczinski. The Polish nobles were divided; some stood for August, others for Lesczinski. In their frenzy, they staged sword-fights in the local Diets and, mustering their adherents from among the small gentry, burnt down each other's villages and estates. In the meantime, King Charles roamed Poland with his troops, living on the population and plundering, ruining the towns and threatening that, once he had brought the whole of Poland to heel, he would turn on Tsar Peter, burn down Moscow and lay the Russian State to waste. After that he would proclaim himself a new Alexander of Macedon. You could say the whole world had gone mad.

Outside the window, with its four small panes, cut deep in the plastered wall, a large icicle fell suddenly with a ringing noise. The brothers turned and saw the fathomless, deep blue, moist sky—such as can only be seen here, on the sea-coast—and heard the rapid patter of the melting snow as it dripped from the roof and the fluttering of sparrows in a bare bush. They began to talk of everyday matters.

"Here are we three brothers," Alexey said thoughtfully, "three wretched bachelors. My orderly washes my shirts and sews on a button when needed, but it's not the same thing. It's not a woman's hand. Besides, that isn't what matters, the shirts can go hang. What I would like is for her to be waiting for me at the window, looking down the street. When you come home tired, chilled to the bone, you throw yourself on your bed with your nose in the pillow, alone in the world like a homeless dog. But where to find her?"

"That's just it—where?" Yakov said, putting his elbows on the table and sending three puffs of smoke out of his pipe, one after the other. "I, my dear chap, am out of the running. I wouldn't marry some illiterate fool, I'd have nothing to talk to her about. And a white-handed lady, whom you dance with at an assembly and to whom you pay compliments on the orders of Peter Alexeyevich, wouldn't want to marry me. So I manage anyhow when the need presses. It's all wrong, of course, it's unclean. But mathematics means more to me than all the women in the world."

"The one doesn't exclude the other," Alexey said to him softly.

"It does, in my view. Now take that sparrow in the bush: he has nothing better to do than jump over his mate. But God has created man so that he should think." Yakov glanced at his youngest brother and pulled on his pipe until it wheezed. "Maybe our Gavrila is talented in this respect?"

Gavrila's face flushed down to the neck. He smiled slowly, his eyes became moist and, in his embarrassment, he did not know where to look.

Yakov nudged him with his elbow.

"Come on, tell us! I like such conversations."

"Go away with you! There's nothing to tell. I'm still too young."

But first Yakov and then Alexey would not leave him alone.

"It's all in the family, you booby, there's no need to be shy."

Gavrila resisted for a long time, then he began to sigh and at last told his brothers the story.

Just before Christmas, towards evening, a messenger from the palace came to Ivan Brovkin's house and said that "Gavrila Ivanovich Brovkin was ordered to present himself immediately at the palace." Gavrila was at first against obeying. Although he was young, he was somebody, in favour with the Tsar and, besides, he was busy inking-in the completed plan of a double-decked ship for the Voronezh shipyard which he wanted to show to his pupils in the navigation school in the Suharev tower, where, on the Tsar's orders, he was teaching young nobles the art of shipbuilding. Ivan Artemyich said sternly to his son: "Put on a French coat, Gavrushka, and go where you are ordered. One doesn't make light of such matters."

Gavrila put on a white silk coat, tied a scarf round his waist, ruffled the lace under his chin and scented his wig with musk. Then, throwing on a cloak that reached to his spurs, he set off for the Kremlin in a sledge drawn by a team of three horses that were the envy of all Moscow.

The messenger led him along narrow staircases and dark passages into the traditional women's quarters that had survived the fire. There all the rooms were low, with vaulted ceilings, painted with a design of plants and flowers on grounds of gold, red and green; there was a smell of wax and stale incense; it was hot from the tiled stoves and, on each stove-bench, a lazy Persian cat lay dozing; jugs and pitchers, out of which Ivan the Terrible had perhaps drunk in his day, glistened behind the mica doors of cupboards; now they were no longer in use. Gavrila made his spurs ring on the carved stone flags in complete contempt for these remnants of the past. At the last door he stooped, took a step forward and was suddenly overwhelmed by beauty as by a wave of scorching heat.

Under the dull gold vault stood a table supported by griffins. On it candles were burning and, in front of them, with her elbows on scattered sheets of paper, a young woman was sitting with a short fur coat thrown over her bare shoulders. The soft light lit up the delicate oval of her face. She was writing. Suddenly she threw down her swan's feather quill, put her hand, covered with rings, to her fair head straightening the thick plait wound round it, and raised her velvet eyes to Gavrila. This was Tsarevna Natalia.

Gavrila did not prostrate himself at her feet, as would have been proper according to the barbaric custom, but, following the rules of French etiquette, he stamped his stretched-out left foot and flourished his hat very low, the curls of his black wig falling over his face. The Tsarevna smiled at him with the corners of her small mouth; she got up from the table, raised the sides of her wide pearl-coloured skirt and made a low curtsey.

"Are you Gavrila, son of Ivan Artemyich?" the Tsarevna asked, looking up at him with eyes that sparkled in the candlelight, for he was so tall that his wig nearly touched the vault of the ceiling. "Welcome! Sit down. Your sister, Alexandra Ivanovna, has written to me from The Hague saying you could be very useful to me in my enterprises. Have you been to Paris? Did you see the theatres in Paris?"

Gavrila had to tell her how the year before last, in company with two navigators, he had gone from The Hague to Paris at carnival time and what wonders—theatres and street carnivals—he had seen there. Natalia Alexeyevna wanted to know every detail and stamped her heel impatiently when he floundered, not knowing how to explain properly. In her delight she moved close to him, looking with wide pupils and even half opening her lips in her amazement at the French customs.

"There," she said, "people don't stay like recluses in their houses, they know how to be gay and bring gaiety to others. They dance in the street and enjoy listening to comedies. We must introduce the same sort of thing here. They tell me you are an engineer. I'm going to get you to alter a room; I've got my eye on it for a theatre. Take a candle and come with me."

Gavrila picked up a heavy candlestick with a lighted candle. Natalia Alexeyevna preceded him, walking with a light step and a rustle of skirts. They passed through vaulted chambers where the Persian cats on the hot stove-benches woke up, arched their backs and lay down again basking in the warmth; where—here and there— the stern faces of Moscow Tsars looked down from the vaults in stern disapproval of Tsarevna Natalia who was drawing herself and this youth—in a wig horned like a devil's—and all the treasured ancient customs of Moscow into the bottomless pit.

On a steep, narrow staircase that led down into the dark, Natalia Alexeyevna felt nervous and slipped her naked arm under Gavrila's elbow. He sensed the warmth of her shoulder, the scent of her hair and of the fur of her coat. She stretched a square-toed little shoe of morocco-leather from under the hem of her skirt, bending forward into the darkness and stepping down with increasing caution. A quick, inner tremor began to shake Gavrila and his voice grew hoarse. When they reached the bottom of the stairs she looked quickly and intently into his eyes.

"Open this door," she said pointing to a low door covered with moth-eaten cloth. Natalia Alexeyevna stepped first over the high threshold into complete darkness and a smell of mice and dust. Raising the candlestick high Gavrila saw a large vaulted hall with four squat pillars. In times gone by this had been a dining-hall where the mild Tsar Mihail Fedorovich used to dine with the National Council. The frescoes on the walls were peeling and the floorboards creaked. On the far wall bast wigs, paper cloaks and other comedians' tawdry finery hung on nails. In a corner, tin crowns and armour, sceptres, wooden swords and broken chairs lay in a heap: all that remained of the German theatre of Johann Kunst, which had been in the Red Square until recently when it was closed down for its silliness and gross indecency.

"I'm going to have my theatre here," Natalia said. "On this side you'll build a raised platform for the actors with a curtain and lamps, and here benches for the audience. The vaults must be gaily painted —if one's going to have entertainment, things shouldn't be done by halves."

Gavrila accompanied Tsarevna Natalia upstairs again the same way they had come and then she dismissed him, giving him her hand to kiss. He got home after midnight and, without undressing, in his wig and coat, threw himself on his bed. As he stared at the ceiling he still seemed to see in the dim light of a guttering candle the oval face with the velvet, attentive eyes, the small mouth shaping words, the delicate shoulders half covered by the scented fur, and he still heard the rustle of the heavy folds of the pearl-coloured skirts that flew before him into the hot darkness.

The next evening Tsarevna Natalia again sent for him and read to him *The Drama of the Burning Furnace,* a comedy, still unfinished, that she had written about three youths. Gavrila listened to her till a late hour as she recited the well-turned verses, emphasising them with a wave of her swan's feather quill, and he thought to himself was he not perhaps one of those three youths, ready to shout in a frenzy of joy as he stood naked in the furnace?

He threw himself eagerly into the job of altering the old hall, although the clerks of the palace Office immediately began to put obstacles in his way and to procrastinate over the delivery of timber, plaster, nails and other things. Ivan Artemyich said nothing, though he noticed that Gavrila neglected his plans and did not go to the navigation school, that at dinner he did not touch his spoon but stared with vacant eyes into space and, at night, when people slept, burnt a whole candle costing an altyn. Only once did Ivan Artemyich, twiddling his thumbs behind his back and chewing his lips, say to his son: "I'll just say this, Gavrushka: you're getting too close to the fire, be careful!"

During Lent, Tsar Peter made a flying visit to Moscow on his way from Voronezh to the Svir. He ordered Gavrila to accompany his brother Yakov to Petersburg to build the port. This put an end to his connection with the theatre.

At this point Gavrila ended his story. He got up from the table, undid the innumerable small buttons of his Dutch coat, threw it open on his chest and, thrusting his hands into his short trousers, as wide as balloons, began to pace the hut from door to window.

Alexey said:

"And you can't forget her?"

"No. And I don't want to forget a thing like that, even if I were threatened with the block."

Yakov rapped his nails on the table and said:

"It's mama who gave us such ardent hearts. Sanka's just the same. You can do nothing about it: there's no remedy for that disease. Let's fill our glasses once more, brothers, and drink to the memory of our mother, Avdotya Yevdokimovna."

At this moment there came a heavy stamping in the passage as someone knocked the mud off his boots. The door burst open and, wearing a black cloak spattered with mud and a black hat with silver lace, in walked the Lieutenant-Bombardier of the Preobrazhensky regiment, Governor-General of Ingria, Karelia and Esthonia, Governor of Schlüsselburg, Alexander Danilovich Menshikov.

2

"My word, you've filled the place with smoke like a bear's den! Don't get up, don't get up, don't stand on ceremony. Well, how are you?" Alexander Danilovich said with rough geniality. "Shall we go and have a look at the river? What do you say?" He threw off his cloak, pulled off his hat together with his great wig and sat down at the table with a look at the well-gnawed bones and the empty bowl. "Things were dull, so I had dinner early and had an hour's nap. When I woke up there wasn't a soul in the house—neither guests, nor servants. They had abandoned the governor-general. I could have died in my sleep, and no one the wiser." He winked at Alexey. "Lieutenant-Colonel, will you offer me some pepper vodka and find me some cabbage, I've got a bit of a headache. Well, how's your business going, brother shipwrights? You've got to hurry things up. I'll go and have a look tomorrow."

Alexey fetched some cabbage and a flagon from the passage. Alexander Danilovich, sticking out a well-kept little finger adorned with a large diamond ring, carefully poured out some vodka for himself alone and picked up a pinch of cabbage with some ice in it from the plate. Screwing up his eyes, he took a pull at his mug, then opened them and began to crunch the cabbage.

"There's nothing worse than Sundays. I get bored to death on a Sunday. Or is it the spring here that's so unwholesome? The whole of my body aches and I feel a sort of yearning. No women—that's the reason. Fine conquerors we are! This is what fighting has brought us! We've built a town—and there aren't any women. By God! I'll ask Peter Alexeyevich to let me off. I've got no use for the governor-generalship, no use at all. I'd far rather be selling something in a Moscow shop, just enough to keep body and soul together. What girls there are in Moscow! Venuses! Mischievous eyes, hot cheeks, all tender and ready to laugh. Well, let's go to the river, it's rather stuffy in here."

Alexander Danilovich could never sit still for long, he never had enough time, as was the case with all who worked with Tsar Peter. It was difficult to adapt oneself to him: he would say one thing, but have something quite different in mind, and he could be dangerous. He pulled on his wig and hat again, threw his sable-lined cloak over his shoulders and left the hut with the Brovkin brothers. The strong, damp spring wind struck them in the face. All over Thomas's Island as it was called in the old days—now the Petersburg Side—pines rustled so softly and yet so powerfully that it was as if a river were pouring out of the fathomless depths of the blue sky. Rooks cawed as they circled over the bare, scattered birches.

Alexey's wood-and-plaster hut stood at the far end of the Troitsa square, which had been cleared of timber and of all stumps and roots, within a short distance of the recently-built rows of wooden shops. Boards were nailed up criss-cross over the shops, for the traders had not yet arrived. To the left, the earth ramparts and bastions of the fortress could be seen, bare of snow. As yet only one of the bastions—that of Bombardier Peter Alexeyev—had been half dressed with stone. There a white flag with a blue St. Andrew's Cross fluttered at the top of the mast: a sign of the expected fleet.

All over the square water rippled in the wind. Alexander Danilovich splashed along in his great topboots without picking his way, making diagonally towards the Neva. The main square of Petersburg existed only in words and on the plans which Peter Alexeyevich drew in his note-book. The only buildings were a little moss-caulked log church—the Troitsa cathedral—and not far from it, closer to the river, the Tsar's hut. This was a two-roomed structure built of neatly trimmed logs, faced on the outside with boards painted to look like brick. A painted wooden mortar, and two bombs made to look as though their fuses were burning, had been set up on the roof-ridge.

On the other side of the square stood a low Dutch house of a very inviting aspect, with smoke constantly curling out of its chimney; pewter pots and plates and hanging sausages could be seen through the dim panes of its window; over the entrance was a painted figure of a terrible-looking navigator with a pirate's beard, a tankard of beer in one hand and a dice-box in the other. The sign that creaked on a pole over the door bore the legend: "Hostelry of the Four Frigates."

When they came out to the river the wind tugged at their cloaks and fluttered their wigs. The ice on the Neva was blue, with large unfrozen patches of water and rough embankments, already well covered with horse dung. Alexander Danilovich broke out in sudden anger:

"Two thousand roubles allotted for all this work! Oh, the inky souls, the stingy mushroom-eaters! I don't give a fig for the clerks, the scribes, all the Offices—in Moscow they grudge every penny and only waste paper. I'm the master here! I've got money, I've got horses, I can get good men, as many as I need, and where I get them is my business. Don't forget, you Brovkins, that you haven't come here to doze. Save time on eating, save time on sleeping—by the end of May all the jetties, booms and warehouses must be ready. And not only on the left bank where you've been ordered to build them. Here, on the Petersburg side, there must be facilities for a large ship to approach and to berth." Menshikov walked quickly along the bank, showing where piles should be driven in and moorings built. "A flagship sails up after a victory at sea, with firing guns and sails pierced by shot—has it got to berth at the mouth of the Fontanka? No, it must berth right here!" And he stamped in a puddle with his topboot. "And if some rich merchant should come in a ship from Holland or England—here's Peter Alexeyevich's house, here's mine —welcome!"

Menshikov's house, or the governor-general's palace, stood some seven hundred feet upstream from the Tsar's hut. It was a hastily constructed building with clay walls and a high Dutch roof visible from far along the river. In the centre of its façade was a portico with a pediment, on the right of whose tympanum was a recumbent wooden gilt figure of Neptune with a trident, and on the left that of a naiad with large breasts, her elbow resting on an upturned pitcher. The initials "A.M.", encircled by a serpent, adorned the centre. The governor-general's personal standard fluttered from a flagstaff on the roof. Two guns stood in front of the portico.

"It's a house one can show to foreigners without feeling ashamed. Aren't those water gods a fine sight? They look just as if they'd come out of the sea to lie down over my porch. And when the fleet from the Svir sails past and we get our cannon smoking. . . . A fine sight, truly a fine sight!"

Menshikov stood admiring his house, screwing up his dark blue eyes. Then he turned and gave a grunt of annoyance as he looked at the distant left bank where the wind swayed a few solitary pines scattered among stumps and bare patches.

"The pity of it! It was a bit spoilt in the hurry." With his cane he pointed out the place where the Fontanka flowed out from the Neva. "What a prospect there was before my windows! A pine wood like a solid wall. One could have built a pleasure house there for the summer. They cut it all down. It's always like that, the devil take it! Well, let's go to my place, we'll find something to eat and have a drink."

"Governor-General," Alexey said. "Look, there seem to be a lot of sledges coming down the Neva. Could it be the Tsar?"

Alexander Danilovich gave one look, cried: "It's he!" and burst into activity. The Brovkin brothers ran off in different directions with orders, while he himself hurried to his house calling to his servants in a loud voice. A few moments later he was again on the riverbank, on the jetty, dressed in his Preobrazhensky uniform with enormous gold-laced red cuffs, a silk scarf across his shoulder and wearing the same sword with which, two years ago, he had boarded the Swedish frigate in the estuary of the Neva.

A long train of sledges was approaching over the swollen ice of the Neva, the sight of which was forbidding enough. Fifty dragoons spurred on their exhausted horses and galloped to the bank in fear of the thawed patches. In their wake a heavy leather-hooded sledge turned and, driving through the water that lay on the ice, stopped at the jetty. No sooner did a long, booted leg stretch out of the depths of the sledge from under the bearskins than the two guns outside the governor-general's house boomed. The boot was followed by two sheepskin sleeves out of which fingers with strong nails freed themselves and gripped the leather apron of the sledge. A deep voice sounded from inside:

"Danilych, help me. The devil—I can't get out."

Menshikov jumped off the jetty into the water which came up to his knees and began to pull Peter out. At the same moment all the bastions of the Peter and Paul fortress gleamed with flashes of fire, wrapped themselves in smoke and a thundering roar rolled along the Neva. The royal standard was hoisted on the flagstaff by the Tsar's hut.

Peter climbed on to the jetty, stretched himself, straightened up and pushed his fur cap to the back of his head. His first look was for Menshikov, at his face flushed with pleasure, his restless eyebrows. Peter took his cheeks in his hand, squeezed them and said:

"How d'you do, my friend? You didn't deign to come to me, though I was expecting you. So now I've come to you. Pull this sheepskin off me. The road is foul. Downstream from Schlüsselburg we were nearly drowned. I'm all bruised with the jolting and I've got pins and needles in my leg."

Turning his round, unshaven face with its untidy moustache to windward, Peter gazed at the swirling spring clouds, at the swift shadows that glided over the puddles and unfrozen patches of the river, at the fierce sun that blazed through the gaps in the clouds beyond the Vasilyevsky island. His nostrils dilated and dimples appeared at the corners of his small mouth.

"A paradise!" he said. "Truly, Danilych, an earthly paradise. You can smell the sea."

People were running across the square splashing in the puddles. Behind them, with a heavy stamping of feet, came the regular ranks of the Preobrazhensky and Semenovsky regiments, in tight green coats and white gaiters, holding their muskets with fixed bayonets before them.

3

". . . in Warsaw, at Cardinal Radzeyevski's, he said at table: 'I won't let a single nutshell through into the Neva. The Muscovites needn't hope that they will hold the coast. And when I've finished with August, taking Saint-Petersburg will be as easy for me as cracking and spitting out a cherry-stone'."

"What a fool he is, the whore's son!" Menshikov was sitting naked on the bench in the bath-house, soaping his head. "If I were to meet him in the field, I'd show this hero some cherry-stones."

"And he also said that he wouldn't let a single English ship get through to Archangel; 'let the goods of the Moscow merchants rot in the warehouses'."

"But our goods aren't rotting, are they, *mein Herz*?"

"Thirty-two English ships, in a convoy, with four escorting frigates have sailed into Archangel, God helping, without any loss. They have brought iron and steel, and cannon-brass, and kegs of tobacco, and much else that we don't need but, nevertheless, had to buy."

"Well, *mein Herz,* we won't suffer any loss. They, too, must have some compensation for their courageous voyage. D'you want some kvass steam? Nartov!" Menshikov called and went to the low door leading to the passage, his bare feet slapping on the wet, freshly planed floor. "What's happened to you? Dizzy with the fumes, Nartov? Bring a jug of kvass and let us have some steam."

Peter lay on the high shelf close to the ceiling, his bony knees raised, fanning himself with a bath-broom. Nartov, the orderly, had already twice steamed him and poured ice-cold water over him, and now he was pleasurably relaxing. He had gone to the bath-house immediately on arrival, the better to enjoy his supper afterwards. The bath-house, built of lime-tree wood, was very pleasant, and Peter was loth to leave it, although guests had already been languishing for two hours in the governor-general's dining-room, waiting for the Tsar's appearance and for supper.

Nartov opened the copper door of the stove and, jumping aside, flung a dipperful of kvass on to the red-hot stones inside. A strong, soft vapour billowed out, heat enveloped Peter's body and there was a smell of bread. Peter grunted with pleasure, fanning his chest with the leaves of the birch-broom.

"*Mein Herz,* now Gavrila Brovkin tells us that in Paris, for instance, they don't understand anything about steam baths, and especially with kvass, and the people are small in size."

"They understand other things there which it wouldn't hurt us to know," Peter said. "Our merchants are real barbarians. The trouble I had with them in Archangel! For them the main thing is to sell rotten goods—they'll lie, they'll swear, they'll weep for three years until the fresh stuff goes rotten too. There's so much fish in the northern Dvina that if you push an oar into the water it stands up of itself—the shoals of herring are so thick. But you can't go past a store-house, the stench is too awful. I talked to them in the Stewards' Chamber, gently at first, but in the end I had to get angry with them."

Menshikov gave a deprecating sigh.

"Yes, that is so, *mein Herz.* Ignorance. If you were to give these traders a free hand, they'd bring the whole country to ruin. Nartov, bring some cold beer."

Peter lowered his long legs and sat upright on the shelf, bending his head. Perspiration streamed from his curly, dark hair.

"It's good," he said. "Very good. That's how things are, my dear friend. Without Petersburg we'd be like a body without a soul."

4

Here, on the edge of the Russian land, by the conquered sea-gulf, new men were sitting at Menshikov's table: those who, in accordance with Peter's order—"henceforth distinction will be awarded according to usefulness"—had made their way by ability alone, out of the chimneyless huts, and exchanged birch-bark sandals for square-toed buckled shoes of Russian leather; who, instead of bitter thoughts— "Why, dear Lord, do you condemn me to howl with hunger in a cold house?"—had willy-nilly begun to think and speak about important affairs of State, as they were doing now, seated before laden dishes. Here were the Brovkin brothers, Fedosey Shliayev and Gavrila Avdeyevich Menshikov—famous shipwrights who had accompanied Peter from Voronezh to the Svir—the contractor Yermolay Negomorsky, a Novgorod man whose eyes glistened like a cat's at night; Terenty Buda, a specialist in anchors, and Yefrem Tarakanov, a very famous woodcarver and gilder.

But there were not only men of low birth gathered round the table. On Peter's left sat Roman Bruce—a red-haired Scot of royal descent, with a bony face and thin, fiercely compressed lips, a mathematician and a great reader of books, as was also his brother Jacob. The brothers had been born in Moscow, in the Foreign Quarter; they had attached themselves to Peter from his early youth and regarded his cause as their own. There was also the eagle-eyed, languid, haughty colonel of the Guards, Mihail Mihaylovich Golitsin, with a moustache shaved to a narrow line under his thin nose, who had won fame in the storming and capture of Schlüsselburg; like all the others he drank a good deal, growing pale and jingling his spurs under the table. There, too, was the vice-admiral of the Baltic fleet, Cornelius Kreis, a sea-rover, with deep, stern wrinkles on his weatherbeaten face and a watery glance, as strange as the cold depths of the sea. There was also Major-General Chambers, thick-set, with a firm face and a hooked nose, again one of those wanderers who believed in Tsar Peter's lucky star and had devoted to him all they possessed— their swords, their courage and their soldiers' honour. And there was also the mild Gavrila Ivanovich Golovkin, the Tsar's chamberlain, a man of a farseeing and cunning mind, Menshikov's assistant in the building of the city and the fortress.

The guests were all talking noisily at the same time, some purposely raising their voices to be heard by the Tsar. The high-ceilinged room smelt of fresh plaster; sconces backed with copper reflectors, bearing three candles each, shed their light from the white walls; there were also many lighted candles on the brightly-coloured tablecloth stuck into empty flagons and set among the pewter and earthenware dishes piled high with everything the governor-general could offer his guests: ham, tongues, smoked sausages, geese and hares, cabbage, radishes, salted cucumbers—all of which had been brought by the contractor Nemogorsky as a present to Menshikov.

The main arguing and shouting was about the allocation of provisions and fodder: who had got more at whose expense. Provisions were brought from Novgorod, from the main Department of Supply —in summer by boat along the Volhov and lake Ladoga, and, in winter, over the newly-cut road through the great forests—to the stores in Schlüsselburg safely guarded by the mighty fortress walls. There, commissioners, sworn agents from among the best men, were in charge of the store-houses. On demand they delivered to Petersburg goods for the army, quartered in the mud-hut town on the Vyborg side, for the various offices engaged in the building, for the provincial peasant-builders who came here in relays from April to September—diggers, woodcutters, carpenters, stonemasons, roofers. The road from Novgorod was a difficult one, the countryside had been ruined by the war and nothing could be obtained locally. The stores were inadequate, and Bruce, Chambers, Kreis and others of less importance all tried to get the lion's share. Now, at table, they had grown heated and were settling accounts.

Peter was served with a hot dish of noodle-soup. One of the soldiers who had been sent out in all directions had succeeded in finding a cock for this soup in a small village on the banks of the Fontanka, and its owner, a Finnish fisherman, had taken advantage of the chance to get five altyns for the old bird. When he had finished eating, Peter Alexeyevich laid his long arms and large hands on the table; following the bath the veins on his hands were swollen. He spoke little and listened attentively. His prominent eyes were stern and somewhat forbidding, but when he lowered them, while filling his pipe or for some other reason, his round-cheeked face with its short nose and small smiling mouth looked good-humoured. If you came up to him boldly, clinked your goblet against his and said: "Your health, Bombardier!" he, according to who it happened to be, either did not answer, or replied with an upward jerk of his head, shaking his fine, dark, curling hair. "In the name of Bacchus!" he would say in a deep voice and drink, as navigation officers and sailors had taught him to drink in Holland—through his teeth, straight into his throat, not touching the goblet with his lips.

Today Peter Alexeyevich felt pleased for a number of reasons: because Menshikov had put up such a fine house with a Neptune and a naiad to spite the Swedes; because all the people sitting at the table were his own men who argued and got excited over a great enterprise, without giving a thought to how dangerous it was or whether it would succeed; and what particularly gladdened his heart was the fact that here, where far-reaching plans and difficult undertakings were concentrated, everything he had entered in an illegible hand in a fat notebook—carried in his pocket, together with a gnawed pencil-stub, a pipe and a tobacco-pouch—had taken visible shape. The wind fluttered the flag on the bastion of the fortress, piles rose out of the marshy banks, everywhere people went about preoccupied with their work, and a town, a real town, was already in existence, not large perhaps, but with all a town's usual features.

Peter chewed the amber mouthpiece of his pipe and heard, without listening, what the infuriated Bruce was muttering to him about rotten hay, what the drunken Chambers was shouting as he tried to reach him with his goblet. This was the long-desired place, the one on which he had set his heart. It was good, of course, on the Sea of Azov, pale and warm, acquired at the cost of such great labour; it was good on the White Sea, whose cold waves rolled under the overhanging fog; but neither of these could compare with the Baltic, with its broad highway to wonderful cities, to rich countries. Here his heart beat as nowhere else, the wings of his thoughts spread out and his energy was redoubled.

Menshikov kept glancing at Peter, noting how *mein Herz's* nostrils dilated wider and wider and how the smoke rose in ever-thickening clouds from his pipe.

"Enough of that!" he cried suddenly to the guests. "You keep hammering away—oats, millet, oats, millet! The Bombardier hasn't come here to hear about oats and millet." Menshikov winked broadly at a small, stout, softly smiling man in a short flared coat. "Felten, pour out some Rhenish wine, you know the one I mean," and he turned expectantly towards Peter. Menshikov had as usual guessed, he had read in Peter's darkened eyes, that the moment had come when everything that had long been working, revolving, tormenting, combining this way and that in Peter's mind was taking definite shape and becoming an unalterable decision. After that you had better not try to argue with him or oppose his will.

Silence fell on the guests at the table. The only sound was the gurgling of the wine as it flowed out of a paunchy flagon into the goblets. Without taking his hands off the table Peter threw himself back in his gilt chair.

"King Charles is brave, but he isn't clever, only exceedingly conceited," Peter began, pronouncing his words slowly, in the Moscow way. "He missed his chance in seventeen-hundred. If he hadn't, we wouldn't be drinking Rhenish wine where we are now. The defeat at Narva served us well. Beating makes iron stronger and men more mature. We have learnt a great deal, much of which we did not even expect. Our generals, together with Boris Petrovich Sheremetev and Nikita Ivanovich Repnin, have shown the whole world that the Swedes are nothing out of the ordinary and can be beaten both in the open field and on the walls of their fortresses. You, children of my heart, have conquered and established this sacred site. Neptune, who stirs the depths of the ocean, has laid himself to rest on the roof of this magnate's house, awaiting the ships on which we have laboured until our hands were calloused. But is it reasonable, once we have firmly established ourselves in Petersburg, to be beating off the Swedes on the Sestra river and on Kotlin island constantly? To wait until Charles, tired of chasing after his dreams and fancies, turns his armies from Europe upon us? If we do that, even the god Neptune may not save us here. Our heart is here, but the place to meet Charles is in the distant marches, in strong fortresses. We must have the courage to take the offensive ourselves. As soon as the ice breaks we must advance on Kexholm and take it from the Swedes, so that lake Ladoga should once again become our lake, as it was in ancient times, and so that our fleet shall be able to sail for the north without fear. We must go beyond the Narova river and take Narva, this time without a defeat. Preparations for the campaign must start immediately, friends. Delay is like death."

5

Through the tobacco smoke, through the small panes of the window, Peter noticed that the three-quarter moon that had been riding among tatters of mist, had come to rest, suspended. "Stay where you are, Danilych, don't come with me. I'll go out and get a breath of fresh air and then come back."

He left the table and went out on to the porch, under Neptune and the big-bosomed naiad with her golden pitcher. He pushed his pipe into his pocket. A man detached himself from the wall of the house, from behind a pillar, fell on his knees and raised a sheet of paper above his head. He was bareheaded and dressed in a rough peasant's coat and birch-bark shoes.

"What do you want?" Peter Alexeyevich asked. "Who are you? Get up! Don't you know the order?"

"Great Tsar!" the man said in low, penetrating tones. "Andrey Golikov, a poor and humble subject, craves a boon. I am perishing, Sire, be merciful!"

Peter snorted, took the petition brusquely and once again ordered the man to rise.

"Are you evading work? Are you ill? Do you get the issue of vodka infused with pine-cones, as I have ordered?"

"I am well, Sire, I don't evade work, I cart stones and dig, and saw logs; but, Sire, I have in me a wonderful power that is being wasted. I am a painter of the Golikov family—icon-painters of Palekh. I can paint portraits like living human faces, that do not age or die and in which the spirit lives forever. I can paint the waves of the sea and ships on them under sail and wrapped in gun-smoke— very well indeed."

Peter snorted again, but this time less angrily, and said:

"You can paint pictures of ships? And how do I know you aren't lying?"

"I ought to go and fetch it to show you, but it's drawn on a wall, and not with paints, but with charcoal. I have neither paints nor brushes. I dream of them. For paints, even in little pots no larger than thimbles, and for a few brushes, Sire, I would do anything for you—I'd throw myself in the fire!"

Peter snorted for the third time: "Let's go!" and, lifting his face to the moon that shone on the thin ice of the puddles crackling under his boots, started off with his usual impetuosity. Golikov trotted to keep up with him, glancing sideways at the Tsar's extraordinarily long shadow and trying not to tread on it.

They passed the main square and, turning off among some scattered pines, came out on to the bank of the Big Nevka where the low turf-roofed huts of the construction workers stood. At one of these Golikov, quite beside himself with emotion, stopped and, bowing and whispering earnestly, opened the slab door. Peter lowered his head and stepped inside. Some twenty men were sleeping on bunks; their bare feet stuck out from under padded coats and bast matting. A man with a large beard, naked to the waist, was sitting on a low stool by the burning cresset patching his shirt.

He showed no surprise at the sight of Peter; he stuck the needle into the shirt, laid it down, got up and bowed slowly, as in church to an icon.

"Tell me what complaints you've got," Peter said abruptly. "Is the food bad?"

"It is bad, Sire," the man replied simply and clearly.

"Are you badly clothed?"

"Clothing was issued to us in the autumn. It got worn out during the winter, as you see."

"Much illness?"

"Many are sick, Sire. It's an unhealthy place."

"Does the pharmacy treat you?"

"We have indeed heard about the pharmacy."

"You don't trust the pharmacy?"

"How can I say it? We seem to get well on our own."

"Where are you from? With which relay did you come?"

"I'm from the town of Kerensk. I came with the third relay, the autumn one. I'm a townsman. In this hut we're all freely hired men."

"Why have you stayed for the winter?"

"I didn't want to go home for the winter, it would only have been to howl with hunger on the stove. I've stayed on as a hired worker, on government keep—we cart timber. Look what bread they issue to us." The man pulled out from under a coat a piece of black bread, pressed it in his hands and broke it with his stiff fingers. "It's mouldy. How can the pharmacy help?"

Andrey Golikov quietly changed the wood splinter in the cresset and it became lighter in the low, clay-plastered hut, white-washed only here and there. A few heads were lifted from under the bast matting. Peter sat down on a bunk and looked searchingly into the eyes of the bearded man.

"And what do you do at home in Kerensk?"

"I'm a mead vendor. But nowadays few people drink mead. Nobody has any money."

"It's my fault, I've robbed everybody? Is that it?"

The bearded man raised and lowered his bare shoulders and the brass cross on his thin chest rose and fell. He wagged his head with a mirthless smile.

"You want to know the truth?" he asked. "Well, I'm not afraid of telling the truth, I've seen trouble enough. Naturally, in the old days the life of the people was easier. There were no such taxes and levies. But today it's all the time: give money for this, give money for that. Formerly, one paid so much on each house, so much on each plough, mainly by mutual guarantee; one could come to some arrangement, make things easier—it was convenient. Now you have ordered everybody to pay a poll-tax, you have registered every single soul, and standing beside each soul there's a commissioner, a country agent demanding payment. And in the last few years, another thing has been added—sending here, to Petersburg, three relays during the summer: forty thousand men from the provinces. That's not easy. At our place they take a man with an axe, an adze, or a shovel, a cross-cut saw from every tenth house. From the other nine houses they collect the money for his keep: thirteen altyns and half a kopek from each house. This money has got to be found. So what's the use of shouting yourself hoarse in the market-place: 'Here's hot mead for you!'? Some good man would be glad to have a drink, but he's got nothing except a 'thank you' in his pocket. You've taken my sons into the dragoons; at home there's my old woman and four girls—one younger than the other. Of course, Sire, you know best what all this is for."

"That's true, I know best!" Peter said harshly. "Give me that bread." He took the mouldy piece, broke it, smelt it and shoved it into his pocket. "When the ice on the Neva breaks they'll bring new clothing and birch-bark shoes. They'll bring flour and the bread will be baked here." He started for the door, having forgotten all about Golikov; but Golikov made such a desperate movement and looked so imploringly at him that Peter said to him with a smile: "Well, icon-painter, show me what you've got there."

Part of the wall between the bunks had been meticulously smoothed, whitewashed and covered with bast matting. Golikov carefully took down the matting, dragged up the heavy cresset, lit another splinter and holding it up in a hand that trembled announced in a high-pitched voice:

"The mighty, glorious sea-victory in the estuary of the Neva on the fifth day of May in the year seventeen hundred and three: the enemy vessel *Astrel* of fourteen guns and the admiral's sloop *Hedan* of ten guns surrender to Bombardier Peter Alexeyev and Lieutenant Menshikov."

On the whitewashed wall there were skilfully depicted, in fine charcoal, two Swedish ships on curling, foamy waves, among clouds of gun-smoke. They were surrounded by boats out of which Russian soldiers were climbing to board the ships. Above the ships two hands issued from a cloud holding a long pennant bearing the legend which Golikov had pronounced. Peter squatted down. "Well, well!" he said. Everything was correct: the rigging of the ships, the billowing sails, the flags. He could even make out Alexander Menshikov, with sword and pistol, climbing up the storm-ladder, and he recognised himself, somewhat too elaborately dressed, but—true enough—he had stood under the very poop of the enemy ship, on the prow of the boat, shouting and throwing grenades. "Well, well! How do you happen to know about this victory?"

"I was one of the rowers in your boat."

Peter touched the drawing with his finger: quite true, it was charcoal. Golikov moaned softly at his back.

"Why, if that's so, I might send you to study in Holland. You won't take to drink? I know you devils."

Peter returned to the governor-general's and resumed his seat on the gilt chair. The candles had burnt low. The guests were already far gone in their cups. At one end of the table the sailors had put their heads together and were singing a mournful ditty. Only Menshikov was quite clear-headed. He had noticed at once that *mein Herz*'s cheek twitched at the corner of his mouth and was swiftly reviewing in his mind what might have caused it.

"Here, taste this!" Peter suddenly shouted at him, pulling out of his pocket the piece of mouldy bread. "Taste this, Governor-General!"

"*Mein Herz,* this is no fault of mine, it's Golovkin who deals with the bread issue, may this piece choke him! The thief, the shameless rogue!"

"Eat it!" Peter's eyes widened with fury. "You feed the men on filth—eat it yourself, Neptune! You are responsible for everything here! For every human soul. . . ."

Menshikov gave *mein Herz* a languid, repentant glance and began to chew the crust, swallowing with exaggerated difficulty as though tears were choking him.

6

Peter Alexeyevich went to sleep in his own hut because the rooms in the governor-general's house had high ceilings, whereas he liked low ceilings and snug rooms. During his stay in Zaandam in the house of the smith Kleist, he had slept in a cupboard where he could not even stretch out his legs, and yet he had liked it.

Nartov, the orderly, had heated the stove well and on the table before the long, low window—through which one had to stoop to look—he had laid out books and notebooks, paper and everything necessary for writing, also sets of drawing, medical and carpentering instruments in thick leather bags, telescopes, compasses, tobacco and pipes. The walls of the room were hung with ships' canvas. A brass lantern, half a man's height, brought for the beacon-mast of the Peter and Paul fortress, stood in one corner. Several anchors for yawls and ice-boats lay about along with tarred ropes and pulleys.

After the bath and the good supper Peter, with a coarse linen night-cap pulled over his ears, should have fallen into a pleasant sleep on the wooden bed with coloured linen curtains, held up by four spiralled bedposts. But he did not feel like sleep. Gusts of wind rattled the roof, howled in the chimney and shook the shutters. His dear friend Alexander Menshikov sat on a felt rug on the floor, with a round iron lantern beside him. He was describing the financial difficulties of King August, which Prince Grigory Fedorovich Dolgoruky, ambassador to his court, constantly mentioned in the reports he sent by special messengers.

King August was completely ruined by his mistresses and there was no money to be had. His Saxon subjects had given him all they could; it was said that in Saxony one could not find even a hundred thalers to borrow. At the Diet in Sandomir, the Poles had refused to give him any money at all. August had sold his castle to the king of Prussia for half its value, and once again the devil, or perhaps King Charles himself, had thrown in his path a lady: the most beautiful woman in Europe, the Countess Aurora Königsmark, and he had spent the money received for the castle on fireworks and balls in her honour. The countess, however, as soon as she had realised that his pockets were empty, had thanked him politely and left him, taking with her a coachful of velvets, silks and silver plate. As for him, he had no money left even for food. He came to Prince Dolgoruky's house, woke him up and wept:

"My Saxon troops," he said, "have been living on dry crusts for over a week, and my Polish troops, having received no pay, have started to loot. The Poles have quite lost their senses; no one can remember such drinking and such feuds as go on in Poland today; the nobles with their followers storm each others' castles and towns, burn down villages and commit worse outrages than the Tatars. The Polish State is the least of their concerns. Oh, unfortunate king that I am! Oh, I had better bare my sword and fall upon it!"

After listening to him, Prince Dolgoruky, who was a kind man, shed tears over such misfortunes and gave him ten thousand thalers out of his own pocket and without asking for a receipt. The king immediately returned home where his new mistress, Countess Kozelska, was raging, and started feasting with her.

Menshikov drew up the lantern, produced the letter and, holding it close to the holes through which the light streamed, read haltingly, for he was still not very good at his letters:

"Here, *mein Herz,* is, for instance, what Prince Grigory Fedorovich writes to us from Sandomir: 'The Polish army fights well in taverns over a mug of beer, but it is difficult to lead it into the field against an enemy. King August's Saxon army is good, but it has no heart for fighting the Swedes. Half Poland has been utterly devastated by the Swedes who have not even spared the churches or the tombs. But the Polish nobles see nothing, each thinks only of himself. I cannot understand how such a State can still exist. It will be of no help to us, unless it be by diverting the enemy'."

"Nor do I rely on any great help," Peter Alexeyevich said. "As for Dolgoruky, I have already written to him that it's up to him to recover his ten thousand thalers from the king; I am not responsible for them. One could build a frigate for that sum." He yawned with a click of his teeth. "Eve's daughters! What don't they do to us! There was one who used to come to me from a tavern in Amsterdam —a liar and a hussy, but not bad. She also cost me a pretty penny."

"*Mein Herz,* how can you compare yourself in this respect with King August? Aurora Königsmark alone cost him half a million. What you gave the tavern wench—I remember it quite well—was either three or five hundred roubles, that's all."

"Five hundred roubles—as much as that? Ay-ay-ay. I deserved a good beating. August is no example for us; we belong to the State, we have no money of our own. Be careful, Alexander, with your 'that's all'—don't hold treasury money so cheap." Peter was silent for a while. "You've got a fellow here carting timber. He has a God-given talent."

"Do you mean Andrushka Golikov?"

"He's being wasted here, it's not the work he's fitted for. He must be sent to Moscow. Let him paint the portrait of a certain person." Peter glanced at Alexander out of the corner of his eye—he was not sure, but the fellow seemed to be grinning. "Take care! I'll get up and give you a taste of my cudgel, that'll teach you to grin. I miss Katerina, that's all. When I close my eyes I see her as if she was there; when I open my eyes, my nostrils feel her—I forgive her everything, all her men, you included—Eve's daughter—that's all one can say about it."

Peter suddenly fell silent and turned to the long window, grey with the dawn. Alexander rose lightly from his felt rug. Outside, a new sound was coming through the noise of the wind—the heavy crash of bursting, breaking, massing ice.

"The ice on the Neva is breaking, *mein Herz!*"

"Really? Then it's no more sleep for us!"

chapter three

The Kexholm campaign was interrupted at the very beginning. The infantry regiments and military baggage-trains that had started in advance were still less than half way to Schlüsselburg, the cavalry had only just crossed the small Ohta river, the heavy rowing barges with the men of the Preobrazhensky and Semenovsky regiments had not even got as far as three miles up the Neva, when a rider burst out of the broken growth of young fir-trees on the bank and desperately waved his hat. Peter Alexeyevich was sailing in a yawl in the wake of the rowing-boat flotilla. Hearing the man shout: "Hi, you boatmen, where's the Tsar? I've got a letter for him!" he shifted the sail and brought the yawl to the bank. The rider jumped off his mount, hurried to the very edge of the water and, touching the crown of his officer's felt hat with two fingers, pushed out his ruddy face with its eager, anxious eyes and said in a hoarse voice:

"From the Lord Equerry Peter Matveyevich Apraxin, Bombardier."

He plucked the letter—stitched through with a thread and sealed with wax—from his soiled red cuff, presented it and stepped back. This was Lieutenant Paul Yaguzhinsky.

Peter cut the thread with his teeth, ran his eyes over the short note, then read it again carefully and frowned. The gaze of his narrowed eyes turned towards the heavily-loaded barges that were advancing with a rhythmical sweep of oars over the sunlit ripples.

"Hand your horse to a sailor and come into the boat," he said to

Yaguzhinsky, and then suddenly shouted at him: "Step into the water, don't you see we are grounded? Push the boat off, then jump in!"

He remained silent all the way to the Petersburg side, to reach which he had to tack against the wind. He skilfully brought the boat alongside the landing-stage. Two sailors hastily hauled down the mainsail, then hurried with a clatter of shoes to the bows where the jammed jib-sail was flapping. Peter glared silently while they furled the sails and put away all the tackle in proper order, according to the rules. Only then did he stride off to his hut. He was joined there immediately by Menshikov, Golovkin, Bruce and Vice-admiral Kreis, all greatly alarmed. Peter opened the window slightly, letting the wind into the stuffy little room, then he sat down and read to them the letter from Peter Apraxin, commander of the garrison in the fortress of Yamburg, which stood some twelve miles to the North of Narva:

"Following your orders, Sire, I marched out of Yamburg in early spring with three infantry regiments and five squadrons of cavalry towards the mouth of the Narova river, and there took up position at the place where the stream Rosson flows into it. Soon after, five Swedish ships sailed up and other pennants could be seen far out to sea. In a slight breeze two warships entered the estuary and began to bombard our baggage-train. Thanks be to God, we replied successfully with our field guns: we smashed one of the Swedish ships with our cannon-balls and drove the enemy out of the estuary of the Narova. For over a week now, since this engagement, the Swedes have remained at anchor in the offing—five warships and eleven transport schooners, which fills me with grave concern. I constantly send out patrols along the whole coast to prevent the Swedes from unloading anything on dry land. And I also send dragoons along the Reval road and up to Narva and destroy the enemy outposts. Prisoners say that they are suffering a shortage of everything in Narva and deplore the fact that on your wise orders we have occupied the mouth of the Narova.

"Our scouts, having stealthily approached the very gates of Narva, captured a messenger in the night from the Governor of Reval to the Commandant of Narva, Horn. He was carrying a letter in code. This special messenger gave his name as Captain of the Guards Stahl von Holstein, of a very noble family and a favourite of King Charles. At first he refused to answer my questions, but after I had shouted at him a little, he told me that in Narva they were expecting Schlippenbach in person soon with a large army, and that the Swedes had already sent a convoy there of thirty-five ships with grain, malt, herrings, smoked fish and salt-meat. The convoy is under the command of Vice-admiral de Proust, a Frenchman, who has lost his left hand and has a silver one fitted in its place. On board his ships he has over two hundred guns and a force of marines.

"I did not know whether to believe Captain Holstein in such an important and formidable matter, but early this morning, Sire, when the darkness over the sea had dispersed, we saw the entire horizon covered with sails and counted over forty pennants. My forces are small, I have very little cavalry and only nine guns, one of which burst the other day during the firing. I expect nothing but disaster. Help me, Sire."

"Well? What do you say?" Peter Alexeyevich asked when he had finished reading.

Bruce pressed his chin fiercely into his black cravat. The weather-beaten face of Cornelius Kreis did not express anything, only his eyes narrowed as though he could see from here the fifty Swedish ships in the bay of Narva. Menshikov, usually quick to find a reply, was now also silent and frowning.

"I ask you, gentlemen of the Military Council, are we to take it that in this cunning game King Charles has won a piece from me: with one clever move towards Narva he has defended Kexholm? Or are we to remain stubborn and lead the Guards to Kexholm, abandoning Narva to Schlippenbach?"

Cornelius Kreis shook his head and, with no regard for his admiral's dignity, took out of his snuffbox a piece of plug tobacco, boiled with Cayenne pepper and rum, and thrust it into his cheek.

"No!" he said.

"No!" Bruce said firmly.

"No!" Menshikov said slapping his knee.

"It won't be hard for us to take Kexholm," Golovkin said in a mild voice, "but during that time King Charles might take a second piece from us, this time the queen."

"Ah!" Peter said.

It was clear, without any words being spoken, that to allow Schlippenbach's corps through to Narva meant giving up the idea of seizing the main fortresses—Narva and Yuriev—without which the approaches to Petersburg remained open. Not even an hour's delay could be afforded. Within a short time messengers were galloping along the Schlüsselburg road and along the Neva to turn the troops and the rowing-boat flotilla back towards Petersburg.

Lieutenant Yaguzhinsky, who had been in the saddle for three days and nights, had only time to coax out of the orderly Nartov a goblet of the Tsar's pepper vodka and a slice of bread with salt, after which he set out for Apraxin's camp again with orders to entrust all his anxieties to God and to stand firm against the Swedish fleet to the last breath. As he was sending off Yaguzhinsky, Peter Alexeyevich took his hand, pulled him towards him and kissed him on the forehead.

"You will tell him by word of mouth," he said, "that in a week's time I shall be at the walls of Narva with all my troops."

2

King Charles was awakened by the lusty crowing of a cock. Opening his eyes in the half-night of the tent, he listened to the cock's persevering efforts. The bird travelled in the baggage-train and at night was set in a cage by the king's tent. Presently a horn sounded a prolonged reveille and the king recalled the misty gorge, the winding of the horns, the barking of the dogs and his impatience to shed the blood of the quarry. Close to the tent a dog yapped; judging by the sound it was a wretched lap-dog of the kind that ladies take with them in their carriages. Someone tried to silence it and the little dog yelped unhappily. The king noted: "Find out where the dog comes from." At the horse-lines nearby, horses began to fight and one of them neighed wildly. The king noted: "It is a pity, but it seems Neptune will have to be gelded." Heavy, measured footsteps passed. The king pricked up his ears to hear the command of the changing of the sentries. Birds flew over the tent with a whistling of wings as they cut the air. He noted: "It will be a fine day." Sounds and voices carried ever more clearly. This cheerful, manly music of a camp awakening was sweeter to him than the strains of violas, harps and clavichords.

The king felt very fit after his short sleep on the camp-bed, under a coat smelling of the dust of the road and of horse's sweat. Ah, yes; it would have been a thousand times more pleasant to be wakened by the cock's crowing with the enemy encamped on the far side of the field and the smell of his campfires drifting across on the damp mist. Then—to jump straight out of bed into his boots and into the saddle. And then, at an easy walking pace, veiling the flashing of his eyes, to ride out to his troops already arrayed in battle order and standing moustached and grim.

The devil take it! After the fatal battle at Kliszow King August, having lost all his guns and banners, did nothing but retreat, retreat for a whole year, dodging like a hare all over limitless Poland. Oh, the coward! Oh, the liar! The intriguer, the traitor, the libertine! He feared an open encounter, he was forcing his opponent to exchange the far-famed glory of his victories at Narva, Riga and Kliszow for a fruitless pursuit of hungry Saxon fusiliers and drunken Polish hussars. He was condemning his enemy to loll in bed all the morning like a courtesan.

King Charles put two fingers in his mouth and whistled. Immediately the flap of his tent was thrown aside and there entered the kammer-junker Baron Björkenheim, who had a little wart on his upturned nose, together with the king's orderly and bodyguard, so tall that his head nearly touched the top of the tent, bringing in the king's polished boots and his dark-green coat, darned in several places where bullets and splinters had torn holes.

King Charles came out of the tent and stretched out his cupped hands into which the orderly began cautiously to pour water from a silver ewer. King Charles had accustomed himself easily to flying cannon-balls but he hated cold water when it ran down his neck and behind his ears. Throwing the towel to the orderly, he combed his cropped hair without a glance into the small mirror which Baron Björkenheim held up for him. He straightened the coat, buttoned to the neck, and looked round at the regular rows of tents on the green field that sloped down to the stream. Behind the tents, the usual bustle was going on at the horse-lines; gunners were polishing the brass barrels of the guns with rags. Charles noted contemptuously: "How much more admirable are mud-splashes on gun-carriages and brass stained with gunpowder smoke!" Down below, on the bank of the stream, soldiers were washing their shirts and hanging them out to dry on the low broom. On the far side, storks, looking like doctors of theology, stalked with dignified steps over the marsh. Still farther out he could see the bare chimneys of a burnt-out village and, beyond it, on a low hill, the twin, peeling towers of a church showing yellow above age-old trees.

King Charles was weary to death of such dull landscapes which he had beheld only too often. Three years spent in marching all over this damned Poland! Three years which could have given him half the world—from the Vistula to the Urals!

"Will Your Majesty please to take breakfast?" Baron Björkenheim said, gesturing gracefully with his well-kept hand towards the open flaps of the tent. Inside, on an empty powder-keg spread with snow-white linen, stood a silver plate with thin slices of bread, a bowl of boiled carrots and another with soldiers' spelt-porridge. That was all. The king entered, sat down and unfolded the napkin on his knees. The Baron took up his position behind his master, never ceasing to wonder at the king's strange fancies: why destroy his health with such poor fare? Perhaps this was necessary for him for future memoirs? The king was ambitious. A gilt goblet—the work of the great Benvenuto Cellini, from King August's collection seized after the battle of Kliszow—held water from the stream smelling of frogs. No doubt about it, world-fame was no easy burden!

"How did a wretched little dog happen to get into the camp? Has someone arrived?" Charles asked chewing a carrot.

"Your Majesty, late last night Countess Kozelska, King August's mistress, arrived in the camp. She hopes you will show her the favour of receiving her."

"Does Count Piper know of her arrival?"

The Baron said yes. Having finished his frugal meal, King Charles manfully drank some water out of the goblet, then crumpled up his napkin and strode out of the tent, pressing on to the back of his head his small three-cornered hat, unadorned by any lace. He asked the whereabouts of the countess's carriage and marched off towards a clump of hazel-bushes, where a gilt Cupid and doves gracing the top of a coach could be seen through the branches glinting in the sunshine.

Countess Kozelska was sleeping in the coach amid cushions and laces. She was a plump, still blooming blonde, with very white skin and fair curls that had worked loose from under her rumpled cap. The yelping of her lap-dog, as it got in the way of the king's boot, woke her up and she opened her large, emerald, Slav eyes—the kind of eyes that Charles despised in men and hated in women. Catching sight of the thin sallow face with a contemptuous, boyish mouth and large, fleshy nose close to the glass of the coach door, the countess let out a scream and covered her face with her hands.

"Why have you come?" the king asked. "Give orders immediately to have your horses harnessed and go back with all speed, in case you are taken for a spy of that dirty libertine, King August. Do you hear me?"

The countess was a Pole and therefore not easy to frighten. Besides, the king had straight away put himself in the wrong by starting with rudeness and threats. The countess took her dimpled hands away from her face—her arms were bare to the elbow—raised herself on her cushions and smiled at him with charming guilelessness.

"*Bonjour, Sire,*" she said gracefully. "Please accept a thousand apologies for frightening you with my screams. It's the fault of Bijou, my little dog. She gives me so much anxiety by getting under people's feet. I let her out of the coach to search for a crust or a chicken-bone. Sire, we are both dying of hunger. All day yesterday we travelled post-haste over a desert, past ruined villages and burnt-down castles; we could not find a morsel of bread, and I offered a gold piece for an egg. The kind Poles who crawled out of dens of some sort only raised their arms to heaven. Sire, I want my breakfast. I want it to make up for all the horrors of the journey, and I appeal to your kindness, to your magnanimity: allow me to have breakfast in your presence."

As she chattered uninterruptedly in a French as exquisite as if she had spent the whole of her life at Versailles, the countess managed to rearrange her hair, paint her lips, powder her face, sprinkle herself with scent and exchange her night-cap for a scarf of Spanish lace. In vain did King Charles try to get in a word, the countess skipped lightly out of the coach and took his arm.

"Oh, my King, all Europe raves about you," she twittered. "No one mentions Prince Eugene of Savoy or the Duke of Marlborough any more; they have been forced to cede their glorious laurels to the King of Sweden. My agitation is pardonable: to see you only for a minute—you, the hero of our dreams—I would unhesitatingly give my life. Accuse me of whatever you please, Sire; I hear your voice at last and I am happy."

The countess caught up the pug-nosed, shaggy little dog that was circling round her feet and gripped the king's arm so firmly that to try to shake her off would have made him ridiculous.

"I eat vegetables and drink only water," he said abruptly. "I doubt whether this will satisfy you after King August's excesses. Come into my tent."

Everyone in the Swedish camp was not a little astonished to see their king drag out of the hazel-bushes a plump beauty, clad in flimsy skirts and laces that fluttered in the morning breeze. The king led her along angrily with his head in the air. Baron Björkenheim, gracefully poised, holding a gold quizzing-glass and wearing an enormous wig, and the loutish, awkward, quietly ironical Count Piper, were standing waiting at the tent.

Charles let the countess precede him into the tent and said through his teeth to Piper:

"It will be a long time before I forgive you for this." Then he turned to Björkenheim: "Find some meat, devil take it, for this person."

The king seated himself on a drum opposite the countess, while she sat on cushions which the baron brought for her. The breakfast served on the powder-keg exceeded all expectations: there was a pâté, goose giblets and cold game, and wine filled Benvenuto Cellini's goblet. The king noted, pursing his lips: "Admirable! Now I know what this rogue Björkenheim feeds on in his tent." The countess did full justice to the meal and threw the bones to her lap-dog, without ceasing to chatter:

"Ah, Jesus, Maria! Why pretend unnecessarily? Sire, you read my thoughts. I came here with a single hope: to save the Polish State. This is my mission, dictated to me by my heart. I want to give back to Poland her lightheartedness, her gaiety, her glorious feasts, her magnificent hunting parties. Poland lies in ruins. Do not frown, Sire; the frivolity of King August is entirely to blame. Oh, how he regrets today that, in an evil hour, he listened to that devil Johann Patkul and became your enemy! Believe me, it isn't August's ill-will that started the war for Livonia, but Patkul alone who deserves to be quartered. Patkul, Patkul alone, created the unnatural alliance between King August and the Danish king and that wild monster, Tsar Peter. But are mistakes irreparable? Is not magnanimity the noblest of all virtues? Oh, Sire, you are a great man, you are magnanimous. . . ."

The countess's Slav eyes became like moist emeralds, though this did not impair her appetite. The thoughts she expressed followed one another so swiftly that King Charles was hard put to it to keep up with them, and no sooner was he prepared to come out with a sharp rejoinder than a new sentence was already demanding a retort. Björkenheim smothered his sighs. Piper smiled shrewdly as he stood in a corner of the tent with his heavy legs set wide apart and his despatch case pressed to his stomach.

"It is peace that King August wants, only peace. He is ready to break the disgraceful treaty with Tsar Peter, for it would be a relief to him. But it is we, women, who are loudest of all in imploring you to make peace. Three years of war and feuds is too much for our brief existence."

"Capitulation, not peace," King Charles said at last, staring at the countess with his almost yellow eyes. "I intend to conduct the talks not here, in Poland—which no longer belongs to King August—but in his capital in Saxony. Have you satisfied your hunger, Madam? Have you no more reproaches to address to me?"

"Sire, I have quite taken leave of my senses," the countess said hastily, licking her pink fingers after having disposed of a perfectly roasted snipe. "I had forgotten the most important part of my mission, the reason why I rushed to you in such haste." She opened a little gold box that hung on her bracelet, took out of it a tiny paper cylinder and unrolled it. "This, Sire, is a despatch received yesterday morning by pigeon-post. Tsar Peter is marching against Narva with large forces. It is my duty to warn you of this dangerous move on the part of the Moscow tyrant."

Count Piper stopped smiling. He moved close to the king and, together, they began to decipher the minute script of the pigeon-post despatch. The countess turned her lovely eyes to Björkenhein, sighed lightly and, raising Benvenuto Cellini's goblet, took a sip of wine.

3

The magnificent King August—who seemed to have been created by nature for sumptuous feasts, for the patronage of the arts, for love affairs with the most beautiful women of Europe, for the vanity of Poland, which wished to have a king in no way inferior to those in Vienna, Madrid or Versailles—was at the moment in a very depressed state of mind. His court had taken up its quarters in the half-ruined castle of the shabby little town of Sokal in the Lvov province, and was suffering from privations. Not even a Sunday market was held in the town, for the Ukrainian population of the neighbouring villages was either hiding in the forests, awaiting the end of the war, or else had gone the devil knew where, most likely to the lands along the Dniepr, from where dark rumours came of a Cossack rising.

To avoid going to bed on an empty stomach, King August was obliged to accept invitations from the local landowners, pay French compliments to provincial ladies and drink execrable wine. Any Polish noble, twirling his great moustache and throwing haughty glances towards the lower, "humble" end of the table, where his dissolute followers rattled their swords and banged their goblets, felt himself more of a king than King August. The Warsaw Diet had dethroned him. It was true that half the Polish provinces had not accepted this but, nevertheless, another Polish king, Stanislaw Lesczinski, now occupied his palace in Warsaw, issued insulting decrees and gave away his—August's—brocade coats and Parisian hose to his servants. The whole eastern part of the country—the lands on the right bank of the Dniepr, from Podolia to Vinnitsa—was aflame with a peasant's revolt, no less bloody than the one in Bogdan Hmelnitsky's time. And, completing the encirclement, somewhere between Lvov and Yaroslav, at no great distance, King Charles was encamped with thirty-five thousand picked troops, cutting August's line of retreat towards his native Saxony.

August lost his self-assurance in his sickening fear of King Charles —that fierce youth in a dusty coat and rusty topboots, with the face of a eunuch and the eyes of a tiger. Charles could neither be bought nor tempted; he desired nothing from life but the thunder and smoke of guns, the clash of crossed blades, the cries of wounded soldiers and the sight of a trampled field, smelling of blood and burning, over which his low-cruppered horse carefully picked its way among the corpses. The only book that King Charles kept under his thin pillow was Cæsar's *Commentaries*. He loved war with all the passion of a mediæval Norseman. He would have preferred to be struck on the head by a twenty-pound cannon-ball than to conclude peace, however advantageous to his kingdom.

That day King August waited for the countess's return. He did not delude himself with the hope that her feminine guile would succeed in persuading Charles to make peace. But the news of Tsar Peter's move received from Lithuania by pigeon-post was so important and so menacing that Charles might well cease to rely on General Schlippenbach's single corps and debate whether to continue the senseless pursuit of August or turn his army to the Baltic provinces. Everybody was urging him to join battle with Tsar Peter: the Austrian emperor, who mortally feared that Charles might form an alliance with the French king and move his troops against Vienna; the French king, afraid of the Viennese diplomats winning Charles over to the cause of the Austrian emperor and suggesting to him a military sortie to the frontiers of France; and the king of Prussia who feared everybody, but most of all the erratic Charles, who could easily invade Brandenburg Prussia, seize Königsberg and wipe him—King Frederick—out of existence.

Later in the day Johann Patkul came to see August. Patkul was in a vile temper, and his ill-fitting Russian general's uniform, green with red cuffs, made him seem fatter than he was. His voice was hoarse, his high forehead, too narrow for his fat and haughty face, was wrinkled in a frown. In atrocious French he complained of the cowardice of Tsar Peter who was avoiding a decisive clash with King Charles.

"The Tsar has two large armies. He ought to invade Poland, and, after joining forces with you, defeat Charles, at no matter what cost," Patkul said, and his mauve cheeks quivered. "This would be a bold and wise move. The Tsar is greedy, like all the Russians. He was allowed to come out on to the Finnish Gulf, where in boyish haste he is building his little town; he received Ingria and two excellent fortresses, Yam and Koporye. He ought to be satisfied and should fulfil his duty towards Europe. But his appetite grows and he wants Narva and Yuriev, he has an eye on Reval. He will want Livonia and Riga next! The Tsar must be kept within limits. But it is useless to speak of this to his ministers. They are rude peasants in wigs of dyed tow. Europe is no more to them than a clean bed to a dirty pig. I may be expressing myself too bluntly and too outspokenly, Your Majesty, but I am suffering. All I want is for my native Livonia to be brought back under the sceptre of Your Royal Majesty. But everywhere—in Vienna, in Berlin and here, in Poland—I meet with complete indifference. I feel at a loss: who is, after all, the greatest enemy of Livonia—King Charles who threatens me personally with quartering, or Tsar Peter, who has shown me such flattering confidence, to the extent of raising me to the rank of lieutenant-general? Yes, I have put on a Russian uniform and shall honestly play my part to the end. But my feelings remain my own. The sorrow in my heart is greatly increased by the torpor and inaction of Your Majesty. Raise your voice, demand troops from the Tsar, insist on a decisive clash with Charles!"

Times were when King August would have simply thrown this impudent fellow out, but today he was silent, turning over his snuffbox in his fingers. At last Patkul went away. The king called the officer on duty—cavalry captain Tarnovski—and told him that he would give one hundred gold pieces (which he did not possess) to whoever was first with the news of Countess Kozelska's return. Candles in a seven-branched candlestick—probably taken from a synagogue—were brought in. The king went up to the mirror and thoughtfully examined his rather drawn face. He never tired of looking at himself, for he could easily imagine how women must love that somewhat sensual mouth chiselled like a classical statue's, that large, aristocratic nose, the gay sparkle of the handsome eyes, windows of the soul. The king raised his wig—yes, there they were —grey hairs! Little lines stretched from the eye to the temple. Damn Charles!

"Allow me to remind Your Majesty," said the cavalry captain who stood at the door, "that Pan Sobeczanski has sent a messenger for the third time to say that he and his wife are waiting for Your Majesty to sit down to supper. Some of the courses are of the kind that will spoil if overdone."

The king took a powder-box out of the pocket of his silk waistcoat strongly scented with musk, passed the swansdown puff over his face, shook the snuff and powder from the lace on his breast and asked casually:

"Are they having anything special for supper?"

"I asked the messenger and he says that since yesterday they've been killing piglets and poultry and stuffing sausages and making stuffing at the Pan's place. Knowing Your Majesty's refined taste the lady of the house has prepared fried leeches with goose blood with her own hands."

"How charming! Give me my sword, I'm going."

Pan Sobeczanski's estate stood not far from the town. A thundercloud hid the fading streak of sunset, and there was a strong smell of road dust and of coming rain as King August approached the mansion in his leather coach that bore many signs of wear and tear due to its master's unhappy experiences. A petty noble who had come galloping along ahead of the king gave warning of his arrival. Torchbearers ran out to meet the coach driving up under the dark branches of the avenue of ancient trees. The coach skirted a flowerbed and, to the howling of watch-dogs, halted in front of a long, one-storied house with a reed-thatched roof. Here too serfs, clad in torn tunics, bare-footed and with wildly tousled hair, ran about with torches. Close to the porch stood a crowd of petty nobles, hangers-on of Pan Sobeczanski—grey-haired veterans of local feuds, whose faces bore terrible sword-scars; big-bellied gluttons, proudly displaying their pomaded moustaches nearly seven inches long and as hard as thorns; youths in shabby second-hand coats, none the less aggressive for that. They all stood with one hand on their hip and the other on the hilt of their sword as a demonstration of their noblemen's freedom. When King August, stooping his big body, got out of the coach, they shouted in chorus a Latin greeting. The elderly Pan Sobeczanski came down the steps of the porch with gestures of welcome: at that moment he was ready, out of lavish Polish hospitality, to present his guest with anything he might wish to have —his hounds, the horses in his stable, all his servants, if he wanted them, his own coat of cornflower-blue cloth edged with fur. Probably the only thing he would not give away was the young Pani Anna Sobeczanska. Pani Anna stood behind her husband, so pretty, so fair, with her little upturned nose and wondering eyes, in a high-crowned Spanish hat with a feather, that all melancholy left King August's heart.

With a low bow he took the tips of Pani Anna's fingers and, slightly raising her hand, as in a figure of the polonaise, led her to the dining-hall. In their wake came the Pan, his eyes moist with pleasure, followed by the chaplain—a barefooted blue-jowled friar, smelling of goats, with a cord tied round his waist—and then the rest of the company, according to rank.

The sight of the table with its tablecloth spread over a layer of hay and strewn with flowers brought cries of admiration from the guests. One tall fellow, in a frogged coat worn over his bare skin, even clapped his hands to his head, swaying and groaning, which aroused general laughter. The dishes of silver, pewter and decorated earthenware were piled high with sausages, roast birds, legs of veal and pork, smoked, boned and pressed fowls, tongues, steeped, pickled and sweet preserves, rolls, doughnuts and flat cakes; there were vodka in Ukrainian bottles of green glass shaped like bears, kegs of Hungarian wine, jugs of beer. Candles were burning and more light came through the windows from the smoking torches held by the house-serfs who watched through the dim panes how gloriously their master was feasting.

King August had hoped that his presence would oblige the host to waive the custom of making the guests drink until not one of them could leave on his own two legs. But Pan Sobeczanski firmly adhered to Polish traditions. He rose as many times as there were guests at the table; smoothing his grey moustache with his hand he named them one by one, beginning with the king and ending with the one seated at the bottom of the table—the same tall fellow who had made them laugh and who turned out to have no boots on his feet—and drank the toast in a goblet of Hungarian wine. The whole company rose to their feet and cried: "Vivat!" Then the host presented a full goblet to the guest who, in return, toasted the host and his lady. When toasts had been drunk to everyone present, Pan Sobeczanski started a new round, proposing toasts first to the Polish State, then to the gracious King of Poland, August—"the only one to whom we will give our swords and our blood." "Vivat! Down with Stanislaw Lesczinski!" the small nobility cried in a frenzy. Then there was an elaborate toast to the inviolate privileges of the nobles. At this point all reason left the heads heated with wine: the guests drew their swords, the table shook, the candles fell. One square-built, one-eyed petty noble shouted: "Thus will our enemies—schismatics and Muscovites—perish!" and with one sweeping blow of his sword, clove in two a great dish of sausages.

On King August's left, on the side of his heart, sat Pani Sobeczanska, flushed like a rose. She managed with great skill to question the king about the entrancing life in Versailles and his amorous adventures there, tinkling with laughter and touching him now and then with her elbow or her shoulder and, at the same time, keeping an eye on her guests, especially those at the "humble" end—where some petty noble, drunk as a lord, was stuffing a smoked tongue or a piece of pressed goose into the pocket of his coarse linen trousers—and, in between, summoning the servants with quick, sharp glances to give them orders.

The king had already made several attempts to clasp the slender waist of his hostess, but every time Pan Sobeczanski offered him a full goblet for some toast: "Into your hands, gracious Sire." August tried to drink only part of the wine or stealthily empty the goblet under the table, but to no avail, for it was immediately replenished by the servant standing behind his chair, or by another who sat with a bottle under the table. At last the famous dish of fried leeches was served to the guest of honour. His hostess filled his plate with her own hands.

"I'm quite ashamed that you should be praising such a rustic dish," she said in innocent tones, though he read something quite different in her eyes. "They are not difficult to prepare. All that is needed is that the goose should be young and not too fat. When the leeches have sucked themselves full of blood, they are put together with the goose into the oven, where they drop off the goose's breast. Then you take them and put them in a frying pan."

"Poor goose!" the king said picking up a leech with two fingers and crunching it between his teeth. "What won't pretty women invent to tickle their palate!"

Pani Anna laughed, and the feather in her high-crowned hat, set on the side of her head, shook alluringly. The king saw that he was making good progress with her and only waited for the dancing to begin to make his declaration without fear of interruption. At this moment, a terrified man in a torn coat, sweating and black with dust, burst into the room, pushing aside the drunken guests in the doorway.

"Pan, Pan, disaster!" he cried throwing himself on his knees before the host's chair. "You sent me to the monastery for a barrel of old mead. I got it all right. But the devil put it into my head to come back along the outskirts of the village, by the main road. I've lost everything—the barrel of mead, my horse, my sword and my cap. I barely saved my soul. I've been completely plundered. An immense army is approaching Sokal!"

King August frowned, Pani Anna dug her fingers into his hand. What army could be entering Sokal now but King Charles's in his unrelenting pursuit? The gentlemen cried wildly: "The Swedes! To arms!" Pan Sobeczanski struck the table with his fist so that the goblets jumped:

"Quiet, gentlemen, if you please! Every one of you who doesn't sober up at once will be stretched out on a carpet and given fifty lashes. Listen to me, you whore's sons. The king is my guest; I will not cover my grey hairs with shame. Let the Swedes come here with their whole army—we won't surrender my guest."

"We won't surrender him!" cried his followers, drawing their swords with a rattle out of their scabbards.

"Saddle the horses! Load your pistols! We'll die, but we won't dishonour the glory of Poland!"

"We won't! Vivat!"

King August realised that the only prudent course would be to jump into the saddle and escape, the night being fortunately dark. But how could he, August the Magnificent, flee like a miserable coward, abandoning a gay supper and a charming woman who still clung to his hand? Charles would not force such humiliation upon him! To the devil with prudence!

"I command you, gentlemen, to return to the table. Let's carry on with the feast," he said, resuming his seat and throwing back the curls of his wig from his hot cheeks. After all, if the Swedes were to come here, these people would hide him somewhere, take him away; no evil befell kings. He poured himself some wine and raised his goblet; his large, shapely hand was steady. Pani Anna looked at him with admiration: one could indeed give a kingdom for such a glance.

"Very good! The king commands us to go on with the feast." Pan Sobeczanski clapped his hands and ordered the nobleman who had hacked the dish of sausages to ride with his fellows to the highway and keep watch there; then he gave orders for the best Hungarian wine to be poured out for everybody, including the "humble" end of the table, until the bottom of the last barrel was dry, to bring everything of the best out of the cellars and storerooms and to call the musicians.

The feast was resumed with renewed enthusiasm. Pani Anna danced with the king. She danced as though she were tempting the apostle Peter himself to open the gates of paradise for her. Her little hat had fallen over one ear, the sounds of the mazurka twined in her curls, her short skirt swirled and clung to her slender legs and her red shoes stamped or flew barely touching the floor. The king too was magnificent as he danced with her: tall, splendid, pale with wine and desire.

"I am losing my head, Pani Anna, I am losing my head! Take pity on me, in the name of all the saints!" he kept saying to her through his teeth, and she replied with a glance which said that it was no case of pity and that the gates of paradise were already open.

Servants' frightened voices and the neighing of horses sounded suddenly in the darkness outside. The music broke off abruptly. No one had time to seize sword or cock pistol. Only the king, before whose eyes everything seemed to be swaying, held Pani Anna close to him and bared his sword.

Two men entered the banqueting hall: one, immense, with only one eye, and a fair drooping moustache under a large nose, wearing a tall sheepskin cap with a gold tassel, and the other, shorter, of noble aspect and a pleasant, mild face, dressed in a dusty uniform with a general's scarf across his shoulder.

"Is His Majesty King August here?" he asked and, catching sight of King August standing with drawn sword in a menacing attitude, took off his hat and made a low bow.

"Gracious Sire," he said, "please accept my report: by order of Tsar Peter Alexeyevich I have arrived to put myself at your disposal with eleven regiments of infantry and five Cossack regiments."

This was the governor of Kiev, commander of the auxiliary army, Dmitry Mihaylovich Golitsin, elder brother of Mihail Golitsin, the hero of Schlüsselburg. The other man, the tall one, in a red caftan and a cloak that reached his heels, was the temporary Cossack Attaman Daniel Apostol. The moustaches of the Polish nobles twitched threateningly at the sight of this Cossack. He stood on the threshold, with one hand laid negligently on his hip, the other playing with his mace; there was a smile on his well-shaped lips, his eyebrows were like arrows and his single eye flashed like the night lit up by the fires of Cossack raids.

King August burst into laughter and, thrusting his sword into its scabbard, he embraced Golitsin and gave the attaman his hand to kiss. The table was spread for the third time. A goblet holding a pint of Hungarian wine was passed round. They drank to Peter, who had kept his promise to send help from the Ukraine, they drank to all the regiments that had arrived and to the destruction of the Swedes. The blustering nobles wished particularly to drink the Attaman Apostol under the table, but he calmly emptied goblet after goblet, merely raising his eyebrows; it was impossible to make him drunk.

At dawn, when quite a few of the gentry had been dragged off into the courtyard and laid out near the well, King August said to Pani Anna:

"I have no treasures to throw at your feet. I am an exile living on charity. But today I am again powerful and rich. Pani Anna, I want you to get into a carriage and follow my army. We must set out immediately, without an hour's delay. I will make a fool of King Charles. Divine Pani Anna, I want to give you Warsaw on a silver plate!" He rose and, with a superb gesture, addressed those who were still sitting at the table with goggling eyes and bristling, pomaded moustaches: "Gentlemen, I suggest that I take you all into my suite and command you to saddle your horses."

No matter how hard Dmitry Golitsin tried, politely and very kindly, to make King August see that the troops needed some three days' rest, that the horses had to be fed and the baggage-trains brought up, there was no holding him. Before the sun had dried the dew he was already back in Sokal, accompanied by Golitsin and the attaman. In all the streets of the town stood waggons, horses and cannon, and weary Russian soldiers slept on the tender grass. Camp-fires smoked. The king looked out of the window of his carriage at the sleeping infantrymen, at the Cossacks picturesquely sprawled out on the waggons.

"What soldiers!" he kept saying. "What soldiers! Heroes!"

At the doors of his castle he was met by Captain Tarnovski who said in a frightened whisper:

"The countess is back. She doesn't want to go to bed. She is extremely angry."

"Oh, what nonsense!" the king said and went gaily into his damp, vaulted bedchamber where the candles were guttering in the discoloured synagogue candlestick. The countess met him standing, looked him silently in the face and only waited for his first words to give him a suitable answer.

"Sophie, at last!" he said more urgently than he intended. "Well? Did you see King Charles?"

"Yes, I saw King Charles, thank you. . . ." Her face seemed to be dusted with flour and looked bloated and ugly. "There's nothing King Charles wants more than to hang you on the first handy aspen, Your Majesty. If you wish to know the details of my conversation with the king, I can give them to you. But at the moment I should like to ask: how would you yourself describe your behaviour? You send me, like the meanest of kitchenmaids, to do your dirty work for you. I suffer insults, on the way I run a thousand risks of being raped, robbed, of having my throat cut. And you, in the meantime, take your pleasure in the arms of Pani Sobeczanska . . . that petty noblewoman whom I wouln't care to have for my maid. . . ."

"What trifles, Sophie!"

This exclamation was unwise on King August's part. The countess came close to him and with the agile movement of a cat's paw, slapped his face.

chapter four

On the hillock where a watch-tower had been erected Peter jumped off his horse and started up the steep ladder leading to the platform. He was followed by Chambers, Menshikov and Anikita Ivanovich Repnin, with Peter Matveyevich Apraxin bringing up the rear—he was greatly hampered by his obesity and dizziness; it was no joke to climb to such a terrible height, some seventy feet above ground level. Peter Alexeyevich, who was accustomed to climbing masts, was not even out of breath; he took a telescope out of his pocket and, setting his feet wide apart, began his survey.

He could see Narva laid out as if on a green dish: all its squat towers, with their gates and drawbridges; the jutting bastions built of square stone at the angles of the walls, the massive bulk of the old citadel with its round gunpowder turret, the winding streets, the pointed spires of the churches raised like spikes into the sky. On the far side of the river rose the eight grim towers, capped with lead, and the high walls breached by cannon-balls, of the fortress of Ivan-gorod, built long ago by Ivan the Terrible.

"The town will be ours!" said Menshikov, who was also looking through a telescope.

"Don't boast too soon," Peter said to him through his teeth.

Below the town, along the river, where Apraxin's earth fort stood on the stream Rosson, baggage-trains and troops were slowly moving, barely discernible through the dust they raised. They crossed a pontoon bridge, and the cavalry and infantry regiments established themselves on the left bank, about three miles from the town. White tents had already gone up, smoke rose in the still air and unsaddled horses wandered in the patches of meadow. There was a sound of axes chopping and the tops of the great old pines trembled as the trees fell.

"We have fenced ourselves in only with waggons and chevaux-de-frise. Won't you give the order to dig ditches and build palisades for greater safety?" Prince Repnin asked. He was a cautious man, wise and experienced in warfare, brave without temerity, but ready—if the great enterprise demanded it—to die without giving ground. In appearance he was not imposing—even though he regarded his lineage as more ancient than Peter's—being puny of body and weak-sighted; but his small eyes with narrowed lids had an exceedingly clever look.

"Ditches and palisades won't save us. We haven't come here to hide behind palisades," Peter growled, turning his telescope farther towards the West.

Chambers, whose habit it was to begin the day by heartening himself with a generous glass of vodka, said hoarsely:

"The soldiers could be given orders to sleep in their boots and with their muskets. But it's unnecessary. If it's true that General Schlippenbach is encamped at Wesenburg he can't be expected to come to the relief of the town before another week."

"I have waited here once before like that for a Swedish relief force. Many thanks, we've learnt our lesson!" Peter replied in a strange voice. Menshikov gave a short, rude laugh.

In the west, towards where Peter was eagerly looking, the sea slumbered in the streams of light; not a breath of air ruffled its grey surface. Straining his eyes, he could distinguish out there, on the clear line of the horizon, a number of ship-masts with furled sails. This was the fleet of de Proust, the admiral with the silver hand, lying becalmed.

Apraxin, gripping the slender rail of the unsteady platform, said:

"How could I help being frightened by such a force, Bombardier: half a hundred ships and such a bold admiral! Truly God saved me by not sending this damned fellow any wind from the sea."

"Oh, what a lot of good things are going to waste!" Menshikov said, counting the masts on the horizon with his finger. "His holds must be chock-full of smoked eels, plaice, sprats, Reval hams. What hams they have, my word! People really eat well in Reval! All his stuff will go bad in this heat, he'll throw it overboard, the one-armed devil. Apraxin, Apraxin, and you sitting by the sea, you landlubber! Why haven't you got any boats? In this dead calm if one were to send a company of grenadiers in boats, de Proust would be cornered."

"A seagull is alighting on the sand!" Peter cried suddenly. "Upon my word, it's alighting!" His face was gay, his eyes round. "I bet ten thalers we're going to have a storm. Who wants to take my bet? Oh, you seamen! Don't grumble, Danilych, it's quite on the cards that we'll have a taste of the admiral's ham."

And, pushing the telescope into the breast of his coat, he ran down the ladder. To Colonel Renne who hastened to help him jump to the ground he said: "Send one squadron ahead and follow me with another." He climbed into the saddle and turned in the direction of Narva. His tall, big-eared bay gelding, a present from Field-Marshal Sheremetev, who had taken the horse in the battle of Erestfär, allegedly from under Schlippenbach himself, was going at full trot. Peter was not very fond of riding and when trotting rose high in the saddle. But Menshikov kept exciting his milk-white stallion, also a prize taken from the Swedes. The spirited horse and his rider seemed to be playing: they would cross a meadow sideways at a short gallop, or the horse would back, sit down on its tail pawing the air with its black hoofs, then rear and start off at full stretch, with Menshikov's crimson cloak thrown over one shoulder streaming out at his back and the plumes on his hat and the ends of his scarf fluttering. It was a lovely day in spite of the heat, and the birds were in full song in the copses and the now abandoned gardens.

Repnin, who was accustomed from childhood to riding Tatar fashion, jogged along easily on his small brisk horse, and turned sideways in the high saddle. Apraxin was streaming with sweat under an enormous wig in which a Russian could find neither comfort nor beauty. Far ahead a squadron of dragoons was scouting among the thickets. Behind Peter and his companions a second squadron rode in military formation, with Colonel Renne prancing at its head. A handsome fellow and a hard drinker, he had, in his quest for fortune, dedicated his sword and his honour to Tsar Peter.

Peter Alexeyevich pointed out to Chambers, who was riding at his side, ditches and holes, high ramparts overgrown with weeds and bushes, and half-rotten poles that stuck out of the earth everywhere.

"Here my army perished," he said simply. "Here King Charles found great glory and we found strength. It is here that we learnt at what end to start, and buried for good and all the antiquated order of things that nearly brought us to final destruction."

He turned away from Chambers and, looking round, caught sight in the near distance of an abandoned hut with a fallen-in roof. He reined in. His round face clouded. Menshikov rode up and said gaily:

"It's that very same hut, *mein Herz*. Do you remember?"

"I do."

Frowning, Peter slapped his horse and again began to bob in the saddle. How could he not remember that sleepless night before the disaster? He had sat then in this hut, his eyes on the guttering candle. Alexander was lying on his felt rug weeping silently. It had been hard for him to master his despair and shame, and his impotent rage, and bring himself to accept the fact that on the morrow Charles would inevitably defeat him. It had been hard for him to reach the decision—so incredible, so unbearable—to leave his army at this hour, to get into a sledge and drive post-haste to Novgorod, there to start all over again from the beginning. Get money, bread, iron; use all manner of shifts and devices, sell everything he had to foreign merchants to buy arms. Cast guns and cannon-balls. And, most important of all, the people, the people, the people! To drag the people out of the age-old swamp, open their eyes, prod them in the ribs. Beat them, lick them into shape, teach them. Rush over thousands of miles through snow, through mud. Break and build. Steer clear of a thousand perils in European politics. And think with horror as he looked back: "What a huge mass that has not been moved yet!"

The foremost dragoons emerged out of the hot shade of the pines on to a broad meadow before the walls of Narva which rose across the moat. The frightened inhabitants, running and shouting, hastily drove their cattle into the town. The meadow was deserted, the chains of the drawbridge rattled as it rose ponderously and banged the gates shut.

Peter rode up a hillock at walking pace. Once again they all took out their telescopes and examined the high, strong walls, with grass growing in the crevices between the stones.

Swedes in iron helmets and leather cuirasses were standing on the top of the gate-tower. One of them, with arm stretched sideways, held upright a yellow banner. Another, a very tall one, came up to the edge of the tower, set his elbow on the parapet and put a telescope to his eye. At first he trained it on one after the other of the horsemen on the hillock, then focussed it directly on Peter.

"What great big fellows they are! When you see them on the tower it's enough to terrify you," Apraxin said in a low voice to Repnin, fanning himself with his hat. "You can see for yourself what I had to endure at Ust-Norova, alone, with nine guns, when the whole fleet set upon me. That long fellow, the one with the telescope—oh, he's an ugly customer! Just before you arrived I met him in the field and tried to capture him. It was hopeless."

"Who's that tall man on the tower?" Peter asked hoarsely.

"That, Sire, is General Horn himself, the military commander of Narva."

No sooner did Apraxin pronounce the name than Menshikov spurred his mount and galloped across the meadow towards the tower. "Fool!" Peter shouted furiously at his back, but the wind whistling in his ears prevented Menshikov from hearing. Close to the very gates he reined in, tore off his hat and, waving it, called out in a sing-song voice:

"Hey, you, on the tower! Hey, Commander! We'll let you out of the town with honours, with your banners, arms and music. Go away amicably!"

General Horn lowered his telescope, listening to what this Russian, decked out like a peacock and prancing wildly on his white horse, was shouting at him. He turned to one of the other Swedes who evidently translated it for him. His stern old face grimaced wryly, as though he had tasted something sour and, leaning over the parapet, he spat in Menshikov's direction.

"That's my answer, you fool!" he shouted. "And now you'll get something stronger."

The Swedes on the tower broke into insulting laughter. There was a flash of fire, a little cloud of smoke puffed up and a cannon-ball rent the air and hurtled with a hiss over Menshikov's head.

"He-e-e-ey!" Repnin shouted in a falsetto from the hillock. "You're not much good at firing, you Swedes. Send us your gunners, we'll teach them!"

This time there was a general burst of laughter on the hillock. Menshikov, knowing full well that he was in for a taste of Peter's whip, curvetted and leapt about on his horse, waving his hat and grinning broadly at the Swedes, until a second ball burst quite close and his mount, shying violently, carried him away from the tower.

On his way back, after he had finished circling the fortress, on the walls of which he counted up to three hundred guns, Peter turned towards the well-remembered hut. There he dismounted and, ordering all the others to wait for him, he took Menshikov with him to the room where, four years ago, he had had to accept shame and dishonour to save the Russian State. In those days there had been a good stove there, but now there was nothing but a heap of sooty bricks, and the floor was strewn with dirty straw: evidently sheep and goats were driven in here for the night. He sat down on the sill of the small broken window. Menshikov stood guiltily before him.

"Remember this well, Danilych. By God, if ever again I see any more of your foolish showing off, I'll take the skin off your back with my whip!" Peter said. "Hold your tongue, don't answer! Today you've made your choice. I was wondering to whom to entrust the command of the besieging troops—to you or to Field-Marshal Ogilvie. In such an enterprise I'd have liked to give preference to a countryman of mine rather than a foreigner. You've spoilt it all yourself, my good fellow, by dancing on your horse like a buffoon in front of General Horn. It was disgraceful! You still can't forget the Moscow market-places. You want to treat everything as a joke, as at my table. But Europe has its eyes on you, you jackass! Hold your tongue, don't answer!" Peter breathed noisily as he filled his pipe. "And another thing: I've had a better look at these walls and I'm worried, Danilych. We can't retreat from Narva a second time. Narva is the key to the whole war. If Charles doesn't realise this yet, I do. Tomorrow we'll surround the town with all our troops, so that not even a bird can escape. But after that, what ought we to do? The walls are strong. General Horn is stubborn, Schlippenbach is hanging on our shoulders. If we mark time here, we'll bring Charles down upon us from Poland with the whole of his army. The town must be taken quickly, but I don't want to spill too much of our blood. What do you say, Danilych?"

"One could, of course, think of some trick. That's easy. But since Field-Marshal Ogilvie is chief here, let him work it out from his books. As for myself, what can I say? Something foolish, in my peasant's way." Menshikov shuffled his feet, mumbled and finally raised his eyes. Peter's face was calm and sad; he seldom saw him like this. He felt a sharp pang of pity. *"Mein Herz,"* he whispered cocking his eyebrows, *"mein Herz,* don't worry. Give me time until night. I'll come to your tent, I'll have found something. Don't you know our people? This is no longer seventeen hundred. Don't worry, trust my word."

2

In the roomy canvas tent the orderly Nartov had carefully laid out on a camp-table cases of mathematical instruments, papers and military maps, just as he used to do in the Petersburg hut. The heat that rose from the earth, as from an oven, came through the raised flaps of the tent, and the crickets chirred so stridently that it hurt one's ears.

Peter was at work, clad only in a shirt wide open at his chest, knee-length Dutch breeches and slippers on his bare feet. From time to time he got up from the table and, in a corner of the tent, Nartov poured a dipperful of spring-water over his head. During these days of the Narva campaign—though it was like that at all times—a great number of urgent matters had accumulated.

Alexey Vasilyevich Makarov, the secretary, an inconspicuous young man only recently appointed to this post, stood close to the table by a pile of papers, handing them to Peter one by one. In a voice loud enough to be heard above the chirring of the crickets he said: "Ukase to Alexey Sidorovich Sinyavin to take charge of the commercial baths in Moscow and other towns", and gently laid in front of the Tsar a sheet of paper on the left half of which the ukase was written in one column. Peter read it running his eyes over the lines, then poked the quill into the inkpot and wrote in a large hand —crookedly and illegibly, leaving out letters in his haste—on the right half of the sheet: "Where possible have barbers' shops attached to the baths to encourage people to shave their beards, also have good experts for treating corns."

Makarov laid before him another document: "Ukase to Peter Vasilyevich Kikin to be in charge of fisheries and water-mills in the whole State. . . ." Peter's hand with a drop of ink hanging on the tip of the quill hung over the paper.

"Who prepared the ukase?"

"It was sent from Moscow by the Prince-Emperor for your personal signature, gracious Sire."

"Moscow's full of parasites, they sit at their windows eating sour gooseberries out of boredom, yet one can't find people to do the work. All right, we'll try Kikin. If he turns out to be a thief, I'll skin him with my whip. Put it just like that in your reply to the Prince-Emperor—say I'm doubtful."

"A report from Lieutenant-Colonel Alexey Brovkin brought by special messenger from Petersburg," Makarov went on. "Six peony plants for your garden on the Petersburg side have been received from Moscow, from Tihon Ivanovich Streshnev, gracious Sire. They have arrived safely but the gardener Levonov died before he could plant them."

"How—died?" Peter asked. "What rubbish!"

"He was drowned bathing in the Neva."

"Oh, drunk, of course. It's always like that; good men don't live long. It's a pity; he was a skilful gardener. Write. . . ."

Peter went into the corner of the tent to have water poured over his head and, blowing and snorting, began to dictate to Makarov who, standing, wrote deftly on the corner of the table:

"To Streshnev. Your peonies have been safely received, though we are sorry you sent so few. Do not miss the right time to send all kinds of flowers from Izmaylovo, especially those with a sweet scent: wallflowers, mint and mignonette. Send a good gardener, with his family so that he will not be lonely. And for God's sake write and tell me how Katerina Vasilyevskaya and Anisya Tolstaya and the others with them are faring in Izmaylovo. Do not forget to write about this more often. Also please inform me how you are getting on with the recruiting for the dragoons' regiments. Get a regiment completed as soon as possible—from among the best men—and send it here."

Peter came back to the table, read what Makarov had written and signed it, smiling to himself.

"What else?" he asked. "Don't give me the papers as they come, give me the most important ones."

"Letter from Grigory Fedorovich Dolgoruky, from Sokal, about the safe arrival of our troops."

"Read it!" Peter closed his eyes, stretched out his neck and laid his large strong hands, covered with scratches, on the table. Dolgoruky reported that, since the arrival of the Russian troops in Sokal, King August was again inspired by excessive valour and wished to meet King Charles in the open field, to take his revenge, with God's help, for his defeat at Kliszow in a decisive battle. He was particularly encouraged in this foolhardy plan by his mistresses, of whom he now had two, and his existence had become extremely complicated. Dmitry Mihaylovich Golitsin had succeeded with great difficulty in making him renounce an immediate clash with Charles (who, like a preying wolf, was waiting precisely for that) and in directing his attention to the road to Warsaw, which Charles had left poorly defended. What the results would be God alone knew.

Peter listened patiently to the long missive and his lip, with its narrow line of moustache, lifted, uncovering his teeth. Twitching his neck he muttered: "A fine ally!" Then he drew a clean sheet of paper towards him, scratched the back of his head and began to write his reply to Dolgoruky, his pen barely keeping up with his thought:

". . . I again remind Your Grace to be untiring in dissuading His Majesty King August from his cruel and fatal intention. He hastens to seek a decisive battle relying on good fortune—in other words, luck, but God alone disposes. As for us mortals, it is wiser to look at what is nearer to us, the things of this earth. In short, to seek a decisive battle is extremely dangerous for him, because in a single hour he might lose everything. If the decisive battle were to end in defeat—from which heaven preserve him, and us too—not only would His Majesty King August be plunged into grief by his enemy, but the furious Poles, who have not the good of their country at heart, will turn him out with ignominy and deprive him of his throne. Why should he bring such calamity upon himself? As for the mistresses Your Grace mentions, in truth there is no remedy for this fever. All you can do is to try to win the good graces of these ladies and make an alliance with them."

It had become impossible to breathe, so thick were the floating layers of tobacco smoke. Peter signed "Ptr" with a splutter of his pen and went out of the tent into the intolerable heat. From this part of the hillock he could see at some distance from Narva a cloud of dust raised by the baggage-trains and troops moving from their camp to their battle positions in front of the fortress. Peter passed his hand over his chest, over the white skin; his heart beat slowly and strongly. Then he turned his eyes towards where Admiral de Proust's ships, invisible from here, were slumbering on the immeasurable, glassy sea, their holds filled with supplies that would have sufficed for the entire Russian army. The earth, the sky and the sea were languid and expectant, as if time itself had stopped. Suddenly a scattered cloud of black birds rushed through the air over the hillock and away towards the forest. Peter threw back his head—it was coming! Filmy veils of cloud were rising rapidly from the Southeast into a sky that blazed like a red-hot sheet of iron.

"Makarov!" he called. "Do you want to bet ten thalers?"

Makarov came hastily out of the tent—sharp-nosed, parchment-coloured from fatigue and lack of sleep. His straight lips held no smile as he pulled a purse out of his pocket.

"At your orders, gracious Sire," he said.

Peter waved his hand at him.

"Go, tell Nartov to prepare my sailor's jacket, sou'wester and sea-boots. And have the tent properly pegged down or it will be blown away. A famous storm is brewing."

The sea always entranced him, ever drew him. Dressed in a loose jacket and a leather cap covering the back of his neck, he rode at a brisk trot towards the beach, escorted by half a squadron of dragoons. (Messengers had been sent to Apraxin at the camp for two guns and some grenadiers.) The sun stung like a scorpion in its death throes. Columns of dust eddied along the roads. Gusts of wind streaked the surface of the sea. A black thundercloud was creeping up from the darkened horizon. And at last the sea sent up its breath, smelling of seaweed and fish-scales. The wind, gathering force, bellowed in Neptune's full voice.

Peter, holding on to his sou'wester, bared his teeth in a happy grin. He jumped out of the saddle on to the sandy beach. The sun glittered for the last time from behind the billowing edge of the thundercloud and the glassy light swept over the curling waves. All at once everything grew dark. The rumbling cloud was lit up from end to end by a lurid glow as though it had been set on fire. A zigzag flash of lightning blinded him as it struck the water quite close to where he stood. The thunder crashed with such force that the men on the beach cowered—the skies seemed to have fallen.

Menshikov turned up at Peter's side, also wearing a sou'wester and a sailor's jacket.

"That's what I call a storm! It's the real thing!" Peter shouted to him.

"How clever of you, *mein Herz*!"

"Have you only just now understood what we can look forward to?"

"We'll get the loot?"

"Not so fast, not so fast!"

They did not have long to wait. By the flashes of lightning they could now see at no great distance Admiral de Proust's warships and merchantmen: the storm was driving them towards the shore, on to the shoals. They seemed to be dancing: the bare masts rocked, torn scraps of sail fluttered, the high poops, with their carved figures of

Neptune and mermaids, tossed. It seemed as if little was needed for the whole scattered convoy to be driven ashore.

"Good man! Good man!" Peter cried. "Look what he's doing! There's a true admiral for you! He's hoisting the flying jibs! Hoisting the stay-sails, the fore-stay-sails! Hoisting the trysails! The devil! Look and learn, Danilych!"

"Oh, he'll get away, he'll get away!" Menshikov groaned.

Whether it was that the wind had slightly shifted, or the admiral's skill had won the struggle with the sea, his ships, tacking with the help of storm-canvas, began to draw away again towards the horizon. Only three heavily-laden barques were still being driven on to the shoals. With a creaking of timbers, a clatter of yard-arms and a flapping of torn canvas, they ran aground some three hundred paces from the shore. Huge waves pounded them and washed over them, sweeping boats and barrels off the decks and smashing the masts.

"Now then, take a shot at them, but make it short, just to give them a fright," Menshikov shouted to the gunners.

The guns barked and the shells threw up a fountain of water close to one of the barques. Pistol shots sounded in reply from the vessels. Peter got into the saddle and drove his horse into the sea. Grenadiers followed him, shouting as they ran. Menshikov was obliged to dismount—his stallion balked—and he too went striding into the turbid waves, spitting and shouting:

"Hey, you, on the barques! Jump into the water! Surrender!"

The Swedes were probably badly frightened at the sight of a horseman in the waves and of the great moustached grenadiers advancing, chest-deep, through the water, to board them, swearing and threatening them with smoking bombs. Sailors and soldiers began to jump off the barques. They gave up pistols and cutlasses, saying: "Moskov, Moskov, friend!" and waded to the shore where the mounted dragoons surrounded them. Menshikov in his turn scrambled up on to a barque with the grenadiers. He took the captain prisoner, but immediately slapped him condescendingly on the back and returned his cutlass to him. Then he shouted:

"Bombardier, the holds stink a bit, but the captain gives hope that the herrings and salt-meat are still fit to eat."

3

The troops investing Narva were disposed in a horseshoe, each end of which rested on the river, one above, the other below the town. On the other bank of the river, Ivan-gorod was invested in the same way. Entrenchments were dug and strengthened with stockades and chevaux-de-frise. The Russian camp was noisy, smoky and dirty. The Swedes looked on grimly from the high walls. Since the storm that had dispersed Admiral de Proust's fleet they were very bitter and fired their cannon even at single horsemen who took a short cut over the meadow past the formidable bastions.

On Peter's orders the barrels of herrings and salted meat, unloaded from the barques, were brought into the camp in full view of the Swedes. In the wake of the waggons decorated with branches, the soldiers carried a fat, naked fellow garlanded with seaweed and yelled a ribald song about Admiral de Proust and General Horn. The barrels were distributed among the companies and batteries. The soldiers brandished a herring or a piece of bacon at the end of a bayonet and shouted: "Hey, Swede, here's a snack!" At this the Swedes could hold back no longer. Trumpets blared, drums rolled, the drawbridge was lowered, letting out a squadron of cuirassiers. With their heads in ribbed helmets lowered and their broad swords set between their horses' ears they came, galloping heavily, at the Russian entrenchments. The Russians had to drop their loot and hit back with whatever came to hand—poles, ramrods, spades. A *mêlée* broke out, accompanied by wild shouting. When the cuirassiers saw the dragoons galloping towards them from the rear and the terrible grenadiers climbing over the stockades, they wheeled. Only a few men remained in the meadow, and for a long time frightened, riderless horses galloped about, chased by Russian soldiers.

Apart from such sorties the Swedes showed little concern. Captured prisoners alleged that General Horn had said: "I'm not afraid of the Russians. Let them dare try to storm the place with the aid of their St. George—I'll give them a better reception than in seventeen hundred." He had enough bread, gun-powder and cannon-balls, but, above all, he relied on Schlippenbach who was awaiting reinforcements to give the Russians a cruel lesson. He was encamped in the small town of Wesenberg on the Reval road, as Menshikov, who had gone himself on a scouting expedition, had established.

The Russian troops were also marking time: the whole of the siege artillery—the great siege-guns and the mortars for starting fires in the town—was still dragging itself along the impassable roads from Novgorod. There could be no question of trying to storm the town without the support of heavy artillery.

The news received from Field-Marshal Sheremetev did not mention any great activity either: he had laid siege to Yuriev, had entrenched himself, had started a sap to breach the wall and was firing bombs into the town. "The Swedes are mightily plaguing us," he wrote to Menshikov in the Narva camp. "To this day I have been unable to silence the enemy's gun and mortar fire. They fire volleys from many guns, curse them, and send ten bombs at a time into our batteries; but mostly they fire at our supply-trains. And although we have tried very hard we have been unable to capture anyone from the town. Only two Finns have come out to us, and they do not know anything for certain and keep ranting about Schlippenbach who has promised to come promptly to relieve the town."

Schlippenbach was, indeed, a thorn in the flesh which ought to be extracted as soon as possible. All Peter's thoughts were concentrated on this problem.

That night Menshikov did not disappoint him. He came to his tent and, after making everybody leave, including Nartov, he disclosed to Peter the ruse he had thought out to discourage General Horn from relying on Schlippenbach. Peter took it badly at first: "Have you been drinking to get such ideas?" But after pacing the tent and puffing at his pipe, he suddenly broke into laughter:

"It wouldn't be a bad thing to make a fool of the old fellow."

"We'll make a fool of him, *mein Herz,* take my word for it."

"This word of yours isn't worth much. And what if nothing comes of it? You'll have a lot to answer for, my fine friend."

"What of it? It wouldn't be the first time. I spend my life answering for things."

"Go ahead, then!"

That same night Lieutenant Yaguzhinsky, fortified by a stirrup-cup, galloped to Pskov where the army depots were. With extraordinary efficiency he brought back in carts, each drawn by three horses, everything necessary for the operation planned. The company and regimental tailors spent two nights altering and adjusting coats, cloaks, officers' scarves, and banners, and edging soldiers' three-cornered hats with white tape. In these two short nights Asafyev's and Gorbov's two dragoon regiments left secretly, squadron by squadron, and with them went the Semenovsky and Ingermanlandsky infantry regiments, with guns the green carriages of which had been repainted yellow. They all took the Reval road and encamped in the wooded area of Terviegi, six miles from Narva. The clothing altered by the tailors was brought into the forest there. The Swedes did not notice anything.

In the clear morning of the 8th of June a sudden commotion broke out in the Russian camp under the walls of Narva. Drums beat an alarming tattoo, the great cymbals boomed, officers galloped about shouting themselves hoarse. Soldiers sprang out of their huts and tents. Buttoning their coats and gaiters and pushing back behind their ears the long hair that hung under their three-cornered hats, they lined up in two ranks. Gunners shouted as they wheeled out their guns and turned them to face the Reval road. Mounted soldiers herded droves of baggage-train horses from the meadows to the camp, behind the waggons.

From the walls the Swedes watched with amazement the desperate confusion that reigned in the Russian camp. Bare-headed, General Horn ascended the gate-tower by the outer stone staircase and directed his telescope towards the Reval road. Two cannon-shots sounded from that direction; within a minute there came two more, and this was repeated four more times. The Swedes realised that it must be the signal heralding the approach of General Schlippenbach, and immediately replied with a royal salute of twenty-one guns. The bells of all the town churches rang out a festive peal.

For the first time since the beginning of the siege General Horn's lips creased in a smile when he saw Menshikov, that most impudent of all the Russians, capering like a goat on his white steed before the Moscow troops that were drawing up in two lines on the far side of the entrenchments. Just as if he were an experienced military commander he flourished his sword, ordering the second rank of soldiers to turn and face the fortress; they obeyed and ran like a herd to take up position in the trenches behind the palisade. Then he reined in his horse, making it rear, and set off at a gallop along the front rank that stood facing the Reval road. All was clear to General Horn, whom years and glorious battles had rendered wise: this coxcomb in his red cloak was going to commit an irreparable mistake; he would lead the thin, straggling line of his infantry to meet the iron cuirassiers of Schlippenbach who would rain cannon-balls on them, cut them to pieces, trample them down and annihilate them. The general drew a deep breath through his hairy nostrils. He had twelve squadrons of cavalry and four infantry battalions arrayed behind the closed gates to be thrown against the Russians from the rear as soon as Schlippenbach made his appearance.

Menshikov, as though hastening to meet his death, quite unnecessarily tore off his hat and waved it, forcing all the battalions that were following the tail of his prancing horse at the double to shout

"Hurrah!" The cry reached the walls of Narva and the old general smiled again. Russian horsemen, speeded by musket fire, began to emerge at a gallop from the pine-wood towards which Menshikov's battalions were moving. And at last, from everywhere among the pines, the companies of Schlippenbach's Guards came into sight in all their glory, marching shoulder to shoulder, as on parade, their muskets with fixed bayonets held in front of them. As they moved, the second rank fired rapidly over the heads of the front rank, while the men in the third rank loaded the muskets and handed them to those who fired. The yellow royal banners, held high, fluttered in the wind. For a moment the old general lowered his telescope and, drawing a linen handkerchief out of his pouch, shook it out and passed it over his eyes. "Gods of war!" he murmured.

Menshikov, holding on to his hat, sped at a gallop along the front and halted his battalions. Guns drawn by six horses each and two powder-carts were galloping up to his flanks. The Russian gunners were efficient; they had learnt something in these last few years. They smartly turned the guns, polished till they shone—eight on each flank—pointing them towards the Swedes (the teams were unhitched and galloped out of the way) and all of them simultaneously threw out tight white balls of smoke—a proof of the good quality of the powder. Before the Swedes had advanced a score of steps, the guns roared out again. The general crumpled his handkerchief in his hand —such rapid fire was astonishing. The Swedes halted. What the devil! It was unlike Schlippenbach to be confused by cannon-fire. Perhaps his intention was to let the cuirassiers through for an attack. Or was he perhaps waiting for his own artillery to come up? General Horn turned his telescope from side to side, searching for Schlippenbach, but the smoke, growing thicker over the battlefield, obscured his vision. It even seemed to him that the Swedes were wavering under the hail of grapeshot. He watched expectantly. At last! Swedish cannon with yellow gun-carriages emerged out of the forest and vigorously gave tongue. Then—he could see it quite clearly—the ranks of Menshikov's men were thrown into confusion. The moment had come! General Horn turned his wrinkled face from the telescope and, baring his yellow teeth to the gums, said to his second-in-command, Colonel Markwart:

"Here are my orders: open the gates and attack the Russians' right wing!"

The drawbridge clattered and, simultaneously out of four gates, the squadrons of cuirassiers rode out, followed at a run by the infantry. Colonel Markwart was leading the Narva garrison in wedge-shaped formation in such a way as to rush and clear the Russians' palisades and chevaux-de-frise, strike at Menshikov's flank from the rear, drive him against Schlippenbach and crush him in an iron vise.

What General Horn saw through his telescope pleased him at first and then disturbed him. Colonel Markwart's force, rapidly and with few losses, scattered the Russians' chevaux-de-frise, cleared the palisades and came out on the far side of the trenches. In its wake the inhabitants of Narva poured out of the gates—on foot and in carts—to loot the Russian camp. Menshikov's battalions, firing their muskets in a desultory fashion, suddenly made an incomprehensible manœuvre: their right flank, on which Markwart was bearing down, began a hasty retreat towards the palisades and chevaux-de-frise, while the left flank—the farther one—rushed with the same haste towards Schlippenbach's Swedes as though to surrender. The cannon on both sides suddenly fell silent. Martwart, attacking brilliantly, found himself in the open field in the fork between Menshikov and Schlippenbach. The squadrons of his cuirassiers, in their shining breastplates, reined in, wheeled in a half-circle and halted in indecision. The infantry that had come up with them halted too.

"I can't understand it! What's happened? The devil take Markwart!" General Horn cried.

"I don't quite understand it either, General," replied Adjutant Bistrem, who stood near him.

Then, moving his telescope with ever-growing haste, General Horn caught sight of Menshikov: the coxcomb was riding full tilt towards the Swedes. Why? To surrender? As he recognised him, Markwart and two cuirassiers galloped to cut him off. But Menshikov outstripped him and, reaching a grass-grown hillock, jumped off his horse by a group of officers; judging from their cloaks and the banner—yellow with a lion rampant—this was Schlippenbach's headquarters. But where was Schlippenbach himself? Another movement of his telescope showed him Markwart in pursuit of Menshikov galloping up to the same group of officers, waving his arm strangely as though defending himself from a spectre, and attempting to turn back. But men ran up to him and pulled him out of the saddle. A horseman was riding up the hillock on a large, lop-eared horse; the banner dipped before him. This could only be Schlippenbach. A tear dimmed the General's vision; he angrily brushed it away and pressed the brass ring of the telescope into his eye-socket. The horseman on the lop-eared horse did not look like Schlippenbach. More than anything he looked like. . . .

"It's treachery, General!" Adjutant Bistrem whispered.

"I can see without your telling me that it's Tsar Peter dressed in Swedish uniform. I've been cleverly taken in. I realise that without your help. Give orders for my cuirass and sword to be brought." General Horn dropped the now useless telescope and, with the agility of a young man, ran down the steep stairs of the gate-tower.

What happened on the field of the mock-battle was what is bound to happen when the military commander has been fooled. The men of the Semenovsky and Ingermanlandsky regiments, dressed in Swedish uniforms, Asafyev's and Gorbov's dragoons, who had remained concealed in the wood biding their time, and Menshikov's battalions on the other side fell upon Markwart's Swedes from both sides at once. Markwart, after surrendering his sword to Tsar Peter, had thrown his helmet on the grass and was standing on the hillock among the Russian officers, his head bowed in shame and despair so as not to see the destruction of his force of picked men, which represented at least one-third of the Narva garrison.

For some time his cuirassiers, who were covering the infantry, retreated in good order, fighting back with short attacks. But when Colonel Renne with his dragoons, who had been lying in ambush in a birch wood, charged down upon their rear, a hand-to-hand skirmish began. All shooting ceased. The only sounds were the furious sharp yells of the Russians as they slashed with their swords, the hoarse cries of the dying Swedes, the clash of blade against cuirass and helmet. Single horsemen, breaking free of the *mêlée,* galloped over the meadow like blind men, crashed into one another and fell, throwing up their arms. The whole Russian army had climbed on to the breastworks to enjoy the sight, as a carnival crowd gathers to watch the baiting of a bear. The soldiers yelled, danced about, threw their hats into the air.

Only a fraction of the Swedish force succeeded in fighting its way back into the town. All General Horn was able to do was to defend the gates to prevent the Russians from breaking into the town in their pursuit. The townspeople, who had come out to loot, drove about distractedly in their carts on the edge of the moat. The soldiers jumped over the palisade and, ignoring the gunfire in the heat of the fray, seized a number of the Narva citizens with their carts and horses and brought them to the camp to sell to their officers.

That evening there was a merry feast in Menshikov's large tent.

They drank Admiral de Proust's fiery rum and ate Reval ham and smoked plaice which few of them had seen before. The fish stank a little but nevertheless tasted good. They slapped Menshikov's back black and blue, drinking to his astuteness.

"You've made a fine fool of the wise Horn! You're the true hero of the day!" Peter said, his shoulders shaking with laughter. He had drunk a good deal and thumped Menshikov between the shoulder-blades with a fist like a sledge-hammer.

"I'll wager you could outwit Odysseus himself!" Chambers cried, thumping the governor-general's back in his turn. "It's hard to imagine craftier people than these Russians!"

The guests, interrupting each other, made several attempts to compose a missive for General Horn bestowing upon him the order of the "Long Nose". The beginning promised well: "Hail! sitting bird of Narva in your wetted breeches, hail! old fool, castrated tom-cat, roaring like a lion. . . ." The suggestions that followed were couched in such strong language that the secretary Makarov did not even know how to put them on paper.

Repnin, when he had bleated his full measure of laughter, said finally:

"Peter Alexeyevich, is it worth while shaming the old man in this way? After all, the business is not yet finished."

The others banged their fists and shouted at him, but Peter took the unfinished letter from Makarov, crumpled it up and thrust it in his pocket.

"We've had our laugh," he said. "That's enough."

He got up, swayed, and gripped Makarov's shoulder. With an effort he composed the relaxed features of his round face into their habitual firmness and, with a jerk of his long neck, as usual, regained complete mastery of himself.

"Enough celebrating!" he said and went out of the tent.

Day was breaking. The grass looked grey with the heavy dew and the smoke of camp-fires trailing over it. Peter inhaled the freshness of the morning deeply.

"Well, may the hour be propitious! It is time!" Immediately Repnin and Colonel Renne detached themselves from the group of officers behind him and moved close to him. "I tell you both once again: I do not want bombastic reports of victory. I don't expect them. The task before you is a hard one. He must be defeated so that he cannot recover. For an undertaking of this kind you must harden your hearts. Now go!"

Anikita Ivanovich Repnin and Colonel Renne bowed and strode knee-deep in the thick grass away from the tent towards the dark forest where the dragoon regiments and the infantry seated in carts—all of them participants of yesterday's mock-battle, now dressed again in their own uniforms—were waiting to march. The task that lay before them was no small one: they had to surround and destroy Schlippenbach's corps near Wesenberg.

4

"And so, gentlemen, ex-King August, whom we believed reduced to a nonentity, has received help from the Russians and is speedily moving towards Warsaw," the young King Stanislaw Lesczinski said as he opened his Military Council. The king was wearied by the affairs of State that had been thrust upon him, and his well-cut, haughty, saturnine face was ashen under the lowered eyelids; he did not raise his eyes because he was sick and tired of the self-satisfied faces of the courtiers and of all the talk about war, money, loans. With an indolent hand he fingered the beads of a rosary. He was wearing Polish clothes, which he detested, but ever since a Swedish garrison, under the command of Colonel Arvid Horn—nephew of the hero of Narva—had been stationed in Warsaw, the Polish magnates and great nobles had hung their wigs on stands, laid aside their French coats—sprinkling them with tobacco against moths—and went about in Polish coats with wing-sleeves, beaver caps and soft boots with jingling and tinkling spurs, and had replaced their swords with their ancestors' heavy sabres.

They led a gay and lighthearted existence in Warsaw under the reliable protection of Arvid Horn, having forgiven his discourteous behaviour when he had forced the Diet to elect to the throne this young man of elegant manners but no birth. The Swedish officers were arrogant and rather coarse but, on the other hand, they could not stand up to the Poles in the matter of drinking wine and mead nor hold a candle to such magnificent mazurka dancers as Vyshnevetski or Potocki. The one trouble was that less and less money came in from the estates ruined by the war, but even this circumstance seemed only a temporary evil; Charles would not lord it forever over Poland and, sooner or later, would go to the East, to deal with Tsar Peter.

And now, out of the blue, a cloud loomed over Warsaw. Without striking a blow, August had seized the rich town of Lublin and was swiftly moving, with a noisy mounted Polish army, along the left bank of the Vistula on Warsaw. The one-eyed monster, Attaman Danila Apostol, with his Dniepr Cossacks, had crossed to the right bank of the Vistula and was approaching Praga, a suburb of Warsaw. Eleven Russian infantry regiments were clearing the towns along the Bug of King Stanislaw's adherents; they had already occupied Brest and were also converging on Warsaw. And approaching it from the West was the Saxon corps of Field-Marshal Schulenburg, who, by a clever manœuvre, had misled King Charles, now looking for him on another road.

"God and the Holy Virgin are my witnesses that I had no ambition to wear the Polish crown, it was the will of the Diet," King Stanislaw said in a contemptuous drawl, without raising his eyes. A white borzoi pedigree bitch was lying on the carpet at his feet with its head on its paws. "So far in my high station I have encountered nothing but difficulties and disappointments. I am prepared to renounce the crown if the Diet wishes it, out of caution and prudence, in order not to expose Warsaw to King August's malevolence. He has, no doubt, good reason to be spleenful. He is ambitious and obstinate. His ally—Tsar Peter—is still more obstinate and crafty, and they will fight until they gain their ends, until we are all brought to final ruin." He laid his foot in its soft morocco leather boot on the dog's back and the dog looked up at him with its violet eyes. "Believe me, I don't insist on anything, I would be delighted to retire to Italy. The studies in the University of Bologna excite my admiration."

Colonel Arvid Horn, with a florid face and fiercely cold eyes, thick-set in his green, well-worn coat, sitting on a folding chair facing the king, said gruffly:

"This is no Military Council. It's a humiliating capitulation."

King Stanislaw gave a crooked smile. Radzievski, the cardinal primate, King August's sworn enemy, did not hear the Swede's insulting remark. He said in that insinuating, humbly masterful tone which has been assiduously taught in the Jesuit Colleges since the days of Ignatius Loyola:

"Your Majesty's desire to avoid a struggle is no more than a passing weakness. The flowers of your soul have been seared by the cruel blast; we are deeply moved. But the crown of a Catholic king, as distinct from a hat, can be taken off only together with his head.

Let us speak with courage of resistance to the usurper and enemy of the Church, for such is August, Elector of Saxony, a bad Catholic. Let us hear what Colonel Horn has to say."

The cardinal turned heavily towards the Swede with a rustle of his sumptuous red silk robe, reflected in the polished floor, and made a courteous gesture as though offering him some delicate dish. Colonel Horn pushed back his chair, spread wide his sturdy legs in tarred topboots (like all Swedes he wore a shabby coat and coarse topboots in imitation of King Charles), coughed drily to clear his throat and said:

"I repeat: a Military Council must be a Military Council, and not idle prattle. I will defend Warsaw to the last soldier—such is the will of my king. I have given orders to my fusiliers to fire after nightfall on anyone who goes outside the gates. I will not let a single coward leave Warsaw: I shall make even cowards fight! It makes me laugh: we have no fewer troops than August. The Great Hetman Prince Lubomirski knows this better than I do. It makes me laugh: August is encircling us! This only means that he is giving us the opportunity to defeat him piece-meal; his drunken cavalry in the south, and to the east of Warsaw the Attaman Danila Apostol, whose Cossacks are lightly armed and won't withstand the onslaught of armoured hussars. Field-Marshal Schulenburg will meet his death before he reaches Warsaw; my king is undoubtedly pursuing him. The only considerable danger comes from the eleven Russian regiments of Prince Golitsin, but while they are plodding along from Brest we shall have destroyed August, and they will be obliged either to retreat or die. I suggest that Prince Lubomirski should, this very night, concentrate all the cavalry regiments in Warsaw. I suggest that before these candles have burnt down in their sockets, Your Majesty should declare the mobilisation of the national militia. The devil take me, if we don't pluck all the feathers out of King August's tail!"

Blowing out his fair moustache Arvid Horn laughed and sat down. Now even the king raised his eyes to look at the Great Hetman Lubomirski, Commander-in-Chief of the Polish and Lithuanian troops. Throughout the whole discussion he had sat in a gilt armchair on the king's left, his forehead cupped in the palms of his hands, so that all that could be seen of him was his round, cropped head with a scalp-lock, as though sprinkled with pepper, and his long, thin, hanging moustache.

When silence fell he sighed and straightened up, as if coming to himself, and slowly laid his hand on the diamond-studded mace stuck in his handsome woven belt. He was tall, bony and broad-shouldered. His aquiline, slightly pockmarked face, with its sunken cheeks and inflamed skin tightly stretched over the cheek-bones, was so aloof and haughtily sombre that the king's eyelids fluttered and he bent down to stroke his dog. The Great Hetman slowly rose to his feet. The long-awaited hour of reckoning was his at last.

He was the greatest of all the Polish magnates, more powerful in his vast domains than any king. When he travelled to the Diet or went on pilgrimage to Czenstohov, no less than five thousand petty noblemen, dressed to a man in red coats with sky-blue linings to their wing-sleeves, rode on horseback, in carriages and carts in front of his coach and behind it. When the national militia was called out—against the mutinous Ukraine or the Tatars—he brought his own three regiments of hussars in steel cuirasses with wings at their backs. As a descendant of the Piasts he had regarded himself as the first candidate to the Polish throne after the overthrow of August. At the time—last year—two-thirds of the delegates of the Diet had shouted, rattling their swords: "We want Lubomirski!" But Charles had been against it, because what he needed was a puppet. Colonel Horn had surrounded the turbulent Diet with his fusiliers, who lighted their fuses and desecrated the solemnity of the place with the rat-a-tat of their drums. Horn, striding up heavily as though hammering in nails with his heels, had approached the empty throne dais and shouted: "I propose Stanislaw Lesczinski!"

Since then the Great Hetman had nursed his resentment. No one had ever dared to offend his honour. King Charles, who probably possessed less arable land and gold plate than Lubomirski, had done so. Shifting his wild, dark glance and scratching the knob of his mace with his nails, he broke into speech, hissing his consonants furiously, like a snake:

"Have I misheard, or is it my imagination? The garrison commander has dared give orders to me, the Great Hetman, to me, Prince Lubomirski! Is it a joke? Or is it impudence?" The king lifted his hand holding the rosary, the cardinal leant forward in his chair and shook his owl-like, bloated face, but the hetman only raised his voice threateningly. "You are waiting for my advice? I have listened to you, gentlemen, and I have consulted my conscience. Here is my answer! Our troops are unreliable. In order to make them shed their blood and that of their brothers, the heart of every nobleman must be set ablaze with enthusiasm and his brain lashed into fury. Perhaps

King Stanislaw knows such a battle-cry? I don't. 'In the name of God, forward for the glory of the Lesczinskis!' They won't move. 'In the name of God, forward for the glory of the King of Swedes!' They'll throw down their swords. I cannot lead the troops! I am no longer Hetman!"

His distorted face flushed darkly up to his shaggy eyebrows. Unable to restrain himself, he pulled the mace out of his belt and threw it at the feet of the boyish king. The white bitch gave a pitiful squeal.

"This is treason!" Horn cried furiously.

5

The term "berserk", or being possesed with frenzy, comes from the hoary past, from the custom of the northern people to intoxicate themselves with the death-cup toadstool. Later, in the Middle Ages, the Norsemen called "berserk" the warriors seized with mad and irresistible fury at the sight of the field of battle: they fought without chain-mail, shield or helmet, clad only in their linen shirts— "baresark"—and were so terrifying that, according to tradition, the twelve berserks, sons of King Canute, sailed in a separate boat because the Norsemen themselves feared them.

In the access of fury which seized him, King Charles could only have been described as berserk, so terrified and overcome were the courtiers who happened to be in his tent at the time. Count Piper even feared for his life. After he had received the pigeon-post missive from Countess Kozelska, Charles, in spite of Piper's advice and that of Field-Marshal Rehnsköld and other generals, had remained unshaken in his vengeful desire to deliver the final blow to August, bring the whole of Poland into submission to Stanislaw Lesczinski, give his troops a good rest and, in the following year, in one summer campaign, terminate the eastern war by a brilliant defeat of Peter's hosts. The fate of Narva and Yuriev gave him no anxiety, for their garrisons were reliable and their walls strong—too hard for the Muscovites' teeth—and there was also the valorous Schlippenbach. But, above all, it would have hurt his pride—he, the inheritor of the fame of Alexander of Macedon and of Cæsar—to change his great plans because of some pigeon-post despatch, delivered, moreover, by a dissolute courtesan.

The news of the arrival in Sokal of the Russian auxiliary force and of August's sudden march on Warsaw—under the very nose of King Charles who, like a replete lion, was in no hurry to bury his fangs in the doomed Polish king—was brought by that same petty nobleman who had hacked the dish of sausages with his sword at Pan Sobeczanski's feast. Count Piper, greatly perturbed, went off to wake the king, for the day was just dawning. Charles was sleeping quietly on his camp-bed with his hands crossed on his chest. The feeble light of a brass night-light lit up his large aquiline nose, his ascetically gaunt cheek and his firmly compressed lips: even in sleep he wanted to be unlike other men. He looked like the effigy of a knight on a tomb.

Count Piper had pinned his hopes on the king's cock, for whom the moment had come to give vent to a full-throated crow. But the cock, who was obliged to share the king's monastic existence, only moved about in his cage behind the canvas of the tent and succeeded in producing no more than a hoarse: "Eh-he-he!"

"Wake up, Your Majesty!" Count Piper said as gently as he could, turning up the wick of the night-light. "Your Majesty, there is unpleasant news." Charles opened his eyes without moving. "August has given us the slip."

Charles instantly jerked out his legs, clad in linen underpants, and dropped his feet in woollen stockings on to the rug. He sat, propping himself up on his fists, and looked at Piper. With a courtier's discretion Piper told him about the change in August's circumstances.

"My boots and my breeches," Charles said slowly, widening still more fearfully his unblinking eyes—they even seemed to flicker, unless it was a reflection from the night-light flame that had begun to smoke.

Piper rushed out of the tent and immediately returned with Björkenheim, whose hastily donned wig was askew. The generals began to assemble in the tent. Charles put on his breeches and his boots, buttoned his coat, breaking two finger-nails in the process, and only then gave vent to his fury.

"You spend your time with dirty whores, you have grown as fat as a Capuchin!" he shouted at the totally innocent General Rosen in a barking voice, because a cramp tightened his jaws and his teeth were chattering. "This day is the day of your dishonour!" he threw at General Löwenhaupt, lunging towards him as though with a sword-thrust. "You should be plodding along as a private in the baggage-train of my army! I learn news of the greatest importance, on which the fate of Europe depends, from some drunken petty nobleman! I learn it from courtesans! I am ridiculous! It's surprising that I haven't been dragged out of my tent in my sleep by Cossacks and taken to

Moscow with a rope round my neck! And you, Herr Piper, I advise you to replace the count's coronet on your coat of arms by a fool's cap! You, guzzler of snipe, partridges and other game, you're a drunkard and an ass! Don't dare to pretend you are insulted! I would gladly break you on the wheel and have you quartered. Where are your spies, I would like to know? Where are your couriers, who are supposed to inform me about events twenty-four hours before they happen? To the devil! I'll abandon the army, I'll become a private citizen! It disgusts me to be your king!"

Then Charles tore all the buttons off his coat. With a kick he burst a drumhead. He tore Björkenheim's wig to shreds. No one dared to address him as he stormed about the tent among the backing courtiers. When the berserk fit began to subside, Charles put his hands behind his back, bent his head and said:

"I command you to give the alarm immediately to the troops. You, gentlemen, I give three hours to get ready. I shall be marching out. You will learn everything from my order. Now leave my tent. Björkenheim, a pen, paper and ink."

6

"It's intolerable. We've been standing here for ages. A little more decision, a good attack, and we might have been spending the night in Warsaw," Countess Kozelska said peevishly, looking out of the carriage at the innumerable camp-fires that formed a wide semi-circle before the city, invisible in the darkness. The countess was faint with tiredness. Her elegant carriage with the gilt Cupid on its roof had broken down at the crossing of some small river, and she had been obliged to accept a seat in Pani Anna Sobeczanska's uncomfortable, jolting, ugly coach. The countess was so annoyed, and Pani Anna seemed to her such a poor creature, that she could even bring herself to be polite to the little provincial noblewoman.

"The king's carriage is standing in front of ours, but he isn't in it. Even God doesn't know what he's thinking about. There are no preparations for supper or rest."

The countess jerked the strap and, with difficulty, lowered the window of the coach. The warm smell of horse-sweat and the appetising smoke of field-kitchens drifted in. The night was filled with camp noises: shouting, cursing, laughter, the stamping of horses, distant gunfire. The countess was bored to death with these delights of army life and she raised the window again, throwing herself back into the corner of the carriage. Everything conspired to annoy her: her rumpled gown, her travelling cloak, the sharp corners of caskets; she felt like biting someone hard enough to draw blood.

"I'm afraid we'll find the royal palace in a terrible state of disorder and loot. The Lesczinski family is famed for its greed, and I know Stanislaw only too well; he's a bigot, mean and narrow-minded. I advise you, my dear, to have some private house to fall back upon, that is, if you have some decent connections in Warsaw. Don't rely too much on King August. My God, what a blackguard he is!"

Pani Anna took great delight in her conversations with the countess—this was the school of good breeding. From early girlhood, ever since charming curves had begun to swell her chemise, Pani Anna had dreamt of an unusual life. She had only to look at herself in the mirror: she was pretty, and not merely pretty, but exciting, and she was intelligent, vivacious and energetic. Her parents' home was a poor one. Her father, a ruined petty nobleman, picked up a living in the markets and at the card-tables of rich noblemen's houses. On the rare occasions when he was at home, he sat at the window in a shabby coat, tired, quiet, with a crumpled face, looking out at his poverty-stricken property. When Anna, his beloved and only daughter, teased him to tell her about his adventures, he would begin with bad grace, but would gradually warm up and then boast of his prowess and powerful connections. Anna listened to both the truth and lies about the wonders and luxury of the Vyshnevetskis, Potockis, Lubomirskis, Czartoryiskis, as to a fairy tale. When her father, having sold his last broken nag to pay a gambling debt and eaten his last chicken, promised her in marriage to the elderly Pan Sobeczanski, Anna did not demur, realising that this marriage was but a convenient stepping-stone to a brighter future. The only thing that annoyed her was her husband's too passionate infatuation, far more passionate than his years warranted. However, she had a kind heart entirely governed by common-sense.

And now, at one stroke, chance had raised her to the topmost rung of good fortune: the King had fallen into her net. Pani Anna did not lose her head as a simpleton would have done; her shrewd wits began to dart about like a mouse in a dark wheat-bin. Everything had to be thought out and foreseen. She tenderly declared to Pan Sobeczanski, who, like most infatuated husbands, saw and understood nothing: "No more country wilds for me! You yourself, Joseph, ought to be happy on my account: I want to be the first lady in Warsaw now.

Don't worry about anything, feast to your heart's content and go on adoring me."

A far more difficult task was that of outwitting Countess Kozelska and quietly getting rid of her, but the most delicate part of all was how to deal with the king: not merely to serve his passing fancy but to attach him firmly to herself.

Feminine charm alone was not enough to ensure success; experience was needed, and Pani Anna lost no time in worming out of the countess the mysteries of seduction.

"Ah, no, dear Countess, in Warsaw I am ready to live in a hut, if only I can be near you, like a little bee near a rose," Pani Anna said. She was sitting with her feet tucked up in the other corner of the carriage and glanced from time to time at the countess's face with its closed eyes: in turn it was rosy from the reflection of the camp-fires and then again melted into the shadow, like the moon in the clouds. "I am still quite a child. I still tremble when the king addresses me, for I am afraid of saying something silly or unsuitable in reply."

The countess began to speak as though in answer to her own thoughts, which were as sour as vinegar:

"When the king is hungry he devours with equal pleasure rye bread and Strasburg pies. In a wayside inn he picked up a pock-marked Cossack woman who was running like a streak of lightning across the yard into the cellar and back into the inn carrying jugs. He thought she was a woman. Nothing else means anything to him. Oh, the monster! Countess Königsmark got hold of him by displaying her garters during the dancing: black velvet ribbons tied in bows over her pink stockings."

"Jesus, Mary! And that has such an effect?" Pani Anna whispered.

"He fell in love like a beast with a Russian lady, Volkova. During a ball she changed her gown and her chemise several times. He rushed into her room, seized her chemise and wiped his sweaty face with it. The same sort of thing happened in the last century to a king of France. But there it ended in a lasting attachment, whereas Volkova slipped away from under his very nose, to everybody's delight."

"I'm terribly stupid!" Pani Anna exclaimed. "I can't understand what a lady's chemise has to do with all this."

"It isn't the chemise that matters, it's the lady's skin, her particular aroma. A woman's skin is the same as a flower's scent. All the little girls in the convent schools know it. With such a depraved creature as your beloved king, it's his nose that determines his inclinations."

"Oh, Holy Virgin!"

"Have you looked at his great nose of which he is so proud, because he thinks it gives him a resemblance with Henry IV? He keeps blowing out his nostrils like a setter that has scented a partridge."

"Then scent, amber powder and aromatic cosmetics are particularly important? Have I rightly understood you, dear Countess?"

"If you have read the *Odyssey* you must remember that the enchantress Circe turned men into hogs. Don't pretend to be so naïve, my dear. But I must say, it's all disgusting, tiresome and degrading enough."

The countess fell silent. Pani Anna wondered which of them had outwitted the other. The head of a horse, with foam dripping from its black lips, appeared at the window of the coach. It was the king who had ridden up. He jumped out of his saddle and opened the door of the coach; his nostrils flared, his large-featured face wore a dazzling smile. In the light of the torch carried by his mounted attendant he was so magnificent, in his light gilt helmet with raised visor and his purple mantle thrown over his shoulders in sumptuous folds, that Pani Anna told herself: "No, no; no foolishness!" The king cried gaily:

"Come out, ladies, you'll witness an historical sight!"

Pani Anna gave a faint cry and immediately flitted out of the carriage. The countess merely said:

"My back feels broken, which is no doubt what Your Majesty has been trying to achieve. I'm not dressed and I'll remain here to doze on an empty stomach."

"If you need a litter I'll send you one," the King replied curtly.

"A litter? For me?" The green flame in her suddenly wide open eyes made August recoil slightly. The countess flew out of the coach as if armed with a lighted fuse. She had a peach-coloured travelling cloak, sparkled with the gems that trembled in her ears and on her fingers, and her coiffure was slightly disarranged, though no less alluring for that. "Always at your service!" she said, thrusting her bare arm into his. Once again Pani Anna recognised the greatness of this woman's art.

All three of them went towards the king's carriage where in the light of torches, a squadron of picked noblemen's cavalry sat their horses in cuirasses with white swans' feathers mounted on iron rims at their backs. August and the two ladies—one on each side of and slightly behind him—took their seats in armchairs set on a carpet. Pani Anna's heart fluttered: it seemed to her as though these tall horsemen who surrounded them, with their wings and their cuirasses and helmets gleaming with the reflections of the fires, were God's angels descended on earth to give back to August his Warsaw palace, his fame and his money. She closed her eyes and recited a short prayer:

"May the king be as a lamb in my hands!"

There came a clatter of horses' hoofs. The squadron parted to make a passage. Out of the darkness the Great Hetman Lubomirski was approaching with his escort: they, too, had wings behind their shoulders, but theirs were of black feathers. The hetman rode up close to the king and reined in with a jerk; then he sprang from his snorting horse, his cloak billowing, and went down on his knee on the carpet in front of August:

"Sire, forgive my treason if you can."

His hot, dark eyes were steady, his inflamed face was sombre, his accents broken. He was humbling his pride. He did not take off his cap with its garland of diamonds, but his thin hands were shaking.

"My betrayal of you was madness, a clouding of my reason. Believe me, however, that not for an instant did I recognise Stanislaw as king. Bitter resentment at the affront was tearing at my vitals. And then at last my hour struck! I threw my mace at his feet. I spat and left him. In the palace courtyard I was set upon by the commander's soldiers. Thank God, my sword-arm is still strong: I sealed my breach with Lesczinski with the blood of the accursed enemy. I offer you my life!"

August, who had been slowly pulling off his iron gauntlets while he listened, dropped them on the carpet and his face cleared. He rose, stretched out his hands and shook them in the air.

"Great Hetman," he said, "I forgive and embrace you with all my heart."

He pressed the hetman's face strongly to his chest, to the chased centaurs and nymphs on his cuirass of Italian workmanship. After holding him like this somewhat longer than necessary, August gave orders for another chair to be brought. But the chair had already been placed. Fingering his bruised cheek, the hetman began a recital of the events in Warsaw after his refusal to take the field against August and the Russians.

There had been a great commotion in Warsaw. The Cardinal-Primate Radzievski, who, in the previous year, at the Lublin Diet, had publicly sworn on his knees loyalty to August and to the freedom of the Polish State; who, a month later, had kissed the Lutheran Bible swearing loyalty to King Charles and had demanded—with foam on his lips—the deposition of August; who had proposed Prince Lubomirski as candidate for the throne, immediately betraying him, too, at the demand of Orvid Horn: this threefold traitor had been the first to flee from Warsaw, taking with him several chests filled with church treasure.

King Stanislaw wandered for three days about the deserted palace; every morning the number of courtiers who presented themselves at the king's levee grew smaller. Arvid Horn did not let him out of his sight; he had sworn to him to hold Warsaw with his garrison alone. As the rules of court etiquette prevented him from being present at the king's table during the king's meals he sat in the next room jingling his spurs. To drown the tiresome jingling, Stanislaw read aloud to himself verses from Apuleius in Latin between the courses. On the fourth night he nevertheless succeeded in slipping out of the palace disguised in peasant's clothes and wearing a false beard, accompanied by his hairdresser and his valet. He drove out of the city gates in a cart with two tar-barrels which contained the whole of the royal treasure. Arvid Horn realised too late that, like a true Lesczinski, King Stanislaw had been busy all these days with other things besides reading Apuleius and wandering aimlessly with his dog about the empty rooms of the palace. Horn tore down and trampled the curtains of the king's bed, ran the palace steward through with his sword and had the chief of the night guard shot. But nothing could now arrest the flight from Warsaw of the noble magnates who were in any way connected with Lesczinski.

August laughed at this recital, banging his fists on the arms of his chair and turning round to the ladies. Countess Kozelska's eyes expressed nothing but cold contempt, but Pani Anna broke into peals of laughter like a silver bell.

"Then what do you advise, Great Hetman? A siege or an immediate assault?"

"Only an assault, gracious Sire. Arvid Horn's garrison is not large. Warsaw must be taken before King Charles has time to come up."

"Immediate assault, the devil take it! A wise counsel!" August cried with a martial clang of his steel-clad shoulders. "For an assault to be successful one must give the troops a good meal of boiled goose, for instance. At a moderate estimate that means five thousand geese!" He wrinkled his nose. "It wouldn't be a bad idea to pay them too. All Prince Golitsin was able to let me have was twenty-thousand thalers. A paltry sum. Where money is concerned, Tsar Peter is not open-handed, no, not open-handed. I was counting on the cardinal's and the palace treasure. All has been stolen!" he shouted and his face became suffused with blood. "After all, I cannot lay a contribution on my own capital!"

Prince Lubomirski heard him out, staring at the ground under his feet, and then said in a low voice:

"My army chest is not empty yet. You have only to give the order. . . ."

"Thank you, I'll be glad to take advantage of your offer," August replied, a little too hastily, but with true Versailles grace. "I need one hundred thousand thalers. I'll repay you after the assault." His face shone and he again embraced the hetman, touching his cheek with his own. "Go, Prince, and rest. We too wish to rest."

The hetman leapt on his horse and, without looking back, galloped away into the darkness. August turned to the ladies.

"Ladies, and so your wearisome journey is going to bring its reward. Only let me know your wishes. The first and the most modest one is, I imagine, to have some supper. Do not think I have forgotten about your comfort and entertainment. It is a king's duty never to forget anything. Allow me to invite you into my carriage."

chapter five

Gavrila Brovkin was driving post-haste to Moscow without stopping to rest. The Tsar's order with which he was provided allowed him to change at every stage the three horses harnessed to his short cart. He was carrying the Tsar's mail and a message to the Prince-Emperor enjoining him to speed up the delivery of all kinds of iron wares to Petersburg. Andrey Golikov was with him. Gavrila's orders were to lose no time on the way. As if he would! His impatient heart was racing miles ahead of his troika. When they drove up to a posting-station Gavrila, covered with dust from head to foot, would dash up the steps of the porch and hammer on the door with his whip. "Commissar!" he would shout rolling his eyes: "A troika immediately!" Then stepping close to the sleepy post-house master, whose only insignia of office was his gold-laced hat—for, owing to the heat, he would be barefooted and clad only in underpants and unbelted tunic —he would demand: "A dipper of kvass, and have the horses harnessed before I have finished drinking."

Andrey Golikov was also in a state of spiritual exaltation. Clenching his teeth, he gripped the sides of the cart to prevent himself from falling and killing himself. With hair streaming over his back and nose thrust forward like a snipe's, he looked at everything with eyes that seemed to have opened for the first time: at the forests, that swam towards them, fragrant with resinous warmth, at the round, swampy lakes, with their poisonously green borders, that mirrored the sky and the summer clouds, at the meandering streams, from whose black waters flocks of all kinds of game-birds rose when the wheels of the cart thundered over a bridge. The bell on the harness-yoke tinkled a plaintive tale of a long, endless road.

The driver kept urging on the horses, sensing with his rounded back the presence of the furious passenger with the whip.

The villages were few and far between. They were very old, with few inhabitants, and the huts were poor with holes covered with bladders for windows and a narrow, soot-covered opening over the low doors. Under a cleft willow there would be a small penthouse with an icon: people had to have something to remind them of God in this wilderness. In some of the villages, only two or three of the huts would be inhabited; in the others the roofs had fallen in, the gates were broken, the yards overgrown with nettles. As for the people: you could seek them in the forest thickets, in the wilds of the north along the Dvina or the Vyga, if they had not fled to the Urals or the lower Don.

"Oh, what poor villages! Oh, how miserably they live!" Golikov whispered, pressing his narrow palm to his cheek in commiseration.

Gavrila would reply sagaciously:

"The people are few while the country is so vast that it would take you more than ten years to travel across it from one end to the other. That's what causes poverty: a great deal is demanded from every man. Now I have been to France. My God! The peasants sway in the wind, they live on grass and sour wine, and not all of them have even that much. Yet when a marquis or the French dauphin himself rides out to hunt, they kill game by the cartload. That's where you have real poverty. But there the reason is a different one."

Golikov did not ask what was the reason why the French peasants swayed in the wind. His mind was unenlightened and he was unable to understand the reason of things; he absorbed the sweet and bitter wine of life through his eyes, through his ears and through his nostrils, and both rejoiced and suffered excessively.

In the Valday hills the countryside became more cheerful: there were clearings where there would be a stack of last year's hay with a kite perched on the top, forest paths that wound out of sight among leafy thickets, tempting one to follow them and pick berries on the way; and the rustling of the forest was different here: soft and rich. The villages, too, were more prosperous, with strong gates and ornamental, carved porches.

They stopped at a well to water the horses and saw a girl of about sixteen, with a thick plait and a birch-bark headdress, every point of which was adorned with a blue bead. She was so pretty that it made a man feel like getting out of the cart and kissing her on the lips. Golikov began to sigh softly. But Gavrila, without paying much attention to such nonsense as a village girl, said to her:

"What are you standing and staring for? Don't you see we've got a broken tyre. Go, call a smith!"

"Oh dear!" she cried out softly and, dropping the yoke with the pails, ran off over the grass with a twinkling of pink heels under the embroidered hem of her coarse linen skirt. However, she must have said something to somebody for, within a short time, the smith made his appearance. Anyone looking at this peasant would have grunted with pleasure: "What a sturdy fellow!" He had strong, regular features and a small, curly beard, his lips wore a smile as though condecension alone had brought him to these travelling idiots; his chest could have stood hammering with a seventy-pound weight and his powerful hands were thrust into the top of his leather apron.

"The tyre's broken, is it?" he enquired with slight mockery in his sing-song bass. "One can see at once it's Moscow work." Wagging his head he walked round the cart, looked under it, then took hold of the tail and easily gave it a shake together with the passengers. "It's all coming to pieces. Only fit for devils to cart wood in."

Gavrila began to argue angrily. Golikov looked at the smith with admiration: of all the wonders this was, perhaps, the most amazing. How could he help yearning for brushes and paints, for fragrant oak boards! Everything, everything flashed past one's eyes, vanished without return into misty oblivion. Alone the painter arrested this senseless destruction by means of his art on the white surface of a board.

"Well, will it take you long to mend it?" Gavrila asked. "Every hour is precious, I'm hurrying on the Tsar's business."

"You can take a long time over it, or you can make it short," the smith replied. Gavrila looked grimly at his whip, then glanced at him.

"All right," he said. "How much will you want?"

"How much I shall want?" the smith laughed. "My work is expensive. If I were to ask the proper price, you wouldn't have enough money to pay. I know you, Gavrila Ivanovich! In the spring you passed through here with your brother and spent the night at my place. Have you forgotten it? Now, your brother is a clever man. I know Tsar Peter well too, and he knows me. Every time he passes along here, he goes to have a look at my smithy. He, too, is clever. Well, drive up to the smithy; we'll do something about it."

The smithy stood on a slope close to the highway. It was a low building of enormous logs, with an earthen roof and three stalls for shoeing horses. All around lay wheels, ploughs, harrows. The smith's younger brothers, in leather aprons and with leather thongs tied round their curly heads, and his elder brother, the hammerman—a sullen, bearded giant—were standing at the door. Without haste, but with easy efficiency, the smith set to work. He unharnessed the horses himself, turned the cart over, took off the wheels and pulled out the iron axles. "Look, they're both cracked. That Moscow smith ought to get tapped on the head with this axle." He thrust the axles into the furnace, emptied a sackful of coals into it and shouted to his youngest brother:

"Vanusha, lively there with the bellows! Eh, when you fell trees, you mustn't spare your arms!" And the brothers got busy. Gavrila stood leaning against the door-jamb, pulling at his pipe. Golikov seated himself on the high doorstep. They had asked whether it would not save time if they helped, but the smith waved them away: "Sit still; take a look for once at what Valday smiths are like."

Vanusha worked the bellows; the sparks flew up in a crackling hurricane to the roof. In their light the bearded elder brother stood like a statue with his hand on the long shaft of his thirty-six-pound hammer. The smith moved the axle about in the hotly breathing furnace.

"Our name is, for your information, we are called Vorobyevs," he said smiling as before into his curly moustache. "We are smiths, gunsmiths and bell-founders. That bell you've got on your harness-yoke, that's our work. Last year Tsar Peter was sitting there, just like you, on the threshold and kept asking: 'Wait,' he said, 'Kondraty Vorobyev —stop hammering—first answer me: why do your bells have such a sweet ring? Why does a sword blade of your work bend without breaking? Why does a Vorobyev pistol shoot twenty paces farther and never misfire?' And I answered: 'Your Majesty, Peter Alexeyevich, the reason why our bells ring so sweetly is that we weigh the copper and tin in a balance, as experienced people have taught us to do, and we cast them without bubbles. And a blade of our work bends without breaking because we heat it till it's crimson and temper it in linseed oil. And our pistols shoot so far without misfiring because when we were small our parent, Stepan Stepanovich, God rest his soul, beat us very painfully with a rod for every mistake and said: "Bad work is worse than thieving". That's how it is.' "

Kondraty snatched the axle out of the furnace with a pair of pincers, brushed the scale off it with a small besom that caught fire, and wagged his beard at his elder brother. The other took a step backwards and started to strike, throwing himself back and falling forwards, wielding his hammer in a circle. Red-hot drops of metal spattered the walls. Kondraty nodded to his middle brother: "Now then, Stepa!" The other took his stand on the other side with a smaller hammer. Then they set up a hammering like a peal of Easter bells: the eldest banged once with his great hammer, Stepa got in two blows, while Kondraty, turning the iron this way and that, tapped swiftly with his small hammer. "Stop!" he cried and threw the welded axle on to the earthen floor. "Vanusha, give us some more heat."

"And so he says to me," the smith went on, wiping off his sweat with the back of his hand. " 'Have you heard, Kondraty Vorobyev, about the Tula smith Nikita Demidov? Today he has his own works in the Urals, and his own mines, and he owns peasants, and his mansion is handsomer than mine, yet he began like you with trifles. It's about time for you to think about a big enterprise, you can't go on all your life shoeing horses by the highroad. If you haven't any money for a start, I'll give you some, though I'm rather short myself. Start a munitions works in Moscow or, better still, in Petersburg. It's a paradise there'. And so well did he describe it all that I felt he was tempting me. 'Oh,' I answered him, 'Your Majesty, Peter Alexeyevich, we live by the highroad as happy as kings. Our father used to say: "A pancake isn't a wedge, it won't split your belly—eat your fill, sleep soundly, work in good harmony". And we follow his precepts. We've got plenty of everything. In the autumn we brew our own beer, so strong that the hoops on the barrels crack, and we drink Your Majesty's health. We put on handsome leather gauntlets, go out into the street and get our fun in fist-fights. We wouldn't want to leave this place'. That's the answer I gave him. At this he got very angry. 'You couldn't have given me a worse answer, Kondraty Vorobyev,' he said. 'The man who is satisfied with everything and doesn't want to exchange the good for the better, will lose all. 'Oh,' he said, 'when will you lazy devils understand this?' Yes, he set me a puzzle."

The smith fell silent, frowned and lowered his eyes. The younger brothers looked at him; they too, of course, wanted to say something on the subject, but did not dare. He shook his head and smiled to himself.

"That's how he stirs up everybody. So we're lazy, are we? But it really looks as though we are."

He turned swiftly to the furnace where the second axle was heating, seized the pincers and called out to his brothers: "To your places!"

An hour and a half later the cart was ready, put together, strong and light. The girl with the birch-bark headdress kept hanging about the smithy. Kondraty noticed her at last.

"Mashutka!" he called out. She swung her plait and stood stock still. "Run and bring some cold milk for the gentlemen to drink before they go."

Gavrila, watching her twinkling heels with narrowed eyes, asked:

"Is that your sister? She's a fine-looking girl."

"She's a nuisance," the smith replied. "It seems a bit early to get her married. But she's no good in the house: won't weave, or milk the cows, or herd geese. All she likes to do is to knead blue clay and amuse herself: she'll fashion a cat riding a dog or an old woman with a crutch, as real as life, true enough. She'll model birds and animals that have never existed. Her room is full of this nonsense. We tried throwing the things out, but she set up a howl. So we leave her alone."

"Dear me, dear me!" Golikov said in a low voice. "We must see these things at once." And he fixed his eyes, open wide as though in sacred awe, on the smith. The smith slapped his thighs and laughed. Vanusha and Stepa smiled slightly, though they would have very much liked to burst into laughter too. The girl in the birch-bark headdress brought a crock of scalded milk.

"Mashka," Kondraty said to her, "this man wants to see your little figures, I don't know why. Show them to him."

The girl grew very pale and the crock with the milk trembled in her hands.

"Oh no, I won't show them!" she cried, and setting down the crock on the grass, she turned and went off as though walking in her sleep. When she had disappeared behind the smithy all the brothers held their sides with laughter and shook their hair. Only Golikov did not laugh. With his nose stuck out he kept looking towards where the girl had vanished round the corner of the smithy.

"Well, how about it, Kondraty Stepanovich?" Gavrila said. "I must, after all, pay you for the job."

"How can you pay me?" The smith wiped his wet eyes, brushed his moustache with his hand and thoughtfully stroked his small beard. "When you see Tsar Peter, give him my greetings. And add yourself whatever is necessary. And tell him that Kondraty Vorobyev begs him not to be angry and says he won't be stupider than other people. The Tsar will understand my answer."

2

A rainbow stretched beyond the billowing fields, beyond the birch-copses, beyond the strips of rye, far beyond the dark blue forest. One of its ends disappeared in the rain-cloud that was drifting away and, where its other end rested on the earth, gold motes flashed and twinkled.

"Do you see it, Andrushka?"

"Yes, I do."

"It's Moscow!"

"Gavrila Ivanovich, it's like an omen. The rainbow has lit it up for us."

"I can't understand myself why Moscow is so brightly lit. And I suppose you are glad to be going to Moscow?"

"Naturally. Both glad and afraid."

"When we arrive, first thing, we'll go to the bath-house. In the morning I'll go and see Romodanovsky. After that I'll take you to Tsarevna Natalia Alexeyevna."

"That's what frightens me."

"Listen, driver," Gavrila said, and this time he even sounded ingratiating. "Whip up your horses, my good fellow, I beg you kindly, whip them up!"

After the rain, the road had become easier. Mud flew from under the horses' hoofs. The leaves on the birches shone. The light breeze was fragrant. From the opposite direction came empty carts with peasants and an unsold cow or a lame horse tied to the cart-tail. A post with an eagle and the inscription "Moscow 34 versts" swam past them. And again they drove past ramshackle huts, placed haphazardly: one sideways to the road, another with its back to it, and a graveyard screened by grey willows with the peeling, tent-shaped roof of a small church. And again a small boy, naked but for a scanty shirt, came running across the road under the very noses of the horses, tossing back his hair and pretending he was a horse. The driver bent down, stinging him with his whip, but the boy only skipped out of the way looking after the cart with round eyes.

And again they drove down one hill and up another. If they looked to the right, where a stream glistened through the bushes, there were bearded peasants in long tunics advancing over a meadow with widely straddled legs, one behind the other, with a simultaneous flashing of scythes. If they looked to the left, there was a herd lying at the edge of the shade of the forest border and a shepherd-boy was running after a piebald bull-calf with his switch, while behind him a clever little dog bounded in the grass with flapping ears. Then again a post—31 versts. Gavrila groaned:

"Driver, we've only covered three versts."

The driver turned his merry face to him with a cheerfully upturned nose that seemed to have found room between his ruddy cheeks merely for the sake of reflecting itself in a glass of vodka.

"Don't go counting versts by the posts, sir," he said. "Count them by the taverns, the posts are unreliable. Look, we'll put on some speed now."

He suddenly gave a prolonged yell: "Oy-oy-oy, my little horses!" leant back and slackened the reins. The large-headed team, unmatched in colour, dashed off at a gallop, swerved sharply and came to a halt by a tavern. This was an old, long log building with a high pole sticking up at the gates and, over the door, for those who could read, the word "Tavern" painted in vermilion on an azure field.

"Do what you like, sirs, but the horses are spent," the driver said gaily and took off his tall felt cap. "Beat me to death, if you like, but better order me a drink of vodka."

The tavern-keeper, dressed in the old fashion in a dark red coat with a collar that stood higher than his bald head, had already come out on to the porch, fresh and welcoming, carrying a tray with three small glasses of vodka and three fancy rolls with poppy-seed. There was nothing to be done; they had to get out of the cart and stretch their legs.

They reached the outskirts of Moscow in the damp twilight. There seemed to be no end to the estates, villages, groves, churches, fences. At times the harness-bow grazed the branch of a lime-tree and raindrops were scattered over the passengers. Lights glimmered everywhere in windows with panes of thick glass or bladder; beggars were still sitting on the church porches; jackdaws cawed in the arches of the belfries. When the wheels began to rattle over wood paving, Gavrila gripped the driver's shoulder and showed him the crooked lane to turn into. "Over there, where there's a man lying by the fence, it's just opposite, in the blind-alley. Stop, stop! We're there!" He jumped out of the cart and knocked at the gate, bound, like a coffer, with bands of tinned iron. At the sound, the famous Brovkin wolf-dogs set up a fierce baying and rattled their chains.

It is good to return to the family home after a long absence. You come in and everything is familiar, you recognise everything afresh. In the cold hall a candle is burning on the windowsill; here, along the walls, are carved benches for the petitioners, where they can sit and patiently wait to be called in to the master of the house; then comes the empty winter anteroom with two stoves, and here a candle set on the floor is guttering in the draught; a cloth-covered door on the left leads to the uninhabited Dutch parlours for notable guests; the door on the right leads to the warm, low-ceilinged rooms; and if you go straight ahead you will wander along passages and steep staircases, up and down, among larders, pantries, bedrooms, closets, storerooms. And the smell in the family home is peculiar to it, pleasant and cosy. The people of the house are overjoyed at the traveller's return, their looks and words are full of affection and they are all eagerness to meet his wishes.

Ivan Artemyich, Gavrila's father, happened to be away on business connected with his manufactures. Gavrila was welcomed by the housekeeper, a portly, sedate woman, as her station required, with a heavy hand and a sing-song voice, by the head clerk—whom Ivan Artemyich himself called a true devil—and by the major-domo Karl, recently engaged from abroad, whose surname no one could pronounce. He was a tall, taciturn man with a full-cheeked face—bloated with idleness and Russian food—a powerful chin and beetling brows which testified to the man's great intelligence. His one defect, which was the reason for his coming to Moscow on a moderate salary, was that in place of a nose he had a small black velvet cap and spoke with a nasal twang.

"I don't want anything, only a bath," Gavrila told them. "For supper let me have some jellied fish and meat-pie, and a goose, and something else of the more solid kind. We've grown quite thin in Petersburg with nothing to eat but smelley salt-meat and dry bread."

The housekeeper threw up her plump hands and then folded them: "Jesus Christ! How could you eat dry bread?" The devil-clerk shook his goat's beard feelingly: "Ay-ay-ay!" The major-domo, who did not understand a word of Russian, stood like a wooden image, disdainful and imposing, with one great flat foot set forward and his hands behind his back. The housekeeper began to collect the change of clean linen for the bath and said in her sing-song voice:

"We'll steam you in the bath, and give you food and drink and lay you to sleep on a swansdown featherbed. Sleep is sweet in the family home. With us everything is well, thank God; misfortunes and worries go past the house. All the Dutch cows have had heifers, the English sows have had sixteen piglets each—the Prince-Emperor himself came to look at them. The berries and cherries in the garden are better than ever before. Your father's home is a paradise, a true paradise! The only pity is that it's empty, ah! ah! Your parent, Ivan Artemyich, keeps walking, walking about the rooms. 'I'm lonely, Agapovna,' he'll say to me. 'Perhaps I'd better go and have a look at my factories'. He's got so much money nowadays that he's lost count of it. If it weren't for Senka," and she winked towards the devil-clerk, "he'd never count it in his lifetime. Our only trouble is this black-nosed fellow. Of course, you couldn't do without such a person in your house these days; they are saying in Moscow that Ivan Artemyich may be granted a title. Well, when this fellow puts a hat with red feathers on his head and raps his mace on the floor and stamps his great feet, it's grand, there's no denying it. He was major-domo to the Prussian king until he got his nose bitten off, or something like that. We were a bit frightened of him at first—after all, he's a foreigner, it's no joke! Ignashka, the groom, taught him to play the balalaika. Since then he strums it all day long, everybody's tired to death of it. And how he eats! He follows me round: 'Mother, give me something to eat'. I've never known such a fool! But perhaps it's what's needed in his calling. On St. John's Day we had a big dinner —Tsaritsa Praskovya Fedorovna honoured it with her presence—and of course we'd have found it difficult without Karl. He put on a coat with at least ten pounds of braid and fringe on it, and buckskin gauntlets with fingers; and he took a golden dish, put a goblet worth a thousand roubles on it and went down on one knee to offer it to the Tsaritsa. Then he took another goblet, better than the first, and offered it to Tsarevna Natalia. . . ."

While the housekeeper was telling her story, the house-serf, who since the appearance of the major-domo was known as the *kammerdiener,* divested Gavrila of his dusty coat and his waistcoat, undid his necktie and began to pull off his topboots, grunting with the effort. Gavrila suddenly jerked away his legs, jumped up and cried:

"The Tsarevna was in our house? What nonsense are you talking?"

"She was, she was, our beautiful Tsarevna! She sat on Ivan Artemyich's left, our lovely Tsarevna. Everybody kept looking at her, forgetting to eat and drink. Her little hands were all covered with rings and bracelets. Her shoulders are like swans and just over one breast there's a little birthmark, the size of a buckwheat grain; everybody noticed it. And her dress was the colour of flax-blossom, lighter than air, very full at the sides, with silk roses along the hem, and on her head she had the tail of a bird of paradise."

Gavrila was no longer listening. Throwing a sheepskin coat over his shoulders, he rushed—his Tatar slippers flapping—along the passages and staircases to the bathroom. In the damp bath anteroom he suddenly remembered:

"Agapovna, where's the man who came with me?"

It appeared that the major-domo had not let Andrey Golikov into the house and he was still sitting in the yard in the unharnessed cart. But he was quite happy there with his own thoughts. Stars were shining over the dark roofs, there was a smell of kitchens, of haylofts and of cattle sheds, all extremely comfortable; now and then the sweetest possible fragrance of lime-tree blossom was wafted to him from somewhere, and it made his heart beat fast. Andrey leant on his elbow and looked at the stars. What were these lights sprinkled so lavishly over the deep lilac sky? Were they very far away and why did they shine there? He did not know and did not trouble his head about it. But peace flowed from up there into his heart. How small he, Andrey, was in this cart! Yes, small he might be, but not as he had been in the days when the elder Nektary beat him: he no longer felt himself a humble worm, a miserable lump of flesh. One would think that a beast could not have endured all that Andrey had had to endure in his short life. He had been humiliated, beaten, tortured, condemned to die of cold and hunger, yet here he was, like a king of kings, with his eyes on the lights of the universe, listening to the secret voice within: go, Andrey, do not lose heart, do not stray from your path! Soon, soon, your wonderful power will rejoice, all will become possible for it; out of ugliness you will create a world transfigured by beauty.

For this devilish voice, in his days with the elder, he would have been chained up for forty days with a dipper of water for all sustenance, and would be secretly smearing his bloody weals with oil taken out of the icon-lamp. The thought made Andrey smile without rancour. He suddenly remembered an occasion when he, the king of kings, had been beaten with particular ferocity in a smoky tavern by some townsmen, who had afterwards dragged him out by the feet and thrown him on the dung-covered snow. Why had they beaten him? He could not remember. It had happened during that terrible winter when the dead streltsi were hanging on the Kitay-gorod and Kremlin walls. In those days, hungry, in a tattered coat over his naked body and barefooted, filled with anguish and despair, Andrey had wandered from tavern to tavern, begging a glass of vodka from the drinkers and secretly hoping that they would finally kill him; at the time he had agonizingly wished it and could have wept with pity for himself. It was there, in a tavern, that he had met the sexton of St. Barbara's Church, a fellow with screwed-up eyes, a cleft nose and a little pigtail sticking up in the air. It was he who had persuaded Andrey to seek saintly peace, to give himself up to the unmerciful torments of the flesh at the hands of the elder Nektary. "Odd creatures!" Andrey murmured. "To torture the flesh! But flesh—ah—how beautiful it can be!" And another memory flashed across his mind: a quiet evening in Palekh, the air full of golden dust, the cows lowing as they turn into their own yards. His mother, a gaunt woman with shoulders like a man's, is going to the gate—the gate has long needed mending —and the yard is poor and neglected. Andrey and his brothers, with a year's difference between each, are sitting on an upturned cart without wheels. They are patiently waiting; with a mother like theirs you couldn't be anything but patient! She opens the sagging gate. Scraping her broad sides against the gate-posts, Burenka, their kind provider, comes in with a short, gentle mooing. Their mother's face is dark, harsh, sad. Burenka's face is warm, her forehead is curly, her nose moist, her eyes large and violet. Burenka would never hurt you. She breathes over the boys and goes to the well to drink. And there, at the well, their mother, seating herself on a stool, begins to milk her. "Shirk-shirk, shirk-shirk" runs Burenka's milk into the pail. The boys sit on the cart patiently waiting. Their mother brings bowls and fills them, pouring the milk in a broad stream out of the pail. "Well, come along," she says roughly. The first to drink the new milk is Andrey. He drinks as long as his stomach can stand it while his brothers watch him; the youngest sighs briefly, because he will be the last to drink. . . .

"Hey, you traveller, get out of the cart!" Andrey came to himself. A lad with an angry face—the *kammerdiener*—stood before him. "Gavrila Ivanovich wants you to come to the bath, to steam yourself. You'd better take off your boots here and throw your coat and cap under the cart. This isn't like a boyar's house—we don't let in people dressed in rags."

Gavrila and Andrey sat down to supper pleasantly relaxed after the bath, with towels round their necks. Agapovna sent the majordomo away to his closet to make things more homely. Her plump, white hands fluttered over the table, piling their plates with the choicest pieces and filling their wine-glasses of Venetian glass, brought out for the occasion, with her best fancy vodkas and fruit liqueurs. When the candles burnt up brightly Gavrila noticed a frame, covered with holland, that stood on a chair in a corner of the room. Agapovna rested her cheek on her hand in a sorrowful gesture.

"I don't know how I am to show this before a stranger," she said. "Your sister Alexandra Ivanovna sent it from Holland for St. John's Day. Our dear Ivan Artemyich hangs it from time to time on the wall, then it distresses him and he takes it down again and covers it up. In the letter she sent with the picture she said: 'Papa, do not hesitate, hang up my portrait in the dining-room; in Europe they hang up more striking things than that. Do not be a barbarian'."

Gavrila got up from the table, picked up a candle and pulled the holland off the thing that stood on the chair in the corner. Golikov half rose; it quite took his breath away. This was a portrait of the boyar lady Volkova of incredible beauty and incredible allurement.

"Well, well!" was all Gavrila said as he held the candle to it. The artist had represented Alexandra Ivanovna on a wave, in the midst of a morning sea; she lay on a dolphin's back naked, as she was born, only covering herself with one hand with pearly nails. In her other hand she held a cup filled with grapes at which two doves, perched on its rim, were pecking. Above her head—to the right and to the left —two fat infants floated upside down in the air blowing into conch-shells with puffed-out cheeks. Alexandra Ivanovna's youthful face, its eyes the colour of sea-water, wore an exceedingly roguish smile that lifted the corners of her mouth.

"There's Sanka for you!" Gavrila said, not a little astonished. "It's to her, in Holland, that we're going to send you, Andrey. Look out that you don't fall into the devil's clutches when you get there. Venus, truly a Venus! No wonder cavaliers fight with swords on her account; and some have got themselves killed."

3

The guardian of Moscow, the Prince-Emperor, lived in his vast, ancestral mansion in the Miasnitskaya, near the Lubianka square. He had a chapel with attendant clerics and choristers, linen workshops, fulleries, tanneries, smithies, stables, cowsheds, sheep-folds, poultry-yards and all manner of cellars and storehouses crammed with goods and provisions. All the buildings were of huge logs, made to last for centuries. The house itself was on the same pattern, with none of the fancy decorations in which Moscow people took so much pride since the days of Tsar Alexey Mihaylovich: it was nothing much to look at, but was solidly built, with a shingle roof, moss-grown with age, and small windows high in the walls. The order and custom of the household were also old-fashioned; but if anyone, taking this for granted, were to come, in the simplicity of his mind, dressed as in the old days in a long-sleeved coat reaching to his heels and wearing his full beard—even though he might be a descendant of Rurik—he would leave the place to the jeers of Romodanovsky's servants: his coat would have been cut to knee-length, tufts of shorn hair would be on his cheeks, while the beard itself would be sticking out of his pocket for him to put in his coffin if he was ashamed to appear without it before his Creator. When the Prince-Emperor gave a feast, many of the guests prepared themselves for the occasion with sighs and lamentations because of the exactions, the indecent frolic and distasteful buffoonery they must expect.

The Prince-Emperor rose early and, dressed in a dark linen tunic, with a narrow belt worn high with a prayer woven into the design, heard a short morning service. When a sunbeam pierced the billowing incense-smoke and the flames of tapers and icon-lamps paled, and the timid priest chanted "amen", the Prince-Emperor dropped ponderously on his knees on the small rug and, grunting heavily, touched the freshly scrubbed floor with his forehead; then, helped up, he rose, kissed the cold cross presented by the priest and proceeded to the dining-room. There, settled comfortably on a bench, he smoothed his black moustache and drank a glass of pepper vodka of such strength that if anyone who was not a Russian had drunk it, he would have stayed gaping for a long while. After that the Prince-Emperor ate a small piece of black bread with salt and then proceeded to his meal. This consisted of cold kvass soup with fish and vegetables, all kinds of jellied, pickled and preserved dishes, noodles and roasts, all of which he ate unhurriedly, in the peasant way. The members of his household, including Princess Anastasia Fedorovna herself—own sister to Tsaritsa Praskovya—remained silent at table, laid down their spoons cautiously and gingerly helped themselves with their fingers from the dishes. In their cages set on the windowsills quail and trained starlings would now begin to give voice; one of them could even say quite clearly: "Uncle, some vodka."

Finally the Prince-Emperor would drain a dipper of kvass, and, after lingering a little, would get up and go out—making the floorboards creak—into the anteroom where they would help him on with his roomy cloth coat and hand him his staff and cap. When his shadow was seen through the dim panes of the covered porch slowly descending the stairs, all those in the courtyard who happened to be anywhere near hastened to make themselves scarce. He went alone across the yard along a brick-laid path. Though he could turn his head only with difficulty because of his thick neck, he noticed everything out of the corner of his protruding eyes: who had run off where, or where he had hidden himself, and any kind of disorder, however small. And he remembered everything. But as he had a great many important State affairs on his hands, he often had no time to attend to trifles. Through an iron wicket-gate in the fence he passed into the neighbouring courtyard of the Preobrazhensky Office. There, in the long half-dark passages, clerks and scribes silently whipped off their caps before him and soldiers stood at attention.

The head clerk of the Preobrazhensky Office, Prohor Chicherin, would meet him at the doors of the chancellery, and when the Prince-Emperor had seated himself at the table near the window, under the mouldy vault, he would immediately begin to report: in the course of the day before, four brass cannon and as many well-cast iron ones had been brought from Tula. Should they be sent on immediately and where: to the camp near Narva or to the one near Yuriev? And yesterday, too, the first company of the newly-recruited regiment had been finally fitted out, though the soldiers were still barefooted; the shoes without buckles would be delivered in the coming week; in the Stewards' Chamber the merchants of the boot guild, Sopliakov and Smurov, were prepared to kiss the cross on it that they would not default. What was to be done? Gunpowder, bullets in bags and flints loose in sacks had been sent to the Narva camp, according to the ukase. It had been impossible to send the grenades because the storekeeper Yeroshka Maximov was drunk for the second day running and would not give up the keys to anyone; they had tried to take them from him by force, but in his frenzy he had threatened the men with a chopper; the kind used to chop cabbage. What was to be done? Many such matters were reported by the head clerk Chicherin. Finally he moved closer to the window under the vault, picked up the records of secret cases (taken down by clerks during interrogations without violence and interrogations under torture) and began to read them out. It was impossible to tell whether the Prince-Emperor, as he sat with one hand resting heavily on the table, was listening or merely dozing, but Chicherin knew very well that he was sure to grasp the gist of the matter.

"In the abandoned bath-house where the unfrocked priest Grishka was hiding, in the grounds of the house belonging to Tsarevnas Ekaterina Alexeyevna and Maria Alexeyevna, a manuscript book has been found under the floorboards, quarto size, half a finger thick," the head clerk Chicherin read from the records in so monotonous a voice that it was as if he were pouring dried peas on one's head. "On the first page there is written: 'Search for every kind of wisdom.' And lower down on the same page there is written: 'In the name of the Father, the Son and the Holy Ghost. . . . There is a herb called *zelezeka* which grows in ravines and burnt-out places, it is small, with nine leaves on its sides, and three flowers at the top: red, purple and dark blue; this herb is very powerful; it must be gathered at the new moon, pounded, infused and the infusion to be drunk thrice—then you will see at your side demons of the air and of the water. Say to them the magic word *nstsdtchndsi* and your wish will be granted'."

The Prince-Emperor sighed deeply and raised his drooping eyelids.

"Say that word again clearly."

Chicherin scratched his forehead, wrinkled up his face and, with an angry effort, barely managed to utter: *"nstsdtchndsi."* He glanced at the Prince-Emperor, who nodded, and went on reading:

"Oh, princes, magnates, oh, tears and sighs! What is it that is desirable? We desire to temper the present times, in their fierceness, so that ordinary times should set in again. . . ."

"That's it, that's it, that's it!" the Prince-Emperor said, moving in his chair, and an ironic gleam of comprehension flickered in his prominent eyes. "It's clear what the herb *zelezeka* stands for. Has the ex-priest admitted that the book is his?"

"Today, in the third hour, after torture, Grishka admitted that it was his. He alleges that he bought it for four kopeks from a stranger in the Kislovka, and when asked why he hid it in the bath-house under the floor, he said it was out of foolishness."

"And did you ask him how one was to understand: 'that ordinary times should set in again'?"

"I did. He was given five lashes and then he replied, saying that he had bought the book for the sake of the paper, to bake church-bread on, and did not read it and does not know what was written on it."

"Ah, the rogue! The rogue!" The Prince-Emperor slowly moistened his finger, turning over the dogeared pages of the manuscript. Some passages he read half-aloud: "The herb *vaharia* is reddish-yellow; if a man has been given a deadly poison, give him an infusion of this to drink, and soon he will be purged from above and from below. . . ." "A useful little herb," the Prince-Emperor remarked and went on, following the lines with his finger-nail: "In Cyril's book it is said: a tempter will come and seduce people. The signs of his advent are: the herb nicotine, otherwise tobacco; orders will be given to burn it and swallow the smoke, and to crush it into powder and smell it, and in place of the singing of psalms they will be continuously smelling this powder and sneezing. Another sign is the shaving of beards." "Well," said the Prince-Emperor closing the book, "let's go and ask him who it is who wishes to temper the present times. The ex-priest is a nimble and experienced fellow. I've known about this book for a long time. He's been through half Moscow with it."

As they went down the narrow brick staircase, worn away by damp, to the torture-room in the cellar, Chicherin, as usual, said deprecatingly:

"This damp comes from under the ground, the bricks are rotten. At any moment you might fall and kill yourself. We ought to have a new staircase built."

"Yes, we ought," the Prince-Emperor replied.

An under-clerk, a scribe, was leading the way with a candle. Like the head clerk he was dressed in foreign clothes, though his were shabby; a brass inkpot hung round his neck and a roll of paper stuck out of his half-torn pocket. When he set the candle on an oak table in the low cellar, several rats scurried off like shadows to their holes in the corners.

"And we've been quite overrun with rats lately," the head clerk said. "I ought to ask for some arsenic at the pharmacy."

"Yes, you ought to," the Prince-Emperor replied.

Two brutal-looking men, stooping under the vaults, dragged in the ex-priest Grishka. His eyes were turned up, his beard matted and his face green with a hanging underlip. Was he really unable to use his legs? When they stood him up under a hook from which a rope dangled, he collapsed softly and lay as if dead. The head clerk said in a low voice:

"I interrogated him without damage to his limbs and he went back on his own two legs."

The Prince-Emperor looked for some time at the bald spot on Grishka's tousled head.

"It has been found out," he said in a somnolent voice, "that the year before last, in Zvenigorod, you ripped off the silver mounts of the icons in the Church of Elijah the Prophet, and broke open the church box in the Church of the Annunciation; and in the same place you stole the priest's sheepskin coat and felt boots from the altar. You sold the things and spent the money on drink. You were arrested and escaped from your guards and went to Moscow, where till this day you hid first in various boyars' houses, and later in the bathhouse in the grounds of the Tsarevna's house. Do you admit this? Will you answer? No? Very well. These doings are only half your trouble."

The Prince-Emperor was silent for a moment. The executioner, a respectable-looking, waxen-faced, hollow-cheeked man, with a large mouth that showed red between his flat moustache and small curly beard, appeared noiselessly behind the brutal-looking men.

"It has been found out," the Prince-Emperor resumed, "that you have been visiting the lay-sister Ulyana in the Foreign Quarter, taking her letters and money from certain persons. And this woman Ulyana carried the letters to Novodevichy, to a certain person. Ulyana took letters and parcels from her and you took them back to the above-mentioned persons. Was that so? Do you admit it?"

The head clerk leaned over the table and whispered to the Prince-Emperor indicating Grishka with his eyes:

"He's on his guard, I can tell by his ears."

"You won't confess? So. You are stubborn. It's a pity. It will only mean more trouble for us and more bodily suffering for you. All right. Now tell me this: to what houses precisely did you go? To whom precisely did you read out of this book about the desire to temper the ferocity of the present times and the desire to bring back ordinary times?"

As though he were waking up, the Prince-Emperor raised an eyebrow and his face swelled. The executioner stepped softly up to the prostrate Grishka, who was lying on his face, touched him and shook his head.

"No, Prince Fedor Yurievich, today he won't speak," he said. "We'd only trouble him unnecessarily. After the rack and the five lashes he's gone numb. We must leave it till tomorrow."

The Prince-Emperor rapped his nails on the table. But Silanty, the executioner, was experienced: if a man had gone numb, you might break him in two, but you would not get the truth out of him. And the matter was extremely important: with Grishka's arrest the Prince-Emperor had got on the track, if not of a downright conspiracy, at least of malicious grumbling and obduracy among Moscow personalities who were still regretting the boyars' privileges of the time of Tsarevna Sophia, still languishing under her nun's cowl in the Novodevichy convent. But there was nothing to be done; the Prince-Emperor rose and went back up the rotten staircase. The head clerk Chicherin remained to hover about over Grishka.

4

The morning was damp, warm and misty. In the alleys there was a smell of wet wooden fences and of smoke coming from stove-chimneys. The horse splashed in the puddles. Gavrila got out of the saddle at the gates of the Preobrazhensky Office and for a long time could not get hold of the officer of the guard.

"Where has he disappeared, the devil?" he shouted to the moustached soldier who stood at the gates.

"Who knows? He was here all along, now he's gone off somewhere."

"Then go and find him."

"I cannot leave my post."

"Then let me in!"

"The orders are to let no one in."

"Then I'll go in myself," and Gavrila pushed the soldier aside to pass through the wicket-gate, but the man said:

"Open that wicket-gate and I'll stick my bayonet into you according to the articles of war."

At last the noise brought out the officer of the guard, who had been killing time in the sentry-box inside the gates. He had a small freckled face and eyes that did not look at anything in particular. Gavrila pounced on him, explaining that he had brought the mail from Petersburg and had to hand it over personally to Romodanovsky.

"Where can I see the Prince-Emperor? Is he at the Office now?"

"I know nothing," the officer of the guard replied, watching a large tabby that was delicately crossing the muddy street. "It's the tom from the Prince's house," he said to the soldier. "What a fuss they made about him being lost. And there he is, the brute."

Suddenly the gates creaked shrilly on their hinges and were flung wide open; four black horses in tandem, with turquoise-blue harness, emerged at a swinging gait. Gavrila had just time to jump back when, through the window of the great shabby gilt coach on low wheels, Romodanovsky glanced at him with his lobster eyes. Gavrila hastily climbed back into his saddle to catch up with the coach. The officer of the guard seized the horse's bridle; the devil knew whether he was obstructive by nature or whether it was really forbidden by the rules to overtake the Prince-Emperor's equipage.

"Let go!" Gavrila cried furiously. He tightened the reins and dug in his spurs making his horse rear; the officer hung on the rein and fell.

"Guard! Catch the rogue!" came the cry far behind him as Gavrila was already riding out on to the Lubiansky Square.

He did not catch up with the coach and, spitting with vexation, turned over the Neglinny bridge into the Kremlin, to the Siberian chancellery. The chancellery occupied a long, low building with a rusty roof, built in the days of Boris Godunov; it stood on the edge of an abrupt rise, higher than the fortress wall, with its back towards the Moskva river. The anteroom and passages were crowded; people were sitting and lying on the floor along the walls. Clerks, in long coats with patched elbows (from continuous rubbing on the tables), and quills stuck behind their ears, kept running out of the creaking doors; they flourished papers and shouted angrily at the grim Siberians who had come over thousands of miles to seek redress against the governor—a malicious taker of bribes, the worst since the creation—or to obtain some concessions for mining, gold-prospecting, fur-hunting or fishing enterprises. An experienced man, after enduring the curses, would wrinkle up his eyes genially and say to the clerk: "Come, my benefactor, let us have a heart-to-heart talk in the provision shop row, or any other place you like." But the inexperienced man would go away with drooping head, to come back on the next day and many days following, wasting his money at the hostelry, to wait and to importune again and again.

The Prince-Emperor was in the department of armaments. Gavrila did not ask whether he could see him. He elbowed his way to the door and, when someone pulled him by the coat—"Where are you going? You can't go in there!"—he pushed him aside with his elbow and went in. The Prince-Emperor was sitting alone in a low, stuffy room with a window half closed by a shutter, wiping his neck with a brightly-coloured handkerchief. A pile of orders, petitions and complaints lay on the table beside him. At the sight of Gavrila he shook his head reprovingly:

"You're a bold fellow, Ivan Artemyich's son! Fancy! The low-born open the doors themselves nowadays. What is it you want?"

Gavrila handed him the mail and then repeated what he had been ordered to convey by word of mouth about the urgent delivery to Petersburg of all kinds of hardware, especially nails. The Prince-Emperor broke the wax seal, unfolded the Tsar's letter with his thick fingers and, holding it at arm's length, began to read, moving his lips. Peter wrote:

"Sire! I inform Your Majesty that an amazing affair happened here near Narva: fools took in clever people. The Swedes had a mountain of pride before their eyes which prevented them from seeing through our trickery. You will hear about this masquerade battle, in which we killed and captured a third of the Narva garrison, from an eye-witness, Lieutenant of the Guards Yaguzhinsky, who will soon be with you. As regards the medicinal herbs for the pharmacy which were to be sent to Petersburg, not an ounce has been sent yet. I have written about this many times to Andrey Vinius who, each time, presented me with a Moscow 'at once'. Please ask him: why is so important a matter, which is a thousand times more valuable than his head, treated so negligently? Ptr."

When he had finished reading, the Prince-Emperor raised the part of the letter where the signature stood to his lips. Then he sighed deeply.

"It's close," he said. "Hot and stuffy. There's a lot of work. In the course of the day one can't get even half of it done. My helpers, ah, my helpers! There are few who want to work hard, all try to skimp it. And to get as much as they can. Why are you dressed up like that, and with a wig on? Is it to the Tsarevna you're going? She's not at the palace, she's at Izmaylovo. When you see her, don't forget to tell her this: in the Petrovka, in a tavern under the arches there's a remarkable starling in a cage in the window. It speaks Russian very well and all who pass stop to listen. I myself listened a while ago from my carriage. It can be bought, should the Tsarevna wish it. Go now. On your way out, tell the clerk Nesterov to send someone to fetch Andrey Vinius and to have him brought to me immediately. Here, you may kiss my hand."

5

In the afternoon it started to drizzle. To keep up their spirits Anisya Tolstaya suggested playing with a ball in the empty throne room where, for many years now, no one had set foot.

Anna and Martha, the Menshikov girls, were always only too glad to play at anything. With ribbons fluttering and dimpled arms stretched out, bare to the elbow, they rushed shrieking after the ball over the creaking floorboards. On this particular day Natalia Alexeyevna felt strangely tearful and the game did not amuse her. When she was quite small the sun had always shone brightly through the small red, yellow and blue panes in all the windows of this room, set high in the wall, and the gilt leather had gleamed on the walls. The leather had now been stripped, leaving the logs of the wall bare with tufts of tow hanging between them. The rain pattered on the roof. She said to Katerina:

"I don't like Izmaylovsky palace. It's big and empty, it's like a corpse. Let's go somewhere and sit quietly."

She laid her hand on Katerina's shoulder and led her downstairs into the small bedchamber—now also abandoned and forgotten—of her dead mother, Natalia Kirillovna. Such a long time had passed, yet the room still held a faint aroma of incense, or perhaps of musk. To the end of her days Natalia Kirillovna had liked oriental scents.

Natalia glanced at the stripped bed with its spiralled posts denuded of curtains, at the dim little square mirror on the wall; then she turned away and pushed open the decayed window-frame, letting into the room the smell of the rain that rustled on the leaves of the lilac under the window, on the burdock, on the nettles.

"Let's sit down, Katia."

They seated themselves by the open window.

"Yes!" Natalia sighed. "Summer will soon be over now. Before we know where we are it will be autumn. What is it to you! At nineteen one doesn't look back at the days; let them fly away like birds! But I—do you know how old I am? I am only one year younger than my brother Peter. Count up how much that makes. My mother married at seventeen, my father was in his late thirties. He was stout, his beard always smelt of mint, and he was always ailing. I don't remember him well. He died of dropsy. One day Anisya Tolstaya had had a drop of fruit brandy and started telling me secrets of bygone days. In her youth my mother was gay, lighthearted, passionate. Do you understand?" Natalia looked with clouded eyes into the eyes of Katerina. "What scandal Sophia's partisans and parasites spread about her! But how can one blame her? According to ancient ideas everything was sinful, it was a sin even to be a woman: a vessel of wrath, the gates of hell. But in our new way of looking at things, it is charming Cupid who comes and pierces people's hearts with his arrow. So what is one to do? Are you supposed to throw yourself into a pond with a stone round your neck one autumn night? It's not the woman's fault, it's Cupid's! Anisya told me that in those days there lived in Moscow a boyar's son, Musin-Pushkin, as handsome as an angel, or rather a devil, fearless, hotblooded, a dashing rider and a hard liver. During Carnival week he challenged any man to a fist fight on the ice on the Moskva river. And he always won. My mother used to drive there secretly in a plain covered sledge and watch his prowess. Later she took him to her court as cup-bearer." Natalia Alexeyevna turned her lovely head towards the stripped bed and a wrinkle formed between her eyebrows. "Then suddenly he was sent as governor to Pustozersk. She never saw him again. But I, Katerina, haven't even got that much."

The gentle rain was still falling. It was close. The great trees that loomed indistinctly through the mist looked strangely unlike the pines of Izmaylovo. All the birds had taken shelter under the eaves and neither twittered nor sang. Only one bedraggled crow flew low over the grey meadow. Katerina watched it with serene eyes; she wanted very much to tell the Tsarevna that the thieving crow was flying towards the poultry-yard and was sure to carry away again a yellow chick, as it had done yesterday. Natalia Alexeyevna put her elbows on the windowsill and her head drooped, heavy with the plaits wound round it. Katerina, looking at her neck and the tendrils at the back of her head, thought suddenly: "Is it possible that no one has ever kissed that? Oh, how bitter it is!" and gave a barely perceptible sigh.

But Natalia heard the sigh. She moved her shoulder impatiently and said, propping her chin on her hand:

"And now tell me about yourself. Only tell the truth! How many lovers have you had, Katerina?"

Katerina turned her head away and whispered:

"Three."

"About Menshikov I know. But before him? Was Sheremetev one of them?"

"No, no!" Katerina replied quickly. "With the Field-Marshal I only had time to make him some soup, a sweet Esthonian soup with milk, and wash his linen. Oh, I didn't like him at all! I was afraid to cry, but I said to myself firmly: 'I'll light the stove and let the fumes choke me, but I won't live with him!' Alexander Danilych took me away from him the same day. I grew to like him very much. He's very gay and he joked a lot with me, and we laughed a great deal. I wasn't at all afraid of him."

"But you are afraid of my brother?"

Katerina pursed her lips and drew her velvet brows together in an effort to give an honest reply:

"Yes . . . But I think I'll soon stop being afraid of him."

"And who was your second lover?"

"Oh, Natasha, the second one was not a lover, he was a Russian soldier, a kind man, I loved him only for one night. How could I refuse him anything when he rescued me from some terrible men in fox-fur caps with curved swords? They dragged me out of the burning house, they tore my dress and beat me with a whip so that I shouldn't scratch them, and wanted to throw me on a saddle. He rushed up, pushed one, pushed another and with such strength! 'Ah, you Kalmuks! You mare's-milk drinkers!' he said. 'How dare you hurt a girl!' He took me in his arms and carried me to the baggage-train. I had no other way of thanking him. It was already dark, we lay on the straw."

Natalia's nostrils quivered and she asked harshly:

"Under a cart?"

"Yes. . . . He said to me: 'It's for you to say, my girl. It is only sweet when the girl is willing'. That's why I regard him as a lover."

"And who was the third one?"

"The third one was my husband, Johann Rabe, cuirassier of His Majesty King Charles, of the Marienburg garrison," Katerina replied gravely. "I was sixteen when Pastor Glück said to me: 'I have brought you up, Elena Ekaterina, I want to keep the promise I gave your dead mother. I have found you a good husband'."

"What about your father and mother? Do you remember them well?"

"No, I hardly remember them at all. My father's name was Ivan Skavroshchuk. He fled when he was still very young from Lithuania, from Minsk, from Pan Sapieha, to Esthonia and there he rented a little farm near Marienburg. We were all born there—my four brothers and two sisters and I myself, the youngest. There was an outbreak of plague and my parents and eldest brother died. Pastor Glück took me into his house; he was a second father to me. I grew up in his house. One of my sisters lives in Reval, the other is in Riga, but where my brothers are now, I don't know. The war has scattered everybody."

"Did you love your husband?"

"I didn't have the time. Our wedding was on St. John's Day. Oh, what a lovely time we had! We went to the lake and made a St. John's bonfire. Then we danced with wreaths on our heads and Pastor

Glück played the fiddle. We drank beer and fried little sausages with cardamoms. A week later Field-Marshal Sheremetev besieged Marienburg. When the Russians blew up the wall I said to Johann: 'Run for it!' He jumped into the lake and started to swim across, and I never saw him again."

"You must forget about him."

"There are many things I ought to forget, but then I forget easily," Katerina said and smiled timidly; her cherry eyes were full of tears.

"Katerina, you have concealed nothing from me?"

"How would I dare conceal anything from you?" Katerina said warmly, and the tears trickled down her peach-bloom cheeks. "I'd remember it and stay awake all night and come to tell you at break of dawn."

"And yet you are lucky," Natalia said, laying her cheek on her hand and looking out of the window like a bird out of its cage. A lump rose in her tender throat. "We Tsarevnas, no matter how gay we are, have only one end: the convent. They don't give us in marriage, and they don't take us for wives. Or else it's—forget all shame in debauchery, like Mashka and Katka. No wonder sister Sophia fought for power like a fierce tigress."

Katerina had just stooped to kiss Natalia's hand with its fine blue veins which, in her distress, she had clenched, when a tall rider on a lean horse appeared in the meadow. The horse's mane was wet, the rider's cloak was drenched and sodden plumes hung from his hat. As he caught sight of Natalia Alexeyevna he jumped out of the saddle and, dropping the bridle, stepped towards the window. Then he took off his hat, bent a knee on the grass and pressed his hat to his breast.

Natalia Alexeyevna rose impetuously. Her thick plait fell on her neck, her face flushed and quivered, her eyes shone and her lips parted.

"Gavrila!" she said softly. "Is it you? Welcome, my friend! Come into the house, don't stand out there in the rain."

Behind Gavrila a dog-cart drove up in which a frightened, sharp-nosed man, protected from the rain with a sack, sat next to the driver. Without taking his dark eyes off Natalia Alexeyevna, Gavrila came close up to the lilac bushes.

"May you live for many years," he said breathlessly. "I have come on an errand for the Tsar. I have brought you a skilful painter with orders to paint the portrait of a certain dear person. After that he is to be sent abroad to study. There he is, in the dog-cart. Permit me to bring him in with me."

6

One servant was sent by Anisya Tolstaya—on horseback—to the Kremlin to fetch all kinds of supplies for supper and sweet-meats —"and candles, many, many candles!"—from the provisions department. Another galloped off to the Foreign Quarter to fetch musicians. Thick smoke curled from the kitchen chimney and cropheaded kitchen-boys set up a clatter of chopping-knives. Girls with tucked-up skirts ran among the dripping weeds chasing chickens. The palace fishermen, who had grown lazy with idleness, went off to the ponds with creels and nets to catch equally lazy carp that lay on their sides on the slimy bottom.

After the rain, mist rose like smoke from the overgrown ponds, veiling the large, rotten bridge which no one used any more, and creeping between the trees over the meadow in front of the palace; and the old building gradually sank in it up to its very roofs.

Old people, house-serfs from the days of the Tsar Alexey Mihaylovich, sitting at the doors of the kitchen by the servants' quarters, watched the hazy glimmer of a candle appear and disappear here and there in the mist-shrouded palace, and listened to the sounds of stamping and laughter. They would not let the old house age and rot in peace, offering its log walls to the storms and its decayed roofs to the heavy rains. Spirited youth, with its new ways, had broken in here too. They were running up and down the stairs from the attics to the basement. But they would finding nothing there: only spiders and mice peeping out of their holes.

Natalia Alexeyevna seemed suddenly to be possessed by an imp of gaiety. Since the morning she had been in low spirits, but after Gavrila's arrival she brightened, her colour rose and she began to devise one amusement after another, allowing no one to sit still for a minute. Anisya Tolstaya did not know which way to turn.

"Tonight we'll have a Belshazzar's Feast," the Tsarevna told her. "We'll have supper in fancy dress."

"Light of my eyes, it's still a long way till Christmas Eve. And then I don't know, I never saw how King Belshazzar feasted."

"We'll search the whole palace, and anything we find that's quaint and fanciful we'll take to the dining-room. Don't cross me today, don't be pig-headed!"

The old stairs creaked, the rusty hinges of doors that had not been opened for a long time groaned. There was a general running to and fro in the palace with Natalia Alexeyevna in the lead, holding up her skirts, followed by Gavrila who carried a candle. His eyes were fixed in an awed stare. This awe had come upon him at the moment when, from his saddle, he had caught sight of Natalia Alexeyevna sitting at the window with her cheek resting sorrowfully on her hand. It was like something from one of the fairy-tales about the Tsarevna Incomparable-Beauty that Sanka used to tell them in his childhood as they sat on the stove. But then Tsarevich Ivan had jumped on his steed "higher than the standing forest, lower than the sailing clouds", up to the casement window and had snatched the ring off Incomparable-Beauty's white hand. . . .

Andrey Golikov was also quite bemused (he had been ordered to join the others). Since the previous night, when he had gazed at the portrait of Gavrila's sister on a dolphin, everything seemed to him halfway between reality and a dream. He was embarrassed to the point of breathlessness by the fair, round-cheeked Menshikov girls, so handsome and full-bodied that not even the ample folds of their dresses could conceal the allure of their curves. And they smelt of apples; and it was impossible not to stare at them.

In the storerooms they found a lot of rugs and furs and clothing and ornaments of the kind that had long been forgotten—enormously wide coats of Byzantine brocade, cloaks, tunics, caftans, pearl headdresses weighing thirty-six pounds each—which the servant-girls carried by the armful to the dining-hall. In one of the basement rooms they saw a small door high up near the ceiling. Natalia took a candle, rose on tiptoe and threw back her head.

"What if he's there?"

"Who?" Anna and Martha cried together in alarm.

"The house-spirit," Natalia said.

The girls clapped their hands to their cheeks, but did not pale, only their eyes grew as wide as they could open them. Fear seized them all. The old man who looked after the stoves brought a ladder and set it against the wall. Gavrila immediately sprang on to the ladder: there was no danger into which he would not have thrown himself at this moment. He opened the small door and disappeared into the darkness. They waited for what seemed to them a very long time; he gave no answer from inside, nor could they hear him move. Natalia said in a terrible whisper:

"Gavrila, come down!"

Then the soles of his boots appeared, followed by the wide skirts of his coat. He came down covered with cobwebs.

"What did you see there?"

"Nothing much. Something grey. It looked shaggy, and something soft brushed my face."

They all gasped. They hurried out of the basement on tiptoe and then broke into a run on the stairs. Only when they were upstairs again did Martha and Anna start squealing. Natalia Alexeyevna suggested playing at looking for the house-spirit. They searched for secret doors, cautiously opened closets under the stairs, peeped under all the stoves, holding their breath with fright. And they were rewarded: in one dark place, spun over with cobwebs, they saw two green eyes burning with a hellish fire. They scuttled away in panic. Natalia tripped and fell on Gavrila's hands. He held her fast so that she even heard his heart beating—slowly, deeply, the way a man's heart beats. She moved her shoulder and said in a low voice:

"Let me go!"

After that they went off to arrange Belshazzar's Feast. The old stove-man, with a yellow beard like the house-spirit's, a brass cross hanging over his tunic and new felt boots on his feet, once again brought the ladder. They hung moth-eaten rugs on the log-walls of the dining-hall, that had been stripped long ago; the table was taken away and the supper laid directly on a carpet on the floor. The orders were for all to sup seated in the Babylonian manner and Gavrila was to be King Belshazzar. They dressed him in a time-worn but still handsome brocade caftan, crimson with golden griffins, and hung a long coat of the kind that used to be worn a hundred years ago over his shoulders; on his head they set a pearl headdress that had apparently belonged to the Tsaritsa, Natalia's grandmother. Natalia was dressed as Semiramis, in a tunic of cloth-of-gold and coloured kerchiefs wound round her heavy plaits. Serving-girls were sent to pluck some handsome feathers out of cocks' tails and they were stuck into her turban.

They wondered whom Martha and Anna would represent. Natalia ordered them to go outside the room, loosen their plaits and take off their skirts and petticoats, remaining in their chemises, as these happened to be long, made of fine linen and quite fresh. The serving-girls ran off again, this time to the pond, and brought back water lilies; these were wound round the Menshikov girls' necks, arms and hair, and the long stems were bound round their waists, whereupon they became naiads of the Tigris and the Euphrates. Katerina was easy to dress as the goddess of flowers and gardens; her Babylonian name was Astarte, in Greek—Chloris. The servant-girls made another excursion and gathered carrots, parsley, green onions and peas, and also brought some unripe pumpkins and apples. Katerina, flushed, with moist lips and eyes round with pleasure, lost her shyness and laughed as usual at every trifle; garlanded with peas and parsley, with a crown of vegetables and a basket of gooseberries and red currants in her hand she looked a veritable Flora.

"And what is the painter going to be?" Natalia suddenly bethought herself. "We've got no Ethiopian. Let him be the Ethiopian king!"

A new miracle began for Andrey Golikov. Women's hands—was it real or only a dream?—pushed him and turned him about, wound silk and brocades round him, blackened his face with soot and pinched his nose in a brass ring, with strict orders to keep it on throughout the feast. It seemed to him that he could not be happier even if God were to give him angel's wings.

Three musicians from the Foreign Quarter—a fiddler, a mouth-organ player and a flautist—entered with low bows. They, too, were made to dress up in one way or another.

"And now for supper! Sit down on the cushions with your feet tucked under and drink mead and wine out of shells."

No one knew exactly how they ought to play at Belshazzar's Feast. They seated themselves before the dishes and the candles and looked at one another and smiled. No one felt hungry. Then Natalia, with a toss of her cock's feathers, began to recite from memory, mouthing the lines, the same verses which Gavrila had heard her declaim on that winter night under the golden vault of the hot room in the women's quarters of the Kremlin:

> "Blissful the ancient gods dwell on a mountain high,
> Yet Cupid at them too lets his cruel arrows fly.
> Great Jove himself complains: 'Alas, I suffer so,
> 'I find no rest, and yet no remedy I know.
> 'My thirst I cannot quench, fire sears my breast with pain.
> 'With love, unhappy wretch, I struggle all in vain.'
> Alas, if even gods succumb to Cupid's darts,
> To whom can mortals look for safety for their hearts?
> Oh, better then make gay! Let us no more repine
> But to the poisoned arrows drink glory in sweet wine."

While Natalia was reciting her face paled below her great turban. She took a sip of wine and went off in a polka with Anisya Tolstaya. The musicians played softly but in a way that made every nerve tingle and sing.

"Dance with Katerina!" Natalia called out to Gavrila with a flash of her eyes.

He jumped up and threw Belshazzar's coat off his shoulders; if need be he could dance for a day and a night without stopping. Katerina's back was hot and pliant, her feet light, and as she whirled, pea-pods and cherries flew off her head and shoulders. Gavrila quickened the measure and so did the musicians. Anna and Martha, too, started to whirl, holding hands. Golikov alone remained on the carpet in front of the candles. He could neither eat nor drink because of the ring on his nose, but this circumstance in no way impaired his happiness; the Tsarevna's verses about the Olympian gods still rang in his ears to the piping of the flute, while before his eyes swam the vision of the naked goddess on the dolphin holding the cup filled with temptation in her hand.

Gavrila was simple-hearted. He had been told to dance the polka with Katerina and he danced without sparing his heels. And though several times it seemed to him as if Natalia Alexeyevna was smiling differently, joylessly, without the former radiance in her eyes, he did not realise that it was high time for him to take Katerina back to her seat among the pumpkins and carrots. He had one more glimpse of the Tsarevna's face with teeth clenched, as if in pain, then suddenly she tottered, stopped and held on to Anisya Tolstaya. The turban with the cocks' feathers fell off her head.

Anisya cried in alarm: "The Tsarevna is dizzy!" and waved at the musicians to make them stop playing.

Natalia Alexeyevna wrenched herself away from her and went out of the room, trailing her mantle. This put an end to Belshazzar's Feast. Anna and Martha felt all at once ashamed in their chemises and, after whispering to each other, they ran out. Katerina resumed her seat in some alarm and started to pluck off the vegetables with which she was decorated. Gavrila, plunged in gloom, stood with feet set wide apart over the carpet with the dishes, blinking at the flames of the candles. Anisya who had rushed out after the Tsarevna returned in a few moments and dug her nails into Gavrila's hand.

"Go to her," she whispered. "Go, knock your head on the floor, you silly fool!"

Natalia Alexeyevna was standing in the passage just outside the dining-hall, gazing out of the open window at the mist lit up by the invisible moon. Gavrila went up to her. He could hear the drops falling from the roof on to the leaves.

"Have you come to Moscow for a long stay?" she asked without turning round. He could manage no answer and only caught his breath. "There's nothing for you to do here. Go back tomorrow to where you came from."

After she had said the words, her shoulders lifted.

"How have I angered you?" Gavrila asked. "God, if you only knew! If you only knew!"

Then she turned round and brought her face with soot-blackened eyebrows close to his:

"I don't want you, do you hear? Go away, go away!"

And as she went on saying "go away, go away", she raised her arms to push him back; but, perhaps because she realised that such a great fellow could not be pushed away, she laid her hands, with a jangling of Semiramis's bangles, on his shoulders and her head drooped lower and lower. Gavrila, also not realising what he was doing, began to kiss the warm parting in her hair, barely touching it with his lips. And she went on saying:

"No, no, go away, go away. . . ."

chapter six

Peter Alexeyevich had thrown off his canvas coat, rolled up his sleeves and tied a crimson kerchief round his head in the manner of Portuguese pirates, which he had learnt from Vice-admiral Pamburg. It was embroidered round the edge with a pattern of vine-leaves; a present from Izmaylovo. In the old days he would have taken off his shoes and stockings too, to feel the warmth of the rough deck under his feet. A light breeze filled the sails, and the two-masted snow *Katerina* glided obediently and easily, as on air. The brigantine *Ulrica* followed in its wake and, in the misty distance, where sky and water met, the frigate *Wachtmeister* was in full sail.

The ships had been recently taken from the Swedes: an unexpected and glorious victory. The Russians had captured twelve brigantines and frigates, the entire robber fleet of Commander Lesjört who, for two years, had prevented even the smallest of boats reaching lake Chud, had plundered the coastal villages and farms and threatened Sheremetev who was besieging Yuriev from the rear. The commander was a bold seaman. Nevertheless, the Russians had succeeded in tricking him. On a dark night during a thunderstorm, for fear of a gale or for some other reason, he had brought his fleet into the estuary of the river Embach and had then heedlessly got drunk on board the flagship *Carolus*. When he opened his eyes at dawn, hundreds of boats and rafts and barrels, lashed together, were hurriedly making their way from the banks towards his ships.

"Fire on the Russian infantry from both broadsides!" the commander shouted.

But before the Swedes could pour gunpowder into the touchholes of the guns or cut the hawsers of the anchors, the Russians had swarmed round the ships and boarded them from their boats, rafts and barrels, throwing grenades and firing pistols. It was an extremely humiliating affair: infantry had captured a fleet! In his rage the commander jumped into the powder-magazine and blew up his ship: flames burst from all the cracks and hatches and, with a thunderous explosion, yard-arms, barrels, men and the commander himself were flung up nearly to the clouds in a huge wave of smoke.

The sun scorched Peter's back, the breeze caressed his face, the shallow waves blinded him with flecks of sunlight. He screwed up his eyes. To cool himself he spread his legs wide as he stood at the helm. The rigging whined and whistled, the seagulls cried harshly at the poop over the ship's wake. The sails, like white breasts, swelled with strength.

Peter Alexeyevich was sailing towards Narva with victory: he was bringing with him Swedish banners heaped together at the foot of the mainmast; the day before yesterday Yuriev had been taken by assault. One more feather had been plucked out of King Charles's tail. Letters had been sent to the Emperor and to the kings of France and England announcing that: "With God's help we have recovered our ancient dominion—the town of Yuriev, founded seven hundred years ago by the great Prince Yaroslav Vladimirovich for the defence of the marches of the Russian land."

Although it had never entered Peter Alexeyevich's head—as in the case, for instance, of his dear brother, King Charles—to liken himself to Alexander of Macedon, and although he regarded war as a hard and difficult business—a matter of bloody toil, a State necessity—this time, under the walls of Yuriev, he had come to believe in his military talent and was proud and pleased with himself. In ten days (having come there from the camp near Narva) he had achieved what had seemed impossible to Field-Marshal Sheremetev and his foreigners—engineers, pupils of the famous Marshal de Vauban.

There was something else too that gave him pleasure: to look at the distant wooded shore and to know that this shore, recently a Swedish possession, was Russian now and that lake Chud was again wholly Russian. But such is human nature that when a man has taken a great deal, he wants more. One might have thought that nothing could be better than sailing on a radiant morning in a beautiful snow, carrying high above the poop, in despite of King Charles, a huge St. Andrew's flag. But no! Precisely today his thoughts were filled with his sweetheart, with a passion that sent tremors through him. There was no other word for her: she was no light-o'-love, no mistress, she was his sweetheart, his darling Katerina. Moving his shoulderblades under his shirt he breathed in the damp air deeply through his nostrils. The water and the boards of the deck smelt like a bathing pool and he seemed to see Katerina bathing on a day as hot as this. It might be that she had woven a spell into the kerchief with vine-leaves and scented it with her feminine charm; the wind at his back blew its ends about and every now and then they tickled his nose and lips. She had known what she was doing, the little Livonian witch, so curly-haired, so gay! In Yuriev the women, half frightened to death, were very good-looking, but not one of them could compare with Katerina; there was not one whose striped skirt swayed so alluringly on firm hips; there was not one woman he would have wanted to take by the cheeks, looking deep into her eyes, pressing his teeth to hers.

Peter Alexeyevich tapped the heel of his square-toed shoe on the deck impatiently. Immediately someone sprang out of the wardroom—evidently jolted awake—and a door slammed. The secretary Makarov came running down the companion-ladder.

"I'm here, gracious Sire," he said.

Trying not to look at his thin, parchment face with red eyelids, so out of place here on board, Peter Alexeyevich gave the order curtly:

"Writing things."

Makarov hastened away and stumbled on the companion-ladder. Peter Alexeyevich hissed like a cat at his back. Makarov quickly returned with a folding chair, paper and inkpot. Several quills were stuck behind his ear. Peter Alexeyevich took one and said:

"Take the helm, grip it tight, you landlubber, and hold it so. If you let the sails flap, I'll give you a taste of the rope-end."

He winked at Makarov, seated himself on the folding chair and laid a sheet of paper on his knee. Then with his head on one side, he looked up at the truck—the cap on the top of the mainmast—where a long pennant was fluttering, and began to write.

On one side of the sheet he inscribed: "To the ladies Anisya Tolstaya and Ekaterina Vasilyevskaya." On the reverse he wrote, spluttering the ink and leaving out letters: "Aunt and mother, may you live in good health for many years. I want to hear how you are. As for me, I live in labour and privation. There is no one to wash and mend for me, but most of all I miss you. Only the day before yesterday we danced a fine dance with the Swedes, which will make King Charles see red. Upon my word, since the time I entered service I have not seen such a fine game. In short, with God's help we have taken Yuriev at the point of the sword. As for your health, do not even think of writing to me about it, but be pleased to come to me yourselves as soon as possible. To save me from dullness. When you reach Pskov wait for instructions about where to go, here the enemy is quite near. Peter."

"Fold and seal it without reading it," he said to Makarov taking over the helm from him. "You will send it at the first opportunity."

He seemed to feel a little easier now. The ship's bell rang the hour with clear double strokes. Immediately a gun thundered from the forecastle and the pleasant smell of gunpowder drifted towards him. The commander of the snow, Captain Nepluyev, a man with a youthful, bony, impudent face, ran up on to the bridge, holding down his cutlass, and lifted two fingers to his three-cornered hat.

"Bombardier, it's the admiral's hour," he said. "Please to accept a glass."

Nepluyev was followed by the short Felten, in a green knitted waistcoat, his shiny face smiling broadly. On board ship in place of a chef's cap he also bound his head, pirate-fashion, with a white kerchief. He held out to Peter a tin tray on which were a silver goblet and a roll with poppy-seed.

Peter Alexeyevich weighed the goblet in his hand then, with a seaman's gravity, swallowed the fiery vodka with its tang of corn-brandy and, hastily throwing pieces of the roll into his mouth, said to Nepluyev, as he chewed:

"We'll anchor for the night by the Narova. I'll sleep on shore. Have you taken the soundings there?"

"In the Narova estuary there's a sandbank near the right bank, near the left bank there's eleven feet."

"Very well. You can go."

Peter Alexeyevich was once more alone on the hot deck, at the helm. The drink sent a pleasant tingling through his body and he began to recall, alternately snorting and smiling, the day before yesterday's glorious action which would make King Charles see red with vexation.

2

Field-Marshal Sheremetev had been conducting the siege of Yuriev in a leisurely fashion, without too much labour either for himself or his troops, hoping to subdue the Swedes by starvation. Peter Alexeyevich crumpled up his discursive letters and threw them under the table. The devil seemed to have changed the field-marshal. For two years he had made war boldly and fiercely, yet today he was mumbling like an old woman before the walls of the Swedes. When Field-Marshal Ogilvie, who, on Patkul's insistence, had been invited from Vienna to take service with Moscow at a high salary—three thousand gold thalers a year in addition to his keep and all manner of supplies, including wine—arrived at last at the Narva camp, Peter Alexeyevich had handed over the command to him and rushed off impatiently to the camp at Yuriev.

The field-marshal was not expecting him. In the noontide heat he was snoring after dinner in his tent set amid the baggage-trains, behind a high earth rampart. He woke up when the Tsar whisked the kerchief that shielded him from the flies off his face.

"You sleep at your ease behind palisades!" Peter shouted and fiercely rolled his eyes. "Come, show me the siege works!"

Fear struck the field-marshal dumb. He did not know how his legs managed to find their way into his trousers. Neither his sword nor his hat was within reach, so he mounted his horse bare-headed. The military engineer Kobert came running to join them, also half-awake, pushing the buttons of his French coat into the wrong button-holes; all the good he had done during the siege was to acquire a pair of fat cheeks on good Russian cabbage soup. Peter angrily nodded at him from his height. The three of them started off to the positions.

There everything displeased Peter. On the east side, from which Sheremetev's troops were conducting the siege, the walls were high, the squat towers had been newly reinforced, the ravelins stood far out into the field, in the form of a star, and the moats before them were filled with water. To the west, the town was well defended by the deep river Embach, and, to the south, by a mossy marsh. Sheremetev had come up to the walls of the town by means of trenches and approaches, but with great caution and not too close for fear of the Swedish guns. His batteries were placed even more foolishly: they had shot two thousand bombs into the town and set fire to a few houses here and there, but had not even scratched the walls.

"Do you know, Field-Marshal, how many altyns each bomb costs me?" Peter asked grimly. "We bring them from the Urals. Would you like to pay for these two thousand wasted bombs out of your salary?" He snatched Sheremetev's telescope from under his arm and moved it to and fro surveying the walls. "The southern wall is old and low. I thought so. . . ." He glanced swiftly round at the engineer Kobert. "The bombs should be aimed here, it is here that the walls and gates must be breached. The town must be taken from here. Not from the east. One should not seek an easy way just because the place happens to be dry. One must seek victory even if it is neck-deep in a marsh."

Sheremetev did not dare to raise any objections. He only mumbled with his thick tongue: "Naturally. . . . You know best, Bombardier. . . . We have been thinking, but hadn't thought of that."

The engineer Kobert wagged his cheeks respectfully but with a deprecating smile.

"Your Majesty," he said, "the southern wall and the towergates, which are called 'the Russian gates', are old, but they are nevertheless impregnable because they can be approached only across the marsh. The marsh is impassable."

"For whom is the marsh impassable?" Peter Alexeyevich shouted. His neck twitched and his leg jerked, making him lose his stirrup. "Everything is passable for a Russian soldier. We aren't playing chess, this is a game of life and death."

He jumped off his horse and spread out the plan of the town on the grass. Pulling a case of instruments from his pocket he took out a pair of compasses, a ruler and a pencil. While he measured and made notes the field-marshal and Kobert squatted beside him.

"Here's where you must place your batteries!" he pointed to the edge of the marsh in front of the "Russian gates". "And add some siege-guns across the river." He deftly drew lines along which the shells from the batteries should be flying towards the "Russian gates". Then he again made measurements with the compasses. Sheremetev mumbled: "Naturally. . . . The distance is accessible." Kobert smiled ironically. Peter said:

"I give you three days to alter the positions. On the seventh of this month I begin the fireworks."

He put the compasses and ruler back into their case and started to stuff it into the pocket of his coat, but the crimson kerchief with the vine-leaf border was there. He pulled out the kerchief and irritably thrust it into the bosom of his coat.

For three days he gave the men neither rest nor sleep. By day, the troops continued the former siege works in full sight of the Swedes, digging trenches under musket and cannon fire and putting ladders together. At night, secretly, without lighting fires, they harnessed oxen to the guns and mortars and dragged them to the new positions at the edge of the marsh and over the pontoon bridge across the river, screening the batteries with fascines and ramparts.

No sooner did the sun show itself above the forest, lighting up the tumbledown roofs on the south wall, and the battlements of the tower of the "Russian gates" stand out above the mists of the marsh and bluish smoke rise from the chimneys in the quiet of the morning, than sixty siege-guns and heavy mortars shook earth and sky and seventy-pound cannon-balls and fuse-bombs hissed and hurtled across the marsh. The batteries across the river added their roar. Screened by the pall of gunpowder smoke, Ivan Zhidok's grenadiers ran with bundles of branches to lay a road across the marsh.

Peter Alexeyevich was with the southern battery. He had no occasion to shout, to give directions or to lose his temper; he barely had time to turn his head as he watched the gunners, repeating over and over again an approving: "Ay-lu-lu, ay-lu-lu!" In less time than it takes to recite the Lord's Prayer at speed, the guns would be cleaned with ramrods, the charges of powder inserted, the balls rammed home, the priming poured into the touch-holes and the guns aimed.

"All batteries!" the short-statured Colonel Nechayev shouted, with bulging, bloodshot eyes. The first volley had sent his hat and wig flying. "Distance as before. Apply the slow-match. Fi-i-ire!" The commanders of the batteries echoed his command with a rolling: "Fi-i-ire!"

They could see the cannon-balls hit their mark and the battlements of the towers crumble; the roof of the wall burst into flames; houses set on fire by the bombs were burning in the town. Bells began to peal in the sharp-spired churches. Swedish soldiers, in short grey uniforms, ran out of the gates, jumping aside at the explosions, and started to throw up a curtain wall, dragging logs, barrels and sacks. In spite of everything, by the end of the day the gate-tower and wall were still standing firm. Peter Alexeyevich gave orders to bring the batteries up closer.

The fireworks went on for six days. Ivan Zhidok's grenadiers were building the road across the marsh, up to their knees, up to their waist in the water, shielding themselves from the enemy's bombs and bullets with mobile fascines—baskets filled with earth. Those who were killed sank on the spot, the wounded were carried out on their comrades' shoulders. The Swedes, who had realised the gravity of the danger, brought up some of the guns from the other towers and daily increased the weight of their fire. The town was veiled. The red sun scorched through the drifting clouds of powder-smoke.

Peter Alexeyevich did not leave the battery. He was black with gunpowder, he did not wash and ate hastily whatever food there happened to be, and he personally handed out vodka to the gunners. He lay down to snatch an hour's sleep to the thunder of the guns, somewhere close by, under an artillery cart. He sent the engineer Kobert back to the main baggage-train because, though a learned man, he was too quiet and "we do not need quiet people here".

At twilight on the 12th of June he sent for Sheremetev. During these last days the field-marshal had been making a noisy diversion with all his troops on the eastern side to frighten the Swedes. Once again he had become active, hardly leaving his saddle, and swearing and using his fists. He found Peter Alexeyevich at the battery that had now fallen silent, surrounded by moustached bombardiers. They were all old acquaintances; men who in the days of the play-army had showered turnips and clay bombs out of wooden cannon in good earnest on the Prince-Emperor's cavalry at the walls of Pressburg. Some had rags tied round their heads and badly torn uniforms.

Peter Alexeyevich was sitting on the gun-carriage of the largest cannon, "Salamander", of Tula-moulded brass; they had had to pour some twenty pails of vinegar over it to cool it and it was still hissing. Peter was chewing bread and discussing the day's work, hurriedly articulating his words. The southern wall had at last been breached in three places, and these breaches the enemy would no longer be able to fill. The bombardier Ignat Kurochkin had sent several red-hot balls, one after the other, into the corner of the gate-tower. "He hammered them in like nails! Didn't he? What?" Peter Alexeyevich cried in a crowing voice. "The whole corner of the tower has fallen in, and the rest of it will come down any moment now."

"Ignat, where are you? Come here!" he said, holding out his pipe with its chewed stem to the gunner. "I'm not giving it to you, I haven't got another on me. But have a smoke. Good man! If we remain alive, I won't forget."

Ignat Kurochkin, a sedate man with a luxuriant moustache, took off his three-cornered hat and carefully accepted the pipe. He dug inside the bowl with his finger-nail and his face creased all over in humorous wrinkles.

"But there isn't any tobacco in it, Your Majesty!"

The other gunners laughed. Peter Alexeyevich took out his tobacco-pouch but there was not a crumb of tobacco in it. At this moment the field-marshal came up. Peter Alexeyevich said eagerly:

"Boris Petrovich, have you anything to smoke on you? We are completely out of vodka and tobacco in our battery." The gunners laughed again. "Be so kind."

Sheremetev, with a bow, proffered courteously a handsome beaded tobacco-pouch.

"Oh, thank you," Peter said. "But give it to Bombardier Kurochkin. I make you a present of it, Ignat, but don't forget to give me back my pipe."

He sent the gunners away and for a while sat loudly crunching a piece of dry bread. The field-marshal stood silently before him with his baton resting on his hip.

"Boris Petrovich, we can't wait any longer," Peter said in an altered voice. "The men are angry. For many days now the grenadiers have been lying in the marsh. It's hard. I'm going to burn tar-barrels and fire all night. And what you must do is to send me immediately a battalion of Moscow fusiliers from Samohvalov's regiment as reinforcement; they're fierce fellows and full of courage. For God's sake, carry on with what you are doing, but don't lose men unnecessarily. At dawn I shall go to the assault."

Sheremetev lowered his baton and crossed himself.

"Go now, my friend," Peter said.

When tar-barrels flared on the edge of the marsh and across the river, all the batteries opened a running fire, the like of which the Swedes had never yet experienced. The gates collapsed. Chunks flew from the curtain, the stockades and the chevaux-de-frise. The Swedes expected the attack in the night: a bristling of bayonets, helmets and banners, rippling in the fitful glare of the burning tar, could be seen through the breaches in the wall. All over the town the tocsin sounded.

Peter Alexeyevich, with knees slightly bent, was looking through his telescope out of the trench sheltered by fascines. Behind him stood Colonel Ivan Zhidok, a man from Orel who looked like a gipsy. His eyes held a dry gleam, his lips quivered and, in his fierce eagerness, he unconsciously ground his teeth. The night was short, the eastern sky above the forest had already taken on a green tint and the stars had faded. It was impossible to wait any longer. But Peter Alexeyevich still tarried. Suddenly Ivan Zhidok heaved an agonizing "O-o-oh!" from the very depth of his chest and shook his drooping head. Peter Alexeyevich gripped his shoulder and said: "Go!"

Ivan Zhidok jumped over the fascines and ran, bent double, across the marsh. Immediately a rocket soared and burst, scattering green lights; it was followed by another and then a third. The guns fell silent. The quiet pressed on the men's ear-drums. They began to rise from among the red-black hummocks of the marsh and to advance heavily—sinking in the mud—towards the gates. The entire marsh was in movement, swarming with soldiers. Companies of Moscow fusiliers, with fixed bayonets, were coming to their aid from the bank. Peter Alexeyevich lowered his telescope, drew a deep breath through his teeth and frowned. "Oh!" he said. "Oh!" From inside the battered curtain the five remaining guns fired point-blank at Ivan Zhidok's attacking grenadiers. A single desperate voice on the marsh shouted: "Hurrah!" Swedes rushed out of the breaches in the walls, running to the encounter with the Russians as if in wild joy. A hand-to-hand battle began in the midst of shouting, roaring, clashing. Up to four thousand men were struggling together at the walls and gates.

Peter Alexeyevich got out of the trench and started off, his heavy topboots squelching in the moss. He kept feeling all over himself as if trying to find the telescope he had dropped, or a weapon. Little Colonel Nechayev caught him up.

"Sire, you can't go there."

They stood looking in the direction of the fighting.

"Send for reinforcements," Peter said to him.

"No need, Sire."

"I tell you, send someone!"

"No need. Our men are already capturing their guns."

"It can't be. . . ."

"I can see it."

True enough: first one, then another gun spouted fire towards the gates. The huge crowd of combatants swayed and poured through the breaches into the town.

Nechayev cried, with tears in his bulging eyes:

"Sire, now the game will start!"

Filled with fury, because it had been so hard for them and so many of them had been uselessly killed by the Swedes, the grenadiers and the Moscow fusiliers thrust and slashed and chased the enemy through the narrow streets to the town square. There, in the heat of the fray, they killed four drummers who had been sent by the commandant of Yuriev to sound the *chamade,* or surrender. It was the trumpeter alone on the castle-tower—bursting his lungs with the hoarse blaring of his trumpet pleading surrender—who brought the massacre to an end, and that only with difficulty and not at once.

3

The *Katerina,* with drooping sails and her sailors clinging to the yard-arms, glided for some time along the shore in the green shade of the forest. A gun was fired and then the anchor-chain rattled. A boat immediately approached the ship. Menshikov was standing up in it, wearing a long cloak and a hat with tall plumes. The handsome fellow's cuffs alone must have taken no less than nine yards of cherry-coloured English cloth. Peter Alexeyevich looked at him from above, leaning his elbows on the bulwarks. Menshikov raised his arm up to his right ear with a flourish, took off his hat and waving it outwards three times, shouted:

"Vivat! Vivat! To the Bombardier, congratulations on the great victory!"

"Wait a minute, I'll be coming down to you at once," Peter Alexeyevich said in a low, deep voice. "And what is the news here?"

"We too are not without a victory."

"That's good. Did you prepare for me what I asked you to in my last letter? Over there we didn't have even the poorest kind of beer."

"Three kegs of Rhenish arrived yesterday!" Menshikov roared. "Our camp isn't managed like Sheremetev's; there's no delay, no lack of anything."

"Go on boasting, go on!" Peter Alexeyevich summoned Captain Nepluyev and gave him orders that tomorrow, as soon as flags were hoisted on the ships, guns should be fired and the signal "Captured with gallantry" be run up; then the Swedish banners were to be taken ashore to the beating of drums. Such orders were an honour for the young captain, and he flushed. Peter Alexeyevich, staring at him to his growing embarrassment, added:

"A fine voyage, Commander!"

Nepluyev turned so deep a red that sweat broke out and his sharp eyes grew moist with excitement; the Tsar was appointing him commander, flag-officer of the squadron. Peter Alexeyevich did not add anything more; stretching out his long legs and scraping his shoes against the tarred side of the ship, he climbed into the boat. He sat down at Menshikov's side and nudged him with his elbow.

"I'm glad you came out to meet me; thanks. So you, too, have had a victory? Have you defeated Schlippenbach?"

"And now we've defeated him, *mein Herz!* Anikita Repnin swooped down on him in carts near Wenden, while Colonel Renne, as I had advised him, barred the way into the town with his cavalry. The Swede was obliged to accept battle willy-nilly in the open field. Schlippenbach got such a drubbing that the poor hero barely managed to escape to Reval with a dozen cuirassiers."

"Still, he got away this time too. Ah, the devil!"

"He's mighty slippery. But it doesn't matter; he's got neither guns, nor banners, nor any army now. Afterwards Anikita Ivanovich, when he was a bit fuddled, lamented: 'I'm not so sorry I didn't capture Schlippenbach', he said, 'as that I didn't get his horse. It's a bird!' I rebuked him for talking like that. 'You aren't a Crimean Tatar, Anikita Ivanovich,' I said, 'to be stealing horses; you're a Russian general and should think like a statesman'. We had a terrible quarrel over it. And another bit of news: a messenger arrived posthaste from Warsaw. King August is sending you a great ambassador. It would be famous to receive this ambassador in Narva itself, in the castle. What do you say, *mein Herz?*"

Peter Alexeyevich listened to his chatter looking with half-closed eyes at the green water and biting his nails.

"What news from Moscow?" he asked.

"More work for you: there was a courier from the Prince-Emperor with a boxful of letters and papers. Gavrila Brovkin was here on his way to Petersburg and brought you a letter from the Izmaylovsky palace." Peter Alexeyevich gave him a quick glance. "I've got it with me, *mein Herz*. And another thing—he brought with him four hothouse melons wrapped in a sheepskin—we'll sample them at supper. He says they're pining for you in Izmaylovo, they've cried their eyes out waiting."

"Now you're lying!" The boat came along shore. Peter Alexeyevich jumped out and climbed up the steep beach where Menshikov's tent stood overlooking the water.

The two of them sat down to supper in the tent alone. Peter Alexeyevich sat on saddle-cushions with shoulders hunched and ate ravenously; Sheremetev's fare had left him hungry. Menshikov helped himself sparingly from the dishes and applied himself mostly to the drink, laying his palm on the broad scarf wound tightly round his waist: bland, red-cheeked, with cunning little lights in his deep blue eyes from the reflection of the candles. He was talking about the new Field-Marshal Ogilvie, taking great care not to provoke the slightest expression of displeasure on Peter's drawn but calm face.

"He's a learned man, there's no denying it. He brought with him from Vienna books in calf bindings, a whole cartful of them, they're lying in a heap in his tent. The first thing he did was to tell us, very haughtily, that he wouldn't eat any of our food. What he wants, when he wakes up, is not vodka with a snack, but chocolate and coffee and white wheaten bread and, for dinner, he must have fresh fish—and not any kind of fish, but only turbot—and game and veal. We were very upset, for since those were the field-marshal's orders the stuff had to be found. I sent a Finn, a scout, to Reval to get the coffee and the chocolate, I gave him five gold pieces out of my own pocket. We've got a cow specially for him, tethered to a peg, and found a nice clean girl to milk the cow and churn butter. We put up a privy behind his tent with a padlock on it. And he never lets anyone have the key."

Peter Alexeyevich hastily swallowed a mouthful and laughed.

"What am I paying him three thousand thalers for? That's why he's teaching you, you Asiatics."

"Oh yes, he does teach us. The next day he summoned the commanders of all the regiments. He didn't ask our names and patronymics, didn't shake hands with anyone, but started to tell us self-importantly how fond the Emperor is of him and what armies he had led and what towns he had besieged, and how Marshal de Vauban said to him: 'You are my best pupil', and presented him with a snuffbox. He showed us all his decorations and this snuffbox; on the lid there's a picture of a girl hugging a cannon. After that he dismissed us. He might have offered us some chocolate out of politeness, but he didn't. 'I'll soon write a disposition,' he said, 'and then you will understand how one must go about taking Narva'. He's still writing it."

"Well, well!" Peter Alexeyevich said, wiping his hands on his napkin. He picked up by the stem a Magdeburg goblet fashioned out of a coconut shell and ornamented with deities in gilt and, gaily puckering his lips—his dark eyes rarely smiled—said:

"Let us, as in the days long past on the Kukuy, give praise, my dear friend, to our father Bacchus and our mother the irrepressible Venus. Now, let me have that letter."

The tiny note, sealed with wax, had the same sweet feminine scent as the kerchief with the vine-leaves. It was from Katerina Vasilyevskaya, but written in the hand of Anisya Tolstaya because Katerina could not write.

"To my Tsar, my light, my joy. I am sending you, Sire, my light, my joy, a present: some melons ripened under glass at Izmaylovo, they are so very sweet. Eat them, Sire, my light, my joy, and may they do you good! And also, light of my eyes, I would like to see you."

"She hasn't written much. But she probably thought over it a long time, and furrowed her brows, and ruckled her apron," Peter Alexeyevich said in a low, slightly mocking voice. He drained the goblet, slapped his knees, then got up and went out of the tent.

"Danilych," he said, "call Makarov and sort the Moscow mail with him. I'm going to stretch my legs."

The evening was close and the black pine-wood smelt of hot resin. The vast sunset gave out no radiance and was fading sombrely. It was the hour for night birds to send out their solitary calls and for bats to flit noiselessly over a man's head. Here and there, camp-fires shone on the meadow, and the horses of the escort that had come with Menshikov jingled their halters. Peter Alexeyevich walked along the river, his stockings wet to the knees with dew. Now and then he stopped to take a deeper breath. At the edge of a small ravine that led down to the river he stopped again: a disturbing smell of damp leaves and honey drifted from there. A light vapour curled mistily —smoke perhaps—and someone's voice carried distinctly, probably that of a trooper, one of those wags who will not let others sleep but makes them listen to his stories. Peter Alexeyevich had turned to go back when suddenly he heard:

". . . It's all nonsense about her being a witch! She was a common servant-girl, unwashed, in a dirty shift. That's how she was when they took her. It isn't every peasant who'd have wanted to sleep with her. Am I right, Mishka? When I saw her, she was already living at the field-marshal's. She'd skip out of the tent, empty the slops and wipe herself with her apron, and then she'd go back to the tent and start going chop, chop with the kitchen-knives. A pretty wench, and sharp. Already at the time I thought: this chit can look after herself. Oh, she's sharp all right!"

A doltish voice asked:

"And what happened to her afterwards, Uncle?"

"Don't you know? It's a true saying that you don't have to cross the sea to find fools. Now she lives with our Tsar. She eats pies and honey-cakes, and sleeps half the day, and yawns and stretches during the other half."

The doltish voice said wonderingly:

"Then she must be made in some special way, Uncle."

"You ask Mishka; he'll tell you how she's made. . . ."

A thick sleepy voice replied:

"Go to the devil, you two! I don't remember her at all."

Peter Alexeyevich's breath came with difficulty. Shame made his face burn. Anger rose in him on a flood of dark blood. For such talk about the Tsar's honour the Prince-Emperor put men in irons. Seize them! The shame of it, the shame! And the laughter! It was his own fault that already the whole army was laughing. "He took the wench from under Mishka. . . ."

With lowered head he advanced towards the large, lazy peasant who had tasted her first sweetness. But it was as though some gentle force stopped him, held his limbs close-bound. He drew a deep breath and laid a hand on his bowed, damp forehead. "A wanton doll, Katerina. . . ." And he felt her there like a tangible vision. Golden-skinned, sweet, warm, gentle, innocent. The devil, the devil! After all, he had known everything about her when he had taken her. About the soldier too.

Stepping high in the damp weeds he went down with dignified bearing into the ravine. Three men rose from behind the smoke. "Who goes there?" one of them shouted roughly. Peter Alexeyevich growled: "It is I." Although fright made them break into sweat, the soldiers picked up their muskets in a twinkling and stood at attention—muskets in front of them, heads cheerfully lifted, eyes staring at the Tsar—ready to face fire and death.

Without looking at them, Peter Alexeyevich poked his shoe into the dead camp-fire.

"Get me an ember!"

The middle soldier—the story-teller and wag—dropped on his knees and raked among the ashes. Snatching up a live coal he tossed it on his palm waiting for the Bombardier to fill his pipe. As he drew at the pipe, Peter Alexeyevich looked from under his eyebrows at the soldier farthest from him. "That was the man. . . ." A great big fellow, strong, well-built. He could not see his face distinctly.

"How tall are you? Why aren't you in the Guards? What's your name?"

The soldier replied according to the rules, but with a Moscow drawl, an impudent drawl which made Peter Alexeyevich's moustache bristle.

"Bludov, Mishka, of the Nevsky dragoon regiment, trooper in the sixth company, recruited in sixteen-ninety-nine, six foot seven inches, Bombardier."

"Fighting since ninety-nine and still a private? Are you lazy? Or stupid?"

The soldier answered tonelessly:

"Yes, Bombardier, I'm lazy and stupid."

"Fool!"

Peter Alexeyevich blew the bit of live coal off his pipe, which was drawing well. He knew that the moment he disappeared in the mist the soldiers would exchange knowing looks; they would not dare to laugh, but they would certainly exchange looks. Putting his thin arms behind his back and holding high his face with the pipe from which sparks were flying, he strode out of the ravine. Back in his tent, he sat down at the table, pushed the candle away from him and greedily drank some wine, for his throat felt parched. Screening himself in the smoke of the pipe he said:

"Danilych, in the Nevsky regiment, in the sixth company there's a soldier fit for the Guards. That's irregular."

Menshikov's deep blue eyes held neither astonishment, nor mischief, only heartfelt understanding.

"Mishka Bludov," he said. "Of course. I've known about him for a long time. He was rewarded with a rouble for the taking of Marienburg. The squadron commander won't let him go—he loves horses, and the horses love him. In the whole of our army there aren't any livelier horses than in the sixth company."

"Transfer him to the Preobrazhensky regiment, right-flank man in the first company."

4

General Horn came down from the tower and went across the market-place, tall, lean-shanked, with flat shoes on his feet. There were, as usual, many people at the stalls, but, alas, each day there was less food to buy: a bunch of radishes, a skinned cat in place of a rabbit, a bit of smoked horse-meat. The angry housewives no longer greeted the general with friendly curtsies, and some even turned their backs on him. More than once he had heard the mutter: "Surrender to the Russians, you old devil! Why do you starve people to no purpose?" But nothing could ruffle the general's composure.

When the town-clock had struck nine times, he reached his clean little house and wiped his feet on the doormat on the step. A neat maid opened the door and, curtseying low, took his helmet from him and the heavy sword that he drew out of his sword-belt. The general washed his hands and made his way with leisurely dignity into the dining-room, where the round, thick panes of the low window, along the whole of one wall, let in only faint yellow and green light.

By the table, awaiting the general, stood his wife, born Countess Sperling—a lady of difficult temper—three round-shouldered little girls with scanty hair and long noses like their father's and a sulky small boy, his mother's favourite.

The general sat down, the other members of the family followed suit and, folding their hands, silently said grace. When the lid was taken off the pewter tureen, steam poured out, but apart from the steam it contained nothing appetising, for it was the usual oat porridge without either milk or salt. The glum little girls swallowed it with an effort, but the sulky boy pushed back his plate and whispered to his mother: "I won't, I won't!" The second course consisted of yesterday's old mutton bones and a few peas. In place of beer, they drank water. The general placidly chewed the meat with his big yellow teeth.

The countess broke into rapid speech, crumbling a crust of bread over her plate:

"No matter how hard I have tried during the fourteen years that I've been married to you, Karl, I have never been able to understand you. Have you got a drop of warm blood in your veins? Have you got the heart of a husband and father? The king sent you from Reval a convoy of ships with ham, sugar, fish, all kinds of smoked and baked provisions. How should the father of four children act, placed as you are? Fight his way, sword in hand, to the ships and bring them to the town. But you preferred calmly to watch the Russian soldiers devour the Reval ham, while my children are obliged to choke on oat porridge! I shall never cease to repeat that you have a heart of stone. You are an unnatural monster. And that ridiculous affair of the mock battle! I'll never be able now to show myself in Europe. 'Oh, you are the wife of that General Horn whom the Russians fooled like a simpleton at the market?' 'Alas, alas!' I'll reply. You don't even know that every market-woman in the town calls you the old crane on the tower. To crown all, our only hope, General Schlippenbach, meets with disaster at Wenden in his efforts to help us, and you sit completely unperturbed, chewing tough mutton as if it were the happiest day of your life. No, I can't stand it any more! You must let me go with the children to Stockholm, to the king's court."

"Too late, Madam, it is too late," Horn said and his pale eyes, turned towards the window, seemed to let in as little light as the thick panes. "We are shut up in Narva as securely as in a mousetrap."

The countess clutched her lace cap with both hands and pulled it down on her face.

"Now I know what you are trying to do; you want to make me and my unfortunate children eat grass and rats!"

The sulky boy laughed suddenly and looked at his mother; the girls tearfully bent their noses over their plates. General Horn was somewhat taken aback. It was unjust; he was in no way trying to make his children eat grass and rats. Nevertheless, he finished his meal with the same composure as before.

For some time already his adjutant Bistrem's spurs had been jingling outside the door. Something had evidently happened. Horn took his clay pipe from the mantelpiece, filled it, struck a spark, lit a spill with the tinder, got his pipe drawing and only then left the dining-room.

Bistrem was holding the general's helmet and sword. He said somewhat breathlessly:

"Your Excellency, a sudden activity has begun in the Russian camp the meaning of which we cannot make out."

General Horn once again crossed the market-place, filled with an alarmed crowd. He carried his head high, not wishing to look into the eyes of the townspeople who called him an old crane. He mounted the worn steps of the tower. It was true: something unusual was going on in the Russian camp. The troops were lining up in two ranks along the entire semi-circle of siege fortifications that closely invested the town. A cloud of dust was swiftly approaching from the east. At first, all that could be distinguished were dragoons galloping along on small horses. At some distance from them rode Peter and Menshikov. The yellow dust raised by the hoofs of the squadron was so thick that General Horn grimaced painfully. Behind the Tsar and Menshikov, soldiers galloped, holding eighteen yellow satin banners aloft. In their fluttering folds eighteen royal lions writhed and indignantly stretched out their paws.

The squadrons, the Tsar, Menshikov, the Swedish banners swept past the entire besieging army which shouted "Hurrah! Victory!" at the top of their barbarians' voices.

5

There was rejoicing in the Russian camp. From the Gloria bastion one could clearly see the guns firing salutes round the Tsar's tent, and it was possible to count by the volleys how many toasts had been drunk. Knowing the boastfulness of the Russians, General Horn was expecting them to send an envoy with some arrogant message; and he was not mistaken. Some forty people poured out of the Tsar's tent, waving goblets and mugs; one of them jumped on to a horse and galloped towards the Gloria bastion with a trumpeter riding to catch up with him. Dodging on his horse this way and that to avoid being shot at, the envoy pulled out a handkerchief, raised it on the tip of his naked sword and reined in at the foot of the tower. The trumpeter, bending far back in his saddle, blew his trumpet with all his might, scaring the flying crows.

"Parole! Parole!" the envoy shouted. "This is Lieutenant-Colonel of the Preobrazhensky regiment Karpov!" He was drunk, his face was red and his curls were dishevelled by the wind. General Horn leaned down from the tower and replied:

"Speak! I am listening. We'll always have time to kill you."

"I have come to inform you," the lieutenant-colonel shouted, throwing back his jovial head, "last Friday, with God's help, the town of Yuriev was taken by assault by Field-Marshal Sheremetev. Condescending to the commander's humble prayer and in consideration of their courageous defence, the officers were allowed to keep their swords and a third of the soldiers to keep their muskets without ammunition. But they were deprived of their banners and music."

Bistrem was translating in a loud voice. The officers who were standing behind Horn exchanged indignant glances, and one of them, beside himself, shouted: "He's lying, the Russian cur!" Lieutenant-Colonel Karpov made a broad gesture indicating the distant tent where the people were still standing with their goblets and said:

"Gentlemen, is not such a peace better than the defeats of Schlüsselburg, Nienschanz and Yuriev? For this reason the Commander-in-Chief Field-Marshal Ogilvie proposes that you surrender Narva by honourable capitulation. Your envoys should present themselves immediately at the tent. The cups are filled and the guns for the salutes are loaded."

"No! I shall fight!" General Horn replied in a harsh voice. His face, with its sunken cheeks and the big nose that age had made more prominent, was bloodless and his veined hands trembled. "Go! In three minutes' time I will give orders to shoot."

Karpov saluted him with his sword and shouted to the trumpeter: "Ride off!" but he himself, instead of galloping away, turned his prancing horse towards the other side of the tower. The officers ran to the parapet and he called out to them:

"Who of you, the rude scoundrel, accused me, a Russian officer, of lying? Interpreter, hurry up and translate! Come on, ride out, if you're bold enough, let's meet in the field man to man!"

The officers raised a shout. One stout fellow turned purple and shook his fists as he struggled to free himself from the others, who sought to hold him back. Musket triggers clicked. Karpov stretched himself out on his horse's neck and galloped away from the tower pursued by shots and the whistling of bullets. At some two hundred paces from the tower he halted and alternately spurring and reining in his horse, waited for his opponent. After some delay the gates creaked on their hinges, the drawbridge fell and the stout officer galloped across the field towards Karpov. He was the taller of the two, his horse was heavier and his Swedish sword was four inches longer than a Russian one. For the duel he had donned an iron cuirass, whereas from under Karpov's unbuttoned coat lace fluttered in the wind.

According to custom, before closing in, the opponents indulged in an exchange of insults, the one barking grim words, the other letting out a rapid stream of fluent Moscow curses. Then they snatched their pistols out of their saddle-holsters, dug in their spurs and rode full tilt towards each other. They fired simultaneously. The Swede stretched his sword out far in front of him. Karpov wheeled away, Tatar fashion, from under the nose of the Swede's horse, circled round him and fired his second pistol. The Swede clicked his teeth and growled, and went in again to the attack with such ferocity that Karpov was only saved by shielding himself with his horse. His opponent's sword drove deep into its neck. "Oh, my horse is lost," he thought. "I won't hold out on foot." But the Swede, as though overcome with sleep, let go the hilt of his sword, and swayed, groping with his left hand for the pistol in the holster. Jumping off his falling horse, Karpov drove his sword several times into the Swede's side under the cuirass and, holding his breath, watched him rock more violently in his saddle. "He's strong, the devil, doesn't want to die!" he thought and ran limping towards his own people.

The shadow of the night covered the field, dew fell, the shooting had stopped long ago, cooking fires were smoking and every creature was settling down to rest, but the Russian camp did not quiet down. At its western edge, where the bridge had been built, more and more lights moved about and sounds came of shouted orders and of the monotonous roar of the voices of men hauling: "Oo-oo-oo-hnem!" Camp-fires, the flames of torches and the lights of lanterns had now spread far out on to the right bank of the Narova up to the walls of Ivan-gorod, and soon these stationary and moving lights became more numerous than the majestic stars in the August sky.

At dawn the watchers on the towers of Narva could see great siege-guns and mortars, drawn by oxen, still driving in over the Yamgorod road. Some drove on across the bridge, but the greater part turned and halted on the right bank in the midst of the massed troops.

That morning General Horn rode into the old town to the Honour bastion that adjoined the river. There he mounted a high ravelin built of brick and considered impregnable. From there he could see with the naked eye and count the brass monsters on cast wheels; he realised without difficulty Tsar Peter's plan and his own mistake. Once again the Russians had tricked him, old and wise as he was. He had overlooked the two weakest spots in the defence: the supposedly impregnable Honour bastion, which would be demolished in a few days by the Russians' siege-guns, and the Victoria bastion, covering the town on the side of the river, which was also brick-built and old, dating back to Ivan the Terrible's time. For two months the Russians had diverted his attention by pretending to prepare for an assault on the powerful fortifications of the new town, but evidently they were even then making ready to attack from this side. General Horn watched thousands of Russian soldiers digging with all possible speed and establishing the siege batteries against the bastions Honour and Victoria and against Ivan-gorod, which defended the river crossings. The Russians were preparing to attack from across the river over pontoon bridges.

"Very well; it's all clear; foolish jokes are at an end. We shall fight!" Horn muttered, pacing along the ravelin with a livelier stride. "For our part we have Swedish valour to oppose to them. It is no small thing."

"Hell will break loose *here!*" he said turning to the group of officers and stamping his heavy boot. "It is here that we shall face the Russian cannon-balls. The Russians are in a hurry, we too need to hurry. I command you to round up in the town everyone capable of using a spade. If the walls fall, we shall fight on the counter-approaches, we shall fight in the streets. I will not surrender Narva to the Russians!"

Late in the evening General Horn returned home and, sitting at the table, chewed the tough meat with his big yellow teeth. The Countess was so alarmed by what the people were saying in the market-place, that indignation choked her into silence. The sulky little boy said, drawing his wet finger along the edge of his plate:

"The boys say that the Russians will kill every one of us."

General Horn took a drink of water, lit his pipe at the candle, crossed his legs and then replied:

"Even so, sonny, the main thing is that a man should do his duty and, for the rest, you must rely on God's mercy."

6

Any other document as long and dull as this one Peter Alexeyevich would have tossed across the table to the secretary Makarov with the words: "Read it and make a comprehensible summary of it." But this was the disposition drafted by Field-Marshal Ogilvie. On the calculation that he had been drawing his salary since the 1st of May and had so far done nothing else, the disposition had cost the treasury seven hundred gold thalers, not counting his keep and other allocations. Sucking at his wheezing pipe and grunting in accompaniment, Peter Alexeyevich patiently read the fruit of the field-marshal's labours, written in German.

Green midges swarmed round the candles; hideous daddy-long-legs swooped in and, scorched by the flame, fell on their backs on the papers scattered over the floor; a death's-head moth, half the size of a sparrow, whirled in, extinguishing the candles and startling Peter Alexeyevich, who disliked strange and useless creatures, especially cockroaches. Makarov snatched off his wig and hopped about chasing the moth out of the tent.

Sitting close to Peter, with his short thighs set wide apart, was Peter Pavlovich Shafirov who had arrived from Moscow with the field-marshal. He was a small man with moist, smiling eyes that expressed a remarkably quick understanding. Peter had had his eye on him for a long time, trying to make out whether he was clever enough to be loyal, whether his astuteness was sufficiently wide in scope and whether he was not excessively greedy. From ordinary interpreter at the Ambassadors' Office Shafirov had lately become an important figure there, although he held no rank.

"More confusion, more meanderings!" Peter Alexeyevich said with a grimace. Shafirov threw up his small hands covered with rings, jumped up and, leaning over the paper, translated the obscure passage quickly and accurately.

"Ha! Is that all? I thought it was some great piece of wisdom," Peter said and, dipping the quill into the inkpot, scratched a few words on the margin of the manuscript. "It's simpler in Russian. Look here, Peter Pavlovich, you've been seeing quite a lot of the field-marshal: is he worth his salt?"

Shafirov's blue-shaven face broadened and looked as cunning as a devil's. He made no reply, not out of caution, but because he knew that Peter's unblinking eyes would read his thoughts without his saying anything.

"Our people complain that he's too haughty," Peter said. "He won't go near a soldier, he's too squeamish. I don't see what there is to be squeamish about with a Russian soldier. Pull up the shirt of any one of them, his body is white and clean. As for lice, only the baggage-train drivers have possibly got them. Oh, these Austrians! I went into his tent this morning; he was washing himself in a small basin: he washed his hands and face in the same water, and spat into it. And yet he finds us offensive. He hasn't been to the baths since he arrived from Vienna."

"He hasn't, he hasn't!" Shafirov said shaking all over with laughter and covering his mouth with the tips of his fingers. "He told me that in Germany, when a gentleman wants to wash, they bring him a basin of water in which he washes whichever part of his body he thinks needs washing. According to him, baths are a barbarian custom. What the field-marshal finds particularly revolting is our habit of eating a lot of garlic—crushed and chopped and plain—serfs and boyars alike. In the first days he used to cover his nose with his handkerchief."

"Fancy that!" Peter said with astonishment. "Why didn't you tell me sooner? It's true we eat a lot of garlic, but it's healthy; let him get used to it."

He threw down the disposition which he had finished reading and stretched himself. Then suddenly he turned to Makarov:

"Barbarian, wipe this mess off the table, all these midges! Tell them to bring wine and a chair for the field-marshal. And another thing: you've got the habit when you are listening of breathing garlic into people's faces. Turn your head away to breathe."

Field-Marshal Ogilvie came into the tent. He was wearing a yellow wig, a white military coat edged with gold braid and soft topboots that fell in creases below his knees. He bowed, raising his hat in one hand and his cane in the other, and immediately drew himself up to his full height, which was considerable. Peter Alexeyevich, without rising, pointed to the chair with his spread out fingers: "Sit down. How are you?" Shafirov glided up and translated with a bland smile. The field-marshal, full of dignity, sat in a slightly sprawling attitude, sticking out his belly and resting his hand on his cane which he held at arm's length. His sallow face was fleshy but morose, with thin lips; his glance, however, was undeniably bold.

"I've read your disposition; it's all right, very sensible, very sensible," Peter Alexeyevich said pulling out the plan of the town from under the table. As he unrolled it, midges and daddy-long-legs immediately fell all over it. "There's only one thing I disagree with: Narva must be taken, not in three months, but in three days." And he nodded, pursing his lips.

The field-marshal's sallow face lengthened as if someone standing behind him had helped in the process; his ruddy eyebrows crept up to the edge of his wig, the corners of his mouth drooped and his eyes expressed indignation.

"Well, well! I was too hasty when I said three days. If we haggle a little we'll agree on one week. But I won't give you more time than that." Peter Alexeyevich irritably flicked the insects off the map with his finger. "You have cleverly chosen the emplacements for the batteries. But, you must forgive me, a short while ago I personally gave orders to turn all the batteries that are across the river against the bastions Victoria and Honour. That's where General Horn's Achilles' heel is."

"Your Majesty!" Ogilvie cried, quite beyond himself. "According to the disposition, we begin with the bombardment and assault of Ivan-gorod."

"It's unnecessary. It's exactly what General Horn is hoping for: that we should be kept busy with Ivan-gorod till the autumn. But it doesn't hinder us in the least; all it can do is to fire a bit at our pontoons. What you say farther on, about the danger of King Charles coming to relieve the town, is very clever, very clever indeed. In seventeen hundred I lost my army at these very same positions because of his coming to the relief. You are preparing a counter-relief, but it's expensive and complicated, and you allow too much time for it. Now the counter-relief I plan is to capture Narva as quickly as possible. To seek victory in speed, and not in caution. Your disposition is the very wise fruit of military science and Aristotle's logic. But I need Narva at once, as a hungry man needs a piece of bread. A hungry man doesn't wait."

Ogilvie pressed his silk handkerchief to his face. He had difficulty in following the young barbarian's reasoning, but his dignity forbade him to agree without argument. Profuse sweat drenched his handkerchief.

"Your Majesty, fortune has favoured me in granting me success in the capture of eleven fortresses and towns," he said throwing his handkerchief into his hat that lay on the carpet. "At the storming of Namur, Marshal de Vauban embraced me and called me his best pupil. And there, on the field of battle, among the groaning wounded, he gave me a snuffbox. In composing this disposition I neglected none of my military experience, everything in it has been weighed and measured. I affirm, in all modesty but with perfect assurance, that the least departure from my deductions will lead to fatal results. Yes, Your Majesty, if I have allowed more time for the siege it is only from consideration of the fact that the Russian soldier is, as yet, not a soldier, but a peasant with a musket. He still has not the slightest notion of order and discipline. One will have to break many sticks on his back before one gets him to obey without reasoning, as a soldier should. Then I shall be confident that, at the wave of my baton, he will take the ladder and climb up the wall under a hail of bullets."

Ogilvie listened to his own speech with pleasure, hooding his eyes with his lids, like a bird. Shafirov translated his bombastic phrases into reasonable Russian. When Ogilvie had finished he looked at Peter Alexeyevich and, with sudden haste, losing much of his dignity, gathered his legs under his chair, pulled in his belly and lowered his hand that held the cane. Peter's face was terrifying: his neck seemed to have stretched to double its length and out of his widened eyes—God forbid, God forbid!—furies seemed ready to spring. He was breathing heavily and his large sinewy hand in its short sleeve lying among the dead insects groped blindly. It found the quill and snapped it in two.

"So that's how it is, that's how it is: the Russian soldier is a peasant with a musket!" he said out of a constricted throat. "I see nothing wrong in that. The Russian peasant is clever, ingenious and brave. And when he's got a musket he is terrifying to the enemy. You don't beat a man with sticks for that! He doesn't know discipline, you say? He knows it! And when he doesn't, it's not he who's wrong, it's his officer. And when my soldier needs beating with a stick, it is I who'll beat him, not you."

General Chambers, General Repnin and Alexander Danilovich Menshikov entered the tent. Makarov handed each a goblet of wine and they sat down where they could. Then Peter, consulting from time to time the field-marshal's manuscript marked with his own notes and, drawing lines and making marks on the map (standing in front of the candles and waving the midges away), read to the Military Council the disposition which, within a few hours, set in motion all the troops, batteries and baggage-trains.

7

Bareheaded women threw themselves at General Horn's horse. They seized hold of the bridle and stirrups and clutched at the tails of his leather coat. Emaciated and blackened by the smoke of burning houses they cried with frenziedly staring eyes: "Surrender the town! Surrender the town!" The grim cuirassiers of his escort were likewise beset and unable to make their way to him. The roar of the Russian cannon shook the houses on the town square, littered with charred beams and broken tiles. This was the seventh day of the cannonade. The day before, the general had rejected Field-Marshal Ogilvie's moderate and courteous proposal not to submit the town to the horrors of an assault and the ferocity of invading troops. For all reply the general had crumpled the letter and thrown it in the envoy's face. This had become known to the whole town.

With eyes as dull as if they were covered by a film, the general looked at the faces of the screaming women, distorted by fear and hunger: such is the face of war. He drew his sword out of its scabbard and, with the flat of the blade, beat their heads while he urged on his mount. There came cries: "Kill us, kill us! Trample us to death!" He swayed in his saddle as they tried to drag him down. At this moment a stupendous roar thundered, at which even his iron heart contracted. A black and yellow column of smoke and flames shot up above the tiled roofs of the old town: the powder-magazines had blown up. The high tower of the old town hall tottered. Frantic voices screamed, the people rushed into the side streets and the square emptied. Holding his sword across his saddle, the general galloped towards the Honour bastion. Balls that swiftly grew in size as they came hurtling in steep arcs from beyond the river fell with a hiss on the roofs of the houses, whose fronts overhung the street, and on to the crooked street itself, where they spun and exploded. The General kept prodding the bloody flanks of his shying horse with his huge spurs.

The Honour bastion was wrapped in dust and smoke. The general could distinguish piles of brick, overturned cannon, horses' legs sticking in the air and an enormous breach in the Russian's direction. The walls had crumbled to their foundations. The commander of the regiment, wounded in the face and grey with dust, came up. The general said: "My orders are not to let the enemy pass!" The commander gave him a look full of reproach, or it might have been derision. Turning away, the general prodded his horse and galloped through narrow alleys to the Victoria bastion. More than once he was obliged to shield himself with his leather sleeve from the flames of burning cottages. As he approached the bastion, he could hear the howling flight of cannon-balls. The fire of the Russians was accurate. The half-demolished walls of the bastion bulged, heaved and collapsed. The general got out of the saddle. The soldier with a round, pink-and-white face who took his horse stubbornly avoided his glance. The general hit him under the chin with his leather-gloved fist and clambered over the piles of brick on to the part of the wall that still remained standing. From here he saw that the assault had begun.

Menshikov was running over the pontoon bridge amongst short-statured fusiliers of the Ingermanlandsky regiment, brandishing his sword and yelling at the top of his voice. All the soldiers yelled at the top of their voices. From the high walls of Ivan-gorod iron cannon thundered at them and bombs plunged into the water, or, heavily rending the air, sped whistling over their heads. As Menshikov reached the left bank, he jumped off the bridge and, turning round, stamped and waved the edge of his cloak: "Forward! Forward!" The fusiliers, looking hump-backed because of their haversacks, ran in close formation across the sagging bridge, but to him they seemed to be merely marking time. "Hurry up! Hurry up!" he shouted and, like a drunken man, burst into a torrent of oaths coined on the spot.

Here, on the left bank, there was little space on the narrow strip between the river and the damp fortress wall of the Victoria bastion; the soldiers who had crossed the bridge crowded together, pressed, slowed down. There was a smell of acrid sweat. Menshikov ran up to his knees in the water to overtake the column. "Drummers, forward! The colours, forward!" The guns of Ivan-gorod were now firing across the river at the column: the cannon-balls splashed close to the bank, drenching the men with water, burst against the walls, scorching them with splinters, hit human bodies with a soft, squelching sound. The foremost ranks, tumbling, throwing up their arms, were already clambering over the rubble of the breach to its crest. Drums began to beat. The shouting grew fiercer along the column of fusiliers who were crawling up to the top. There, beyond the crest, a voice yelled hoarsely in Swedish. A volley exploded. The fusiliers poured over the crest of the breach into the town.

The second assault column was marching past General Chambers. He sat on a tall horse that nodded its head in rhythm with the drums. He was wearing a brass cuirass polished with brick dust, which he donned only on solemn occasions, and he held his heavy helmet in his hand to allow the soldiers a clear sight of his blood-suffused, hook-nosed face, that resembled a red-hot bomb. He kept repeating in a hoarse and expressionless voice: "Brave Russians—forward! Brave Russians—forward!"

At the head of the column, advancing at the double across the meadow towards the Honour bastion, was a battalion of the Preobrazhensky regiment, tall to a man, moustached, well-fed, in small three-cornered hats pulled down to their eyebrows, with bayonets screwed on to their muskets, because the order was not to shoot, but to thrust and stab. Lieutenant-Colonel Karpov led the battalion. He knew that the eyes of his own people and those of the Swedes lurking in the breach were upon him. He strode with his chest smartly thrown out like a pigeon's, his head well in the air, without turning round towards his men. Behind him, four drummers beat a poignant tattoo. Fifty paces remained to the wide breach in the deep brick wall; Karpov did not quicken his step, but his shoulders lifted. Seeing this, the soldiers pressed on, losing step, those in the rear jostling those in front. "Rrrrra-ta, rrrra-ta!" the drums rolled. Iron helmets and musket barrels slowly rose in the breach. Karpov shouted: "Drop your arms, carrion! Surrender!" and ran towards the volley with his sword in one hand and his pistol in the other. There was a flash and a roar, and gunpowder smoke hit him in the face. "Is it possible I'm alive?" he thought happily. And the fear he had been overcoming, and that had made his shoulders rise, left him. Now he was thirsting for the fight. But the soldiers had out-distanced him and he vainly sought someone to attack with his sword. He could see only the broad backs of the Preobrazhensky men who wielded their bayonets like pitchforks, peasant fashion.

The third column—that of Anikita Ivanovich Repnin—hurled itself with storm ladders to the assault of the half-demolished Gloria bastion. The defenders on the walls kept up a running fire, hurled down stones and logs and set fire to tar barrels to pour the burning liquid on the attackers. Repnin stamped about on his little horse at the foot of the gate-tower in a fever of impatience. His huge cuffs were turned up and he shook his small fists and shouted in his reedy voice, encouraging his men for fear that they might falter on the ladders. One, and then another, and several more, bruised and stabbed, fell off the very top. But—God was kind—the soldiers kept swarming up fiercely in thick clusters. The Swedes did not have the time to overturn their flaming barrels; the Russians were already on the walls.

The countess clutched at her children's hands as if each time she were counting them. She would start up and listen: shots and the wild shouts of the combatants sounded ever nearer. She stretched out her arms, wringing her clasped hands and whispered hotly with writhing lips: "You wanted this, you monster, you; you stubborn, heartless man!" The girls pleaded, weeping: "Mama, don't, don't!" The boy crammed his fist in his mouth watching his crying sisters.

Wheels rattled quite close. The countess rushed to the window: a limping horse with a broken leg was dragging a cart loaded with household goods and behind it ran women with bundles. "To the castle! To the castle! Run for safety!" they were crying. Four soldiers went past carrying a stretcher. More and more stretchers followed with waxen-faced wounded. Then she saw a round-shouldered old man with a sack—a well-known rich pawnbroker—shuffling hastily along in his slippers and carrying a small squealing pig under his arm. Suddenly he dropped both the sack and the pig and took to his heels. From somewhere quite close there came the tinkling of breaking glass. "Oh-o-oh!" moaned an agonized voice. She caught sight of General Horn at the far end of the square. He was waving his arm and pointing somewhere. Cuirassiers rode past him at a heavy gallop. Horn several times struck his staggering horse with the flat of his sword; in his blackened face all his teeth showed like a wolf's.

Then, bobbing high in his saddle, he disappeared at a gallop down an alley.

"Karl! Karl!" The countess ran out into the hall and opened the street door: "Karl! Karl!"

And then she saw the Russians: they were skirting the houses in the deserted square and glancing up at the windows. They had broad faces, long hair and there were brass eagles on their hats.

The countess was so frightened that she stood and watched them approach, pointing at her and at the commander's flag over the door. The soldiers surrounded her, gesticulating and talking in angry, excited voices. One flat-faced fellow pushed past her into the house. When he pushed her as if she were a common woman in the marketplace, all her long, pent-up hatred exploded: hatred of her old husband who had spoilt her life and hatred of these Russian barbarians who had brought so much suffering and fear. She clutched at the flat-faced fellow and pulled him out of the hall, hissing and choking with broken words, clawing at his cheeks and eyes, biting him, butting him with her knees. The bewildered soldier defended himself as best he could from the demented woman. They fell together in a heap on the stones. His comrades, wondering at such fury in a woman, tried to pull her away and, finally getting angry, fell on the two and separated them. But when they stepped aside the countess was lying prone, her head twisted round and her face an unpleasant blue colour. One of the soldiers pulled her skirt down where it had ruckled up over her legs, another turned angrily towards the three girls and the boy who had appeared in the doorway. The boy was stamping with his mouth wide open to scream, but he had neither voice nor tears. "To the devil with these brats!" the soldier said. "Let's get away from here, lads."

In three-quarters of an hour all was finished. The Russians broke like a hurricane into the squares and streets of Old Narva. It was impossible either to stop them or to throw them back. General Horn ordered his troops to retreat towards the earth rampart that separated the old town from the new. This rampart was high and broad and he hoped to make Tsar Peter's regiments pay a heavy toll in blood on its steep slopes.

The general sat on his horse whose head drooped down to its very hoofs. His personal black-and-yellow pennant flapped on its high staff in the fresh breeze that had risen. Fifty cuirassiers sat their horses in a grim and motionless semi-circle at his back. From the high rampart the general could see down several streets. It was along these streets that the troops should have been retreating, but they were deserted. He watched and waited, chewing his wrinkled lips. At last, at the far end, first of one street, then of another, small figures came into sight, running. He could not understand who these figures were and why they were running across the streets. At his back the cuirassiers growled deep in their throats. A rider appeared galloping frantically; he jumped off his horse at the foot of the rampart and, supporting his bloodstained left hand with his right, climbed up the steep incline. This was adjutant Bistrem, without his sword, without his pistol, hatless and with a tail of his coat torn off.

"General!" he cried lifting his wild face to him. "General! Oh, my God, my God!"

"I am listening to you, Lieutenant Bistrem. Speak more calmly!"

"General, our troops are surrounded. The Russians are running wild! I have never witnessed such a massacre! General, hurry to take cover in the castle!"

General Horn found himself at a loss. Now he understood who those figures were running across the streets in the distance. His slow-moving thoughts that always led him to a firm decision were confused. He could not make up his mind. His feet slipped out of the stirrups and hung below the horse's belly. Even the rumbling, alarmed exclamations of his cuirassiers failed to rouse him. From both sides, along the broad rampart, bearded Cossacks, in terrifying, tall sheepskin caps pulled down over one ear, were galloping full stretch with strident yells, brandishing their curved swords and pointing their arquebuses. Bistrem pressed his face against the General's horse to shut out this horror. The cuirassiers, looking round at each other, started to unsheathe their swords, throwing them on the ground, and to get out of their saddles.

Colonel Renne, hot with excitement, was the first to gallop up; he seized the General's horse by the bridle.

"General Horn! You are my prisoner!"

Then, as though in a trance, the General lifted his sword and Colonel Renne had to force open the fingers gripping the hilt to take it away from him.

Had it not been for the presence of Field-Marshal Ogilvie, Peter Alexeyevich would have long ago rushed off to join his troops; in three-quarters of an hour they had achieved that which he had been preparing for four years and which had worried and preoccupied him like an unhealing ulcer. But—the devil take it!—he had to behave as befitted a monarch according to European custom. Dressed in a Preobrazhensky uniform, white scarf and new, shaggy, three-cornered hat with a cockade, Peter Alexeyevich sat gravely on a white horse, his right hand holding a telescope resting on his hip—there was nothing more to look at from this hillock—with an expression of imposing majesty on his face. This was an affair of European importance: it was no joke to capture by storm one of the most impregnable fortresses known.

From time to time officers galloped up and when Peter Alexeyevich directed them towards Ogilvie with a movement of his chin, they reported the progress of the battle to the field-marshal. So many streets and squares had been occupied. The Russians were advancing like a crushing wall, the enemy was everywhere retreating in disorder. Finally, three officers emerged from the broken gates of the Gloria bastion and approached as fast as their horses could carry them. Ogilvie raised a finger and said:

"Ah! Good news, I imagine."

The first to reach them was a Cossack cornet who flew out of his saddle before his horse halted, and roared, raising his black beard towards Peter:

"The Commander of Narva, General Horn, has surrendered his sword."

"Excellent!" Ogilvie exclaimed. Then, with a graceful gesture of his hand in a white buckskin glove, he invited Peter, saying:

"Your Majesty, please to proceed: the town is yours."

Peter strode impetuously into the vaulted hall of the castle. He seemed taller than usual, his back stiff, his chest heaving stormily. In his hand he carried a naked sword. He glanced furiously at Menshikov. Menshikov's steel cuirass was dented by bullets, his narrow face was drawn, his hair damp, his lips parched. From him, Peter's eyes went to the small Repnin, who was smiling mildly with his narrow eyes; then to the ruddy Colonel Renne who had already managed to drain a goblet of wine and, finally, to General Chambers, who looked as pleased with himself as though this were his birthday.

"I want to know," Peter shouted at them, "why the massacre in the old town has not been stopped yet? Why is looting going on in the town?" He stretched out his hand that held the sword: "I struck one of our soldiers. He was drunk and was dragging a girl along." He threw the sword on the table. "Bombardier Lieutenant Menshikov, I appoint you governor of the town. I give you an hour to stop the bloodshed and looting. You'll be responsible for this, and not with your back but with your head."

Menshikov paled and immediately went out, trailing his torn cloak. Anikita Repnin said softly:

"The fact is that the enemy was very late in asking for mercy, that's why it's difficult to restrain our soldiers, they are so furious. The officers I sent grab them by the hair, drag them away. As for the looting, it's the townspeople themselves who are looting."

"Seize them and hang them to drive fear into the others."

Peter Alexeyevich sat down at the table but immediately got up again. Ogilvie entered followed by two soldiers with an officer leading General Horn. Complete silence fell; the only sound was the slow jingling of Horn's star-shaped spurs. He approached Tsar Peter, lifted up his head, looking past him with dull eyes and his lips twisted in a mirthless smile. Everybody saw Peter's hand jerk up off the red cloth of the table and knot itself into a fist (Ogilvie in alarm took a step towards him) and his shoulders move with disgust. He remained silent for so long that the others became weary of holding their breath.

"You shall not get honourable treatment from me," Peter said without raising his voice. "You fool! You old wolf! Bloodthirsty, obstinate man . . . !" He flashed a glance at Colonel Renne. "Take him to prison, on foot, across the whole town, that he may see his sorry handiwork."